I'll Be Home
for Christmas

I'll Be Home for Christmas

True Stories for the Season

Deseret Book Company
Salt Lake City, Utah

Library of Congress Cataloging-in-Publication Data

I'll be home for Christmas : true stories for the season

    p.   cm.

  ISBN 1-57345-437-0 (hardbound)

  1. Christmas—Miscellanea. 2. Mormons—Miscellanea. 3. Church of Jesus Christ of Latter-day Saints—Miscellanea. I. Deseret Book Company.

  BV45.I45   1998

  263'.915—dc21

98-29419
CIP

Printed in the United States of America

18961-6369

10 9 8 7 6 5 4 3 2 1

CONTENTS

Contents

INTRODUCTION

We often think of Christmas as a warm, exciting time, when our families gather 'round us and we all revel together in the peace and joy (and noise and bustle!) of the occasion.

But sometimes we can't be home for Christmas.

What happens when we're in a faraway place during this special season . . . or we're "home" but not at our *family home* . . . or we find ourselves at Christmastime under particularly trying circumstances, not experiencing the holiday the way we'd hoped?

"I'll be home for Christmas" the old standard song says—but sometimes it's "only in [our] dreams."

CHRISTMAS IN THE HOLY LAND

Lloyd and Karmel Newell

Now that I think about it, we *were* home on Christmas Day in 1992. My wife and I were up late packing. Christmas music played in the background while we squeezed choir tapes and ties, name badges and dresses into suitcases, which were labeled in blue like every other bag that would find a place on the chartered aircraft. We were leaving with the 325 "singing ambassadors" of the Mormon Tabernacle Choir (and their guests) early in the morning. Ours was a goodwill "mission" for the next ten days in the Holy Land. Having signed an agreement not to proselyte or discuss the doctrines of the Church with the people of Israel, we sensed that this tour would be different from any other the choir had undertaken.

We had been to the security briefings; we knew something of the miracle of the BYU Jerusalem Center—but how could we be fully prepared for the experience we were about to have? We were coming as emissaries of peace; our music would be a balm to those who heard it. The love that radiated from our group would invite age-old enemies, Muslims, Jews, and Christians alike, to sit down together and worship God. Our hope was that, for a moment at least, some of these ancient animosities could be softened, and we would be instruments in the Lord's hands as we, through music, "spoke comfortably to Jerusalem" (Isaiah 40:2). The message was simple and powerful.

My wife and I had been on tour with the choir before. We had seen how audiences are set on fire with the choir's spirit and song. We knew about the rigorous performance schedule, the 5:00 A.M. bag checks, and the unrelenting pace. We were accustomed to wearing dresses, ties, and name badges from morning until night.

But we had never been expectant parents before—not at home or abroad. My wife was five months pregnant with our first child. She was in good health, and we were in good spirits. It was Christmastime. We were leaving family and friends behind, but we were together, and we were with our "family" of dear choir members. Even though we would soon be many miles away from home, we had an inclination that we would not feel like strangers to a land we had read about from our earliest years. We were traveling to Israel; we were going "home" for Christmas.

> Israel, Israel God is calling,
> Calling me from lands of woe . . .

The Christmas story was so much a part of my consciousness that December morning, almost like a song you just can't stop singing, and the events of that first Christmas kept playing in my mind. Thoughts of Mary, the mother of Jesus, were unavoidable as I reached for my wife's hand mid-flight. I noticed how Karmel was adjusting her weight. She didn't—wouldn't—complain, but I knew she must have felt uncomfortable by now. We had been sitting for such a long time. Soft and accommodating though our seats were, I, too, was feeling the need to move around a little.

And then I considered Joseph's plight. How he must have ached to provide even minimal comforts for his wife, so "great with child" (Luke 2:5). How the bumps of that dusty road to Bethlehem must have dually pained him—for his dear Mary and for his inability to relieve her. What could he do but pull the donkey forward? What could I do but wish the hours away? The journey had to be made; not out of necessity like Mary and Joseph, but out of a marvelous opportunity to sing glad tidings of great joy.

> Oh, come, all ye faithful,
> Joyful and triumphant!
> Oh, come ye, oh, come ye to Bethlehem.

Here we were eating, reading, resting on our way to Bethlehem. Consider, in contrast, the way Mary and Joseph traveled. Did they pack enough bread and goat cheese? What kind of bedding might they have carried? Were they hungry as well as tired? Did Mary bring swaddling cloth along with her, or did they have to borrow that as well? And what about the uncertainty of it all?

Karmel and I knew just where we would be staying when we arrived. We knew the hotel, its address, telephone number—even our room number before we ever touched ground. Several doctors were on board, should we require any medical assistance en route. But Mary and Joseph. Joseph and Mary.

They must have known before they ever arrived that the village inns would be filling fast, if they were not already full. And every time the baby shifted in his mother's womb, Mary might have wondered: who would assist with the birth? Where would they lay him? Would the accommodations they found be good enough for their newborn King?

Although they were traveling to the little town of Bethlehem, a land of their kin, still "There was none to give room in the inns." (JST, Luke 2:7) Although alone, concerned, and without the most basic comforts, Mary—and Joseph—must have already felt that "peace . . . which passeth all understanding" (Philippians 4:7). Quite literally, the peace of God had already been born and nurtured in their souls.

> Joy to the world,
> The Lord is come;
> Let earth receive her King!

Every time I turned around, someone was asking about Karmel and sharing in our excitement. "Your first child!" "We're so happy for you. Do you know if you're having a boy or a girl?" "Let us know when the baby is born." The smile these comments put on my face always lingered. Months before our baby was born, I was already feeling like a proud and excited father. I just couldn't contain my joy.

But Joseph, how alone he must have felt in his sacred perspective—and joy. Certainly, he couldn't have explained all he understood. How did he respond to the probable questions and whisperings regarding their situation? And Mary. This sweet and holy virgin, favored above all others, what did her friends and kinsfolk think? Were there celebrations, congratulations— or anything of the like? Was her immense and exalting joy not to be shared except with Elisabeth, and Joseph? Who would be there to welcome her King of kings?

> Silent night! Holy Night!
> All is calm, all is bright
> Round yon virgin mother and Child.
> Holy infant, so tender and mild,
> Sleep in heavenly peace . . .

I reached for the itinerary in my carry-on bag. Karmel had closed her eyes. She looked like she was intent on sleeping. I tried not to disturb her as I turned the pages. The choir would be performing for the first time at Galilee, the Garden Tomb, the Mount of Olives, shepherds' field, and many other sacred and historic spots. Miraculous negotiations and circumstances

had led the way for permission to be granted for the choir's singing and recording a video of their performances at these holy sites. What a thrill to take part in this!

I could already picture the footage of the choir singing in the fields where shepherds had once heard heavenly hosts proclaim Christ's birth. I couldn't help but wonder if some of these talented and faithful choir members had been among those who sang anthems of glory on that blessed night so long ago.

And then I thought of something I hadn't previously considered. Mary and Joseph may not have heard any of those angelic choruses. The shepherds most likely told them about the glad tidings they had received. But like many who would not be able to find a seat in the choir's packed concerts, Mary and Joseph probably didn't even hear the heavenly angels sing. And the star that shone above them. Did they notice its newness and luster?

Certainly, they must have been so enraptured by their Holy Child, this incomprehensible gift from God, that they needed no further declaration—or even celebration of His birth. He was miracle enough. He was Savior of all, even of Mary and Joseph.

> God be with you 'til we meet again
> By his counsels guide, uphold you;
> With his sheep securely fold you . . .

The choir was singing farewell to the crew of our aircraft. I couldn't believe we were already making our descent into the

Holy Land. I started to sing along with the choir, but emotions were welling too forcefully inside me. I had felt the story of Christ's birth at a depth I did not know was possible. Christmas had happened in my heart, a day after it was celebrated and days before we ever toured in Bethlehem. The Christ child had entered in, and I could not contain the love I felt. This was the love that we would share with His children in Israel. This was the light of Christmas that we had come to ignite.

Lloyd and Karmel Newell live in Utah with their three children. Lloyd is the author of two books and is the spokesman for "The Spoken Word," which is broadcast with the Mormon Tabernacle Choir each week to millions of homes around the world. Karmel has a masters degree in English from the University of Utah and serves on a general Church writing committee.

I WAS A STRANGER

Lael Littke

It was on an early November day, four months after we were married, that George came home and said, "Guess what! I've been offered a fellowship to complete my Ph.D., and even better, a job goes with it. Do you think we should accept it?"

"Of course," I said without hesitation. "Isn't that what we've been hoping for?"

I looked around our cozy Denver apartment on the third floor of what had once been a silver baron's mansion. I loved that spacious, pretty apartment—our first home together. "Will we be staying here in Denver?" I asked hopefully.

George shook his head, grinning.

"Okay, where?"

"New York," he said. "City."

"New York City?" I howled. "The Big Apple? Baghdad on the Hudson? Give my regards to Broadway? *That* New York City?"

"That's the one," George said. "The offer comes from New York University."

Scenes from movies passed through my mind. Narrow, crowded, shadowed streets lined with tall buildings. Endless traffic. Wall-to-wall people. Gangsters.

I gulped. It would take a while to adjust to this idea. "When do we have to leave?"

"Classes start in January," George said, "but I'll start work on December 6."

I slumped. We had expected to spend Christmas, our first as a married couple, with our parents in Idaho and Salt Lake City. We already had plans for family parties and sleigh rides.

I had never been away from home on Christmas before.

"So?" George asked.

"Whither thou goest," I said limply.

We arrived in The City on December 4, a Saturday. We didn't know a single soul among those millions of people. We drove our old Dodge, loaded to the top with clothes and wedding gifts, forlornly along the streets, wondering where we were going to sleep that night. Finally we turned into a parking garage and asked the attendant if there was a restaurant nearby where we could eat.

"Sure thing," he said cheerfully. (Weren't New York parking garage attendants supposed to be surly and sullen?) "Right across the street is Mama Maria's where they have the best lasagna in the city. I'll keep an eye on your car while you go have a bite."

His accent sounded strange to our ears. Could we trust him? Would he clean out our car while we were gone? And what was lasagna? This was the Fifties. Who had heard of lasagna?

Tired, hungry, and suspicious, we decided we had to go eat regardless of the consequences. Wondering if we'd ever see our car again, we trudged across the street to Mama Maria's, where Mama herself greeted us and sat us down at a window table covered with a spotless red-checked tablecloth. The lasagna was delicious and comforting, and our car was still there when we got back to the garage. The friendly, helpful attendant told us the location of an inexpensive hotel in a safe area and turned down a tip saying, "You probably need it more than I do right now."

This was New York City?

That first day was upbeat, but we had no family there. No friends. How could we spend Christmas in such a place? Couldn't we have waited to come until the springtime?

The next day we attended church in the Manhattan Ward chapel on West 81st Street. It was old and a bit shabby, but warm and welcoming. So were the people. A man named Jack greeted us at the door, shaking our hands and asking, "Are you just passing through or are you staying?"

"We'll be here for at least a couple of years," we admitted.

A huge smile split his face. "We have *jobs* for you," he said.

We met a number of nice people that day, many of them young couples like ourselves, who had come to New York City for educational purposes. We were impressed by the quality of the speakers and by the professional-sounding choir. Apparently a number of the ward members were in the city to develop their talents.

After the meeting, the choir director invited us to join if we liked to sing. "We're beginning work on our Christmas music," he said.

Maybe that would help. We promised we would be there for rehearsal the next Sunday.

That afternoon we looked for an apartment, since George was to begin work the next day, and I had to find a job. As we climbed endless flights of stairs to look at drab rooms we could barely afford, I couldn't stop thinking about our sunny Denver apartment. Not even a Christmas tree could cheer up some of the places we saw. There was one whose rent was right, but it was just one medium-sized room, with a kitchen counter along one wall and a Murphy bed built into the opposite one. We would have to pull down the bed each night, then fasten it back into the wall in the morning, just to move around.

"Not this one," I whispered to George. "Very likely the guy next door works nights and pulls that bed into his room to sleep in the daytime."

We giggled together and gave up our search for the day. When we got back to the hotel, one of the couples we had met at church called and invited us to stay with them in their apartment across the East River in Astoria until we found a place. We accepted.

They had a small child, and their Christmas tree was already up and decorated for his benefit. We slept on a pull-out couch right next to the tree, and in the dark of night, I breathed in its fragrance and could almost believe I was home in Idaho.

The next week brought a job for me on Madison Avenue in Manhattan and a big-windowed, one-bedroom, unfurnished apartment in the same complex where our new friends lived. We bought a bed, a table and chairs, and a skinny Christmas tree.

"I want to go home," I said, looking at its bare branches.

George produced a small German ornament he had bought during his mission to West Germany. "It won't be so bad," he said, hanging it on an upper branch.

I thought of the familiar bright balls and bells that had decorated our Christmas trees at home throughout my childhood. I thought of the familiar faces of my family gathered in the comfortable living room of our farm home. I thought of the snowy mountains and frozen creeks.

"Maybe we'll be home next Christmas," I said.

I could live through this one if I hung onto that thought. Of all times to be away from home, Christmas was the worst, I decided. How could we feel its spirit when we were thousands of miles away from everything we knew?

The next couple of weeks were busy as we settled into our new jobs. Sundays were best, when we crossed the Queensboro Bridge, drove up along Central Park, then through it to look for a parking place on 81st Street, near the chapel. Having a car was almost a handicap in the city. There weren't many places to park.

On the other hand, it was an asset to be able to give rides to people and get to know them. One of our riders invited us to a party on Christmas Eve. We had originally been scheduled to attend George's huge extended family Christmas Eve party in Salt Lake City where I was supposed to get acquainted with all the relatives. The abundance of food and the congeniality of the people at this party were legendary, and I was depressed that we would miss it. Our new friend's party would be an adequate substitute, and we were grateful for the invitation.

Shopping at Macy's and Gimbels, as well as in Greenwich Village, was exciting, and we mailed huge boxes of gifts home to our families. The annual sky-tall Christmas tree went up in the plaza of Rockefeller Center where George worked. We spent a couple of evenings wandering through the area, eating roasted chestnuts bought from street vendors and looking at the store windows along Fifth Avenue, with their animated Christmas scenes. This was all new to me. Who would have thought New York City could be so much fun?

We bought a sofa for our Christmas present so we could invite someone over to share our Christmas dinner, although the thought panicked me. I had never cooked a holiday meal alone before. What could I serve? What did I know how to make?

Before we had a chance to invite any-

body to dinner, George's boss asked if we would like to join him and his wife and two little kids on the big day. They lived up along the Hudson River, in Westchester County. We accepted the invitation. It would be our first venture out of the city since we had arrived.

Christmas Eve and Christmas Day would be taken care of. It wouldn't be like being home, but it was much better than being alone.

Our choir sang lovely Christmas music, including selections from *The Messiah* with professional-sounding soloists, on the Sunday before Christmas. It was a snowy day, and I felt strangely content as we came out after the meeting. Gathering up several people who would otherwise catch the subway, we started home, delivering them on our way. We all laughed together as we shared funny tales of living in one of the biggest cities in the world.

My office had a Christmas party on Thursday, and I got better acquainted with my co-workers. They were curious about a Mormon girl from beyond the hills of Idaho and started conversations without my having to think up subjects for small talk. I liked them.

On Friday morning George and I decided to do tourist things, like riding the elevators to the top of the Empire State Building. I was impressed by the enormous city spread out below us. Now that we knew a few people, it didn't seem quite as intimidating as it had on our first day.

7

I still couldn't help but think of my friendly little town back home where the carolers would be going out that night in horse-drawn sleighs.

Our friend's party in her small, crowded apartment that evening was fun. We laughed endlessly as we ate spaghetti and played a game with the $1 gifts we had each brought. We felt as if we had found several more new friends.

The next morning was the hardest as George and I sat beside our skinny, bare tree with its lone ornament and read from St. Luke, then opened the gifts our families had sent. Before we left the apartment, we called home to talk to our parents. That brought them much closer.

After a lovely dinner at George's boss's home, we drove back along the banks of the Hudson River. "This is where Washington Irving lived," I said. "In the spring, I want to come back here and see the sights." It was exciting to look forward to.

As we approached the city and saw the tall buildings looming up ahead, I had a strange feeling. What was it? Pride? Excitement? Anticipation? Surely not contentment! I laughed. "Can a girl from Mink Creek, Idaho, find happiness in a city like New York?" I said, paraphrasing the opening lines of an old radio soap opera.

"Absolutely," George said.

I couldn't believe it. The day I had dreaded had been a delight, just as the events leading up to it had been. I had come to realize that there isn't just one way to celebrate Christmas, nor just one place. I thought of the old saying, "Home is where the heart is," and I decided the heart can be in several places at once. Part of mine was back in Mink Creek; a slice of it at Utah State University where I had gone to college; a chunk in Denver. I knew I would leave bits and pieces in every place I would live from that day on.

At that very moment, the biggest part of my heart was right there in New York, the vast city that I had been so afraid of just three weeks earlier.

I thought of one of my favorite quotations from Him whose birth we were celebrating. "I was a stranger," I said, "and ye took me in." (Matt. 25:35.)

I was, after all, home for Christmas.

Lael Littke has published thirty-three books for young people; she enjoyed thirty-six Christmases with her husband, George, before he passed away in 1991.

THE SCARLET FEVER CHRISTMAS

Alan Barnes, as told to
Kathleen H. Barnes

It was the winter of 1942, and Christmas was fast approaching. The world was at war, but it did little to dim the excitement I felt as a seven-year-old boy, anticipating the arrival of Santa. I loved everything about Christmas: the biting cold that created the icicle swords hanging from our roof; the familiar colored glass ornaments that hung each year on our tree; my mother's rich pink fruitcake that was more fruit than cake; and the wood logs that we hauled from the basement to replenish the fire in the living room grate.

Christmas brought with it a coziness of home and family and safety and love. It was filled with fun evenings of storytelling and games and puzzles and music. Everything from "'Twas the Night Before Christmas" to "Luke, Chapter 2" was read while we sipped hot chocolate and listened to "Silent Night" on the old Victrola. We could always count on a rousing game of Rook or Monopoly. I was the reigning "King of Hearts" and looked forward to defending my crown during this game-playing season. Mother

was the queen of puzzles, and she would often stay up too late, trying to fit just one more piece into the maze. Christmas was everything and I could hardly wait!

School had been dismissed for the holiday break. I was eagerly looking forward to endless days of play and excitement. There would be snow forts and sleigh riding. There would be trips to the store and the visit with Santa Claus and parties and friends and everything wonderful that comes with Christmas.

The excitement was mounting. My plans for fun were escalating—until I awoke one morning feeling sick. As the day wore on, I felt increasingly worse. With a sense of alarm, mother consulted with the doctor. Her greatest fears were confirmed. I had contracted scarlet fever.

This was one of the dreaded diseases of the time. Its complications could be serious, even fatal. The highly contagious nature of this disease required reporting, and by mid-afternoon, the Board of Health had placed a sign in the window that read "Scarlet Fever." Our house was suddenly under quarantine. According to the public health standards set at that time, no one approached a quarantined home.

It was as if the Scarlet Letter had been stamped on our foreheads. Those in the house were to remain in the house, and those not in the house were not allowed to return. My mother and my twelve-year-old sister Maureen were with me when the sign went up. My father and my older brother

Ray were at work. They would not be allowed back in the house until the quarantine was lifted.

It was determined that Dad and Ray would live in our ill-equipped basement. Any supplies mother needed would be left on the back step but nothing could leave our quarters. They would be required to live independently of us and their belongings.

Our basement was typical of most basements at the time. It was roughly finished with exposed beams and pipes. My brother and I had rigged up a shower by hanging a piece of hose over a beam and connecting it to a faucet in the washtub. A daybed had been placed in the corner of the room where I sometimes slept when the heat of the summer forced us to the cooler lower level. A small wood-burning monkey stove provided heat, and our food storage was the basis for their meals. However, the basement was sorely lacking in bathroom facilities. "We'll solve that," my dad said. The church was just up the back alley and he made arrangements to use their bathroom facilities morning and night.

So this routine began. Dad and Ray lived downstairs. Mother and Maureen and I lived upstairs. We communicated by phone during the day, and occasionally in the evening, they would come to the window and wave to us.

Suddenly it was Christmas Eve, and the impact of the quarantine began to surface. Even in my feverish state I wondered,

"What does a quarantine do to Santa? Does this mean he cannot come?" I imagined it so. I began to worry. Everything I had ever felt about Christmas began to wash away. No Dad, no brother, no stockings by the fire, no Christmas Eve stories, no friends, no Christmas dinner, no presents, no Santa! In other words, "no Christmas."

As the sun began to set on the day, I gazed from my bed through the window, looking into the night sky. Santa would be riding tonight. He had probably already left the North Pole. I wasn't sure of his route, but I knew he would arrive in our city before too long. A deep sadness fell over me. If I had to have scarlet fever, couldn't it have come after Christmas?

While staring into the night, I suddenly saw him. I was sure of it. He passed by my window as if in a dream and yet so real. His white beard reflected against the dark sky. His red, rounded suit bounced as he moved swiftly past my window. Santa was here. He was in our city. He was by my house. Maybe, just maybe, he would find a way to leave something on Christmas Eve for a small boy with scarlet fever. If the quarantine meant "no Santa," he might think to leave something on the front porch. I went to sleep with a glimmer of hope and childlike faith.

Christmas morning dawned. I awoke with mother standing over me, feeling my fevered brow. She grinned as I roused. "It's Christmas," she said, "and it's just possible that Santa found a way to leave a few gifts for you. Let's go see." Maureen joined us as we went into the living room. The fire in the fireplace brought warmth to the room. The lights on the tree seemed to twinkle "good morning," and beneath the tree, by some mystical magic, Santa had carefully placed presents wrapped in shiny paper. My heart leaped. "He did it!" I exclaimed. "He came into our quarantined house and left us gifts."

In the magic of the moment, I forgot about those of the family outside of the quarantine. A little rap on the window diverted my attention. There, bundled in coats, hats, gloves, and scarves, stood my dad and Ray, looking in with their noses pressed against the glass.

My little boy heart tugged as I realized that we were separated by illness. The coldness of their breath clouded their faces as they wistfully watched us enjoying the comforts of our warm, cozy room.

Mother began distributing the gifts. As we unwrapped each one, we held it up so Dad and Ray could give their nod of approval. The cold of the morning finally forced them indoors and back to the basement. Such was Christmas morning.

The rest of the day remains a blur. If our traditional breakfast of waffles and homemade fruit cocktail was served, I have no memory of it. The usual storytelling and game playing became victims of a Christmas cut short by illness. Amidst the dullness of the day, the memory that remains vivid is that of returning to my sick bed satisfied

that Santa had defied the boundaries of mortal man and could do just about anything. There was nothing left to do but wait out my days of recovery.

In the years since, I have often reflected on the events of that Christmas. It must have been hard on my mother. Her preparations were suddenly brought to a halt when she became confined to the house. There was no last-minute shopping. Even her traditional baking came to a halt, since nothing could leave the house to go to neighbors or friends. Her added responsibility of caring for a very sick child must have caused her great concern.

Since that time, I have become sensitive to the feelings of my father and brother, who stood in the cold that Christmas morning and watched the day unfold without them. I have come to understand that loneliness can be a state of the heart, not just of place. I have come to appreciate in a greater way the blessings and comforts of home and family.

Many Christmases have come and gone since then. They have been spent in all parts of the world. Some have been wrapped in the sweet confines of family and friends. Others have been spent far from the familiarity of home, but there are a few memories of a seven-year-old child that remain vivid. Each year as the season approaches, I am riveted back to that little home with its bundles of memories and soft warm feelings. I can feel mother's gentle hands caring for her sick child. I can see my family, separated by glass, trying in some small way to share a Christmas morning. Each Christmas Eve I look out the window, scanning the sky for Santa. I know he's there, because once long ago, perhaps in a feverish state, I saw him fly across the sky on his way to the home of a little boy whose Christmas could have been ruined by a quarantine.

So much has changed since that time. My adult skepticism has replaced some of the childlike faith and fantasy, but there shall always remain with me the feelings, the magic, and the memories of that "Scarlet Fever Christmas."

Alan Barnes works with the Salt Lake Olympic Organizing Committee, is active in community affairs, and serves as a bishop.

Kathleen H. Barnes is a wife, mother, and grandmother. A graduate of the University of Utah, she owns her own business and is active in Church and community affairs.

OUR FIRST CHRISTMAS IN UTAH

Carolyn J. Rasmus

Having never married, I felt an unspoken expectation that I would spend Christmas each year with my parents and my brother's family in Ohio. In fact, it never really occurred to me that I would have Christmas anywhere else. So for fifty plus years, I packed Christmas presents, boarded crowded planes, and headed for the snowy Midwest. While I loved the family reunion time, I dearly wanted to have Christmas in my own home—especially the year I purchased a new home. I started suggesting a "Utah Christmas" a year in advance and began the "hard sell" in July. Finally, Mother and Dad relented; they would come to *my* home, and we would have Christmas in Utah.

Of course, I wanted *everything* to be perfect, and I began planning months in advance for a wonderful and memorable Christmas celebration in my home. We would spend Christmas Eve with a large family in my ward. After dinner their children would act out the Christmas story, complete with bathrobes, draped sheets, necktie head pieces, *and* a newly born baby.

I knew it would be a contrast from the midnight, candlelight services in the Lutheran Church, but I wanted my parents to see how Latter-day Saints celebrated Christmas. I was grateful they would be in Utah the Sunday before Christmas so they could come to sacrament meeting with me. I wanted them to hear our choir and to feel the special spirit of our ward.

I decorated my home with gusto, bringing out decorations from my childhood, each with a special story that I knew would spark as many memories for Mother and Dad as they did for me. I even draped evergreen roping on the antique corner cupboard, which had been in our family for four generations, just the way I remembered Mother doing it when this heirloom was in her home. Candles were everywhere, and I dreamed about the "perfect Christmas" every time I hung an ornament or bought groceries for our Christmas dinner. I was especially thoughtful as I purchased presents, hoping each would evoke a memory of Christmases past.

The most special event of all would be on Christmas Day. After reading the Christmas story from the second chapter of Luke and singing a few Christmas carols (I'd even had the piano tuned), we would open presents and enjoy a traditional turkey dinner, for which I hoped Mother would agree to make her special giblet dressing. Then the *big* surprise—we were going on a "mystery trip"—first to see the manger scene on Temple Square in Salt Lake City and then a quiet stop at the Christus statue in the visitor's center. For the "grand finale," I had made a reservation to take my parents for a horse-drawn buggy ride down the beautifully decorated streets of the city! I was as eager as a young child for Christmas Day to arrive!

Believe it or not, everything was even better than I had planned. Who would have imagined that a light snow would begin falling just as we boarded the carriage! Instead of a blanket, the driver covered my parents and me with a large animal skin, which immediately evoked childhood memories for Mother. We returned waves to the passersby as Mother and Dad told me of childhood experiences from long ago.

By the time Christmas Day came to a close, I found myself looking forward to Mother's and Dad's return to Ohio. Being a "perfect" hostess was exhausting! They were scheduled to leave the morning of December 28, and I would fly to Hawaii the following day for a series of Know Your Religion lectures and a little rest and relaxation.

Nothing could have prepared me for what happened the day after my perfectly planned Christmas. Dad fell coming up the basement steps. His forehead was severely cut, and he was extremely disoriented. A physician friend came to our home and suggested we take Dad to the hospital immediately. Days of tests confirmed that in addition to the Parkinson's disease from which he suffered, he had had a slight stroke. He would remain hospitalized for at least a week, then be in a care center where he could receive therapy. I grudgingly canceled the Hawaii trip. I spent days and nights with Dad and tried to assure Mother that all would be well, while I secretly wondered how things really would turn out. I struggled to know how to respond as I watched my parents become my children.

Too quickly, I was back at work, trying to juggle its obligations with my parents' needs. Memories of my best Christmas ever quickly faded, and uncertainty and fear overshadowed my feelings of excitement and joy. I began to question why I had ever suggested that we have Christmas in Utah.

One night in February when I was physically tired, emotionally drained, and feeling especially sorry for myself, I tried to understand my feelings of anger and resentment. I wrestled with hard questions. Did I want to share only happy times with my parents? Was being with them an event, something carefully planned and executed— or were the everyday circumstances and challenges of life the things that really made family members important in each other's lives? Is the celebration of Christmas only a seasonal thing? What does it mean when we covenant to "take His name upon us"?

It was one of those times when the whisperings of the Holy Ghost prompted a desire for repentance and a true change of heart. What if I could see each day as a gift to Mother and Dad? Could I come to see these current circumstances as an opportu-

nity to demonstrate love for my parents instead of feeling sorry for myself? As I searched my soul, I began to come to an increased understanding not only of Christ's birth, but of the significance of his life and atonement and what it can mean every day in our lives.

I can't say that everything became easy and that challenges ceased, but I began to understand that the love and peace and joy so celebrated at Christmastime is something we should seek for daily. What happened to me that night changed my mind, but more importantly, my heart. I began to realize that I was passing by the most important gift I could ever give my parents—the gift of time and caring and unconditional love. I came to understand that through prayer, Christ gives us the ultimate gift—a change of heart. He can help us see disappointments and frustrations as opportunities for growth.

My parents were with me for about three months. There were many occasions for simple acts of kindness and genuine sharing, even times of celebration. I began to learn that the best presents are not the kind that are wrapped and placed under a tree, but are the gifts of the heart. I learned that quiet time spent enjoying one another can be more valuable than the perfectly planned events which had seemed so important.

The house seemed especially quiet when they returned home to Ohio in late March. I turned quickly to the notebook I had gotten for Mother so she could jot down memories of her childhood while she was alone during the day. Though she had often shared her writings at the end of the day, her first entry was one I'd never seen. It was entitled, "Christmas 1986." Mother wrote, "Our first visit to Utah for Christmas. What a wonderful day we had! We celebrated the birth of the Christ child by reading Luke 2:1–20. . . . We had an early dinner, then drove to Salt Lake City to see the beautifully decorated Temple Square with a quarter of a million lights on the trees and shrubs. Then the highlight—the beautiful Christus room. The figure seemed alive, asking all to come to Him. Finally, what a surprise, a ride through the decorated streets in a horse-drawn carriage. What a wonderful birthday party for our Savior. Thank you, Carolyn."

No, Mother, thank *you*. Thank you for reminding me of the lights, of His light, and of His invitation "to come unto me." You are right, Christmas is a "birthday party for our Savior." Think what would happen if I tried to make everyday a celebration of His birth by following His ways.

Carolyn J. Rasmus was born two days after Christmas and named by her father, who announced proudly, "I'm carolin' for joy!" Carolyn recently retired from full-time teaching at the Orem Institute of Religion but plans to continue living life to its fullest.

A TAHITIAN CHRISTMAS

Donald R. Marshall

All it takes is that first scent of a plump green lime being sliced or the juicy taste of a ripe mango, its sensuous fruit a rich reddish-orange. Even a whiff of jasmine or frangipani perfume can bring it all back—especially when I can conjure up in my memory and mix with it the headier scent of strips of coconut oozing oil in the noonday sun. The sultry spiciness of it all is inevitably borne by humid evening breezes across the lagoon and out to sea, signalling that the islands are near, even before the first faint, jagged outline becomes visible, jutting up like a pale and hazy emerald on the horizon.

Any one of these luscious appeals to the senses—whether coconut, jasmine, mango, or lime—can instantly transport me back to Tahiti.

There were times when, in Tahiti as a missionary in the 1950s, a certain image or sound or smell would momentarily take me back to America, where after watching Gene Kelly and Leslie Caron at the drive-in movie, we would go for milkshakes and cheeseburgers, served by carhops on roller skates, while Frankie Laine, Patti Page, and the Four Aces sang to us from the juke box.

Especially at Christmastime, my memories frequently meandered back to the United States. With no snow and nothing much resembling an actual Christmas tree, even a Tahitian version of "Silent Night" would set me longing for New England church spires and sleighbells jingling down snowy country lanes.

Now, almost half a century later, the memories are working the other way. A decorated tin box of assorted cookies I glimpsed in ZCMI caught me off guard and sent me reeling back forty-three years to a rambling old house, its corrugated roof and dilapidated veranda overlooking the lagoon on the island of Raiatea.

We had done our best to give the place some kind of festive holiday touch. It was, after all, not only where we lived, but also where our straggling little branch would be meeting that Christmas Sunday as they had every other Sunday since missionaries established themselves on the island. We had no Christmas lights to string along the big porch outside and no pine boughs or holly wreaths or even a fireplace mantel to arrange them on.

We had found a scrawny three-foot tree, and though it was actually a flimsy little semi-tropical bush with exotic green leaves, rather than a pine or blue spruce, we had strung it with red and green star and bell cut-outs we had made. It may have seemed only a token effort, but we felt we had done the best we could, given our limited resources on this little palm-covered island in the heart of Polynesia.

On the afternoon of the day before Christmas, we were tidying up our house for Sunday's services when we heard the familiar clankity-clack of a bicycle in need of repair. We glanced up at each other with the look that meant, "sounds like old Mimi." A glance through the big glassless window, its flap-like covering propped open by a long pole, told us we were right.

Mimi Oaoa was a large—not fat, just large—Polynesian man of about fifty, whose frail little Chinese wife, Mimi Vahine, faithfully scrubbed, ironed, and folded every piece of clothing brought to her each Saturday by the missionaries. Mimi himself had held a number of odd jobs, most recently loading and unloading the different cargo ships that regularly docked at Raiatea's smelly wharf. Due to a freak accident that had caused several heavy crates to fall on him and crush one of his legs, Mimi's dock activities—as well as work of almost any kind—had become drastically limited. The big man, now left with a severe limp, mainly got around with a cane or by riding, somewhat clumsily, the rattling and creaking family bicycle, usually with one or two of his barefoot children balanced on the handlebars or on the back.

Mimi and his wispy little wife had ten children—all of whom were still young and at home—from the fifteen-year-old Flora, who wanted to learn English and become a school teacher, to a little boy barely two years old. Today none of the Oaoa children accompanied Mimi on the bike. He had pedaled there by himself along the three- or four-mile road between his little house and our big rambling one.

Mimi was at present our branch president. He was a dear man, soft-spoken, kind, and well-meaning, if not as schooled in the gospel and in matters of leadership as one might have hoped. Nevertheless, he was the best we had at that point and had come a long way once the mantle of leadership had been placed on his shoulders. He did, however, have one vice, and though it didn't show itself often, it had cropped up a time or two since he had been set apart as leader of the branch: Mimi drank.

It went back to his teenage years, before he became a member of the Church. It had also been a part of his life during the first years of his marriage. Since joining the Church, Mimi had suffered only a few occasional lapses. Some of them were fairly recent, due perhaps to the pain he felt in his leg, to the depression brought on by his disablement, or perhaps to the feeling of camaraderie brought on whenever he lingered at the wharf in the evening with his co-workers and former drinking companions.

Because there was always much remorse, followed by tearful repentance, this sweet, soft-spoken man inevitably won our hearts with his promises and renewed resolutions, and we, in turn, had always decided to give him yet another chance. I'm not sure why we were a little nervous about Mimi's surprise visit that afternoon. It probably had something to do with the upcoming holiday and our worries about the temptations Mimi might face if he were to run into any of his old buddies planning—or even having—a Christmas celebration at the docks.

There seemed to be no hint of liquor on the man's breath, no guilt-filled confessions, no promises and resolutions, and not even any requests for our extra prayers on his behalf. There was one request: could we possibly give him a little money—just a few dollars—so that he might buy a few simple presents for his family?

"Eiaha te tahi mau mea rahi roa," he told us. Not a lot of things; just something for the children—especially the little ones.

My companion murmured something to me about the chance of Mimi's taking the money and getting drunk with it. I think I mumbled something back about the seeming impossibility of helping him buy presents, even if his motives were perfectly pure, when there were other families in our branch in similar predicaments. How could we help one household without helping the others?

"We're really sorry, Mimi," we finally told him after a few more questions to him and a few more mumbled comments in English to each other. We certainly wanted to help him, we said, but it just wouldn't be possible.

He nodded his head quietly, but still didn't leave immediately. He had one more request: "*Na reira ïa. Tera râ, hoê mea toe: e nehenehe anei ia'u ia tarahu hoê pereoo, ia nehenehe i to'u utuafare e haere mai i te pureraa ananahae, hoê taime, hoê tere?*" Would it be possible then for him to hire a truck-taxi to bring all twelve of them—him, Mimi Vahine, and the ten children—to church on Christmas morning, therefore arriving all at once, instead of one starting two or three hours early, with two or more on the old bicycle, then riding back alone to pick up another load, and so on, until all twelve of them were there?

The repeated request for a few dollars made us both a little nervous—and suspicious. Though we talked about Mimi's particular problem of living so far down the road, having such a large family, and owning only one bicycle, we again felt that it was not something we could do for one family without offering the same assistance to everyone else in our little branch. It hurt to tell him no, but it seemed the right thing to do.

"We're sorry," we told him, "but we just can't."

I'll never forget his sigh and his sad and resigned whisper, "*Na reira ia.*" Then so be it.

We felt terrible as we watched him awkwardly get on the old bicycle and ride it off down the long dusty road. We eased our

consciences by saying something like, "Now the poor guy probably *will* take whatever money he has and go get drunk."

The next morning, hardly before we had time to get ourselves ready, grab a bite of cooked wheat cereal, and get the narrow little cots we slept on made up to serve as additional benches for our Christmas services, the Oaoa children had begun to arrive. Colette and Florence came first—our favorites, at nine and ten years old. Their older sister, eleven-year-old Olivette, left on the bicycle to go back and bring another load.

We were still just cleaning up our cereal bowls and spoons from the little table out on our veranda when Colette and Florence, bright-eyed and scrubbed, their dark hair neatly braided, came and stood by our table.

"Joyeux Noël," they said in French, beaming, with their hands behind their backs.

Did we dare bring it up or not? One of us did: "Well, did you have a good Christmas?" we asked in Tahitian.

"Yes," they said again, their eyes still sparkling. Papa Noel, they told us, had not forgotten them. They then brought their hands from behind their backs, one girl holding a small tin box of assorted cookies, and the other, an imported package of Ritz crackers.

"This is what we got," they said excitedly.

We nodded and smiled, faking enthusiasm for their new possessions left by Papa Noel.

"But Florence and I have decided," Collette went on, brightly, "and we want you missionaries to have our gifts."

I have relived that moment many times—that moment and those moments the day before—when Mimi Oaoa came with his lame leg and his squeaking bicycle and visited us. Most of the time, I try to forget both of those moments, but it never works.

We kept the cookies. We had to because of the startled looks on the girls' faces when we tried to protest. We shared them as best we could with the whole branch. Whatever was left, I have a hunch, we never finished.

I think often of Tahiti and of that little island of Raiatea. Just the smell of a lime will take me back there. Or the taste of a mango, or the smell of jasmine.

Or the sight and smell and taste of a box of cookies.

Dr. Donald R. Marshall is a professor of Humanities at Brigham Young University, where he is also director of International Cinema. He is the author of four books— The Rummage Sale; Frost in the Orchard; Zinnie Stokes, Zinnie Stokes; *and* The Enchantress of Crumbledown—*and is just completing a new novel.*

ONE MORE CAR

*J.K. "Trapper" Hatch,
as told to Jo Ann Hatch*

I grew up during the Great Depression in the little town of Taylor, Arizona. In those days there were no jobs around Taylor, so when I was seventeen years old, a couple of friends and I decided we would hitchhike the 250 miles to Phoenix to find some kind of work.

It was the first week in December of 1933, and we rode part of the way in the back of a cattle truck. We had to get down between the cows to keep warm.

When we arrived in Phoenix, we found out that there was no work to be had. Many men were standing in lines waiting for the free soup the government was giving out to those in need. You could buy hotcakes for ten cents, but we didn't have a dime; so after a while we joined the soup line.

We looked for work and somehow survived for two weeks; then Christmas drew near. One of my friends had a sister who lived not too far away, and he and my other friend decided to go to her house for Christmas. But I was determined to go home.

Early the next morning, the day before Christmas, I started hitchhiking.

I didn't get to Flagstaff until 5:00 in the afternoon. That was halfway home. The sky was steel gray and it was bitterly cold, with eight inches of snow on the ground. There were holes in both of my shoes, so I found some cardboard and cut pieces to fit inside to keep my feet a little drier. Then I started down the highway again, trying to get another ride.

Since it was Christmas Eve, there wasn't much traffic. It grew darker and colder, and I became more and more dejected as the few cars swished by in the snow and the chill of the night penetrated my thin coat.

By 10:00 P.M. I had become so cold and numb that I began to wonder what it would be like to freeze to death. I was so tired that I knew I'd never make it unless someone stopped soon. Several more cars passed me by, and I had to talk to myself to keep going. "One more car," I said. "If the next car doesn't stop, I'll lie down under a tree and let it happen. One more car."

In a short while I could hear an engine in the distance. "This is it," I told myself, taking a deep breath as I held out my thumb. Swish. The car went by me. I closed my eyes and sank to my knees in total despair.

In my misery, everything was shut out of my mind for several seconds; but then I heard a sound. The car had stopped and was backing up! I struggled to my feet, heart pounding. In the car were two men from my hometown of Taylor. They had recognized me as they passed.

At about 1:00 A.M. I was safely deposited at the front door of my home. I could see there was still a light on, and as I came quietly through the door, there sat Dad and Mom with their heads in their hands, praying. When I spoke I was greeted with joyful cries and tears. Mom told me they had been praying all evening and into the night for my well-being and safe return home.

There were no presents that Christmas. Dad killed an old rooster the next morning, and that was our Christmas dinner. Yet I have never felt the spirit of Christmas more strongly than I did that day as I sat with Dad, Mom, and my brothers and sisters and felt the warmth and love of our family.

Trapper Hatch passed away in April 1983. He was a high priest in the Taylor Ward, Taylor Arizona Stake.

Jo Ann F. Hatch is a family historian and certified genealogist. She is a member of the Pinedale Ward, Showlow Arizona Stake.

CHRISTMAS IN ROME, 1944

Leonard J. Arrington

As a soldier in the United States Army during World War II, I was stationed in North Africa for fifteen months in 1943–44 and in Italy for another fifteen months in 1944–45. This meant three Christmases away from my wife and family. In December 1943, I was in Bizerte, Tunisia, and the primary "treat" for Christmas was a day's pass to Tunis, where I spent most of the day reading histories and listening to the records of favorite operatic arias. The final Christmas, in 1945, was spent serving K.P. (kitchen police) duty for officers and men awaiting their return trip to the United States after the war had ended. Something worth remembering occurred while I was in Rome, Italy, during the Christmas season of 1944.

I was working as a T-5 corporal on behalf of the Allied Commission for Italy, as a "controllore" for the Italian Central Institute of Statistics. Several dozen of our regiment were lodged in a hotel the Allies occupied in that Eternal City. I was friendly with another occupant of the hotel, Corporal Jay Chaffin, a congenial person with interests and values similar to my own. As we approached Christmas in 1944, he suggested that we go to the Vatican for Christmas Eve. There would be important happenings there, he said. So we put on our khakis (it was still warm in Rome), and we walked the several miles from our hotel to Vatican City.

The event was precedent-shattering. For the first time in history, a pope publicly celebrated Christmas Mass at St. Peter's Basilica. One of the greatest crowds in Roman history, an estimated 150,000 Italians and Allied troops, converged on the Vatican to take part in the observance. Not more than a third of these were able to get into the Basilica. Because of the enormous unregulated crowd, there was not only pomp and ceremony, but also some hysteria as families became separated; and women and children screamed as they were bruised and stepped on. There was pushing and fainting. It was a clear, brilliantly moonlit night. As one writer reported, "The dense multitude seethed and swirled like the waves of an uneasy sea."

Jay and I wormed our way through the crowd to get at the center of the action. Despite the surging crowd, this was not hard to do because we were American soldiers, clearly identifiable in an occupied city. Everybody was courteous to us and allowed us to pass forward.

Somehow, in the process of moving up, Jay and I became separated. In getting to the center of things, near the entrance to St.

Peter's, I had gotten into a group of about thirty or forty khaki-clothed soldiers that I thought at first were Americans, but that proved to be former Italian prisoners of war. These were Italian army troops who had volunteered, after the occupation of Rome, to work with Allied soldiers. They had been cleared by our military to constitute a force of volunteers aiding the American war effort. They were also clothed in American khaki, so I was indistinguishable from them.

I did not know what the Italian Volunteers were doing there as a unit, but it soon became clear. There was in process an international radio broadcast program from the Vatican, and the Italian Volunteers had been requested to sing as part of that program. Soon a leader appeared in front of us and motioned us to sing. They broke out with "Tu Scendi delle Stelle"—"You Came Down from the Stars," a favorite Italian Christmas hymn that I had learned while I was with an American prisoner of war processing unit in Ber Rachid, Morocco, during the fall of 1943. There followed another song or two, the names of which I do not recall. The leader of the group then pushed the crowd of onlookers aside as he led us into St. Peter's to observe the performance of mass by the reigning pope, Pius XII.

At 11:30 P.M., or thereabouts, Pope Pius XII entered the Basilica in a procession led by the red-plumed Swiss Guard, as silver trumpeters, perched on the balcony, played a triumphal march. The Pope was carried aloft in the gestatorial chair. The crowd applauded, waved their hats, and shouted "*Viva il Papa!*" ("Long Live the Pope!") The Pope gave his benediction as his procession moved across the Basilica to the central altar, the magnificent Bernini bronze canopy. There, His Holiness put on the golden chasuble and celebrated low mass to the accompaniment of motets sung by the Sistine Choir and Christmas songs sung by Allied soldiers in their own languages. At the completion of the mass, to which the Italians and I were front-line observers, Pius XII himself came down to offer Holy Communion to the several hundred persons around the altar, who included diplomats, Roman nobility, Allied officers, members of the Italian government, and our little group of singer-soldiers. While I was contemplating the uniqueness of the occasion, the Pope was suddenly in front of me. Instead of kissing his ring, as most were doing, I shook his hand, which he gladly proffered. He looked at me genially and said, in broken English, "You are an American, aren't you?" I replied, "*Si,*" and said I appreciated meeting him. He moved on.

There was a certain humor in the situation. Unknown to the Pope and the Volunteers around me, this Italian-speaking American was part of the group—and a Mormon at that!

My feeling of exhilaration was tempered by the wish that I could be home, where I might have spent the evening in a Latter-day Saint meeting, listening to the story of the birth of the Savior given by a

Latter-day Saint brother or sister, and having the opportunity of partaking of the holy sacrament. This was a keen feeling because in all my thirty months in North Africa and Italy, I never was able to locate an LDS meeting in an area where I was billeted.

The Pope celebrated a second mass, which took about half an hour, then resumed his seat in the gestatorial chair and the procession exited, with the Pope giving his benediction to the throng, as once again they shouted and cheered.

It was a long evening, and I did not reach my hotel until about 2:30 in the morning. This happy experience did not occur to my friend Jay, who nevertheless had been delighted with his own presence at the Vatican on that Christmas Eve in 1944.

In recollecting the event, which I have not had occasion to tell publicly, I felt (and feel) nothing incongruous in having been in a group blessed by the Pope. Indeed, I later was present at a papal reception for soldiers, where I took with me two sets of beads for the Pope to bless. I gave one of them to my secretary at the Instituto Centrale di Statistica; the other I brought home with me in January 1946. In the spring of 1945, when U.S. troops moved north to occupy northern Italy, I was stationed in Milan as an Allied representative with the Committee on Price Control in Northern Italy. I remained there until the Christmas of 1945, when I joined a group of soldiers awaiting transportation back to the United States.

During the school year 1958–59, I was appointed Fulbright Lecturer on American economics for Italy and traveled around the country giving talks in city centers, universities, and at special festivals. At Christmastime we were in Rome, where I renewed acquaintances with many friends. There was no LDS congregation in all of Italy at the time, so in our rented apartment in Rome, we had our own family Christmas Eve and Christmas Day celebrations. We were reminded of our Savior by the constant tolling of bells. We felt blessed to sing our own songs and tell our own stories. A day after Christmas, I took our family to St. Peter's, where we watched as the new Pope John XXIII was consecrating bishops. We saw him at close range as he conveyed blessings to us and other observers. We were blessed in being participants in sincere, devout ceremonies.

Leonard Arrington is a former Church Historian and professor of history at Brigham Young University. He is author of more than two dozen books, including The Mormon Experience: A History of the Latter-day Saints *(1979, with Davis Bitton) and* Brigham Young: American Moses *(1985).*

WHAT I WANTED WAS *HOME*

Beppie Harrison

We had always been home for Christmas, until that year. We were both in our early twenties, and each of us had spent every Christmas of those twenty-plus years at home—no, wait, I'm forgetting. My English husband, Geoffrey, had come to the United States as an architectural student for a year. (It was during that year that we met.) But every other year each of us had spent at home until our marriage, and in the two Christmases since then, we had divided our united presence with scrupulous fairness. The first Christmas we spent in Lancashire with his family; the second Christmas we flew back to the States to spend Christmas with mine.

So this would be the third. We were living in London. That year we had bought our own house just off the village green in the suburb of Kew Gardens, but it was still very sparsely furnished. We had a bed, a stove, a refrigerator (a little counter-height one, which was the typical English fridge back then), a rocking chair made from a kit sold by one of the Sunday newspapers, a dining room table made of a flat piece of plywood (supported by trestles) that was painted a wonderfully rich aquamarine green, and four red folding wooden chairs. And we were going to have a baby in January.

We had decided sensibly early in the pregnancy that there was no way in which we could do anything but stay in London for Christmas. The airlines (even if we could have afforded tickets) had rules forbidding the transportation of women due to deliver fairly imminently, so America was out. We did have a little car, but driving from one end of England to the other—London is in the southeast; Lancashire is in the northwest—was slow and complicated. Back then, the motorway network that now keeps much of England in perpetual gridlock was only partially completed, and the traffic that now fills all four lanes in each direction was distributed end-to-end along the ordinary roads at Christmastime. The trains would be equally packed, and that would have been expensive, too. Besides, in the lazy warmth of summer, staying alone together in our brand new home for Christmas sounded not only practical but delightful.

It felt different when Christmas got closer.

For me, the difference began with the Christmas cards. We went out to choose them in early November, as soon as they appeared in the shops. We couldn't afford to airmail the cards to the States, so we had to be organized about it. We had more problems selecting the cards than I had initially expected. One of the adjustments of early marriage was the discovery that my husband preferred architectural purity in design (interior arrangements, furniture, Christmas cards), and I liked coziness, which he described as "stuff." Since he's Lancashire-born, this was pronounced "stoouf" in a gloomily disapproving manner. Trying to find a cozy Christmas card with acceptable stoouf was time-consuming, but in the end, manageable. I don't remember precisely what the stoouf was, but I do remember that part of it was snow. Splendidly atmospheric snow and a great big Christmas tree, just like the Christmas trees we always had at home. A great, big, up-to-the-ceiling Christmas tree.

It was while I was writing the Christmas cards that I remember the first real twinges of doubt that Christmas on our own was going to be—well, was going to really be *Christmas.*

Looking at the cards with the snow and the Christmas tree, I asked cautiously, "Does it snow in London for Christmas?"

My husband glanced over from where he was working on the drawing board balanced at the other end of the plywood dining table and said, equally cautiously, "Dunno. I expect it might sometimes."

"Oh," I said. Snow wasn't really necessary, I told myself briskly. I had had green Christmases. We didn't have to have snow.

The Christmas tree was the next hurdle. We had gone together to Harrod's,

that splendid emporium that sells everything from very fresh fish to nannies' uniforms, trouser buttons, and fine china. Up on the top floor they had their Christmas decorations, and they were magnificent. We chose some of the more modestly magnificent ones—although we could not resist a golden angel suspended within a glass globe. (She lives on our tree still, every Christmas.) This meant that our tree-topping angel had to be very modest indeed, and so she was. But we had a tree topper, which was the important part.

We then went to get the tree.

It was cold walking down to Kew Station, which was where our local shops were. All the way down the curving road that led to the station, I told my husband about how I liked Douglas firs best, because they smell so nice. Wouldn't he like to get a Douglas fir, for our first tree? He didn't say much, which I didn't understand until we got to the shops. Then it all became clear.

Christmas trees in England were then sold by the greengrocers, which meant that you bought a tree along with your potatoes and onions and Brussels sprouts. Once I looked at the stock available, it was obvious that in England a tree was a tree was a tree. There was no choice of tree variety: they were all anonymous. Worse, there were only a few, and those they had were little. At our greengrocer's shop down by the station, it turned out we could choose among about seven or eight very small trees and two taller ones. (The taller ones were less than five feet tall.) One of the taller ones had a substantial gap between the halfway-up branches and the top ones, while the other one had an interesting bend in its spine.

I stood there looking at those two forlorn trees, and all I could see was Christmas-tree shopping excursions back at home, with the whole family spread out around the Christmas tree lot, each of us choosing the absolutely perfect tree and then arguing enthusiastically with everyone else about who had the best of the best. I refocused on my husband, who was watching my face anxiously, and I swallowed everything I was on the point of saying. I beamed—or at least tried to—and pointed at the one with scoliosis.

"That one?" I asked.

He carried it home. (I took the bag with the potatoes and vegetables.) At least we had plenty of ornaments for a tree that size, and the tree-topper angel was very easy to admire. It was right down there where you could see it. If we turned the tree just right, you hardly noticed the bend in the spine at all. And it *was* our very first Christmas tree. Our neighbors on either side (newly married couples, both of them, just like us) came in during the decorating process to appreciate the splendor, and to bring an ornament to hang. Neither couple was putting up a tree of their own that year—they were both going home to spend Christmas with their families—so our tree became the communal tree, shared by all

for the time being, and was extravagantly admired. It was officially declared absolutely lovely.

And so December wound down toward the day. Our packages for the families at home had long since been dispatched, and brown paper packages arrived for us. The ones from my family had customs declarations that had to be torn off and burned, unread; the ones from my husband's family were undeclared but securely wrapped. My mother-in-law believes that any package might spontaneously fall open in the post, so the English parcels arrived swathed in multiple layers of brown paper with sticky tape wrapped vertically, horizontally, and around all corners. Our address was written clearly in large letters on the front, back, and sides of the parcel and on at least two pieces of paper tucked into the inner wrappings so that should all the adhesive suddenly and miraculously fail to hold, the package could still be delivered accurately. And indeed, absolutely intact, it was delivered. So we had presents under our tree.

Christmas Eve arrived quietly. The English are not given to the extravagant lighting displays of American suburban neighborhoods. We did have carolers, but since in England carolers are traditionally given some money by way of thanks, we had one official group that was fundraising for a charity and three or four entrepreneurial children who were clearly bawling only part of a song to raise funds for sweetshop shopping down at the corner. They had scampered further down the street by the time my husband came home from work. He went upstairs to change and, downstairs by myself, I suddenly fully realized that this was what Christmas was going to be: the two of us, all by ourselves. The house lay around us, quiet. I could hear him walking around on the bare bedroom floor overhead, but there were no friendly neighborly noises—our neighbors on both sides were now gone. We were most definitely on our own.

I went and turned on the television, but it wasn't the same. The living room, with the rocking chair and the plywood table— even considering the Christmas tree by the window—seemed bleak and uninhabited. What I wanted was bustle and confusion and voices and rolls of Christmas wrapping paper and people looking for scotch tape and the delicious suspense of knowing that something wonderful was going to happen. What I wanted, I knew with an overwhelming wash of homesickness, was *home.* I was a great big, enormously pregnant, adult woman with a good life and a wonderful husband, and all I wanted was to be back home with my mother and father, and my sisters, and my house, and my absolutely familiar Christmas. I was thoroughly ashamed of myself, but I still wanted more than anything else to sit down and howl with all the abandon of a two-year-old.

I don't remember exactly what happened next. What I do remember is when everything changed.

We had had dinner. We had lamb chops (which we have had every Christmas Eve since) because they were cheap then in England, and because we love them. It was a good dinner. We found some Christmas music on the radio, and, after all, we *were* together. Then the doorbell rang. We opened the door, and there was one of the men that my husband worked with. He had come with three or four of his children. (It was a big Catholic family). They were on their way to midnight mass, but they had stopped by our house to visit and to bring us fresh, home-baked buns and some flowers. They were all clearly having a wonderful time, and everyone was talking at once. Suddenly our house, too, was full of happy voices and noise and confusion and—when they talked about the Christmas mass service they were looking forward to—the knowledge that something wonderful was going to happen.

Some carolers passed by as they were leaving. They didn't come to our door, possibly because we were obviously in the middle of a departure, but they waved from the road. We stood there with our friends, listening to the voices singing of the miracle that all of us were remembering—that Christ came to our ordinary imperfect world to bring us all the promise of love and eternal life. We were all remembering it, in our different ways: the carolers with their song, our families at home, our friends on their way to midnight mass, even my husband and I, working tentatively to establish our own home and traditions.

"Yes," I thought, as the baby, who would a month later be our daughter, chose that moment to thrash around inside me, "this is the important part." Christ was born and brought us the promise of returning to our real home, our only home. Like my baby that was coming, Christ was born. And recognizing that miracle, we can celebrate it in a thousand different ways, and all of them can be splendid. It doesn't matter. Christmas will always be Christmas, wherever it is spent. Whether we celebrate with Christmas trees big or little, stoouf or architectural purity, surrounded by lots of people at home or on our own abroad, even whether there's snow or not, the miracle is the same.

But on Christmas morning that year, as we opened our presents, it snowed.

Beppie Harrison, who now feels at home on both sides of the Atlantic, is presently living in Michigan. She writes books, teaches business school, and celebrates white Christmases with her husband and her four children.

TRAGEDY AND THE TRUE MEANING OF CHRISTMAS

Linda Gappmayer Reed

It was going to be our best Christmas ever. Little did we know that a tragedy would make it one we would never forget.

Dad was a high school geography teacher, and money was scarce. We three children heard the words "we can't afford it" much too often. We could hardly believe it—and certainly had little appreciation for the sacrifices involved—when Dad and Mom announced that we were going to take a vacation at Christmastime.

Even more unexpected was the news that we would be buying our first-ever new car—a yellow 1963 station wagon with mock wooden trim and a luggage rack on top—for the trip. The only items missing were the optional seat belts that Dad had wanted installed before the trip. Since they hadn't arrived at the car dealership in time for our departure, we left without them.

Time and scenery passed quickly as we listened to Christmas carols on the car radio and tried to stifle our giggles and whispers as we speculated about the gaily wrapped packages peeking out at us from their hiding places in the back of the car. I was hoping for what every ten-year-old girl was hoping for that year—a Barbie doll, complete with wardrobe and blue vinyl carrying case. Eventually the rhythm of the road and the stillness of the dark lulled us children into happy dreams.

I awoke instantly, with confusion all about me. I felt as if I were one of a hundred puzzle pieces, tossing and whirling, unable to come together as a whole. I remember screams and cries, the sound of the radio, darkness, and things flying past me and hitting me. When I reached out to try to avoid the jarring bumps, I briefly felt the smooth inside of the roof of the car.

Then, as suddenly as it had begun, everything stopped moving, and for just an instant, there was silence. The road had been covered with patches of black ice, invisible and treacherous. We had hit some ice, lost control of the car, and now we were at the bottom of a steep incline a few miles outside of Lovelock, Nevada. In the darkness of the early morning, I could see that my father was conscious, but was bleeding from several cuts in his scalp. Mother had been thrown free of the car and was unable to move. Paul, the baby, was screaming with fright. I was unhurt. Sam, my seven-year-old brother, was missing.

Dad wiped the blood from his eyes and prayed quickly for help. He and I began searching for Sam, while Mom called out

continually, "Have you found him?" We did, finally, lying in a pile of shattered glass and rock. He had been thrown an incredible distance, taking with him the curved back window of the station wagon. He looked so small and cold, lying very still in his blood-soaked pajamas. The sight made Dad cry out in despair, "He's dead! We've lost him!"

As I looked about, I saw our belongings. One whole side of our beautiful new car was now smashed as flat as an aluminum can. Our luggage had been thrown open, and the contents were scattered all over the hillside. Christmas presents were everywhere, with wrapping paper torn or missing—and I could see the corner of a blue vinyl carrying case where the paper had been ripped away.

In those few moments I grew up quickly. I realized, with a growing sense of urgency, that none of those things mattered now. More than anything, I wanted my family around me, healthy and happy. I was already feeling the sense of loss and incompleteness Sam's passing would leave in my life.

It was not likely that we would be spotted from the highway by a passing car, so someone needed to climb the steep embankment to flag down help. Dad stayed at Sam's side while I climbed up. Ice and snow hurt my bare feet—I was wearing only pajamas—but I was warm inside as I considered the trust that Dad had placed in me. I prayed out loud as I waited several minutes with no sign of other traffic.

When help arrived, it was indeed an answer to prayer. The first car stopped. Inside were a doctor and his wife, a nurse, and they had blankets and medical supplies in the trunk of their car! Seconds later, a truck driver stopped and called ahead for an ambulance.

The doctor examined Sam and found faint, hopeful signs of life. His wife wrapped Paul and me in blankets and treated the worst of Mom's abrasions. Then, while we were waiting for the ambulance, they helped us sort out our belongings and packed them into their car for the trip into town. The ambulance arrived and we were loaded inside, but the drive was no faster than a crawl because of the icy road.

The sun was just coming up as we came into Lovelock. Since a bus had overturned earlier, resulting in several deaths and critical injuries, the hospital was already filled to capacity. Paul was taken to an empty crib in the nursery, and Dad's cuts were quickly cleaned and stitched. Mom and Sam were examined on gurneys in the hallway: Mom had suffered severe ligament damage, and Sam had a badly fractured skull. His open head wound was filled with dirt and broken glass, and the doctors were concerned about possible infection, blood loss, and brain damage. Later, when Sam was conscious, Dad and I were allowed to see him briefly. The doctor asked him if he recognized us. Sam said nothing, but his eyes revealed his fear and confusion.

Dad and I collected our luggage, left the hospital, and checked into a nearby motel, where we washed our dirty, blood-stained clothing in the bathtub. I was still barefoot and in my pajamas, so we sorted through the remnants of our belongings for warmer attire. I found a sweater and a pair of jeans to wear but could find only one shoe. For the next three days, I walked to the hospital and back in my stocking feet— until my other shoe was discovered in the wreckage of the car.

That night at the hospital we were relieved to see that a room had been made available for Mom and Sam, but we were surprised to discover that they had company. Somehow, members of the Lovelock Branch had discovered our plight and had sent us the Christmas spirit. Two brethren had brought a small decorated Christmas tree and gifts for each of us. I received a pink powder mitt made of flannel with a blue satin bow. When I opened it, I cried for the first time since the accident and allowed myself, for a little while, to be a tired, frightened little girl.

The men assisted Dad in administering to Mom and Sam. Through their kindness, the priesthood blessing, and the whisper of love from the Lord, we finally found peace and reassurance. In less than twenty-four hours, our emotions had come full circle, and we were once again filled with Christmas hope.

Looking back, I realize that my father was younger then than I am now. Throughout our experience, he set an example for me of calm strength and faith in the will of the Lord. Although it must have been difficult to face each day with only the companionship of a ten-year-old child, he made me feel useful and important.

Mom and Sam were recovering slowly, but it would be some time before they would be able to travel. Since Dad had to get back home for work after a few days, he made the difficult decision to leave them in the hospital, borrow money to fly home with Paul and me, and then return for Mom and Sam when they were able to travel again.

At home, neighbors and ward members readily stepped in to help. Paul and I were taken into the homes of ward members, and someone loaned Dad a car so he could get to and from work.

Finally, Mom and Sam were strong enough to come home, but they couldn't travel by air. Some friends offered their station wagon and fit a mattress into it. Another friend took time off work to be the driver.

What a joyous reunion we had! Mom was soon on her feet again, and Sam recovered quickly, showing no signs of the trauma he had so recently survived. During a routine checkup several months after the accident, the doctor couldn't believe that Sam had ever suffered a severe skull injury; there was only a small external scar, and the X-rays revealed no internal scarring or

damage. When he saw the original X-rays, he said, "Well, I've seen a miracle!"

My blue vinyl Barbie case was one of the few gifts that survived that Christmas. Today, as I watch my four little girls playing with it, I wish I could pass on to them the other, more important gifts I received that year: a greater appreciation for life and family relationships, faith in my parents, faith in the compassion of friends and strangers, and, most important, faith in God and in the power of his priesthood.

If I could, I would shield my little ones from the hurts of life that will inevitably come to them. Certainly all of their trials may not have the happy outcome my tenth Christmas ultimately did, but I will watch over them and encourage them as they experience both the joys and the sorrows of this life. And I will pray that from their experiences, they too will recognize and accept the best gifts.

Linda Gappmayer Reed, a member of the Stockdale Ward, is currently serving as the Primary president in the Bakersfield California Stake. She and her husband have five children and one granddaughter.

CHRISTMAS IN PRAGUE, 1948: 50-YEAR-OLD REFLECTIONS

Stanley B. Kimball

It was 1948, and I was a twenty-two-year-old missionary living behind the Iron Curtain with my companion in a single room with one window, a small coal stove, and no plumbing. We were lucky to have that. It was in a part of Prague called Holesevice. I had been in Czechoslovakia (now known as the Czech Republic) since that October and was just getting used to the stress of living under Communism. Christmas was approaching. We were also cold; oh, it was so cold. Our room was above a vacant shop, so no heat came from below.

Three other elders and myself had been the last missionaries allowed into the country. Several others were later sent, but not permitted to enter. Because of this, all of us missionaries—elders and sisters—realized how precious and limited our opportunity to tell the story of the Restoration might be. This caused us to draw closer to the

Spirit than we might otherwise have done. Somehow we had to try to offset the counterfeit "religion" of Communism.

The Christmas of 1948 was the first one under Communist rule in Czechoslovakia; therefore, many of the old ways and practices lingered on. While many of the ancient yuletide customs prevailed, there was something in the air signaling that this would be the last of the old Christmas celebrations. Regrettably, a year later, official atheism had eliminated many Czech Christmas traditions, and several months later our mission was shut down. (I was ordered to leave by February 21, 1950.)

The normal Czech Christmas season lasted about a month. It started early, on December 6, *Svaty Mikulas* (St. Nicholas' Day, from which the name Santa Claus comes), and lasted until Epiphany, the traditional day of the arrival of the Three Wise Men, on January 6. On December 6, all the Christmas bazaars opened and people officially started celebrating. Our mission president, Wallace F. Toronto, and his wife, Sister Martha, went along with this custom and hosted a branch party at the mission home in an area called Stara Stransnice.

After light refreshments, it was gift exchange time. The custom was to give small gifts, called "Jesicek" (little gifts from Jesus); therefore, the presents were given anonymously. There was some friendly competition among the missionaries as to who would receive the most gifts. (I received twenty.) I remember one gift was a pair of suspenders. I figured someone thought my pants hung too low. In those days we did not eat very well, for we were issued nonworker's ration books, and non-workers were considered parasites, so I had lost some weight. Once in a rare while, however, we had been served duck or goose, and I wondered just what a proper Christmas feast might feature—pheasant maybe? Well, not exactly.

Sometime in mid-December, members and investigators began to proudly show us their Christmas meal. What we saw was a fish, a carp, swimming around in the bath-tub! Carp for Christmas? This made no sense to me until I learned that a fish had been an ancient symbol for Christianity. (The Greek word for fish is *Ichthus,* and the letters of this word stand for "Jesus Christ, God's Son, Savior" in Greek. I did not like carp—baked, boiled, in soup, leftovers, or any other way at all—but I said nothing. Another Christmas treat I had trouble with was black bread with a quarter inch of goose grease spread on it.

Fortunately, in the mission home in Salt Lake City before we had been sent abroad, a wise physician addressed us. He warned us that we would be expected to eat all kinds of strange things. Then he said, "Elders and sisters, I am now informing you that you are all allergic to many kinds of food. So when you are served something strange in the mission field, you can politely tell the hostess that your physician told you you were allergic to that."

One day we stopped and heard some Christmas carols sung by a group of little girls near a downtown church. It was very comforting for us to know that this was still allowed. I recognized only two carols, "Silent Night" and "Come All Ye Shepherds" (often titled "Old Bohemian Carol"). (Incidentally, the "Good King Wenceslaus" of the carol was a real thirteenth-century Czech king.)

One evening while we were visiting some investigators, there was a knock at the door. There stood someone dressed as St. Nicholas and a small boy dressed as a little devil. The former was looking for good lit-tle children, and the latter was looking for naughty children—naturally, he found none at that address. This had all been pre-arranged by the parents for their two small children, who were thrilled to see St. Nicholas. It was like a visit to Santa Claus in the States.

My companion and I bought a little Christmas tree (maybe two-feet high); then we went to one of the many Christmas bazaars and purchased some Czech-made ornaments and decorated it. (For ages, the Czechs have been famous for their glass work.) We also put candles and sparklers on the tree and very carefully lit them. It was not much, but it helped us remember home and what Christmas was all about. More importantly, it reminded us that we really were in the right place at the right time, doing the right thing. What else mat-tered? The Communists could never take that feeling, that assurance from us—not even when I was shadowed and twice interrogated by the Secret Police. I found an old cake or candy tin somewhere and later packed away my ornaments. (I still have them and put them on our tree every year.) I also bought a cardboard manger or *creche* scene done in the Czech style and displayed it back home for years.

On Christmas Eve, my companion and I walked through the beautiful falling snow, across town and the great Vltava River, through the Disney-esque medieval Old Town, and up Castle Hill to the splendid St. Vitus Cathedral to attend midnight mass. After this beautiful and uplifting experience, where we worshipped with many people of different faiths, we slowly trudged our way back through the snow to our freezing room. We were full of the Christmas spirit and determined to work even harder to spread the message of the Restoration.

The next morning, Christmas Day, we slept in late and then visited twelve families of members and investigators. Every place we went, we had to have some carp and sweet things—what a combination. The kind Czechs always served the best to the missionaries. Among the homes and apartments we visited was one built into the wall of a six hundred-year-old castle, which was exceptionally Middle-Aged and fascinating—except to the people who had to live there.

Finally that evening, all the Prague mis-

sionaries showed up at the mission home, where we had a typical American Christmas dinner and entertainment, including songs, skits, and games. Afterward, President Toronto had a special treat for the missionaries. We went into his office, and he told us we could ask any questions we wanted about the gospel, anything at all. We could even talk about the mysteries, and he would answer us as best he could. (It reminded me of a meeting we missionaries had had in the Salt Lake Temple while in the missionary school.) I felt that I had the best of both worlds. I had celebrated a Czech Christmas with my beloved brothers, sisters, and friends and an American Christmas with our small "American colony."

On one day during this period, I received a CARE (Cooperative for American Remittances to Europe) package of food from my mother. The word went out, and a few days later all local missionaries met with the elders who had the nicest rooms. Everybody brought whatever food they could scrounge up, and we prepared a real feast—and counted our blessings. My companion and I took some of the food back to the people we rented from. Sadly, they could not eat it for it was too rich for them—their daily fare had been so limited for so long.

I shall never forget my two Christmases in Prague, the special spirit we all enjoyed, and our efforts to plant a few good seeds to keep the Restoration alive. Our work was cut short, and the mission closed in April

1950, but we left behind a solid body of the faithful.

After I finished my mission in England, I earned a Ph.D. in East European History with a concentration in Bohemian/Czech studies, and over the years revisited Prague seven times. I did research by day and visited members by night, trying to fan glowing embers into a flame. Over the decades many of the Czech saints held to the "iron rod." Their faithfulness was rewarded when the Czech Mission reopened in 1990. Today there is once again a flourishing Czech Mission, and one of my original three companions from 1948, Edwin B. Morrell, is the president.

Stanley B. Kimball, born in Farmington, Utah, is now professor of Western American History, with emphasis on Mormon Trails, at Southern Illinois University, Edwardsville. He is in the O'Fallon Stake Sunday School presidency.

I WANT TO GO HOME

Janene Wolsey Baadsgaard

I want to go home," Dad said, sitting up straight in his hospital bed then swinging his legs to the side, ready to hop down onto the cold tile floor. "I want to go home."

I wondered if Dad meant his brown brick home in Springville or his heavenly home. I had never seen anyone die before. I didn't know what to expect. I have been present shortly before or after the death of those I loved, but until the Christmas season of 1994, I had never been in the same room when someone important to me took their last breath.

My father-in-law, Esbern Baadsgaard, had been in and out of the hospital many times in the past few years, initially for quadruple by-pass surgery and later for serious bleeding problems caused by liver failure. In 1993, after the open-heart surgery and subsequent discovery of his damaged liver, the surgeon ushered my husband and me from Dad's hospital room into the hall, where he told us the bad news.

"Your father has about a year left," the doctor said. We would not have performed the heart surgery if we had known what shape his liver was in."

At first it seemed a cruel thing to tell us, but after we allowed the news of Dad's impending death to settle in our minds and hearts, we both decided it was a gift—a gift of time and knowledge. We had time to express our love, time to listen to Dad's stories and laugh at his corny jokes. We had one short year to resolve any unfinished business, to forgive and celebrate—a beautiful year to say good-bye.

Mom and Dad Baadsgaard were married on December 20, 1944, in the Salt Lake Temple, a few months before the end of World War II. Now fifty years later, all their seven daughters and only son could make it home for Thanksgiving.

The children decided to surprise their parents with a fiftieth wedding anniversary party that Thanksgiving holiday weekend. They secretly invited Mom's and Dad's extended family members and old friends to attend. We all wrote a tribute to Mom and Dad in the form of personal letters of gratitude. Little did we know that those same tributes—our last gifts—would be used at Dad's funeral just days before Christmas.

Dad was not a man easily given to tears, but he cried openly at the anniversary party that night. He warmly greeted his old buddies with big bear hugs and watched his house fill to the brim and over the brim with grown children and their spouses, his fifty-something grandchildren and great-grandchildren, and a large assortment of neighbors, ward members, cousins, nieces and nephews. Circulation problems had left Dad feeling chronically cold; after the party he said it was the first time in years he had felt warm.

Esbern was a hard-working farmer, bricklayer, and real estate agent by trade. He did not take well to sickness and dependency, but those last few years of health problems softened Dad, and I often heard him express, "My family means everything to me."

About two weeks after the surprise anniversary party and during those hectic pre-Christmas days, we rushed Dad to the Utah Valley Regional Medical Center once again for another emergency. All the medical procedures Dad had endured those past months to stop his bleeding had left his esophagus severely damaged. Bacteria filled his lungs. After the doctors drained his lungs, they told us they couldn't fix him anymore. They took the family members into a private room and told us Dad would die that night.

Once again we were given the gift of time so we could call all the children and grandchildren living nearby to come and say good-bye, to hug their grandpa one last time. Dad was alert and able to respond. We even had enough time to call the two daughters who lived out of state and give them time with Dad on the phone.

My father-in-law was a large, strong man—six-feet-four-inches tall and over two hundred pounds—and not easily affected by suffering. Later that night as the pain and fear grew too great to bear, he reached for his only son, Ross, and humbly asked him for a priesthood blessing.

"I want to go home," Dad said after the blessing as he sat up in the hospital bed. "I want to go home."

My husband, Ross, sat next to Dad on the hospital bed, wrapped his broad arm around his father's shoulders, and gently replied, "We're working on it, Dad. We'll get you there as soon as we can."

Dad relaxed in his son's arms as Ross helped him back into bed and pulled the warm blankets up to his chin. Then Ross reached up and stroked his father's moist forehead, just as he had stroked mine in those anxious hours before I gave birth to our nine children. That's when the gentle realization came to me that our entrance into and exit from this life are sacred moments of light and wonder, but only after the benediction of pain. I wondered if family were gathered on the other side, joyfully anticipating Dad's arrival, as we gathered in sadness to see him go. I wondered also if at the moment of our birth, family members on the other side gather in that same mix of joy and sadness as they watch us leave for our life here on earth. I did not know until that moment that birth and death are so connected, so sacred.

Respiration, heart, and blood pressure readings on the various monitors surrounding Dad's bed gradually grew lower and lower, slower and slower as the hours ticked

by on that long December night. As I watched the mechanical readings in the dim light of the hospital room, I remembered the monitors surrounding my bed as my labor contractions intensified. The monitor readings in those hours before giving birth grew higher and higher, faster and faster. I realized that the same feelings of love, anticipation, fear, pain, joy, and sadness mixed together at both birth and death, that beginnings were really endings and endings were really beginnings, depending on your point of view. In the eternal order of things, there is no beginning or end.

I watched Mom as she sat in a chair next to the hospital bed, cupping Dad's huge hands in her tiny, frail fingers, shaking from Parkinson's disease. She kissed his palms.

"I love you," Mom whispered. "I'm going to miss you, Ez."

Each child and their mate spent the last hours of that long night surrounding Dad's bed, stroking his arms, rubbing his feet, kissing his brow, and quietly whispering words of love and reassurance. There were no dry eyes, for none of us could hold back our overwhelming feelings of loss and gain.

When the nurse discontinued the blood pressure medication at the doctor's instruction, Dad drifted into a deep sleep. His breathing grew slower and more labored as the hours ticked away. He struggled to get comfortable. Finally his breathing gradually slowed, then stopped. In the quiet of the predawn hours, Dad was gone. A reverence filled the room as if time were held suspended for just a moment. As I stood next to Dad's bed and watched him take his last breath, I felt the same gentle peace that surrounds me when I'm standing in the celestial room of the temple.

The nurses asked us all to leave the room while they unhooked Dad from the medical monitors; then they invited us back into the room to linger as long as we desired before the people from the mortuary came. The warmth of his body flowed first from his fingers and toes, then traveled inward, until his body was cold and hard and not like Dad at all. In a breath, what made him Esbern was gone.

The room suddenly felt crowded, as if we were sharing the small hospital space with Dad's family members on the other side. I felt encircled with love. With reluctance, we finally left the room and let him go.

Dad didn't make it home to Springville for Christmas. We spent the holidays without him that year, but somehow even in his absence we knew Dad got his wish.

"I want to go home," Dad whispered just hours before his death.

Now we understand that Dad made it home for Christmas after all.

Janene Wolsey Baadsgaard is the author of Is There Life after Birth?, Families Who Laugh . . . Last, *and many other books and magazine articles. She lives near Spanish Fork, Utah, with her husband, Ross, and their nine children.*

GIFTS OF CHRISTMAS

Shirley Sealy

The large snowflakes were beginning to stick to the roads, and the night lights on the freeway were almost blurred out. I was driving home alone after a memorable brunch party I attended with Lori, our son Dev's wife, and a final day of shopping in the city. I arrived at home a few minutes later, opened the back door, and let myself in. Passing through the front room, I could see the outside Christmas lights still twinkling through the front windows. The shimmering, slender, green-and-gold Christmas tree, laden with presents wrapped in gold paper and shining green bows, was still glowing on the inside too, in front of the big window. I went into our bedroom and found my husband Milt asleep. Changing into my nightshirt and white furry slippers, I made my way back to the front room to sit and unwind on the couch in front of the Christmas tree.

My mind was full of wonderful thoughts. I was still feeling Lori's words as she had told of her most memorable Christmas at the brunch party. At last I had found out the secret of a Christmas ten dollar bill that I had almost forgotten, and about their first Christmas in Atlanta, Georgia, several years earlier.

In October of that year, our son Devro and his wife, Lori, had put their new home up for sale and, with their two small sons, moved to Atlanta, where Dev had accepted a new job. There hadn't been time to sell their home in Utah and still meet the deadline for starting the new job. Dev had found a house to rent, but they had had many unexpected expenses, and the new job hadn't come through with the promises the company had made. They experienced a very difficult time with finances.

"It was the most memorable Christmas we have ever had," Lori said, as she stood up at the brunch. "I will never forget it. We were poor. We had never been so poor, as far as having money and material gifts are concerned. We had barely been able to pay the essential bills, like rent, water, and lights. We had only a little food storage left and no cash. We had each other, we were well, and we kept reminding each other how blessed we were. We knew we wouldn't have a glamorous Christmas, and we knew there was no way we could give the kinds of gifts we were used to getting for our children or each other.

"We knew our parents would help us if we asked or told them, but we wanted to be on our own. We didn't want to borrow any money or have any more debts. We knew we were all right; we just didn't have any money for Christmas.

"When we arrived in Georgia, we immediately became active in our new ward. As Christmas approached, the bishop called and asked us to handle the Sub-for-Santa service assignment that year. There was a family in the area that needed help. They weren't members of our church. The woman was pregnant, they had several children, and the father had been in prison. Dev and I contributed our share to the fund to start the collection of money, food, and material things to give to this needy family.

"At first, I was a little resentful," Lori said. "I didn't think we should be giving to that needy family what we needed for ourselves. No one knew the things we were doing without, but the money and items we collected for that family from friends, neighbors, and ward members were things we needed ourselves, right then. I felt we needed those items as much or more than that family did, but we did the collecting and organizing as the bishop asked us to. We gathered food, clothing, toys, and money and put it all together to deliver to that family on Christmas Eve. Ironically, I was wishing that maybe someone would deliver a gift like that to us.

"In the meantime we prepared our own Christmas. It was the most creative Christmas we ever had. We decorated the house with remnants from past Christmases and bits of colored paper and tree branches. We made the gifts we sent home to our family members out of materials we had on hand. We knew the children were too young to understand very much. We had one little soft toy for Shea that a four-month-old boy could unwrap, hug, and eat. He would be just fine. We had one nice present for Kylee—a Fisher-Price tape player—that I had bought before we moved that summer. He was four, and he would love it. Of course, we would have a few things from exchanging names in the family.

"'We'll be all right,' Dev and I told each other as we looked at our wonderful children and felt the warmth of our rented home. As it came time to deliver our 'Santa's helper items,' Dev and I had everything taken care of except a gift for each other. We decided that we would have to be creative. At the last minute, we were able to squeeze out five dollars each from our bottle where we saved small change for family treats. That's all we had to buy a gift for each other. We made coupon books for each other without the other one knowing; then we added little things we could make or put together and filled our stockings. Mom's letter to Kylee had arrived. It contained a ten dollar bill and a note."

I remembered. Just a few days before that Christmas, as I wrote out a few last-minute Christmas cards, I decided to send one to Kylee. I slipped in a ten-dollar bill and wrote him a little note of instruction:

Dear Kylee,
     This money is for you to take shopping to buy a little surprise for your mother, father, and your little brother for Christmas. Can you ask your mother and father to take you to the store so you can spend this money for Christmas surprises? I love you, Grandma.

"Mom," Lori went on, looking at me, "You couldn't have known, but right then that was the biggest ten dollar bill I'd ever seen. That year we really learned how big a little money can look. We did what you asked and took Kylee to the store. We let him buy a small, inexpensive gift for each of us and himself, then we spent the rest of the ten dollars to make Christmas dinner.

"We were so grateful, but what we felt was only part of what made that Christmas so memorable. Something happened to us that Christmas, as we took our boys and delivered all the things we had gathered to the needy family. A feeling came over us, something we both felt deep inside as we looked into the faces of that family. They were so excited and happy. In a way Dev and I have never really been able to explain, we felt the same kind of excitement because we were part of making them happy, and it made us happy too. It was as if we suddenly began to understand the true meaning of Christmas. We were so grateful that we had a place to live, food, and mostly, each other and our wonderful children. When we left that small dirty house, we were different people than when we arrived.

"We went home that Christmas Eve and read the story of Christ's birth, as we had every Christmas, but now it had new meaning. There was a lump in my throat, and I knew Dev was having trouble with tears too, as we read the Christmas story to each other and our two little boys. I no longer harbored any resentment for giving away what we could have used ourselves. We were grateful to that needy family for what we now felt about Christmas and for what the story meant to us as we read about the shepherds, the angels, and the wise men that visited and brought gifts to the baby Jesus in that lowly manger. The setting of the manger and the cattle lowing had suddenly become very real to us. Mostly, we were aware of how much it meant to have each other. I don't suppose I will ever be able to explain the depth of the feeling we had that Christmas. It is one of those things each person has to experience before he or she can understand.

"That night as we said our prayers together, we felt our Heavenly Father's blessings as a family. We knew he loved us even more than we loved each other. We were a family, not only an earthly family, but part of a heavenly family. We realized so clearly how we were Heavenly Father's children. After our prayers, we put on a record of Christmas carols and tucked the children in bed to wait for Christmas morning.

"We spent Christmas Day at home with our children—just the four of us. I don't think there has ever been another Christmas when we didn't leave our home all day.

We found unwrapped small gifts in our Christmas stockings and the envelopes we had exchanged with coupons for service as gifts. We laughed when we found we had given similar coupons to each other. Dev loved his back-scratch coupon. There was a foot rub, a movie of our choice from the change bottle once it was built up again, a coupon for a breakfast in bed, and a dishwashing break. Many little acts of kindness were pledged to each other.

"After stockings and breakfast, we played games with our children and made things together. We fixed creative food dishes and laughed and took care of each other all day. It was a feeling we enjoyed together that I will never be able to forget." Lori stopped to clear her throat before she went on.

"We have had many wonderful Christmases since that time," Lori said as she wiped her eyes. "We have known times of prosperity with many gifts under the tree. We have traveled to many places, sometimes taking a cruise as part of Christmas with our family, but that one difficult, happy Christmas became a symbol to us of how important it is to be together, no matter where we are or what activity we choose.

"Dev and I recall that Christmas often, and we think of it as the year we found out that money isn't the most important part of Christmas or of giving. Gifts of Christmas are the togetherness of each individual family, plus the feeling of togetherness with

those who are away who send home their
love—that makes Christmas in our hearts.
We feel that perhaps it is close to what
Mary and Joseph felt that first Christmas,
looking at their newborn son. They were
away from home, on their own, when their
baby Jesus was born. He was born in a
manger but brought the gift of peace and
love into the world. They were not gifts of
money but gifts of feeling. We learned quite
a lot about the gift of peace and love on our
first Christmas away from home, on our
own, in Atlanta, Georgia."

The feeling of Lori's story stayed with
me. I felt it now, here, surrounded by the
atmosphere I had enjoyed creating for the
children to enjoy when they came for
Christmas dinner. It was a dinner, I
reminded myself, that had cost a lot more
than what was left of a ten dollar bill.
Would the children and their children, as
they came together in this setting, feel what
I felt as Lori told her story?

"It isn't a feeling of poor or rich in a
material way," I said to myself, as I folded
the comforter and prepared to go to bed.
"It's the feeling of family togetherness,
being together, doing things together in
peace and love. As long as we remember
these are the gifts of Christmas, we can find
them in any circumstance." The thought was
comforting.

It was late and I knew I'd be getting up
early. I walked to the front door and turned
off the Christmas lights. Making my way
into the bedroom, I remembered that I still

had a few last-minute preparations to make
in the morning before the family arrived in
the evening.

*Shirley Sealy is the author of fifteen published books.
She and her husband, Milton, reside in Utah and are the
parents of five children, twenty-five grandchildren, and
seven great-grandchildren.*

An Unexpected Christmas Celebration

Francis M. Gibbons

When Helen Bay and I were married on June 7, 1945, it seemed unlikely we would enjoy the next Christmas together. At the time I was in the Naval Amphibious Forces, stationed aboard the *USS Chilton* in San Francisco, California. Our ship, which had been damaged at Okinawa by a Japanese kamikazi plane, had been ordered to return to the United States for hull repairs. Since the *Chilton* was to be in dry dock for several weeks as the damage was mended, members of the crew were given ten-day leaves in rotation. After I flew to Salt Lake City, we were married in the temple, enjoyed an abbreviated honeymoon, and looked forward to an uncertain future, dictated by the war in the Pacific. The tenacious way the Japanese had waged their defensive withdrawal, island by island, did not augur well for an early end to the war. So when we parted in mid-June, neither of us held any hope of spending the next Christmas together.

Returning to Okinawa, our days were spent providing support for the army in its mopping-up operations on the island, guarding against more kamikazi and suicide swimmer attacks and helping to fill out the details of the plan for the expected invasion of the main islands of Japan. In the midst of this came the surprising news on August 6, 1945, that an atomic bomb had been dropped on Hiroshima. Three days later Nagasaki was similarly bombed; and a few days after that the Japanese capitulated. It was incredible. The speedy end to the war suddenly opened up the prospects of a prompt demobilization and the possibility that we might be home for Christmas, a little more than four months away. It was a heady prospect.

The celebratory mood which settled on the fleet after Japan surrendered was enhanced by a victory dinner served aboard ship. Our cooks went all out to provide a feast. They figuratively cleaned out the pantry in providing a dinner the likes of which none of us had seen while in the navy. It was a time of rejoicing and thankfulness that a terrible war had at last ended, making it possible for those on both sides to return to peacetime pursuits and the simple joys of family life.

However, all this was prelude to a strange happening which no one had expected. Some pilots in the Japanese air force refused to accept surrender. These warriors mounted a series of unauthorized kamikazi attacks on the fleet around Okinawa. When radar revealed the approach of enemy aircraft, all ships were ordered to "make smoke," a maneuver executed by small craft that circled the ships, emitting clouds of heavy, black smoke that hid the fleet from enemy pilots. While this limited the accuracy of the kamikazis, it increased tension among the ships' crews. The smoke had an acrid smell that burned the eyes and hindered breathing. Because it filtered into all parts of the ship, there was no place one could go for relief. When the alert was in force for several hours, cheerful Christmas thoughts were far from the minds of the crew. The situation was made more irksome by frequent newscasts that described the elation at home caused by the end of the war. It was easy to feel deprived.

When the pool of rebel pilots was exhausted, the suicide attacks ended. Then began a delayed celebration throughout the fleet, along with animated discussions about the timing of our return home. There was little agreement between the policy makers and the rank and file in the fleet. We were ready to go home the next day, but there were still chores to be performed to bring the war to a formal end. Aware of the eagerness of reservists to go home, along with their need for a time frame on which to build their plans, the Joint Chiefs of Staff devised a formula to determine when separation from the service would occur. Under this formula, points were earned according to age and months of active service. Then tentative target dates for discharge were set according to accumulated point totals. By

this formula, it was possible I would be discharged near Christmastime, four months away. It seemed unreal to us and was exciting to think about. Helen and I began to make plans. The lifting of naval censorship a few weeks later added a privacy to our correspondence we had not known before and made our planning more personal and specific.

With an end of naval service in sight, the winding up duties given to the fleet did not seem burdensome. Indeed, they proved to be interesting. The *USS Chilton* was the flagship of Commodore Thomas Britton, who directed an amphibious squadron of twenty ships, plus escorts. The squadron's first post-war assignment was to transport a marine division from the Ryukyu Islands to Darien, Manchuria. This voyage took us through the East China and Yellow seas. En route, the Commodore received word that Russian troops had already occupied Darien. He was then ordered to take the marine division to Tientsin, China, west of Darien across the Gulf of Chihli. There we anchored near shore from where the marines and their gear were off-loaded by Chinese lighters. A dense fog shrouded the coast, which prevented even a binocular scan of the area. Also, security concerns caused by the conflict between Mao Tse-Tung and Chiang Kai-shek prevented any naval personnel from going ashore.

Our next assignment was to transport an army division from Okinawa to Korea. In returning to the Ryukyu Islands from

Tientsin, we encountered a typhoon in the East China Sea. The turbulence it created was severe, complicating normal routines. Meals, for those interested, featured canned Spam and bread. Hot drinks were too hazardous to serve, given the lurchings of the ship. Most work was suspended. Sleep was hardly possible. A peaceful calm followed the storm as steps were taken to restore order aboard ship and to prepare for boarding the army division.

There was much excitement as the *Chilton* approached the Inchon harbor on the western coast of Korea. A Korean pilot was taken aboard to guide us through the tricky outer channels as we neared the harbor. He was dressed in a baggy, well-worn suit, white sneakers and an American-style baseball cap. He eyed us with the same curiosity we bestowed on him. Once we anchored inside the harbor, we immediately began the work of unloading. Such haste was dictated by the extreme fluctuation of the tides at Inchon. When the tide is out, mud flats are exposed in the harbor, so a seagoing vessel must work quickly and leave promptly at the risk of being grounded. This oddity made General Douglas McArthur's surprise landing at Inchon during the Korean War even more surprising.

A liberty at Inchon (sometimes called Jinsen) created several mental images, both surprising and enduring—the enormous strength of the lean Korean stevedores working on the docks; the dejected Japanese prisoners, wearing white masks to ward off disease, who waited to board some of our ships; the gracious Catholic chapel, quiet and peaceful, where we removed our shoes in reverence to honor an ancient Asian custom; a German and a Russian whom we met, businessmen who spoke fluent English and who wondered what the war's end would do to their businesses; a huge ox-drawn cart, carrying human waste, winding its way through the city's crowded streets; and the heavily armed troops who did not linger in Inchon, but who moved at once to Seoul, sixty miles inland.

While on the way to the Ryukyus after leaving Inchon, the Commodore received orders to proceed directly to Manila in the Philippines. The purpose was to refit our ships to accommodate Chinese troops. As we entered Manila Bay, with the Bataan Peninsula to our left and Corregidor to the right, we saw remnants of the naval battle that had been waged there, with bare mastheads showing above the water line. On shore, we found the devastation of Manila to be almost complete. Only a few buildings had been left standing from the Japanese air attacks, and these were seriously damaged. All else was rubble. Among the ruins, enterprising merchants had set up tawdry businesses, most of them dealing in cheap trinkets or liquor. One bar, for instance, advertised its fetching "Atomic Revue." Some of these bars were declared off-limits soon after the fleet arrived because they sold poisoned liquor.

Once the ships had been refitted, we

sailed directly to Hong Kong. There we loaded a division of Chinese Nationalist troops and their equipment. Arriving at the docks, we found the troops sitting cross-legged on the ground, their new helmet liners glistening in the sun. Their arrival was complicated by the red tape of British authorities in clearing them to enter the colony. We wondered how we would have reacted if, for instance, we'd had to get approval from a foreign power, as American troops, to enter San Francisco and march to the Embarcadero. The age of these soldiers ranged from the teens to the seventies. Several of them died and were buried at sea on the way to Tsingtao, China. After unloading, we returned to Hong Kong and boarded another Chinese Nationalist Division. It was transported to Chinwangtao, not far from the terminus of the Great Wall of China. Ostensibly, we were returning these troops to the north to be near their homes, but it was reported that within hours after debarking, they were fighting Mao's communist troops inland. Some have wondered how history in the Far East would have changed if the United States had continued to give overt support to the Chinese Nationalist regime as it was doing in the autumn of 1945.

When we landed the Chinese division at Chinwangtao, our post-war duties in Asia were ended. We were then ordered to return to the United States, perhaps in time for Christmas. On the way, we were to stop at Nagoya, Japan, to board American troops who were going home for discharge. It would be difficult to imagine a happier group of men than these. As they boarded, they were jovial, back-slapping comedians. Whatever cares they may have had were swallowed up in the euphoria of demobilization. They were on their way home and nothing, seemingly, could mar their happiness. Two days later you would not have recognized them. They had become glum and snappish. A rough sea had made the change. Our voyage from Nagoya followed the northern Pacific route, which can be turbulent, especially in winter. Two days out, we encountered a series of giant, parallel waves moving southward. When in a trough between two of these waves, the *Chilton* rolled sharply, causing small landing craft griped into the ship at the third deck level to dip into the sea. This and gale-force winds created much turmoil aboard ship. In the chaos, all things not anchored to the deck or bulkheads were strewn about haphazardly. Several men suffered broken bones when they were thrown to the deck or down ladders. Spam and bread again became the menu of the day.

As we neared the Washington coast, the sea calmed, the wind subsided, and the sun came out. With that, our passengers emerged from their gloom. Their joy and celebration were ecstatic. As we neared the naval base at Tacoma, snow-capped Mount Rainier came into view, and a small boat spraying water, with a band and dancers aboard, came alongside the ship to welcome us home. All this created an indelible memory as the *Chilton* listed to starboard when the crew and passengers crowded the railing to see the show.

The *Chilton*'s crowded schedule during its post-war duties complicated mail deliveries. This had made it impossible to advise Helen precisely when I would reach a home port. After arriving in Tacoma, with Christmas only a few days away, I decided not to call or wire, but to surprise her. With a thirty-day leave in my pocket and a few gifts I had purchased for her in Hong Kong stowed in my seabag, I boarded a train in Tacoma, heading for Salt Lake City and the bride with whom I had spent only a week as husband. The thought of sharing Christmas with her and of having an entire month together was a wealth beyond computing. The only regret I had as the train rolled on was that I had been unable to stay long enough in Tsingtao to pick up the teakwood chest I had ordered for her from a Chinese businessman, Joseph T. Zee, whom I had befriended there.

Helen had seen a notice in the Salt Lake newspaper, unknown to me, that said the *USS Chilton* had docked in Tacoma. Excited about the possibility that we would be reunited for Christmas, she had met trains from the northwest for several evenings, hoping to find me there. She had gone early on December 23, 1945, but again was disappointed. When I arrived at the Union Pacific Depot on a later train that night, I carried my seabag to our little apartment on West North Temple across the street from today's Church Museum. When Helen answered the door with tears streaking her cheeks, the months of uncertainty and waiting seemed to dissolve in that first, warm embrace.

In terms of yuletide sparkle, this was a low-voltage Christmas. Helen had decorated a small tree, which sat on the card table we had received as a wedding gift. The apartment was crowded and plainly furnished. There was none of the glitter and abundance that marked some of the later Christmas celebrations in our home. But in terms of love and gratitude for the Savior and his matchless gift to us, and in terms of the joy of being together as a family in peace and security, none can compare.

Francis M. Gibbons, a former secretary to the First Presidency and former member of the Seventy, has written fourteen published books on the lives of presidents of the Church. He continues to write and is now involved in three projects: A historical novel based on the life and times of Martha McBride Knight, charter member of the Relief Society and widow in succession of Bishop Vinson Knight, the Prophet Joseph Smith, and President Heber C. Kimball; a biography of the columnist, Jack Anderson, written in collaboration with a daughter, Suzanne Burton; and a compilation of fifty conversion stories, written with a son, Daniel Bay Gibbons.

CHRISTMAS IN ISRAEL

Kathleen Lubeck Peterson

Frequent flier miles, a gift from a kind friend, brought me to Jerusalem. My friend would be in Egypt much of the time and had arranged for me to share an apartment with a Belgian student, LDS, who was studying at Hebrew University. I was looking forward to a spiritual feast, being in Jerusalem during the Christmas season. I would be writing a couple of magazine articles there, one about the BYU Jerusalem campus presently under construction, and another featuring how LDS teens celebrate Christmas in Israel.

As I took the cab with my friend from Tel Aviv to Jerusalem, I wondered if David, Solomon, Lehi and Sariah, even Paul had passed by the orange groves, eucalyptus trees, and stands of pines I saw on the way. Perhaps they were too new—only a few centuries old. I was entering a dimension where old and new were inseparably mingled, the realization of prophetic words spoken throughout the dispensations of time.

My first glimpse of the city bore the look of an unfinished masterpiece awaiting completion. The landscape was a patchwork quilt of bright new buildings and worn, weathered structures, interspersed with rocky lots and ravines, a jumble left by thousands of years of inhabitants. The city was white with buildings and walls shaped from limestone, the rock mandated by law for all buildings.

The apartment I was staying in was small and spare, but clean and functional. The walls were white, the rock floor cold. To warm the water for a shower, I had to turn on a switch. It took about an hour for the water to warm up. Heat in the apartment came on only from 7 to 10 P.M. It was a cold time of year.

My new roommate, Ingrid, had helped warm up the apartment with symbols of Christmas. She had decorated a tiny Christmas tree sparingly with wooden ornaments carved from olive wood, six silver glass bulbs, and delicate, lacy, silver garlands. A sprig of pine and red pyracantha berries tied together by a red ribbon was hanging on the wall.

I was curious to see what Christmas in Israel would be like. Would I feel closer to the Spirit in the Holy Land as I rejoiced at the Savior's coming to earth?

The next day I went walking through the city. I found no festive twinkling lights, no Christmas trees, no carols being piped into department stores, no advertisements for presents, no Santas spotted anywhere.

I knew then that I would like Christmas

in Jerusalem. None of that was there when the Savior was born either.

Christmas in the Mormon community was its own unique celebration. D. Kelly Ogden, the branch president, invited me to join the branch members at the annual "Mormon shepherds' field" event, an outing taking place outside Bethlehem, where Church members speculated the angels may have visited the shepherds on the night of the Savior's birth. He kindly offered to take me there, so I piled into his van with various other visitors who had decided to attend.

We arrived. The evening air was cool and quiet, the ground rocky and terraced with limestone walls, the hillside scattered with olive trees. The sky was flooded with brilliant gold light, tinged with orange, just as the sun touched the edge of the earth. It looked as if the sun had melted, washing its liquid colors across the horizon. An elderly Arab shepherd, bent with age, staff in hand, walked slowly across the rocky fields, leading a dozen or so shaggy sheep across the uneven terrain. As he leaned into his staff he seemed ageless, as if he could have lived at this time or many centuries ago. The man and the sheep disappeared into the distance.

This night I was thinking of some other shepherds who had been in these fields some twenty centuries ago—the night the angel of the Lord came to the shepherds, and the glory of the Lord shone round about them. The angel said to them, "Fear not: for behold, I bring you good tidings of great joy, which shall be to all people. For unto you is born this day in the city of David, a Saviour, which is Christ the Lord." (Luke 2:10–11.)

That night the angels sang praises to God in the shepherds' field, full of joy that the Savior was to be born, in Bethlehem. This night the branch members would sing with joy. The stars were starting to pop out like diamonds against a black, velvet-lined jewel case. The stillness of the night and joyful purpose of the meeting drew a veil of quiet solemnity over those gathered. It was once again a holy night.

A prayer was offered. A branch member spoke of the significance of these fields where they were gathered. These were the fields where the widowed Ruth had gleaned wheat after faithfully following her mother-in-law, Naomi, to Bethlehem. Ruth was converted and joined Naomi in worshipping the God of Israel. She married Boaz and was the great-grandmother of David, through whose lineage the Savior was born.

The branch president read Luke's account of the Savior's birth, how Joseph went to Bethlehem to pay his taxes, and how Mary, who was expecting a child, came too. I looked over to Bethlehem and marveled at the beautiful, yet cold, hard terrain surrounding us. The wilderness sheltered no romance—it did not portray the symbolic image I had of the nativity scene. The night the Savior was born, I doubt that Mary was sitting demurely veiled in a crisp headdress with the baby Jesus in her arms. I suspect she was exhausted from the traveling and exhausted from childbirth. There was perhaps no hot water, no comfort the rocky soil would yield. Mary gave birth to a child—a painful ordeal even in ideal circumstances—in a cave or area that couldn't have been sterile, and certainly was not quaint.

Yet, her joy must have filled her soul to profound depths as she saw through spiritual eyes the significance of her son sired by God the Father. As the Savior passed through the veil into mortality, so great was the joy in heaven and in nature that the angels slipped through the veil in song and the night sky refused to be darkened.

My heart burst with joy as I sang with saints lit by the brilliance of the fire that night. I wept silently, hoping no one would notice.

I rode back to Jerusalem with Kelly Ogden, thinking of the Savior's birth, his ministry, his death and resurrection, and the centuries, past and future, tied to the day of his birth.

"Tell me about the BYU Jerusalem Center," I said to Kelly. "I've heard there's been trouble."

He told me.

Some people in Israel did not want the BYU Center built. They were Orthodox, observant Jews. I found out later that some were afraid that if the entire nation of Israel were not observant of the Law, the Messiah would not come.

It had not been easy for those closely involved in the construction of the center.

Picketers had been in front of the Galbraith's and Ogden's homes each day (David Galbraith was director of the center). Bomb threats had been made, along with other threats against the Galbraiths and Ogdens.

"We pass it off," said Kelly, "but it's intimidating."

The next day David Galbraith and his son Joel took me to visit the site of the BYU Jerusalem Center. I shot some photos for the article I would be writing. The saints were determined that the center would be finished.

In the afternoon I drove to Bethlehem with a friend. We walked to a church where the Savior was supposedly born. Different parts of the church were run by separate denominations. The interior was dark and incense filled. Later, I read in the newspaper that the mayor of Bethlehem was glad this year that there was no bloodshed during the annual cleaning of the shrine. Typically, the denominations would literally fight over who got to clean it, since cleaning and refurbishing suggested ownership, which was in dispute.

I spent the rest of the day wandering by myself through windy streets of the Old City of Jerusalem. I loved watching the people, Arabs and Israelis. The children of the city captured my heart. Sometimes they were pawns for the parents to make a buck; sometimes they were carefree school children. They were all little charmers, some tougher than others. A group of four girls laughingly greeted me, shouting "Shalom!"

and giggling off down the street. I stopped in a bakery, where the baker pulled an ancient version of an Egg McMuffin from a wood-fired oven, egg cooked over chewy bread, and offered it to me. The McDonalds' version lost by a long shot.

As I walked home, an old man and a young man were drinking tea off in a grove of trees and invited me to join them. I said, "no thanks," and they asked if I were Mormon. I said yes. The young man answered, "You must be David's friend." I nodded.

When I reached the apartment, my throat started aching. The next day, it was on fire. It was December 24. I stayed home in bed and started taking some antibiotics I had brought along.

The Galbraiths had invited me over for Christmas Eve, but I felt too sick to go. They had shown remarkable kindness to me, even though they had known me for less than a week. I left a message on their answering machine that I had to cancel the evening with them. I cooked a can of Israeli chicken soup that did not look appetizing to me. I couldn't gulp it down anyway. I felt cold and tired. I missed my family and clean sheets and a warm house. I decided to go to bed early, luxuriating in my misery.

The phone rang. It was Frieda Galbraith who said, "It doesn't matter if you're sick, you shouldn't be alone tonight. Joel is coming over right away to pick you up," and he did.

There was always room at the Galbraith home. I was not the only visitor there; the house was crowded. The Galbraiths had prepared a turkey dinner for their guests. David said a prayer on the food that evening and thanked the Lord for abundant blessings, the birth of our Savior, and for the Savior's love for each of us.

The group sang Christmas carols. (My throat was too sore for singing.) The Galbraiths then passed out presents, visitors first. They gave me a tiny box wrapped in cheery Christmas paper with two pink soaps inside, and a souvenir rock from the BYU Center.

After the presents had been passed out, David told us that he had just spoken to Elder Howard W. Hunter of the Quorum of the Twelve. Elder Hunter said, "Don't worry about the bomb threats. Your name is in the temple. The Lord is protecting you."

I left the gathering at about nine o'clock, as they were just putting in a video of *It's a Wonderful Life.* I walked the few blocks home in the Jerusalem night, thinking about temples, the warm mantle of the Savior's love that protects us, the stone cut out of the mountain without hands, and the kingdom that will never be destroyed.

When I reached the apartment, it was warmer than when I left—the heat had come on. I snuggled into bed and listened to Handel's Messiah on my Walkman. I wept all the way through it.

Two days later, a story on the BYU Center in Jerusalem ran on Israeli television. It contrasted Christmas carols of peace playing in the Galbraith home with demonstrations against the Jerusalem Center simultaneously taking place in front of the home. That night the Galbraiths' telephone was jammed with calls from outraged Israelis, embarrassed by the opposition to the center. Surely this time there was room in the inn.

Kathleen Lubeck Peterson is a former director in the Public Affairs Department of the Church. She has served on the Young Women General Board and the General Activities Committee, and has written many magazine and newspaper articles.

THE YEAR CHRISTMAS CAME TO ME

Sandra Drake

J ust after I turned twenty-one, I was re-admitted to the hospital for more intravenous antibiotic treatment of an infection that had been plaguing me for five years. I didn't really mind, however, because Christmas was a month away. My doctors would have four weeks to clear the infection. Having spent three of the previous four Christmas seasons in the hospital, I felt nothing was as important as just being home with my parents for the holidays.

Unfortunately, the weeks passed by quickly with little improvement in my condition. On Friday, December 19, my doctors announced that I wouldn't be spending Christmas at home after all. My hope for a Christmas filled with warmth and love seemed to disappear.

At the same time, however, a friend of mine from my hometown of Logan, Utah, was planning an excursion with some youth from her stake to Salt Lake City, where I was hospitalized. Their final destination was to be Temple Square, with its grounds aglow in lights and holiday decorations. Thinking that a detour in their trip might add joy to my Christmas, Rae Louise contacted the nurses who cared for me at the university hospital.

On the Saturday before Christmas, a large group of young women squeezed into my room at the hospital. Christmas carols rang out and changed my frown to a smile. Little did these youth know that their visit was only the beginning of my most inspiring and memorable Christmas ever.

For their concluding number, the youth sang "I Am a Child of God." Tears rolled down my cheeks as I remembered that I, too, was a child of God, that he loved me and would take care of me. Suddenly, just knowing this fact made me feel better about staying in the hospital at Christmas. I wouldn't be home in Logan, but I would be loved.

For family home evening the following Monday night, my sister (who was teaching school in Salt Lake City) and her roommates kidnapped me—with my doctor's permission, of course. For two hours we cruised along the residential streets of the city, enjoying the lights strung from the many rooftops and the nativity scenes on numerous lawns. Though it banged continually against the back window, my IV bottle survived the evening.

Tuesday at noon, my lunch tray failed to arrive on schedule. I didn't think too much about it until fifteen minutes later, when the women from my doctor's clinic walked in with pizza and garlic bread—the works.

After four weeks of hospital food, that pizza tasted good.

Wednesday was Christmas Eve. Though many people had already done much to make my Christmas in the hospital special, I still awoke feeling discouraged. I was going to miss the traditional family Christmas that I loved.

At six o'clock that night, however, my family walked in carrying a ham dinner with all the trimmings. They had brought the dinner eighty miles from home, and I enjoyed it as much as I would have in Logan. While I slept later that night, the nurses brought in my stocking and attached it to my IV pole. It was filled with gifts and goodies, and as always, it had the traditional orange in the toe. Mom and Dad hadn't forgotten anything!

On Christmas morning my family arrived early to open packages and spend the entire day at my bedside. It couldn't have been much fun for them, but I have never heard any complaints about that Christmas. Each of us learned that it is not the glamour and glitter or the bows and packages that are important. If love is shared, Christmas can be celebrated almost anywhere.

Though further infections led to total deafness, Sandra Drake continues to listen from within. A frequent speaker to LDS and civic groups along Utah's Wasatch Front, she currently resides in Logan, Utah.

STRANDED IN A SMALL TOWN

Frank W. Olsen,
as told to Kathleen Olsen

Christmas Eve in Wyoming was about as cold and wintry as late December can be, but this didn't dampen our excitement as we prepared to make the four-hour drive to Spanish Fork, Utah, to celebrate Christmas with our other family members.

It was already dusk when we started out with our four children. The wind was blowing across the empty, rolling hills and the mercury was steadily dropping when, some distance east of Evanston, Wyoming, I saw blue smoke billowing out from behind our car. We stopped immediately. The motor had thrown a rod, and the car could take us no farther. The dark and cold settled down around us.

We tried unsuccessfully to get anyone to stop. Traffic was sparse. The wind-chill dropped the temperature to nearly 70 degrees below zero, and the car was rapidly losing heat. The children were starting to shake from the cold. Kai, our five-year-old son, suggested we pray to Heavenly Father and ask him to send us some help.

Taking my son's advice, we offered a prayer.

After a few minutes a car approached, and my wife jumped out of our car and stood in the middle of the road, frantically waving down the oncoming vehicle. The car stopped, and a man inquired what we wanted. He agreed to transport us into Evanston. All the way into town he kept muttering, "I can't imagine what made me stop—I never stop for anybody along the road."

He let us out at one of the few restaurants still open on Christmas Eve. Calling my father in Spanish Fork, I explained our plight and asked if anyone would be willing to drive to Wyoming and pick us up. He promised to see what he could work out. I gave him the name of the restaurant where we waited.

As we settled into a booth for the long wait, Troy (then seven) wandered over to a neighboring booth and engaged a young couple in animated conversation. Soon our plight became known, and they approached us with an invitation to join them at their motel room, where we could relax comfortably during the long wait ahead.

Who could refuse such goodness? Leaving word of our location with the manager of the restaurant, we headed for the comfort of the motel. The couple, though strangers, opened their hearts to us and showered our children with Christmas treats.

We had just settled the children to

watch a Christmas television program when a knock came at the door. When we opened it, a weather-beaten ranch hand stood there holding a set of keys.

"Here's the outfit for you," he said, nodding to a truck parked behind him.

"What do you mean?" I asked in utter amazement.

"I dunno what it's all about. My boss lady just told me to bring her four-wheel-drive truck in for you to take to Spanish Fork. Just drop it off on your way back through when you get your own rig fixed."

Tipping his hat, he disappeared into the dark wintry night.

Puzzled, my wife and I stared at the keys and at the truck parked outside. Shaking our heads in disbelief, we bid our kind hosts good night and drove out of town to pick up our suitcases and continue our trip.

When we arrived at Spanish Fork, my father explained that after the phone call he had turned to the family and announced that he was driving to Wyoming to pick us up.

"No need for that," said my Uncle Charlie. "I have a friend just outside Evanston who will help. I'll just call her."

He called an elderly widow who owned a large sheep ranch and explained the situation to her. She agreed to help, wished him a Merry Christmas, and sent a ranch hand into town with the truck.

For us, it was a night filled with unexpected, unforgettable acts of service from many people, for we were strangers, and they took us in (see Matt. 25:35). Their many thoughtful acts on that cold winter night many years ago were gifts of Christmas kindness that have warmed our hearts and brightened our memories ever since.

Frank W. Olsen serves as Scout committee chairman for the Kanab Sixth Ward, Kanab Utah Kaibab Stake. Kathleen Olsen serves as Laurel adviser in the Benjamin First Ward, Spanish Fork Utah West Stake.

CHRISTMAS AT CHINA BEACH

Marion D. Hanks

Christmas, and the warmth and wonder and sweet memories and tender emotions it recurrently awakens in me, is always associated in my grateful mind with home—the home I grew up in and the homes our family has been blessed to live in and enjoy across the span of major oceans and many years.

Of tenderly recalled events that occurred far from American shores during the holiday seasons, two come back into focus on the bright screen of recollection as the remote control focuses on faces and occasions out of the past.

One picture: a tiny, nearly toothless, teary-eyed refugee mother looks with wonder in her eyes at a gracious lady missionary from Utah, who (with her companions) was in the refugee camp in humanitarian service. They were there offering cultural orientation and helping these tragically offended people learn English in order to be qualified for life in America, their land of promise. They had fled from their own country, the home, the village in which they lived, which none of them expected to ever see again. Many of them had lost family as "boat people" and they were reliant and totally dependent upon these attractive, young foreign ladies for help to prepare them for a future for which many had long since abandoned hope.

This day, Christmastime, they have witnessed the sweet pageant portraying the journey far from home made by Mary and Joseph and the baby Jesus. Like many others in these last-stop camps along the Thailand and Cambodian borders, the refugee mother had not heard this account before. So her comment to the lady missionary from Utah who played the part of Mary, tenderly rocking a little brown baby selected to represent the Jesus child, is fully understandable.

"Why," she said, "this story of Jesus and his folks is a *refugee story,* isn't it! Those people must not have known who Mary and the baby Jesus were or they would have given them their bed!"

How gentle and moving that memory.

Another event that most forcefully focuses on my recollection screen with thoughts of home and Christmas occurred in Vietnam on the day before Christmas Eve at the height of that sad war. I had spent the full month between Thanksgiving Day and Christmas with our Latter-day Saint troops and their friends from one end of Vietnam to the other, sustained by President McKay's personal charge to me when I had visited him at his invitation prior to leaving for Southeast Asia. Warmly and tearfully he had congratulated our family for supporting and encouraging their husband and father in this assigned undertaking far from home. He understood the challenge of our separation from each other in our young family, and the importance of the visit in encouraging and comforting our troops in their much more lengthy and difficult absence from loved people and places at the holiday season. President McKay said, "What an honor for you and your wife and little children to have you making this difficult journey at this holiday time!"

President McKay had given me an encouraging message to convey to our troops, and at a special meeting in northern South Vietnam I endeavored to deliver that message to a large group of LDS servicemen and friends assembled for this holiday gathering. Some of those in attendance were called on to speak in the meeting. One of those who spoke provided a highlight for me of many choice experiences over years of association with our people serving in America's military forces in Europe and Asia and elsewhere in the world.

The Mormon officer who spoke that night was serving as commander of a gunship squadron and had been particularly pleased as a personal friend to learn well ahead of time that I was coming to meet with them. He reported that the previous day, after his unit had fulfilled a very difficult assignment and he was preparing to leave for the eagerly anticipated LDS meetings, he was summoned by his superior offi-

cer in the battle area and told that his group had just been called to meet another emergency. He responded to this announcement with a strong protest. He reminded his commander that he had been cleared to attend these Church meetings. He was told that this order was not an option. It had come through the chain of command. His unit was assigned to the line, and he went angrily out to join them.

Our brother shared with us as he reported in our meeting that night that he felt he perhaps had approached his unit too gruffly as they prepared for their assignment. The men were all standing near their aircrafts waiting for him to issue orders to begin the dangerous mission. The blades of the whirlybirds were rotating when the commander was approached hesitantly by a young enlisted man from the crew of one of the airplanes. He brusquely asked the crewman why he had not boarded his plane.

"Sorry, sir," he said. "Some of us were wondering whether you've had time to pray this morning."

Humbled by the nature and spirit of the question, the commanding officer replied that, yes, he had had time to talk to the Lord.

"Thank you, sir," said the young man, relieved. "The guys and I hoped we wouldn't have to take off on this mission before you had had time to pray."

There had been no overt prayers or conversation with the group and no sermon or lesson on the subject, but the word was out among the men that their outfit had something special going for them because their commanding officer was a man who prayed to God. They believed they had been helped on that basis, and they were blessed again on this assignment.

Everyone present joined Major Allen in his emotional sharing of this memorable moment.

In our special Christmas meeting that night, two handsome young men—boys, really—their rifles in the nearby stack, stood before this large group of their comrades at China Beach, near DaNang, South Vietnam, and sang "Silent Night." They had no accompaniment, but the sweet, clear ring of their voices touched every heart. Tears flowed freely and eyes were averted as emotions were touched with thoughts of home and loved ones.

Not many hours later that night there was a faint knock on the door of the private quarters assigned to me. I was organizing notes and messages to be dictated early the next morning and conveyed out of the country to a faithful secretary, who would transcribe them for delivery to the homes and families of the men who had been present at the meetings.

There at the door stood one of the young men who had sung so sweetly that night. He had his helmet on his arm. He was fully equipped for a "search and destroy" mission, grenades hanging from his belt, rifle in hand. He apologized for awak-

ening me and I replied that I would not have heard his soft knock had I been sleeping. He then explained that these missions were always perilous and very difficult. Then he said, "Brother Hanks, I wonder if I could shake your hand one more time before I go." I put my arms around him and blessed him and sent him on his way.

It was not the Sabbath activity he would have chosen; he was disappointed not to be able to worship with fellow Latter-day Saints in the scheduled meetings that day; but he went out to fill his assignment. I returned to my bedside to plead again with the Lord for these dear, young, loyal agents of their God and country.

With the dawn, I again began dictating notes to parents and wives and children, reporting my visits with their loved ones in our special worship services the day and night before.

Across the earth over the long span of years I have since met many of those loved ones, who mentioned with gratitude the comforting assurance that their dear one was yet alive and well and participating in sacred worship.

Marion D. Hanks was called to serve in the First Council of the Seventy in 1953 at age thirty-one and served thirty-nine years before being made a General Authority Emeritus in 1992. Since that time he has continued to inspire and lead the work of local groups seeking to provide community service in Africa, the Philippines, and other Third World countries.

JUST THE RIGHT GIFT

Lillian Thatcher

It was three days before Christmas, and shoppers were hurriedly buying the perfect last-minute gifts. There was an almost tangible air of festivity all around, with Christmas music playing in nearby stores and with street lights and store windows colorfully decorated with pine boughs, holly, and mistletoe.

My mother and I were going shopping, trying to find "just the right gifts" for our families. I was carrying my warmly wrapped baby as we got out of the car and walked along Main Street in Logan, Utah. The ankle-deep snow crunched under our feet, and the icy wind caused our eyes to water.

Suddenly we noticed a young girl, maybe fifteen or sixteen years old, running down the street in our direction. As she approached, we saw in her arms a tiny baby, wearing nothing but a diaper and an undershirt. The young mother herself had no coat, only a thin white T-shirt and blue jeans. The baby not only had no other clothes on, but did not have a blanket either.

It seemed almost unreal and created a "what's wrong with this picture" feeling—the stark contrast of warmly dressed shoppers laughing and talking with each other, carrying colorful packages, music playing, and sparkling decorations all around, and in the middle of the scene a young mother and baby, alone and in tragic circumstances, running almost unnoticed through the crowd. It was so shocking and unexpected that it took a few seconds for the reality to register in our minds.

My mother and I both stopped, our mouths gaping in astonishment, as the young mother came nearer, her head bowed down protectively over her baby, her small young hand trying to shield the baby's ear and head from the bitterly cold wind.

As the young girl rushed past us, my mother lashed out angrily at her, "Why don't you even have a blanket on that poor little baby—it's *cold!* What is the *matter* with you that you would bring a tiny baby out like that?"

The girl looked up briefly, her eyes frantic and worried, and she gestured with her head to a Greyhound bus at the corner. "I've got to get on that bus!" she cried breathlessly.

She had no suitcase, no diaper bag for her baby, no belongings whatsoever. We watched as she boarded the bus, just as it pulled away. We kept watching, speechless, until it turned the corner and went out of sight. We turned to each other, horrified at what we had just seen. We realized that any mother and baby out on the street in bitter cold without a coat or blanket, running frantically to catch a bus, must certainly be in a desperate situation.

My mother, wiping tears from her eyes, said, "Oh, that poor girl—and that cold little baby."

We stood there on the street corner trying to think of all the possible circumstances that might have brought the young mother to this point. Was she leaving home at Christmas—or trying desperately to get back? Had she been running for her life from an abusive boyfriend or husband? Was she a young runaway, having left home because she was pregnant and afraid to tell her parents, but finally at rock bottom and desperate enough to go home? Or was she in some kind of trouble, fleeing to the next town to live on the streets, homeless and alone in the world, doing what she could to feed herself and her baby?

We hoped that wherever she was going, there would be someone to meet her with warm embraces and welcoming smiles— and help. We knew that the probability of this was unlikely. Whatever the circumstances, this young mother and baby needed our *assistance,* not our criticism.

"Oh, why did I say those things to her?" my mother cried as we talked about the various possibilities. "Why didn't we think to give her this warm flannel quilt Lisa is wrapped in. We had another quilt in the car!"

I added, "And our coats, we could have given her our coats!" We both had others at home.

"I had twenty dollars in my purse I could have given her!" my mother said tearfully.

Everything had happened so fast that we hadn't had time to think clearly, but we both felt sharp regret that we had failed to give a helping hand to someone so obviously in need. We had made matters worse with our harsh criticism and had "kicked her when she was down."

I like to think that given a few more seconds, we would have thought to run after her and offer our assistance. We could have taken her to our warm car or home while we tried to find resources to help her with her problems.

This sad incident was burned into our memories; it haunted us for years. My mother's grief over the plight of the young mother and her baby did not dim, and gradually I began to realize why. It was because my mother had seen herself in this young woman's desperate situation.

My mother, too, had been alone, recently divorced with two young babies during the Great Depression. It was a time of mass unemployment and general poverty and despair. An excellent nurse, my mother had found work in a small hospital, but her meager paycheck was not enough to hire a babysitter while she worked twelve-hour shifts. She did the best she could by parking her old car near the window with her two little ones in it. While she worked, she went to them frequently to feed and comfort them, trying to keep them warm and safe. The memory of that time was so painful that, even fifty years later, she wept whenever she spoke of it.

Especially at Christmastime, whenever we passed the corner where we had seen the young woman, my mother would tearfully recall the incident and wonder what happened to her. We would discuss it again, and each time we would feel new regret that we had done nothing to help her. We would ask for the hundredth time, "Why didn't we hand her that warm quilt and the diaper bag and our coats?"

Until the peach-colored quilt that my baby had been wrapped in finally wore out, my mother would see it on her visits to us, pick it up, clutch it to her, bury her face in its softness and say, sorrowfully, "Wouldn't that little mother have loved this quilt?"

Often, the best gifts come without wrapping. The most wonderful gift we could have given that Christmas would have been a helping hand, an understanding heart, a used coat, and that warm flannel quilt.

These simple things would have been "just the right gift."

Lillian Thatcher is a registered nurse; she and her husband, Robert, are the parents of six children. After living for twenty-five years in Logan, Utah, they recently moved to Salt Lake City.

FIFTY YEARS AGO: MEMORIES OF THE CALIFORNIA MISSION AT CHRISTMASTIME, 1948

James B. Allen

The Christmas season of 1948 was truly special for me. Not that I had never been away from home for Christmas; in fact, I had just spent three years in the U.S. Navy. On September 6, after I had served in the California Mission for just over two months, my companion, Elder Grant Carlisle and I attended a special meeting in Carlsbad. There, President Oscar W. McConkie called the missionaries to begin immediately traveling "without purse or scrip." We needed more faith, he explained, and the Spirit told him that this was the way to accomplish it. The next day we were to give up our apartments, store our baggage wherever we could, and take off, as I wrote in my diary that night, "for parts unknown." We were to "wear" ten dollars (i.e., keep some money in our wallets), so that we would not be picked up for vagrancy, but we were to rely totally on the people we met for the food we ate and a place to sleep. In exchange, we were to give them the gospel. "It is rather strange," I also wrote, "to think that right now I have no idea whatsoever where I'll sleep tomorrow night. This experience is certainly going to humble us all and teach us to put our faith and trust in the Lord." By Christmastime I could think back over the past four months and see President McConkie's promise literally fulfilled. Those thoughts were especially strong at a remarkable missionary conference held in Los Angeles just before Christmas.

There is not enough space here to tell all the stories related to our missionary work, but there is enough to set the tone for what happened at the conference. On Sunday, September 19, I wrote the following in my journal. The entry, unfortunately, is all too sparse—but at least it catches the spirit of what was happening:

> Well, it's now been two weeks since we started without purse or scrip, and it's been quite an experience so far. It is strange to start out early in the morning, not knowing where we're going to eat or sleep that night. The first night out we slept in a tool shed, in which there was an old bed fixed up. By contrast—last Wednesday we slept in a mansion way out in the country. And it was really a man-

sion—we had a large, beautiful bedroom, private bathroom & shower, private outdoor veranda—and the lady of the house sent her little dog to wake us up the next morning.

> This has certainly made us do a lot of walking. We average ten miles some days, and in hot California, that's no picnic. . . .

> As far as missionary work goes, we are making a lot of friends and meeting a lot of people. In the course of each day, however, it's easy to become discouraged because there are very few people who will be interested enough to invite us in and talk to us. And, of course, it's sometimes after dark before we find a place to stay that night.

If such an entry sounds a bit discouraging, it is only because of the physical difficulties we sometimes felt. The entry really masks the deep spiritual growth that gradually came to me, and I assume, to all the California missionaries as we worked our hearts out to fulfill what was expected of us. Elder Carlisle and I worked, for the most part, in rural areas, ranging from Escondido, where we were officially assigned, to Julian, a little town way out in the eastern hills of San Diego County. We made friends, worked with missionaries from another district to open up a little Sunday School for investigators in Poway, and eventually got our own Sunday School started in Santa Ysabel, a tiny community not far from Julian. The remarkable thing to me was that no matter where we were, Elder Carlisle and I never went without a place to sleep, nor did we ever miss being on time to a meeting or an appointment—no matter how far away it was. We were not allowed to hitchhike. We could only walk along the road hoping someone would pick us up. Invariably, even if our meeting was twenty miles away and we thought we might not make it, someone would stop and ask us if we wanted a ride, and we would get to our destination on time. On December 12, I noted: "I haven't gained any weight lately. Neither, however, have I lost any, so I'm satisfied. The Lord has been very good to us."

We did not have a lot of baptisms, compared to what is happening in the mission field today, but the friends we made for the Church and the deeply spiritual, sometimes miraculous, experiences we had gave me much to think about at Christmastime and made me appreciate the gospel more than ever before in my life. Though we were invited to eat and sleep in a palatial home once in a while, more often we spent our nights with humble, ordinary folks who were truly interested in what we had to say, even though not many joined the Church. I will never forget the marvelous evenings spent in the humble home of Brother and Sister Bailey in Santa Ysabel. After our first contact, they invited us to come back often. Our bed was a fold-out living room couch, and our meals sometimes consisted of nothing more than bread and gravy, but to me

the meal was a feast. The love of the Baileys for us and for what we were teaching them filled every void. We soon got permission to open a little Sunday School in their home. They did not immediately join the Church but finally, in June 1949, they were baptized. The joy of that occasion, for all of us, simply could not be matched.

I suppose that all the California missionaries had experiences such as these, for by the time the December missionary conference came along, they were ready for one of the most spiritually uplifting meetings they (or, at least, I) had ever attended. It was the conference that made that whole Christmas season so memorable.

It was held in Los Angeles on Friday, Saturday, and Sunday, December 17–19. The first day was a fast day, and the meeting, which lasted from 8 A.M. to 4 P.M., was a testimony meeting. All two hundred missionaries, it seemed, were filled with the Spirit, wanting to tell of their experiences and express gratitude for their blessings. From the moment the meeting began, two or three missionaries at once tried to get the floor, and President McConkie finally had to designate who would be the next speaker. It took me five tries before I could bear my testimony. "Many missionaries," I wrote in my journal later, "told of miraculous healings, of being led by the Lord to someone who needed the gospel, of miraculous help received while traveling without purse or scrip, and many more inspiring and faith-promoting experiences and testimonies. . . . I saw a number of missionaries sitting there with tears in their eyes as they heard these testimonies, and even I, as hard-hearted as I think I am, felt moisture in my eyes a number of times during all the meetings."

Our Saturday meetings consisted mainly of instructions from President McConkie—instructions that I thought were both powerful and inspired. On Sunday morning Elder Carlisle and I went to church in a Glendale ward, after which our host took us to visit the famous Forest Lawn cemetery, with its outstanding "Last Supper" stained glass picture. On Sunday afternoon, President McConkie conducted another testimony meeting, which lasted for three hours with sometimes six or seven missionaries at a time trying to share their testimonies.

Words on paper cannot really capture the power we felt at that conference, but how appropriate it was that such an experience came just the week before Christmas, when we would celebrate the birth of the Savior, whom we were there to serve.

The following Saturday was Christmas, but in a way it was anti-climactic. Earlier in the week we made our way back to Santa Ysabel, where we visited the Baileys. We were delighted that they were reading the Book of Mormon and that they had a lot of questions we could answer for them. We spent Christmas Eve and Christmas Day at the home of the branch president, where I probably bothered some people as I spent

several hours learning to play the new harmonica someone gave me. The following day I even talked with my parents on the telephone. All this was wonderful, but what really made this Christmas season special was the fact that in taking seriously the challenge President McConkie had given us on September 6, I not only grew in spiritual strength, but I knew more fully than ever before how precious the gospel of Jesus Christ really is and how important it is to share that knowledge with others. This was another Christmas away from the home and family that I loved, but it was also a Christmas fully at home with the love of Him whose birth we celebrated that day.

James B. Allen, a native of Logan, Utah, received his Ph.D. degree from the University of Southern California in 1963. He taught in the seminary and institute programs of the Church from 1954 to 1963. He joined the BYU faculty of religion in 1963, and then moved to the department of history in 1964, where he stayed until he retired in 1992. From 1972 until 1979 he also served as assistant Church historian. He currently volunteers his time at the Joseph Fielding Smith Institute for Church History at Brigham Young University. He is the author of The Story of the Latter-day Saints *(with Glen M. Leonard), as well as numerous scholarly articles on the Church and western American history. He and his wife, Renee Jones Allen, have five children.*

On Movin' On

Emma Lou Thayne

Saturday, December 13, last year was not easy. It was the day to put up Christmas. And I did not like it.

It started in an empty house. Never had Christmas come quietly, so having not a soul around to breathe it in and put it up was more than strange. Mel had to go to a meeting and three out of our five daughters lived away. The other two had busy days of their own just as I had had at their stage, with young children and preseason rushing to do it all.

Mel set the quite beautiful, pungent fir in the usual corner and dashed through the path of its needles, inhaling his skim milk and banana on his way to the car, waving.

And there we were, the tree and I, in that quiet chaos, wondering what in the world to do with each other.

Music. That had to be the answer. Turn through the house the 1962 stereo, played till it needed pliers to work its switches. Out with the Christmas records, the choir, the strings of the Philharmonic, Barbra Streisand, the Carpenters. They were warm and scratched with familiarity. And they were a disaster. In their grooves lay little-girl voices and candles for Santa, Patty Play

Pals and new skis, bikes painted in secret places, beds refinished for surprises on Christmas morning.

"Joy to the World" rang through another time. I was in the same house getting ready for our moving in on a Christmas Eve twenty-nine years before, me in my paint coveralls in an echo-y living room, bare then of carpet and drapes, like the fir in the corner; projects arrayed like packages; my still-little family asleep; me young and able, working into the night alone with possibility and preparation, listening in some very happy region to the joy indeed and to "Beautiful Savior" on our old portable hi-fi.

That Saturday morning, "Jingle Bells" and "It's Beginning to Look a Lot Like Christmas" sent me frayed and rumpled downstairs for stashed goods in the storage room piled with girls' wedding gifts still waiting for places to live. The light seemed too dim and me too short to tell which boxes were full of old ornaments and which of new. Always someone else had rummaged and reached, pulled down and carried up to me balls or demitasse and miniatures to boughs, the stockings to mantel, the creche to prominence. Now my cheek, injured that summer before, hurt bending down, my back, fused fourteen years ago, ached carrying up.

The record that flopped onto the others to invite the wobbly needle was the Jay Welch Chorale singing "Do You Hear What I Hear?" Marilyn Wood, my crazy, wonderful friend, was singing on it, the last gift she and Dick brought to our door the Christmas before she died of cancer six and a half years ago.

I set down the carton of Santa mugs, their eyes washed away after twenty-five years of hot chocolate, and attacked the job of balancing the cookie tree and its twelve days of Christmas as Johnny Mathis and "I'll Be Home for Christmas" told me that Megan, our youngest, could not be home this year, and nothing anywhere was the same.

I sat at the kitchen table, strewn with Christmas lists and empty places, and let despair flood me with tears. I was sixty-two, and coming back to life was excruciatingly different from a year ago, let alone from five, twenty, or from thirty-seven years before, when on the twenty-seventh of December I had been a bride off to California with a new husband and a life full of every kind of promise.

Seven months earlier, in May, that now-older husband had had heart surgery, a triple bypass. One day we were playing tennis, and he was short of breath; two days later an angiogram showed his left main artery ninety-five percent occluded. At any moment, he could have had a heart attack that most certainly would have been fatal. But he was saved. By making some changes, big ones, not only in those arteries, which someone else changed for him, but in his diet, and his way of life.

When he was barely recovered, just before the Fourth of July, I'd had my encounter with a crowbar that crashed through the windshield into my face and temple, barely missing my eye. I was riding along the freeway with our son-in-law, Jim, returning from camping with his family and Mel—Mel's first outdoor adventure since his heart surgery. Suddenly, my whole life changed. That crash, a split in the windshield, my hand full of blood, eight fractures in my face, temple, jaw. No one believing that I could have survived. Plastic surgeons put together the eight fractures around my eye and in my cheek, temple, and jaw, using screws and plates, most of the surgery done through my mouth to avoid scarring. But scarring was the least of my concerns. I wanted to be alive and able to see. And to be around, with my family and those precious others, for a lot of July Fourths and Christmases to come.

So this was one heck of a way to start spending a day, let alone the whole Christmas season, maybe forever, feeling sorrier for myself than I ever could remember. I felt drowned in deprivation, victimized by time. I hated it.

As usual, it was people who saved me. I wrestled myself to the phone, found a dear friend dying to put up someone else's tree, since she never liked to for herself in her house alone. I called oldest grandkids Nick and Richard, twelve and ten, offering eggnog and the fun of hanging ornaments from Siberia before emptying the Ping-Pong table for a game.

In half an hour all of us were humming "Rudolph" and "Away in a Manger" as we scurried new candles into old holdings and scolded reluctant light clips onto prickly branches.

Of course there was not enough time. They had to leave, and I had to meet a man at my studio to fix my ailing computer printer. We left a terrible mess of straw from the manger, unusable bows, boxes to be loaded back downstairs, the half-arranged tree skirt and stockings. But it was all right. All that could be cleared up easily. We had launched the present season, and they had saved me from the past.

But more than that had happened. By evening, when I had been at my keyboard working, even half seeing, on *Russia,* a two-and-a-half-year, five-hundred-page project—had taken time to be alone in a fashion that made sense—I came back to the mess cleared up by Mel, home in late afternoon from his meeting and keyed up by it for new ways to operate his business and his life. He'd always helped, with changing diapers, wringing out floods, making Christmas happen. Despite his busyness away from it, that home has never been anything but very much his too, and he has attended me with loving regard and companionship. But time had stalked his moments there like a starving tiger. And, born of his parents' Depression mold, fear—of depletion.

We talked about change, aging, and spending, mostly about the shutters in the living room that I had ordered and put up without his knowing—a total switch in the way we had always managed. We have very different ideas about spending at any age, always have had. He wants to have money to save; I figure resources are to spend, personal or monetary. And my father's motto, "Things work out," also out of the Depression, had kept me buoyant even in the days when we were too student-poor to own a stove with an oven.

Now we are in a new place and time. And we'd better look at how we expect to spend ourselves on it before it spends us into depletion and tears. We must each do what we do and be who we are, alone as well as together, or growing old in the same household could be like the pulling of blinds for one or the other—or both.

I have always recognized that, thanks to Mel and his ways of earning and saving, I am a privileged woman, never needing to work for financial security, only for the wholeness in the working. And the luxury of having earnings that I can spend for surprises like a snowblower—a welcome convenience given his ailing back—or a cabin on the mountain or shutters for the living room. More, I have had the health and energy to work hard at home to earn that prerogative of working wherever else demand and fancy have taken me. Meanwhile, we both—and the household—have benefited in my being able to operate mostly from home, thanks to Mel. Now we sidle into a new era.

No, I will not have children to decorate

with, nor my committee of daughters to cook with, nor a husband, well but nervous even in a time of plenty and semi-retirement, not headed out the door to the office. Neither will I have the litheness to go for the low boxes or branches. And certainly I can't expect a return in anything but memory of other capacities and dears from a past I so adore.

What I have now is a life I have waited far too long to harness, given me indeed by Grace. What I can do is what I can do best, what I have learned about from all those sixty-two years—using my head and my heart and my fingers where my strength and circumstances and even temporary incapacity will no longer let me. Gratefully and without guilt. Yes, even with a lovely modicum of serenity in the means and joy of finally being free to choose.

Of course I can cook if I want to, or put up a tree, or clear up a mess. Goodness knows I've served my apprenticeships, have loved the serving and the learning how. But I realize I'm simply accepting now what I've raced toward every day of that other lifetime—a chance to be the self that has waited to come alive.

Beyond that, after my accident, when I couldn't read, work, or put my face down for several months, I learned to listen to a distant music, to pay attention as I never had to the divine in humanness. I had been to another home and had returned. I wanted a life trimmed and useful in new ways. What I had to give was different from

what it had been. And the same had to be true for Mel.

Unlike a woman in her home, Mel and my brothers have the right to retire from offices and labs, not to take on what they did at thirty-five or even fifty. All too often women are expected—or, more truly, we expect it of ourselves—still to be playing in that playhouse we fashioned in our twenties. Only with no dolls to be put to bed, and yet the routines that included the dolls to be continued.

Time is short and days precious. This Christmas season I will not do things the same as I always have. I will spend myself more on ideas and promulgating them than on open-faced sandwiches and distributing them. Peace on earth, good will to all must be more than a Christmas bromide. "And let it begin with me" must be in my heart and in my home if peace is to be a valid concern anywhere else in my life or my world. That peace must be part of everything I am in on. Yes, even in a lovely modicum of serenity—of faith and having enough to give away.

I will have more of my grandchildren, one at a time, to talk and spree with than in hordes to try to get through to. Not that I would ever want to miss the celebrations or catastrophes, no matter the size, that involve my people. But I will enjoy more time year-round with my family and friends without crowding, either in time or numbers, and let that be the gift to both them and me at Christmas.

Most of all, I will enjoy the accessible silence of these years—if the phone doesn't ring—a silence that lets my head loose and my heart find its way to new settlings that I realize I've waited too long to explore.

Grateful for the resources and the inclination, I would like to stay solvent by spending myself on what is yet to come. It just may be the only way to grow older without growing old. After all, at sixty-two, what in this world do I want to save for?

Today I am young again, intrigued by a future that tells me, regardless of anything, that I would not go back a finger's worth. Not even for a Christmas like those in our home movies, even on video now, that we never seem to have time to see all the way through. I like now. And I like that Mel is able to be a new part of now, to enjoy as he never has the fruits of his so eloquent labors over the years. Life is just beginning for both of us.

And I love the privilege of getting to be in on it alive and almost well—and wiser by far than I was thirty-seven years or even twenty-four hours ago.

Come home for Christmas, everyone who can. Be as always part of me and my house that is not your home as it used to be, any more than it is mine. But oh, how I love it to be filled with you. You'll play your violins, piano, and flute for me; and I'll probably cry as I always have when you play "Danny Boy" and "Silent Night" and "Movin' On." But it will be all right. We'll have a just fine time together—and apart. And not one tear will be for what waits out there for all of us—a new year and a new way to go. As I'm very certain it was meant to be.

Emma Lou Thayne is a widely published poet and writer living in Monument Park Third Ward in Salt Lake City with her husband, visited often by five daughters and sons-in-law and nineteen grandchildren. She authored the words to the hymn "Where Can I Turn for Peace?" with music by Joleen Meredith, and is fed by friends of many faiths around the world. This story was originally published in As for Me and My House *(Salt Lake City: Bookcraft, 1989).*

THE CHRISTMAS OF CHOICE

Sherrie Johnson

This is a Christmas story, but it began on a hot July 24 that started out like any Utah Pioneer Day with a parade and a celebration at the park. The rest of the day wasn't so ordinary. By the time the sun went down, I'd given birth to our second daughter, who arrived two weeks early, and my husband, Carl, had been drafted into the United States Army.

Ten days later, Carl left me with a good case of postpartum depression to go to Fort Lewis, Washington, to be trained as a soldier. I was twenty-one years old, and this had not been part of our plan for life together. It was 1969, and all around us lives were being ended and changed by the Vietnam War.

For the next five months, I lived alone with the new baby, Talena, and her sister, Laresa, who was fourteen months older. Slowly the lonely days and nights, filled with fears both real and imagined, passed. Finally, Carl came home for Christmas, packed us up, and drove us to San Antonio, Texas, where we lived while he completed his medical training.

Together again, we became more hopeful, but questions still hovered like ghosts over our lives, haunting everything we thought and did. Would Carl be sent to Vietnam? If so, would he return? I'd had a close friend killed in Nam, and we knew others who had lost their lives there. In addition, many of our new friends had been to Nam. It was encouraging to know that soldiers did come back. However, each of them was still battling terrible psychological wars. At any social gathering, the conversation eventually turned to the atrocities they had witnessed and endured while in Nam. Many were overwhelmed with the fact that they had killed other human beings—something so foreign to their natures that it was torturous to live with.

We listened and waited for what everybody said was inevitable, but to our surprise, Carl was miraculously assigned to stay at Fort Sam Houston. We relaxed and began making plans to finish our time in Texas. That was a mistake. Four weeks later, Carl received a letter telling him to report the next morning for new orders.

That night every story we had heard about Nam came back to us. Assaulted by raw emotions, we spent the night praying, and crying, and praying some more.

The next day I waited, jumping at any sound, ornery, tired, unable to concentrate on anything. Finally, the phone rang. I listened as Carl explained how he and two hundred other men and women had arrived, been given packets with orders, and marched into a room where the sergeant began giving instructions as to when they would ship out and how to prepare for Nam. The sergeant was about ten minutes into the lecture when a soldier sitting next to Carl whispered, "Hey, your orders have an APO address. You're not going to Nam." Just then the sergeant stopped. "Oh, I forgot," he said. "Five of you aren't going to Nam. If you have an APO address, you're excused to report to the desk where you'll receive your instructions."

At the desk Carl was told he was going to Bremerhaven, Germany. That night we were again on our knees, this time with gratitude and tears of joy.

The next few days tumbled with decisions. The girls and I could go, but since Carl would not be serving a full tour of duty in Germany, the Army wouldn't pay our expenses or let us live on the base. When he was drafted our salary had been cut by more than half, and we were barely making it financially. I had lived alone and couldn't even think about doing it again, so before Carl left for Germany, he drove us back to Utah. The girls and I stayed there with my parents until I sold everything we owned in order to buy airfare. Five weeks later, after a traumatic thirty-six hour journey with two children and eighty pounds of luggage, I arrived in Bremerhaven. It was a cold, cloudy Sunday morning, the Sunday before Thanksgiving. We had nothing—not even an idea as to how we would make it through the next year—but we were together and that's all that mattered.

Carl had found us a quaintly furnished apartment, but it would not be ready for three weeks. The Joel Johnson family came to our rescue and let us stay with them. Another family, the J. C. Connells, invited us for Thanksgiving dinner. People in the branch loaned us dishes, and we were able to borrow a high chair and bedding from the base.

The weeks passed and we moved into our apartment. The last year had been turbulent. We had plummeted to the depths with worry and fear and soared to the heights with joy and gratitude. All of our friends who had been drafted, without exception, had gone to Vietnam. I could not possibly take for granted the blessings of being together and Carl's having escaped the war. However, as we began to settle in, I experienced another low.

It had been more than twenty-five years since World War II, but I was surprised to find that some people had never stopped fighting. One day I walked into a bakery and asked for a loaf of bread. As I spoke, the shopkeeper turned away. I assumed he hadn't understood and repeated my request. This time he straightened and glared into space with icy eyes. "We would have won the war," he spit the words through clenched teeth, "if we hadn't been bound by the Versailles Treaty you Americans imposed on us."

Stunned by his intensity, I left.

After a few of these encounters, I was

almost afraid to speak in public, and yet I understood. Besides the war that had filled Germany with hatred, there had been years of "ugly Americans" plaguing these people. Most of the Germans who were angry had their reasons. Still, I felt helpless and frustrated. I wanted to say that not all Americans are bad, that I held no ill feelings, and that if we could let go of the past, the future would be brighter, but I had trouble asking how much an item cost—let alone expressing any emotion. All I could do was smile and hope my feelings could be seen in my eyes. However, the people who were filled with anger refused to look me in the eye.

What I had thought would be the end of the emotional roller coaster turned out only to be a new ride. Carl's shift work meant that I still spent some long days alone. We had no telephone or even a stroller to take Laresa and Talena for a walk. The apartment included a television, but everything was broadcast in German. On the other hand, the new sights, sounds, smells, and tastes were exciting. I loved the storks on rooftops, the bellow of the ships in the harbor, the church bells on Sunday morning, the spicy mustard, the clop of horses on the cobblestone street. Nevertheless, as Christmas approached, I began to miss my parents, brothers, and sister.

Mother always made Christmas such an occasion! There were traditions and decorations and music and food and especially the warmth of a close family. I was homesick. I wanted to be back in a safe place where peo-

ple loved me. This was intensified by our financial situation. We decided we would have to do without a tree or decorations and that we wouldn't give each other presents. We did splurge, however, and bought the girls one small toy they could share.

Despite the way I clung to the feeling of gratitude at being together, the closer it got to Christmas, the more I began to feel sorry for myself. I throbbed with feelings of guilt. Thus, the pity and guilt teetered back and forth until I was dizzy. Finally, three days before Christmas, I told Carl that I had to have a tree. I needed something to make it feel like Christmas, more like home. I'd go without bread or eggs, but I had to have a tree. He agreed, and we counted our coins and walked to a tree lot several blocks from our apartment.

When we arrived, we were at a loss as to what to do. We didn't know how to ask for the cheapest tree on the lot, and we had found that the Germans thought every American was rich. Sometimes when they knew you were American, they would raise the price. There was no way we could pay more than the three marks I had in my hand.

We walked around the snowcovered lot and finally found the scrawniest tree we could. Surely it would be the cheapest. We took it to the salesman. He was old. Obviously he'd lived through World War II. I approached him timidly and asked how much the tree cost. He smiled, and I relaxed. His eyes glistened gently under thick gray eyebrows as he answered, but I couldn't understand what he said. I asked him to repeat it and patiently he did, but still I couldn't understand. Finally I held out my hand and let him take what he wanted. As he did, I was overwhelmed with the desire to speak to him, to respond to his kindness. I stammered a moment watching my warm breath rise in the cold air. "Danka. Danka," I repeated over and over, hesitating to leave. I could tell Carl was feeling the same. We nodded. The man nodded as if he, too, wanted to speak, but there were no words. It was Christmas, the time of peace and love and good will. As badly as we wanted to share those feelings, we couldn't. In frustration, we turned and began to walk away. Behind us we heard footsteps and knew he was following. Tears began to well in my eyes and I prayed to be able to say something—anything—when suddenly a word from my grade school days came to mind.

I stopped and turned back. "Gesundheit. God bless you," I said. His face broke into a smile. "Gesundheit," he repeated softly and waved as we walked away with the feeling that somehow our hearts had been eternally tied to his.

We took our tree home and propped it in a corner since we had no tree stand. I spent the next four hours excitedly threading popcorn to make a chain for a decoration. I had never made one before and didn't realize how hard it is to keep the popcorn from breaking. Finally, with needle-pricked fingers, I proudly wound the chain around the tree. To add the finishing touch, I wrapped aluminum foil around three cardboard toilet paper rolls and hung them on the tree.

While I was making the popcorn chain, the missionaries had come by. An hour later we answered the door and found a box of ornaments. I put the six glass balls on the tree and thought it was the most beautiful tree I'd ever seen. Somehow it represented everything good from the past year, and I had to tear myself away from it to make supper. I had been in the other room only about fifteen minutes when I came back to steal another look at the tree—and discovered that the girls had eaten every single piece of popcorn, leaving only the black thread. My first thought was to cry, but then I looked at the thread and toilet paper rolls on what had to be the scrawniest tree ever and began to laugh at how out of place the six beautiful glass ornaments looked. Now, more than ever, it was a symbol of our past year.

The next day, the operating room staff at the hospital where Carl worked was having their Christmas party. Even though I wasn't invited, I was excited. It was the only Christmas party either of us would be going to, and Carl would get a Christmas present—the only Christmas present either of us would receive besides those my parents had given us before we left home. The people in Carl's unit knew he was LDS and that he didn't drink. They also knew he was the only one in the unit that had children. I don't think, however, that they knew how little we had or what the Christmas present meant to us. At any rate, Carl came home that day with the news that for his gift they had given him a bottle of wine. They had laughed and thought it was a great joke. He had left the wine under the Christmas tree and had come home empty handed.

On Christmas Eve, Carl had to work a twelve-hour shift from seven P.M. to seven A.M. I played with the children awhile, read them the Christmas story, said prayers, put them to bed, then climbed into bed myself, but I couldn't sleep. Every time I closed my eyes, I'd think about home and what I knew my family was doing. I was the oldest and the only one married. The others would be gathered in the family room after a turkey dinner; a fire would be blazing; they would be unwrapping a pair of pajamas, putting the wrapping in the fire and dressing in the pajamas. Then they would line up in front of the tree for a picture, read the Nativity, have family prayer, giggle and joke as they arranged a plate of cookies and a glass of milk for Santa; then they would go to bed and fall asleep listening to the hum of mom and dad's voices. Here I was without even enough pans or money to bake Christmas treats! Tears filled my eyes and then the horrible guilt feelings came. How dare I be so ungrateful when I had been so blessed? That night, I couldn't stop the self-pity even with that thought. My feelings coasted up and down as I lay in the dark waiting for seven o'clock to come.

Suddenly the doorbell buzzed. I looked at the clock. It was 11:00 P.M. Who would be coming at this time of night? Frightened, I got out of bed and wondered what to do. Outside, the street, which was normally quiet at this time of night, was full of drunks and rowdy celebration. I waited, shivering. The doorbell buzzed again. Still, I was unsure what to do. I heard rattling against the second-story window pane. Someone was throwing pebbles against the glass. My heart raced as I ran to the window and peeked out. Standing on the cobblestone street, two men bundled in hats, coats, and scarves waved to me through the falling snow. It took a moment before I recognized Brother Connell and a friend. They yelled for me to come downstairs. By the time I got to the door, they were gone, but on the porch was a large cardboard box. I carried it upstairs and found one present for each of us, a card game for the family, and some Christmas goodies.

I put the wrapped gifts under the tree and then curled up on the couch and cried. There is no way those families will ever know how much those small gifts meant to me. For a long time, through a blur of tears, I stared at the tree with its black thread, gilded toilet-paper cardboard, and six beautiful baubles.

At first my mind was full of everything we had endured: worry, fear, war, poverty, injustice, bigotry, and hatred. But then other thoughts began to come. The Johnsons' hospitality. The missionaries. The man at the tree lot. The members of the branch who had shared with us in love.

As I looked at my tree—an evergreen tree—I remembered that it was a symbol of everlasting life, but without water my tree was turning brown. The floor was covered with falling needles, and the ones still on the tree were brittle. My scrawny little tree was dead and so was my innocent perception of the world.

Somehow I understood that I was at a crossroads in my life. I could dwell on the dead tree, believing in the reality my eyes at that moment could see and ignoring the unseen promise Christ had given me of a life after death. I could choose to be bitter at the injustices of the world, the hardships we had been forced to endure, the unkindnesses. Or I could look to the Savior, whose birthday the tree celebrated, whose light our friends reflected, and trust in His promise that somehow, some way He would eventually make everything right. He would dry every tear, comfort every sorrow, mend every broken heart, correct every injustice, eliminate every frustration, reunite every loved one—but most of all, He would establish peace.

That cold Christmas morning, in a city still plagued by the wars of men, I chose the Savior. I have never regretted it.

Sherrie Johnson has published sixteen books and more than one hundred articles and short stories. She lives in West Bountiful, Utah, with her husband, Carl; they are the parents of ten children and eight grandchildren.

NEXT CHRISTMAS IN BETHLEHEM!

Daniel H. Ludlow

"Next year in Jerusalem!" has been the cry of the Jews since they were forced from their sacred lands in the first centuries after the crucifixion of Jesus Christ. This same cry also became my personal wish shortly after Israel became an independent nation again in 1948—"Next year in Israel. Next year in Jerusalem."

My insatiable desire to visit Jerusalem was not fulfilled until 1963, when I visited the Holy Land for the first time during the spring and summer months. At that time Israel was still a land divided. Most of the areas immediately around Jerusalem were still part of the Hashemite Kingdom of Jordan, including Jericho to the east, Ramallah immediately to the north, and Bethlehem immediately to the south. I had arranged to visit these Arab-controlled areas before entering Israel, since I knew it was impossible to visit on the same passport any of the Arab lands after having visited Israel. Jerusalem itself was a divided city, with the eastern section in Jordan and the western section as part of Israel.

My 1963 trip to the Holy Land was

followed by another in 1964. After another visit in 1968, the trips became annual, and by 1972 they had become semiannual. By then my old wish of "Next year in Jerusalem" had faded somewhat, and my new wish was "Next Christmas in Bethlehem."

The wish to be in Bethlehem at Christmas time was not realized until 1973. That year, the Brigham Young University Travel Study Department chartered a stretch DC-8 airplane to take 250 people, including six tour directors, to visit Israel. The itinerary called for all of the groups to arrive in Israel on December 24 and to be in Bethlehem on Christmas Eve. My wife, Luene, and I were privileged to be chosen as one of the tour directors to accompany the group.

The official title of the tour was "Christmas in the Holy Land, December 22, 1973-January 1, 1974." The eleven-day tour included visits to both Greece and Israel, and the itinerary for the first four days provided the essentials of the events leading up to our two visits to Bethlehem:

> *December 22, Saturday* (Salt Lake City/Athens): Depart Salt Lake City for Athens on charter flight #31502 at 12 noon.
>
> *December 23, Sunday* (Athens): Arrive Athens at 13:30 and transfer to hotel. Balance of day free (sacrament meeting). Dinner at hotel.
>
> *December 24, Monday* (Athens/Tel Aviv/Jerusalem/Bethlehem): Break-

fast at hotel. Morning tour to Acropolis. Take El Al flight #31419 at 13:00 to Tel Aviv. Arrive at 14:45 and travel to hotel in Jerusalem. Dinner at hotel. In evening take bus to Bethlehem.

> *December 25, Tuesday* (Jerusalem/Bethlehem): Breakfast at hotel. Morning tour of old city. *Afternoon tour of Bethlehem.* Dinner at hotel.

So, at long last, the day arrived for my visit to Bethlehem on Christmas Eve, and I was looking forward to the fulfillment of a life-long dream. As indicated in the itinerary, the day started with a morning tour of the Acropolis in Athens, followed by a plane flight to Tel Aviv and then an hour's bus ride to our hotel in Jerusalem. Although everything went according to schedule, we had very little time at the hotel—just enough time to eat a quick dinner and then change into warmer clothing for our short seven-mile trip to Bethlehem.

To help you appreciate (or at least better understand) the description of the events on this particular Christmas Eve, the following facts might be useful:

> The Christmas season is one of the highest peaks of visits by tourists to Israel, along with Easter and the Passover.
>
> The small village of Bethlehem lies in the tops of the hills of Judea, about 2,700 feet above the level of the Mediterranean Sea, which is some fifty miles away.
>
> In the northern hemisphere,

where Israel is located, the days of late December have the fewest hours of daylight of any days of the year.

The weather in late December in Bethlehem can range from moderately cool to downright cold, with occasional winds and rainstorms possible.

The weather on that Christmas Eve of 1973 was inclement. Wisps of brisk wind and occasional rain made the already chilled air even colder. By the time our bus approached the outskirts of Bethlehem, we found the road ahead of us clogged with tourist buses of every size and color. We parked about one mile (the equivalent of eight Salt Lake City blocks) away from our destinations—Manger Square and the Church of the Nativity. Manger Square is located in the heart of Bethlehem, bordered on two sides by businesses related to the tourist industry, on a third side by the local police station, and on the fourth side by the Church of the Nativity. This church is one of the holiest spots in all of Christendom since it is built over the cave where it is believed Jesus Christ was born of His Virgin Mother, Mary. The square usually serves as the parking lot for visitors to the holy sites in Bethlehem, but on Christmas Eve the square is reserved for the numerous choirs that come from throughout the world to perform on this holiest of nights.

As our group left the warmth and protection of our bus, we found ourselves in a drizzling rain on an already darkening night, with a wind that seemed to cut through our light coats. As we headed toward the small town, we immediately discovered we were competing with thousands of other tourists who were wending their way along the narrow roadway up toward the top of the ridge where Bethlehem is located.

Some of us who had been there before had the advantage of having in our mind's eye what might await us—the rather spacious Manger Square with armed Israeli soldiers standing guard on the rooftops surrounding the square; a crowded Church of the Nativity with a long line of people waiting to visit the Grotto of the Nativity; the relatively steep and narrow steps leading down into the grotto, with equally steep and narrow steps leading out of the grotto on the other side; the small, cramped confines of the grotto, where only a few visitors are permitted to enter at one time.

In retrospect, I have wondered what might have been in the minds of those who had never been to Bethlehem before and who were now waiting in the rain for their very first visit. They had plenty of time to wonder, for the crowd on the narrow road was soon compressed into such a mob that it was virtually impossible to move forward. In fact, those moving along the road at a snail's pace were just as apt to be pushed from side to side, or even backwards, as they were to move forward.

Soon, simultaneous communication with our entire group proved impossible; we were able only to shout a message to the nearest tour member and have it passed along. (This was before the introduction of individual headsets for participants in BYU tours!). Fortunately, our group had previously been organized into seven "family" groups, ranging from five to eight members each. A "family" leader was responsible for keeping his members together and for giving an accounting of his group when its name was called out. (Appropriately, the chosen "family" names of the groups were Adam, Eve, Enoch, Jacob, Moses, Ruth, and Jonah.)

The minutes that ordinarily should have been sufficient for the walk to Manger Square turned into hours. As midnight approached, we finally made it to the edge of the square. It then became evident that we would never be able to work our way even to the outside of the Church of the Nativity, let alone proceed into the grotto itself.

Finally, the decision was made to try to get the group back to the bus, where at least we could have protection from the weather and could discuss the importance of the events of the night we had come here to commemorate. Before we left the bus, I had instructed the driver to turn it around so we could leave as soon as possible after our return.

It was after midnight when we gathered again in the bus and the driver was able to depart from Bethlehem on a side road. I directed the driver to a location about one mile north of Bethlehem, where we could

have a good view of Bethlehem from the bus. When we arrived at this spot, the rain had ceased, so we left the bus and seated ourselves on rocks on a hillside that has since become known as "Mormon Shepherds' Field." There the peaceful, calm spirit of Christmas soon permeated and engulfed the group, as we read by flashlight the familiar scriptures pertaining to that first Christmas, and sang from memory the verses of the hymns and carols concerning the birth of the Holy Child of Bethlehem.

The next day, as scheduled, we returned for our regular tour of Bethlehem, walking leisurely around Manger Square and visiting the Church of the Nativity and the sacred Grotto with moderate-sized crowds from other touring groups.

Since 1973, I have read and pondered the experiences of some of our Church leaders as they visited in the area of Bethlehem. President David O. McKay recorded his visit to Bethlehem on Tuesday, November 1, 1921, as follows:

"Although it was nearly 3:30 o'clock, we concluded that we still had time to drive to Bethlehem, six miles south of Jerusalem. . . . The cold west wind blowing this afternoon and evening made us realize more keenly what hardships Mary would have endured had she entered Bethlehem 'late' as we were. . . . Fortunately for her, it was in the month of April." (*Cherished Experiences from the Writings of David O. McKay*, Clare Middlemiss, comp. [Deseret Book Co.: Salt Lake City, 1955], 120–21.)

President Spencer W. Kimball recounted the visit he and Sister Kimball made to the Holy Land with Elder and Sister Howard W. Hunter:

"On Christmas Eve we were mingling with thousands of religionists and curious from around the world. We bent over to get through the small aperture into the Church of the Nativity and inched our way in turn to the crypt where some churches claim are the sacred spots of the manger and the birth of the Savior. . . . We [went] to the hill overlooking the shepherds' field. . . . Before us is the undulating area where shepherds once watched their sheep. On the brow of the hill is a cave opening out over the little valley. There, tradition says, the shepherds slept and watched on that eventful night. An open cave could protect them from the night's coolness, yet still they could watch their flocks. There, gazing into the valley, the only place near Bethlehem where we could find privacy, we stood in the dark, looking out into the starry sky as did the shepherds. . . .

"We seemed to hear singing in unison, the never-to-be-forgotten melody, the cry of the ages: 'Glory to God in the highest, and on earth peace, good will toward men' (Luke 2:14).

"As the strains of the heavenly words merged with our hearts, we four sang. After singing, 'Far, far away on Judea's plains, shepherds of old heard the joyous strains,' we stood close together in the star-lighted night with our wraps pulled tight about us—physically close, mentally close, spiritually close, emotionally close; and we communed. No lights but the twinkling lanterns in the heavens, no sound but the whispering of our subdued voices. Our Father seemed to be very near. His Son seemed close. We prayed. More in unison than a single voice, our four hearts poured out love and gratitude that rose to mingle with the prayers of all mankind that night." (*Ensign,* Dec. 1980, 3, 9.)

President Gordon B. Hinckley recorded his visit to the Bethlehem area with President Harold B. Lee in 1972 as follows:

"We . . . journeyed to Bethlehem, not with apprehension as did Joseph and Mary; but, with appreciation for the marvelous events that occurred here. In our minds again, we saw the shepherds in the field, and heard again the heavenly chorus. We, too, in thought and contemplation, visited the manger and marvelled at the condescension of God, that He, the Creator of Heaven and Earth, should be born in circumstances so humble." (*Church News,* Dec. 16, 1972, 5.)

Christmas in Bethlehem in 1973 did not turn out exactly the way I had dreamed and hoped, but the memory of the experiences and feelings in shepherds' field, where we seemed to sense the actual presence of our Savior, will be cherished forever. Also, I gained some valuable insights from the experience: you don't need to be in Bethlehem, nor with large crowds, to feel the true spirit of Christmas; and, as the Savior promised, "where two or three are gathered together in my name, there am I in the midst of them." (Matt. 18:20.)

Since 1973 I have spent several Christmas Eves in the fields of the shepherds near Bethlehem, and each time I have felt the true spirit of Christmas. I have also felt this spirit in the same fields in early April (which is the true time of the birth of the Savior as revealed to Latter-day Saints—see Doctrine and Covenants 20:1), when the temperatures and climate are more moderate and when appropriate scriptures and songs can turn the thoughts readily to the birth of the Son of God.

I have now visited Israel more than sixty times. During each visit I have gone to Bethlehem and to the other major sites associated with the birth, life, mission, and atonement of Jesus Christ. Each time I thrill as I visit these traditional sites and sense a spiritual feeling. However, I have also come to appreciate and more fully understand the remarks of President Spencer W. Kimball regarding visits to these places, including Bethlehem:

"To visit the places where such momentous happenings affected the eternities of us all was most interesting and intriguing and added color to our picture, but we did not need to walk through the Holy Land to know eternal truth.

"We realized it is not so important to know whether Mt. Hermon or Mt. Tabor was the transfiguration place but to know that on the summit of a high mountain was held a great conference of mortal and immortal beings where unspeakable things were said and authoritative keys were delivered and approval was given of the life and works of his Only Begotten Son when the voice of the Father in the overshadowing cloud said: 'This is my Beloved Son, in whom I am well pleased.' (Matt 17:5.)

"Not so important to know upon which great stone the Master leaned in agonizing-decision prayers in the Garden of Gethsemane, as it is to know that he did in that area, conclude to accept voluntarily crucifixion for our sakes. Not so needful to know on which hill his cross was planted, nor in what tomb his body lay, nor in which garden he met Mary, but that he did hang in voluntary physical and mental agony; that his lifeless, bloodless body did lie in the tomb into the third day as prophesied; and above all that he did emerge a resurrected perfected one—the first fruits of all men in resurrection and the author of the gospel which could give eternal life to obedient man.

"Not so important to know where he was born and died and resurrected, but to know for a certainty that the Eternal, Living Father came to approve his Son in his baptism and later in his ministry, that the Son of God broke the bands of death and established the exaltation, the way of life, and that we may grow like him in knowledge and perfected eternal life." (*Teachings of Spencer W. Kimball,* ed. Edward L. Kimball [Bookcraft: Salt Lake City, 1982], 22.)

Thus, my wish related to Christmastime is no longer "Next Christmas in Bethlehem." My wish is now that wherever I may be, "Next Christmas seek earnestly for the spirit of Jesus Christ, and be thankful for the good news of his birth and his gospel."

Daniel H. Ludlow taught religion for many years at Brigham Young University, where he also served as dean of the College of Religious Instruction. He has served as the director of Correlation for the Church and as editor-in-chief of the Encyclopedia of Mormonism. *He is the author of several books and many magazine articles. He and his wife, Luene, are the parents of nine children, forty-two grandchildren, and fifteen great-grandchildren.*

THE CHRISTMAS PRESENT

Layne H. Dearden

Three of the interns had already told me that I was well enough to leave the next day—the day before Christmas—and then come back to the hospital after a short holiday respite. I was sure that I would get final confirmation of this pleasant news from Dr. Sherman, department chief of staff, when he made his usual rounds later in the day. He finally appeared and stopped at my bedside. His examination was routine; in fact, it was too routine.

"You're doing fine, just fine," he assured me, and turned to leave the room, but he said nothing to me about leaving the hospital for Christmas.

I gulped down my alarm and asked, "I'll be leaving tomorrow for a few days, won't I?"

The only indication of his surprise was the way his gray eyebrows lifted themselves a little higher on his forehead. He slowly answered, "I'm sorry, son, but you're not going anywhere for at least two more weeks."

His voice was kind, but it was also firm

and definite. I lay there speechless as he left the room. The one thing I had been holding to for the last few days was gone. My one firm hope had just been stepped on, crushed.

It wasn't fair—none of it was fair! I had been on my mission for over a year when it happened. I was happy in my calling. Teaching the gospel in New York City was challenging and exciting. Lately it had begun to be productive—our labors were being blessed with success. I had been blessed with good health—at least until two weeks earlier, when my right arm suddenly became paralyzed for a few minutes and my ability to speak was gone for more than two hours.

No one knew what had happened to me, so I had been brought to this hospital in the Bronx to find out. No one at the hospital seemed to know for sure just what had happened to me either. I had overheard whispered conversations about strokes, seizures, tumors, and syndromes. Dozens of inconclusive tests had left me exhausted and more ill than when I had entered the hospital. It just wasn't fair for me to be wasting my time in the hospital when there were investigators to be taught. It wasn't fair that the mysterious affliction had appeared in the first place.

I called my folks in Utah almost every night, assuring them that I was all right and that there was nothing to worry about. My mother wanted to fly out to be with me, but I knew that they couldn't afford it and

that I would feel even more self-conscious about my hospital stay if she were to come. So I joked about my mysterious malady over the phone and carefully acted the role of a nonchalant victim so they would not worry about me so much.

The small hospital in the Bronx, famous for its work with neurological problems, had to be the most desolate and cheerless place on earth; I was sure of it after spending just one night in the place. As the days became weeks, my hopes of leaving for the Christmas holidays had made my suffering bearable. Thoughts of yuletide excitement and activity alleviated the boredom and discomfort.

"You're not going anywhere for at least two more weeks." Dr. Sherman's pronouncement lodged in my mind and filled it with a sense of nostalgia and finality. As a child, I would dream of Christmas for months ahead. As a young man, I found that my childish pleasure had been only partially replaced with a deeper appreciation of friends, family—and Jesus Christ.

I lay unmoving in the hospital bed for at least fifteen minutes before I shifted position enough to reach the radio and turn it on. It had been the only pleasure and diversion in my lonely room since coming to the hospital. Now even listening to it made my mood darken. My disappointment had been replaced with resentment and anger; I was totally miserable. I felt it within me, discoloring my personality from some corrupt inner well.

Still, I stubbornly listened to the radio, preferring it to the routine sounds from the corridor and the nearby kitchen. Every station seemed to be blasting me with Christmas carols. Happy voices proclaimed joy to the world. Singers reminded me again and again that "there's no place like home for the holidays."

I wasn't full of joy. I wasn't home. I wouldn't even be going home to my missionary and member friends here in New York. For me there would be no Christmas this year.

December 23 slowly passed and became December 24. Then it was Christmas Eve. The hospital was hushed and quiet. Many of the patients had been allowed to go home for Christmas, but not me; I was alone. I was lonely, small, and unimportant.

I glumly lay in bed, listening to the radio carols, mocking them in my mind and fervently wishing that the night would quickly pass. Around 8:00 P.M. there was a knock at the door. Ed Cazakoff, one of the recent converts I had helped teach, walked into the room. His arms were full of packages, and his face was covered with a big grin. He greeted me with a cheery "Merry Christmas," put down the packages, and warmly shook my hand.

It was astonishing to see him away from his family tonight. This was not just Christmas Eve—it was Hanukkah, a special family time in Judaism. There had been much family difficulty because of Ed's conversion to Christianity and the restored gospel, and he spent as much time as possible with his family to reassure them of his continued love and loyalty.

Ed's face was radiant as he talked with me that evening. His warmth and enthusiasm and vulnerability made him seem younger than his twenty-four years. He smiled continually as he talked about his Church work, his delight in the gospel, and his concern and love for our mutual friends and for his family. For several hours we talked, listened to the radio carols, and opened the gifts he had brought with him. Some were from him; others had been gathered and sent by other friends.

After he left, I thought about the hours he would now spend waiting for the subway and traveling home this wintry night. I looked around at the once bleak room. Holiday paper tumbled from the wastebasket, a small stack of opened gifts graced the solitary chair, and a row of red-and-white candy canes paraded around the sides of my bed. More than the room, I must have looked vastly different. My heart had been touched; his happiness and radiance had warmed my soul. I had been wallowing in momentary concerns when I should have been thanking God for the rich blessings I could enjoy forever.

This had been Ed's first Christmas Eve, and he had given it to me. His sincerity and loving concern exemplified true Christianity. He had sacrificed for me; he had cared. He had been deeply aware of the significance of Christmas, and I had been ignoring it. The pleasures I had lamented about missing weren't really important at all. They were, by themselves, artificial and shallow.

For the next several hours, I lay there in the darkness and listened to the radio carols with a humble awareness of their meaning. I thought of a night many years before in a land across the sea. I delighted in the life of the child born that night and thrilled at the spirit of the approaching day. I peacefully fell asleep, grateful for the Christmas presents I had been given by two of my brothers.

Layne Dearden, a native of Henefer, Utah, lives in Rexburg, Idaho, where he teaches public speaking and interpersonal communication at Ricks College. He and his wife, Helen, are the parents of three sons and three daughters. After thirty years, the visit of Ed Cazakoff to his hospital room is still "a cherished watershed moment and blessing" in his life. Ed's widow, Gladys Cazakoff, lives in Kew Gardens, Queens, New York.

THE FLAVOR OF FAITH

Carma Rose de Jong Anderson

In the southern hemisphere, the days grew hotter and more humid each week in October and November of 1947. In the romantic beauties and bustle of subtropical São Paulo, Brazil, Daddy and I were spending another evening of camaraderie with the students and teachers at the *Union Cultural, Brasil / Estados Unidos.* He was a cultural and linguistic expert for the U.S. State Department, lecturing in English and Portuguese on North American culture, and I was his adventurous chum, his motherless seventeen-year-old daughter. São Paulo was an hour's ride away from our apartment in Santos, where I was hired as an English teacher and librarian at the U.S. Cultural Center near the beach.

Gorgeous Brazilians were my friends that year, making Utah boy- and girl-friends look rather dull and pale. Brazilians were tall, especially 6'4" Euvaldo Nacimento, who could perform a beautiful waltz with me, and very short, like our undernourished but adorable little janitor, named Joao; and they were medium height, like the average Latino and Asian. They were black, brown, and blond-haired, extremely bright and fun, and learning English with both eagerness and anxiety, to get ahead in the modern world. They came from mostly Portuguese, some Spanish, and a lot of Native Indian ethnic sources, their population originally having a heavy infusion of French culture before North America became an ideal. There were great quantities of very interesting, upwardly mobile Italian and Asian immigrants, all of whose blood was somewhat mixed with the descendants of the African slave population first brought to Brazil to work the massive *fazendas*—the coffee plantations in the north—and to work on cattle ranches and as domestics. The black culture, with its powerful forces of music and dance rhythms, was easily incorporated into that very Catholic and minimally Protestant society, not feared and hated as in the United States. Black blood was an eighth, sixteenth, or thirty-second part of perhaps two-thirds of all the people in Brazil's greatest "melting pot of the world." It was certainly present at the U.S. cultural centers, where the aggressive business and professional people and their teenagers congregated.

One of my boyfriends, who determinedly taught me to dance the Samba, was one-half black and a truly elegant and brilliant young man. When I finally was brave enough to really dance at the Centro parties, my best girlfriend, a doctor's daughter who feared she was growing too old at twenty-four to be marriageable, commented wryly that I had learned to dance *como uma Preta!* (like a black girl!) It was simple jealousy since I had long red hair and was identifiable in a crowd.

Daddy, the first dean of fine arts and professor of modern languages at BYU, was asked by the U.S. State Department to take a year to direct the new *Centro Cultural Brasil/Estados Unidos* in the resort city of Santos. Twenty-eight *Uniões* and *Centros* were set up all over South America for various levels of English classwork, with American literature and music libraries, visiting lecturers from the United States, and a full social life of youthful students trying to converse in English. These Americanizing institutions were deemed very effective in 1947 for hemispheric understanding and democratic solidarity in a world still shocked by World War II and tottering on the edge of tremendous political upheavals. There was a deathly fear of Naziism rising in Argentina, and worse, the spread of Communism in many countries. The United States really needed democratic friends.

There was another young businessman of about twenty-six, who often talked with me in good English, preferably away from the crowded gatherings. I met Theodore, an émigré to Brazil in his teen years, while visiting São Paulo. He was like a wonderful brother to me, which I had never had, a very serious thinker on many important subjects of life, but he had a smile in his big blue eyes and beautiful curls of red hair all over his head. He was Jewish, from a smart Jewish family who had recognized the growing Nazi threat to Germany and especially the Jewish population. His Simons family, like many other European Jews, were clever and courageous enough to get out of Germany in 1935 at the first signs of threats, not waiting until the desperate times of 1938 and after!

Ted and I visited back and forth between São Paulo and Santos, where I kept house. Daddy and I would make expeditions through the lush banana groves of the coastal plain, climbing in a huge modern bus to the high, drier plateau where the hard-working Paulistas lived (São Paulo was building the fastest growing megalopolis in the world). We would go up on Sundays, when Daddy could get away, so we could attend the tiny branch of the church there with President Beck's family and beg for two of the rare missionaries in that land (which is far bigger than the United States) to open up Santos for teaching the gospel. Finally, we received two missionaries, and with the four of us and one lukewarm investigator, we established the first LDS church in Santos in our little apartment. Five years later they had a chapel! From then on, it was one Mormon explosion after another!

We made one kind of special trip because Ted had written to me (which he did all the time, in his lovely, artistically scrolled handwriting) wanting to invite me to his São Paulo home to meet his parents at a social gathering, a coffee evening. I surmised what that meant! I was going to be evaluated by his nearest and dearest. Of course, I felt that marriage was out of the question—since I was missing my junior year at BY High School to live in Brazil! I had always intended to do a lot more with my education than *just dating* before I would ever pick out a husband! I was very choosy, to my widower father's great relief.

It was a stiff social event, meeting Ted's siblings and friends and his very formal and suspicious parents dressed in the European fashion of black clothing. It was something of a fiasco because my Portuguese was not yet to the point that we could really communicate. Although I did a big lesson out of a textbook almost every day with Daddy's critique, I still could not handle delicate nuances of social conversation, even breaking out in Spanish on occasion when frustrated with the new language. So I spoke very little in Portuguese. I gave all the compliments I could in English, which Ted dutifully translated into German for his family, but both the German (which I had not yet studied) and the French-saturated Brazilian social graces had strong linguistic patterns which were complicated necessities, and taboos, in ordinary speech. This was one of the few times in my life I knew when to shut my mouth.

Ted had his mother primed to serve this Mormon girl (whatever she thought that was) hot chocolate instead of strong, syrupy

Brazilian coffee or liquor, which everybody else drank. They sat me precariously on a tiny velvet chair amidst the porcelain bric-a-brac. Over my suddenly extra-long legs, I was trying to balance the boiling-hot cocoa in a fragile demitasse cup and receive cookies with the polished elegance of my miserably sunburned hands, without scalding my thighs and standing up screaming. I couldn't understand anything anyone around me was saying—but his mother's cookies communicated with me.

The cookies! Enveloped as I was in rich fumes of chocolate, I tasted one of the white sculptured cookies. The flavor wafted me back to my fifth year, a Christmas long, long before in my childhood. I didn't know what came over me, but I must have sat there in a trance for some moments, searching through my past to identify that unique flavor so laden with the emotions of a family Christmas.

My sisters and I were climbing out of the back seat of the old Hudson in front of the Seiters' house. Our family was invited for a special evening, so my father had brought home a huge paper sack of then expensive oranges. They were piled so high in the sack that I eagerly suggested Daddy leave some of them in the car. "Oh, no," said Mama, "the Seiters need them! They don't have many friends and almost no one in this whole town of Provo can speak to them in German." "This is a *gift*," Daddy said. I chased the falling oranges when they rolled down the icy walk and Daddy wedged them

back into the bursting sack as we rang the bell.

(Years later, I could interpret from that scene the phrase from a patriarch about God's blessings to me, "the measure of His giving shall be heaped up and running over.")

In the small parlor was a very large Christmas tree with wax candles and ornaments on the branches. It almost filled the room. In that little home in Provo, the old couple dressed in black were bowing and smiling and excitedly speaking German with my father that night in 1935 (just as the Simons family later surrounded me with the German language in Brazil). In the dimly lit room with plush chairs, I couldn't understand anything anyone was saying, but I was sipping hot chocolate and nibbling artfully sculptured cookies. What was that fairy-tale flavor I had never before savored?

It was close to Christmas Eve when they would light the candles on the tree, each one clipped onto a tiny tin holder. Then I discovered under the Christmas tree the greatest wonders I had ever seen in my five years, the artful symbols of faith of German carvers—perhaps of some of Brother Seiter's own ancestors. In my scratchy organdy best dress I dropped to the floor, gazing with astonishment for a long time at the beauty of the minuscule wooden figures in scenes all around the base of the tree. Instinctively I picked up a charming goose and was told by my mother to carefully put it back. Longing to hold it, I saw how it was finished exquisitely, realistically, and painted so delicately! I had never seen anything like those little figures, only two inches tall, at most: milk maids with milk pails, magistrates with books, wood choppers with tools, wood carvers leaving their work bench, old grandpas and grandmas with umbrellas and canes, and all kinds of children with baskets of offerings and kerchiefs tied around their gifts—wending their way to the nativity creche. Here were herds of geese, horned goats, and white-faced sheep, mothers with brooms, lumbering cows and donkeys with carts, and lumbering grand ladies with servants and cats, all making the pilgrimage to see the newborn Jesus.

I lay there on my stomach, elbows roughened by the threadbare carpet, with my patent leather slippers waving over the back of my white ruffled dress, oblivious to the babble of foreign words. The sweet tiny face of Jesus smiled up from his bed of golden hay. There was something wonderful about him that I could not describe, even to myself. He was so beautiful! So beautiful compared to the garish celluloid Santa and sleigh for which my sister and I had entreated our parents in Woolworth's. Here in the soft shadows, shepherds were lovingly placed on spring green hills, and Mary and Joseph received them quietly in the hush of candlelight.

We saw no presents wrapped in tissue on display at the Seiters'. It was the home of immigrants with special presents to be brought out as surprises, and there was little money for luxuries. But smiling Sister Seiter could make divine Springerle cookies flavored with miraculous anise seeds, so valued in biblical times, and Brother Seiter had brought the precious carvings out of Germany, with their legacy of faith in the Lord. With such care he carried them and his family a great distance from his homeland to Utah, when they joyously found Another Testament of Jesus Christ.

Later, during difficult times in Brazil, when I needed an explanation of my life, the flavor of anise seeds brought me back to Truth, to Peace, and my Savior.

Carma Rose de Jong Anderson is a designer / producer of historic clothing and interiors for LDS historic sites, and teaches costume at the department of theatre and media arts, Brigham Young University.

CHRISTMAS IN BULGARIA

Saren Eyre

The following story is comprised of selections from my missionary journal that relate to the Christmas I spent in Bulgaria.

DECEMBER 10, 1993

It's so cold here. Day after day it's gray and overcast and the cold eats right through your clothes no matter how many layers you have on. Everything looks so dead—gray concrete apartment blocks, gray sky, little patches of dead brown grass mixed with vast expanses of mud, broken playground equipment and car "carcasses" scattered between the buildings, brown, pollution-choked air. Beat-up, mud-stained cars and buses mix helter-skelter on the roads. Figures bundled in old, dark clothing dart between them, scurrying from one place to another. The monotony of the color scheme is broken up by the blue or orange-dyed hair that so many old ladies have. It's so funny! I guess that dying your hair is one way to make a stand against the grayness that surrounds you!

Everyone is so poor. Bread is getting expensive. More and more products are available—we even saw some peanut butter in the market today! But fewer and fewer people can afford what is available. This morning, I saw an old lady with an amazingly wrinkled face sitting on the ground by the bus stop. Displayed in front of her were four shriveled carrots and a jar of pickled cabbage. I see old people like her all the time, sitting out in the freezing cold selling whatever they can to supplement their tiny government pension. So many people here now remember the days of communism with nostalgia as they talk about how everyone used to be assured a job and a place to live.

This is a crazy country. No one enforces any sort of rules. Last week the bus I was on ran into a car. The bus driver and the driver of the car got out and yelled at each other, flailing their arms, for about fifteen minutes, causing a traffic jam. Then some people helped the car driver pull his mangled car off the road and all the people gradually got off the bus and walked to the next bus stop. The police never came. They never do. People park their cars all over the sidewalk and there is a lot of crime. Bulgarians fought long and hard for democracy but it seems as if what they have achieved so far is anarchy.

Speaking of crime, a couple of elders got beat up a few days ago. There have been a lot of little incidents, but this one was the worst one so far. There is starting to be a lot of persecution of the Church here because people associate our church with all these weird sects that poured into the country when communism pulled out. There have been full-page articles in the paper that say all sorts of weird things about the church. We've been accused of everything from encouraging suicide to eating babies. I guess I don't blame people for being scared of us! It breaks my heart to see people look at me with such fear in their eyes and move away quickly before I can even talk to them. It's been a little easier since we stopped wearing our name tags a couple of weeks ago. We've been trying to approach people with a Christmas message. But Christmas doesn't seem to strike a chord with many people here.

I'm afraid Christmas isn't much of a holiday here. The Communists weren't much for religious holidays, so for forty years, people have done some major celebrating for the new year instead. In preparation for the big New Year's festivities, everyone has been throwing "bombichkee" (firecracker things) off their balconies. Every few minutes, a huge explosion goes off. It sounds like we're living in a war zone or something with the sounds echoing off all the concrete buildings. It can *hurt* when one lands relatively near you and about deafens you! It gets pretty annoying after a while. So far these lovely noises have been the only signs that it's a holiday season.

It doesn't feel like Christmas at all. This is going to be really hard for me. Christmas is my favorite time of year—and here I am in the most un-Christmasy place imagina-ble, trudging around in the mud and trying to talk to people who don't want to have anything to do with me.

DECEMBER 15, 1993

Sister Derabeva and I had a great planning meeting this morning. We're both feeling pretty homesick and pretty unmotivated about the work. But we set some goals and decided to make this the best Christmas ever. There's so much Christmas spirit to be had in giving!

We talked to the Relief Society today about doing a clothing drive for a home for disabled children that the service missionary couple told us about. The Relief Society sisters were a little confused about the idea at first. People here don't do service projects. Under communism, the government was supposed to do everything for everyone. When we told them about the children's specific needs, they started talking together about all the stuff they could give and seemed to get more excited. People here save everything, and they all have tons of good winter clothes their children have outgrown.

There still aren't many signs of Christmas around here! On the radio in a taxi this morning, "Little Drummer Boy" was playing randomly. We saw some red and green Christmas lights in a window. It made me so happy to see them! On the way home tonight, we bought a sad little twig of a tree. It's smashed in the back so it goes nicely against the kitchen wall. We decorated it with popcorn chains and some candy canes we found. It looks pretty cute!

DECEMBER 18, 1993

We have set up a party for the kids in the orphanage. The ladies at the orphanage were so excited about the idea. They said they've never done anything for Christmas before. We're going to get our district to come with us, and maybe some of the young women. It'll be fun to share those wonderful kids. Today we got to see Vessie take her first steps! It's seriously a miracle. When I first met her in September, she could barely sit up and Dr. Petcheva told me that she would never walk. The tumor she has in her head is so large that it throws her off balance, and they say she's too little to have an operation to remove it. These kids all have such strange and sad physical problems, but they have an amazing will. They flourish even under the little love and attention we give them when we go there every week.

We talked to our district leader about caroling as a district to our investigators and giving them holiday treats. At first he didn't seem too excited about the idea, but I think we're going to do it.

DECEMBER 21, 1993

The last couple of nights, our district has been doing some serious caroling. We contacted virtually all our investigators and inactive members. We practically *ran* everywhere. Our caroling turned out to be a bit

like trick or treating! The six of us would stand in a semi-circle at the door and ring the bell. They would open the door, we would start singing, and their looks of puzzlement, annoyance, or frowns immediately melted into smiles as soon as we started singing. Then they would usually run inside, leaving us singing to an empty doorway. They would come back with more family members and assorted treats to give us. Some people joined in the singing, and some stood there with their hand on their heart and their eyes closed as they listened. Others living in the entryway would stick their heads out of their doors to see what was going on. Our songs really echoed through the buildings. They would frown and then smile and stand there listening. When we finished singing, we gave people cookies and an invitation to our branch Christmas party on Thursday. We would try to leave, but they would insist on giving us something. We protested, saying that we just wanted to give *them* something, but Bulgarians don't take "no" for an answer when it comes to giving. We ended up with pockets stuffed with apples, holiday sweetbread, olives, walnuts—you name it.

When we got to the door of one apartment, we could hear the family in there totally yelling at each other. Elder Hanson said, "I'm not going to interrupt that!" but Elder Outz reached over and pushed the bell. He got a glare from Elder Hanson. The door opened and the whole family was standing there. We sang with our biggest smiles, and they seemed so pleased—the Spirit rushed right in.

We really got in the Christmas spirit. We established contact with a lot of less-active members, and we laughed a lot. We tried not to laugh when dogs frequently tried to harmonize with us. We laughed when we tried to cram all six of us into the scary little elevators they have here while we held our huge plate of cookies above all of our heads. We climbed and ran down countless stairs and felt some serious "good-will to men." It was a definite success. I love Christmas!

Sister Derabeva and I are trying to do this sort of "Sub for Santa" thing for Sashka's kids. They live in this little shack out in the gypsy village. They are the cutest kids: Sonia, Rumiana, and Kristo. We shopped for them on P-day. I decided to use my birthday money. We found some cute sweaters and toys. We really need to do Christmas for Lubka and Maria and their mom too. They don't even have food to put on the table. There's so little time! And I don't have much money left. I did get Brother Vasilev to go over to their house and see if he could fix their stove. He was over there for ten hours, and not only did he fix the stove, he also fixed all their wiring, which has been messed up for years. We arrived at their house to carol just as Brother Vasilev was leaving. He was so excited to tell us about all the work he'd done and what joy he'd had in serving them. We caroled to Maria and Lubka and their

mom as they stood in their now well-lit front entryway and cried and cried. Oh, I love them! I love it when we can serve and help others experience the joy of service!

December 22, 1993

It snowed last night, just a tiny bit. It was gone by noon, but it was so fun to wake up to everything all frosted in white.

Some of the greatest women are in this branch! Tonight at homemaking meeting, the Relief Society folded and sorted all the clothes they have collected for the home for disabled children. They have so much good stuff: tons of sweaters, some good coats, and lots of hats and scarves. Almost everything is in really good condition. Baba Katia knitted three pairs of beautiful, colorful new mittens to donate. We talked to everyone about the project less than a week ago, but that woman has knitting needles like lightning! We ended up with ten huge trash bags full of clothes, and there are only about fifteen women in the branch. The sisters brought in stuff from their own homes and asked friends and neighbors for donations. Projects like this have to help the Church's image here in time. I wish all Bulgarians could have been there tonight to see the love and excitement in that room as these beautiful women chatted, laughed, sorted, and packed clothes.

December 24, 1993

Today, finally, people started getting into the holiday spirit. People were bustling through the markets and poking everyone with little Christmas trees as they crowded onto the buses. We shopped all day for stuff for our two families. Elder and Sister England (the service couple) heard about what we are trying to do and gave us some extra money so we could do this right.

This morning we visited Maria and Lybka. They said they had a surprise for us. They led us into their kitchen and it was *clean!* They spent all day yesterday cleaning the place. They threw out literally hundreds of bags of junk accumulated from so many years of depression and hopelessness. They said they threw out *buckets* of dead cockroaches. That place was so disgusting! They said that after Brother Vasilev fixed their lights, they just felt like cleaning. It's amazing what love can do!

We gave them a nice little Christmas lesson. We talked about how God loves us all and how when things look black, we have to keep going and praying and watching. They were sad today. Their father came home drunk again and beat their mother. They couldn't pick up their unemployment checks because the place ran out of money—typical! So they have *nothing* for the holidays—no food, let alone presents. They felt so bad that they couldn't offer us anything to eat. I'm so excited to bring them the presents and big food basket that we have for them tomorrow! They will be so happy and they deserve it so much!

We had so much fun yesterday at the orphanage. Our whole district plus a couple of the young women went. They had the kids all dressed up and sitting at little tables when we arrived. We dressed Elder Hanson up as Santa, sang songs and played instruments, gave them treats, and made the kids laugh a lot. Oh, I love them! They are so beautiful!

We had three "Budnee Vecher" (Christmas Eve) meals tonight. That was the smallest number we could get away with. I'm so full I think I might die! Tanya (one of our young women) really needed to talk to us, so we went over there and her mother *made* us eat all this pumpkin baklava. Then we went to Virginia's and had the official Christmas Eve dinner with her and her family. She has such a funny, great family. We had all the traditional "fasting" Christmas foods: rice wrapped in pickled cabbage leaves, bean soup, special sweet bread, pumpkin baklava, and lots of fruit. It's a tradition to eat no meat for forty days before Christmas, but people generally follow the "no meat" idea only on Christmas Eve. They put a coin in the sweetbread and whoever gets it is supposed to have good luck all year. I didn't get it. Oh, well. The father carried incense into every room of the house, "blessing" the home, another Christmas tradition. We talked about how great Virginia's baptism was last week and ended up committing her mother to baptism!

Next, we went over to Rositza's, hoping just to drop off a little card and gift, but she had a huge meal all prepared for us. We had all the same stuff to eat. She didn't want to be alone on Christmas Eve. I'm so glad we could be with her. She is the most wonderfully intelligent, cultured lady, and she's lived so long that she has wonderful stories.

DECEMBER 25, 1993

It's Christmas! I'm sitting in a sun-soaked room, listening to one of my presents—a tape of Christmas music—and feeling just a touch sad that I'm here in this weird little apartment rather than home with my family. But I don't have long to feel this way. We have to wrap up all our stuff for our two families and deliver them soon.

I woke up really early this morning to the phone ringing—my family. It was so great to talk to them! Then my companion, roommates, and I read the Christmas story by candlelight and sang some of our favorite Christmas songs. We opened our presents. Mom is *so* sweet! They sent me a lot of nice stuff. I got a new white blouse. It just looks so amazingly clean and white compared to everything in my wardrobe and everything in this country. The best thing I got was a packet of special letters from everyone in the family with their testimonies of Jesus Christ—such beautiful, sweet testimonies from all the kids, a perfect poem from Dad, and a tear-bringing, testimony-dripping letter from Mom. Oh, a mission sure makes you appreciate your family!

After we opened presents, we did my family's Christmas tradition and had an eggs benedict brunch. My companion and room-

mates were a little skeptical, especially as I made hollandaise sauce from a packet, fried rather than poached the eggs, used bread instead of English muffins, and green beans instead of asparagus. It actually turned out to be delicious and everyone loved it.

DECEMBER 26, 1993

Ok, I'll tell the rest about Christmas.

Sister Derebeva and I spent all afternoon wrapping gifts for our Sub-for-Santa thing. We found some really great stuff over the last few days and chose some of our most un-American-looking Christmas presents to give away. We don't want anyone to ever guess that this stuff is from us! We ended up with make-up sets, shirts, skirts, and jewelry for Lubka, Maria, and their mom, slippers for their dad, and a lot of food—basic staples plus special Bulgarian holiday foods. For Sashka's kids, we had a new sweater, a little toy, and a bag of candy for each kid, plus a bunch of fruit and food for the family. We found some nice wooden crates to put all our stuff into. It looked so festive!

We loaded the stuff into a taxi and went to pick up the Englands so they could see what their money had bought. First we went out to Sashka's. The taxi just about got stuck in the deep, nasty mud out there. It rained all day yesterday so it was worse than usual. We sneaked up to their door, set the stuff down, knocked and ran as fast as we could. It was pretty hard running in ankle-deep mud! We both just about fell flat on our faces! (Whenever I think of Bulgaria, I think I'll always think of *mud*.) Anyway, we heard them open the door as we ran away. They yelled "Dyado Koleda!"—Father Christmas! I don't think they saw us.

We then went to Maria's and Lubka's. We picked up a little Christmas tree on the way and put some decorations on it. We lodged the tree in the box with all the other stuff, put it outside their door, knocked, and ran.

Well, at church today, Maria and Lubka came in beaming, all decked out in their new clothes. They came up to me as I was struggling through the prelude on the piano and told me how they woke up early on Christmas Day and read the Christmas story by candlelight as the sun rose. I asked them what else they did for Christmas and they said that late at night their dad opened the door to head out and find something to drink (I guess they hadn't heard our knock) and there was Christmas waiting for them on their doorstep! They excitedly told us about the wonderful presents they received and all the good food. They were so happy to show off their new clothes and jewelry. Maria said, "You were right. God *does* care about us!" They thought the stuff was from the social services. Sometimes really poor families used to get holiday packages from social services. They said they were shocked that they got anything, let alone such nice stuff, since social services seems to be out of money these days. They were *so* excited! I'm so glad they didn't suspect us! Success!

We then saw Sashka's kids. Rumiana came running up and accused me of giving them their stuff. I promised that it wasn't me (not really a lie—it was really God's idea). She decided I could prove it by writing down the words "Father Christmas" and she took out the card that had been with the presents so she could compare the handwriting. I wrote in block letters rather than the cursive I'd written on the card. She looked up at me with this incredulous look in her big brown eyes, "I guess it really was Father Christmas then!" She and Kristo told me that after they had opened their presents and eaten some of their candy, they decided it would be fun to "play Father Christmas." They talked about how *much* stuff they had and how the kids who lived next door probably had nothing for Christmas. They wrapped up some of their candy and oranges, put the package on their neighbor's doorstep, knocked, and *ran*. They had this total delight in their eyes and voices as they excitedly talked over each other, trying to tell me the story at the same time. What precious children of God! They have so little, yet it just seemed so natural and fun for them to share what they had.

I couldn't have asked for a better Christmas. I want to do service like this every year! I've never felt so close to Christ or seen the light of Christ in so many other people's lives as I watched them give and receive. I love this country. I love the Lord. I even love the mud and the cold and the gray. It makes warm smiles and good will and the Christmas spirit stand out so much more. I'm so grateful for so many amazing opportunities to feel close to the One whose birth we celebrate at this bleak time of year.

Saren is the oldest child of Richard and Linda Eyre. She has attended Harvard University for a masters degree in education, served a mission to Bulgaria, and managed national volunteer recruitment efforts for The Points of Light Foundation.

ONE MIRACLE AT A TIME

Brad Wilcox

This Thanksgiving is going to be wonderful," my cousin Jan told me. Jan had never been one to prepare a huge feast, because when our huge family gets together everyone brings a food assignment so it isn't too much work for anyone. However, this year was different. Jan and her husband, Russ, were planning to have their Thanksgiving together with only their three children. After all, this year there was so much to be thankful for—Dustin was home.

Five-year-old Dustin, a curly-haired boy with bright blue eyes and a quick smile, bounced through life the way most children bounce on a trampoline. In fact, he was on a trampoline when I first noticed what was later diagnosed as a cancerous tumor.

It was April and we were having a family get-together between Saturday sessions of general conference. Dustin was jumping on the trampoline with my son Russell, who is his same age. With each jump, the boys spread their arms and legs wide and soared happily into the springtime air.

As Dustin bounced, his shirt flew up,

and I couldn't help noticing his tummy protruding. I commented to my mother standing nearby, "Dustin's beginning to look like one of those malnourished children you see in the magazine pictures."

"No chance of that," Mom laughed. "I'm afraid he must have just inherited the family appetite." We both chuckled and turned our attention to cleaning up after the picnic. Soon however, we would no longer be chuckling. On April 22, 1990, Dustin was diagnosed with Wilms' Tumor Cancer, and surgery was scheduled for the following day to remove his right kidney and adrenal gland.

That morning, family and ward members began fasting and praying for Dustin. The surgery took six hours. For Jan and Russ, the wait was agonizing. When the doctor finally finished and came to talk with them, he reported that the invasive tumor had grown to be the size of a Nerf football and weighed almost four pounds. No wonder Dustin's little tummy had protruded.

In the recovery room, Dustin was surrounded by monitors and tubes. This little boy, who so recently had been rocketing to the sky from his trampoline launch pad, was now fighting simply to stay alive. Slowly, he began waking from the anesthetic. Jan leaned forward and said, "Dustin, it's Mommy. Do you know Mommy is here?" He nodded yes.

Word of the successful surgery spread quickly throughout the family. My Aunt Wyla summed up our feelings when she said, "We're grateful for the miracle." However, more phone calls soon came with additional news—this time not so positive.

The tragedy of Wilms' Tumor is that it is difficult to catch in its early stages because it has virtually no noticeable external symptoms. By the time it is diagnosed, the cancer has usually spread, and Dustin's case was no exception. Doctors had found eleven detectable cancer spots on Dustin's lungs. It was determined that he needed to begin radiation and chemotherapy as soon as possible. We were all stunned. Again, Aunt Wyla summed up family feelings when she said, "It looks like we'll just have to take this one miracle at a time."

Jan, Russ, and their two older children were suddenly thrust into a new world. Over the next few months, Dustin was hospitalized five separate times. His treatments were brutal, with drugs causing nerve damage, muscle pain, loss of coordination, tissue burning, hair loss, mouth sores, nausea, and vomiting, to list a few of the side effects. It was a lot for a five-year-old to handle. It was a lot for his family to handle, too.

Jan and Russ felt they were plunging into an uncontrollable tailspin. It became a challenge to balance Russ's work and the needs of the older children, while caring full-time for Dustin. Jan and Russ felt frustrated by encounters with thoughtless people who tactlessly criticized their choice to put Dustin through chemotherapy. On the other hand, they were strengthened by the show of support they received through get-well cards, phone calls, gifts, meals, balloons, flowers, and much-needed financial donations.

Jan spent many hours in prayer expressing gratitude and pleading for blessings. And there were tears—countless tears of anger, grief, and exhaustion. But now she cried happy tears. Her prayers had been answered. It was November. Dustin's treatments had been going well, and this would be a Thanksgiving to remember.

Jan busied herself in the kitchen, preparing stuffing. Grandma always made it look so easy. Now that Jan was trying it on her own, she was about ready to give up and use the box mix. Suddenly, from the family room, Dustin cried out, "Mommy!"

"I'm coming," Jan called, quickly wiping her hands on a dish towel. "Mommy's here." As Jan came around the corner and approached the couch she could see the gleam of Dustin's perspiration. "Not again," she panicked, as she hurried to kneel by his side. She felt his forehead—now bald as a result of his treatments. He was flaming with fever.

Once again, Jan and Russ rushed their youngest son to the hospital. He was frail—almost lifeless. Their hopes and spirits plummeted. Forget the homemade stuffing. Forget the box mix. Their Thanksgiving dinner was prepared in the hospital cafeteria and served in Dustin's somber room.

During the weeks that followed there was no time for Christmas decorations—no

lights, no tree. After the disappointment of Thanksgiving, Jan secretly decided not to get her hopes up for Christmas. One day Dustin would feel better. The next day he would struggle again. On one of the good days, Dustin felt well enough to sit on the knee of a visiting Santa Claus. Despite everything he had been through over the last year, Dustin's eyes were still bright and his smile quick. There was talk of toys and games, but it didn't take Santa long to figure out what this bald five-year-old and his parents really wanted for Christmas. Of course, Dustin's recovery was not something Santa could promise. It was entirely out of the realm of usual requests.

Dustin's December treatments were scheduled for the eighteenth through the twentieth. Jan knew that if he responded as he had in November, they would probably be eating Christmas dinner from cafeteria trays, just as they had for Thanksgiving. That night she prayed, "Dear Heavenly Father . . . " She had said those words so often in the last year. They were usually followed with thanks and petitions, but tonight no more words would come. There were just feelings—intense longings that words could not begin to express. Stress and helplessness, bottled up inside during the last year, exploded. She broke down in sobs from the depths of her soul.

"That's when I felt it," Jan says. "An incredible peace that filled me completely. I wish I could say it was a peace that all would be well according to my wishes, but it wasn't like that. I simply felt a peaceful assurance that Heavenly Father knew what our family had been through, that he knew Dustin, and that he cared. Come what may, I knew Dustin was in Heavenly Father's hands."

From then on the Christmas spirit hit Dustin's home full strength. Despite the lack of time for traditional preparations, the Christmas season had never felt sweeter. "This year more than ever," Jan wrote in the annual family Christmas newsletter, "we appreciate the gift of Heavenly Father's son Jesus Christ to the world. We celebrate His birth with a new sense of meaning and joy."

Dustin's December treatments went well. He responded better than he had in previous months. By December 24 Dustin was still doing fine. That night he came to our traditional family party and reclined in his mother's lap. He sang "Rudolph the Red-Nosed Reindeer" along with all the children. When Grandma passed out bells for everyone to ring during "Jingle Bells," Dustin picked out two and rang them with gusto. When Uncle Wayne read from Luke in the Bible, the children acted out the nativity. In his small bathrobe, Dustin was already costumed as a shepherd.

By the time we had the family gift exchange, Jan could no longer hold back tears. She watched her youngest son rip into the package on his lap and tried to memorize the joy she saw in his eyes at that moment. She looked at her other two children, and other family members all around.

She saw the miniature lights from Grandpa's Christmas village along the window sill and the olive-wood figures of Grandma's favorite nativity set on top of the piano. Suddenly it all became a blur as she lowered her head and wept.

Dustin turned and saw his mother crying. "What's the matter, Mom?" he asked. "Didn't you get what you wanted?"

Jan began to laugh. "Oh, yes," she replied happily, brushing tears. "I got exactly what I wanted."

Note: Dustin's recovery has not been easy, and he must still have regular checkups. However, he is currently in eighth grade and doing great. He loves sports, Nintendo, and pizza, and still enjoys jumping on the trampoline with Russell.

Brad Wilcox is an assistant professor of Teacher Education at Brigham Young University and currently serves as bishop of the BYU 138th Ward. He is the author of Tips for Tackling Teenage Troubles. *He and his wife, Debi, have four children and live in Provo, Utah.*

I Won't Be Home for Christmas . . .

Barbara B. Jones

I couldn't believe it when our daughter Wendy decided to go on a mission; at age sixteen as her older brother John left on his mission to Argentina, she announced, "Well, you'll never see me going on a mission."

When she called us from Provo, Utah, to tell us that she had turned in her mission papers, we were shocked. Then she added, "I even asked Heavenly Father to send me on the hardest mission."

I remember thinking, "Be careful what you pray for." Sure enough, she was called to Honduras, a Third World country. She would need to learn Spanish, one of her worst subjects in high school.

Wendy had always been a social butterfly in high school. She was a cheerleader, a member of the prom committee, and a runner on the track team, but her grades had never been the greatest, especially in Spanish. I wondered how she would be able to learn the language in eight short weeks, plus be able to cope with the changes that living in a Third World country would bring. As Wendy's mother and the one who knew her the best, I knew that one of her most difficult challenges would be her first Christmas away from home.

Christmas at our home was Wendy's favorite time of the year. Each year our Christmas tree was Wendy's personal masterpiece. She would string literally hundreds of colorful twinkle-lights on first, then place the ornaments we had collected over the years on each branch. Next, she would string garlands of popcorn and candies. The final touches were a huge cluster of wide shiny red satin bows on the top and two big mechanical dolls that, when plugged in, seemed to be decorating the tree. It would take her hours and hours to complete the project.

In addition to her Christmas tree masterpiece, Wendy loved getting presents. Now you're saying, "Who doesn't?" But, you don't understand. Wendy really *loved* presents! I could never keep them hidden from her. Even when she was six, she managed to hunt everywhere until she found her gifts hidden in the trunk of my car. I knew that for Wendy the first Christmas on her mission would be very different, but never would I have believed that her first Christmas away from home would turn out to be one of the most memorable Christmases of her life—and mine, too.

The two months Wendy spent in the Missionary Training Center trying to learn a foreign language were stressful but also incredibly spiritual. The missionaries in her district were enthusiastic about going out into the world to teach the gospel, but when Wendy arrived in Honduras, she was not quite ready for the culture shock. Her letters each week were filled with the frustration of not being able to communicate in Spanish. She had so much that she wanted to tell their investigators, but the language just wasn't getting any easier. Her frustrations led her to start bending the mission rules, which led to even more frustrations and less success.

The final straw came in November. She broke her ankle, was put in a cast, and was sent to the mission home as an invalid for three weeks. During this period, another sister missionary also broke her ankle, so the two of them were convalescing at the same time. Both girls were so depressed that their mission president allowed each of them to call home.

When I received the phone call from Wendy, she said, "Mom, I just can't believe this is happening to me. I wanted so much to come here and be a successful missionary. I have struggled so hard with the language, and now this! Christmas is coming! [By this time, I could hear the tears in her voice.] And we won't even have a tree, and there won't be any presents. I just feel horrible. Our mission president says our families shouldn't try to send us packages because most of the time the packages just get confiscated.

"And, Mom, everyone here in Villa Florencia has been so wonderful to us, especially the bishop and his family. We go there for almost all of our meals, and they have thirteen children. They treat us just like family. I wish I could give the entire family Christmas presents."

To take her mind off her situation, I asked, "So Wendy, if you could get them anything, what would it be?"

"Oh, Mom, I'd get the bishop a model airplane. That's his hobby. And I'd get dolls for all the girls, and toy dishes and coloring books—all the things you used to get for me when I was little. His wife is such a sweetheart. She always takes care of us when we're sick. She's an absolute angel."

As we finished our conversation, I was wishing there were a way I could personally thank the bishop and his family for all they had done for my daughter. If only there were a way to send Christmas presents from America. There must be a way. Maybe Heavenly Father would hear the prayers of two depressed and struggling sister missionaries and at least one very grateful mom. Yes, that's what we needed—a "mini" miracle.

On December 1, the two sister missionaries had their casts removed and were released from the mission home to return to their area and to serve together as companions. Now it was time for some changes. During their recovery time in the mission home, they promised Heavenly Father that if he would help them with the language, they would do everything in their power to be better missionaries, to follow every rule, and to give Heavenly Father a "white"

Christmas. In this case, "white" did not mean snow. It meant investigators dressed in white and ready for baptism. Yes, they would work their very hardest to give the best gift to the Savior on his birthday—bringing souls unto him.

Meanwhile, back in America, I had several speaking assignments across the United States. The first weekend in December, I spoke in a Relief Society in an area of California where many migrant workers live and attend church. During my final workshop, I felt prompted to share the story of my missionary daughter. At the end of the conference, a woman came up to me and said, "Sister Jones, I'll take a gift to your daughter. I'm going to Honduras for Christmas. My family lives there."

I was so excited that I could hardly contain myself. What a great surprise for Wendy. I would send her a new camera since hers was broken. Or should I send the backpack she needed? Or the hair dryer? Her companion needed to have a gift also. What about the bishop and his family? In my enthusiasm, I started collecting things. First, I bought a small tree about a foot high complete with twinkle-lights, ornaments, and a star for the top. Next came the stockings and paper decorations for the walls of their room, backpacks, and perfume. I bought a model airplane kit for the bishop, dolls for the little girls, coloring books, crayons, a tiny set of toy dishes, and small gifts for their investigators.

After purchasing all the items, I suddenly felt numb. I could never get all of this into one box. I had enough things to fill an entire suitcase. Would the sister who was going to Honduras be overwhelmed if I asked her to take an entire suitcase? I got up the courage to call her. "Isabel, I'm so sorry to ask you this, but could you take an extra suitcase with you to Honduras. There were just so many things I needed to send."

She was very gracious and said she would be happy to take the suitcase with her. If, however, the Honduran customs officials opened the suitcase during their random spot checking, they would most likely confiscate everything.

I prayed harder than ever that the suitcase would make it, and somehow deep down inside me, I felt that it would. During the days that followed, I would catch myself thinking of all the possible ways that the suitcase would make it to Wendy's doorstep. I wondered if she would recognize the old brown tweed suitcase that used to belong to my Aunt Barbara. Would Wendy be at home when the suitcase arrived, or would she just find it after it had been mysteriously left on her doorstep? A million scenarios passed through my mind, and with each one I found myself with the biggest Cheshire cat grin on my face. The smile was for the anticipated happiness of someone I love. My daughter was learning a lesson that all parents hope their children will learn as they reach adulthood: serving the Lord brings enduring happiness.

So what happened to the suitcase?

Wendy gave me permission to share some of her journal pages:

Dec. 15—We have been working so hard, harder than I have ever worked. We really have some great investigators. I am really seeing the blessings you receive when you work really hard.

It's incredible. I thank my Heavenly Father so much for helping me make this great change on my mission. I guess if I had to be put in a cast for a month to kick me into shape, well then, I am very grateful! The secret to successful missionary work is simple, and it's only two words—WORK HARD! Put in all your heart, might, mind, and strength. I know with the Lord at my side, I can do anything. I really am so happy and very grateful to be here on my mission in Honduras. I can't believe Christmas is so close. No tears! I don't want to be sad because I'm not home. What a difference. It's 85 degrees outside, and it's Christmastime!

Dec. 23—Wow, what a day today was. We had seven investigators at church, and Miriam Dias, the great girl who was baptized last week, sat in the front. Then in the evening, Manuel Solano, a boy age 10, was baptized. Denni Ulloa told us that he will be baptized on Christmas Day. He said it was going to be his Christmas gift to Jesus. It truly is a "white" Christmas after all. What an incredible feeling that really can't be described on paper.

Then we came home tonight, and they told me that they had a suitcase for me. A suitcase? I couldn't believe my eyes. I recognized the suitcase. It was from home! Mom had sent a suitcase all the way from home! But how did it get to me? No one seemed to know very much about the stranger who had appeared in the doorway with the suitcase. She had not even left her name. (I'm sure she must have been an angel in disguise.) Hermana Knight and I quickly carried the suitcase into our room, and we were both in shock as we opened it up. Tons of stuff! Even a Christmas tree with lights and ornaments. By now we were both laughing and crying at the same time. Hermana Knight and I got stockings and tons of presents that were marked, "Do not open until Christmas." There were presents for us to give to the bishop and all of his family, plus gifts for the people. Dad even sent us some money to buy things that could not fit into the suitcase. We are going to be major Santa Clauses. What fun! Mom even sent us both Santa hats. What a Christmas to remember! I just have the most wonderful parents in the whole world. How could I have been so blessed in my life? Thank you, Heavenly Father, for everything, especially for my parents. They do so much for me, just like you do. I am so grateful to be on a mission. This will probably be the most memorable Christmas of my life.

Dec. 25—I have experienced Christmas in Honduras—the fireworks at midnight were spectacular. The children in our neighborhood, plus children from everywhere, came to see our little Christmas tree all the way from America. We visited the families in our branch and our investigators. Everywhere we went we wore our Santa hats and gave out presents. Our bishop was so thrilled to get a model airplane kit from America, and the little girls loved the dolls that Mom picked out. It was so much fun! This was truly the greatest Christmas of all time. I am meeting the most beautiful people, changing, learning, and growing so much.

Please let my parents have a wonderful Christmas alone together. I love you, Heavenly Father.

Barbara Barrington Jones is an author, professional speaker, and international image consultant. She is a member of the President's Roundtable at BYU–Hawaii, and directs the worldwide women's program, "A New You."

THE ANGEL ON THE AMMO CAN

John L. Meisenbach

Each year I feel the Christmas spirit in our home as we get out the decorations. The nativity scene is put in its usual place, and the stockings are hung above the fireplace. The reindeer and elves are put on the stair rail. And always, when we place the Christmas angel in her traditional spot, my mind wanders to a place halfway around the world.

It is December 22, 1970. I am in a jungle near the village of Song Be, South Vietnam. We can hear the re-supply choppers coming. We prepare the landing zone and wait to receive supplies: food, water, ammunition, and, most important, letters and packages from home.

I make sure the men under my command have received their rations and have all their mail and packages. Then I take some time to read my own letters. My mind wanders, and many things trouble me as I read the letters—some of them mailed over four weeks ago. I've been in Vietnam for 335 days, most of them spent in the field. I feel hardened and frustrated with life. Here it is—three days before Christmas—and the one thing I'm thinking of is that I have only twenty-nine days left until I'm on my way home. I hope my last missions will go well, that I'll be able to leave my responsibilities and my men well, and that my replacement will be the best one they could receive.

There are no thoughts of Christmas or of my Savior's birth until I open the package with the beautiful white angel inside. She's about twelve inches tall, dressed in white clothes, with golden hair. I put her on top of an overturned ammunition can and begin to read the letter from my dear mother.

In her own words she tells me the story of the birth of our Savior and bears a quiet, sweet testimony. I feel myself being lifted spiritually. My mother told me this story over and over when I was a child, but never did I feel the Spirit of Christ so close before.

I glance up from the letter and notice some of my men looking at the white angel. I wind her up and no one says a word as "Silent Night" fills the air, and the Christmas angel brings special emotions out in each one of us. Some tears are shed and feelings exchanged as the Spirit of Christ touches each of us.

Later, as I pack and prepare to move out, I wrap the angel carefully and place her in my rucksack. I think of home, family, and loved ones, but most of all I think of Jesus and all that he has done for me.

John L. Meisenbach is presently serving as bishop of the Tustin Fifth Ward, Orange California Stake.

CHRISTMAS EVE MIRACLE

Alda McDonald Strebel

I can still hear my mother's soft voice as she related this Christmas Eve miracle. The experience was sacred to Mama; she told it only on special occasions, such as the evening my sweetheart asked for my hand in marriage.

The story began on a crisp autumn day in October 1923. The huge barn behind our home in Heber City, in northern Utah, was heaped to the rafters with fresh hay. The loft was filled with the happy laughter and shouting of romping children. I was among them, unaware of the tragedy about to strike. I found an inviting hay hill and got ready to slide down. Suddenly, I was falling headfirst through a chute. Down I shot to a cement floor in a feeding manger at the bottom of the barn.

I still remember the startling sensation of regaining consciousness, and the horrible frustration of not being able to cry. My brothers ran for Papa. How comforting and secure his sturdy, strong arms felt as he lifted me out of the hay manger and carried me into the house. Gently, he placed me on my bed.

Several days later, my headache had not subsided. The condition became even more complicated when I contracted a severe cold. To this day I remember the nightmare of the accompanying high fever. Later one afternoon when the doctor made his routine call, he shook his head as he read the thermometer, and Mama knew it was time to take action. She sent for Papa, and we prepared to leave for Provo, forty miles away, where I could be hospitalized. Neighbors and relatives gathered to offer their assistance and to assure us that my four small brothers would be well cared for.

The journey through the winding roads in Provo Canyon was long and hard, as Papa pushed his Model T Ford through herds of sheep on the roadway. We arrived at the hospital late that night.

The pain was severe behind my left ear, and after two more days of high fever, the doctors operated and discovered a deep-seated mastoid infection. By this time it had entered my bloodstream. The next week the surgeons were compelled to lance my left arm, and the next week my right leg. For seven long weeks I endured the grueling ordeal of many operations.

Three days before Christmas, the doctors called my father into the office and told him they could offer little hope for my recovery. Knowing of my intense longing for my brothers and home, my parents decided to take me home for Christmas. They located a truck to take me to the train

(there were only a few trucks in the entire town) and lifted me onto a cot. In the hallway, the hospital personnel gave me a lovely doll dressed in a pink, hand-knit sweater and cap. I clutched the doll close to my body under the blankets, and when we came out into the refreshing night air, I was hysterically happy. I thought I was leaving the whole ordeal behind me in that hospital.

Slowly the truck made its way to the depot. We boarded, the conductor shoveled a huge lump of coal in the potbellied stove in the caboose, and the train began its three-hour journey home. The sleeping powder the doctor had administered before we left the hospital soon took effect, and I slept most of the way. When the train stopped, Papa stepped to the door of the car, then bent over me chuckling.

"You would never believe the crowd that is out there to welcome us," he said. "My goodness, you would think a celebrity was getting off this train." He chuckled again as he pulled a warm cap over my head. Mama tucked the covers under my chin, and my cot was lifted to Uncle Dode's bobsled. Sleighbells tinkled as the horses pranced down Center Street over the smooth, icy roads.

When we reached the tabernacle corner, the sleigh stopped with a merry "whoa." In the middle of the main street was a large Christmas tree, adorned with electric tree lights, the first I had ever seen. How colorful and sparkly they were! The children of my Primary class stood beneath the tree, welcoming me with the sacred strains of "Silent Night, Holy Night." With all the faith and meekness of a child, I felt the love of our Savior in the hearts of many gentle people. Mama's tears were mingled with the soft snowflakes that fell on my face.

A short time later, at our own front door, Mama laughed and cried as she hugged her four little sons. Seven weeks without a mother had seemed an eternity to them. Then, with hushed excitement, they led the way into my bedroom, which they had adorned with red-and-green paper chains. A large, deep-red tissue bell hung from the single light globe. "Oh, see! The Christmas elves have been here!" Mama exclaimed, hugging the boys again. As the exertion of the trip took its toll, I realized the pain and suffering had not ended. By Christmas Eve my situation was critical, and the doctors told my parents that my chances of surviving the night were small. The elders administered to me, and for the first time, my parents had the courage to say, "Thy will be done."

After the blessing, a special peace descended over the household. Papa and Mama went into the living room with the four boys and helped them hang their Christmas stockings; then they tucked each one into bed, assuring him that Santa was on his way.

Knowing that she was going to need strength for what lay ahead, Mama was per-suaded to retire to an upstairs bedroom. I loved to hear her tell of lying in the stillness of the night, and of the peace that came over her as she fell into a sound sleep. She was awakened, startled, just as dawn was breaking Christmas morning. She turned to my bedroom door, a silent prayer on her lips. Papa was coming out, his tired face bathed in a relieved smile. A miracle had happened. I had been given strength to sur-vive the night, and Mama could even see a slight sparkle in my tired eyes.

"Has Santa been here yet?" I asked.

"You bet he has," she cried, tears streaming from her eyes. "It looks like Santa just stumbled into our living room and all the toys fell out of his bag."

"But the most precious gift of all," Mama would say whenever she retold the story, "was the Savior's gift to us that hal-lowed Christmas Eve."

Although the illness left me with a physical handicap—one leg was much shorter than the other—I have been privi-leged to lead an active life. In 1977, before he passed away, my husband, Dr. George L. Strebel, and I served in Europe, where he was coordinator of English-speaking semi-naries and institutes. I now have four hap-pily married children and fifteen beautiful grandchildren.

Several years ago I had total hip surgery and one-and-a-half inches were added to my leg. I am now walking without crutches and with only a slight limp. My leg is getting better all the time—a modern installment to the miracle that began that Christmas Eve.

Alda M. Strebel, a retired school teacher and mother of four children, celebrated her eighty-fifth birthday in March 1998. She continues to serve in Church assignments in the Murray Hillside Ward (Murray, Utah), and rejoices in her large posterity.

THE HORSE THAT SAVED CHRISTMAS

Jane Brooking Flint

On our tree each Christmas hangs a little horse-shaped ornament made of dough. To my family, it is the horse that saved Christmas. How did a four-inch tall, cream-colored rocking horse with a glittered bridle save our Christmas? It's a story we will never forget.

Christmas had always been special when we lived in Kentucky, full of traditions and memory-making hours with cousins and grandparents. Christmas Eve was spent with my husband's parents, opening gifts, then listening as Granddaddy Sullivan read the Christmas story by flickering candlelight. We would then travel to my mother's house, where we would spend the night. Christmas morning meant children running down her long staircase to find what Santa had left, followed by a day playing with twenty cousins who lived in the area. Aunts and uncles, sisters and brothers, "in-laws and outlaws," as Mother called her seven children and their spouses, spent the day enjoying each other's company.

Then came the year that a recession in Kentucky forced us to move to Texas, where my husband was able to find a construction job. We spent Christmas that year in Texas with only our immediate family.

"Next Christmas we will go to Kentucky and spend it with Mammy Mae in cousinland," we promised the children.

Next fall came, and with it the Texas monsoon. The weekly paychecks were small because of workdays missed. When December arrived, our savings were depleted and there was no obvious way we could make the trip to Kentucky for the holidays.

We paid our tithing rather than using the money to make the trip, knowing that Christmas in Kentucky would not be worth withholding from the Lord to get there.

The next week brought more rainclouds to match the one brooding over my head. In despair I went to our bedroom, closed the door, and on my knees poured out my heart to my Father in Heaven. "Please, Father—I need a miracle. We have five little ones who are counting on us to take them to Kentucky for Christmas. They have three loving grandparents who are counting on us to get them there too. I can't leave my babies and get a job. I pray that I might know what to do!"

Immediately I felt a surge of energy, and with it came a plan. In my mind I saw the little cream-colored rocking horses I had made for my oldest son's fifth-grade class the year before. They were salt-dough ornaments I had cut out, water colored, then dipped in varnish. The horses were personalized with a name across the rocker.

I had learned the craft in a Relief Society Homemaking class, and the ornaments were inexpensive to make. I knew, with ten willing hands to help and with the Lord on our side, we could make more of the ornaments and sell them.

We met in family council and agreed we would need to sell three hundred horses at one dollar each. Our total cost for the project would be twenty dollars. The three school-aged children each took a horse to school the next day to show to their teachers. Word spread, and it seemed everyone had a dollar to spend for a cream-colored rocking horse.

Our kitchen became an assembly line, with each family member taking part in painting, glittering, or dipping each ornament in varnish. By December 15 we were well on our way to reaching our goal. A friend at the bank got one hundred orders. Eli, our eleven-year-old, sold sixty-five. Jacob, the nine-year-old, sold twenty-five, and even seven-year-old Mae sold twenty-one horses. Still, we were almost ninety horses shy of our goal.

That weekend, I was scheduled to speak at the Saturday evening session of stake conference about "living within our means." I felt inspired to include in my talk the story of our family's project to let the members know how the Lord was helping us meet a financial goal. After the meeting, a brother from another ward whom I had never met approached me and asked, "Do you have any more of those horses?"

"Oh, yes, we still have to sell about ninety to reach our goal," I answered.

"Good. I want a hundred," he said.

We delivered the one hundred horses Monday afternoon and started discussing who we wanted to see first after we crossed the Kentucky state line.

Our project taught us many lessons. We learned that family members grow closer as they work and sing together, and that honest work is the answer to a financial need. We also learned that the Lord will inspire us when we worthily plead for ideas, and he will help us to fulfill our righteous desires.

That Christmas the children made the most of every minute they spent in Kentucky. We gave Mammy Mae twenty-six rocking horses, each one bearing a grandchild's name. It was our last Christmas with Granddaddy Sullivan. He passed away the following summer.

I am thankful to Heavenly Father for the wonderful Christmas we enjoyed as a result of his inspiration to make a little cream-colored rocking horse.

Jane Brooking Flint now lives with her husband, Rod, and their children in the 100-year-old farmhouse where she grew up near Kevil, Kentucky. An English and journalism teacher, she publishes her high school's newspaper and yearbook.

Coming Home, Going Home

Mary Ellen Edmunds

How he wanted to come home for Christmas! It would take too long to explain why he was away from home in the first place, but he was. He hadn't been in the hospital too many days, and he wouldn't be there much longer, but even *one hour* seems too long when you'd rather be home. The decorations and pictures we had put in the room were no substitute for the real thing. Even our frequent visits didn't quite do it, though he very much appreciated having us there.

What a glorious time we had on that Christmas Day of 1997 when my brother John brought Dad home. It was a Thursday. We rejoiced when we saw Dad in his own chair, with his family surrounding him.

He had celebrated many Christmases since his first one in 1902 in the little community of Wales, Utah, but this one seemed best of all. All eight of us children and our families had gathered, including almost all of the thirty grandchildren (the youngest, Jill Ella, had been blessed by her grandfather a few days earlier in his last priesthood ordinance) and eleven great-grandchildren (including "brand new" Sydney) were there to enjoy this remarkable day.

With the miracle of the "pocket talker" we all had a chance to tell him "Merry Christmas," to report on Christmas morning, and to ask him questions and hear his wonderful answers. Little ones looked into his bright blue eyes as they sang about Rudolph, told him what Santa had brought, and gave him their special Christmas gifts and greetings. No visit from Santa Claus could have come close to the feeling of having Dad right where he belonged for this Christmas Day.

Memories of so many previous Christmases came flooding back: Christmas Eve pageants, with our "towel-and-robe" costumes and whatever animals were on hand— always at least one dog, and usually a guinea pig or two; the times when Dad got his violin out, invited us to get our different instruments, and we played Christmas hymns together; the village on the mantle with cotton for snow and little lights in the windows of the tiny cardboard homes; the tree, the presents, the story from the Book of Luke.

I remembered my own homesickness as I spent so many Christmas seasons in faraway places with strange-sounding names. How I cherished the letters from home, reminding me that I was missed.

At the end of that perfect Christmas day, my brother Paul and his son had the tender task of taking Dad back to the rehabilitation center. First he wanted to sit on the "church bench" near the front door and have his sweetheart Ella sit beside him. He kissed her sweetly and said goodbye. Looking back, we realize that perhaps he knew what was happening and why that particular goodbye was so important to him.

On Friday it seemed that Christmas had been almost "too much." My sister Charlotte visited Dad early in the morning and called to say that he was "zonked" and not responding much to anyone. On Saturday he was able to visit with us, as bright and alert as ever. Most of us had the chance to visit him that day. I was there for a while in the afternoon, and it seemed as if he didn't want me to leave. Did he have some idea of what was coming? I think perhaps he did.

I watched as the kind respiratory therapist gave him the treatments that made him cough a lot, then Dad turned, saw me, and welcomed me so warmly. I talked to him, hugged him, got him water to drink, and tried to adjust his bed to where he felt comfortable. He was so sweet as he asked, "Try it a little bit higher." I would crank it a little bit (the bed didn't have the push-button way of being raised and lowered), wanting to make it just right. Almost apologetically he would say, "maybe a little lower." When I finally left, just as Charlotte and her daughter Mary arrived, he said, as always, "Thank you for your visit." Always the perfect gentleman and gentle man.

Early on Saturday evening, shortly after my sister Ann and her boys had left, something drastic happened to Dad. With his many years of experience as a physician, he knew exactly when, and he knew exactly what. There was a rupture in his intestine with the inevitable excruciating pain.

Dad was taken to the emergency room, and the rehab center people tried to get in touch with Charlotte. She wasn't home, but they got her husband, Art, and he went down there immediately. When Dad saw him he asked, "How did *you* know?" Sweet Dad! John arrived after Dad had been put on a gurney, and Dad looked up at him and said "Finally you've come!" Meanwhile Charlotte found out and went quickly to the hospital.

It seemed that everything took such a long, long time. There were X-rays, lab tests, an I.V., and so on. When the surgeon came and looked at the X-rays, he called Charlotte and John aside. He showed them the X-rays and explained that the situation wasn't very good. He told them he would do surgery if they pressed him, but on a scale of zero to ten (as to how Dad would fare), Dad was at zero. The surgeon said that if it were *his* Dad, he'd keep him very comfortable and "let him go." He talked to them about this being the way it happens— we get old and things wear out and it's time to go. He talked of how Dad had lived a *good* life for ninety-five wonderful years.

Charlotte told me this was the most difficult part, to see the look on Dad's face as John helped him understand. She said John was so kind and gentle with Dad as he

explained what the surgeon had said. Still, it was Dad's decision whether to have the surgery. He told John and Charlotte several times, "I'm so nervous." There was such sweetness and honesty as the inevitable began to settle in on them—there was no way Dad could survive surgery, and there was no way he could survive without surgery.

My brother Frank had arrived by then and worked with John and Charlotte in loving and helping Dad. They did all they could to comfort and support him.

Dad did not want to make the decision alone as to whether or not to have surgery. He wanted the rest of us there. No words could describe the agony of realizing that surgery really wasn't an option. It was time for our dear father to go Home.

My phone call came at 12:40 on Sunday morning, December 28. The phone itself didn't awaken me entirely, but I heard my brother's voice coming from the answering machine in the other room. When I finally heard "the still, small voice" tell me to get up and listen to that message, I knew something huge was happening. I called the emergency room and talked to both John and Frank. They said that Dad might be facing something we really didn't know how to handle. I dressed quickly and drove to my youngest brother's home.

Richard and his wife, Glenda, responded to my knock, and all I could say was, "I think Dad's going Home." I briefly explained where Dad was and that we were all gathering. Richard offered to pick up our sister Ann on his way to the hospital.

It was time to get Mom. My sister Susan was about to leave as I drove up and wondered if she should wait for us. I told her that it was all right for her to go ahead.

I went in quietly, not wanting to jar Mom awake with the sound of knocking or the doorbell. The instant I touched her shoulder, she sat up and looked into my face with a question she couldn't ask. I told her, "Mom, Dad's going Home, and we're all gathering." I helped her get ready, and we headed for the hospital to join the others.

I knew I couldn't fully understand what it was like to have spent sixty Christmases with someone who loved you as much as our father loved our mother, then realize that you would have to say goodbye for a while.

A cold wind was blowing across the snow as we went out to the car. Mom looked around and said, "It's a beautiful night." Yes, a beautiful, silent, holy night.

The drive to the hospital was so quiet. There were many things Mom needed and wanted to say as she prepared for this experience—the one you think or hope will never come.

The emergency area was busy even though it was the middle of the night. I pointed to the cars that belonged to my brothers and sisters and said to Mom, "Look, all your children are here."

Dad had not been taken to a room, but curtains were drawn so that we could have some privacy. There has not been a time when it felt more important or sweet to see every brother and sister gathered around our dear parents. As I looked at each of them and their companions and realized how seldom we were all in town at the same time, it seemed that Dad may have asked for the timing, if not the method. There we were, sealed together because of the covenants of our patriarch, our precious father, who now needed to leave us for a little while.

He was in pain but aware of what was happening. We could sense how much it meant for him to see his sweetheart, Ella—his favorite nurse—and all of his children by his side.

Paul offered a most beautiful and comforting prayer, while Dad listened through the pocket talker and the rest of us stood with our arms around each other. We each had a chance to tell him of our love, to thank him for being such a wonderful father, to tell him good-bye, and to send our messages of love to those whom Dad was soon going to see. And yes, there were angels 'round about to bear us up, waiting to accompany him on his journey. I quoted Doctrine and Covenants 84:88 for him, knowing he was much more aware of the angels than I. He looked at us from time to time, especially at Mom.

We waited for arrangements to be made for a room somewhere in the hospital. We kept talking to him. "We're all here, Daddy. We won't leave *you,* but you can leave us when you need to." "Angels are all around you." "Please come and visit us *anytime,* Daddy." "Thanks for the good name you've given us and all you've taught us." "We love you because you first loved us." "Rest now, Daddy." "Merry Christmas."

It was time to move to a room on the sixth floor where we could be with our dear father for his final day of mortal life, this last Sunday of the year, this Christmastime. It was about 4:00 A.M. when we went to room 617. There were many unforgettable moments during the next twelve hours. Everyone helped each other as we took turns coming and going.

At 7:00 A.M., just as a spectacular sunrise was coming over the mountains, Ann and I went to the rehabilitation center to get Dad's belongings. It was especially hard when we put things like his cane and clothing in the car. I noticed how simple his surroundings were, just like at home. He and Mom often said to me, "Our wants are few; we have everything we need." I remembered Dad telling us about one of his favorite Christmases as a child—there was one orange for all the children to share.

Back in his hospital room, we took turns sitting by Dad, holding his hand and talking to him. A grandchild read scriptures to him. A great-grandchild sang "I Am a Child of God." One little one called to ask her dad, "Is Grandpa still alive?" "Yes, Tina." "Does he still love me?" "Oh yes." A grandson shared his feelings: "Thanks for being my Grandpa. I remember all the times you

played Parcheesi with me for hours and hours, and you never got tired of me."

The nurses and other staff members were so kind. They came regularly to check on Dad. We noticed that his blood pressure was slowly but surely going down. A group of doctors arrived from the family practice clinic, and when they said it would be "two to three days," Charlotte turned to me and quietly shook her head. She knew it wouldn't be that long.

There were such tender comments from the little ones: grandson Paul telling his mother, Kathy, that his dad, Frank, "can make Grandpa better—he's a *doctor!*" Later, when Dad had gone, grandson David told his parents, Richard and Glenda, that "he died because he didn't have enough hair," and then, with a very sad face, "now I won't see him for *two hundred years!*" And Christopher telling his parents, John and Melanie, that "it's Angels' Day."

I know Dad was listening to us, aware of our love and tender feelings. He squeezed our hands as we held his. We wanted to make sure we were always touching him, that he always knew we were right there, and that he wasn't alone. He certainly *wasn't* alone, and I'm not just talking about "earthlings."

Once I leaned over to kiss and hug him and said into the little pocket talker, "Dad, it's me, it's Sweetie." He opened his eyes and looked right into mine with pure love.

Frank thought that was wonderful and took his turn. "Dad, it's Frank." No response. (At least Dad didn't open his eyes). Then Frank asked, "Dad, are you ignoring me?" His gentle humor helped us all through this difficult experience.

We spoke of those who would be waiting for Dad, including his own dear father whom he had not seen since he was nine years old, and his mother, brothers, and sisters, Susan's dear husband, Wendell, who was close to Dad before going Home just two years earlier, and so many others. It was as if we could sense them getting ready to welcome him as soon as we were ready to let him go.

Family members came and went. Many who had been up all night had gone home to rest, to care for their children, and to prepare to spend the night back at the hospital. We had planned to be with Dad in shifts, at least two at a time. At 3:00 P.M. everyone had gone except Charlotte and me.

If we had known what would happen next, no one would have left.

The moment everyone had gone but us, Dad's breathing changed. Charlotte noticed it first, looked at me, and said, "He's going." We knew it, but didn't want it to be true. We hugged and kissed our sweet Daddy, and I kept asking, "Are you going, Daddy? Is it time for you to go?" Charlotte leaned over and said, "You can go, Daddy, you can go now."

I think that's what he needed to know—that it was all right for him to respond to the angelic beckoning of which he most certainly was aware.

We kept talking to him. I promised him that we would take good care of Mom.

It was about 3:20 on that Sunday afternoon when he didn't breathe anymore.

One of the things Paul had prayed for was that Heavenly Father would bring Dad back to Him gently, and that's exactly what happened. Quietly, tenderly, gently our Daddy slipped away from us. We knew, and yet I kept talking to him. "Have you gone, Daddy?" I couldn't help saying to Charlotte that Dad must be shaking his head, watching as his two daughters who were nurses couldn't seem to understand that he had gone. Is anything more sacred or holy than hugging your Daddy as he slips from your loving arms to those of his own daddy and mother, brothers and sisters, Savior and Heavenly Parents?

We called for the nurses who were on duty to come and make sure of what we knew, and then we called our family to come back. We gathered around our sweet Daddy once again, shedding our tears, hugging and comforting each other, mourning with those who mourned.

And so, Daddy came home for Christmas. And then he went Home forever.

Mary Ellen Edmunds is an author and teacher. She served as a member of the general board of the Relief Society and was a director of training at the Missionary Training Center.

CROSSING THE SWEETWATER OF OUR HEARTS

*Scot Facer Proctor and
Maurine Jensen Proctor*

For some time we had been worried about our high school son Eliot, a worry that ate at our peace of mind and sometimes kept us talking into the night, restless and edgy, wondering what we could do to help him. We remembered so many tender things about him—the way he used to leave a minute's worth of kisses for Maurine on the answering machine when he was little, the funny story that he had written about a monster in first grade, the way he remembered birthdays and Christmases with unique presents. As he had grown up we could see he had a gift with people, a charisma that attracted friends to him in hordes, but for all the good things about him our relationship had become strained. Our love for him was laced with fear, for we had come to worry about his choices. His priesthood leader said he always skipped out on meetings; he sluffed seminary; and he had told us, his words dripping with sarcasm, that we couldn't shove "our religion" on him.

The more we saw these changes, the more we worried, and nothing degenerates a relationship between parent and child quite like fear. Where was he headed? Would he reject the things that matter most? Was he throwing away his opportunities, his life? This is what we thought while we asked instead, "Where are you going tonight?" Fear made our questions to him too pointed, too insistent. Fear obliterated casual conversation. And the fear in our hearts, unbeknownst to us, also edged into resentment. How can this boy trample the values that are dearest to us? And even more, we wondered at our own feeling: "I love you and I don't recognize you."

It was in this state of mind that Scot went to Wyoming to take several photographs of Martin's Cove and the Sweetwater River. He recorded this of his experience:

Gray, wintery days are miserable for photographers whose lives are spent chasing the light. An aching hollowness seems to stalk the halls of the creative mind and heart as he looks for definition, for light and shadow in the rocks, the trees, and the streams he is trying to shoot, and finds none. Such was the kind of day I faced as I stood alone on the banks of the Sweetwater River in the highlands of Wyoming and within echoing distance of the famous Devil's Gate.

Sometimes I will wait for hours for the light to change, for cloud cover to move over, for the angle of the sun to increase—waiting for that moment when all the elements from the heavens work together and my immense task is to use my index finger to press the shutter. It is during these times that I ponder and pray, wander in memories, meditate the things of eternity.

The Sweetwater was cold and swift that day as I stood beside an S-curved shoreline. With the camera locked on the tripod and the meter set, I took a moment and dipped my hand in the icy water. A shiver went up my spine and my hand immediately throbbed and ached, "Now that is cold water," I said aloud. The horses in the field nearby seemed to hear my voice.

In that terrible, early blizzard of 1856, members of the Martin Handcart company had been forced to cross the Sweetwater near this very spot where I was standing with my camera, an intolerable idea given their haggard, hungry, already-frozen condition. I thought of Patience Loader as she described her feelings when she saw that the river must be crossed again, "I could not keep my tears back. . . . One of these men who was much worn down, asked in a plaintive tone, 'Have we got to go through there?' On being answered yes, he was so much affected that he was completely overcome. That was the last strain. His fortitude and manhood gave way. He exclaimed, 'Oh dear! I can't go through that!' and he burst into tears."

My mind wandered to those brave teen-aged boys, C. Allen Huntington, George W. Grant, David P. Kimball (and the less-known Stephen W. Taylor) who had arrived with the rescue team to do what they could to try to save the Martin Handcart Company. Seeing the plight of the people, they willingly plunged their bodies into this icy river scores of times all through the day to carry the freezing and hopeless pioneers one by one to the other side—across what seemed to the pioneers an uncrossable chasm.

A slight breeze picked up and changed the face of the water before me. How had their parents instilled such goodness in them? Where had these young men found such nobility of spirit? I then thought about Eliot and my spirit took a bit of a dive as I stood there by the Sweetwater and thought of the pain I felt in parenting this child. I thought of his anger and how he seemed to thwart every effort for good we attempted.

My ponderings became vocal as with almost cynical doubt, I blurted aloud, "If Eliot had been here at this spot in 1856, would he have helped these Martin Handcart saints across this freezing river?" Then came a surprise. At that second, the Spirit whispered to me in a startling, gentle, heart-piercing voice, "Of course he would have." Tears came to my eyes. "Of course, he would have." I knew that the Spirit testifies of the truth of all things. I knew that God cannot lie. My feelings for this seemingly hardened teenager were softened and it appeared that mine was the heart that had been cold.

In the year and a half that followed, we changed and so did Eliot, and in the flurry of life we didn't think much more about Scot's experience in the snow until our son had been in the Ukraine Donetsk Mission for over a year. Winter in Ukraine is bitter with winds that sweep off the Arctic and blow across the Russian steppes with a ferocity that slices into the very bone marrow, and as young American missionaries tramp the streets their eyelashes and nostrils freeze and their muscles numb to the point that words fall out of their mouths in a mumble. Anything they had known of cold in the past dims before this blast which teaches them new levels of endurance. Because there is no snow removal, the ice on the walks builds with every storm until is it four or five inches thick, cutting into boots and making missionaries fall. Eliot said the record number of falls in his mission in one day was fourteen. "It is so weird," he said, "to be walking along and have your companion suddenly fall to the ground, unable to keep his footing."

Yet missionaries in Ukraine can't find much comfort by slipping into public buildings for a moment of warmth either. Even here their breath still pants out in frozen clouds and their face never thaws, for it costs money to heat buildings and in the depressed economy, heat is a luxury. The first building in Donetsk where Eliot attended church was an old barn of a Communist rally center where for three hours in layers of thermal garments, thermals, shirt, sweater, coat, down parka, gloves, wool socks and hat, he froze, partaking of the sacrament with fingers stiff with cold.

While the discomfort was bad, the toll upon the less fortunate was worse. One week the temperature plunged to 35 below zero and the missionaries were advised to stay inside, but outside, Eliot learned, people froze in the streets, their life slowly ebbing out amidst an inhuman chill.

When Christmas came, the bleakness of the city was hardly lifted, and Eliot stomped through the streets feeling the grimness seeping into his soul. The buildings seemed identical in their gray and tan drabness. They were either of five stories or nine, with the only essential difference being that the five-story apartment buildings had no elevator. In both, water and heat were intermittent and appliances were clanky and rusted. Now, in this season of lights, there were none. The only vestige of Christmas that Eliot found was a straggly tree in the city center with a couple of strands of Christmas lights and a drunk Santa Claus and a Snow Princess who charged two dollars to have their picture taken with you.

"All of us missionaries had expected that our mission field Christmases would be our best ever, and we were so let down. The difference between here and home was indescribable. Not one person we knew even mentioned that Christmas was coming, and when I received a new companion from Estonia on Christmas Day, he asked casually, totally unaware of the holiday, 'What's the date today?'"

It gradually became clear to Eliot that if there was to be any Christmas cheer for the missionaries in his district and the neighboring one, he would have to rally. He couldn't bear to think of how the missionaries' spirits would sag without a little remembrance of the season. A few days before Christmas, he and his companion were shopping at the market, putting potatoes and cabbage into a nylon bag, when a Christmas tree for sale caught his eye. Though his hands were already full, he bought this eight-foot tree, put it on his back and dragged it home, the top trailing in the ice behind him. A couple of times he had to stop and rest, but it gave him time to hatch the entire plan. He would give a Christmas dinner for the missionaries at his apartment!

Though he had always hated shiny balls, suddenly he was thrilled to find them for sale by a street hawker, and he got tinsel from a little woman at the side of the road. He broke his only knife trying to saw off the bottom of the tree, and when he stuck it in a bucket, the only adequate weight to keep it from toppling was an old pair of missionary boots stuck in with the trunk.

Dinner was equally inventive as he divided up assignments amongst the mis-

sionaries. Some brought potatoes, some vegetables, but Eliot made an apple cake and plucked a turkey to bake. Midway through the preparations, Eliot had to go to the office to pick up his new companion, and when he got back another elder was trying to cut the turkey. "Didn't you ever watch your parents cut a turkey?" Eliot asked. "This is how you do it." "It felt so good to cut a turkey," he later confided to his journal.

The missionaries drew names to exchange gifts with each other, and Eliot pulled items from his own Christmas box to fill in the gaps of those who had nothing to give.

As parents we delighted in hearing about this Ukrainian Christmas from a distance on the telephone that Christmas night. We felt a tenderness for this dear son who had tried to make Christmas fun for his fellow missionaries, and we listened on the other line while his three-year-old sister, Michaela, sang "Jingle Bells" to him. He had not cried talking to us, but now we heard him sniffing as she mispronounced the words in great glee to him.

It was only a few weeks later that Eliot sent us a poignant letter. The bleak midwinter weather had begun somewhat to relent, and the buds were on the trees. Easter was coming when Eliot and his companion came upon a man swaggering on the street in drunkenness. They had been here long enough to know that the drunkenness was only the symptom of a deeper ill—a hopelessness that came with the inability to find work.

The missionaries asked the man where he lived. He was too incoherent to answer, and they knew that he was in danger of becoming another statistic—another forgotten soul found dead on the road. Finally, learning from a neighbor where he lived, Eliot picked him up, staggering a little under his dead weight, and ploddingly, painfully carried him home. "My arms are in pain from the weight of his body, even though he was not that big," Eliot wrote home. "This man was completely helpless. Without us carrying him home, who knows what would have happened? We are all like this middle-aged man who, on the wayside of life, are utterly helpless without the atoning blood of our Savior Jesus Christ. I am so grateful for his love for us."

It was when we read of this event that Scot's moment on the Sweetwater came back to us. "Would Eliot have helped these Martin Handcart Saints across the freezing water?" Scot had asked, and the Spirit had answered, "Of course, he would." Scores of memories came rushing to us. A neighbor telling us that Eliot had seen her carrying heavy boxes as he drove by in a car. He had stopped to ask if he could help. An elderly woman at a grocery store in Idaho couldn't make her boxes fit on the wheeled vehicle she had brought shopping. Eliot had run across the parking lot to steady them. A baboushka on a winter's day in Donetsk was shoveling a pile of coal. Eliot had taken the shovel from her and done her work. A bunch of missionaries needed a Christmas dinner and Eliot plucked a turkey. A drunken man needed to find his way home and Eliot carried him.

We are grateful that in a manger of Bethlehem lies the promise of the Garden of Gethsemane, that the Christ who was born for us also atoned for us, knowing both our pain and our possibilities intimately. And we are grateful that the Spirit cannot lie, for on a winter's day on the Sweetwater, our hearts made a crossing as we were told something about our son that we had forgotten—who he really was.

Before he went on his mission, Eliot had a movement in his soul, but so did we. We thawed.

Scot Facer Proctor and Maurine Jensen Proctor are a husband-and-wife creative team who produce outstanding pictorial books, including The Gathering, Witness of the Light, Source of the Light, *and* Light from the Dust. *Maurine has enjoyed more than twenty years as a free-lance writer. She graduated from the University of Utah in English and received a master's degree in teaching from Harvard University. Scot has a background in filmmaking, photography, and writing. He graduated from Brigham Young University in motion picture and television production and received a master's degree in instructional technology from Utah State University. Both Scot and Maurine teach institute part time and have been editors of* This People *magazine. They are the parents of eleven children.*

ALL I WANT FOR CHRISTMAS IS SOMETHING SMALL, ROMANTIC, AND EXPENSIVE

Louise Plummer

The first year Tom and I were married, thirty-four years ago, we made a decision—I suspect it was his idea—not to exchange Christmas presents. The thinking was that we were both full-time university students struggling to build a life together and too poor to buy Christmas gifts for each other.

We weren't poor. We had a couple of thousand dollars in the bank and we each worked part-time. Tom had a senior scholarship that paid all of his tuition and books. Plus, the dollar was actually worth a dollar then, instead of the twenty-five cent value it carries today. Given our age and circumstances, we were loaded. Still, I was twenty-two and making a pretense at maturity, and mature people hung onto their money even at Christmastime. How else would I have agreed to such an odious plan?

On Christmas morning, I awoke hoping that my new husband had set me up, so that he could surprise me with something small, romantic, and expensive. He hadn't and he didn't. I was disappointed, but I was also mature and smiled my way through the day telling myself that Christmas dinner with loved ones and watching others open *their* presents was satisfaction enough for an old married woman. Besides, I anticipated that evening when my parents would surely give me, their oldest child, something wonderful, maybe even frivolous.

Tom and I sat on the sofa together and opened our gifts from them—both packages exactly the same size—both packages containing temple clothes! I loved the temple, but temple clothes were not my idea of a fun gift. There's nothing fun about temple clothes. If you own them, you have to wash and iron them and carry them in a funny suitcase that looks like you're going to stay overnight at Grandma's house. If you rent them for a couple of bucks, someone else washes and irons them for you. Seems like a no-brainer to me. But you can't say this to parents who lived through the Depression and World War II in occupied Holland. I smiled and thanked them profusely, as if I were mature and grateful. I was neither.

The following year, our lives changed radically when Tom began graduate studies at Harvard while I worked full-time at the Freshman Seminar Program. We travelled back and forth on electric buses from

Harvard Yard to our apartment on Commonwealth Avenue in Boston. We ate lunches at Brigham's or ordered out at Cardullo's and learned to order tonics instead of soda pop and frappes instead of shakes. We learned that the proud Massachusetts name of Peabody was pronounced Peabuddy with the accent on pea. We browsed in Design Research. We attended church in the Cambridge Ward on Longfellow Park and found added spiritual uplift at the Isabella Stewart Gardner Museum, where we discovered the American painter, John Singer Sargent, for the first time. We were happy and, more importantly, *knew* we were happy.

That second Christmas of our married life and our first year in Boston, we agreed to exchange presents. This, too, was Tom's idea. "I thought last Christmas was boring," he said. "Let's not ever do that again." I don't remember my reaction, but whooping and hollering sounds about right.

"Let's not make any lists," I said. "Let's surprise each other."

"Are you sure? Don't you want to give me at least a few hints?" he asked.

"No, I want to be surprised."

"Scary," he said.

We both set about to do our individual shopping. I bought him the conventional tie and a sweater and a Chinese Checkers game, but I began to sweat the really "fun" present. I thought of fishing gear, records, blah, blah, blah. Not "fun" enough. Finally, one day I passed a music store on Boylston Street and

went in. Initially, I was looking for Cole Porter songbooks but ended up in front of a case of wooden recorders in varying sizes. The recorder, it seemed to me, was a friendly instrument, portable, even charismatic. Think of the Pied Piper. Surely he played a recorder when leading all those children out of Hamblin. In my mind, the Pied Piper looked remarkably like Tom in a green elf suit. I had played the flute growing up, and Tom was a pianist, so I was confident looking at the fingering and scales that we could learn to play in one day. I bought two recorders, one for him and one for me with a book *Teaching Little Fingers to Play the Recorder* and a second book, *Easy-to-Play-Christmas Carols.— Duets for Soprano and Alto Recorders.* I had it all gift-wrapped and made my way home.

"I bought you the most wonderful present," I said, coming into the apartment. "You're going to have so much fun on Christmas Day." He stood in the vestibule.

"What?" I asked, seeing his face.

"I bought *you* several wonderful presents too," he said, smiling like Bambi's mother.

I turned to look at our Christmas tree, but there was nothing under it. (There was nothing *on* it either, except one strand of stringed popcorn which I had tediously strung together one night. It reminded me too much of failed sewing projects for me to continue).

"They're not under the tree," Tom said, following my gaze. "I've hidden them. You'll have to find them on Christmas morning."

Probably, I squealed, "This is going to be so fun!" I liked these kinds of games. If he had disappointed me the year before, he was not disappointing me now.

"I'll hide yours too. You're going to love what I got you. You're just going to love it!"

"Give me a hint."

"No, and don't touch them either. Don't even look at them."

"The red one looks like it might be a game. Is it a game?"

"Don't guess either. Don't even."

On Christmas Eve, we ate dinner and sat in front of our woefully undecorated tree. "In my family, Santa Claus came on Christmas Eve. That's when we opened our presents," Tom said. "Why don't we do that?"

"That's not any fun," I said. "All the anticipation goes out of it. In my family, we kids couldn't sleep and we'd sing all night and then send the youngest one to Mother and Dad's room to ask if we could get up now—at four in the morning."

"Is that what we're going to do? Sing all night?"

"No, Silly."

We went to bed early and played guessing games. Did you get me clothing? *No. I wouldn't dare buy you clothes.* Did you get me cologne? *No.* A book? *No.*

We sang too, our voices in a tentative harmony—"God Rest Ye Merry Gentlemen—"

Then came periods of silence broken by, "Are you asleep?"

"Yes, are you?"

"Yes." Muffled guffaws.

"You'll love what I got you."

"*You'll* love what I got *you.*"

At two in the morning, we still had not slept. Tom pushed the blankets back. "I can't stand it," he said, sitting up.

"Actually, it *is* officially Christmas," I said.

"Let's do it!" We both leaped out of bed.

"I have to go down to the car," Tom said. "I hid your presents in the trunk."

"You were going to let me search all over this apartment?"

"Yes, but I can't stand to wait any longer." He put on his bathrobe and padded down the hallway.

I pulled his presents from their hiding places—the best being in the electric frying pan under the lid.

Tom returned delightfully burdened with gifts.

He loved the cardigan sweater and the tie. He loved the Chinese Checkers, which he played with his grandmother growing up. He loved the recorder and the music and began learning scales immediately.

I loved the oil paints, the easel, the canvases. I loved the pink suit, a suit I would never have bought for myself. A polyester suit. A suit that made me look more like a goose than a swan. "You can exchange it if you want. Honestly, I don't care. I can't believe I even dared buy you a suit."

"I love this suit," I said holding it against

my nightgown. "I love it because you bought it for me." I kissed him. I was twenty-three years old and goofy with love for my young husband who had ventured into a woman's shop and risked all confidence to buy me a bad suit. A suit I wore gladly for years, because I sensed that to return it would mean he would never again risk buying me a surprise present.

There are photographs of us playing recorder duets on that Christmas Day in front of our forlorn tree. "Jingle Bells" was our first piece. We had it down cold by ten in the morning. Tom is wearing his new cardigan and tie. I am wearing a pink poly-ester suit with a cowl neckline, and I look quite mature for my age.

Louise Plummer is an assistant professor of English at Brigham Young University as well as a writer. Her latest novel is The Unlikely Romance of Kate Bjorkman. *She and her husband, Tom, have four sons and live in Salt Lake City.*

OTHER TITLES OF INTEREST FROM ST. LUCIE PRESS

Organization Teams: Building Continuous Quality Improvement

Team Building: A Structured Learning Approach

The Motivating Team Leader

The New Leader: Bringing Creativity and Innovation to the Workplace

Total Quality in Managing Human Resources

Total Quality in Research and Development

Total Quality in Marketing

Total Quality in Purchasing and Supplier Management

Focused Quality: Managing for Results

The Executive Guide to Implementing Quality Systems

Sustaining High Performance: The Strategic Transformation to a Customer-Focused Learning Organization

How to Reengineer Your Performance Management Process

Deming: The Way We Knew Him

For more information about these titles call, fax or write:

St. Lucie Press
100 E. Linton Blvd., Suite 403B
Delray Beach, FL 33483
TEL (407) 274-9906 • FAX (407) 274-9927

S^t_L

Total Quality in
INFORMATION SYSTEMS AND TECHNOLOGY

The St. Lucie Press
Total Quality Series™

BOOKS IN THE SERIES:

Total Quality in HIGHER EDUCATION

Total Quality in PURCHASING and SUPPLIER MANAGEMENT

Total Quality in INFORMATION SYSTEMS and TECHNOLOGY

Total Quality in RESEARCH and DEVELOPMENT

Total Quality in MANAGING HUMAN RESOURCES

Total Quality and ORGANIZATION DEVELOPMENT

Total Quality in MARKETING

MACROLOGISTICS MANAGEMENT

For more information about these books call St. Lucie Press at (407) 274-9906

Series Editor • Frank Voehl
Series Development Editor • Sandy Pearlman

Total Quality in

INFORMATION SYSTEMS AND TECHNOLOGY

By
Jack Woodall, MBA
Vice President and COO
Management Systems International
Boca Raton, Florida

Deborah K. Rebuck, MBA
CEO and Founder
Maximum Business Automation
Tampa, Florida

Frank Voehl
President and CEO
Strategy Associates, Inc.
Coral Springs, Florida

S_L^t

St. Lucie Press
Delray Beach, Florida

Phone: (407) 274-9906
Fax: (407) 274-9927

$S{}_L^t$

Published by
St. Lucie Press
100 E. Linton Blvd., Suite 403B
Delray Beach, FL 33483

TABLE OF CONTENTS

SERIES PREFACE

The St. Lucie Press Series on Total Quality originated in 1993 when some of us realized that the rapidly expanding field of quality management was neither well defined nor well focused. This realization, coupled with America's hunger for specific, how-to examples, led to the formulation of a plan to publish a series of subject-specific books on total quality, a new direction for books in the field to follow.

The essence of this series consists of a core nucleus of eight new direction books, around which the remaining books in the series will revolve over a three-year period:

- Education Transformation: *Total Quality in Higher Education*
- Respect for People: *Total Quality in Managing Human Resources*
- Speak with Facts: *Total Quality in Information Systems and Technology*
- Customer Satisfaction: *Total Quality in Marketing*
- Continuous Improvement: *Total Quality in Research and Development*
- System Transformation: *Total Quality and Organization Development*
- Supplier Partnerships: *Total Quality in Purchasing and Supplier Management*
- Cost-Effective, Value-Added Services: *Total Quality and Measurement*

We at St. Lucie Press have been privileged to contribute to the convergence of philosophy and underlying principles of total quality, leading to a common set of assumptions. One of the most important deals with the challenges facing the transformation of the information systems and technology area for the 21st century. This is a particularly exciting and turbulent time in this field, both domestically and globally, and change may be viewed as either an opportunity or a threat. As such, the principles and practices of total quality can aid in this transformation or, by flawed implementation approaches, can bring an organization to its knees. A total of $60 billion a year is spent in this area.

As the authors of this text explain, the total quality orientation redefines managerial roles and identifies new responsibilities for the traditional function to come to grips with. The information systems/information technology professional's role now includes strategic input and continual development of the strategic planning system to increase customer satisfaction both now and in the future. The full meaning of these changes is fully explored in light of the driving forces reshaping the systems environment.

As Series Editor, I am pleased with the manner in which the series is coming together. Its premise is that excellence can be achieved through a singular focus on customers and their interests as a number one priority, a focus that requires a high degree of commitment, flexibility, and resolve. The new definition of the degree of satisfaction will be the total experience of the interaction—which will be the determinant of whether the customer stays a customer. However, no book or series can tell an organization how to achieve total quality; only the customers and stakeholders can tell you when you have it and when you do not. High-quality goods and services can give an organization a competitive edge while reducing costs due to rework, returns, and scrap. Most importantly, outstanding quality generates satisfied customers, who reward the organization with continued patronage and free word-of-mouth advertising.

In the area of abstracts, we are indebted to Richard Frantzreb, President of Advanced Personnel Systems, who has granted permission to incorporate selected abstracts from their collection, which they independently publish in a quarterly magazine called *Quality Abstracts*. This feature is a sister publication to *Training and Development Alert*. These journals are designed to keep readers abreast of literature in the field of quality and to help readers benefit from the insights and experience of experts and practitioners who are implementing total quality in their organizations. Each journal runs between 28 and 36 pages and contains about 100 carefully selected abstracts of articles and books in the field. For further information, contact Richard Frantzreb (916-781-2900).

We trust that you will find this book both usable and beneficial and wish you maximum success on the quality journey. If it in some way makes a contribution, then we can say, as Dr. Deming often did at the end of his seminars, "I have done my best."

Frank Voehl
Series Editor

AUTHORS' PREFACE

This book breaks tradition in its treatment of information technology, also known as information systems. Its purpose is to educate business and technical personnel at all levels on how to bridge the communication and quality gaps between their respective areas. The intent is to provide a guideline for actions to be taken before getting into the "nuts and bolts." Acting before preliminary planning costs money, especially when expensive technology is involved.

Many business managers believe the technology area should be excluded in company planning. Traditionally, technology has been viewed as a costly overhead area that rarely delivers on time or within budget. Properly used, technology is an investment rather than an expense. On the flip side, many technicians invariably want the newest technology regardless of cost. Our intent is to show how a company can gain a competitive edge when the technical and business areas work in harmony. This book covers proven, successful methods.

We would like to acknowledge and express our gratitude to organizations and individuals who provided additional information and experiences. A special thanks to the Data Processing Management Association, Dr. Roger McGrath, Jr., University of South Florida, Penn State, University of Miami, Warfields Business Record, American City Business Journals, and the Data Interchange Standards Association. There were other individuals who provided support (they know who they are), but an extra special thank-you to Pat Woodall and Joe Burke for their patience.

We encourage you to contact us to share your success and concerns.

Jack Woodall
Deborah K. Rebuck
Frank Voehl

THE SERIES EDITOR

Frank Voehl has had a twenty-year career in quality management, productivity improvement, and related fields. He has written more than 200 articles, papers, and books on the subject of quality and has consulted on quality and productivity issues, as well as measurement system implementation, for hundreds of companies (many Fortune 500 corporations). As general manager of FPL Qualtec, he was influential in the FPL Deming Prize process, which led to the formation of the Malcolm Baldrige Award, as well as the National Quality Award in the Bahamas. He is a member of Strategic Planning committees with the ASQC and AQP and has assisted the IRS in quality planning as a member of the Commissioner's Advisory Group.

An industrial engineering graduate from St. John's University in New York City, Mr. Voehl has been a visiting professor and lecturer at NYU and the University of Miami, where he helped establish the framework for the Quality Institute. He is currently president and CEO of Strategy Associates, Inc. and a visiting professor at Florida International University.

On the local level, Mr. Voehl served for ten years as vice chairman of the Margate/Broward County Advisory Committee for the Handicapped. In 1983, he was awarded the Partners in Productivity award for his efforts to streamline and improve the Utilities Forced Relocation Process, which saved the state of Florida some $200 million over a seven-year period.

THE AUTHORS

Jack Woodall, MBA, is vice president and chief operating officer of Management Systems International in Boca Raton, Florida. As a consultant in total quality management, he participates in the assessments of clients' total quality management needs, identification of initial and successive interface areas, and total deployment programs.

Mr. Woodall received his Masters in Business Administration from the University of Miami and attended the Program for Management Development at the Harvard Business School.

His strong management skills are enhanced by his involvement as a major contributor in the development and implementation of FPL's total quality management system and the Deming examination. He is an expert in total quality management deployment technology and methodologies.

Mr. Woodall assisted in the implementation of the University of Miami's Institute for the Study of Quality in Manufacturing and Services and served as a director for the institute. He participated in study missions and steering committee meetings in Japan and has studied under Drs. Asaka, Kano, Kondo, Kuragane, and Makabe. He has also served on numerous committees and held positions of leadership within professional and user computer organizations.

Deborah K. Rebuck, MBA, is the CEO and founder of Maximum Business Automation in Tampa, Florida. Her firm specializes in planning, management, training, and bridging the gap between the business and technical worlds. The company provides personnel who can address both technical and business issues. Ms. Rebuck is a results-oriented business and computer professional with solid experience and achievements working within various corporate environments. She has over fifteen years of solid management experience with major Fortune 100 companies. Her background includes both domestic and international experience in major projects.

Ms. Rebuck received her Masters in Business Administration, magna cum laude, and Bachelor of Science, summa cum laude, in management and marketing from Tampa College in Tampa, Florida. She also holds a certificate in computer programming from Lear Siegler in Washington, D.C.

Her experience in key troubleshooting roles has earned her a reputation as a results-oriented individual. She focuses on business solutions, using information technology as an enabler, rather than letting technology drive the solution.

CHAPTER 1

HARNESSING THE POWER OF INFORMATION TECHNOLOGY THROUGH TOTAL QUALITY: AN OVERVIEW OF TECHNOLOGY, QUALITY, AND INFORMATION

TECHNOLOGY: THE GREAT ENGINE OF CHANGE

Technology is arguably the most powerful and definitive force in the development of modern civilization. Fueled by scientific development and discovery, the evolution of technology is synonymous with the history of man's struggle to improve his condition on the planet, his sheer will and desire to reach beyond the limitations of the day and create altogether new, unprecedented ways of traveling, treating the ill, communicating, working, creating, and entertaining. Technology has transformed, and continues to transform, the way we live and move and think. Quite succinctly, technology has and continues to transform *what we are*.

Technology is so deeply embedded in the human psyche that it is an extension of man himself, of his desire to exercise control over the environment and wield the materials of the world to his advantage. Beginning with the first flint and stone, the first rudimentary wheel, technology has shaped the way we think of ourselves, the way we interact with one another, and the way we control the natural environment. It is as much a cause as an effect of human and planetary evolution. It is used by the good to build and create and by the evil to destroy and violate.

Technology is not static. It moves in spurts and sometimes waves of discovery and innovation. Like a tornado, its course is often unpredictable and dangerous. Like shattering glass, it can break off in a thousand directions, spawning a huge network of subinnovations and spinoffs, each with its own unique shape, form, and application. How, for example, can we begin to assess the impact of Gutenberg's printing press, Watt's steam engine, or Franklin's lightning conductor on the development of civilization?

Technology rarely acts alone. Discoveries, advances, and innovations often merge and combine to engender new applications, new products that would not be possible without the important contribution of each separate technological development. Guns, for instance, would never have come into existence if gunpowder, formerly used by the Chinese for fireworks, was not combined with the matchlock, the flintlock, and subsequent advances in gunpowder-ignition mechanisms. Electricity, without developments in generation, transmission, and distribution, would never have found its way into almost every household in the developed world. And oil, the precious fuel of the industrial age, would never have become so vitally important apart from the combustion engine, would never have even been extracted in mass quantities apart from drilling technologies, would never have been refined without processing technologies, and would never have been consumed on a mass scale apart from the literally thousands of parallel technological developments undergirding the commercialization of energy and oil-powered transmission and travel.

Technology has the power to ravage old inventions on a global scale, rendering them useless and obsolete, while simultaneously laying the groundwork for entirely new ways of constructing, moving, communicating, and living. Who, for example, in today's gas-powered society remembers the horse and buggy? Who can fathom survival without the toilet, the calculator, or the telephone? While all these innovations were spawned in the spirit of their archaic precursors—the outhouse, the slide rule, the telegraph—they represent quantum, nonlinear leaps in how sewage is disposed, numbers are crunched, and messages are sent. How many of us still use the Morse code?

Clearly, technological innovation has the power to change the lives of millions in one overarching swoop. In fact, the economic destinies and living conditions of entire nations have been and continue to be radically altered by significant technological breakthroughs. As technology evolves, mutates, and permeates the world, it holds great potential and possibility for the future and, for better or for worse, leaves the lives of millions, even billions, hanging in the balance.

THE BEHAVIOR OF TECHNOLOGY

Sometimes technology develops in increments and sometimes by leaps and bounds, a phenomenon we can trace by looking briefly at the history of building materials and techniques from pre-industrial to industrial times. From earth to timber to clay to stone to iron to steel, a quick study of this evolution affords us a glimpse into the behavior of technology—how it sometimes progresses in small, linear steps and how sometimes, in one large, quantum leap, it jumps beyond itself, breaking through all the old assumptions and their concomitant constraints.

In early times, Paleolithic men, when caves were not available, made cave-like dwellings built into the ground from timber, earth, and, some believe, animal bones. Later, Neolithic men made above-the-ground structures from timber and animal hide and bones. In the Near East (which had less timber), dried clay, reeds, and palm leaves were used to construct entire villages east of the Tigris and in Jericho during the Stone Age, a time when various uses of clay were developed and proliferated as a staple element of construction.

Further developments in building technology awaited the introduction of stone by the Egyptians, who cut out and transported large blocks as heavy as 1,000 tons for use in the construction of pyramids and temples. According to T.K. Derry and Trevor Williams,[1] authors of A *Short History of Technology*, stone was also used later, in the first millennium B.C. by Assyrian king Sennacherib, to build a stone canal through which water was transported to Nineveh from a point 50 miles away.

These developments in stone-based construction did not replace earlier clay- and wood-based techniques overnight, much as modern-day technological developments do not instantly replace their predecessors. As with any new technological development, there is an incubation period during which the new technology is applied experimentally and sporadically. After this initial period of development, when the new materials and techniques are tested and refined, there comes a time when the new surpasses the old, at first overshadowing it and, eventually, rendering it secondary or obsolete. At just the right time, when the market is ready, the emerging technology is catapulted to the forefront.

In the case of stone, for hundreds of years it was combined with clay and brick and wood in construction. The Cretans, for example, used stone rubble for the bottom of their palace walls, sun-dried brick for the upper part, stone piers for the first-floor supports, and timber for the frame. Eventually, however, due to superior strength and durability, incremental accelerations in stone- and cement-based construction technologies during the Renaissance and post-Renaissance periods largely replaced the early clay-based building materials.

The introduction of iron, on the other hand, represented a leap in building and construction. Used for framework, roofwork, cement reinforcement, and, as early as 1779, for bridge building, iron ushered in a new era of building materials. At a time when multi-story mill buildings were made with solid plank floors and wooden beams and posts, the use of iron greatly reduced the threat of fire (and the cost of fire insurance!) and introduced an element of strength and flexibility theretofore unachievable. The cast-iron frame, sometimes reaching 70 feet, foreshadowed the modern type of structure that in no way relied on the walls to bear the weight of the structure.

Finally, cheap steel, even stronger and less rigid than its iron predecessor, was introduced as a structural material in the 1870s. While at first most steel was consumed by the railways for track, later it was approved by the British Board of Trade for use in bridge building. In America, the world's leader in cheap steel output, the innovative new material was used at first in the upper stories of enormously tall buildings as high as 14 stories and later in the construction of all-steel-framed skyscrapers, some as high as 386 feet. So revolutionary was this new-age material that the 21-story Masonic Temple built in 1892 in Chicago was described as one of the 7 wonders of the world.

In much the same way as earlier advances, the advent of steel combined with related technological advances to yield entirely new ways of constructing buildings and civil infrastructures. The invention of reinforced concrete for foundations and hydraulic lifts for elevators, for example, combined to make possible that stretching, formerly unimaginable structure we now call a skyscraper. It is this "technological clustering" phenomenon that has transformed society with such menacing power and sheer force and that promises to continue its upward trend for as long as humans inhabit the earth.

The legacy of building materials is, of course, long and detailed enough to fill many more pages. It is only mentioned here, with the aid of a simple, pre-industrial age example, to illustrate the developing nature of technology: how it moves, jumps, and clusters to change the way we live and make our living.

Technology is an essential and foundational element of virtually every facet of life, including building and construction, travel and communications, energy, entertainment, and industry. As such, the way it is managed and applied becomes a matter of critical importance that has far-reaching implications for consumers, businesses, and society at large. But before we discuss these implications and explore how total quality and technology, specifically information technology, work together to create competitive advantage, let us for a moment explore the power of technology.

THE POWER OF TECHNOLOGY

With the advent of industrialization and urbanization, the sheer number of technological developments multiplied and proliferated as rapidly as the very populations inhabiting our burgeoning city-states, the great symbols of modern civilization.

In architecture and construction, travel and transportation, tools and devices, agriculture, medicine, and communications, industrial-age advances were made at a pace and on a scale never before witnessed by human life. What we see with the advent of industry, in short, is an acceleration of change that is explosive beyond comprehension. In his seminal work, *Future Shock*, futurist Alvin Toffler[2] quotes eminent economist and imaginative social thinker Kenneth Boulding, who asserts: "The world of today [1970]…is as different from the world in which I was born as that world was from Julius Caesar's" (p. 13).

What Toffler is trying to get across is that during the industrial era, the pace of life quickened so dramatically that the world was literally transformed in the span of just one single person's lifetime. In an era when the mode of transportation went from the automobile to the rocket in just 40 years, technology had asserted itself as an undisputed engine of change and had set in motion a never-ending cycle of development that would change the world, and change it again, and change it again.

Although much of the key technological innovations of the past century are hidden from the view of the common person, they have the power to influence and shape our very consciousness, the way we act and interact, the way we view ourselves, raise our children, organize socially, transact business, retire, and, in short, live on the planet.

Who, for example, contemplates the vast and complex communications networks spanning our globe? Yet who is not affected by the ability to pick up a telephone anywhere in the world and call wherever they want to? Who thinks about the system of roads, railways, shipping lanes, and airways—the distribution channels—encircling the industrialized world? Yet who is not able to sit down and, all in one meal, enjoy meat from Argentina, wine from Italy, cheese from France, strawberries from California, and coffee from Jamaica? Who can fathom the intricate systems of water treatment, sewage, and drainage that lie just below the surface of our great metropolitan cities? Yet how many go one day in America without washing or bathing or without flushing unwanted waste down the toilet? And what person considers the vast and powerful electrical systems that energize our planet; the subways, tramways, and mass transit systems that lace our cities; the cables that run under our oceans or the pipelines that carry oil across vast distances? These are the core elements, the infrastructure of the industrial age, that have shaped and defined our planet and the lives of its inhabitants.

At a very basic level, then, technology forms and shapes the way we view ourselves, our role in the world, our relationships with others, and our view of nature and the world. Sometimes driven by very deliberate, planned developments and sometimes by unexpected, serendipitous ones, the grand scheme of technological progress unfolds before our very eyes and rages forward at ever-increasing speeds, changing and transforming and leaving in its wake new realities.

Yet in all their wondrous glory, the techno-developments that have been discussed heretofore are what futurist Alvin Toffler calls "second wave" innovations—foundational and key elements of industrial society. They do not approximate or come close to the technological explosion of the information era, the third great wave of human history that has been forming slowly since the 1950s and at blinding speed since around the mid-1980s.

It is on these information-age developments that this book will focus— how they shape and define the economic environment, how they literally structure and restructure whole industries and businesses, how they change the structure of competition, and how they affect the way we manage, the decisions we make, and the operating environment in which we make those decisions. From the way we plan to the way we communicate to the way we hire, train, design, purchase, produce, deliver, and distribute—technology and total quality work hand in hand to achieve organizational objectives and priorities.

Technology, however, does not develop in a vacuum. It is both a cause and result of a rapidly changing and evolving world, and it is inextricably connected to social and organizational developments and developments in the theory and practice of management. (For additional information, see Abstract 1.1 at the end of this chapter.)

THE RISE OF ORGANIZATIONAL SOCIETY, MANAGEMENT THEORY, AND TOTAL QUALITY

Industrial-era technological advances were paralleled by other important advances in the size of markets, the scale of production, the organization of productive enterprise, and the science of management. Together, these coalesced to spark the birth of quality control and to establish an economic system that, in order to function and sustain itself, required higher levels of standardization and control all along the value-added chain.

What we witness in this period is a series of explosions—in population, markets, technology and know-how, scientific discovery, organizational and institutional sophistication, and management methodologies. We see the train of development set in motion during the Renaissance gathering momentum and progressing with ever-increasing, even exponential, speed. If

Galileo Galile, Rene Descartes, Francis Bacon, and Leonardo DaVinci defined and paved the way for the new society, those who came later—Isaac Newton, Adam Smith, Frederick Taylor, Walter Shewhart, and Edwards Deming—made it happen. What we see, in short, is a new society unfolding before us.

Essentially, a flurry of productive activity occurred in the mid-18th century, fueled by the collision of multiple factors: the further organization and institutionalization of European society, the continuing emphasis on humanism and the role of man in exercising power and control over the environment, the proliferation of scientific thinking and methods, the increasing influence and exponential effect of technological innovation, such as steam power, and increased demand for industrial output (England's population doubled between 1750 and 1820).

Output of rubber from Brazil (the world's main supplier of the raw material) grew, for example, from 31 tons in 1827 to 27,650 in 1900, a dramatic rate of growth brought on in part by the advent of vulcanization, advances in transportation and distribution, and rapidly increasing demand. Similar order-of-magnitude advances were made in mining, agriculture, textiles, iron and steel, chemicals, industrial machinery, pottery and glass, printing and photography, canning, refrigeration, and food processing and preservation—to name a few. In literally hundreds of areas, the face and inner workings of industry were transforming.

Around the late 19th and early 20th century, the locus of work shifted from the family to the factory, and the beginnings of large-scale production took root. To meet demand—the sheer volume of output—industrialists sought economies of scale and restructured the production process to include greater division of labor, more centralized discipline and regulation, and hierarchical planning and control. New products, new processes, new machinery, new production techniques, new markets, and new management and organizational forms combined to fashion a new world order and undeniably instituted new requirements for controlling the uniformity and quality of inputs and outputs throughout an ever-lengthening value chain. In short, an increasingly complex production process required greater organization and coordination, more varied human skills (labor and management), and new methods and techniques of quality control.

And so began the legacy of total quality: in close connection with concurrent developments in technology, production, organization, and management. As we enter the future, then, the challenge for total quality is to maintain and improve this important relationship between technology; the tools, techniques, and raw materials of production; and the management methods employed to organize, bridle, control, and plan the value-added process of information-intensive businesses and business functions.

Before delving into the specifics of total quality—what it is, how it developed, and how it is applied in an information systems environment—

let's explore the characteristics of the emerging information society, the new applications of information technology, and the challenges facing organizations as they do business in an increasingly information-driven economy.

THE AGE OF INFORMATION

If the world was transformed by industry, it was transformed yet again by information. In today's environment of techno-wizardry, the innovations of yesterday—the printing press, the cotton gin, the telegraph, the railroad, the combustible engine—evoke a languid response and wane greatly in comparison to the present onslaught of information-age innovations bombarding our minds and lives at every juncture.

With all their power to transform the world, most industrial-age technological innovations relied primarily on mechanics, not information. With the rapid rise of the service economy and information-driven technology, however, the information quotient has grown exponentially and continues to increase at breakneck speed.

Already, the world is well into what futurist Alvin Toffler calls the third great phase of human history—the information age—about which he eloquently penned the following words in *The Third Wave:*[3]

> For Third Wave civilization, the most basic raw material of all—and one that can never be exhausted—is information, including imagination. Through imagination and information, substitutes will be found for many of today's exhaustible resources although this substitution, once more, will all too frequently be accompanied by drastic economic swings and lurches.
>
> With information becoming more important than ever before, the new civilization will restructure education, redefine scientific research and, above all, reorganize the media of communication. Today's mass media, both print and electronic, are wholly inadequate to cope with the communications load and to provide the requisite cultural variety for survival. Instead of being culturally dominated by a few mass media, Third Wave civilization will rest on inter-active, de-massified media, feeding extremely diverse and often highly personalized imagery into and out of the mindstream of the society.
>
> Looking far ahead, television will give way to "indi-videon"—narrow-casting carried to the ultimate: images addressed to a single individual at a time. We may also eventually use drugs, direct brain-to-brain communication, and other forms of electro-

chemical communication only vaguely hinted at until now. All of which will raise startling, though not insoluble, political and moral problems.

The giant centralized computer with its whirring tapes and complex cooling systems—where it still exists—will be supplanted by myriad chips of intelligence, embedded in one form or another in every home, hospital, and hotel, every vehicle and appliance, virtually every building-brick. The electronic environment will literally converse with us.

With eerie accuracy, Toffler's words, articulated in 1980, pinpoint the reality of 1995 and beyond. From outer space to cyberspace in just one generation, the world of the past 30 years has seen, and absorbed, more change than all previous generations combined! In essence, the transition from industrial society to information society, now complete, is a revolution unprecedented in human history. With ever-quickening modes of transportation, ever-pervasive networks of data communications, and ever-increasing options, the world as we once knew it is changing before our eyes: it is becoming smaller, more personalized, and more interconnected and the boundaries of space and time are blurring. (For additional information, see Abstract 1.2 at the end of this chapter.)

Information and its by-product, knowledge, have firmly established themselves as the undisputed engines of the new economy. The spectacular productivity improvements of the past 50 years, in conjunction with the rapid rise of service- and information-intensive businesses and business functions, have caused tectonic shifts in the structure of the world economy that have hurled information into center stage and relegated labor- and capital-intensive businesses and business functions to a secondary, even tertiary, position in the economic pecking order.

Eminent management guru Peter Drucker,[4] in *Post-Capitalist Society,* offers the following comments about the decline of manufacturing and labor-driven business activity:

> When Frederick Taylor started to study work, nine out of ten working people did manual work, *making or moving things;* in manufacturing, in farming, in mining, in transportation. Forty years ago, in the 1950's, people who engaged in work to make or move things were still a majority in all developed countries. By 1990, they had shrunk to one fifth of the workforce. By 2010, they will form no more than one tenth. The Productivity Revolution has become a victim of its own success. From now on, what matters is the productivity of non-manual workers.

Essentially Drucker has articulated the end of capitalism, or at least capitalism in its original form. He and others, like Alvin Toffler, Robert Reich, and Tom Peters, have made it their business to understand the stream of change that promises to turn into a flowing river and, at some point not far in the future, a gushing rapid of info-possibility—cybernetic galaxies yet unexplored.

In this brave digital world, information will replace capital and labor as the primary factor of production. Already, the presence and availability of information technology is transforming formerly labor- and capital-intensive industries such as farming and manufacturing. Italian businessman Vittorio Merloni, whose company makes 10 percent of all washing machines, refrigerators, and other household appliances sold in Europe, says, "We need less capital now to do the same thing. The reason is that knowledge-based technologies are reducing the capital needed to produce, say, dishwashers, stoves or vacuum cleaners"[5] (p. 89). Among other applications, Mr. Merloni is using information technology to reduce high-cost inventory and speed factory responsiveness to the market.

In hundreds of thousands of companies, information is assuming a greatly expanded role. Even in Germany, where manufacturing is still king, information technology has made its way into the center of business life. At premier toolmaker Trumpf, although apprentices still devote most of a year to hand-filing metal, one-third of the company's research staff is comprised of software engineers, according to Tom Peters.

In *Liberation Management*, Peters[6] (pp. 113–114) outlines a few examples of how information technology is changing or more accurately—radically altering—the way business is conducted. Among these are the following:

- *Business Week,* July 1991—"In the future, U.S. apparel factories will need automated sewing equipment to remain competitive with overseas competitors. But one question that raises is quality control. Now, researchers at the Georgia Institute of Technology in Atlanta have designed electronic 'ears' that enable sewing machines to supervise their own work and check for mistakes….Broken or worn needles have a distinctive sound, or acoustic signature. Computer analysis of those signatures reveals that the amplitudes increase in proportion to how badly the needle is worn. When the sewing machine hears this, they trigger a flashing light that notifies a human operator that maintenance or adjustments are necessary."

- Consultant Stan Davis and professor Bill Davidson in *2020 Vision*—"Cattle were sold in stockyards in the industrial economy, but video auctions on an electronic network could mean that stockyards would go the way of the old-fashioned cattle drive. Superior Livestock Auction of Fort Worth uses satellite transmission, television cameras and computerized buying networks to auction steers that never leave the ranch until they are sold."

- A Coors promotional stunt reported in the *Toronto Globe and Mail,* May 26, 1992—"A microchip inside a container nestled within a can of Coors Light enables it to 'talk.' When exposed to light, it is supposed to say, 'You win!,' and then describes the prize, items like stereos and compact disks, valued in excess of $1 million."

The business of sewing machines, cows, and beer will never be the same. All will be transformed, in one way or another, by the power of information technology.

Even in the grocery business, information technology has become a core and essential element, a prerequisite for survival. Through optical scanning technology, long checkout lines and errors in accounting have been minimized. The Universal Product Code or bar code (the small black box of lines and numbers that appears on everything from applesauce to laundry detergent) has forever changed the way products are packaged, distributed, stocked, sold, and ordered. According to Toffler, bar coding has become nearly universal in the United States, with fully 95 percent of all food items marked by the distinctive little symbol. In France, by 1988, 3,470 supermarkets and specialty department stores were using it. In West Germany, 1,500 food stores and 200 department stores employed scanners. From Brazil to Czechoslovakia and Papua New Guinea, there were 78,000 scanners at work as far back as 1988.[5]

As with virtually any application of information technology, however, the examples above represent only the infant stages of the information age, the first babbling expressions of just-born technology. In supermarkets and retail stores, for example, consumers may soon find themselves navigating their way through aisles lined with "electronic shelves." Instead of paper tags indicating the price of items, they will find blinking liquid crystal displays with digital price readouts. The implications are staggering. In addition to automatically changing thousands of prices from a remote location, the new displays would provide nutritional and other information at the touch of a button and even elicit market research information from the consumer.

In retail, Wal-Mart is setting the electronic pace by requiring all its vendors to be tied into its system of electronic data exchange. Simply through the use of integrated computer-to-computer systems, Wal-Mart's suppliers know when the retailer is running low on specific products and send new inventory automatically—without any order being placed, without any unnecessary handoffs or steps in between.

What we are moving toward is a seamless connection between consumers and manufacturers. According to George Fields, chairman and CEO of ASI Market Research (Japan), "distribution no longer means putting something on the shelf. It is now essentially an information system." Distribution, he notes, "will no longer be a chain of inventory points, passing goods along the line, but an information link between the manufacturer and the consumer"[5] (p. 105).

In this environment, "prosumers"—a term coined by Alvin Toffler[3] in *The Third Wave*—become actively engaged in product design. Using CAD/ CAM software, for instance, the day when prosumers will be able to participate in the design of their vehicles at the dealer's workstation may not be too far off in the future. A prosumer can preselect the body structure, drive train components, and suspension components and can tailor the car's lighting system or instrument panel layout to fit personal preferences. And, perhaps most impressive, the car can be delivered within three days after the order is placed.

In countless instances, across the board, information technology is redefining how companies conduct business and succeed in the marketplace. From the development of new information-related products and services such as personal computers and software development; to the design of new noninformation-related products such as automobiles, stereo systems, and razor blades; to the construction of prototypes; to the invention of new products; to the "smartening" of everything from sewing machines to elevators to shopping carts to machine tools to buildings, the role and economic significance of information technology are rapidly expanding.

Information is, in short, taking over the world. According to Davis and Davidson,[7] authors of *2020 Vision*, by the year 2020, 80 percent of business profits and market value will come from that part of the enterprise that is built around info-businesses. In this world of heightened info-possibility, those who know how to develop, acquire, and utilize information for their companies and their customers will outpace and outsmart their competitors and win in the game of global competition. Today's business leaders unequivocally understand that when it comes to information, there are no options: either you get it, develop it, and use it to your best advantage or fall into the abyss of a forgotten age.

Consider the following words of Alex Mandl, an executive in the transportation company CSX, as quoted in *Powershift*, by Alvin Toffler:[5]

> The information component of our service package is growing bigger and bigger. It's not just enough to deliver products. Customers want information. Where their products will be consolidated and deconsolidated, what time each item will be where, prices, customs information, and much more. We are an information-driven business (p. 76).

Everywhere, the importance of information is growing, even exploding. In every sector of the economy and in every business function and activity, information is creeping, and sometimes leaping, into center stage. The rules of the game are changing. Restructuring, reengineering, revitalization, and even total quality management methods are of little help in today's high-tech society without the speed and power of information technology and information systems. In boosting productivity and profitability, in improving quality and reliability, in lowering costs, and in increasing customer responsiveness, information is critical.

In a world where antiballistic missiles can, at a speed of more than several thousand miles per hour, hone in and make final real-time trajectory adjustments while in flight before obliterating their moving targets; where, in the United States alone, more than 400 million customers book flights on daily domestic flights annually; where entire libraries full of data are transmitted over great distances in a matter of minutes; where, all in the space of 12 seconds, the word *moshimoshi* is spoken in Japanese and translated into Japanese text by one computer, which then passes it on to another computer that translates it into English and sends it via modem to yet another computer, which reads the text and synthesizes the English word "hello"; in this world, the role of information technology—and its possibilities—is skyrocketing.[5,6]

So deeply and significantly has information changed the corporate landscape that the very character of the organization and the way it produces and delivers value is changing too. Old paradigms are tumbling, falling by the wayside. Outmoded concepts of work, rigid organizational hierarchies and structures, excessive division of labor, and large-batch production—once the hallmarks of industry—are now going the way of the dinosaur.

A new era is upon us, one in which organizations are flat and flexible; bureaucracies, hierarchies, and rigid structures are dissolving; labor and business activity is increasingly cross-functional; and production is fast and made-to-order in small batches—all trends made possible and undergirded by the presence and proliferation of information-based technologies. What we are witnessing, in a nutshell, is the integration of previously separated, disjointed market and organizational functions. The boundaries are blurring—between consumers and producers, between suppliers and customers, between departments and functions within the organization.

In this environment, the average life span of new products is drastically declining, cycle times of everything from invoice processing to field repairs are falling sharply, and the time required to complete value-added activities continues to plummet. In this environment, Japanese automakers are actively pursuing the "72-hour car"; Citicorp Mortgage is processing loans in 15 minutes; Sony Corporation is churning out a different model of its Walkman about once every three weeks; market and competitive intelligence data are gathered, processed, and acted on in week-long cycles; and salesmen in the field are digitally connected with the production floor so that as soon as orders are placed, production begins. Developing before us is a new organizational culture, fueled and driven by information, where there is a premium on speed and flexibility and where, all at once, the needs and wishes of greatly varied customers—from housewives to Hare Krishnas—can be met with accuracy, precision, and impeccable timing. (For additional information, see Abstract 1.3 at the end of this chapter.)

THE CULTURE OF CHANGE

The world, and the corporation, is becoming less static and more dynamic. "We do not seek permanence," says Matsushita Corporation's Chief of Design Masatoshi Naito. "...Consumption is a continuous cycle of new products replacing old products, everything is in a process of change, nothing endures"[6] (p. 3). Indeed, today, the only constant is change. Even change itself has changed: it happens faster, its implications reach further, and its power to render today's products and services obsolete is growing stronger by the day. "The nineties will be a decade in a hurry, a nanosecond culture," says vice-chairman of Northern Telecom David Vice. "There'll be only two kinds of managers [and organizations]: the quick and the dead"[6] (p. 59).

Throughout the developed world, the culture of change is taking root and shaping the way we think, plan, make, sell, service, and structure our organizations and value-added networks. The creation, coordination, transmission, management, and use of information and information-based technologies will keep pushing the world toward one huge, interconnected economic system already foreshadowed by the rising regional economies of the Pacific Rim, the European Union, the Americas, and several other regional economic alliances.

The challenge, then, for information systems executives is to apply their craft and develop their systems in a way that will best perpetuate and facilitate the fluid and open business environment we find unfolding before us. It is in this permanently ephemeral world that the instruments and intelligence of the information age find life and purpose and are employed to ensure the continued success of the ever-transforming corporation. And it is in this culture of perpetual change and permanent flexibility that the instruments and methods of total quality are applied in conjunction with the proliferating information technologies and their myriad applications.

Before we discuss how total quality and information technology work together to maximize organizational effectiveness, let's go one step further in our overview of information technology in the information age. Let's look briefly at a few of the key emerging technologies—how they are impacting individual consumers; how they are being used by companies to create competitive advantage; how, in short, they are altering the present and forming the future.

NETWORKS, SATELLITES, AND SUPERHIGHWAYS

Like the railroads, highways, canals, and electrical and telephone systems of the industrial age, the emerging information networks promise to rewrite the rules for doing business in the information age. Networks have always been at the center of technological and civilizational progress, have always spurred drastic changes in the way goods and services are brought to market, and, at a fundamental level, have changed the way business is transacted.

Can we attempt to describe what kind of coordination and control is necessary to run today's enterprises—modern railways, airports, telecommunications networks? Since 1850, the world population has more than quadrupled, the speed at which man can travel has increased from 100 miles per hour to more than 18,000, and systems—from power to transportation to telecommunications—have proliferated, grown in complexity, and forever reconfigured the course of civilization.

Today, the new information networks are rewiring the planet. Although these emerging networks build on the cables and wires laid and strung during the industrial era, they are changing, improving, and replacing these systems with altogether new ones that promise to hurl the world—and all that is in it—into a new reality. Known to many as cyberspace, the emerging reality is one in which previously only imagined possibilities are materializing in our midst.

Consider TRON Pilot Intelligent House, for example, located in Tokyo. You approach the TRON house, located in the heart of Tokyo, and the lights turn on. You drop your briefcase in a bin in the closet, and it is whisked away by a conveyor belt and stored in the basement. Later, you turn on a video monitor and scroll through pictures of as many as ten similar cases, each containing a unique set of contents, and pick the one you want. You select it and, presto, it is whisked back into your closet bin. The house is so sophisticated that you can draw your bath by phone before leaving the office. Cooking a meal is as simple as punching a couple of buttons on the combination oven/VCR, with a video showing you how to prepare the meal. Sprinklers automatically turn on and water the plants. There is even a "smart" toilet that adjusts the strength, direction, and temperature of the water spewing from the bidet, and the attached computer conducts a detailed urinalysis and blood-pressure test. Controlled by wires, cameras, and sensors running through the walls and ceilings, the pilot smart home is a product of collaboration between 18 Japanese companies, including Nippon Telegraph & Telephone Corporation, Mitsubishi Electric Corporation, and Seibu Department Store Ltd.[6]

But the smart home is only the beginning, a narrow slice of the burgeoning info-sphere. Also just over the horizon lies the much-publicized "interactive, multimedia revolution," the great confluence of television, computers, telephones, faxes, and video cameras. Inside this smart home, so the vision holds, there will be an electronic epicenter, a section of the living room parceled off for nothing more than the electronic machinations of those family members who are young enough or technologically astute enough to navigate themselves through the cybernetic world invading their homes.

Want to call up a movie from a library of thousands using a menu displayed on the television screen? Want to buy a wedding gift by selecting the wedding department, searching for gifts in a certain price range, paying for your selection, and arranging for pickup or delivery all with the touch of a few buttons on your telephone or remote control device? Want your phone calls digitized and your callers pictured in a little box on your TV screen? Want to study the third baseman during a ball game, while others view the batter? Play Street Fighter or NBA Jam with another video game junkie located hundreds of miles away? Surf 500 channels? Replay that action scene? Design and customize your own clothing?

Well, say the experts, in the not-too-distant future, you will be able to do all this and more. It will be made possible by glass fibers that can carry as much as 250,000 times more data than the old copper wires, space satellites that beam information in large batches to regional earth stations, and home-based "smart boxes" that manage and coordinate incoming and outgoing data. The electronic superhighway is on its way.

Yet as much as the so-called Infobahn or I-way is giving birth to a cornucopia of novel applications and possibilities for the private user, the real potential lies in the corporate sector, where businesses and organizations are capitalizing on the commercial opportunities presented by the unfolding information age.

In retail, trade, manufacturing, electronics, construction—in virtually every business sector—the growing data-sphere is revolutionizing how market and customer data are gathered and used and how products and services are made, distributed, sold, and serviced. Some companies, such as those in telecommunications, computers, and fiber optics, are transforming the marketplace while at the same time transforming themselves. MCI, for example, while building the new communications infrastructure also expects to employ that infrastructure in conducting its business. Similarly, Corning Glass Works, maker of fiber-optic cables, will benefit from the very cables it makes and sells. And Intel, maker of the much ballyhooed Pentium chip, will use it to run its own personal computers.

More than any other, however, the software companies stand to cash in on the coming revolution, for it is they that will shape and define the underlying structure of the emerging business environment. It is their contributions that promise to be even more important and impressive than the fibers, cables, and satellites through which their bits and mips race at raging speeds. It is for the brain of the information economy that the coming commercial battles will be fought, for it, more than anything, will determine the character and course of the coming cyber-culture.

All these companies—MCI, Corning, Intel—and thousands more are the pioneers of the information frontier, the engineers of the information age. They are on the vanguard of change, and it is their special contributions that will raise the entire economic machinery—from market research to product and service design to raw material extraction and processing to production, sales, and after-sales service—to a new level. It is their contributions that will enable companies in all sectors to design more quickly, produce more efficiently, and simply do what they do better. (For additional information, see Abstract 1.4 at the end of this chapter.)

The real revolution, then, is not taking place in our living rooms. It is being shaped and formed in the boardrooms, from England to Japan. It is changing the way companies do business, the way they act and interact with their suppliers, customers, shareholders, regulators—every last constituent, institution, or organization with which they come in contact. In a nutshell, information is transforming the very heart of the modern corporation.

While there is not space enough here to cover the entire spectrum of new systems, applications, products, machines, robots, tools, gadgets, and devices used in business and brought on by the information revolution, a few examples of current corporate information infrastructure developments are in order. These are the networks and mega-networks that undergird and make possible the budding info-revolution.

Local Area Networks

Local area networks are popping up everywhere, connecting PC users in one building or complex. From the tiny business with two or three computers to larger ones that employ hundreds, local area networks are revolutionizing the way people communicate and work together. Through electronic mail, for example, Richard Pogue, a managing partner of a global law firm, keeps communications "personal, collegiality high and far-flung offices part of the team." E-mail, according to Pogue, lets people converse with him who otherwise might be too intimidated to drop by his office. And while a memo may sit in his briefcase for weeks, the psychology of wanting to wipe that screen clean impels Pogue to respond almost instantly to his 35 to 40 daily electronic messages.[6] From quarterly financial data to information about the wellness program, E-mail is changing the way people communicate within the corporation.

Bulletin Boards and Databases

Bulletin boards and databases covering such diverse interests as new legislation, stock market performance, education for the handicapped, and the weather are available for online perusal and interaction. With only a PC and modem, these networks allow the individual user to tap into specific sources of information and, in many cases, download that information onto a floppy or hard drive. Through a small window the size of a monitor, bulletin boards and databases enable the user to view and experience vast infoscapes and to interact with any of the hundreds of thousands of other users planet-wide.

Just one such available information utility is Minitel, a system developed by France Telecom, a government-owned telephone company. With 18 percent of all French households hooked up to Mintel through terminals provided free of charge, citizens can access a variety of paid services: travel information, news, banking interest rates, online shopping, and the wildly popular "messagerie rose," an adults-only fantasy line.[8]

Of course the network of networks, the ultimate bulletin board, is Internet, an interconnected group of networks connecting academic, research, government, and commercial institutions from within the United States and in more than 40 countries worldwide. Research house Dataquest reports: "Somewhere between 20 and 30 million people around the globe use the Net more or less regularly. The graphical portion called the World Wide Web is stocked with more than 22 million pages of content, with over 1 million more pages added each month."[9]

Collaborative Networks (Computer-Augmented Collaboration)

These are special electronic tools designed to support the process of collaboration so vital in the present business climate, where there is a premium on team power—the process by which people unite their minds and skills to tackle problems and issues, design new products, configure new systems, or write business plans. For example, computer-generated shared space is a good way to get people to participate playfully in meetings. A large screen becomes a community computer screen where everyone can write, draw, scribble, type, or otherwise offer information for community viewing. It is shared space. People can produce on it or pollute it. Traditional conversational etiquette does not apply here. One person may write a controversial message on the community screen while another talks about something else. Ostensibly, this may not seem revolutionary, but exploring ideas and arguments in the context of shared space can completely transform conversation. The software injects a discipline and encourages people to create, visually and orally, a shared understanding with their colleagues. The technology motivates people to collaborate.[6]

Electronic Data Interchange Systems

The object here is intimacy, or connectivity. The means is electronic data interchange (EDI) systems—electronic connections that greatly ease the burden of interacting with suppliers, customers, and other entities within and external to the organization. By electronically integrating key functions, such as invoicing, scheduling, and material requisitions, the value-added chain is made tighter and stronger at key linkage points. Inventories are reduced, engineering data are exchanged, work scheduling is improved, distribution networks are streamlined, market feedback and research are collected, and many of the former costs associated with coordination, communication, and linkage are greatly reduced. More and more companies are bringing EDI systems on line. The big auto companies, for instance, now refuse to do business with suppliers that are not equipped for electronic interaction.

Expert Systems

These systems are able to do much more than store and organize data in rigid categories, recall facts and figures, and package outputs for the user. Through extensive programming, expert systems can approximate *intelligence.* In addition to storing facts, they determine and change the relationships between those facts. As new information becomes available, the knowledge base (the database of the expert system) can reorganize and repackage its outputs to reflect the new input obtained. Although still far from perfect, expert systems have saved millions of man-hours and dollars in fields as diverse as medicine, manufacturing, and insurance.

For example, Digital Equipment Corporation's XCON, perhaps the most successful expert system in commercial use today, has been configuring complex computer systems since 1980. The system's knowledge base consists of more than 10,000 rules describing the relationship among various computer parts. It reportedly does the work of more than 300 human experts, with fewer mistakes. Other expert systems include MYCIN, a medical system that outperforms many human experts in diagnosing diseases.[8]

Parallel Systems and Neural Networks

In the quest for speed and power, parallel processing machines use multiple processors to work on several tasks at the same time. The technology is especially promising for such applications as speech recognition, computer vision, and other pattern-recognition tasks. Some supercomputers, called Connection Machines, use as many as 64,000 inexpensive processors in parallel to execute thousands of instructions simultaneously in the achievement of complicated tasks, such as those required by expert systems.

One complex parallel system is the neural network, which utilizes thousands of simple processors called neurons and which approximates the parallel structure of the human brain. Instead of processing information in linear, sequential steps according to a set of rules, neural networks are able to process information concurrently and distributively and, in doing so, learn by trial and error—somewhat like the way humans learn. In effect, they train themselves and form habits based on their past experience. Some neural networks, for example, are intelligent enough to narrow or widen themselves as a function of how much electronic traffic they find pulsing through their systems. That would be like an interstate widening and narrowing itself automatically based on how many cars it found rolling across its surface!

Already, neural networks are being used at banks to recognize signatures on checks and at financial institutions to analyze complicated correlations between hundreds of variables and the performance of the Standard and Poor's 500 index. In the future, researchers are hopeful that the nets may provide hearing for the deaf and sight for the blind.

Corporate Virtual Workspaces

The information revolution is so important that it may end up redefining every aspect of corporate life, including the very space in which companies operate. The corporate competitive advantage will lie in the acquisition and use of information. Companies have the ability to be dispersed geographically and replace existing physical facilities. Employees can now work from home or other mobile locations. Permanent office space will no longer be a necessity. Sales and marketing can take place using the information highway, otherwise known as cyberspace.

Corporate virtual workspaces, neural networks, expert systems, EDIs, the Internet—these are the elements of the information infrastructure that promises to change the way we conduct business in the post-capitalist age. These are the systems that will define the structure, character, and behavior of the info-corporation. Add to these the throngs of information-based technological innovations—computer-integrated manufacturing, computer-aided design, digital image processing, optical character and automatic speech recognition, three-dimensional modeling, virtual reality, hypermedia, digital video, computer vision, xerography, and liquid crystal and plasma displays—and you have an info-society complete with info-products from the most commonplace to the most advanced and bizarre. How many are aware, for example, that scientists have constructed tiny robots the size of large insects to handle maneuvers in spaces too small for human involvement, or that in the field of microtechnology, scientists have already produced motors no more than the width of two human hairs? Some day, they say, these microscopic machines might be crawling around inside the human body, searching out and destroying aberrant cells like those that cause cancer.

From the living room to the local ATM to the factories and offices of corporate America—and everywhere in between—the power and presence of information are linking up the planet, connecting and integrating people, companies, and nations and changing and redefining the very foundation upon which modern civilization was built and upon which the economy of industrial society was formed. Today, we rely not so much on railroads, highways, airways, and shipping lanes (the infrastructure of the industrial age) as we rely on satellites, optical cables, computers, and modems (the infrastructure of the post-industrial age). Like an expansive convolution of interlocking spider webs girdling the globe—networks within networks within networks—the new information infrastructure is becoming something like the neurological system of the planet.

Just how vast and pervasive the cyber-frontier will become is not a question for the novice or recreational thinker; it is a question asked by tough-minded businesspeople whose destinies are certain to be swept into the swirling vortex of information-driven change and whose futures will depend on their ability to navigate and manage their way through the ever-thickening info-sphere. (For additional information, see Abstract 1.5 at the end of this chapter.)

THE NEXUS OF INFORMATION TECHNOLOGY AND TOTAL QUALITY

Background and History

Without detailing the history and legacy of total quality (a topic addressed in Chapter 4), it is enough for our purposes here to simply establish that, from the beginning, the quest for quality has influenced our behavior and the outputs of our labor. From the terra-cotta sculptures of Babylon to the pyramids of Egypt to the self-contained cities of Greece and Rome—and beyond—the quest to create and maintain quality has permeated the tasks to which man has applied his hands. As the architects of civilization, and as the perpetuators of art and industry, humans have always been galvanized by the drive to produce works of distinctive form and function. The quest for quality is, in short, embedded in the human soul.

It is the evolving soul of man, then, that has driven and defined the course of quality throughout the ages. In ancient times, the quality of man's products was guided by a sense of enchantment, wonder, myth, and mysticism; the gods were in complete control, and the work of humans merely reflected their omnipresence and omnipotence. In Classical times, the quality of art and industry reflected an increasing emphasis on technological know-how, in addition to a continuing emphasis on the spiritual verities of existence, as evidenced in the great temples and ornate and intricate shrines of Greece and Rome.

During the Renaissance, we begin to see a dramatic shift in the nature of man and, commensurately, in the nature and application of quality. With growing attention to material life and science, man's sense of quality began to shift from the spiritual to the practical. Instead of applying his aesthetic sensibilities to works of art, he increasingly applied his analytical sensibilities to the accelerating sciences. In the important pursuits of medicine and invention, for example, quality was becoming increasingly synonymous with utility and function, not beauty and form.

Yet it was not until the advent of industry that quality began to grow into a science unto itself. Spurred by the advent of mass production and hierarchical organizations, the quest for quality turned completely material and reflected the nature and character of the unfolding industrial culture. Quality, like everything, began to conform with the scientific paradigm. In accordance with developing markets, production methods, organizational structures, and management theory, quality, like the whole of society, grew out of the tinkering stage and passed into the stage of economic necessity. The age of mass production and consumption—the consumer society—had arrived, and with it came the imperative to manage and control the processes by which products were churned off the production line.

From this point on, we are quite familiar with the trajectory of quality control. It was first applied in the form of statistical process control to ensure product uniformity and to prevent defects. Next, it was expanded to include the people-oriented processes of quality circles and quality teams. After this, the blossoming methods and techniques of quality control were applied in the nonproduction areas, such as procurement, delivery, and other services, including information systems. And finally, as pioneered by the Japanese in the 1950s, quality methods and principles had become so pervasively applied that they evolved into what is today called total quality management, or total quality.

Integration through Total Quality

Why is total quality so important in today's world, where at the touch of a few buttons we can launch rockets into outer space, where our factories are populated with robots and smart machinery, and where soon we will be able to use our television sets to get an education, pay our bills, and participate in town meetings?

The answer is that as smart as our machines are and as powerful as our information might be, we still live in a world dominated by the behavior and movement of people and the organizations to which they belong. Computers, although they can help us perform complex, detailed analyses and tasks, cannot think strategically, consider the moral implications of their actions, or even begin to comprehend the work to which they are applied. In short, they cannot manage.

Total quality, on the other hand, encompasses the whole. It is an overall management framework through which to integrate the various elements of a successful organization: strategy, policy, planning, information systems, project management—all the activities required to run today's large, complex organizations. In this capacity, total quality plays the role of integrator, focusing the entire organization in one direction, coordinating the plans and actions of hundreds of otherwise fragmented organizational sections and functions, controlling the processes and outputs all along the value-added chain, and improving the business by increments and, when necessary, by leaps and bounds.

There is, then, a unique synergy between total quality and information technology: when they are properly applied together, they can catapult an organization into new levels of market strength. Total quality and information systems work together to reduce defects, decrease cycle time, improve safety, improve delivery, increase reliability, and increase customer service and satisfaction.

The power and miracle of information technology is simply only as good as the structures and processes of the organization in which it is applied. Many companies are implementing high technology merely to become technical innovators or leaders. They are doing so without rethinking their corporate goals and objectives. They are using technology as the instant business solution without matching technology to their corporate strategy and plans. Without aligning new technology with the corporate strategy, the solution often becomes more complex and expensive.

The danger we encounter with technology is that if we do not change the way we do business at a fundamental level, it only allows us to do the *wrong things* faster. According to Michael Hammer,[10] the nation's forerunning expert on business reengineering, technology without business process redesign is, at best, a poor allocation of resources and, at worst, a good way to automate yourself out of business. The irony is that although we have made great and amazing advances in technology, many of us still follow business processes that were invented long before the advent of the computer, modern communications, and other technological innovations.

Many business processes and methods were designed to compensate for a time when we lived in relative technological poverty. Although we are now technologically affluent, we often find it difficult to break out of the old way of thinking: that certain processes, certain methods by which business is conducted—methods that were invented decades ago—are set in stone. The practical result, according to Hammer, in the information technology industry is that many of these archaic assumptions are now deeply embedded in automated systems.

The key point about technology and total quality, then, is that both need to reflect the possibilities of an advanced technological age, not the constraints of an age gone by. When this occurs, the results can be staggering. Consider the following organizations that used total quality in conjunction with information technology to gain an edge in the marketplace:

- IBM Credit reduced the amount of time it takes to approve a customer's credit application from seven days to four hours while achieving a hundredfold improvement in productivity.[10]
- Federal Mogul, a billion-dollar auto parts manufacturer, reduced the time to develop a new part prototype from 20 weeks to 20 days.[11]
- Mutual Benefit Life, a large insurance company, halved the costs associated with underwriting and issuing policies.[11]
- The IRS achieved a 33 percent rise in the amount of tax dollars collected from delinquent taxpayers with half its former staff and a third fewer branch offices.[11]
- Ford reduced the number of people involved in paying vendors from 500 to 125. In some parts of the company, like the Engine Division, the head count for accounts payable is just 5 percent of its former size.[10]
- Eastman Kodak slashed its product development process for its 35-mm single-use camera nearly in half while reducing its tooling and manufacturing costs by 25 percent.[10]

For additional information, see Abstract 1.6 at the end of this chapter.

What we learn from these companies, and what we will demonstrate in the chapters that follow, is that the role of information technology in a total quality effort is secondary, not primary. It is a means to an end, not an end in itself. We will learn that, like a thoroughbred horse, information technology must be bridled and harnessed by the effective application of total quality principles and methodologies. We will learn how executives and corporate leaders apply total quality to the information technology function and how information technology, in turn, supports the company's strategic intent and improvement objectives.

ENDNOTES

1. Derry, T.K. and Williams, Trevor I. (1961). *A Short History of Technology.* New York: Oxford University Press.
2. Toffler, Alvin (1970). *Future Shock.* New York: Bantam.
3. Toffler, Alvin (1981). *The Third Wave.* New York: Bantam.
4. Drucker, Peter F. (1993). *Post-Capitalist Society.* New York: HarperCollins.
5. Toffler, Alvin (1990). *Powershift.* New York: Bantam.
6. Peters, Tom (1992). *Liberation Management.* New York: Alfred A. Knopf.
7. Davis, Stan and Davidson, Bill (1991). *2020 Vision.* New York: Simon and Schuster.
8. Beekman, George (1994). *Computer Currents.* Redwood City, CA: Benjamin Cummings.
9. "Taming the Internet." *U.S. News and World Report.* Spring Tech Guide, April 29, 1996.
10. Hammer, Michael and Champy, James (1993). *Reengineering the Corporation.* New York: HarperCollins.
11. Davenport, Thomas (1993). *Process Innovation: Reengineering Work Through Information Technology.* Boston: Harvard Business School Press.

ABSTRACTS

ABSTRACT 1.1
ACHIEVING TOTAL QUALITY THROUGH INTELLIGENCE

Fuld, Leonard M.
Long Range Planning, February 1992, pp. 109–115

Information—in whatever form—can empower employees to make continuous improvements in product and process, contends the author, by monitoring customers, competitors, and suppliers. He describes the complexities of information sharing at Corning, where 25,000 employees at 90 locations throughout the world must communicate about 60,000 products and services. A "Corrective Action Team" was formed to conduct an information audit. This resulted in a computer-based "Information Exchange Intelligence System" that allows information entry and access throughout the company. Cost per user is lowered by making the system accessible to all employees, and instead of funneling all information through the company's information systems department, data can be entered by any system user in a standard format. By creating a personal electronic file folder, any time new information that matches a user's request is fed into the system, it is entered into the user's folder for viewing the next business day. A sidebar to the article, based on a survey of over 200 large companies, highlights six principles for building an information system for total quality. The bulk of the article discusses the way information flow is important to the five key factors assessed by Baldrige Award examiners:

1. Customer focus

2. Meeting commitments

3. Process management and elimination of waste

4. Employee involvement and empowerment

5. Continuous improvement

The author gives examples from a number of companies, such as Xerox, M&M Mars, Johnson & Johnson, IBM, GTE, and Milliken.

ABSTRACT 1.2
KEIRETSU IN AMERICA

Kinni, Theodore B.
Quality Digest, December 1992, pp. 24–31

The author is a well-known business writer who presents a concise and intriguing look at one of the key features of Japan's success—an integrated marketing and sales/purchasing/supplier quality management system: *keiretsu*. The opening frame sets the stage with a simple well-directed statement: "Corporate Communism? Industrial war machines? As U.S. business comes to terms with dealing with Japan Inc. on home turf, it's time we understood how our new neighbors do business." The reason, according to Kinni, is that Japanese business interests hold a sizable stake in over 1,500 U.S. factories, a fact which is confirmed by the Japan External Trade Organization.

Keiretsu is the Japanese system of conglomerates which cross-market and trade heavily with one another, dating back to the Meiji Restoration of 1868. The author quotes Robert Kearns in describing how an American *keiretsu* structured along the lines of the Mitsubishi or Sumitomo group might operate: "Such a group would be worth close to a trillion dollars. Each of the 30 or so lead companies would own a piece of each other, would do business among themselves and meet once a month for lunch and discuss matters." *Keiretsu* members share in the economies of large-scale operation, says the author, such as low-cost capital at rates of 0.5 percent to 1.5 percent interest. Membership in a *keiretsu* virtually guarantees a market for one's goods, since other member companies own large stakes in each other's companies, and the value of their investments depends on the long-term success and growth of the member firms. According to Kinni, "the *keiretsu* system is an ideal structure for rapid and secure economic growth and a major reason for Japan's economic success since World War II." After describing how the system operates, the author turns to examples of the *keiretsu* way, which means allowing a foreign group to eventually own about 30 percent of one's company stock and, to some extent, dictate the organization's future. Some U.S. companies, like Timken Co., are building structures reminiscent of the *keiretsu* on their own, such as the "supplier city" in Perry Township, Ohio, which will bring its suppliers within arm's reach. What does the future hold?

Invasion or evolution? The author uses observers and "experts" to sum up the final arguments. "As the Japanese investments in this country mature, their plants and equipment will age, their employees will grow more expensive, and the playing field will level. Perhaps the *keiretsu* will learn a new respect for the individual and will begin to temper its authoritarian structures." On the other hand, he believes that U.S. corporations can learn much from the business practices of the *keiretsu*, with its efficient cross-marketing and supplier relationships. The best way to come to terms with *keiretsu*, he concludes, is to think of it as an immigrant, not an invader, with gifts to offer and lessons to learn—for those wise and gracious enough to know how to use them.

Overall, this is a most worthwhile article on an often misunderstood topic. As America moves further along in its understanding of the "extended enterprise," businesses will see themselves as members of a global network, whose aim will be to optimize the value chain through mutual relationships built on trust. Illustrations and models are provided, although the citations are from 1978 and 1986 material.

ABSTRACT 1.3
THE LAW OF PRODUCING QUALITY

Wollner, George E.
Quality Progress, January 1992, pp. 35–40

Most large-scale efforts to bring total quality (TQ) into organizations fail, says the author. Top leadership commitment is the key to success, he contends, and commitment is determined by appropriate incentives. The author expounds two important laws of producing quality:

- Achieving TQ is a matter of incentive.

- More quality is produced when it brings organizational leaders more of the success they desire.

He cites Soviet production policies as examples of disincentives. "While TQ can be an effective tool for redesigning or eliminating nonproductive processes," he says, "the first step has to be in the elimination of the wrong incentives." Almost every failed TQ effort results from an organization's perception that the TQ process is not worth it, he concludes. The key is for the leader to "consistently and continuously measure the three TQ success objectives (increasing customer satisfaction, increasing employee satisfaction, and decreasing unit costs) and link employees' important rewards to their achievements." He mentions the power of noneconomic incentives such as employee empowerment, recognition, self-esteem, and pride in work, as well as monetary incentives. The author introduces the term "incentive controller" as the person or group who has the power to provide or withhold the prized incentives that an organization or individual seeks. "When the incentive controller and the end consumer are the same, and competitive conditions prevail, the market produces quality well," he says. But when incentive controllers are stockholders or politicians, for example, short-term gain can rob long-term advantage. The author discusses the role of TQ leaders in realigning the organizational incentive system. In every case of successful TQ, he says, three critical events occur:

1. The leaders of the organization experience an irresistible incentive to improve product quality.

2. They transform this challenge into a compelling vision that is attractive to the work force.

3. They make it in everyone's best interest to use TQ as the way to achieve the vision.

The article concludes with a simple "TQ Success Forecaster." (©*Quality Abstracts*)

ABSTRACT 1.4
THE NEW SOCIETY OF ORGANIZATIONS

Drucker, Peter F.
Harvard Business Review, Vol. 70 Issue 5, September/October 1992, pp. 95–104

Peter Drucker opens this article with gusto in the opening sentence of the first paragraphs: "Every few hundred years throughout Western history, a sharp transformation has occurred. In a matter of decades, society altogether rearranges itself—its world view, its basic values, its social and political structures, its arts, its key institutions." Our age is such a period of transformation, which began with the G.I. Bill of Rights, giving to each American soldier returning from World War II money to attend a university, something that Drucker feels would have made no sense at the end of World War I. This signaled the shift to a knowledge society, in which land, labor, and capital become secondary and knowledge became *the* product. For Drucker's managers, the dynamics of knowledge imposes one clear imperative—every organization has to build the management of change into its very structure. Every organization must learn to exploit its knowledge to develop the next generation of applications from its own successes, and it must learn to innovate.

If the organization is to perform, it must be organized as a team. For more than 600 years, no society has had as many competing centers of power as the one in which we now live. Change is the only constant in an organization's life. Drucker is always the master storyteller, with his tales of Japanese business development (the soccer team), the Prussian army vs. Henry Ford's assembly line (models of teams), PTAs at suburban schools (perfunctory management), university freedom (the autonomous centers of power), who will take care of the common good (unresolved problems of the pluralistic society), and the failure of socialism/communism (leading to cohesive power of knowledge-based organizations). This is Drucker's thirtieth article for *Harvard Business Review* and undoubtedly one of his best.

ABSTRACT 1.5
THE NEW BOUNDARIES OF THE "BOUNDARYLESS" COMPANY

Hirschhorn, Larry and Gilmore, Thomas
Harvard Business Review, Vol. 70 Issue 3, May/June 1992, pp. 104–115

The opening lines of the first two paragraphs clearly set the stage for this interesting and thought-provoking article on organizational boundaries which are meant to be defined in the eyes of the beholders: the institutional leaders and IS/IT support staff. "In an economy founded on innovation and change, one of the premier challenges of management is to design more flexible organizations. For many executives, a single metaphor has come to embody this managerial challenge and to capture the kind of organization they want to create: the corporation without boundaries." From this vision of Jack Welch to the "data feelings" of the alert IS/IT manager, a wide variety of challenging topics are covered: (1) challenges of flexible work; (2) remapping organizational boundaries of authority, tasks, politics, and identity; (3) the authority vacuum; and (4) downsizing with dignity.

The authors point out, however, that managers should not assume that boundaries may be eliminated altogether. Once the traditional boundaries of hierarchy, function, and geography disappear, a new set of boundaries become important and must be dealt with. These new boundaries are more psychological than organizational, and instead of being reflected in a company's structure, they must be enacted over and over again in a manager's *relationships* with bosses, subordinates, and peers. The four new important boundaries are the authority boundary, task boundary, political boundary, and identity boundary. The article ends with a plea for getting started and is enhanced by an interesting mini-study on "The Team that Failed." The implications for IS/IT are for renewed networking within as well as outside of the enterprise. A shortcoming is that references are not provided.

ABSTRACT 1.6
HEROES ON THE HELP DESK: REDEFINING THE STRATEGIC ROLE OF SUPPORT

Murtagh, Steve and Sheehan, R. William
Fortune, April 15, 1996, pp. 69–85

Although positioned as an advertisement/editorial, the authors and principals of Renaissance Partners, Inc. have put together a provocative piece of reading on how effective IT support services are saving their client organizations millions and improving customer satisfaction at the same time. Although help desks have been around for almost 20 years, assisting customers and internal staff with PC and other technical problems, not everybody is happy with the concept. As computers have made their way from the glass palace to the desktop, the cost of supporting the infrastructure has risen faster and higher than anyone expected, contend the authors. Global expenditures for technical services and support have exceeded $175 billion in 1995, and the percentage of the IT budget that goes to support services, rather than to operations and development, averages 57 percent and is climbing.

Clearly, a new approach is required, one that strategically redefines and repositions the help desk to sit astride not one but three critical processes: contacts, incidents, and problems. Thus, the function must be reengineered to best satisfy these three processes. A number of companies are profiled and their attempts documented:

- *Clorox*—Reengineered IT support services to create measurable strategic value and short-term tactical results, with a goal of reducing the hidden cost of IS/IT support services by 50 percent.

- *Florida Power & Light*—Developed a training program to familiarize employees with basic PC/LAN concepts, resulting in a reduction of calls by some two-and-one-half times.

- *IBM*—Created a special support service for external customers to provide effective help desk functions such as assessment, automation services, integration support, and operations assistance.

- *Vantive Corporation*—The fastest growing publicly traded software company in the customer interaction market and the leading provider of integrated customer interaction software covering automated sales, marketing, customer service, defect tracking, field service, and internal help desk functions.

- *Software Artistry, Inc.*—Develops and markets a product called SA-Expertise which provides support management tools required to link operations such as help desk, network management, asset-change management, and end-user empowerment.

- *Clarify, Inc.*—Provides systems to assist clients with product support call management, help desk management, product change requests, and inventory control.

- *Entergy Corp.*—Used the Quality Action Teams approach, coupled with natural work teams, to completely reengineer its 13 help desk operations in three states into a single "Command Theater" operation and double the number of calls processed with a 15 percent reduction in staff.

- *Taco Bell*—Used the SCORE system to separate help desk support from the IT group in order to become more focused on the business of supporting restaurants.

- *Magic Solutions, Inc.*—Has worked with over 27,000 organizations worldwide, including the White House, to improve help desk operations, and recently rated number one by *Software Digest.* Features embedded artificial intelligence to assist help desk professionals in solving complex problems and shorten the support cycle.

- *Remedy Corporation*—Developed the Action Request System to help track and resolve support requests in the over 2,000 PC and UNIX computing environments in 35 countries, involving some 1,000 customers.

- *NASCO*—Used the Bendata HEAT software system to centralize and revamp its help desk operations, including the education of customers on tools, services, correct usage, and options available.

CHAPTER 2

UNDERSTANDING THE INFORMATION TECHNOLOGY ORGANIZATION

Technology is often known for its jargon, acronyms, and newly created word definitions. The term "information technology" usually creates confusion because it has various names and functions. There are no set naming rules or conventions. A company's senior management will usually name a departmental area based upon preference. The "buzz name" is not important; the function performed and the results realized are.

Before proceeding, let's clarify some confusing interchangeable terms and their usages. The first are information technology (IT) and information systems (IS). Some say that IT is the technical equipment used, and IS is the method of delivering the information. One accepted definition of IT is the application of technology to business processes, gathering data and creating information that is valuable to managers who make business decisions.[1] It does not matter whether a company calls the function IT, IS, data processing, or some other name, as long as everyone in the company uses the same terminology. IT will be used in this text, but some endnotes refer to IS. The two terms are interchangeable.

Other perplexing terms are data and information. Again, these are basically the same. The primary difference is their usefulness. One definition of data is "a representation of facts, concepts, or instructions in a formalized manner suitable for processing."[2] Information is defined as data assembled in a usable form and beneficial to person(s) using it. Purists are specific about the usage of these terms, but most individuals use them interchangeably. Technology is not necessary to generate information, and some information is best derived manually. Information was being created long before computers were invented.

Technology has developed over time and will continue to change. The functions and roles of IT are continually changing as a result of this revolution and evolution.

REVOLUTION AND EVOLUTION OF INFORMATION TECHNOLOGY

The First Computers

Data-processing devices have progressed over the centuries, from counting on fingers and toes to the abacus to slide rules to calculators to electronic computers. The first computers were primarily used for scientific purposes and have advanced over the years from business to personal use.

Calculating and computing devices exist in digital and analog forms. The difference between the two forms is that the analog device measures and the digital device counts. Analog computers were subject to systematic errors but were very fast. The first mechanical analog computers were introduced in the 1920s, but it was not until the mid-1940s that digital computers were introduced. IBM and Harvard University teamed in 1938 to build a general-purpose digital computer, the Automatic Sequence Controlled Calculator, also known as the Mark I. The Mark I computer was installed in 1944 as the first fully automatic computer. It was huge (it filled a room) and consisted of thousands of relays connected by mazes of wire. This computer was considered a success, but it was also a failure because it was slow—the Mark I was only a hundred times faster than a human using a mechanical calculator. The Mark I was put to work calculating gunnery tables during World War II.

Computers have continually improved since the Mark I was introduced. The computer evolution has caused a continual change in technology and the business environment. The computer age can be thought of as two eras.

Era One

The first technology era was from the 1950s to 1980s. Until the 1980s, technology was primarily used to automate *existing* business functions and reduce clerical costs. The basic IT structure was hierarchical, with walls built within functions and between companies. IT systems were designed to support individual companies and their business functions with minimal or no cross-company integration of information. It was a rare occasion for companies to share software with customers or team with a competitor to enhance industry technology. This era can be subdivided into five generations, each of which provided major technical advancements.

First Generation: Late 1940s to Late 1950s—The computers were large, required a controlled room temperature, and operated using vacuum tubes. The input methods were paper tape or punch cards. These computers were primarily used for scientific calculations.

Second Generation: Late 1950s to Mid 1960s—Transistors replaced vacuum tubes, which allowed for a smaller, modular-designed computer. The ability to teleprocess and transmit data to another computer via telephone lines was introduced. The development of large databases with long-distance linkups connected by terminals also began. Major corporations, which were the only ones that could afford a computer, started using it for business purposes.

Third Generation: Mid 1960s to Late 1960s—Major changes occurred during this generation. Miniature integrated circuits replaced transistors. The computer became smaller, and processing speeds were reduced to billionths of a second. Other advancements were optical scanners, magnetic ink character readers, and larger storage devices.

Computers were enhanced by the addition of additional languages and a "multi-programming" capability which made the computer capable of handling simultaneous processing of independent functions. The remote processing concept was introduced, which allowed a terminal to directly access the computer from various off-site locations.

Fourth Generation: Early 1970s to Early 1980s—This was the personal computer (PC) age. Microprocessors replaced integrated circuits and allowed the computer to become smaller, faster, and more powerful. The mini- and micro-computer era began. Smaller businesses were now able to consider purchasing computers and automating their business processes.

Fifth Generation: Early 1980s to Late 1980s—Manufacturers developed "chips" customized for each computer's specific needs. The PC was given the power of mainframe computers. Costs came down, and the computer became affordable for most businesses and some individuals. This generation saw the development of robotics and the growth of electronic data interchange (EDI).

Era Two

The second era started in the late 1980s, and it is difficult to see when it will end. Technology has now come to play an important role in supporting business development. Technology advances have enabled companies to interact. In a special supplement about the second era in IT, *Business Week*[3] mentions that the traditional IT system should be changed to reflect the new enterprise. Like the new enterprise, it is open and networked. It is modular and dynamic and based on interchangeable parts. It technically empowers users by distributing intelligence and decision making. Yet, through standards, it is integrated, moving enterprises beyond system islands (and their organization equivalents) of the first era. It works the way people do, ignoring boundaries among data, text, voice, and image, and provides a backbone for team-oriented business structures. The IT paradigm shift is bringing about fundamental change in technology in just about everything regarding the technology itself and its application to business. *Organizations that do not make this transition to the new paradigm will fail.* They will become irrelevant or cease to exist. The new IT enables enterprises to have a high-performance team structure, to function as integrated businesses despite high business unit autonomy, and to reach out and develop new relationships with external organizations—to become "extended enterprises."

This text provides the foundation to support the IT Era Two. Firms must start using technology to develop new business opportunities and include the IT functions when reviewing business processes. Basically, they must rethink how to better utilize technology *effectively* to enhance company growth and profits. (For additional information, see Abstract 2.1 at the end of this chapter.)

Technology Trends

Computers and the methods used to gather and process data will continue to improve and change. Technology touches every individual, whether at work, play, or home. With the technical advancements being made, hardware is waiting for the software and peripheral devices to catch up. Peripherals include data storage devices and various input/output devices. It is impossible to predict the technological future except to say that "electronic communications" appear to be the next trend. The technical area is wide open for innovation and creativity, as people are becoming more imaginative as to the application of technology.

Business functions such as accounting and inventory control have been around for centuries, and people have had time to adjust to them. However, the slow development of such functions cannot be compared with the technical advances that have occurred over the past 50 years. Small wonder that people do not fully understand the rapidly developing technology of our own era. Rather than inculcate training and development of personnel to accommodate an ever-changing technology, most companies simply try a new method, and if it is unsuccessful, they try something else.

Change should be an improvement. Often it is merely an extension of an earlier method or technique. Only the name is changed to reflect a new and improved version of an old method, even though the old method was inefficient. An example is object-oriented design, an approach where a reusable, modular design is to be created. Although the term "object-oriented" is new, it is actually the modular, reusable program routines in use since the early 1970s.

Well-known management consultant Peter Drucker had the following to say about business executives and computer technology:[4]

> There are still a good many businessmen around who have little use for, and less interest in, the computer. There are also still quite a few who believe that the computer will somehow replace man or become his master. Others, however, realize by now that the computer, while powerful, is only a tool and is neither going to replace man nor control him. The trick lies in knowing both what it can do and what it cannot do. Without such knowledge, the modern executive can find himself in real trouble in the computer age.

This statement was made in 1966. It still holds true today, even with all the advances made over the past 25 years.

INFORMATION TECHNOLOGY ORGANIZATIONAL FUNCTIONS

Organization Overview

A popular conception of IT is, "All those expensive machines and people are overhead! They speak a language all their own." This is partially true. It does cost time and money to invest in machines and people. But that is not overhead; it is an investment in the future. The IT profession is a specialty and requires skilled expertise. Compare IT professionals with accountants or lawyers; they also speak a unique language. The IT profession is even more complex as there are multiple professions and functions within it. There is an additional communication barrier between the functional units within IT. Application programmers speak a different jargon than telecommunications specialists, and they become frustrated with one another, just as a businessperson does when dealing with a "techie."

From the outside, the IT organization looks like a single entity, but it is actually comprised of separate functional units. Each functional unit plays a distinct role, and all need to work together as a cross-functional team.

FUNCTIONAL UNIT DESCRIPTIONS

The IT area basically consists of four functions (Figure 2.1), regardless of the size of the company. The number of people supporting IT usually depends on the size, budget, and work volume of the company.

The four basic IT functions are:

- Telecommunications
- Data center
- Applications support
- Information administration

The name of the functional unit and work responsibilities performed vary from company to company. For example, the applications support function has been called information systems, management information systems, business systems development, data processing, etc. The point is that no one name is correct; it is the job function being performed that is critical.

Telecommunications

This functional unit adds to and maintains any technically driven communications. The telecommunications function usually installs the company telephone system and keeps it working. When a company is involved with electronic interchange, whether it be installing workstations or transmitting data from one location to another, this functional area is involved. Whenever telephones, cabling, wiring, or computer networks are included, this functional unit should be an active participant. This unit includes two subfunctional units:

Communications (Voice and Data)—Monitors and installs telephones and any data communications devices. Evaluates and installs cables to connect workstations or terminals, for example.

Computer Networks—Builds and maintains the network that is used to transmit data or information from one location to another. Makes certain the different computers can "talk" to one another and determines the best route for the data to travel for security and expediency.

Data Center

This function maintains the computer facilities. The data center includes the computer hardware, peripherals, and the software that tell the computer what to do (not to be confused with application business software). Data center subfunctions include:

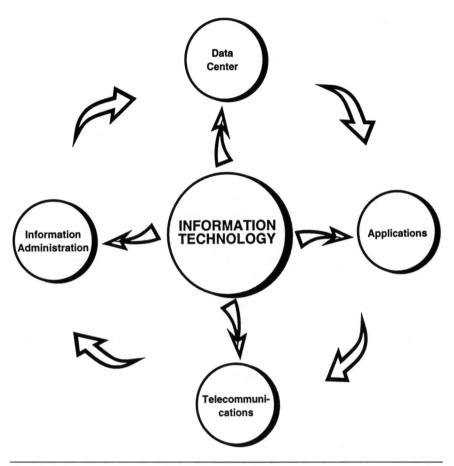

Figure 2.1   Information Technology Basic Functions.

Operations Support—Monitors the computer and ensures that there are no computer processing interruptions to the business.

Systems Support—Improves computer efficiency, maintains the computer operating software, and stays abreast of new advances. Includes monitoring space, where data are stored, and data security.

Production Support—Plans and schedules the work to be completed by the computer. Ensures all data inputs are prepared and the outputs are distributed on time to the customers. This unit is often responsible for ensuring that computer-related documentation is completed and for enforcement of standards.

To further complicate matters, it is important that cross-functional team-work occurs *within* the data center functional unit. For example, production support informs the operations support area what work must be processed, when it must be completed, and how it is to be delivered to the customer.

Applications Support

This functional unit is usually the one most visible to the business customer (also known as the end user). Applications support is responsible for build-ing and maintaining business support computer software, such as payroll, inventory, accounts payable, sales forecasting, and so on. Depending on the size of the company and the number of business computer systems, the traditional applications support area is divided into subgroups which sup-port computer systems in various business departments (e.g., all the financial computer systems are under one subgroup which supports the financial department. This provides better customer support but hinders an integrated process team approach. The subfunctions include:

Business Support—Interacts with the business and represents the business applications processing. Consists of the analysts, programmers, and project team managers who design, code, test, and implement projects and changes for the company.

Data Base—Administers, maintains, and analyzes data and information used by the business applications processing in an integrated, centralized manner.

Information Administration

Information administration is usually a separate functional unit in larger companies, but it should be considered a necessary function for small firms. The smaller company usually handles this function within applications sup-port. This functional unit is the central location for business and technology coordination. It provides computer assistance (also known as the help desk) to the centralized business user. It integrates information, plans technical strategy, provides security, and does business recovery planning. This unit is the central technical watchdog and helper.

Help Desk—Provides assistance when business or technical units require any help relating to a technical concern. A centralized contact point.

Security/Audit—Monitors the information and regulates who can access what information in the computer systems.

Business Recovery—Maintains a contingency plan supporting how business will be conducted if the automated systems should become unavailable. This function includes planning for a temporary interruption to business and major disasters for all IT support functions and business processes.

Strategic Planning—Works with the company to define the vision and goals in order to generate a technology strategic plan.

Miscellaneous Support Systems

Over the years, various miscellaneous information support systems have evolved. They are generated by business users to avoid the IT organization, especially for ad hoc reporting. These areas are referred to as "private sand boxes," and they cause great difficulty for the IT area. They generally develop in response to business users' impatience with IT's long response times. There is nothing wrong with having different support systems, but when it comes to business recovery planning, security, data integrity, and information integration, they create a nightmare for IT and business decision makers. These functions include but are not limited to decision support systems, executive support systems, and expert systems.

The term decision support system was coined in 1971. It allowed organizations to distinguish between the bulk of structured data-processing activities (such as sales orders or managing payroll) and the use of information and IT to support the less structured tasks of managers.[5] Additional versions of decision support systems were spawned as vendors sold new products and decided to call them something else. Other names include, but are not limited to, executive information systems and group decision support systems. Results range from a spreadsheet to graphical displays.

Information should be under a central control. Total quality is sacrificed with multiple information centers. Multiple centers of information lead to redundant information, unpredictable results, reporting inconsistencies, and poor to no security (or business recovery planning). A firm cannot be forced to keep all support system functions under IT, but the importance of coordination with IT cannot be overstated. This is where teamwork comes into play. If a department has the funds to purchase software and hardware, then it should work as a team with IT to coordinate effort and receive support. IT should adopt a positive attitude and begin offering solutions to the end user. Without teamwork, communication breaks down and inefficient use of technology will be a recurring difficulty until organizational barriers come down.

DESCRIBING THE INFORMATION TECHNOLOGY PROFESSIONAL

An IT professional is defined is anyone who works in or is employed in a technical field profession. This can be within any of the functional units. Each person within IT is considered a professional, regardless of position or function.

Image Projected by Information Technology

Unfortunately, a stereotypical image of the IT professional is someone who is:

- Egotistical
- Nontraditional
- Loyal only to the computer
- Highly paid compared to other business functions
- Unconventional in appearance
- Speaks a strange language
- Acts strangely

The following is a true story about a management misunderstanding as to what IT work entails. A senior manager walked through the computer department and asked why a particular person just sat there, staring into space. The senior manager voiced the opinion that this person ought to be reprimanded and told to get to work immediately. The individual in question was a programmer, one of the best, who was thinking through a programming problem. The individual had been called in to work on a problem that had to be corrected before the start of the business day. He had been on-site from 1:00 a.m. to 3:00 a.m. The senior manager did not understand that most IT work is not observably busy, but requires thinking, planning, and off-hours support. This adds to the complexity of managing or working with IT professionals; sometimes it is difficult to know if they are working. This should be judged by the work produced and its quality.

Role and Characteristics

The IT professional must be a visionary in order to anticipate future technological trends. No one really knows what new and great product will be introduced next. Professionals must continually stay abreast of marketing trends and future product announcements. IT should design and implement systems using modular methods and offer flexibility to meet changing business needs.

Each IT professional should possess the following general characteristics:

- Team player
- Friendly
- Open-minded
- Accept change and challenge
- Trainable
- Business and technical solution oriented
- Ethical and moral
- Patient
- Good communicator (oral and written)

This seems like a tall order, but the IT professional of the future must interact with the business and technical functional areas to provide what is best for the entire company instead of just what is best technically or personally. The ethical and moral necessities are included because the individual has access to secure data and other confidential information. The concept of total quality stresses teamwork, being innovative, and customer service ("users"). If IT professionals do not possess these characteristics, a company cannot succeed in implementing total quality.

IT managers generally advance from the technical ranks and thus do not have the same leadership and management expertise as business managers. This is changing as IT managers realize the need for business management education and training. To properly function with business managers, IT managers must articulate technical issues in a meaningful way to those who control the business, understand how to solve the problems of others, and motivate subordinates to work as a team.

Types of Positions

The IT profession has created new specialized job types. Each is its own specialty and requires continual training due to constant technical advancements and changes. They are listed by functional unit but could report elsewhere in a company. The exhibits at the end of this chapter detail the possible skill descriptions for IT professionals. This is far from an inclusive list but touches on the most common job types. Table 2.1 shows a comparison between manufacturing and IT positions when generating a product. (For additional information, see Abstract 2.2 at the end of this chapter.)

Information Technology Manager—This position in larger companies is sometimes called the chief information officer (CIO) or IT director. This person is responsible for coordinating and leading *all* IT functions in the organization.

Table 2.1 Position and Function Comparison: Manufacturing to Information Technology

IT position	Manufacturing position	Function performed
Systems analyst	Design engineer	**Designs** the product
Programmer	Production engineer	**Builds** the product
End user	Customer	**Uses** the product

Telecommunications

Telecommunication Analyst—This relatively new position is the position of the future. This person should be responsible for the company's computer networks in terms of security and business recovery, system and network tools, and wireless technologies.

Telecommunication analysts are involved with electronic data interchange, distributed processing, and are data "traffic cops." Data networks become congested, similar to highway systems, but the result is "data jams" instead of "traffic jams."

Data Center Support

Computer Operator—Monitors the computer and ensures that all is functioning properly.

Production Control Analyst—Responsible for the day-to-day data center scheduling and ensures that work is completed on time.

Applications Support

Project Team Manager—Responsible for a team of IT personnel who support a project. Interfaces with the business customers. Prepares status reports and project plans. Interfaces with the other IT functions.

Systems Analyst—A person with analytical skills, a problem solver. Interfaces with the end user, obtains business requirements, designs the computer system, and assists with testing and system conversion planning. This individual must know the company products and services, policies and procedures, and regulatory considerations. Systems analysts interact with the other IT functional units and work with the programming team(s).

Programmer—Designs, codes, and tests software programs. The programmer of the 1990s is a computer analyst who is also becoming a business analyst who interfaces with the business users.

Data Analyst—Plans and designs the technical data base. Maintains and secures any data dictionary or software support that involves the data.

Information Administration

Systems Integrator—This individual ensures that technical and business needs are met. This position is a liaison between technical functional units, the company, its suppliers, and the business users. Systems integrators make certain that information is integrated and that all financial and legal ramifications are considered. This position could be part of the role of the systems analyst (explained above) in smaller firms.

Strategic Planner—Responsible for developing a company-wide operating plan and a long-term strategic plan by optimizing the return on investment of technical resources. Provides guidance and direction to implement the overall technical goals and objectives of the company.

Performance Measurements

Firms usually look at company profitability as the primary measurement criterion for performance evaluations and offering incentives. This trend appears to be changing. Celia Berk, who heads employee programs and training for Reuters company operations in North and South America, has stated:[6]

> ...we decided that if you measure yourself just by financial results, you can't tell if you're creating an opportunity for rivals. Now the company measures itself on client satisfaction, employee effectiveness and satisfaction, operating efficiency, and contribution to shareholder value, in that order.

Performance measurement criteria are changing and in many instances are being forced to change. With more employees working at home, thanks to technology, the former scenario of showing up for work on time, working hard, and receiving a good review will no longer hold true.

IT employees should be evaluated on their willingness to learn new techniques, the quality of work produced, their business knowledge, customer (end-user) satisfaction, and their teamwork abilities. If someone is working an excessive number of hours, the reason why should be investigated. For example, is the extra time due to problems not uncovered until the project was installed as a result of poor testing? In this case, the person should be given a poor review for generating poor quality results.

In some companies, the direction of performance reviews is to evaluate performance based upon the entire team. The team result is the individual result. One reason for this trend is the belief that team members will support each other and "force" everyone to participate and carry their own weight. The verdict is still out on this. One concern in this type of review is that sometimes one individual's performance outshines all others. It is not always fair to that individual when others do not carry their weight on the team. Another concern is the uneven distribution of individual talent among teams. Until these concerns are addressed and a standard in place, there is the potential risk of unfairness when solely using team reviews.

Future Career Opportunities

Technology in the computer arena is reshaping the workplace and is giving data processing professionals, long a mysterious priesthood, new power and prominence. Computer scientists and systems analysts will be among the fastest growing occupations through the year 2005. Employment of programmers is expected to grow faster than the average for all occupations through the year 2005 as computer usage expands.[7]

This presents a good news/bad news scenario. The good news is that there will be greater opportunity and better jobs for IT professionals. The bad news is that IT retains the image of a "mysterious priesthood." IT cannot become part of strategic planning if viewed as a necessary but alien function. The IT professional must embrace the language of business, and businesspeople must learn to communicate with the IT professional. The success of IT, total quality, process engineering, or any business/technology plan is heavily dependent on the success of this cross-communication.

IT professionals, who for years experienced a certain job security, are now beginning to fear for their jobs. Many companies are shrinking IT functions by outsourcing them to external companies in order to save money. The external company has the option of hiring existing staff, but many IT management positions disappear. Technology, hardware, and software have also changed, and many firms replace older individuals, who have outdated technical skills, with younger individuals who have learned newer technologies, do not require retraining, and are lower salaried. The dilemma is: *Will the company want young, up-to-date technical professionals or will it train the older, experienced IT personnel in the newer technology?* No one can predict what companies will do in this situation; every company will respond differently.

Another concern is the career path for IT professionals. Initially, the only way to climb the corporate ladder or advance was to go into management.

Fortunately, this is changing; now excellent technicians who would be ineffective managers can receive the same status and remuneration as managers and still remain technicians.

Information Technology Cross-Functional Roles

The IT organization traditionally has been hierarchical and consisted of different specialized areas. These special areas are necessary because technological advances are ongoing and no one person can be an expert in everything. Examples are applications programmers and telecommunication analysts. Each area of expertise requires its own unique language, has its own skill set, and is continually changing. Each functional area has its own unique hardware and software. *It is important that individuals within IT gain a basic knowledge about other IT functional units to support one another and work as a team.* The applications support area should not implement a new project unless the data center (and in today's world, the telecommunications area) is involved from the beginning.

INFORMATION TECHNOLOGY INFRASTRUCTURE

The IT organization should be customized based on how a firm conducts business and how processes are used to meet business goals and objectives. The intention of this section is to stress that the IT organization consists of multiple functional units configured to support overall business goals and objectives. There is no "right" or "wrong" IT structure; what is right is what works for your company.

Why an Infrastructure?

Every organization needs leadership and communication. They are a means to direct and coordinate activities and a way to monitor and evaluate performance.

Total quality stresses teamwork, customer service, service reliability, efficiency, and innovation. Without an infrastructure, the different functional areas within a company (or within IT) would be unable to effectively communicate with one another.

Structuring an Information Technology Organization

When structuring or restructuring the IT organization, the same considerations must be followed as when structuring the overall organization:

1. Decide what type of organization (centralized, decentralized, or combined) best fits the goals and objectives of the company.
2. Establish the goals and objectives of the IT organization.
3. Prioritize the goals and objectives.
4. Determine the precepts that apply.
5. Define the services to be offered.
6. Determine functions and job families.
7. Decide on a location.

The IT organization should be in a position to handle continual and rapid change. This not only preserves a competitive edge in the market but also promotes internal business support. When company management turnover occurs, IT is affected, as business processes usually change and the information needed for decision making changes.

The IT organization should be structured in manageable functional pieces in order to monitor budgets and schedules, as well as evaluate performance and provide feedback at the departmental and individual levels.

There is not now, nor will there ever be, a standard organization that fits every firm or even a majority of users. Each organization has its own unique constraints and variables; thus, a single solution cannot possibly work for all.[8]

Types of Organization

There are two key considerations when deciding on the type of organizational structure for IT:

1. To whom will the organization report and be accountable?
2. Where are the computer facilities (equipment and people) to be located *and* will there be multiple locations?

There are many variations and types of organizational structure. The common IT types are:

Centralized—The IT organization's management representation is on the same level as the other business functions reporting to senior management. *All* the IT functions throughout the company are managed through this one central point and location. Equipment, facilities, and personnel are all at a central location. There is no duplication.

Decentralized—The IT organization is spread out over multiple locations, each with its own staff, management, and equipment.

Partial Centralized and Decentralized—IT functions are split throughout the company. The data center and telecommunications support functions are located at one central site, but the applications, management, and equipment are divided throughout the company.

Placing Information Technology in the Company

The IT organization must represent the entire company and all of its entities. IT should be in a position to *fairly* provide support to all business functions. One suggested approach is for IT management to report directly to senior management at the same level as other business managers. IT would then be a provider for the *entire* company. The current business direction is geared toward interorganizational systems that have integrated information and processes that cross corporate entities. The American Airlines SABRE system and American Hospital Supply's ASAP order-entry system are examples of the potential competitive advantage of interorganizational systems.[9] IT can better support the company when reporting to top management and when top management makes a commitment to IT.

When IT reports directly to one functional department, there is sometimes a barrier between supporting the entire company versus supporting one function. As an example, when IT reports to the chief financial officer (CFO), the CFO is interested in saving money (and technology costs money). In such circumstances, IT often feels budget cuts before other departments.

Business integration becomes difficult when everyone is "doing their own thing" with technology without coordination. Without the coordination of a company-wide team to consider all technical needs, funds are spent over and again for the same software and hardware without standards. One way to avoid this is to use cross-functional teams, where representatives from the different units meet and compare notes. Departmental responsibility, control, and budgeting are needed, but no project should be implemented without company-wide IT/business consultation. (For additional information, see Abstract 2.3 at the end of this chapter.)

EXTERNAL SUPPORT CONSIDERATIONS

Defining External Support

IT is an area where a single function or entire functional units could be external to the company or, using today's terminology, "outsourced." There is a fine line between the term "outsourcing" and its use. For our purposes, outsourcing is using a specialized outside company to provide a particular service. Other names are time-share (buying computer time) and insourcing (offering more than temporary staffing but less than full outsourcing). All this adds to the confusion. The bottom line is that a firm seeks outside assistance; the level of services provided can and will vary. It can consist of temporary help, including people and equipment, or printing at a remote location. Multi-sourcing is the term used when a firm outsources multiple functions.

Why Consider Outsourcing?

Each IT functional unit can be considered a separate business. IT functional units could function independently but must remain coordinated and integrated to ensure quality and consistency.

The trend is for organizations to use outside companies to conduct IT activities and support. This is called a value-added or strategic business partnership. A value-adding partnership is a set of independent companies that work closely together to manage the flow of goods and services along the entire value-added chain.[10] The value-adding partnership is becoming popular and gives small firms the opportunity to compete with and work with larger firms. This is one example of teamwork, a key total quality principle.

What Can Be Outsourced?

Any company, large or small, can consider going outside to replace an IT activity and save money on value-added services. Almost every large corporation has used external help in IT at some time or another, especially for software support. The imagination is the limit, but managers must remember to be reasonable and think the situation through. Sending an activity to an outside firm may save dollars, but it necessarily gives up some control.

Many activities take place within IT functional units. When outsourcing, it is recommended that the activities going outside be grouped modularly by function and not divided. This activity can vary from firm to firm as each has its own organization and work functions. There are no set rules. A sampling of IT functions and activities that are candidates for external support are:

Data Center—Facilities management, computer hardware, equipment maintenance, printing, imaging, or remote location IT needs.

Telecommunications—Computer network usage, including voice and data communications support.

Applications Support—Maintenance support for existing systems, programming, design, and new project development.

Information Administration—Help desks, office automation, workstation maintenance, strategic planning, business recovery planning, documentation writing, and training.

Some firms often outsource separate business support computer systems such as:

- Payroll
- Human resources benefit packages (i.e., pensions)
- Sales analysis
- Financial ledgers
- Accounts payable

A firm may already have an in-house IT support organization, but it is sometimes feasible to contract an outside company to provide the IT area with information which can be integrated into the in-house system. Payroll is an excellent example of a process that continually requires mandatory changes and may be more beneficial to outsource.

Another area often outsourced is education and training. Firms often have an outside firm write their procedure manuals and then conduct the business-user and technical training for a project.

Within IT, one area where it might be feasible to outsource is the data center facilities (while retaining in-house programming support) because of costs associated with hardware upgrades. A company should analyze the cost–benefits of new technology to determine whether outsourcing IT functions is appropriate. This analysis is usually done by experienced outside advisors. By going outside, a company ensures an objective study, without internal, emotional, or political considerations. The main criterion is what will be best for the firm.

Without knowing all the facts and conducting a feasibility study, it is impossible to know whether or not a company should outsource.

Why Go External?

Most companies decide to go outside to reduce the full-time employee head count and to obtain quick savings. In the past, financially unstable firms were the main users of outsourcing, but current trends indicate that healthy companies are now following suit. Xerox (considered a "healthy" firm) is outsourcing IT functions. A Xerox spokesman indicated that although the company expects to achieve considerable savings, "it was motivated to outsource by other reasons as well: to speed the rate that it can move to new technologies and to free management to focus on strategic information management issues instead of on day-to-day concerns."[11]

There are risks in outsourcing entire IT functions, and the bottom-line dollars and cents should not be the sole determining factor. Reasons a company might consider outsourcing include:

Pace of Technical Change—Technology is constantly changing; by outsourcing, a firm does not need to continually invest in hardware that becomes outdated almost before a project is implemented. The outside company would assume the expense of upgrading hardware and software.

Free Up IT Management and Personnel—One difficulty may be that the IT staff is too busy supporting antiquated, day-to-day business systems and unable to devote effort to new development. By outsourcing, existing management and staff would be able to devote time to focusing on strategies, learning new tools and techniques, and becoming active participants in business reengineering efforts. The existing staff, who understand the business, would be better qualified to assist with new development efforts than would outside new development experts.

Reduce Workforce—When a firm outsources, it does not require additional support staff and can sometimes eliminate employees. The outside firm may even hire part or all of the company's staff.

Eliminate Layoffs—At times, additional support staff may be needed temporarily. There are many specialized skills within the IT function, and it is often advantageous to obtain outside help. Outsiders, usually referred to as contractors or consultants, perform temporary tasks for a limited duration of time. This saves a firm from having to hire additional employees and release them when a project is completed.

Risks of Going External

In addition to bottom-line costs and savings, there are other factors a company should consider before deciding whether or not to go outside. Risks include:

- Legal ramifications
- Employee loyalty and morale
- Customer service impacts
- Quality standards
- Security and confidentiality
- Turnaround time and costs
- Stability of outsource firm

A price must be put on all the above factors when considering the feasibility and risks of outsourcing.

Legal Ramifications—Before outsourcing, a firm must consider any legal implications. Considerations include liability for inaccurate information, not meeting mandatory schedules, licensing agreements, and existing contractual agreements.

Employee Loyalty and Morale—Employees may take an "I don't care" attitude and feel that their jobs will be eliminated no matter what. This attitude ripples from unhappy employees to customers, adversely affecting customer service and quality. A firm should also consider security, since an unhappy employee will sometimes join the competition. The loss of key IS employees can have a devastating effect on an organization's ability to use IS to support in-house activities.[12]

Customer Service Impacts—Consideration should be given to how customer service will be affected by having an outside firm provide a service. This includes outside analysts interfacing directly with both business users and customers.

Quality Standards—It is important that standards and measurements be established and strictly enforced. When dealing with an outside firm, a company (client) encounters multiple risks. Sometimes, especially when contracting programming, the outside firm assigns inexperienced personnel. This lack of experience affects the overall quality and usually extends the completion time. Another risk is that the employees of the outside firm may be temporary or may have minimal loyalty to the client and, in some instances, the outside firm. This generates an added risk in that those employees may leave the outside firm during the project. The client company must ensure that the outside firm follows the agreed upon standards and measurements. The results should be continuously monitored. It is suggested that the client company have at least one employee act as a liaison with the outside firm.

Security and Confidentiality—When a company uses outsourcing, someone outside the company becomes responsible for the security of company information. Outside individuals have access to information which some competitors may want. When going outside, the hiring company *must* be certain that it does not give up control of its information. A firm also does not want an outsider to be responsible for generating information used for decision making.

Turnaround Time and Costs—When a company outsources all or a portion of its IT function, it becomes additionally important that technology considerations be part of overall business planning. It is no longer possible to "go down the hall and ask Joe Tech for a report." Users must formally go outside the company for requests and pay for each request. While many companies have internal charge-backs for technical services, this money is transferred from one budget to another but remains within the company. When outsourcing, the firm pays *another* company for technical support services. The funds then leave the corporate entity, which can result in lower profits.

Outsource Firm Stability—Firms must examine performance records and potential longevity of potential outsourcers; without proper planning, IS performance is likely to be diminished if the outsourcer goes out of business.[13] It is important to make certain the outside firm can and will deliver what the company needs.

Whether outsourcing or not, someone must lead or facilitate. When going outside, it is even more important to have a technology plan that is integrated into the business strategic plan. A company must have someone in house to represent its best interests and coordinate the technology activities. A formalized sign-off process should be in place before accepting any changes an outside firm makes. Without this extra monitoring, a firm could well lose control of its business. (For additional information, see Abstract 2.4 at the end of this chapter.)

ENDNOTES

1. Daniels, N. Caroline (1994). *Information Technology. The Management Challenge.* Wokingham, England: Addison-Wesley and The Economist Intelligence Unit, p. 36.
2. Frates, Jeffrey and Moldrup, William (1984). *Introduction to the Computer.* Englewood Cliffs, NJ: Prentice-Hall, p. 535.
3. Tapscott, Don and Caston, Art (1993). "Information Technology Enters a Second Era." *Business Week.* October 25 (special supplement).
4. Drucker, Peter F. (1966). "What the Computer Will Be Telling You." *Nation's Business.* August, p. 84.
5. McGee, James V. and Prusak, Laurence (1993). *Managing Information Strategically,* The Ernst & Young Information Management Series. New York: John Wiley & Sons, p. 180.
6. O'Reilly, Brian (1994). "What Companies and Employees Owe One Another." *Fortune.* June 13, p. 47.
7. Occupational Outlook Handbook, 1994–95 Edition. Bulletin 2450. Washington, D.C.: Bureau of Labor Statistics, U.S. Department of Labor, p. 226.
8. Hoyt, Douglas B. (1978). *Computer Handbook for Senior Management.* New York: MacMillan Information, p. 31.
9. McGee, James and Prusak, Laurence (1993). *Managing Information Strategically,* The Ernst and Young Information Management Series. New York: John Wiley & Sons, p. 76.

10. Johnson, Russel and Lawrence, Paul (1988). "Beyond Vertical Integra-
     tion—The Rise of the Value-Adding Partnership." Reprinted in *Revolution
     in Real Time Managing: Information Technology in the 1990's*. Boston: Harvard
     Business School, 1991, p. 17.
11. Halper, Mark (1994). "Xerox Signs-Up EDS." *Computerworld*. March 28,
     p. 8.
12. Arnett, K. and Jones, Mary C. (1994). "Firms that Choose Outsourcing: A
     Profile." *Journal of Information Systems Applications*. April, p. 182.
13. Arnett, K. and Jones, Mary C. (1994). "Firms that Choose Outsourcing: A
     Profile." *Journal of Information Systems Applications*. April, pp. 179–188.

EXHIBITS

EXHIBIT 2.1 INFORMATION TECHNOLOGY MANAGER SKILL DESCRIPTION

Job Title: Information Technology Manager

Department: Information Technology

Duties and Responsibilities:

1. Coach and lead IT personnel
2. Plan and maximize IT resources (people, equipment, time, costs) to the fullest
3. Establish measurements and monitor IT performance within IT and business support group(s)
4. Perform routine administrative tasks such as planning, scheduling, budgeting, and leading
5. Interface with business management and provide superior technical solutions for the business direction
6. Prepare and monitor IT budget
7. Develop salary structures, training plans, and career paths for staff
8. Maintain IT disaster contingency plan; ensure security for information and the data center
9. Foster a cooperative, friendly working relationship between IT personnel and all IT customers (i.e., business users, suppliers)
10. Provide the company's technical services at all levels
11. Confirm that the technical strategic plan complements the company's vision, mission, goals, and objectives

Desirable Qualifications:

1. Minimum ten years of strong management experience
2. College graduate with degree in business administration
3. Excellent oral and written communication skills
4. Gregarious; able to interact with all levels of business and management
5. Technical exposure, with hands-on technical background a plus
6. Capable of selling senior management on technology by working with business processing teams and communicating technical data in plain language
7. Politically "savvy"
8. A visionary and leader

EXHIBIT 2.2 PROJECT TEAM MANAGER SKILL DESCRIPTION

Job Title: Project Team Manager

Department: Information Technology

Duties and Responsibilities:
1. Coach and lead IT projects and personnel
2. Plan and maximize IT resources (people, equipment, time, costs) to the fullest for assigned projects
3. Establish measurements and monitor IT performance within IT and business support group(s) for assigned projects
4. Perform routine administrative tasks such as planning, scheduling, budgeting, and leading
5. Interface with business and provide superior technical solutions for the business direction
6. Prepare and monitor IT budget for assigned projects
7. Interview and hire IT team individuals for assigned projects
8. Prepare performance evaluations and feedback for team members
9. Foster a cooperative, friendly working relationship between IT personnel and all IT customers (i.e., business users, suppliers)

Desirable Qualifications:
1. Minimum five years of technical and team leadership experience
2. College graduate with degree in business administration or computer science
3. Excellent oral and written communication skills
4. Able to interact with all levels of business and management
5. Technical exposure, with hands-on technical background a plus
6. Capable of selling business management on technology by working with business processing teams and communicating technical data in plain language
7. A visionary, coach, and leader
8. Knowledge of existing IT systems, tools, procedures, and standards
9. Responsible, with a "can do" attitude

EXHIBIT 2.3 SYSTEMS ANALYST SKILL DESCRIPTION

Job Title: Systems Analyst–Project Lead

Department: Information Technology/Applications Support

Duties and Responsibilities:
1. Coach and lead IT project team on assigned projects
2. Participate as team member on the business cross-functional team representing technology
3. Plan resources and schedule IT tasks for assigned projects
4. Establish measurement norms and monitor IT performance on assigned projects
5. Offer innovative solutions to existing systems and business processes
6. Verify standards are being met
7. Design systems and write specifications based upon business needs and what is best for the business
8. Liaison with all IT functional areas for projects (i.e., programming, data center, telecommunications, and administrative information)
9. Assist with testing of assigned projects
10. Coordinate with IT customers on assigned projects
11. Measure work progress and report status to management
12. Coordinate training and education requirements for new projects
13. Assist project group members in overcoming difficulties with their work
14. Monitor conversion and final installation of assigned projects
15. Prepare contingency plan for projects being installed in case installation cannot proceed
16. Obtain and analyze feedback on newly installed projects
17. Develop and maintain a business disaster recovery plan and coordinate with other IT functional areas

Desirable Qualifications:
1. Over five years of working experience in technical and business analysis
2. College graduate; preferably a degree in business administration or computer science
3. Excellent oral and written communication skills
4. Enjoy working with others and able to interact with all levels of business support and management
5. Ability to lead, organize, and gather information
6. Previous programming background a plus
7. Capable of communicating as a business analyst and computer analyst
8. Understanding of the company and its business
9. Creative, innovative problem solver
10. Knowledge of existing IT systems, tools, procedures, and standards
11. Responsible, with a "can do" attitude

EXHIBIT 2.4 PROGRAMMER SKILL DESCRIPTION

Job Title: Programmer

Department: Information Technology/Applications Support

Duties and Responsibilities:
1. Receive system specifications from systems analyst lead
2. Determine effort and time needed for programs and testing with the systems analyst lead
3. Prepare test data
4. Conduct and participate in all testing
5. Check testing results and review with systems analyst lead
6. Design and code programs in a modular fashion with maintainability in mind
7. Prepare documentation and ensure it meets IT standards
8. Report progress to lead programmer or systems analyst lead
9. Conduct program walk-throughs with others on the IT project programming team
10. Interface with business users and other IT customers as needed for clarification, testing, and installation support on assigned projects
11. Meet agreed-upon project delivery dates based on quality and time
12. Evaluate software and hardware and make recommendations
13. Maintain existing programs

Desirable Qualifications:
1. Minimum two years of programming experience, preferably on the same type hardware as in the organization
2. High school graduate, technical programming school or college a plus
3. Above average oral and written communication skills
4. Enjoy working with others and able to interact with all levels of business users
5. Logical approach to solving problems
6. Detail-oriented individual
7. Responsible and motivated
8. Willing to work odd hours, as needed
9. General knowledge of the company and its business
10. Function as a team player and offer technical solutions

EXHIBIT 2.5 COMPUTER OPERATOR SKILL DESCRIPTION

Job Title: Computer Operator

Department: Information Technology/Data Center

Duties and Responsibilities:

1. Receive and review work schedules from operations manager
2. Ensure that security procedures for the data center are being met
3. Verify that scheduled work is completed and distributed to all internal and external customers on time
4. Monitor the computer equipment and report any interruptions of service to IT management immediately
5. Participate in conducting the business recovery plan testing at off-site locations, verify its results, and document any procedural changes

Desirable Qualifications:

1. Minimum two years of computer operations experience, preferably on the same type of hardware as in the organization
2. High school graduate
3. Team player who can interact with all levels of users
4. Follow directions and procedures
5. Responsible, with a sense of schedule
6. Basic knowledge of the company and its business

EXHIBIT 2.6   STRATEGIC PLANNER
SKILL DESCRIPTION

Job Title: Strategic Planner

Department: Information Technology/Administrative

Duties and Responsibilities:

1. Develop and maintain a technical strategic plan which ensures that the IT organization and company are working toward the same vision, mission, goals, and objectives

2. Verify that resources allocated to IT meet company plans for competitive positioning and growth

3. Review IT proposals to ensure they meet company goals and objectives and do not adversely affect existing technical strategic plans

4. Participate with the company strategic planning team to offer state-of-the-art technical data

5. Optimize the return on investment for the IT resources and systems

6. Develop and maintain a business disaster recovery plan that covers the business functional units in addition to the IT functional units

Desirable Qualifications:

1. Minimum five years of planning experience

2. College graduate with a degree in business administration

3. Work well with others and able to interact with all levels of business users and top management

4. Innovative and creative

5. Responsible and highly motivated

6. Strong knowledge of the company and its business

7. Technical expertise, preferably as a systems analyst

EXHIBIT 2.7 TELECOMMUNICATIONS ANALYST SKILL DESCRIPTION

Job Title: Telecommunications Analyst

Department: Information Technology/Telecommunications

Duties and Responsibilities:

1. Support the telephone and data communications functions within the company
2. Keep abreast of new technical communications in the marketplace
3. Ensure security and business recovery for existing communication networks
4. Coordinate activities with the other IT functional areas and business processes
5. Provide technical advice and solutions pertaining to communications
6. Optimize the return on investment for IT communications (voice and data)
7. Develop and maintain a business disaster recovery plan covering the telecommunications function and coordinate with other IT functional areas and business departments

Desirable Qualifications:

1. Minimum four years of telecommunications experience with the IT platform the company uses
2. College graduate with a degree in computer science or engineering
3. Get along well with others and able to interact with all levels of business users and management
4. Innovative, dedicated, and self-motivated
5. Responsible; do what is needed without direction
6. Basic knowledge of the company and its business
7. Understand data requirements for developing networks
8. Strong knowledge of LANs (local area networks), WANs (wide area networks), voice response, and video conferencing

EXHIBIT 2.8 DATA ANALYST SKILL DESCRIPTION

Job Title: Data Analyst

Department: Information Technology/Administration

Duties and Responsibilities:

1. Document the data and the structure used throughout the entire company
2. Analyze data requirements for new projects and determine whether the data are new or existing
3. Regulate data access by system and security
4. Coordinate activities with the other IT functional areas and business departments
5. Provide data recovery
6. Ensure data are integrated for the entire company and easily accessible to the business processes and top management
7. Confirm standards are being met and each data element is given a definition, owner, and a list of users by business process, function, and IT system
8. Develop and maintain a business disaster recovery plan covering the data recovery function and coordinate with other IT functional areas and the business areas

Desirable Qualifications:

1. Minimum four years of data analyst experience with the IT platform the company uses
2. College graduate with a degree in computer science
3. Interface well with others and able to interact with all levels of business users and management
4. Innovative, dedicated team player
5. Know the job and do it efficiently
6. Good knowledge of the company and its business
7. Superior analytical skills

EXERCISE

EXERCISE 2.1   CAREER PATH: PERSONAL VISION AND MISSION

Each IT associate must have a vision and mission in order to create a career path that provides personal growth and development. The following are questions to ask yourself and examples for various positions within the IT organization.

- What career path do I want to take (i.e., remain technical hands-on or pursue a management position)?

- Do I want some management responsibility and some hands-on?

- Do I want to remain in IT management, possibly with a larger company, or do I want to progress to company top management?

- Do I have the aptitude, education, and patience for the position?

INFORMATION TECHNOLOGY MANAGER
John, 47 years old, started in computers 25 years ago. He obtained a four-year college degree in business administration while attending college nights and working full-time days. He began his career as a computer operator, advanced to programmer, progressed into systems analysis, and within ten years was the IT manager for a mid-sized company. He has worked for the same company for five years and has functioned in the same role while the company has increased its use of technology. Over the years, he was oriented toward technical management, but when he became a manager, his management knowledge was acquired on the job.

Five-Year Vision: John reevaluated his career direction choices and decided he could: (1) remain in IT management and move to a larger company, (2) progress to a business management top position, (3) remain where he was and continue growing the company, or (4) go back to a hands-on position, possibly telecommunications. John decided to remain with the company and progress to a business top management position, where he felt his technical expertise would bring down communication barriers associated with technology. He will take additional MBA executive training to enhance his business management knowledge.

SYSTEMS ANALYST
Cathy is 28 and a 4-year college graduate with a B.S. in computer science. She started as a programmer trainee and advanced into systems analysis after four years with the same large corporation. Her responsibilities have become more oriented toward administrative management.

Five-Year Vision: Cathy is at the stage where she must decide whether to pursue a full-time management position or continue to function in her current role. She is young and aggressive, and her career ambition is to become an IT manager, where her technical skills can be used to a company's advantage. To move in this direction, she will need to expand her business management skills and continue to stay current with technical developments to provide technical solutions to business problems.

PROGRAMMER

Joe is 23 and has been a programmer with the same company for two years. He enjoys the technical aspect, hates talking with people, but loves a challenge. Joe is an excellent programmer, logical and detail oriented.

Three-Year Vision: Joe analyzed his strengths and weaknesses. A possible three-year career path for a programmer would be lead programmer/analyst, systems analyst, data analyst, or telecommunications analyst (any of which would be a specialty change). He decided to remain in the programming arena since he dislikes interviewing business users and solving business problems. In the future, however, he may need to change professions, as the company direction is for programmers to become more involved with the business. The IT organization has a career path for people who are not management material and want to remain technically focused. Joe decided to remain with the company another two years and then determine whether he would be interested in management. He will learn the newest technology tools and techniques and remain abreast of advancements in technology.

COMPUTER OPERATOR

Linda is 20 and has been a computer operator for one year. She is a high school graduate and has not attended college. Linda is at the point where she must determine what career direction she wishes to pursue.

Five-Year Vision: Linda decided to remain in the IT organization. She is not certain what she wants and has decided to remain hands-on and reconsider management in five years. Her logical career path would be as a telecommunications analyst, data center manager, programmer, or data analyst. The opportunities within IT are many. Linda decided to become a telecommunications analyst.

ABSTRACTS

ABSTRACT 2.1
BETTER INFORMATION MEANS BETTER QUALITY

Ashmore, G. Michael
Journal of Business Strategy, January–February 1992, pp. 57–60

What role can information systems play in achieving total quality? This article examines three main areas where information technology can play a very important role.

1. *Process monitoring*—This takes many forms: collecting performance data, modeling possible scenarios, or tracking the results of quality efforts. By monitoring a process closely, it is possible to detect and fix problems early.

2. *Customer service*—The author gives the example of a software company whose goal was "to make it as easy as possible for the customer to do business with it and to work with its product." A 50 percent share of a very competitive market was the result of the company's efforts. Quality in customer service refers to every interaction that might take place between the customer and the company, from the moment of purchase, to delivery, maintenance, etc. Quality is solving your customers' problems. "Information systems," says the author, "can play a critical role in providing answers quickly and accurately, in every aspect of the service strategy." He then enumerates many ways in which this can be done.

3. *Production*—Production systems can contribute to quality in two ways: (1) production support, which includes yield, productivity, and cost control, and (2) cross-functional information exchange between production and other basic business functions.

Information systems can have a great impact in making total quality a reality. Applying the total quality philosophy to the information systems themselves increases their capacity to be more responsive to the needs of "customers (both internal and external) and the quality needs of the business."

ABSTRACT 2.2
IS THIS WORKPLACE HEAVEN? NO, IT'S QUAD/GRAPHICS

Simmons, John
Journal for Quality and Participation, July–August 1992, pp. 6–10

Quad/Graphics has become large by thinking small, according to CEO Harry Quadracci, subject of this interview. The essence of thinking small, he believes, is fostering close personal relationships—with one another and with clients. This is encouraged by "Think Small Dinners" and "Think Small Activities" to promote communication. Quad/Graphics also emphasizes an egalitarian organization. Managers wear the same uniform as other employees; employees share in the company by owning 70 percent of the company stock. Employee ownership, says Quadracci, allows the company to think more long term than short term. Another key is beginning with inexperienced new hires (who haven't learned bad habits elsewhere) and immersing them in a culture which is proud of its high quality and builds self-esteem. Quadracci sees Quad/Graphics as a value-based company. While peers communicate the culture to new hires these days, Quadracci remembers when he had to implant the culture forcibly: either you do this or you're fired. Since then, he has nurtured the culture by communicating values to employees in ways which might seem a little corny. "The typical American executive is too sophisticated to do it," he says. Quadracci sees money as a demotivator; rather, adequate pay with proper recognition of each employee's contribution produces motivated workers. Quad/Graphics does not benchmark. They have a saying, "keep your eye on the customer, not the competition," and they empower employees to go to extraordinary lengths to satisfy the needs of the customer.   (©*Quality Abstracts*)

ABSTRACT 2.3
MAKING TOTAL QUALITY WORK: ALIGNING ORGANIZATIONAL PROCESSES, PERFORMANCE MEASURES, AND STAKEHOLDERS

Olian, Judy D. and Rynes, Sara L.
Human Resources Management, Vol. 30 Issue 3, Fall 1991, pp. 303–333

Throughout this article, four survey sources are used: the KPMG survey of 62 companies, two Conference Board surveys of 149 firms and 158 Fortune 1000 companies, and the AQF/Ernst & Young study of 500 international organizations. The cornerstone of this 30-page article revolves around the authors' statement: "The goals of total quality can be achieved only if organizations entirely reform their cultures. Total quality (TQ) is increasingly used by companies as an organization-wide system to achieve fully satisfied customers through the delivery of the highest quality in products and services. In fact, TQ is the most important single strategic tool available to leaders to effect the transformation of their organizations. Traditional management, operations, finance and accounting systems are reviewed against changes that are needed in organizational processes, measurement systems, and the values and behaviors of key stakeholders to transform the status quo and shift to a total quality culture that permeates every facet of the organization."

Total quality must reflect a system-wide commitment to the goal of serving the strategic needs of the organization's customer bases, through internal and external measurement systems, information and authority sharing, and committed leadership. In this sense, the objectives are very similar to ISO 9000 readiness for registration. Therefore, the concepts presented by the authors are also valid for those TQM organizations that are seeking ISO 9000 certification. The article contains the following pertinent data: (1) organizational synergies critical to achieving a pervasive culture, whether it be for TQM, ISO 9000, or other types of quality assurance; (2) the essentials of TQ; (3) organizational processes that support TQ; (4) establishing quality goals, including a look at Six Sigma and benchmarking; (5) training for TQ; (6) recognition and rewards; (7) measuring customer reactions and satisfaction; (8) developing four areas of measurement: operation, financial, breakthrough, and employee contributions; and (9) getting stakeholder support. Of significant added value are over 60 references on the subjects discussed, which are reason enough to obtain a copy of this extremely worthwhile article, in spite of its formidable length. This is highly recommended reading for IS/IT organizations seeking to implement total quality.

ABSTRACT 2.4
ALIGNING VALUES WITH VISION: ENHANCING THE TOTAL QUALITY PROCESS

Witmer, Neil T. and Sherwood, Stephen
Continuous Journey, October–November 1992, pp. 30–35

Values, say the authors, are deep-seated pervasive standards that influence all aspects of our behavior—our personal bottom line. Values are especially critical in times of change, when normal policies and habits no longer apply. After discussing how personal values are formed and changed, the authors turn to the importance of corporate values. They present a hierarchy-of-values graphic which shows a *vision of desired values* at the top of a pyramid, below which are *shared corporate values,* then *group values* of various groups in the corporation, followed by *personal operating values and behavior.* "Ultimately," the authors contend, "shared corporate values can unify the efforts of disparate groups and the behavior of employees." After discussing a three-step methodology for assessing values, the authors offer suggestions on how to align company values. Then they identify four types of employees which emerge in a TQM process: (a) those who already possess the desired values and behave accordingly (20 percent), (b) those who easily learn desired values as part of the TQM process (40 percent), (c) those who successfully shift their values with considerable effort and hands-on leadership (20 percent), and (d) those who cannot change their values (20 percent). The last group "will probably have to be outplaced or moved to a more appropriate assignment before they cause costly damage," say the authors. Finally, they discuss some specific strategies to maximize value shifts in a TQM effort:

- Top leaders must keep their fingers on the pulse of the changing norms and culture, identify informal leaders and "gatekeepers" to create a "critical mass" of change, and "walk the talk."

- The company vision, mission, and values must be kept visible through constant communication and storytelling by key leaders.

- Goals and objectives must be clearly specified and understood by all employees.

- Customers must have an open channel of communication and feedback to the organization.

- A well-designed management process should be used to give recalcitrant managers an honest look at their versatility, maturity, confidence, self-awareness, and attitudes.

- People's competencies should be matched to their jobs and career expectations.

- A continuous improvement strategy should continue to develop and reexamine desired values, corporate values, and personal operating values, while the CEO meets regularly to seek input and discuss problems. (©*Quality Abstracts*)

CHAPTER 3

ROLE OF INFORMATION TECHNOLOGY

IDENTIFYING TECHNOLOGY GROUND RULES

New technical innovations are giving small and large companies the opportunity to grow and improve profits. The following are a set of "ground rules" that have grown out of the ever-evolving use and evolution of technology:

1. Information technology (IT) is necessary to gain and maintain a competitive edge.

2. IT personnel must be both business analysts, who provide business solutions, *and* computer analysts, who provide computer solutions.

3. Information planning must be part of all business plans, and not simply the province of the IT department. IT functions must be supportive corporate-wide.

4. Integrating various IT functions, such as personal computers (PCs), E-mail, communications, programming, analysis, etc., is a responsibility of business management, as well as the responsibility of IT management.

5. Hardware and software are becoming more affordable and are of advantage to areas where heretofore automation was not cost effective.

6. High technology plays a significant role in almost every product life cycle. This includes education, healthcare, food production, publishing, and related services.

7. From the time a product or software/hardware is off the drawing board until it is available, a new and improved technology has been introduced.

Understanding these "ground rules" helps eliminate the "black hole" label often associated with IT. Integrating total quality with IT is difficult because IT is rapidly changing and difficult to quantify. Software or hardware recommended today may not be the best tomorrow. The number of lines of program code produced per day should not be used to determine programmer productivity; the quality of the results of the code is what is important, as well as how the programmer interacts with the business.

Technology gains are being achieved every day. Without a vision and plan to provide a systematic method for business improvement which includes managing change and training, a company is only "spinning its technology wheels" and not improving its information flow to become more competitive and profitable. New technical breakthroughs are inevitable. Everyone should learn to accept change and work with technology as a team.

The bottom line is that IT should not be used solely to save money or for convenience. It can, and should, be used to make money *and* expand the business. Just because technology is installed and works does not mean it is optimal. A business can have the newest and best technology, but what good is it if it does not improve the company's quality and service?

It is human nature to treat knowledge "like a jewel," hiding it, protecting it, and keeping it to ourselves. Individuals must stop hoarding knowledge and not sharing it with others, as we have in the past. *All* business functional departments must work together and determine what is best for the company instead of just a particular department or area. Each business department must work to eliminate emotional, selfish concerns. The aim is to function as a corporate team and eliminate the mindset of "my department is bigger than yours and I'm only concerned about my functional area." Obviously, one does want to be concerned about one's own department, but *responsibilities must be shared when sharing improves company-wide quality.* One of the primary rules of total quality is *teamwork*, and without it, the quality process will fail, no matter how great the information or technology.

The following statement was made by Jacques Maisonrouge, a former IBM executive:

> But technology is not an end in itself; its essential function is to permit the manufacture of better products that allow us to find a quicker and more satisfactory solution to the problems encountered by men and women in every profession.[1]

COMMON INFORMATION TECHNOLOGY ROLES

IT personnel wear many different hats, and based on a company's industry and size, the processes and type of technology vary. Companies must consider IT a valuable partner and stop thinking of IT as a support function that costs money. IT plays many common roles in business:[2]

- Automates existing processes
- Builds communication infrastructures both within the company and externally
- Links a company to its customers and suppliers
- Supplies decision support
- Quickly calculates large quantities of information

The above IT roles should be found in any company, regardless of size or type of industry. Another important role of IT is gathering information that gives a firm a competitive edge. Peoples Express Airline, which is now defunct, is an example of a company that failed to use IT for business information in order to stay ahead of its competition. Its competitors (such as American Airlines) were changing their information systems, but Peoples Express opted to remain unchanged.

IT offers advantages to small businesses as it gives them an opportunity to compete with larger companies. A small business can be made to look larger by forming strategic alliances with other firms when completing certain technical functions. Hardware prices have dropped considerably over the past years, and as the PC has become as powerful as older mainframes, small businesses are able to compete. *The key is proper business and technology planning before getting into the "nuts and bolts" of the process.*

Another small business advantage is that larger companies have antiquated computer systems which will take years to replace due to corporate and geographic barriers. This gives the smaller firm a chance to outshine a larger company by offering customers more modern technology, as small firms need not stay tied to older systems.

IDENTIFYING INFORMATION TECHNOLOGY CUSTOMERS

IT has many "customers." The generic definition of a customer is "one who buys." A customer, per our definition, is defined as anyone, whether a company, individual, or business process, that uses or interfaces with technology. The IT customer is not necessarily "buying" something but nevertheless expects the highest quality product, service, or support to be delivered.

Customers can be categorized according to four perspectives:

1. Internal within the IT organization
2. Internal within the company
3. Direct external
4. Indirect external

Internal Customers

Internally within a company, IT customers are the individuals, business departments, processes, or entities that represent the same company IT supports. Figure 3.1 presents an example of the interaction between IT and its internal customers. Basically every functional department and individual

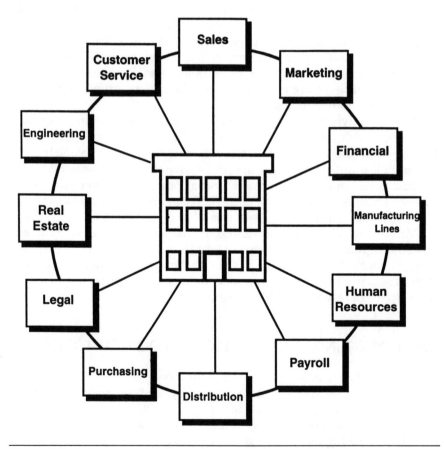

Figure 3.1 Information Technology Internal Business Customers.

within the company is a customer of IT and should be treated in the same manner as an external customer. IT provides a product (automated systems) and service supporting that product. For example, telephone support is usually a responsibility of the telecommunications IT function.

When an outside firm is used to deliver any IT organizational function, as in outsourcing, it is expected to deliver quality products and service or risk losing its reputation and future business. Why should an IT organization within a company be treated or respond any differently?

Internally within the IT organization, customers are the various IT functions and individuals who support each other (Figure 3.2). IT has many specialized functional areas that interact with each other. For example, a programmer who needs additional computer time becomes a customer of the scheduler in the data center. The programmer requests additional time from the scheduler, and the scheduler responds to the customer (programmer) as

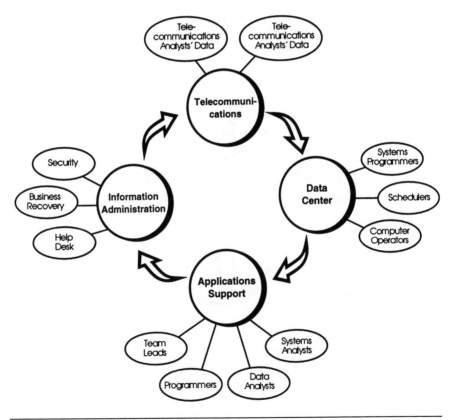

Figure 3.2 Information Technology Internal Customers.

to when the service can be provided. Unless a company is small and has a one-person IT organization, there is always interaction between the functions as services are provided. Each IT functional area and its staff must interact with and support one another if quality service is to be provided. This internal IT customer service is also a key to helping achieve overall company goals.

External Customers

External customers are interests or individuals outside of the company. Figure 3.3 displays an example of IT external customer interaction. Direct external customers are outside recipients who are provided information or service as a result of the products and services provided by IT. For example, when a supplier inquires about an invoice, availability of information, timeliness, and accuracy are the result of IT.

Indirect external customers are firms and individuals who may never directly interact with a company but are affected by the information provided by IT. Shareholders would be considered indirect external customers who are affected by IT since they expect stock dividends. This is basically a

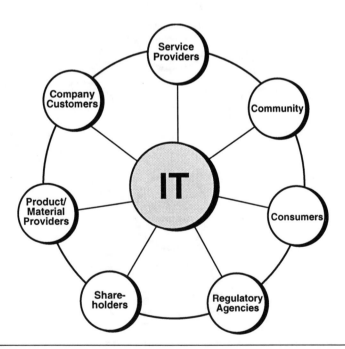

Figure 3.3 External Business Customers.

ripple effect; when the buying customers are happy, sales go up, which increases profits, which are distributed as dividends. IT does not interface directly with shareholders but indirectly affects them. The community and regulatory agencies are also indirect external customers. For example, a firm might decide to expand, based upon information received from IT. The community would benefit, since new jobs would be created, which would generate revenue to the local economy. IT must satisfy regulatory and government agencies (local, state, federal, and international), which indirectly are "customers" in that their information needs must comply with regulations or requirements.

Customer Needs

Customer-identified needs play a vital role in corporate strategic planning, which in turn affects the direction of technology. Table 3.1 displays various IT customers and their needs. IT should team with "internal users," which consist of the business functional departments and the processes responsible for providing services or products to external customers (i.e., marketing, sales, field engineering, customer service, etc.). The role of IT is to support the team by offering its technical input so that the company can consider options which will support customer needs. Automated processes are designed based on customer needs analysis; it is helpful for IT to understand how business processes interface with and support customer needs.

Reduced product-to-market cycles and increasing competition demand that IT functions keep pace with internal and external customer needs and provide processes that are responsive to ever-changing market needs.

TECHNICAL STRATEGIC PLANNING

What Is a Technical Strategic Plan?

A technical strategic plan defines a vision, mission, and goals for technology efforts within a company. This plan is a "road map"; it takes a company from where it is to where it wants to be by using technology. The technical strategic plan should be developed and maintained corporate-wide. The basic objective is to provide a means for technology to establish an efficient return on investment using its resources: human, hardware, and software.

Why a Technical Strategic Plan?

Every business that utilizes technology should have a technical strategic plan. However, unless there is a separate technical budget, this does not

Table 3.1 Information Technology Customer Needs

Type of customer	Needs
Internal customers	
IT employees	Knowledge, skills, and abilities to pursue professional goals; enjoy working with others, sharing knowledge, and learning
IT management	Leadership, continuous personal growth, providing knowledge to and coaching others
IT functional units	Continuous improvement, cooperation, and information exchange
Internal customers within the business	
Business employees	Services provided when needed or requested, questions answered and support given; personal growth and training
Business functions and processes	Continuous improvement, information exchange, teamwork, and cooperation
External customers—direct	
Customers/clients	Quality service and products, dealing with knowledgeable individuals
Suppliers/vendors	Capable, informative individuals with whom to interface
Competitors	United effort to establish industry guidelines and standards
External customers—indirect	
Shareholders	Ethical, profitable firm
Regulatory agencies	Compliance with government regulations/requirements
Community	Competent and reliable involvement with area services

occur. A business, no matter how large or small, will only have a plan for IT if it represents a substantial part of its budget.[3] *Every* technology organization needs a vision, mission, and direction, or funds will continually be wasted. The plan does not need to be lengthy or involved, but the technology direction must be well designed. Decisions about whether outside expertise or additional resources are needed for anticipated projects are based on the business strategic plan. The results are then used when preparing the technical budget.

The technical strategic plan assists IT by defining objectives and responsibilities more explicitly and helping IT personnel to understand their roles. Without knowing its objectives and vision, IT is functioning in a vacuum and cannot be a full contributor. IT must play a role in a firm's strategic and tactical planning. After developing company goals, senior management must prioritize them. Then company management must determine how to assist IT in meeting any priority tasks. Just like any other business unit, IT must have a direction and develop priorities in order to function efficiently. It is difficult for the IT area to effectively plan and budget for growth without knowing the business direction.

A corporation cannot afford "islands of technology" within the business; all resources must be combined into an integrated network. Without integrated information, a company has fractured information at multiple locations. This causes inconsistencies and makes accurate change–response difficult for IT. Isolated information "sandboxes" have multiple "business owners"; this forces IT to respond individually and interface with each entity before making any change. (For additional information, see Abstract 3.1 at the end of this chapter.)

There is also an audit/security concern which could bring on disastrous results. When information is located at multiple locations and no one location claims "ownership," an arbiter is needed to determine access or who can alter information. Auditors abhor separate, redundant information for which no manager is responsible. On the security side, an irate employee may decide to internally sabotage a company. When information is not integrated and secure, such an employee can destroy or contaminate data and cause crippling damage. Information can also be illegally pirated from company computers and confidential information sold to a competitor for someone's personal gain. Another concern is software "viruses," which can completely destroy information.

BUSINESS MANAGEMENT AND INFORMATION TECHNOLOGY INTERACTION

Why Business Management Support?

When top management endorses and uses technology, lower levels will follow. For example, when senior managers use electronic mail (E-mail), others are forced to use it when communicating with the top (the ripple effect). When top management does not use or support IT functions, then the system is doomed to fail, as the lower levels feel they do not have to use it or make a commitment to support IT. A considerable number of systems have languished or failed because of this.[4] Top management support and teamwork from all levels and departments are important in order for IT efforts to truly succeed and meet total quality requirements.

Business management must start thinking of IT as a means to make money and gain a competitive edge. *Everyone in the company, both IT and*

business staff, should be a contributor in finding new ways to improve the process.
Business users (customers) too often presume that the IT area knows what is
needed. On the other hand, IT assumes that because a user did not ask for
something, he or she does not want it. Business management and IT management must endorse the concept of IT and business functions working together in supporting the business processes. Each must stop thinking of
functional boundaries, look at the business process, and involve all functional units.

Well-known management consultant Peter Drucker had the following to
say about management's role in IT:

> Executives and professional specialists need to think through what
> information is for them, what data they need: first, to know what
> they are doing; then, to be able to decide what they should be
> doing; and finally to appraise how well they are doing. Until this
> happens MIS departments are likely to remain cost centers, rather
> than become the result centers they should be.[5]

Products and systems are increasingly more dependent on software and
hardware. Every department must be computer literate. Engineering resources in the manufacturing process must become software dependent.
Companies must provide cross-functional business/computer usage training to improve employee productivity. IT must solicit input from users when
developing or enhancing automated systems, because it is the departmental
personnel who utilize these systems to serve the company's customers.
When users participate in developing systems, they have pride of ownership,
are less resistant to change, and welcome rather than resist new technology.

Why It Helps Information Technology to Understand the Business

When a company practices total quality, the needs of the customer drive
decisions. IT employees must know who the outside customers are and
understand the functions of all the internal processes as well as the departments they support. IT must learn the business "whys" in order to become
a member of the business cross-functional team and an accepted partner in
the organizational strategy.

Most businesspeople do not understand the technologies available, either now or in the near future. In some cases, they may know just enough to
be dangerous! Many simply consider the computer a means to "crunch
numbers" and do not look for improved ways to conduct business. Some
business users do not understand the time and cost ramifications of automating an entire process around an exception that happens once a year. IT can

assist by sharing its technical knowledge and by working with the business user to find a better solution. Each can learn from the other. Compare a lawyer writing a contract and a technician designing a system for business needs; both should offer advice for making improvements and avoiding potential pitfalls. When developing new systems, the technician must review the existing computer systems that support the business, However, it is important to remember that there may be a better way to conduct business— by changing the processing flow of the existing system.

Business Involvement

IT can be thought of as a business in itself. As such, it requires the same disciplines as a company. When a company uses an outside firm for technical support functions, it is even more important that technology be considered. The company is now spending money to purchase technical services; without proper planning, procedures, and controls, the company will lose control, which will cost more money due to miscommunication and rework. IT should be an active participant in the following key activities since technology considerations are usually involved:

- Corporate business planning
- Change management
- Continual improvement
- Business reengineering

Corporate Business Planning

IT can usually respond to changing business demands by becoming part of the overall business planning process. Suppose a firm is planning a merger but does not inform the IT organization until the press is notified. Management then expects IT to implement all changes due to the merger within a month, even though it took two years for the merger to become final. Had IT been informed earlier, IT management could have planned for the merger and responded quicker.

When IT is not included in the planning process, then those in IT management should take it upon themselves to alert senior management about the potential IT has to offer the business. When senior management realizes the value-added benefit of involving IT, it will be more likely to include IT in the planning process, but *IT will need to prove its worth to the company before it is considered part of the business team.*

The corporate vision can be be expanded to include new business opportunities when top management is made aware of technical advancements available. CEOs have various "extreme" attitudes toward IT, which range from completely ignoring technology to believing they know all about it. Somewhere between the extremes is the CEO who knows enough to be involved by setting an appropriate direction for information systems (IS) and involving IT management because the CEO has sufficient confidence in the IS manager's abilities to contribute to the firm's strategic direction.[6] Simply put, IT must earn the respect and trust of the business.

IT should incorporate its technical strategic plan into the overall corporate plan, which is based upon company strategic and tactical plans. This eliminates any potential confusions about the growth and direction of IT and ensures that the business and technical worlds are working together and using the same blueprint. (For additional information, see Abstract 3.2 at the end of this chapter.)

Change Management

Changes impact IT personnel as well as business users. IT personnel often must learn a new tool or technique that alters the way they perform a task, such as new programming languages, revised project development tools, and computer hardware. Both business users and IT staff handle change in similar ways; after all, people are people. Although technical people should be used to change, they have also been known to resist new methods and techniques. IT personnel, like business users who have always performed a task a certain way, also build a comfort factor when using a certain technology. They usually dislike dealing with change, especially when deadlines do not allow for learning the new technology. IT staff can compare themselves to business users who receives a new computer system without education or involvement before installation. IT personnel should remember that they themselves usually resist change when proper training and communication do not take place before implementing new technical tools and techniques. Think of the reverse situation. Can you blame business users for resisting technical change when they were not involved?

Ways to Overcome Change

Change is inevitable. It is human nature for individuals to become comfortable with methods they use every day, but these "comfort zones" must be changed if only to keep up with competition. No human advancement would have occurred if everyone had accepted things as they were.

Suggested approaches for overcoming resistance to change include:

- Keep everyone informed and communication lines open
- Make certain all staff are involved from start to finish

- Receive, and be receptive to, feedback
- Conduct thorough training sessions before a change is implemented
- Explain the reasons for a change
- Refrain from "changing a change"—one thing at a time

The above suggestions pertain to technology modifications or any type of change.

How to Handle Change

The following suggestion is offered as a means to handle fear of change:[7]

> The best way to deal with fearful employees is to address these fears openly at the outset. Make it clear that the computer applications you will ask them to use do not require advanced mathematics or technical abilities. All employees will be given the opportunity to learn the programs, at their own pace, and from their own level, without negative performance appraisals if it should take them longer to learn.

Introducing new technology causes fear because of a management perception that more technology means less staff. People are not receptive when they believe a change can cost them their jobs. But technology can be used to create new positions. The people using the old processes should welcome the opportunity to learn new skills and to become more valuable as a result. By using this "carrot," the company expands its market, retains the same staff, and improves both employee skills and company morale, resulting in higher productivity and profits.

IT personnel are also concerned about job security because many firms outsource IT functions. They fear that new user-friendly languages and end-user systems will eliminate their functions and place information access directly in the hands of the end users.

Technology is rapidly and continually changing. People (even those in IT) have difficulty keeping up with all the new leading-edge technologies and are not receptive to the continuous changes. IT is more a matter of culture than machines. If great gains seem possible, IT might choose to risk trying new technology, but the risk must be carefully considered and a contingency plan prepared in the event of failure. All too often, a vendor sells a company "vaporware" (a product as yet unavailable but promised for a specific date). Then, when the company needs the technology on the promised date, the vendor says that it is not available yet. In such cases, the business and its schedule are held hostage by the vendor.

Information Technology Resources Change Control Process

IT needs to have a formalized change control process when implementing technical resource (i.e., software and hardware) changes, in addition to handling people concerns. The objectives of the change control process are to plan, coordinate, monitor, and provide a consistent means to control modifications involving IT resources. A formal change process will enable IT to have a visible means to measure system change activity and results, such as maintenance versus new project development, nature of the changes, systems affected, business risks, successes versus failures, and how many changes are made.

A change control process can be an aid when IT prioritizes its workload. For instance, two major stand-alone projects, which happen to overlap business processes and were assigned to different project team leaders, were being scheduled for implementation the same weekend. The change control process caused the project managers to realize that the same date had been chosen to implement both projects, but neither manager was in a position to change the date. Management then became involved to decide which project was to be given higher priority and implemented on the original date. In this example, a potential conflict was resolved before customer-deliverable commitments were made, allowing IT to save face and provide quality customer service.

One suggested approach is to form a team with a minimum of one representative from each IT functional area to enhance the communication between functions. This helps ensure that all parties are aware of planned changes. The change control process can be as simple or complex as the team feels is needed. Some larger companies have a weekly change review meeting where representatives from each IT functional area discuss any planned change activity affecting IT resources. Every company currently has some type of change process, but it should become formalized. When a change will impact a particular business process, it is important that the customer be involved and made aware of the change.

It is also strongly recommended that a testing environment be built separate from the production environment. It is risky to make modifications directly to the existing production systems until new change requests have been thoroughly tested and their implementation has been carefully planned. For example, suppose a programmer is changing program code that is currently being used in a production environment. A test environment does not exist and no back-up version of the program is made before the programmer starts making changes and testing the program. A production problem occurs that affects the program being modified. How does the programmer distinguish the original program code from the changes he or she has made? Basically, the programmer has two choices: (1) try to remember the changes and temporarily delete them from the program or (2) take a chance and implement the program with the untested changes. Let's take this example one step further. Programmer A is making changes to a program and programmer B is also making changes to the same program, unaware of programmer A's changes. This situation can be pretty scary when you consider the potential business impacts when program coding is inadvertently overlaid. A formal change process and test environment would help overcome such difficulties.

Commitment from IT and business management is a must before implementing a formal IT change control process. Benefits of this process are hidden. Until a major error occurs, there is no visible monetary payback. The only return on investment is determining the cost of having a set change process by asking, "If an error occurred, how much would this impact customer service and our company's quality indicators?" Similar to a disaster recovery plan, there is no payback until a disaster occurs, but without such a plan, an organization could be destroyed or suffer a severe setback.

Our purpose is not to try to outline how a change control process should be implemented. It is suggested that the change control process be assigned as an IT total quality project and a formalized team created to define a vision, goals, and deliverables which support improving the change control process. To be successful, it must be aligned with the business strategy. An outside advisor may be consulted to assist in implementing a formalized change control process. Each company is unique, and there is no one right or wrong approach, as long as quality is being maintained; however, as a firm grows, a standard change process will provide a common direction and means of competitive cost benchmarking. (For additional information, see Abstract 3.3 at the end of this chapter.)

Continuous Improvement

The automated systems that IT creates and operates become an integral part of all business work processes. This is viewed as a plus in the beginning, but difficulties arise as IT's company-wide responsibilities grow and the time needed to make changes to the systems increases. Continuous improvements drive the organization toward constant change. IT may receive an avalanche of change requests, become backlogged, and be slow to respond. IT is then perceived as a barrier and not part of the company team. When IT personnel are part of a management planning effort, they often overcome this perception through creative and/or innovative methods. However, even if IT cannot handle all requests as fast as others might like, being in contact with all levels of management involves everyone in developing a solution.

IT pressures and backlogs can be understood and managed by various means, such as cross-functional management priority committees, joint business planning, user funding of suggestions, and downloading information to

PCs. All are useful. Thus, IT can relieve pressure for requests by interacting with user departments. The obvious benefit is that business users become guardians and advocates of their systems and IT becomes a valuable friend.

Business Reengineering

What Is Reengineering?

Reengineering is reviewing existing business processes and finding more efficient ways to handle them. It may radically change the way a company operates. Reengineering really is moving to a process-managed organization as opposed to simply improving performance.[8] Authoritative management and rigid organizational structure become teams and shared responsibility. Reengineering technology solutions should not be thrown at problems. Applying IT to business reengineering demands *inductive* thinking—the ability to first recognize a powerful solution and then seek the problems it might solve, problems a company probably does not even know it has.[9]

Total quality and reengineering go hand in hand, continually improving processes, seeking innovation, building teams, and finding new business solutions.

Who Is Reengineering?

Basically, all types of companies are reengineering. Refer to Figure 3.4 for additional information about the types of industries that are reengineering. Approximately 25 percent of the larger companies are reengineering. Their efforts usually involve one or two projects and are not widespread implementations. Japan, the nation that used the "made in America" concept of total quality management to rebuild its war-shattered economy, is now eyeing another American notion: business reengineering.[10] The Japanese have realized that a business must be looked at by process versus function and are including technology to maximize any business reengineering effort.

Business areas considered prime reengineering targets are the back-office processes, sales support, marketing, and accounting.

Implementing Reengineering

IT, in some companies, must modify its thought processes and change itself. This section provides the information and steps that should be followed when reengineering a business.

Two important reengineering rules IT **must** remember are:

1. Reengineering a business process is **not** rewriting the existing computer systems using a new and improved technology *or* designing a new computer system using the existing business processes.

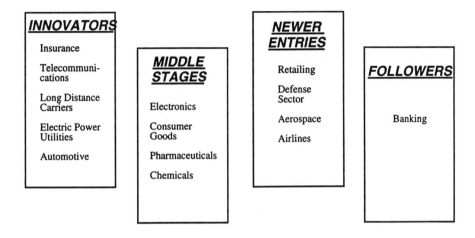

Figure 3.4 Reengineering Status by Industry. (Source: Maglitta, Joseph (1994). "One on One with Michael Hammer." *Computerworld*, January 24, p. 84.)

2. The business process changes should be implemented gradually using a modular and pilot plan approach. This decreases the risk of failure by thinking the process through in pieces and lessens user resistance to change.

Technology and customer demands have changed over the years. What is needed to support a business and how this will be accomplished usually differ from the original systems implemented years ago. Too many people still think the answer is computer-aided software engineering (CASE) tools or other such Band-Aids.[11] A company can have the best tools and techniques, but if IT and the business processes and their functional units are not working together, there can be no great success story.

IT cannot be the leader in driving any reengineering effort; it is merely a helper. A firm's senior management must take the initiative, or IT management must persuade senior management to recognize the business problem and take steps to resolve it. IT personnel have important roles to play in the reengineering activity itself because they understand processes, they are accustomed to change, and they are oriented to new technology.[12] Some business managers envision IT personnel as the reengineering leaders and expect them to intuitively know the customer needs. IT personnel are there to help but should not make any business decisions alone. The business reengineering effort involves IT and the business working together as a team. IT is there to support the business and help it improve, but it should not take responsibility for determining how the business should be run.

In a *Computerworld* interview, Michael Hammer, one of the authors of

Reengineering the Corporation, states that reengineering projects fail due to three major reasons:[13]

1. Lack of management commitment to push it through.
2. A firm says it is going to reengineer, doesn't get results, and then says it failed at reengineering when it never tried it in the first place.
3. People do not know how to go about it and improvise.

To quote Michael Hammer when asked about how reengineering affects an organization:

> Re-engineering is basically taking an ax and a machine gun to your existing organization. One company said, "Through re-engineering we have saved the business and destroyed the organization." That just puts it perfectly.

Implementing Business Involvement and Information Technology

Strategic planning is the building block used for determining the company's policy management. The definition of policy management for our purpose is directing an organization to identify, solve, maintain, and improve its corporate priorities. This provides a way to accomplish corporate short- and long-term strategies and "achieve the vision."

Policy management, commonly referred to as the company steering or priority committee, plays a key role in achieving total quality and continuous improvement. Policy management is a blueprint for a company using continuous improvement techniques. Other total quality processes help achieve the goals of the company. Policy management provides a forum to instruct the entire firm as to what is important to customers, stockholders, regulators, management, and employees. The IT organization benefits from this since it is given a direction in terms of what the business is doing and is able to plan for future technical activities. The policy also assists IT in knowing what should be worked on, monitoring the number of requests, and prioritizing tasks, since everyone wants their requests completed now.

INFORMATION ARCHITECTURE

What Is Information Architecture?

An information architecture is a set of models and plans that represents the flow of information throughout the business.[14]

Before defining the architecture, a company must identify the information and consider:

- *Value*—How important is it or is it needed?
- *Usage*—Who will use it and where?
- *Storage*—What way will it be accessed and when?

Value

Companies are realizing that information (or data) is a valuable resource and should be treated as a useful ally. The value of any information system for top management depends on the quality of the data—its timeliness, accessibility, accuracy, and completeness.[15] This holds true not only for top management, but for anyone using the information, whether to make internal decisions or to provide customer support. According to a popular saying, information is only as accurate as what is entered into the computer system. When a customer's name is spelled incorrectly or an address is inaccurate, it was usually entered into the system incorrectly. Customers become irritated when their names are spelled wrong or they receive late payment telephone calls for bills they never received. A company can have all the information in the world, but if it is untimely or inaccurate, customer service and quality will be affected.

In order to be effective, there should never be an overabundance of information that is not used. The costs of gathering and retaining information must be considered. The cost of obtaining information must not exceed the value of that information.[16] Sometimes the expense of capturing, processing, and storing information far exceeds the benefits gained in using the information for decision-making analysis. The information should be given to people who can use it and react.

When IT functions are outsourced, it becomes even more critical to define information needs and the value of information. The outsource firm must have a clear, concise understanding of who can access information and when the information will be accessed in order to meet customer requirements. A company that hires an outsource firm should keep control of its information. After all, it is the company's information base that is used for decision making.

Usage

Access to and the use of information ought to be standardized, integrated, process driven, and "user owned." Information should never be redundant or processed or stored without a clear, concise idea of its use—even between vendors, suppliers, and internal customers. Each piece of information, called a data element, must be clearly defined and a "business owner" identified. A determination must be made for each data element as to who is allowed to create, view, or alter it for integrity and audit/security reasons. An internal individual or business process must accept responsibility for the ownership, accuracy, and security of information.

Information use has changed dramatically over the years, but the data elements remain the same. Defining the base requirements, standardizing data elements, and providing user-oriented definitions for elements help in the planning of future systems. The business user should be involved in establishing data element definitions. Data, properly identified and tied to other tools, makes new IT development faster and more accurate. Examples of other tools include data dictionaries, repositories, and productivity programming languages (report writers). These shorten IT's response time for system changes and reporting requests. It is much easier to make changes or issue reports, and there is less risk of error, when the data is documented with such information as where it is used throughout the IT systems, what business processes use it, and a definition.

Measurement

The measurement of IT and technology planning is required for the proper budgeting of computer investment. However, there has been an inability to measure effectiveness and accurately quantify benefits. This leads to problems in productivity measurement, because you can't measure what you can't define. Many experts feel that conventional ratio analysis and critical success factor methods only yield partial answers. The value-added approach seems to offer better ways to measure quality and productivity, as discussed in Abstract 3.4. For a discussion on measurement, see the article at the end of this chapter.

Storage

Keeping data in a central location will expedite IT's response time in delivering business requests. The following quote is based on a company's complaint about IT service and what could have been done to improve it:

> If the company had maintained all its computer-readable data in a single pool or bank—in a so called "data base"—and if the company had structured this base of data so that a program for virtually any feasible use could have been run from this data base, then it would have been a matter of sheer expertise and flair for a good, experienced programmer to concoct a program that pulled the desired information together.[17]

Many business departments start their own user information base, which causes a mish-mash of information inaccuracy and redundancy. IT has the capability, thanks to PCs and computer networks, to distribute data to business departments or processes which will allow them to generate additional information or models. A central base is the key to adding and maintaining consistency. An example showing how the same information is fragmented is a customer address. Sales and marketing has the address in its system and the order department has the same address in its separate system. A customer informs the company of her address change, but only the sales/marketing area receives the change. Since only one department changes the address, the frustrated customer, who knows she sent the company an address change, must notify the company again.

Data can be stored and easily accessed in various ways, but to be readily accessible for IT, data should be stored via some type of electronic medium, such as disk or tape. Many a businessperson has requested information and become upset when the IT organization informs him or her that the data are not being captured or there is no way to automatically access the information. This relates back to the importance of determining the information a company needs when defining system requirements. It is difficult for IT to respond to customer requests unless it has the data.

Databases or files can be designed in modular segments that can be woven into new applications and processes. The data should be tied to customer needs, have key measure indicators, and allow for future usage. Having a readily available source with a clear data element definition and knowing who uses the data helps the IT professional solve business problems in a dependable and timely manner and at a reasonable cost.

COMMUNICATION

Understanding a company's organizational structure is important, but it is just as vital to understand the functional interactions that make the structure work. When interacting with customers and reviewing business processes, business users and IT professionals should follow a few simple communication rules:

- Don't become insulted or defensive when suggestions are made about a type of technology or a revised business process.

- Speak in understandable terms (technicians should not use technical jargon). In the same vein, businesspeople such as accountants and lawyers should also explain their jargon in simpler terms.

- Follow the Keep It Simple (KIS) philosophy—Don't make something more complex than it has to be.

Timothy Edwards, chief operating officer of Matewan National Bank, had the following to say about the interaction between IT and the business:

> Operations and IS must be looking at the total picture together, as a team. Turf battles are non-productive. There's no time for internal conflict; it'll drag down the whole organization and kill you in today's market.[17]

Before the communication barriers can come down, IT management *and* business management must understand each other and work together. Table 3.2 shows typical business and technical managers' thinking roles. When they realize they must cooperate and work as a team, the effect ripples throughout the organization. When business management and IT management become allies, they can approach top management, as a team, to obtain the support they may need to improve the process.

Other ways to keep everyone in the company informed about new technologies or projects are to:

- Distribute a newsletter

- Provide project updates

- Circulate information for everyone to review and provide feedback to the project team

Table 3.2 Why Information Technology and Business Management Disconnect

The chief operations officer (COO) and chief information officer (CIO) usually have different approaches to their roles:	
COOs	CIOs
Short-term oriented	Long-term oriented
Dislike having technology forced upon them	Must introduce new technologies
Fear encroachment of IT into their territory	Fear involvement by COOs threatens their jobs
Underestimate strategic role of IT	Most adopt business-oriented strategies

Source: Menagh, Melanie (1994). *Computerworld.* February 28, p. 87.

These techniques can be used for IT internal coordination, but it is recommended that they be introduced company-wide. There is no such thing as too much communication or too much awareness of changes that are taking place.

SUMMARY

The IT organization must become part of the business planning process to effectively support the corporate goals and objectives. In large companies, IT should provide support based on the entire corporate business process and not just by business functional unit. Change is inevitable, and a formalized process should be introduced to aid in improving controls and eliminating resistance.

IT should be viewed as the creator and maintainer of information systems and technology. Business users should claim ownership of information and be responsible for its usage and integrity. IT should become part of the overall business cross-functional team and offer technical solutions that will benefit the business. IT personnel must project an image that indicates they really care about business-user requests and when they will be completed. The driving force behind reengineering should be the business and not IT, whose role is to contribute technical expertise. When reengineering any existing process or system, it should not be rewritten simply by using a newer technology. This defeats the purpose of reengineering, which is re-evaluating and improving the business process.

Communication barriers between the business and technical worlds must come down. If this means bringing in outside help, then that must be done.

ENDNOTES

1. Maisonrouge, Jacques (1985). *Inside IBM, A Personal Story*. New York: McGraw-Hill, pp. 283–284.
2. Daniels, Caroline N. (1994). *Information Technology—The Management Challenge*. Wokingham, England: Addison-Wesley and The Economist Intelligence Unit, p. 20.
3. Winfield, Ian (1991). *Organisations and Information Technology Systems, Power and Job Design*. Oxford: Blackwell Scientific, p. 157.
4. Eliot, Levinson (1984). "The Implementation of Executive Support Systems." Working Paper No. 119. Cambridge, MA: Center for Information Systems Research, Sloan School of Management, MIT, October, p. 68.
5. Drucker, Peter (1988). "The Coming of the New Organization." Reprinted

in *Revolution in Real Time, Managing Information in the 1990's*. Boston: Harvard Business School, 1991, p. 9.

6. Arnett, Kirk P. and Jones Mary C. (1994). "Firms that Choose Outsourcing: A Profile." *Information and Management Journal*. April, p. 180.

7. Shore, Joel (1989). *Using Computers in Business*. Carmel, IN: Que Corporation, pp. 35–36.

8. Maglitta, Joseph (1994). "One on One with Michael Hammer." *Computerworld*. January 24, p. 85.

9. Champy, James and Hammer, Michael (1993). *Reengineering the Corporation*. New York: Harper Business, p. 84.

10. Alter, Allan (1994). "Japan, Inc. Embraces Change." *Computerworld*. March 7, pp. 24–25.

11. Maglitta, Joseph (1994). "One on One with Michael Hammer." *Computerworld*. January 24, p. 84.

12. Ibid., p. 85.

13. Ibid.

14. Daniels, Caroline N. (1994). *Information Technology—The Management Challenge*. Wokingham, England: Addison-Wesley and The Economist Intelligence Unit, p. 44.

15. DeLong, David W. and Rockart, John F. (1988). *Executive Support Systems: The Emergence of Top Management Computer Use*. Homewood, IL: Dow Jones-Irwin, p. 189.

16. Shore, Joel (1989). *Using Computers in Business*. Carmel, IN: Que Corporation, p. 32.

17. Brandon, Dick (1970). *Management Planning for Data Processing*. Princeton, NJ: Brandon/Systems Press, p. 228.

18. Menagh, Melanie (1994). "Crossfire." *Computerworld*. February 28, p. 87.

ARTICLE

BUILDING THE MEASUREMENT SYSTEM FOR INFORMATION SYSTEMS AND TECHNOLOGY

If you can't measure it, you can't manage it.

Peter Drucker

While many IS/IT organizations are embarking on some form of a total quality program, few have implemented a measurement system which can be used to figure out how good of a job is being done. Because so few have done this well enough to be examples for industries to follow, it is difficult to do any real benchmarking in this area. From the studies conducted on the practices of excellent IS/IT operations, however, some operating models have resulted. One of the most useful is a variation of the Corporate Measurement System (CMS) approach, based upon the work of Jack Rockart of MIT and others.* This model suggests the use of a vital few critical success factors (CSFs), which are linked to the business objectives and processes, around which the corporate indicator system is built.

What formerly took three years or more to accomplish can now be done in six to nine months using available software programs such as COMSHARE or PILOT. In addition to implementation speed and economy, the CMS approach is extremely flexible in terms of environment, future needs, and changes.

What IS organizations need is a measurement system that is simple and flexible in design, easy to use and modify, and integrated into key functions and processes. The information provided needs to be timely and accurate and must be perceived by the employees as truly useful and not just another "Big Brother is watching" type of system. Instead, what is needed is a

*The work of Rockart and others is detailed in a technical report titled "Building the Corporate Measurement System," published by Strategy Associates, Miami, Florida, 1992. The basic premise is that an effective measurement must not only be comprehensive and screen input from many constituencies, but it must also be selective in considering only the critical information. Without this, the system may become so cumbersome that it will not be effectively utilized to make IS decisions.

measurement system that IS professionals can use to manage their efforts better and to link all areas of the company, from the computer in the field or office to the corporate vision.

The following attributes are needed in an IS/IT measurement system:

- Simple system that is easy to understand
- Analyst/programmer commitment and motivation
- Specific objectives, procedures, and guidelines for use
- Consistent, continuous monitoring
- Assignment of specific responsibility and accountability
- Top management interest and support
- Timeliness
- Good lines of communication
- Good monitoring staff who provide competent analysis
- Periodic reports
- Useful and relevant information
- Accurate, reliable information linked to strategy and business objectives

PRINCIPLES AND OBJECTIVES

There are two guiding principles to follow when developing an IS/IT measurement system: (1) people on the information lines of the organization respond best to information relevant to their piece of the world and (2) when people have relevant information about things they deem important and can influence, they become very committed to using the information.

The following is a summary of the objectives of an IS/IT measurement system:

- Translate the vision to measurable outcomes all staff can understand
- Focus and align the direction of staff based on measurable results
- Track systems-related breakthrough and continuous improvement results
- Foster accountability and commitment
- Integrate strategic plans, business plans, quality, and benchmarking
- Provide standards for benchmarking
- Problem-solve IS business problems
- Provide basis for reward and recognition
- Create individual and shared views of performance

IMPLEMENTATION OVERVIEW

There are three types of measures that must be considered when implementing an IS/IT measurement system: outcome (or macro) measures, just-in-time process (or micro) measures, and upstream control (predictive) measures.

Outcome measures are often called macro due to their broad nature which generally reflects an after-the-fact type of indicator. Examples are return on investment, or equity, overall customer satisfaction, program/project savings, etc. Micro, or process, measures represent work-in-process types of situations and are often used to stop the project or program when bugs and/or rejects occur. Predictive measures are used for "upstream control" or prevention of problem situations. Most effective measurement systems have an effective combination of macro, micro, and predictive indicators.

Micro measures act as trip wires by enabling us to look at programs and see if we can increase speed of actions and decrease time, cycle, and steps. Whereas macro measures help us to focus on measuring the results of leadership on the corporate outcomes and to work the vision to see if the message is getting out there, micro measures help focus on the day-to-day routines. Conversation needs to be created among technicians in the field to help determine if the programming attribute corresponding to a particular corporate function enhances or inhibits the ability to create external customer satisfaction. In other words, do the programs, functions, routines and processes enhance or inhibit the journey along the path of total quality?

CATEGORIES OF IS/IT MEASURES

There are seven general or broad categories into which most measures can be classified or rolled up: accuracy or reliability, responsiveness, timeliness, customer satisfaction, cost, maintainability, and implementation responsibility.

The first three—accuracy or reliability, responsiveness, and timeliness—refer to the manner in which and the speed with which the IS organization conducts its business transactions and the way its programs and services perform. The fourth category—customer satisfaction—can also include employee satisfaction when IS employees are viewed as internal customers. The fifth and sixth categories—cost and maintainability—can be broken down into a wide variety of subcategories. The final category—implementation responsibility—is often replaced in larger organizations with a more relevant category relating to the competition, such as competitive marketing intelligence.

Templates, or flowcharts, are used to first link all existing measures to the corporate vision and objectives. Once existing indices are linked, then gaps and missing indices are identified and added to the system where appropriate. Decisions are also made about modifying or eliminating existing indices as new ones are added. Overall, there are generally between 25 to 100 detailed indicators that roll up into the seven broad categories.

GENERAL SYSTEM DESIGN

The IS/IT measurement system model consists of 26 major milestones which are used for the successful implementation of most measurement systems. These 26 milestones can be compared to running a marathon, which consists of 26 miles. These milestones are organized into three phases.

Phase 1: Linking to Business Objectives/CSFs

Activity/milestone	Estimated man-hours
1. Prepare getting started plan and obtain approvals	5
2. Communicate the plan to corporate executives	1
3. Meet with design team and do initial training	9
4. Management workshop	4
5. Follow-up design team and consolidate documentation	6
6. Assemble CSF rollout plan using available templates	3
7. Hold CSF workshop and work with design team on gathering CSF data	21
8. Coordinate with design team and conduct second round of CSF interviews	21
9. Coordinate with design team and finalize corporate data profiles	3
10. Hold focusing workshop with management	8
11. Complete preliminary system design	10
Total man-hours	91

Phase 2: Decision Scenarios

Activity/milestone	Estimated man-hours
12. Plan and hold key indicators workshop for design team rollout	19
13. Design team discusses indices with key user areas and assists with format indices, screens, and data	14
14. Plan and conduct decision scenario workshop and help design "what if" scenarios	21
15. Help finalize general design	20
Total man-hours	74

Phase 3: Prototyping The System

Activity/milestone	Estimated man-hours
16. Define prototype in terms of info templates	10
17. Define in which areas to pilot the prototype and which IS measurement systems functions to include	20
18. Complete draft of detailed specs	25
19. Investigate application software alternatives	20
20. Review and document coding structure required to implement CMS	2
21. Conduct interviews to resolve open points	12
22. Select a software package for CMS	12
23. Perform programming coordination and also perform unit testing	10
24. Complete prototype system testing using test data	3
25. Load/convert live data, finalize testing, and go live with system prototype	15
26. Project management and coordination	64
Total man-hours	193

SUMMARY OF BENEFITS

The following ten benefits can be realized by using well-defined measures which are part of an IS measurement system:

1. Identify the current capabilities of the IS/IT organization
2. Highlight opportunities for process improvement and reengineering
3. Facilitate goal-setting
4. Mark progress toward goal attainment
5. Benchmarking comparisons with other organizations
6. Improve job satisfaction and morale by enabling staff to work more effectively
7. Strong emphasis on employee technical involvement
8. Emphasis on process, not people
9. Produce higher quality products and enhance pride in delivering them
10. Lower cost and increase productivity by harnessing the intelligence of everyone in the organization

Overall, the effective use of a well-designed corporate measurement system should yield a payback ratio of four to one or greater over a one-year period following implementation.

ABSTRACTS

ABSTRACT 3.1
ELM: A HOLISTIC APPROACH

Teresko, John
Industry Week, June 20, 1994

The author is a well-known business writer who presents a concise look at one of the key features of how to use information technology to more successfully coordinate logistics throughout the organization in order to more reliably deliver goods and services to customers. ELM stands for Enterprise-Logistics Management, which is an important new step in the passage of manufacturing from art form to science. The author often quotes author Thomas Gunn, using excerpts from his book *Age of the Real-Time Enterprise: Managing for Winning Business Performance Through Enterprise Logistics Management* (Oliver Wight Publications). Gunn defines ELM as a holistic approach to managing operations and the value-added pipeline (total supply chain), from suppliers to end-use customers.

The author discusses three drivers to achieve competitive position: (1) a relentless quest for customer satisfaction, (2) recognition of the need for real-time management, and (3) ability to perform in a world-class manner. Additionally, superior logistics management is increasingly being cited as the new strength of the Japanese manufacturers, instead of just-in-time (JIT) alone. The post-JIT environment places an emphasis on information systems and technology, including electronic production-control systems. According to Professor Jichiro Nakane of the Systems Science Institute, Tokyo, the key is to achieve superior management of the flow of information, from customer order to the delivered product or service, with an integrated enterprise-wide system.

The shortcomings in today's software solutions are discussed in terms of the inability of MRP products/vendors to execute distribution resource planning at the front end and a lack of procurement applications at the back end. The inability to track material through the entire manufacturing process results in poorly tracked plans and schedules. When computing is diffused throughout the entire organization, it is difficult to collect and understand cost allocation trends attributed to open, distributed architecture. The author concludes with the premise that there is ample evidence that the total cost of spending on information systems in a typical company may represent 30 to 40 percent of its capital spending. And a company may be surprised to learn that in the catch-up mode, it is not spending nearly enough. This article is worthwhile reading in spite of the absence of references.

ABSTRACT 3.2
IS DATA SCATTER SUBVERTING YOUR STRATEGY?

Lingle, John H. and Schiemann, William A.
Management Review, May 1994

The main premise of this article is that lots of organizations have information available from many sources to let them know how they are doing. The authors argue that the problem is the poor coordination of this data and its frequently nebulous connection with the organization's purpose. The solution lies in systems and processes for overcoming "data-scatter."

When viewed from the perspective of information systems, most organizations are Balkanized environments—bits and pieces scattered in often conflicting jurisdictions such as MIS, marketing, finance, sales, human resources, and so forth. They have a 21st century computing capacity and a 1960s approach to transforming data into useful information. Data-scatter results from the poor job that organizations do in managing and transforming data into integrated information needed to drive success.

The symptoms of data-scatter that signal possible trouble are:

- *Strategy silos*—Each executive defines the future in terms of his or her own self-image, which is suboptimized to the overall detriment. The authors pose five useful questions to test for symptoms.

- *Data wars*—Knowledge is power and weapons pointed at colleagues often start a family feud. Bootleg databases abound.

- *Decision jerk*—Occurs when management zigs and zags with each piece of data, continually shifting priorities or piling on new initiatives. Chunks of data are used to make decisions resulting in multiple misguided efforts.

The authors offer five measures of success with the key word as "focus":

1. Strategically anchor gauges
2. Reflect the outcomes, not the activities
3. Create a counterbalance
4. Ensure responsiveness to change
5. Exhibit strong signal-to-noise characteristics

They point out that winning organizations focus their measures around a balanced scorecard type of system in a family of measures approach. To maintain focus, it is important that organizations track a limited number of gauges, which are updated regularly and available to all the people in the work force. To the extent they can avoid data-scatter, organizations will be able to tap into that storehouse of information and convert it to new knowledge for serving customers in a more innovative way than the competition. This is a thought-provoking piece for the business community. No references are provided.

ABSTRACT 3.3
HOW TO IMPLEMENT COMPETITIVE-COST BENCHMARKING

Markin, Alex
Journal of Business Strategy, May–June 1992, pp. 14–20

"Competitive-cost benchmarking," says the author, "is a powerful bottom-line tool that uses and assimilates quantitative and financial information on competitor performance to upgrade production capabilities, set measurable targets for process improvement, identify markets where competitors are vulnerable, and improve the realism of strategic decision making." This article begins with several case studies of chemical producers (resin, caustic, soda/chlorine, and polymer) that conducted competitive-cost benchmarking against significant competitors and then used the information gained to make strategic decisions. The author gives tips on how to carry out this type of benchmarking:

- *Multifunctional team*—The benchmarking process should be carried out by a coordinated multifunctional team composed of business analysts and managers from the various functions, as well as outside consultants.

- *Quantitative thrust*—The author gives a list of nine areas of questions to research concerning competitors, such as: "How are products, coproducts, and byproducts integrated with other company business?"

- *Quantitative thrust*—He suggests ways to show detailed cost stacks for each competitor using spreadsheets. In addition, he gives sources for learning about competitors.

- *Refinement of data*—"As the analysis progresses and input is reviewed and assimilated," the author says, "care should be taken to validate key assumptions and findings and understand the reasons for cost differences."

- *Action plan preparation*—He observes that research may show points of vulnerability, or it may lead a company to consider joint ventures, or even to phase out an operation.

- *Presentation of findings*—Information and recommendations are now distilled into a simple format. (©*Quality Abstracts*)

ABSTRACT 3.4
PARADIGM SHIFT: THE NEW PROMISE OF INFORMATION TECHNOLOGY

Tapscott, Don and Caston, Art
McGraw-Hill, New York, 1993, 337 pp.

This is an exhaustive and highly recommended work, based upon investigations of more than 4,500 business and government organizations. The authors offer profiles of organizations such as Toys 'R' Us and Fedex to illustrate how new information technology can be of assistance and help leaders and business managers take action to gain and maintain competitive advantage. Throughout, the authors focus on how organizations achieve long-term success with IS/IT. The major breakthrough areas covered are enterprise computing, interenterprise computing, and team/work cell computing. It can be used as an effective companion piece to *The New Paradigm in Business: Emerging Strategies for Leadership and Organizational Change* (Ray and Rinzger, World Business Academy, Tarcher/Perigee, 1993), which is a collection of essays by leading-edge business managers and thinkers on business in the new age of connectivity and vision. Contributors include Warren Bennis, Peter Senge, Willis Harman, and others. Both volumes can be purchased for $39 total.

CHAPTER 4

OVERVIEW OF
TOTAL QUALITY

Frank Voehl

WHAT IS TOTAL QUALITY?

Introduction

During the past five years, there has been an explosion of books in the field of total quality. Yet in all of the thousands of books and billions of words written on the subject, there is an absence of three essential ingredients: a good working definition, a comprehensive yet concise history, and a clear and simple systems model of total quality. This overview of total quality is intended to fill that void and provide some interesting reading at the same time.

Understanding the Concept of Total

Total quality is total in three senses: it covers every process, every job, and every person. First, it covers *every process*, rather than just manufacturing or production. Design, construction, R&D, accounting, marketing, repair, and every other function must also be involved in quality improvement. Second, total quality is total in that it covers *every job*, as opposed to only those involved in making a product. Secretaries are expected not to make typing errors, accountants not to make posting errors, and presidents not to make strategic errors. Third, total quality recognizes that *each person* is responsible for the quality of his or her work and for the work of the group.

Total quality also goes beyond the traditional idea of quality, which has been expressed as the degree of conformance to a standard or the product of workmanship. Enlightened organizations accept and apply the concept that quality is the degree of user satisfaction or the fitness of the product for use. In other words, *the customer determines whether or not quality has been achieved in its totality.*

This same measure—total customer satisfaction—applies throughout the entire operation of an organization. Only the outer edges of a company actually have contact with customers in the traditional sense, but each department can treat the other departments as its customers. The main judge of the quality of work is the customer, for if the customer is not satisfied, the work does not have quality. This, coupled with the achievement of corporate objectives, is the bottom line of total quality.

In that regard, it is important, as the Japanese say, to "talk with facts and data." Total quality emphasizes the use of fact-oriented discussions and statistical quality control techniques by everyone in the company. Everyone in the company is exposed to basic quality control ideas and techniques and is expected to use them. Thus, total quality becomes a common language and improves "objective" communication.

Total quality also radically alters the nature and basic operating philosophy of organizations. The specialized, separated system developed early in the 20th century is replaced by a system of *mutual feedback and close interaction of departments.* Engineers, for example, work closely with construction crews and storekeepers to ensure that their knowledge is passed on to workers. Workers, in turn, feed their practical experience directly back to the engineers. The information interchange and shared commitment to product quality are what make total quality work. Teaching all employees how to apply process control and improvement techniques makes them party to their own destiny and enables them to achieve their fullest potential.

However, total quality is more than an attempt to make better products; it is also a search for better ways to make better products. Adopting the total quality philosophy commits a company to the belief that there is always a better way of doing things, a way to make better use of the company's resources, and a way to be more productive. In this sense, total quality relies heavily upon value analysis as a method to develop better products and operations in order to maximize value to the stakeholder, whether customers, employees, or shareholders.

Total quality also implies a different type of worker and a different attitude toward the worker from management. Under total quality, workers are generalists rather than specialists. *Both workers and managers are expected to move from job to job, gaining experience in many areas of the company.*

Defining Total Quality

First and foremost, total quality is a set of philosophies by which management systems can direct the efficient achievement of the objectives of an organization to ensure customer satisfaction and maximize stakeholder value. This is accomplished through the continuous improvement of the quality system, which consists of the social system, the technical system, and the management system. Thus, it becomes a way of life for doing business for the entire organization.

Central to the concept is the idea that a company should *design quality into its products,* rather than inspect for it afterward. Only by a devotion to quality throughout the organization can the best possible products be made. Or, as stated by Noriaki Kano, "Quality is too important to be left to inspectors."[1]

Total quality is too important to take second place to any other company goals. Specifically, it should not be subsidiary to profit or productivity. Concentrating on quality will ultimately build and improve both profitability and productivity. Failure to concentrate on quality will quickly erode profits, as customers resent paying for products they perceive as low quality.

The main focus of total quality is on *why*. It goes beyond the *how to* to include the *why to*. It is an attempt to identify the causes of defects in order to eliminate them. It is a continuous cycle of detecting defects, identifying their causes, and improving processes so as to totally eliminate the causes of defects.

Accepting the idea that the customer of a process can be defined as the next process is essential to the real practice of total quality. According to total quality, control charts should be developed for each process, and any errors identified within a process should be disclosed to those involved in the next process in order to raise quality. However, it has been said that it seems contrary to human nature to seek out one's own mistakes. People tend to find the errors caused by others and to neglect their own. Unfortunately, exactly that kind of self-disclosure is what is really needed.[2]

Instead, management too often tends to blame and then take punitive action. This attitude prevails from front-line supervisors all the way up to top management. In effect, we are encouraged to hide the real problems we cause; instead of looking for the real causes of problems, as required by total quality, we look the other way.

The Concept of Control

The Japanese notion of *control* differs radically from the American; that difference in meaning does much to explain the failure of U.S. management to adopt total quality. In the United States, control connotes someone or something that limits an operation, process, or person. It has overtones of a "police force" in the industrial engineering setting and is often resented.

In Japan, as pointed out by Union of Japanese Scientists and Engineers counselor and Japanese quality control scholar Noriaki Kano, *control* means "all necessary activities for achieving objectives in the long-term, efficiently and economically. Control, therefore, is doing whatever is needed to accomplish what we want to do as an organization."[1]

The difference can be seen very graphically in the Plan-Do-Check-Act (PDCA) continuous improvement chart, which is widely used in Japan to describe the cycle of control (Figure 4.1). Proper control starts with planning, does what is planned, checks the results, and then applies any necessary corrective action. The cycle represents these four stages—Plan-Do-Check-Act—arranged in a circular fashion to show that they are continuous.

In the United States, where specialization and division of labor are emphasized, the cycle is more likely to look like Fight-Plan-Do-Check. Instead of working together to solve any deviations from the plan, time is spent arguing about who is responsible for the deviations.

This sectionalism, as the Japanese refer to it, in the United States hinders collective efforts to improve the way things are done and lowers national productivity and the standard of living. *There need be nothing threatening about control if it is perceived as exercised in order to gather the facts necessary to make plans and take action toward making improvements.*

Total quality includes the control principle as part of the set of philosophies directed toward the efficient achievement of the objectives of an orga-

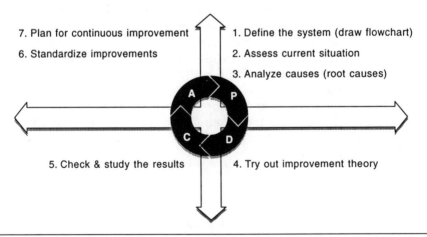

Figure 4.1 PDCA Chart. System improvement is the application of the Plan-Do-Check-Act cycle to an improvement project.

nization. Many of the individual components of total quality are practiced by American companies, but few practice total quality as a whole.

TOTAL QUALITY AS A SYSTEM

Introduction

Total quality begins with the redefinition of management, inspired by W. Edwards Deming:

> *The people work in a system. The job of the manager is to work on the system, to improve it continuously, with their help.*

One of the most frequent reasons for failed total quality efforts is that many managers are unable to carry out their responsibilities because they have not been trained in how to improve the quality system. They do not have a well-defined process to follow—a process founded on the principles of customer satisfaction, respect for people, continuous improvement, and speaking with facts. Deming's teachings, as amplified by Tribus,[3] focus on the following ten management actions:

1. Recognize quality improvement as a system.
2. Define it so that others can recognize it too.
3. Analyze its behavior.
4. Work with subordinates in improving the system.
5. Measure the quality of the system.
6. Develop improvements in the quality of the system.
7. Measure the gains in quality, if any, and link them to customer delight and quality improvement.
8. Take steps to guarantee holding the gains.
9. Attempt to replicate the improvements in other areas of the system.
10. Tell others about the lessons learned.

Discussions with Tribus to cross-examine these points have revealed that the manager must deal with total quality as *three* separate systems: a social system, a technical system, and a management system. These systems are depicted as three interlocking circles of a ballantine,[4] as shown in Figure 4.2.

Overview of the Social System

Management is solely responsible for the transformation of the social system, which is basically the culture of the organization. It is the social system that

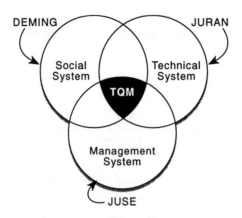

Figure 4.2 Implementing Total Quality Management—System Model.

has the greatest impact on teamwork, motivation, creativity, and risk taking. How people react to one another and to the work depends on how they are managed. If they enter the organization with poor attitudes, managers have to reeducate, redirect, or remove them. The social system includes the reward structure, the symbols of power, the relationships between people and among groups, the privileges, the skills and style, the politics, the power structure, the shaping of the norms and values, and the "human side of enterprise," as defined by Douglas McGregor.

If a lasting culture is to be achieved, where continuous improvement and customer focus are a natural pattern, the social system must be redesigned so as to be consistent with the vision and values of the organization. Unfortunately, the social system is always in a state of flux due to pressure from ever-changing influences from the external political and technological environments. The situation in most organizations is that the impact of total quality is not thought through in any organized manner. Change occurs when the pain of remaining as the same dysfunctional unit becomes too great and a remedy for relief is sought.

As shown in Figure 4.3, six areas of strategy must be addressed in order to change and transform the culture to that of a quality organization:

- Environment
- Product/service
- Methods
- People
- Organizational structure
- Total quality management mindset

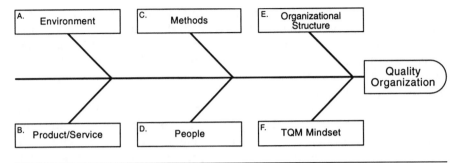

Figure 4.3 Strategic Areas for Cultural Transformation.

Each of these areas will be covered in some detail in the chapters in this book. Of the six, however, structure is key in that total quality is about empowerment and making decisions at lower levels in the organization. Self-managing teams are a way to bring this about quickly.

The Technical System

According to Tribus,[5] "The technical system includes all the tools and machinery, the practice of quality science and the quantitative aspects of quality. If you can measure it, you can probably describe and perhaps improve it using the technical systems approach." The technical system thus is concerned with the flow of work through the organization to the ultimate customer. Included are all the work steps performed, whether by equipment, computers, or people; whether manual labor or decision making; or whether factory worker or office worker.

The technical system in most organizations contains the following core elements:

- Scientific accumulation of technology
- Pursuit of standardization
- Work flow, materials, and specifications
- Job definitions and responsibilities
- Machine/person interface
- Number and type of work steps
- Availability and use of information
- Decision-making processes
- Problem-solving tools and process
- Physical arrangement of equipment, tools, and people

The expected benefits from analyzing and improving the technical system are to (1) improve customer satisfaction, (2) eliminate waste and rework, (3) eliminate variation, (4) increase learning, (5) save time and money, (6) increase employee control, (7) reduce bottlenecks and frustration, (8) eliminate interruptions and idle time, (9) increase speed and responsiveness, and (10) improve safety and quality of work life.

The three basic elements of every system are (1) suppliers who provide input, (2) work processes which add value, and (3) output to the customer. High-performing units and teams eliminate the barriers and walls between these three elements. A standard problem-solving process is often used by teams, such as the quality control story, business process analysis, etc.[6]

The Management System

The third system is the managerial system, which becomes the integrator. Only senior managers can authorize changes to this system. This is the system by which the other two systems are influenced. It is the way that practices, procedures, protocols, and policies are established and maintained. It is the leadership system of the organization, and it is the measurement system of indicators that tell management and the employees how things are going.

The actual deployment of the management system can be visualized in the shape of a pyramid. As shown in Figure 4.4, there are four aspects or intervention points of deployment: strategy management, process management, project management, and individual activity management. A brief overview of these four aspects is as follows:

- *Strategy management*—Purpose is to establish the mission, vision, guiding principles, and deployment infrastructure which encourage all employees to focus on and move in a common direction. Objectives, strategies, and actions are considered on a three- to five-year time line.

- *Process management*—Purpose is to assure that all key processes are working in harmony to guarantee customer satisfaction and maximize operational effectiveness. Continuous improvement/problem-solving efforts are often cross-functional, so that process owners and indicator owners need to be assigned.

- *Project management*—Purpose is to establish a system to effectively plan, organize, implement, and control all the resources and activities needed for successful completion of the project. Various types of project teams are often formed to solve and implement both process-related as well as

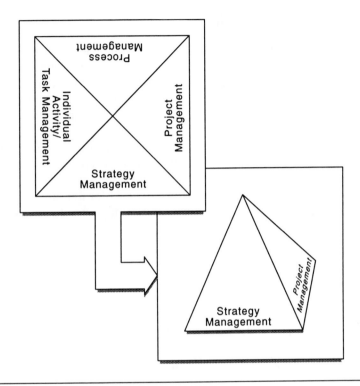

Figure 4.4 Management System Pyramid.

policy-related initiatives. Team activities should be linked to business objectives and improvement targets.

- *Individual activity management*—Purpose is to provide all employees with a method of implementing continuous improvement of processes and systems within each employee's work function and control. Flow-charting key processes and individual mission statements are important linkages with which all employees can identify. A quality journal is often used to identify and document improvements.

Various types of assessment surveys are used to "audit" the quality management system. Examples include the Malcolm Baldrige assessment, the Deming Prize audit, and the ISO 9000 audit, among others. Basic core elements are common to all of these assessments. Their usefulness is as a yardstick and benchmark by which to measure improvement and focus the problem-solving effort. Recent efforts using integrated quality and productivity systems have met with some success.[7]

The House of Total Quality

The House of Total Quality (Figure 4.5) is a model which depicts the integration of all of these concepts in a logical fashion. Supporting the three systems of total quality described in the preceding section are the four principles of total quality: customer satisfaction, continuous improvement, speaking with facts, and respect for people. These four principles are interrelated, with customer satisfaction at the core or the hub.

As with any house, the model and plans must first be drawn, usually with some outside help. Once the design has been approved, construction can begin. It usually begins with the mission, vision, values, and objectives which form the cornerstones upon which to build for the future. The pillars representing the four principles must be carefully constructed, well posi-

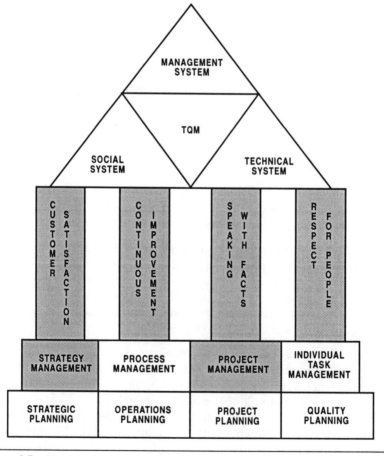

Figure 4.5 House of Total Quality.

tioned, and thoroughly understood, because the success of the total quality system is in the balance. As previously mentioned, many of the individual components of total quality are practiced by American companies, but few practice total quality as a whole.

HISTORY OF TOTAL QUALITY

In the Beginning

About the year one million B.C., give or take a few centuries, man first began to fashion stone tools for hunting and survival.[8] Up until 8000 B.C., however, very little progress was made in the quality control of these tools. It was at this time that man began assembling instruments with fitting holes, which suggests the use of interchangeable parts on a very limited basis. Throughout this long period, each man made his own tools. The evidence of quality control was measured to some extent by how long he stayed alive. If the tools were well made, his chances of survival increased. A broken axe handle usually spelled doom.

Introduction of Interchangeable Parts and Division of Labor

A little over 200 years ago, in 1787, the concepts of interchangeable parts and division of labor were first introduced in the United States. Eli Whitney, inventor of the cotton gin, applied these concepts to the production of 10,000 flintlock rifles for the U.S. military arsenal. However, Whitney had considerable difficulty in making all the parts exactly the same. It took him ten years to complete the 10,000 muskets that he promised to deliver in two years.

Three factors impacted Whitney's inability to deliver the 10,000 muskets in two years as promised. First, there was a dramatic shortage of qualified craftsmen needed to build the muskets. Consequently, Whitney correctly identified the solution to the problem—machines must do what men previously did. If individual machines were assembled to create each individual part needed, then men could be taught to operate these machines. Thus, Whitney's application of division of labor to a highly technical process was born. Whitney called this a *manufactory*.

Next, it took almost one full year to build the manufactory, rather than two months as Whitney originally thought. Not only did the weather inflict havoc on the schedule, but epidemics of yellow fever slowed progress considerably.

Third, obtaining the raw materials in a timely, usable manner was a hit-or-miss proposition. The metal ore used was often defective, flawed, and pitted. In addition, training the workers to perform the actual assembly took much longer than Whitney imagined and required a considerable amount of his personal attention, often 15 to 20 hours a day. Also, once the men were trained, some left to work for competing armories.[9]

To compound these factors, his ongoing cotton gin patent lawsuits consumed a considerable amount of his highly leveraged attention and time. Fortunately for Whitney, his credibility in Washington granted him considerable laxity in letting target dates slip. War with France was no longer imminent. Thus, a quality product and the associated manufacturing expertise were deemed more important than schedule. What was promised in 28 months took almost 120 months to deliver.

Luckily for Whitney, the requirement of "on time and within budget" was not yet in vogue. What happened to Whitney was a classic study in the problems of trying to achieve a real breakthrough in operations. Out of this experience, Whitney and others realized that creating parts exactly the same was not possible and, if tried, would prove to be very expensive. This concept of interchangeable parts would eventually lead to statistical methods of control, while division of labor would lead to the factory assembly line.

The First Control Limits

The experiences of Whitney and others who followed led to a relaxation of the requirements for exactness and the use of tolerances. This allowed for a less-than-perfect fit between two (or more) parts, and the concept of "go–no-go" tolerance was introduced between 1840 and 1870.[10]

This idea was a major advancement in that it created the concept of upper and lower tolerance limits, thus allowing the production worker more freedom to do his job with an accompanying lowering of cost. All he had to do was stay within the tolerance limits, instead of trying to achieve unnecessary or unattainable perfection.

Defective Parts Inspection

The next advancement centered around expanding the notion of tolerance and using specifications, where variation is classified as either meeting or not meeting requirements. For those pieces of product that every now and then fell outside the specified tolerance range (or limits), the question arose as to what to do with them. To discard or modify these pieces added significantly to the cost of production. However, to search for the unknown causes of defects and then eliminate them also cost money. The heart of the problem was as follows: how to reduce the percentage of defects to the point where (1) the rate of increase in the *cost of control* equals the rate of *increase* in *savings*, which is (2) brought about by *decreasing the number of parts rejected.*

In other words, inspection/prevention had to be cost effective. Minimizing the percent of defects in a cost-effective manner was not the only problem to be solved. Tests for many quality characteristics require destructive testing, such as tests for strength, chemical composition, fuse blowing time, etc. Because not every piece can be tested, use of the statistical sample was initiated around the turn of the century.

Statistical Theory

During the early part of the 20th century, a tremendous increase in quality consciousness occurred. What were the forces at work that caused this sudden acceleration of interest in the application of statistical quality control? There were at least three key factors.

The first was a rapid growth in standardization, beginning in 1900. Until 1915, Great Britain was the only country in the world with some type of national standardization movement. The rate of growth in the number of industrial standardization organizations throughout the world, especially between 1916 and 1932, rose dramatically.[11] During that 15-year period, the movement grew from one country (Great Britain) to 25, with the United States coming on line about 1917, just at the time of World War I.

The second major factor ushering in the new era was a radical shift in ideology which occurred in about 1900. This ideological shift was away from the notion of exactness of science (which existed in 1787 when interchangeability of parts was introduced) to probability and statistical concepts, which developed in almost every field of science around 1900.

The third factor was the evolution of division of labor into the factory system and the first assembly-line systems of the early 20th century. These systems proved to be ideal for employing an immigrant work force quickly.

Scientific Management and Taylorism

Frederick Winslow Taylor was born in 1856 and entered industry as an apprentice in the Enterprise Hydraulics Shop in 1874. According to popular legend, the old-timers in the shop told him: "Now young man, here's about how much work you should do each morning and each afternoon. Don't do any more than that—that's the limit."[12]

It was obvious to Taylor that the men were producing below their capacity, and he soon found out why. The short-sighted management of that day would set standards, often paying per-piece rates for the work. Then, when a worker discovered how to produce more, management cut the rate. In turn, management realized that the workers were deliberately restricting output but could not do anything about it.

It was Taylor's viewpoint that the whole system was wrong. Having studied the writings and innovations of Whitney, he came to realize that the concept of division of labor had to be revamped if greater productivity and efficiency were to be realized. His vision included a super-efficient assembly line as part of a management system of operations. He, more than anyone at the time, understood the inability of management to increase individual productivity, and he understood the reluctance of the workers to produce at a high rate. Because he had been a working man, it was apparent to him that there was a tremendous difference between *actual* output and *potential* output. Taylor thought that if such practices applied throughout the world and throughout all industry, the potential production capacity was at least three or four times what was actually being produced. When he became a foreman, Taylor set out to find ways to eliminate this waste and increase production.

For more than 25 years, Taylor and his associates explored ways to increase productivity and build the model factory of the future. The techniques they developed were finally formalized in writing and communicated to other people. During the early years of this experimentation, most who knew about it were associated with Taylor at the Midvale Steel Company and Bethlehem Steel.

Other famous names began to enter the picture and contribute to the body of science of the new management thinking. Among them were Carl G.L. Barth, a mathematician and statistician who assisted Taylor in analytical work, and Henry L. Gantt (famous for the Gantt chart), who invented the slide rule. Another associate of Taylor's, Sanford E. Thompson, developed the first decimal stopwatch.[12] Finally, there was young Walter Shewhart, who was to transform industry with his statistical concepts and thinking and his ability to bridge technical tools with a management system.

At the turn of the century, Taylor wrote a collection of reports and papers that were published by the American Society of Mechanical Engineers. One of the most famous was *On the Art of Cutting Metals*, which had worldwide impact. With Maunsel White, Taylor developed the first high-speed steel. Taylor was also instrumental in the development of one of the first industrial cost-accounting systems, even though, according to legend, he previously knew nothing about accounting.

Frank G. and Lillian Gilbreth, aware of Taylor's work in measurement and analysis, turned their attention to mechanizing and commercializing Taylorism. For their experimental model, they chose the ancient craft of bricklaying. It had been assumed that production in bricklaying certainly should have reached its zenith thousands of years ago, with nothing more to be done to increase production. Yet Frank Gilbreth was able to show that by following his techniques and with proper management planning, production could be raised from an average of 120 bricks per hour to 350 bricks per hour, and the worker would be less tired than he had been under the old system.

The Gilbreths refined some of the studies and techniques developed by Taylor. They used the motion picture camera to record work steps for analyses and broke them down into minute elements called "therbligs" (Gilbreth spelled backwards). Their results were eventually codified into the use of predetermined motion–time measures which were used by industrial engineers and efficiency experts of the day.

By 1912, the efficiency movement was gaining momentum. Taylor was called before a special committee of the House of Representatives which was investigating scientific management and its impact on the railroad industry. He tried to explain scientific management to the somewhat hostile railroad hearings committee, whose members regarded it as "speeding up" work. He said:

> Scientific management involves a complete mental revolution on the part of the *working man* engaged in any particular establishment or industry...a complete mental revolution on the part of these men as to their duties toward their work, toward their fellow man, and toward their employers.
>
> And scientific management involves an equally complete mental revolution on the part of those on *management's side*...the foreman, the superintendent, the owner of the business, and the board of directors. Here we must have a mental revolution on their part as to their duties toward their fellow workers in management, toward their workmen, and toward all of their daily problems. Without this complete mental revolution on both sides, scientific management does not exist!
>
> I want to sweep the deck, sweep away a good deal of the rubbish first by pointing out what scientific management is not— it is not an efficiency device, nor is it any bunch or group of efficiency devices. It is not a new system of figuring costs. It is not a new scheme of paying men. It is not holding a stopwatch on a man and writing things down about him. It is not time study. It is not motion study, nor an analysis of the movements of a man. Nor is scientific management the printing and ruling and unloading of a ton or two of blank forms on a set of men and saying, "Here's your system—go to it."
>
> It is not divided foremanship, nor functional foremanship. It is not any of these devices which the average man calls to mind when he hears the words "scientific management." I am not sneering at cost-keeping systems—at time-study, at functional foremanship, nor at any of the new and improved schemes of paying men. Nor am I sneering at efficiency devices, if they are really devices which make for efficiency. I believe in them. What I am emphasizing is that these devices in whole or part are *not* scien-

tific management; they are useful adjuncts to scientific management, but they are also useful adjuncts to other systems of
management.[12]

Taylor found out, the hard way, the importance of the cooperative spirit.
He was strictly the engineer at first. Only after painful experiences did he
realize that the human factor, the social system, and mental attitude of people
in both management and labor had to be adjusted and changed completely
before greater productivity could result.

Referring to his early experiences in seeking greater output, Taylor described the strained feelings between himself and his workmen as "miserable." Yet he was determined to improve production. He continued his
experiments until three years before his death in 1915, when he found that
human motivation, not just engineered improvements, could alone increase
output.

Unfortunately, the human factor was ignored by many. Shortly after the
railroad hearings, self-proclaimed "efficiency experts" did untold damage to
scientific management. Time studies and the new efficiency techniques were
used by incompetent "consultants" who sold managers on the idea of increasing profit by "speeding up" employees. Consequently, many labor
unions, just beginning to feel their strength, worked against the new science
and all efficiency approaches. With the passing of Taylor in 1915, the scientific management movement lost, for the moment, any chance of reaching its
true potential as the catalyst for the future total quality management system.
Still, the foundation was laid for the management system that was soon to
become a key ingredient of organizations of the future.

Walter Shewhart—The Founding Father

Walter Shewhart was an engineer, scientist, and philosopher. He was a very
deep thinker, and his ideas, although profound and technically perfect, were
difficult to fathom. His style of writing followed his style of thinking—very
obtuse. Still, he was brilliant, and his works on variation and sampling,
coupled with his teachings on the need for documentation, influenced forever the course of industrial history.

Shewhart was familiar with the scientific management movement and its
evolution from Whitney's innovation of division of labor. Although he was
concerned about its evolution into sweatshop factory environments, his
major focus was on the other of Whitney's great innovations—interchangeable parts—for this encompassed variation, rejects, and waste.

To deal with the issue of variation, Shewhart developed the control chart
in 1924. He realized that the traditional use of tolerance limits was short-
sighted, because they only provided a method for judging the quality of a
product that had already been made.[13]

The control limits on Shewhart's control charts, however, provided a ready guide for acting on a process in order to eliminate what he called *assignable causes*[8] of variation, thus preventing inferior products from being produced in the future. This allowed management to focus on the future, through the use of statistical probability—a prediction of future production based upon historical data. Thus, the emphasis shifted from costly correction of problems to prevention of problems and improvement of processes.[14]

Like Taylor, Shewhart's focus shifted from individual parts to a systems approach. The notion of zero defects of individual parts was replaced with zero variability of system operations.

Shewhart's Control System

Shewhart identified the traditional act of control as consisting of three elements: the act of specifying what is required, the act of producing what is specified, and the act of judging whether the requirements have been met. This simple picture of the control of quality would work well if production could be viewed in the context of an exact science, where all products are made exactly the same. Shewhart knew, however, that because variation is pervasive, the control of quality characteristics must be a matter of probability. He envisioned a statistician helping an engineer to understanding variation and arriving at the economic control of quality.[15]

Shewhart's Concept of Variation

Determining the *state of statistical control* in terms of degree of variation is the first step in the Shewhart control system. Rather than specifying what is required in terms of tolerance requirements, Shewhart viewed variation as being present in everything and identified two types of variation: *controlled* and *uncontrolled*.

This is fundamentally different from the traditional way of classifying variation as either acceptable or unacceptable (go–no-go tolerance). Viewing variation as controlled or uncontrolled enables one to focus on the causes of variation in order to improve a process (before the fact) as opposed to focusing on the output of a process in order to judge whether or not the product is acceptable (after the fact).

Shewhart taught that controlled variation is a consistent pattern of variation over time that is due to random or *chance causes*. He recognized that there may be many chance causes of variation, but the effect of any one of these is relatively small; therefore, which cause or causes are responsible for observed variation is a matter of chance. Shewhart stated that a process that is being affected only by *chance* causes of variation is said to be *in a state of statistical control*.

All processes contain chance causes of variation, and Shewhart taught that it is possible to reduce the chance causes of variation, but it is not realistic or cost effective to try to remove them all. The control limits on Shewhart's control charts represent the boundaries of the occurrence of chance causes of variation operating within the system.

The second type of variation—uncontrolled variation—is an inconsistent or changing pattern of variation that occurs over time and is due to what Shewhart classified as *assignable causes*. Because the effects of assignable causes of variation are relatively major compared to chance causes, they can and must be identified and removed.[16] According to Shewhart, a process is *out of statistical control* when it is being affected by assignable causes.

One of Shewhart's main problems was how to communicate this newfound theory without overwhelming the average businessman or engineer. The answer came in the form of staged experiments using models which demonstrated variation. His *Ideal Bowl Experiment*[17] with poker chips was modeled by his protege, W. Edwards Deming, some 20 years later with his famous *Red Bead Experiment*.

Another major contribution of Shewhart's first principle of control was recognition of the need for operational definitions that can be communicated to operators, inspectors, and scientists alike. He was fond of asking, "How can an operator carry out his job tasks if he does not understand what the job is? And how can he know what the job is if what was produced yesterday was O.K., but today the same product is wrong?" He believed that inspection, whether the operator inspects his own work or relies on someone else to do it for him, must have operational definitions. Extending specifications beyond product and into the realm of operator performance was the first attempt to define the "extended system of operations" which would greatly facilitate the production process.

The Shewhart System of Production

Shewhart's second principle—the act of producing what is specified—consists of five important steps (Shewhart's teachings are in italics):

1. **Outline the data collection framework**—*Specify in a general way how an observed sequence of data is to be examined for clues as to the existence of assignable causes of variability.*

2. **Develop the sampling plan**—*Specify how the original data are to be taken and how they are to be broken up into subsamples upon the basis of human judgments about whether the conditions under which the data were taken were essentially the same or not.*

3. **Identify the formulas and control limits for each sample**—*Specify the criterion of control that is to be used, indicating what statistics are to be com-*

puted for each subsample and how these are to be used in computing action or control limits for each statistic for which the control criterion is to be constructed.

4. **Outline the corrective actions/improvement thesis**—*Specify the action that is to be taken when an observed statistic falls outside its control limits.*

5. **Determine the size of the database**—*Specify the quantity of data that must be available and found to satisfy the criterion of control before the engineer is to act as though he had attained a state of statistical control.*[8]

The Shewhart system became a key component of the technical system of total quality. The works of Deming, Juran, Feigenbaum, Sarasohn, Ishikawa, and others who followed would amplify Shewhart's concept of quality as a *technical system* into its many dimensions, which eventually led to the body of knowledge known as total quality.

The Shewhart Cycle: When Control Meets Scientific Management

From the "exact science" days of the 1800s to the 1920s, *specification, production,* and *inspection* were considered to be independent of each other when viewed in a straight-line manner. They take on an entirely different picture in an inexact science. When the production process is viewed from the standpoint of the control of quality as a matter of probability, then specification, production, and inspection are linked together as represented in a circular diagram or wheel. *Specification and production* are linked because it is important to know how well the tolerance limits are being satisfied by the existing process and what improvements are necessary. Shewhart compared this process (which he called the Scientific Method) to the dynamic process of acquiring knowledge, which is similar to an experiment. Step 1 was formulating the hypothesis. Step 2 was conducting the experiment. Step 3 was testing the hypothesis.[18] In the Shewhart Wheel, the successful completion of each interlocking component led to a cycle of continuous improvement. (Years later, Deming was to popularize this cycle of improvement in his famous Deming Wheel.)

Shewhart Meets Deming

It was at the Bell Laboratories in New Jersey where Shewhart, who was leading the telephone reliability efforts during the 1930s, first met Deming. Shewhart, as discussed earlier, was developing his system for improving worker performance and productivity by measuring variation using control charts and statistical methods. Deming was impressed and liked what he saw, especially Shewhart's intellect and the *wheel*—the Shewhart cycle of control. He realized that with training, workers could retain control over their work processes by monitoring the quality of the items produced. Deming also believed that once workers were trained and educated and were empowered to manage their work processes, quality would be increased and costly inspections could once and for all be eliminated. He presented the idea that higher quality would cost less, not more. Deming studied Shewhart's teachings and techniques and learned well, even if at times he was lost and said that his genius was in knowing when to act and when to leave a process alone. At times he was frustrated by Shewhart's obtuse style of thinking and writing.[19]

In 1938, Shewhart delivered four lectures to the U.S. Department of Agriculture (USDA) Graduate School at the invitation of Deming. In addition to being in charge of the mathematics and statistics courses at the USDA Graduate School, Deming was responsible for inviting guest lecturers. He invited Shewhart to present a series of lectures on how statistical methods of control were being used in industry to economically control the quality of manufactured products. Shewhart spent an entire year developing the lectures, titled them *Statistical Method from the Viewpoint of Quality Control*, and delivered them in March of 1938. They were subsequently edited into book format by Deming and published in 1939.

In a couple of years, both Deming and Shewhart were called upon by the U.S. government to aid the war effort. As David Halberstam recounted, the War Department, impressed by Shewhart's theories and work, brought together a small group of experts on statistical process control (SPC) to establish better quality guidelines for defense contractors.[20] Deming was a member of that group and he came to love the work.

Origins of Deming

Who was Dr. W. Edwards Deming, the man who was to take Shewhart's teachings, popularize them, and even go beyond? He was born on October 14, 1900 and earned his Ph.D. in physics at Yale University in the summer of 1927, which is where he learned to use statistical theory. As a graduate student in the late 1920s, he did part-time summer work at the famous Western Electric Hawthorne Plant in Chicago. It was at this plant that Elton Mayo some ten years later would perform his experiments later known as the Hawthorne Experiments. While working at Hawthorne, Deming could not help noticing the poor working conditions of this sweatshop environment, which employed predominantly female laborers to produce telephones. Deming was both fascinated and appalled by what he saw and learned. It was at Hawthorne that he saw the full effects of the abuses of the Taylor system of scientific management. He also saw the full effect of Whitney's second great innovation—division of labor—when carried to extreme by ivory tower management uncaring about the state of the social system of the organization. So what if the work environment was a sweatshop—the workers were paid well enough! "The women should be happy just to have a job" seemed to be the unspoken attitude.

When Deming Met Taylor(ism)

A couple of years before meeting Shewhart, when Deming encountered Taylorism at Hawthorne, he found a scientific management system with the following objectives:

- Develop a science for each element of work.
- Scientifically select a workman and train and develop him.
- Secure wholehearted cooperation between management and labor to ensure that all work is done in accordance with the principles developed.
- Divide the work between management and labor. The manager takes over all work for which he is better suited than the workman.

It was the fourth point, which evolved out of the division of labor concept, that Deming found to be the real villain. In practice, this meant removing from the worker basic responsibility for the quality of the work. What Deming disliked was that workers should not be hired to think about their work. That was management's job. Errors will occur, but the worker need not worry—the inspector will catch any mistakes *before* they leave the plant. In addition, management could always reduce the per-piece pay to reflect scrap and rework. Any worker who produced too many inferior quality pieces would be fired.

The problem with Taylorism is that it views the production process mechanistically instead of holistically, as a system which includes the human elements of motivation and respect. Taylorism taught American industry to view the worker as "a cog in the giant industrial machine, whose job could be defined and directed by educated managers administering a set of rules."[21] Work on the assembly lines of America and at Hawthorne was simple, repetitive, and boring. Management was top-down. Pay per piece meant that higher output equals higher take-home pay. Quality of work for the most part was not a factor for the average, everyday worker.

This system found a friend in the assembly-line process developed by Henry Ford and was widely incorporated into America's private and public sectors. Taylor's management system made it possible for waves of immigrants, many of whom could not read, write, or speak English (and at times not even communicate with one another), to find employment in American factories. Taylor's ideas were even introduced into the nation's schools.[22]

Edwards Deming had various colleagues at the time, one of whom was Joseph Juran, another famous quality "guru." They rebelled at the scientific management movement. They felt that the authoritarian Taylorism method of management was degrading to the human spirit and counterproductive to the interests of employees, management, the company, and society as a whole.[23] Mayo and his Hawthorne research team confirmed these feelings with their findings: good leadership leads to high morale and motivation, which in turn leads to higher production. Good leadership was defined as democratic, rather than autocratic, and people centered, as opposed to production centered. Thus began the human relations era.

Post-World War II

When the war ended, American industry converted to peacetime production of goods and services. People were hungry for possessions and an appetite developed worldwide for products "made in the U.S.A." The focus in the United States returned to quantity over quality, and a gradual deterioration of market share occurred, with billions of dollars in international business lost to Japanese and European competitors. These were the modern-day phoenixes rising from the ashes of war. America became preoccupied with the mechanics of mass production and its role as world provider to a hungry people. What followed was an imbalance between satisfying the needs of the worker and a lack of appreciation for and recognition of the external customer. America moved away from what had made it great!

The Japanese Resurrection

Japan first began to apply statistical control concepts in the early 1920s, but moved away from them when the war began.[24] In 1946, under General Douglas MacArthur's leadership, the Supreme Command for the Allied Powers (SCAP) established quality control tools and techniques as the approach to effect the turnaround of Japanese industry. Japan had sacrificed its industry, and eventually its food supply, to support its war effort. Subsequently, there was little left in post-war Japan to occupy. The country was a shambles. Only one major city, Kyoto, had escaped wide-scale destruction; food was scarce and industry was negligible.[24]

Against a backdrop of devastation and military defeat, a group of Japanese scientists and engineers—organized appropriately as the Union of Japanese Scientists and Engineers (JUSE)—dedicated themselves to working with American and Allied experts to help rebuild the country. Reconstruction was a daunting and monumental task. With few natural resources available or any immediate means of producing them, export of manufactured goods was essential. However, Japanese industry—or what was left of it—was producing inferior goods, a fact which was recognized worldwide. JUSE was faced with the task of drastically improving the quality of Japan's industrial output as an essential exchange commodity for survival.

W.S. Magill and Homer Sarasohn, among others, assisted with the dramatic transformation of the electronics industry and telecommunications. Magill is regarded by some as the father of statistical quality control in Japan. He was the first to advocate its use in a 1945 lecture series and successfully applied SPC techniques to vacuum tube production in 1946 at NEC.[25]

Sarasohn worked with supervisors and managers to improve reliability and yields in the electronics field from 40 percent in 1946 to 80 to 90 percent in 1949; he documented his findings for SCAP, and MacArthur took notice. He ordered Sarasohn to instruct Japanese businessmen how to get things done. The Japanese listened, but the Americans forgot. In 1950, Sarasohn's attention was directed toward Korea, and Walter Shewhart was asked to come to Japan. He was unable to at the time, and Deming was eventually tapped to direct the transformation.

In July 1950, Deming began a series of day-long lectures to Japanese management in which he taught the basic "Elementary Principles of Statistical Control of Quality." The Japanese embraced the man and his principles and named their most prestigious award for quality the Deming Prize. During the 1970s, Deming turned his attention back to the United States. He died at the age of 93, still going strong. His 14 Points go far beyond statistical methods and address the management system as well as the social system or culture of the organization. In many ways, he began to sound more and more like Frederick Taylor, whose major emphasis in later years was on the need for a *mental revolution*—a transformation. Deming's Theory of Profound Knowledge brings together all three systems of total quality.

The Other "Gurus" Arrive

What began in Japan in the 1950s became a worldwide quality movement, albeit on a limited basis, within 20 years. During this period, the era of the "gurus" evolved (Deming, Juran, Ishikawa, Feigenbaum, and Crosby). Beginning with Deming in 1948 and Juran in 1954, the movement was eventually carried back to the United States by Feigenbaum in the 1960s and Crosby in the 1970s. Meanwhile, Ishikawa and his associates at JUSE kept the movement alive in Japan. By 1980, the bell began to toll loud and clear in the West with the NBC White Paper entitled "If Japan Can Do It, Why Can't We?" The following are thumbnail sketches of the teachings of the other gurus.

Joseph Juran

Joseph Juran was the son of an immigrant shoemaker from Romania and began his industrial career at Western Electric's Hawthorne Plant before World War II. He later worked at Bell Laboratories in the area of quality assurance. He worked as a government administrator, university professor, labor arbitrator, and corporate director before establishing his own consulting firm, the Juran Institute, in Wilton, Connecticut. In the 1950s, he was invited to Japan by JUSE to help rebuilding Japanese corporations develop management concepts. Juran based some of his principles on the work of Walter Shewhart and, like Deming and the other quality gurus, believed that management and the system are responsible for quality. Juran is the creator of statistical quality control and the author of *The Quality Control Handbook,* which has become an international standard reference for the quality movement.

Juran's definition of quality is described as "fitness for use as perceived by the customer." If a product is produced and the customer perceives it as fit for use, then the quality mission has been accomplished. Juran also believed that every person in the organization must be involved in the effort to make products or services that are fit for use.

Juran described a perpetual spiral of progress or continuous striving toward quality. Steps on this spiral are, in ascending order, research, development, design, specification, planning, purchasing, instrumentation, production, process control, inspection, testing, sale, service, and then back to research again. The idea behind the spiral is that each time the steps are completed, products or services would increase in quality. Juran explained that chronic problems should be solved by following this spiral; he formulated a breakthrough sequence to increase the standard of performance so that problems are eliminated. To alleviate sporadic problems, which he finds are often solved with temporary solutions, he suggests carefully examining the system causing the problem and adjusting it to solve the difficulty. Once operating at this improved standard of performance, with the sporadic problem solved, the process of analyzing chronic and sporadic problems should start over again.

Juran pointed out that companies often overlook the cost of producing low-quality products. He suggested that by implementing his theories of quality improvement, not only would higher quality products be produced, but the actual costs would be lower. His Cost of Quality principle was known as "Gold in the Mine."

Juran is known for his work with statistics, and he relied on the quantification of standards and statistical quality control techniques. He is credited with implementing use of the Pareto diagram to improve business systems as well.

Juran's concept of quality included the managerial dimensions of planning, organizing, and controlling (known as the Juran Trilogy) and focused on the responsibility of management to achieve quality and the need to set goals. His ten steps to quality are as follows:

1. Build awareness of opportunities to improve.
2. Set goals for improvement.
3. Organize to reach goals.
4. Provide training.
5. Carry out projects to solve problems.
6. Report progress.
7. Give recognition.
8. Communicate results.
9. Keep score.
10. Maintain momentum by making annual improvement part of the regular systems and processes of the company.

Ishikawa and the Japanese Experts

Kaoru Ishikawa studied under both Homer Sarasohn and Edwards Deming during the late 1940s and early 1950s. As president of JUSE, he was instrumental in developing a unique Japanese strategy for total quality: the broad involvement of the entire organization in its *total* sense—every worker, every process, and every job. This also included the complete life cycle of the product, from start to finish.

Some of his accomplishments include the success of the quality circle in Japan, in part due to innovative tools such as the cause-and-effect diagram (often called the Ishikawa fishbone diagram because it resembles a fish skeleton). His approach was to provide easy-to-use analytical tools that could be used by all workers, including those on the line, to analyze and solve problems.

Ishikawa identified seven critical success factors that were essential for the success of total quality control in Japan:

1. Company-wide total quality control and participation by *all* members of the organization
2. Education and training in all aspects of total quality, which often amounts to 30 days per year per employee
3. Use of quality circles to update standards and regulations, which are in constant need of improvement
4. Quality audits by the president and quality council members (senior executives) twice a year
5. Widespread use of statistical methods and a focus on problem prevention
6. Nationwide quality control promotion activities, with the national imperative of keeping Japanese quality number one in the world

7. Revolutionary *mental* attitude on the part of both management and workers toward one another and toward the customer, including welcoming complaints, encouraging risk, and a wider span of control

Ishikawa believed that Japanese management practices should be democratic, with management providing the guidelines. Mission statements were used extensively and operating policies derived from them. Top management, he taught, must assume a leadership position to implement the policies so that they are followed by all.

The impact on Japanese industry was startling. In seven to ten years, the electronics and telecommunications industries were transformed, with the entire nation revitalized by the end of the 1960s.

Armand Feigenbaum

Unlike Deming and Juran, Feigenbaum did not work with the Japanese. He was vice president of worldwide quality for General Electric until the late 1960s, when he set up his own consulting firm, General Systems, Inc. He is best known for coining the term *total quality control* and for his 850-page book on the subject. His teachings center around the integration of people–machine–information structures in order to economically and effectively control quality and achieve full customer satisfaction.

Feigenbaum taught that there are two requirements to establishing quality as a business strategy: establishing customer satisfaction must be central and quality/cost objectives must drive the total quality system. His systems theory of total quality control includes four fundamental principles:

- Total quality is a continuous work process, starting with customer requirements and ending with customer satisfaction.
- Documentation allows visualization and communication of work assignments.
- The quality system provides for greater flexibility because of a greater use of alternatives provided.
- Systematic reengineering of major quality activities leads to greater levels of continuous improvement.

Like Juran and Deming, Feigenbaum used a visual concept to capture the idea of waste and rework—the so-called Hidden Plant. Based upon studies, he taught that this "Hidden Plant" can account for between 15 and 40 percent of the production capacity of a company. In his book, he used the concept of the "9 M's" to describe the factors which affect quality: (1) markets, (2) money, (3) management, (4) men, (5) motivation, (6) materials, (7) machines and mechanization, (8) modern information methods, and (9) mounting product requirements.

According to Andrea Gabor in "The Man Who Discovered Quality," Feigenbaum took a nuts-and-bolts approach to quality, while Deming is often viewed as a visionary. Nuts and bolts led him to focus on the benefits and outcomes of total quality, rather than only the process to follow. His methods led to increased quantification of total quality program improvements during the 1970s and 1980s.

Philip Crosby

Unlike the other quality gurus, who were scientists, engineers, and statisticians, Philip Crosby is known for his motivational talks and style of presentation. His emergence began in 1961, when he first developed the concept of zero defects while working as a quality manager at Martin Marietta Corporation in Orlando, Florida. He believed that "zero defects" motivated line workers to turn out perfect products. He soon joined ITT, where he quickly moved up the ranks to vice president of quality control operations, covering 192 manufacturing facilities in 46 countries. He held the position until 1979, when he opened his own consulting company, which became one of the largest of its kind with over 250 people worldwide.

He established the Quality College in 1980 and used that concept to promote his teachings and writings in 18 languages. It has been estimated that over five million people have attended its courses, and his trilogy of books are popular and easy to read. It is in these works where he introduces the four absolutes of his total quality management philosophy:

1. The definition of quality is conformance to requirements.
2. The system of quality is prevention of problems.
3. The performance standard of quality is zero defects.
4. The measurement of quality is the price of nonconformance, or the Cost of Quality.

The fourth principle, the Cost of Quality, is similar to Feigenbaum's Hidden Plant and Juran's Gold in the Mine. Like Deming, he has 14 steps to quality improvement. Also like Deming, he has been very critical of the Malcolm Baldrige National Quality Award, although his influence (like Deming's) can be seen in virtually all seven categories.

He departs from the other gurus in his emphasis on performance standards instead of statistical data to achieve zero defects. He believes that identifying goals to be achieved, setting standards for the final product, removing all error-causing situations, and complete organizational commitment comprise the foundation for excellence.

ISO 9000 and the Quality Movement

At the turn of the century, England was the most advanced nation in the world in terms of quality standards. During World War I, England led the charge and during World War II was at least the equal of the United States—with one exception. England did not have Shewhart, Deming, and the other American quality gurus. It was not until the Common Market accepted the firm touch of Prime Minister Margaret Thatcher that the European movement was galvanized in 1979 with the forerunner of ISO 9000. It was Thatcher who orchestrated the transformation of the British ISO 9000 series for the European community. In less than 20 years, it has become the worldwide quality standard.

ENDNOTES

1. During the course of the Deming Prize examination at Florida Power & Light in 1988 and 1989, Dr. Kano consistently emphasized this point during site visits to various power plants and district customer service operations. The concept of worker self-inspection, while new in the United States, has been a practiced art in Japan over the past 20 years.

2. Whethan, C.D. (1980). *A History of Science*, 4th edition. New York: Macmillan.

3. Tribus, Myron (1990). *The Systems of Total Quality*, published by the author.

4. The total quality ballantine was developed by Frank Voehl to illustrate the three-dimensional and interlocking aspects of the quality system. It is loosely based on the military concept of three interlocking bullet holes representing a perfect hit.

5. Tribus, Myron (1990). *The Three Systems of Total Quality*, published by the author; referenced in Voehl, Frank (1992). *Total Quality: Principles and Practices within Organizations*. Coral Springs, FL: Strategy Associates, pp. IV, 20.

6. The use of a storyboard to document the various phases of project development was introduced by Dr. Kume in his work on total quality control and was pioneered in the United States by Disney Studios, where it was used to bring new movies to production sooner.

7. For details, see Voehl, F.W. (1992). *The Integrated Quality System*. Coral Springs, FL: Strategy Associates.

8. Shewhart, W.A. (1931). *Economic Control of Quality of Manufactured Product*. New York: Van Nostrand.

9. Olmstead, Denison (1972). *Memoir of Eli Whitney, Esq.* New York: Arno Press.

10. Walter Shewhart on the "go–no-go" concept: If, for example, a design involving the use of a cylindrical shaft in a bearing is examined, inter-

changeability might be ensured simply by using a suitable "go" plug gauge on the bearing and a suitable "go" ring gauge on the shaft. In this case, the difference between the dimensions of the two "go" gauges gives the minimum clearance. Such a method of gauging, however, does not fix the maximum clearance. The production worker soon realized that a slack fit between a part and its "go" gauge might result in enough play between the shaft and its bearing to cause the product to be rejected; therefore, he tried to keep the fit between the part and its "go" gauge as close as possible, thus encountering some of the difficulties that had been experienced in trying to make the parts exactly alike.

11. Walter Shewhart was the first to realize that, with the development of the atomic structure of matter and electricity, it became necessary to regard laws as being statistical in nature. According to Shewhart, the importance of the law of large numbers in the interpretation of physical phenomena will become apparent to anyone who even hastily surveys any one or more of the following works: Darrow, K.K. (1992). "Statistical Theories of Matter, Radiation, and Electricity." *The Physical Review Supplement.* Vol. I, No. I (also published in the series of Bell Telephone Laboratories reprints, No. 435); Rice, J. (1930). *Introduction to Statistical Mechanics for Students of Physics and Physical Chemistry.* London: Constable & Company; Tolman, R.E. (1927). *Statistical Mechanics with Applications to Physics and Chemistry.* New York: Chemical Catalog Company; Loeb, L.B. (1927). *Kinetic Theory of Gases.* New York: McGraw-Hill; Bloch, E. (1924). *The Kinetic Theory of Bases.* London: Methuen & Company; Richtmeyer, F.K. (1928). *Introduction to Modern Physics.* New York: McGraw-Hill; Wilson, H.A. (1928). *Modern Physics.* London: Blackie & Son; Darrow, K.K. (1926). *Introduction to Contemporary Physics.* New York: D. Van Nostrand; Ruark, A.E. and Urey, H.C. (1930). *Atoms, Molecules and Quanta.* New York: McGraw-Hill.

12. Matthies, Leslie (1960). "The Beginning of Modern Scientific Management." *The Office.* April.

13. Walter Shewhart on the use of the control chart: Whereas the concept of mass production of 1787 was born of an *exact* science, the concept underlying the quality control chart technique of 1924 was born of a *probable* science, which has empirically derived control limits. These limits are to be set so that when the observed quality of a piece of product falls outside of them, even though the observation is still within the limits L_1 and L_2 (tolerance limits), it is desirable to look at the manufacturing process in order to discover and remove, if possible, one or more causes of variation that need not be left to chance.

14. Shewhart noted that it is essential, however, in industry and in science to understand the distinction between a stable system and an unstable system and how to plot points and conclude by rational methods whether they indicate a stable system. To quote Shewhart, "This conclusion is consistent with that so admirably presented in a recent paper by S.L. Andrew in the *Bell Telephone Quarterly*, Jan., 1931, and also with conclu-

sions set forth in the recent book *Business Adrift,* by W.B. Donham, Dean of the Harvard Business School. Such reading cannot do other than strengthen our belief in the fact that control of quality will come only through the weeding out of assignable causes of variation—particularly those that introduce lack of constancy in the chance cause system."

15. As the statistician enters the scene, the three traditional elements of control take on a new meaning, as Shewhart summarized: "Corresponding to these three steps there are three senses in which statistical control may play an important part in attaining uniformity in the quality of a manufactured product: (a) as a concept of a statistical state constituting a limit to which one may hope to go in improving the uniformity of quality; (b) as an operation or technique of attaining uniformity; and (c) as a judgment."

16. Deming refers to assignable causes as being "specific to some ephemeral (brief) event that can usually be discovered to the satisfaction of the expert on the job, and removed."

17. Shewhart used what he called the *Ideal Bowl Experiment* to physically characterize a state of statistical control. A number of physically similar poker chips with numbers written on them are placed in a bowl. Successive samples (Shewhart seems to prefer a sample size of four) are taken from the bowl, each time mixing the remaining chips. The chips removed from the bowl are drawn by chance—there are only chance causes of variation. In speaking of chance causes of variation, Shewhart proves, contrary to popular belief, that the statistician can have a sense of humor. "If someone were shooting at a mark and failed to hit the bull's-eye and was then asked why, the answer would likely be *chance.* Had someone asked the same question of one of man's earliest known ancestors, he might have attributed his lack of success to the dictates of fate or to the will of the gods. I am inclined to think that in many ways one of these excuses is about as good as another. The Ideal Bowl Experiment is an abstract means of characterizing the physical state of statistical control." A sequence of samples of any process can be compared mathematically to the bowl experiment and, if found similar, the process can be said to be affected only by random or chance causes of variation or can be characterized as being in a *state of statistical control.* Shewhart states: "It seems to me that it is far safer to take some one physical operation such as drawing from a bowl as a physical model for an act that may be repeated at random, and then to require that any other repetitive operation believed to be random shall in addition produce results similar in certain respects to the results of drawing from a bowl before we act as though the operation in question were random."

18. It may be helpful to think of the three steps in the mass production process as steps in the Scientific Method. In this sense, specification, production, and inspection correspond, respectively, to formulating a hypothesis,

conducting an experiment, and testing the hypothesis. The three steps constitute the dynamic scientific process of acquiring knowledge.

19. The following story was related at one of Deming's now-famous four-day quality seminars: I remember him [Shewhart] pacing the floor in his room at the Hotel Washington before the third lecture. He was explaining something to me. I remarked that these great thoughts should be in his lectures. He said that they were already written up in his third and fourth lectures. I remarked that if he wrote up these lectures in the same way that he had just explained them to me, they would be clearer. He said that his writing had to be foolproof. I thereupon remarked that he had written his thoughts to be so darn foolproof that no one could understand them.

20. Halberstam, David (1960). "The War Effort during WWII." Lectures, Articles and Interview Notes.

21. This is a general consensus feeling among many historians and writers as to the inherent "evil" of Taylorism—machine over man. Walter Shewhart, to his credit and genius, tries to marry quality control and scientific management. In the foreword to his 1931 master work referred to in Endnote 8, he writes, "Broadly speaking, the object of industry is to set up economic ways and means of satisfying human wants and in so doing to reduce everything possible to routines requiring a minimum amount of human effort. Through the use of the Scientific Method, extended to take account of modern statistical concepts, it has been found possible to set up limits within which the results of routine efforts must lie if they are to be economical. Deviations in the results of a routine process outside such limits indicate that the routine has broken down and will no longer be economical until the cause of trouble is removed."

22. Bonstingal, John Jay (1992). *Schools of Quality.* New York: Free Press.

23. The Hawthorne Experiments, Elton Mayo, 1938.

24. Voehl, F.W. (1990). "The Deming Prize." *South Carolina Business Journal.* pp. 33–38.

25. This was first pointed out by Robert Chadman Wood in an article about Homer Sarasohn, published in *Forbes* in 1990.

26. Figure 4.2 ©1991 F.W. Voehl. Figure 4.3 ©1992 Strategy Associates, Inc.

ARTICLE

THE DEMING PRIZE VS. THE BALDRIGE AWARD*

Joseph F. Duffy

The Deming Prize and the Baldrige Award. They're both named after Americans, both very prestigious to win, both standing for a cry for quality in business, both engaged by their share of critics. One is 40 years old; the other a mere four. One resides in an alluring, foreign land; the other on American soil. One is awarded to the paradigm of Japanese business, individuals and international companies; the other to the best of U.S. business. One has grown in what a psychologist might call a mostly safe, nurturing environment; the other amongst a sometimes sour, sometimes sweet, bipolar parental image of government officials, academia and business gurus who seem to critically tug every way possible. One represents a country hailed as the world leader in quality; the other is trying to catch up—trying very hard.

A battle between Japan's Deming Prize and the Malcolm Baldrige National Quality Award would be as good a making for a movie as *Rocky* ever was: You have the older, wiser Japanese, who emanates a wisdom that withstands time, against the younger, quickly maturing American who has an outstanding reputation for being a victorious underdog. Who would win? We took the two awards to center ring, made them don their gloves and have a go.

ROUND 1: HISTORY

Although residing almost half a world apart, the Deming Prize and the Malcolm Baldrige National Quality Award are bonded by influence. After the ravages unleashed during World War II took a ruinous toll on Japan, W. Edwards Deming came to aid this seemingly hopeless land. With his expertise in statistical quality control (SQC), Deming helped lift Japan out of the rubble and into the limelight by having Japanese businesses apply SQC techniques.

---

* This article is reproduced from *Quality Digest*, August 1991, pp. 33–53. In it, the author interviewed four individuals representing organizations with a reputation for being involved in the formation of the Baldrige Award. While no conclusions are drawn, the topics are central to total quality and worthy of debate.

In 1951, the Union of Japanese Scientists and Engineers (JUSE) created an accolade to award companies that successfully apply companywide quality control (CWQC) based on statistical quality control. In honor of their American quality champion, JUSE named the award the Deming Prize.

Not until 31 years later did a similar prize take root in the United States, mainly due to the efforts of Frank C. Collins, who served as executive director of quality assurance for the Defense Logistics Agency and has formed Frank Collins Associates, Survival Twenty-One—a quality consulting firm; he also serves on the board of directors of the Malcolm Baldrige National Quality Award Consortium.

Collins, after many trips to Japan, based his U.S. quality award idea on the Deming Prize. "That's where I got the idea for the Malcolm Baldrige Award," he explains, "although I never in my wildest dreams expected it to be connected to Malcolm Baldrige."

Malcolm Baldrige, Secretary of Commerce in the Reagan administration, was killed in a rodeo accident in 1987. Reagan chose to honor Baldrige by naming the newly created award after him.

"The original concept was that it would be the National Quality Award," says Collins. "It would be strictly a private sector affair. The government would have no part in it other than the President being the awarder of the recognition."

ROUND 2: PROCESS

The Deming Prize has several categories: the Deming Prize for Individual Person, the Deming Application Prize and the Quality Control Award for Factory. Under the Deming Application Prize are the Deming Application Prize for Small Enterprise and the Deming Application Prize for Division. In 1984, another category was added: The Deming Application Prize to Oversea Companies, which is awarded to non-Japanese companies.

The Deming Application Prize has 10 examination items and is based on CWQC—the Prize's main objective.

A company or division begins the Deming Prize process by submitting an application form to the Deming Prize Committee, along with other pertinent information. Prospective applicants are advised to hold preliminary consultations with the secretariat of the Deming Prize Committee before completing and submitting the application.

After acceptance and notification, applicants must submit a description of quality control practices and a company business prospectus, *in Japanese*. If successful, the applicant will then be subject to a site visit. If the applicant passes, the Deming Prize is awarded.

Sound easy? Sometimes the applicant's information can fill up to 1,000 pages, and the examination process for U.S. companies is expensive.

The Baldrige Award applicant must first submit an Eligibility Determination Form, supporting documents and $50. Upon approval, the applicant must then submit an application package—running up to 50 pages for small business, 75 pages for a manufacturing or service company—and another fee. Among seven categories, 1,000 points are awarded. No particular score guarantees a site visit.

Each of the three categories—manufacturing, service and small company—are allowed up to two winners only.

ROUND 3: PURPOSE

The American obsession for winning is enormous. From Watergate to Iran-Contra, the American Revolution to Desert Storm, Americans have shown that they love to win no matter what the cost. So it's no wonder that as soon as quality awards and prizes have an impact, they fall under scrutiny. But most critics of these two world-class quality awards think these coveted prizes are mostly pristine in purpose.

Frank Voehl, *Quality Digest* columnist and corporate vice president and general manager of Qualtec Inc., a Florida Power & Light Group company, oversees the implementation of the total quality management programs within Qualtec's client companies. In 1987, Florida Power & Light (FPL) became the first and only U.S. company to win the Deming Prize. Through his work with hundreds of Japanese and U.S. companies, Voehl feels that there are seven reasons why companies quest for the Deming Prize or the Baldrige Award.

"The first general comment that a number of companies that I've talked to in Japan that have applied for the Deming Prize said was, 'We did not apply for the Deming Prize to win but to drive us toward better quality control,'" says Voehl. "Second is applying for and receiving the examination had more meaning than did winning the Prize." Voehl's other five reasons are:

- The audit or the exam itself helped point out many areas of deficiencies and continuous improvement activities that they hadn't noticed.

- Since the Deming Prize dictates a clear goal and time limit, quality control advanced at an extremely rapid rate.

- The company going for the quality award was able to accomplish in one or two years what would normally have taken five or ten years.

- There was a unification of a majority of the employees.

- They were able to communicate with a common language to the whole company. This is where the cultural change takes place.

Robert Peach, who was project manager of the Malcolm Baldrige National Quality Award Consortium for three years and now serves as a senior technical advisor to the administrator, feels the Baldrige Award "is not an award for the sake of the award—it is the 200,000 guidelines and applications that go out that matter, not the handful that actually apply."

And the companies that experiment with and implement the Baldrige criteria, as well as the Deming criteria, can only learn from their endeavor. However, for the companies taking it a step further and committing to win the prize, it isn't Little League, where the profits extracted from learning and having fun are supposed to outweigh the benefits of scoring more points than the other team. The Deming and the Baldrige are the Majors, where going for the award may mean 80-hour work weeks, quick hellos and goodbyes to spouses and missing your child's Little League games.

ROUND 4: GOING TO WAR

So your boss comes up to you and says, "Get ready—we're going for it." How you react may depend on the attitude of your senior-level management and the present quality state of your company. Ken Leach, a senior examiner for the Baldrige Award and founder of Leach Quality Inc., implemented the quality system at Globe Metallurgical—1988 winner of the Baldrige Award's small company category. He says winning the Baldrige was easy because its quality system was in place well before the birth of the Baldrige Award criteria.

"We got into it before Baldrige was even heard of, and we got into it at the impetus of our customers—Ford and General Motors in particular," explains Leach. "So we implemented a number of specific things to satisfy the customer, and you don't have a choice with them—you have to go through their audit system. We did that and did it very well. So that gave us the base to apply for the Baldrige and win it the very first year without trying to redo what we were already doing."

Leach says that because Globe was in such a readied state before the inception of the Baldrige Award, the company did not add any people or spend large sums of money on the implementation of a quality system. In fact, Globe was so advanced in its quality system that Leach claims he took the Baldrige Award application home after work on a Friday and returned it complete by the following Monday.

But even Leach agrees that Globe was exceptional and that not all companies can implement the Baldrige criteria as smoothly as Globe did.

Yokogawa-Hewlett-Packard (YHP) won the Deming Prize in 1982. Unlike Globe and its easy conquest of the Baldrige, YHP claims the quest for the Deming was no Sunday stroll. The company released the following statement in *Measure* magazine:

"Japanese companies compete fiercely to win a Deming Prize. Members of a management team typically work several hundred extra hours each month to organize the statistical charts, reports and exhibits for judging."[1] YHP also says that "audits had all the tension of a championship sports event."[2]

Voehl calls these extra hours and added stresses "pain levels and downside effects" and found that they were typical of most companies going for the Deming Prize. And because the Baldrige Award is a "second generation" of the Deming Prize, Voehl says the Baldrige Award is no exception to possible disruption. He explains that the quest for winning becoming greater than the quest for quality is a "natural thing that occurs within these organizations that you can't really prevent. Senior management focuses in on the journey and the overall effects that will happen as a result of going for the examination and the prize."

Voehl adds, "Getting ready for the examination and the site exams brings a tremendous amount of pressure upon the organizations, whether it's the Deming or the Baldrige, because of the implications that you should be the one department that results in the prize not being brought home."

William Golomski, who is the American Society for Quality Control's representative to JUSE, says deadline time for the award may be a time of pressure.

In the case of the Baldrige, there have been a few companies that hired consultants to help them get ready for a site visit after they've gone through an evaluation by examiners and senior examiners," recalls Golomski. "So I can understand that people who are still being asked to go through role playing for a site visit might get to the point where they'll say, 'Gosh, I don't know if I'm interested as I once was.'"

Collins looks at customers in a dual sense: your internal customers—employees or associates—and your external customers—the people who pay the freight to keep you in business.

"To me," Collins says forcefully, "when you *squeeze* your internal customer to win an award, you're really making a mockery of the whole thing."

But for the companies that take the Baldrige application guidelines and implement them without competing, Peach says the quality goal remains the biggest motivator.

"In my exposure both to applicants and other companies that are using the practice and guidelines independent of applying, I feel that they have the right perspective, that companies identify this as a pretty good practice of what quality practice should be," expounds Peach. "And they're using it that way. That's healthy; that's good."

Deming says it best: "I never said it would be easy; I only said it would work." And this piece of wisdom can pertain to the implementation and competing processes of both the Baldrige Award and the Deming Prize. But although sometimes not easy to pursue, these awards spark many companies to the awareness and benefits of a quality system. But as more companies win the Baldrige, more critics are discussing which accolade—the Baldrige or the Deming—holds more advantages over the other.

ROUND 5: ADVANTAGES VS. DISADVANTAGES

With a U.S. company capturing the Deming Prize, U.S. businesses are no longer without a choice of which world-class quality award to pursue. Motorola, before it went for the Baldrige Award, contemplated which award would improve Motorola's quality best, according to Stewart Clifford, president of Enterprise Media, a documentary film company that specializes in management topics. In a recent interview with Motorola's quality staff, Clifford asked if Motorola was interested in questing for the Deming Prize.

"I asked them the question about if they were looking at applying and going for the Deming," remembers Clifford. "And they said that they felt frankly that while the Deming Prize had some valuable points for them, the reason why they liked the Baldrige Award better was because of its much more intense focus on the customer."

But Voehl claims this is a misconception and that both approaches focus heavily on the customer. "Florida Power & Light really got a lot of negatives from our counselors that we weren't zeroing in on the external and internal customers enough," recalls Voehl. "We had to demonstrate how our quality improvement process was a means of planning and achieving customer satisfaction through TQC."

Section Seven of the Baldrige Award covers total customer satisfaction, and it's worth more points than any other section. In the Deming criteria, total customer satisfaction may seem lost among the need for applicants to document, document, document and use statistical approaches.

One reason Collins says he would compete for the Baldrige instead of the Deming is the Deming's unbending demand to have everything documented. "If you say something, you have to have a piece of paper that covers it," he jokes. "Having worked for the government for 33 years, I see that as a bureaucratic way of doing things. And the Japanese are extremely bureaucratic."

And in an open letter to employees from James L. Broadhead, FPL's chairman and CEO, printed in *Training* magazine, his employees confirm Collins' beliefs: "At the same time, however, the vast majority of the employees with whom I spoke expressed the belief that the mechanics of the QI [quality improvement] process have been overemphasized. They felt that we place too great an emphasis on indicators, charts, graphs, reports and meetings in which documents are presented and indicators reviewed."[3]

However, Collins says that what he likes about the Deming Prize criteria that's missing in the Baldrige Award criteria is the first two examination items of the Deming Prize: policy organization and its operation.

If you want people to understand what you mean by quality, you have to spell it out, you have to define it as policy, explains Collins. As far as objectives go, he remembers asking a Japanese firm what their objectives were. The president of this company said, "First to provide jobs to our company." "How many American firms would say that?" asks Collins. Organization and understanding its operation is extremely important. He says, "Those two criteria are the bedrock foundation of the Deming Prize that makes it somewhat stronger and of greater value than the Malcolm Baldrige National Quality Award."

Another point that may persuade a U.S. company to compete for one of the two awards is cost. All things considered, U.S. companies going for the Deming Application Prize to Oversea Companies seems more costly than U.S. companies competing for the Baldrige Award. Leach describes Globe's venture as very inexpensive: "It doesn't have to cost an arm and a leg for the Baldrige. You don't have to reinvent the wheel of what you're already doing." Peach worked with a small-category company that spent $6,000 on its Baldrige Award venture, and that included the application fee and retaining a technical writer for $1,000.

But these are small companies with 500 employees or fewer. FPL, on the other hand, with about 15,000 employees, spent $1.5 million on its quest for the Deming Prize, according to Neil DeCarlo of FPL's corporate communications. And there are some Baldrige applicants that have spent hundreds of thousands or even millions of dollars on their quality quest, according to *Fortune* magazine.[4]

But no matter how much the Baldrige applicant pays, whether it be $6,000 or millions, it still receives a feedback report as part of the application cost. In comparison, those companies not making it past the first level of the Deming Prize criteria may pay JUSE for counselors, who will come into the company and do a diagnostic evaluation.

Because FPL was a pioneer in the oversea competition, many of the costs that would have otherwise been associated with this award for an overseas company had been waived by JUSE, according to Voehl. But still, FPL dished out $850,000 of that million-and-a-half for counselor fees, says DeCarlo—an amount Voehl claims would be three or four times more if FPL had to hire a U.S. consulting firm.

One of FPL's reasons to go for the Deming award was because in 1986, when it decided to go for a quality award, the Baldrige Award did not yet exist. In fact, what many people, including some FPL critics, don't know is that the company heavily funded the activities leading to the Baldrige Award. FPL agreed not to try for the Baldrige Award for five years to deter any conflict of interest, says Voehl. Also, FPL had an excellent benchmarking company in Japan's Kansai Electric, which had already won the Deming Prize.

The Deming Prize puts no cap on the number of winners; the Baldrige allows a maximum of two winners for each of the three categories. Leach contests that by putting a limit on the winners, you make the Baldrige Award a more precious thing to win. Peach agrees. "I think there should be a limit," he says. "You just don't want scores of winners to dilute this."

Voehl disagrees. "We should take the caps off," he argues. "I think we'd do a lot more for the award, for the process if we didn't have a win–lose mentality toward it."

ROUND 6: CONTROVERSY

"The Baldrige is having such an impact," asserts Peach, "that now people will take a look at it and challenge. That will always happen—that's our American way." And at four years old, the Baldrige Award has already received a fair share of controversy. One of the most disturbing criticisms aimed at the Baldrige Award comes from Deming himself. Deming called the Baldrige Award "a terrible thing, a waste of industry" in a recent issue of *Automotive News*. The article states: "Among the reasons Deming denounces the award is its measurement of performance and the effects of training with numerical goals, which he cites as 'horrible things.'

"'It's a lot of nonsense,' he said. 'The guidelines for 1991 (make that) very obvious.'"[5]

Golomski says that Deming is unhappy with two parts of the Baldrige guidelines. One is the concept of numerical goals, which Deming believes can cause aberrations within companies. "I don't take quite as strong a stand as Deming does," Golomski explains. "He makes another statement about goals and that far too often, goals are set in the absence of any way of knowing how you're going to achieve these goals."

Leach does not know what to think of "Deming's non-supportive or active disregard for the Baldrige Award." He finds it ironic that "a company could very much have a Deming-type philosophy or a Deming-oriented kind of company and could do quite well in the Baldrige application. I'm sure that Cadillac [1990 Baldrige Award winner] must have had a number of Deming philosophies in place."

Even if Deming is trying to be the burr under the saddle and spark U.S. companies into a quality quest, Leach doesn't think that Deming's "serving the pursuit of quality in general or himself very well by making public statements like that."

But Voehl agrees with some of Deming's points. "Cadillac got severely criticized by the board of trustees of the Baldrige because Cadillac took the Baldrige Award and General Motors tried to use it as a marketing tool," he

Deming Prize Application Checklist: Items and Their Particulars

---

1. Policy

- Policies pursued for management, quality and quality control
- Methods of establishing policies
- Justifiability and consistency of policies
- Utilization of statistical methods
- Transmission and diffusion of policies
- Review of policies and the results achieved
- Relationship between policies and long- and short-term planning

2. Organization and Its Management

- Explicitness of the scopes of authority and responsibility
- Appropriateness of delegations of authority
- Interdivisional cooperation
- Committees and their activities
- Utilization of staff
- Utilization of quality circle activities
- Quality control diagnosis

3. Education and Dissemination

- Education programs and results
- Quality-and-control consciousness, degrees of understanding of quality control
- Teaching of statistical concepts and methods and the extent of their dissemination
- Grasp of the effectiveness of quality control
- Education of related company (particularly those in the same group, subcontractors, consignees and distributors)
- Quality circle activities
- System of suggesting ways of improvements and its actual conditions

4. Collection, Dissemination and Use of Information on Quality

- Collection of external information
- Transmission of information between divisions
- Speed of information transmission (use of computers)
- Data processing, statistical analysis of information and utilization of the results

5. Analysis

- Selection of key problems and themes
- Propriety of the analytical approach
- Utilization of statistical methods
- Linkage with proper technology
- Quality analysis, process analysis
- Utilization of analytical results
- Assertiveness of improvement suggestions

6. Standardization

- Systematization of standards
- Method of establishing, revising and abolishing standards
- Outcome of the establishment, revision or abolition of standards
- Contents of the standards
- Utilization of the statistical methods
- Accumulation of technology
- Utilization of standards

7. Control

- Systems for the control of quality and such related matters as cost and quantity
- Control items and control points
- Utilization of such statistical control methods as control charts and other statistical concepts
- Contribution to performance of quality circle activity
- Actual conditions of control activities
- State of matters under control

8. Quality Assurance

- Procedure for the development of new products and services (analysis and upgrading of quality, checking of design, reliability and other properties)
- Safety and immunity from product liability
- Process design, process analysis and process control and improvement
- Process capability
- Instrumentation, gauging, testing and inspecting
- Equipment maintenance and control of subcontracting, purchasing and services
- Quality assurance system and its audit
- Utilization of statistical methods
- Evaluation and audit of quality
- Actual state of quality assurance

9. Results

- Measurement of results
- Substantive results in quality, services, delivery, time, cost, profits, safety, environment, etc.
- Intangible results
- Measuring for overcoming defects

10. Planning for the Future

- Grasp of the present state of affairs and the concreteness of the plan
- Measures for overcoming defects
- Plans for further advances
- Linkage with long-term plans

says. "And that's not the intention. Those sort of things do not do the Baldrige Award any good because it seems like all you're interested in is public relations."

Cadillac has fallen under scrutiny from many critics for taking home the Baldrige Award.

After returning from consulting in Israel, Collins heard that Cadillac had won the Baldrige Award. "I couldn't believe my eyes," Collins exclaims. "Cadillac has gotten so much bad press over the last decade—transmission problems, difficulty with their diesel engines, their service record—a whole number of things that to me when they said Cadillac won it, I said, 'Impossible. They couldn't win it. Somebody's pulling a cruel joke.'"

Deming is not the only quality guru criticizing the Baldrige Award. Philip Crosby says in *Quality Digest* (February 1991) that customers should nominate the companies that compete for the Baldrige, not the companies themselves.

It is difficult to come by harsh criticism about the Deming Prize since few Americans are familiar with it. However, Collins questions FPL's quest for winning as superseding their quest for quality.

"There's no question in my mind that Florida Power & Light's John Hudiburg was intent on leading Florida Power & Light in a blaze of glory," insists Collins. "And money was absolutely no consideration as far as winning the Deming Prize. I don't know what the final tab on it was, but he bought the prize—there's no question about it."

Collins' comments do not go without backing. A number of articles on FPL's quest contain complaints from disgruntled employees who worked long hours to win the Deming Prize.

"If the goal is to win an award, then the cost of winning the award is not worth the award itself," Voehl admits. "The focus needs to be on the outcomes for the organization." And Voehl feels that FPL's quality outcomes very much outweigh the cost put forth.

ROUND 7: CONSULTANTS

With the two awards, there's a big difference in the use of consultants or counselors, as they're called in Japan. In the case of the Deming Prize, a successful applicant uses counselors trained by JUSE throughout the examination, explains Golomski. "For the Baldrige, you're on your own or you use whomever you wish to help you—if you think it's worth it."

"Considering the tremendous number of brochures I get every day," says Collins, "it appears that everybody and his brother is an expert on the Malcolm Baldrige National Quality Award. And my experience tells me that there *ain't* that many experts on the Malcolm Baldrige National Quality Award."

So, are some consultants or counselors using the Baldrige Award to prey on aspiring companies? Voehl says he sees it happening all over and calls it "absolutely preposterous and absurd and unethical."

Voehl compares it to just like everybody jumping on the TQC bandwagon. "Everybody from a one-man or two-man mom-and-pop consulting company to a 1,000-employee consulting arm of the Big 8 seems to be an expert in TQM," he says. "It's like a dog with a rag: They're shaking it and shaking it, and they won't let it go because they see it can mean money to their bottom line. It's giving the consulting field a terrible black eye. It's giving the people who bring in these consultants the expectations clearly that they are going to win the award. These are false expectations, false hopes and false starts. They shouldn't even be looking at winning the award; they should be looking at implementing a quality system that can ensure customer satisfaction."

But there are good reasons to have consultants help you through the Baldrige quest. Leach points out that if a CEO of a company needs to change his or her approach on something, an employee will probably be intimidated to approach the CEO; instead, a consultant can do this. Also a consultant may carry in an objective view that brings different ideas to the company.

Deming Prize counselors, however, have a reputation to guard. That's why Golomski feels FPL had no chance to "buy the Prize."

"The counselor simply wouldn't agree with them that they [FPL] were ready," Golomski argues. "The counselors help an organization improve itself, but if they don't think the company is ready for the big leagues, they simply won't recommend it."

ROUND 8: MODIFICATIONS

The Baldrige Award criteria are constantly modified to meet changing expectations. This is how it grows stronger, becomes more mature. When awarded the Baldrige Award, recipients must share their knowledge of total quality, but Golomski wants to see better ways of technology transfer.

Collins thinks we will probably have a follow-up award similar to the Japan Quality Control Prize—which is awarded to Deming Prize winners if they have improved their quality standards five years after winning the Deming Prize and pass rigorous examination—but not until the Baldrige Award can be further improved.

Peach feels the Baldrige criteria are at a position where modifications will be in smaller increments. He says cycle time might become important enough to be emphasized more.

The possible modifications of the Deming Prize are hard to predict. However, modifications of the Baldrige Award may be based on the Deming Prize's influence.

ROUND 9: SAVING FACE

Junji Noguchi, executive director of JUSE, was contacted for an interview for this article. When he learned of the subject matter—comparing the two world-class quality awards—he declined to answer. He said, "I am sorry I have to reply that I cannot answer your interviews. That is because the contents were not preferable and that they are not what I was expecting."

Noguchi continued, "Awards or prizes in the country have been established under the most suitable standards and methods considering their own background of industries, societies and cultures. We do not understand the meaning of comparing awards in different countries that have different backgrounds."

Noguchi is displaying some of that ancient wisdom and showing a difference in our cultures that even Americans find difficult to explain. Is this why their award has been going strong for 40 years and why the Baldrige Award is a 4-year-old child growing much too fast thanks to our intrinsic desire to slice it up, examine it and try to put it back together more completely than before? Maybe. But as a result, our U.S. quality award will always remain provocative and exciting and keep the people talking. And this is good.

REFERENCES

1. "YHP Teamwork Takes the Prize," Measure (January–February 1983), 3000 Hanover St., Palo Alto, CA 94304, pg. 6.
2. Measures, pg. 6.
3. James L. Broadhead, "The Post-Deming Diet: Dismantling a Quality Bureaucracy," Training, Lakewood Building, 50 S. Ninth St., Minneapolis, MN 55402, pg. 41.
4. Jeremy Main, "Is the Baldrige Overblown?" Fortune (July 1, 1991), Time & Life Building, Rockefeller Center, New York, NY 10020-1393, pg. 62.
5. Karen Passino, "Deming Calls Baldrige Prize 'Nonsense,'" Automotive News (April 1, 1991), 1400 E. Woodbridge, Detroit, MI 48207.

CHAPTER 5

THE HOUSE
OF QUALITY

The basic concepts and principles associated with total quality are represented by the House of Total Quality (Figure 5.1). As in a well-built house, the major components of the House of Total Quality are (1) the *roof*, or superstructure, consisting of the social, technical, and management systems; (2) the *four pillars* of customer satisfaction, continuous improvement, speaking with facts, and respect for people; (3) the *foundation* of four managerial levels—strategy, process, project, and task management; and (4) the *four cornerstones* of mission, vision, values, and goals and objectives.

As in building any house, the plans must be developed first, usually by experienced individuals working together—a team. Once the plans are approved, construction (implementation) can begin.

Total quality efforts frequently fail because the individuals responsible for the efforts (i.e., management) are unable to carry out their responsibilities. They do not recognize the importance of systems thinking and do not have a well-defined purpose and process to follow. That is why Deming, *kaizen*, and the Baldrige Award focus on the following ten management guidelines[1] as part of the implementation process:

- Recognize quality improvement as a system.
- Define it so others can recognize it, too.
- Analyze its behavior.
- Work with subordinates in improving the system.
- Measure the quality of the system.
- Develop improvements in the quality of the system.

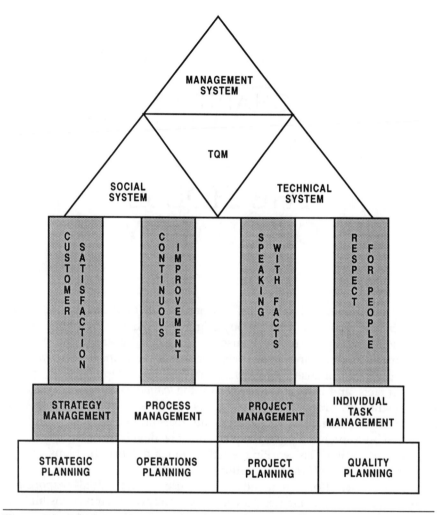

Figure 5.1 House of Total Quality. (Source: ©1992 Strategy Associates, Inc.)

- Measure the gains in the quality, if any, and link these to customer delight and quality improvement.
- Take steps to guarantee holding the gains.
- Attempt to replicate the improvements into other areas of the organization.
- Tell others about the lessons learned.

These guidelines, when implemented, will assure success because of their impact on all aspects of the enterprise. They are also reflected in the House of Total Quality, which illustrates the universality of the basic principles and procedures for carrying out total quality. Use of the House of Total Quality does not negate, but rather supports, the works of Deming and the Baldrige Award. Throughout this chapter, the 14 principles of Deming and the seven categories of the Baldrige Award are presented within the context of the House of Total Quality.

SYSTEMS AND TOTAL QUALITY

The superstructure of the House of Total Quality involves a system composed of three subsystems held together by total quality (Figure 5.2). The three subsystems are social, technical, and management. Their interdependencies are depicted in the three interlocking circles of a ballantine, as shown in Figure 5.2. The successful implementation of total quality and continuous improvement efforts requires the redefinition of management to recognize the importance of the systems. As Deming[2] states, "The people work in a system. The job of the manager is to work on the system, to improve it continuously, with their help." Within the House of Total Quality, the manager must work on the three systems.

The Social System

The social system includes factors associated with the formal and informal characteristics of the organization: (1) organizational culture (the values,

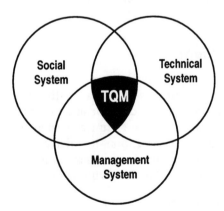

Figure 5.2 Implementing Total Quality Management System Model.

norms, attitudes, role expectations, and differentiation that exist in each organization); (2) quality of social relationships between individual members and among groups, including reward structures and symbols of power; and (3) behavioral patterns between members, including roles and communication. It is the social system that has the greatest impact on such factors as motivation, creativity, innovative behavior, and teamwork. Managers have a major responsibility for the nature and character of the social system.

The social system may or may not have a planned function within the organization. Many managers would like to deny, or at least ignore, the existence of cultures, roles, or organizational values. However, social systems exist, and they exert influence, both positive and negative, on the activities of an organization.

To achieve total quality, a social system must be developed in which constituent or customer satisfaction, continuous improvement, management based on facts, and a genuine respect for people are accepted practices of the enterprise. Frequently this requires a substantial change in the social system, and change does not come easily for most organizations. Change usually occurs when the cost (disadvantages, lost opportunities) of remaining the same becomes greater than the benefit of an alternative condition.

Figure 5.3 represents a fishbone diagram (also known as a causal analysis diagram) of the social system characteristics that help create a total quality organization. As shown in Figure 5.3, six areas of strategy must be addressed in order to change and transform the culture of an organization to a quality-driven organization: (1) the environment, (2) product or service, (3) methods, (4) people, (5) organizational structure, and (6) mindset of total quality improvement. Thus, in organizations driven by total quality, people feel they belong, feel pride in their work, learn continuously, and work to their potential. Each of these major areas will be covered in some detail in the following sections.

The Technical System

According to Tribus,[3] "The technical system includes all the tools and machinery, the practice of quality and the quantitative aspects of quality. If you can measure it, you can probably describe and perhaps improve it using the technical systems approach." The technical system is concerned with the flow of work through the organization. It is driven by two primary guides: fulfillment of its mission and service to the customer. In most organizations, the technical system contains the following core elements:

- Accumulation of technology
- Pursuit of standardization
- Workflow, materials, and specifications

- Job definitions and responsibility
- Machine/person interface
- Number and type of work steps
- Availability and use of information
- Decision-making processes
- Problem-solving tools and processes
- Physical arrangements and equipment, tools, and people

Technology in the information technology (IT) world has even more of an impact. Yesterday's promises are finally being fulfilled through the advances of technology. The following technological advances are making the extended enterprise a reality.

Communication Networks and Associated Technologies—In today's environment, separation of data from text, graphics, images, and voice is not acceptable. Technology is available to integrate all of these components and allow employees to work in the most natural setting possible to achieve greater productivity and customer satisfaction.

Integration of Processes and Systems—The ability to provide timely information to any and all levels of a highly leveraged task team organization, as compared to the hierarchical organization, requires complete integration of many functions. The historical boundaries of organizations are being destroyed. The new organizations are not only crossing functional lines of historical organization, but are also creating strategic alliances with vendors. Partners are acting as strategic partners with their customers. Highly visible teams are assigned tasks that cross all boundaries of an organization, and teams are empowered to solve problems or create solutions. The systems and the organization must be designed to complement, not retard, these types of functions. Data collection, data storage, and data availability must be completely rethought to meet these demands. The old paradigm of control and knowledge by a few is gone. The new paradigm is to provide information to all who need to know in a timely manner. The entire concept of proprietary systems that prohibit the open flow of information within an industry and within an organization is dead!

Open Architecture

Hierarchical organizations controlled information. Command-and-control techniques from the early 1900s influenced the design of the IT industry, and most systems in the industry sector were designed to honor this time-proven methodology. Proprietary software and hardware designed to only comple-

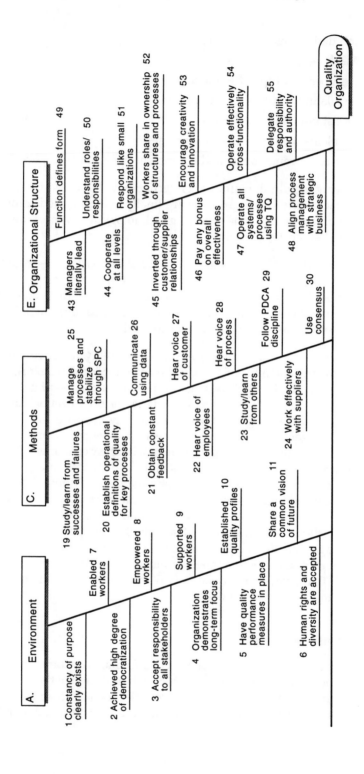

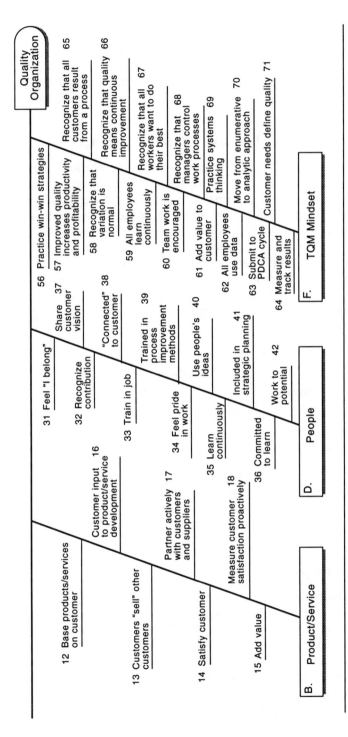

Figure 5.3 Social System Characteristics of a Total Quality Organization (Fishbone Diagram).

ment selected software were the trademark of all IT services. The designers of corporate systems followed suit and made system fortresses out of the smokestack organization. Knowledge, culture, and financial investment have made it difficult for the IT industry to break the old paradigms and move toward the open systems necessary to support today's enterprise.

Client/Server and the Open Systems Concept

The open systems concept has been a major contributor to an organization's ability to reengineer its business. It places information in the hands of the people who need the information without extra steps and cost. Customer-centered organizations without tall hierarchies are providing truly enabled employees at the point of contact and providing enriched jobs for those who have the information, knowledge, and responsibility to satisfy the customer.

Knowledge is distributed to the worker, not just the control points. This promotes a team approach and a greater opportunity for motivated people to provide greater innovation and ideas for improvement.

The expected benefits from analyzing and improving the technical system(s) are to:

- Reduce (eliminate) waste and rework
- Reduce (eliminate) negative variation
- Increase learning
- Reduce (eliminate) interruptions and idle time
- Save time and money
- Increase employee control over the work process
- Reduce bottlenecks and frustration
- Improve safety and quality of work life
- Increase speed and responsiveness
- Improve customer satisfaction

The Managerial System

The managerial system includes factors associated with (1) the organizational structure (formal design, policies, division of responsibilities, and patterns of power and authority); (2) the mission, vision, and goals of the organization; and (3) administrative activities (planning, organizing, directing, coordinating, and controlling organizational activities). Management provides the framework for the policies, procedures, practices, and leadership of the organization. The management system is deployed at four levels: strategy, process, project, and personal management. These comprise the foundation of the House of Total Quality and will be briefly discussed later in this chapter and more thoroughly in Chapter 6.

As stated at the beginning of this chapter, the Deming principles and Baldrige categories are an integral part of the House of Total Quality. Deming's first two principles and the third category of the Baldrige Award address the superstructure and the three systems described above.

Deming Principle 1—Create a constancy of purpose toward improvement. Deming is saying that we need to look to the future in terms of the business for which we are responsible. Items such as training of employees and investment in long-term projects, more often than not, do not yield returns in the short term.

Deming Principle 2—Adopt the new philosophy. This is a difficult area, and changing a culture can take years. Management must have the courage and the vision to understand the new philosophy and live up to the challenge.

Baldrige Category 3—Strategic quality planning examines the planning process of the enterprise and how all key quality requirements are integrated into an overall plan. Also examined are short and longer term plans, as well as how quality and performance requirements are deployed to all work units.

Quality and service are the means, but value for the customer is the end. The final judge of an organization's performance is the customer. As we exercise many means to achieve customer satisfaction, we must not lose sight of the fact that the ultimate goal is that our customer perceive that the product or the service we have rendered provides value. Cost, quality, scheduling, and reliability are all valid items to improve and provide powerful means to achieve our value-added goal.

The effectiveness of an organization is measured by its managerial systems. Most people, however, do not take time to understand the power of their managerial systems. It is here that an organization can gain the most important advantage. Deming states that "80% of the problems with American business is management." Actually, that is a misstatement; the figure is probably closer to 90 percent.

The managerial system consists of three subsystems (Figure 5.4). Each subsystem is divided into other systems. Management systems are composed of three major processes: policy management, quality assurance (ISO 9000), and daily management.

Policy Management

Policy management (Figure 5.5) is a business planning process used to formulate, deploy, and achieve business objectives by concentrating resources

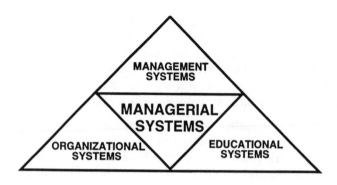

Figure 5.4 Subsystems of the Managerial System.

on high-priority items. This method of management links business activities to the long-term view of the company and provides the system that propels a company toward its vision, while increasing the opportunity for competitive advantage.

It is here that the talkers are separated from the doers. We can talk about principles, give token training to our employees, or say that people are our most important resource. We can even start a few quality circles, but it is only through implementing the systems changes that focus on those items that are critical to the success of the organization and its stakeholders that we start the journey toward improvement.

Policy management is called many things and involves many different functions. True policy management in the total quality management (TQM) arena is the *systematic process needed to direct an organization toward priority issues of the organization*. It provides the vehicle to accomplish the corporate

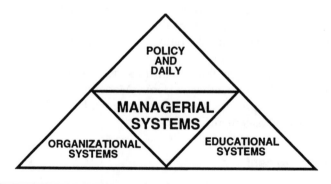

Figure 5.5 Policy and Daily Management.

short- and long-term strategies and achieve customer satisfaction. Policy management provides a blueprint to the organization for how and what is required to achieve its goals.

Policy management also provides a system of indicators, used for tracking progress and results, as well as outlining the strategic plan framework. (For additional information, see Abstract 5.1 at the end of this chapter.)

Improved communication within an organization is also a very important factor and results from the deployment of the policies identified in the policy formulation stage. It provides a clear road map for where the organization is going and what is important to all the stakeholders. This road map is used by teams and individuals to focus their energy on the areas that can best help the organization achieve its goals. The cumulative benefits of the creativity, innovation, and increased productivity of the organization's employees is wonderful, and the cost is recognition, training, and appreciation—a bargain in any business calculation. Managers who listen to their employees and act on their ideas and contributions—what a unique concept! (For additional information, see Abstract 5.2 at the end of this chapter.)

Daily Management

Daily management is a business planning process that provides a systematic focus for day-to-day or repetitive activities not handled by policy management. Examples include processing of sales orders, preparation of certain reports, etc. It involves the aspects of control, promotion of improvement, and review and is founded in the concepts of efficiency and continuous improvement.

Continuous improvement through daily management activities helps accomplish and maintain the gains made through policy management. It also provides the processes and tools to make improvements in our daily activities and builds teamwork within the organization.

Daily management does not receive as much attention as policy management, but it is a very critical part of the TQM journey. Daily management provides a means to improve the daily, routine functions and the gains an organization makes through continuous improvement activities. It also controls the gains made through policy management.

The next important part of the management systems is the organizational systems (Figure 5.6), or how the organization utilizes its personnel to accomplish tasks.

Cross-Functional Management—Management teams formed to carry out company initiatives that cross departmental or functional lines. Key customer concerns are generally cross-functional in nature and require coordination.

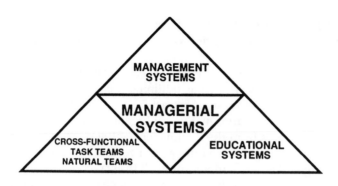

Figure 5.6 Organizational Systems.

Task Teams—Teams formed for a specific purpose, either in the area of policy management or for a major departmental concern. Membership is determined by expertise and organizational background, and individuals are selected by management.

Natural Teams—Similar to quality circles, natural teams have a more homogeneous membership and concentrate their efforts on department production processes. This concept implies that all departmental efforts can be viewed as process and results in the production of something.

The educational system is closely aligned to the social system and must reflect the values and principles of the organization, as shown in Figure 5.7.

Statistical Thought Process—Applying the concepts of priority and variation to the task of management at all levels. Suggested areas for concentration include the seven basic statistical tools (check sheet, Pareto analysis, cause-and-effect diagram, histogram, control chart, scatter diagram, run chart). Additional tools include the graph, process decision program chart, arrow diagram, matrix data analysis, affinity diagram, relations diagram, and systematic diagram) and more advanced techniques such as multivariate analysis, multiple regression, fault tree analysis, etc.

Human Thought Process—The concept of valuing employees and treating them as the most valuable resource encompasses the human thought process. It is in this area that the techniques of team building and consensus are introduced to the organization and the underlying principle of *respect for people* is woven into the fabric of the management system.

The value system or principles of an organization support the managerial, technical, and social systems, which in turn protect the principles and values of the organization.

Figure 5.7 Educational System.

THE PILLARS OF QUALITY

TQM in any organization is supported by four driving forces, or pillars, that move the organization toward the full application of quality service. The four pillars of the House of Total Quality (see Figure 5.1) are customer service, continuous improvement, processes and facts, and respect for people. All are distinct but equal in potential strength. All four must be addressed; minimizing one weakens the others. By not addressing one, the entire House of Total Quality will fall.

Serving the Customer (The First Pillar)

Peter Drucker has said that "The business of business is getting and keeping customers." This philosophy in the House of Total Quality is the first pillar—serving the customer (Figure 5.8). In today's complex business world, it is difficult to clearly identify the "customer." In the world of IT, we must understand the internal customer as well as our ultimate customer. To focus on customer satisfaction places the responsibility for quality in each step of the process and leads us to recognize that the next process is our customer.

While this sounds like an easy philosophy to follow, all too often we take the concept of "product out" instead of considering our customer's needs and evaluating those needs in a "market in" attitude. A "market in" attitude means that we listen to our customers and design the system, product, or service based on their real needs and not our perceived evaluation of their needs.

In order for organizations to be successful, IT must provide systems that are responsive to both the internal and external customers' needs. The sys-

Figure 5.8 Serving the Customer.

tems must be open and allow decisions to be made at any level of the organization, as defined by needs. Today's applications require real-time access by many to critical information.

All too often, management states that the goal is to provide total customer satisfaction but does not have the systems to achieve it. Nor does management take the time to define who its customers are or what quality characteristics are required to meet their needs. This should be a priority of management. By understanding the needs of the customer, management can develop the systems and provide the necessary training and resources to meet those needs.

One of the main issues the technologist faces is how to improve personal service for the customer while applying new technologies.

Why should we take the time to understand our customers and try to satisfy them? A study by the U.S. Office of Consumer Affairs reveals that only 4 percent of unhappy customers complain. The remaining 96 percent never give you a chance to correct the problem; they just tell nine other people about the problem, and 90 percent of the dissatisfied customers never purchase the product or service from the company again. The study goes on to say that 22 percent of the issues that you do not hear about are serious problems.

Continuous Improvement (The Second Pillar)

Continuous improvement (Figure 5.9) is both a commitment (continuous quality improvement) and a process (continuous process improvement). The Japanese word for this second pillar is *kaizen*, and it is, according to Imai,[4] the single most important concept in Japanese management. The commitment to quality is initiated with a statement of dedication to a shared mission and vision and the empowerment of all participants to incrementally move toward the vision. The process of improvement is accomplished through the initiation of small, short-term projects and tasks throughout the organization which collectively are driven by the achievement of the long-term vision and mission. Both are necessary; one cannot be done without the other.

Continuous improvement is dependent on two elements: learning the appropriate processes, tools, and skills and practicing these newfound skills on small achievable projects. The process for continuous improvement, first advanced many years ago by Shewhart and implemented by Deming, is *Plan-Do-Check-Act* (PDCA) (Figure 5.10), a never-ending cycle of improvement that occurs in all phases of the organization. While no rigid rules are required to carry out the process, the general framework of each step can be described.

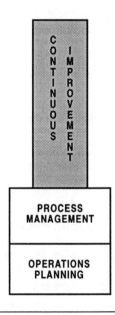

Figure 5.9 Continuous Improvement.

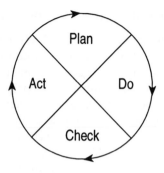

Figure 5.10 Plan-Do-Check-Act.

The first step, *plan*, asks such key questions as what changes are needed, what results are needed, what obstacles need to be overcome, are data available, and what new information is needed. *Do* is the implementation of a small-scale change or pilot test to provide data for answers. *Check* is the assessment and measurement of the effects of the change or test. *Act*, the final step, first asks whether the data confirm the intended plan, whether other variables are influencing the plan, and whether the risks in proceeding are necessary and worthwhile. Then, based on these answers, the project or task is modified and moves into the *plan* stage again, where the iteration continues, expanding knowledge and implementing further improvement. Ideally, this process would continue indefinitely.

Two of Deming's principles and two Baldrige categories address this important aspect of total quality:

Deming Principle 3—Cease dependence on inspection and testing to achieve quality. Reduce the need for inspection by building quality into the programs and services in the first place. Within IT, cease dependence on testing to achieve quality. Provide learning experiences that create quality performance.

Deming Principle 5—Improve constantly and forever the system of program quality and service in order to improve quality performance.

Baldrige Category 5—*Management of process quality* is the key element of how the organization develops and realizes the full potential of the work force to pursue its quality and performance objectives. Also examined are the efforts required to build and maintain an environment for quality excellence that is conducive to full participation and personal organizational growth.

Baldrige Category 6—Quality and operational results examines quality levels and improvement trends in operational performance of IT and supplier quality, as well as the current quality and performance levels of competitors.

In the development of systems, the concepts of continuous improvement come into play in two significant processes. The first is in the development of systems and the second is in the support of systems.

The first part of the *plan* cycle of PDCA in the system development cycle is the requirements phase. This phase, tied to the concepts of customer satisfaction, builds the plan for the product based on customers' valid needs. Focus groups, customer councils, user groups, and partnerships help define the needs of the chain of customers that most systems must serve.

The second part of the *plan* cycle involves the analysis and design phase, where technologies and customer needs are married. This portion of the *plan* phase also requires interface with customers to assure compliance and understanding.

The *do* stage is the development cycle in the system. A clear definition of the quality measurements of the system is required before the development begins. Items include considerations such as:

How to measure customer satisfaction:
- Capability
- Performance
- Availability
- Training
- Reliability
- Changeability
- System documentation
- Flexibility
- Ease of use

Quality of product delivered:
- Timeliness
- Cost
- Ease of installation
- Backlog of errors
- Fit to specification

These are some of the major items that should be understood at the beginning of the development cycle. Measurement processes should be considered and designed prior to beginning the project.

The *check* functions may include:

- A quality system plan
- Performance design points
- Prototyping
- Nine cycle change control systems
- Development of change control systems
- Publications change control systems
- Training
- Documentation
- Quality assurance review
- Unit testing plan
- Integrated testing plan
- Field test

The *act* cycle is the driver for change. It is easy to forget the fact that PDCA is a cycle and that within the individual parts we must PDCA each of the activities with which we are dealing. The metrics of performance must be continually monitored, and these items must be acted upon as opportunities for continuous improvement.

The life cycle system an organization develops with its customers should be its road map to appropriate change and control.

The second significant use of PDCA is the support activity, also known as the maintenance phase of the system. The *kaizen* approach to customer satisfaction means continuing improvement in all aspects of the life of a product or service. (For additional information, see Abstract 5.3 at the end of this chapter.)

Managing with Facts (The Third Pillar)

Deming, paraphrasing the axiom "In God we trust, all others bring cash," noted the central tenet of this third pillar (Figure 5.11): *In God we trust. All others bring facts.* Too often, the management of a program is based on intuition, influence, hunches, or organizational politics. External and internal forces require the elimination of this precarious managerial approach. Stable or diminished funding; the increasing cost of salaries, supplies, and services; the increased number of women and minorities at all levels of the organization; and continuous competition will force *all* organizations to be driven by decisions and actions based on facts, rather than only partial awareness of the issues, reliance on traditional networks, and/or just doing what has always been done. Tom Peters, paraphrasing the axiom "If it isn't broke, don't fix it," repeatedly states, *"If it isn't broke, break it!"*

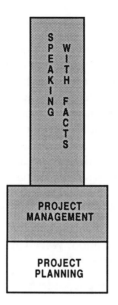

Figure 5.11 Managing with Facts.

This requires a substantial shift in many areas to a process of carrying out continuous improvement (the second pillar—Plan-Do-Check-Act) and effective process management through the extensive use of a variety of tools designed to gather and analyze data and make decisions based on facts (the third pillar). Seven basic, highly effective tools were identified early in the history of the total quality movement: fishbone diagram (cause-and-effect diagram), check sheet, control chart, histogram, Pareto diagram, run chart, and scatter diagram; the control chart, cause-and-effect diagram, and Pareto diagram are the three tools most commonly used in the total quality process.

None of the Deming principles or Baldrige categories directly apply to this pillar. Managing with facts requires two actions. First, collect objective data so that the information is valid. Second, whenever possible, manage according to this information and not according to instinct, preconceptions, or other nonobjective factors. Managing with facts is important because *people* collect and use the facts, providing a common framework for communication and understanding what is being done and what needs to be done. Thus, not only does it provide a solid base of objective data upon which reliable decisions can be made, but it also contributes to empowerment of and respect for the people within the organization (the fourth pillar of the House of Total Quality).

Respect for People (The Fourth Pillar)

For whom does one work? No one works just for the customers and the company. In the end, each individual works for himself or herself, trying to create a meaningful and satisfying life in the best way possible. Fortunately, quality of output goes hand in hand with quality of work. The only way total quality will be attained is through total commitment and participation.

Every employee must be fully developed and involved. The result will be an empowered individual—a value-added resource, with loyalty to the program, the team, and the entire organization. Respect for people (Figure 5.12) often boils down to such simple things as:

- Creating a sense of purpose in the workplace so that people are motivated to do their best

- Keeping people informed and involved and showing them how they are a part of the bigger picture

- Educating and developing people so that they are the best that they can be at what they do

- Helping people communicate well so that they can perform their jobs with peak effectiveness

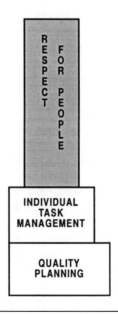

Figure 5.12 Respect for People.

- Delegating responsibility and authority downward so that people are not just doing what they are told, but are taking the initiative to try to make things work better

It is not enough to just go through the motions. These behaviors work well when they are part of a genuine attitude of respect and caring for other people. Managers who do not have this attitude of respect and caring cannot pretend for very long that they do.

It is to this fourth pillar that Deming directed 8 of his 14 principles. It reinforces the reason he retains the opinion that most organizations are unable to truly implement total quality because of their pervasive attitude that people are an expense to be controlled rather than an asset to be developed.

Deming Principle 6—Institute education and training for everyone: management and all employees.

Deming Principle 7—The goal of supervision should be to help people use procedures, techniques, machines, and materials to do a better job. Leadership of management and employees is in need of a general overhaul.

Deming Principle 8—Drive out fear, so that everyone can work effectively for the organization. Create an environment in which people are encouraged to speak freely.

Deming Principle 9—Break down barriers between corporate entitles and all departments. Each area must work as a team (work teams and cross-functional teams). Develop strategies for increasing the cooperation among groups and individuals.

Deming Principle 10—Eliminate slogans, exhortations, and targets that promote perfect performance and new levels of productivity (e.g., write X lines of code, reduce expenses by X percent). Exhortations create adversarial relationships. The bulk of the causes of low quality and low productivity belong to the system and thus lie beyond the control of employees.

Deming Principle 11—Eliminate performance standards (quotas) for employees. Eliminate management by numbers and numerical goals. Substitute leadership.

Deming Principle 12—Remove barriers that rob employees of the right to take pride in and enjoy the satisfaction of personal performance and productivity. This means, among other things, abolishing annual or merit ratings and management by objectives. The focus of responsibility for all managers must be changed from quantity to quality.

Deming Principle 13—Institute a vigorous program of education and self-improvement for everyone.

THE FOUNDATION AND CORNERSTONES

The roof and four pillars rest upon a foundation and cornerstones which consist of four managerial and planning processes. This discussion has evolved from a broad systemic framework, i.e., the three TQM systems (social, technical, and managerial), to the four principles that guide these systems (customer satisfaction, continuous improvement, managing with facts, and respect for people), and now to the procedural functions that make the systems and principles operational. The roof (the systems) is the most theoretical, with the principles providing guides for actualizing the system but still not making it operational. It remains for the managerial and planning processes to be put into action in order to actualize the quality improvement process. Therefore, with the metaphor of the House of Total Quality, it is appropriate that these functions are the foundation and cornerstones of the entire house. It is here where the construction begins. It is also here where you get your hands dirty!

Strategy Management—Quality planning is the broadest of the managerial levels. It establishes the organization-wide TQM strategy and framework. It is a top-down strategy, initiated by senior management but developed with everyone involved through a variety of consensus, team-building, and brainstorming activities. The outcome is a three- to five-year plan that contains the mission, vision, guiding principles or values, and goals and objectives for the organization. "Ownership" of the plan is achieved when everyone acknowledges the focus of the plan and accepts its potential to help the organization move in a common direction.

Process Management—Operations planning assures that all key processes work in harmony with the mission and meet the needs and expectations of the constituents or customers by maximizing operational effectiveness. Its key components are continuous improvement problem-solving methods. Efforts at this managerial stage are often cross-functional, as many functions cross departmental boundaries. This requires interdepartmental collaboration, with process and indicator functions appropriately assigned. The outcome is a common process and language for documenting and communicating activities and decisions and for realizing success in eliminating waste, redundancy, and bottlenecks.

Project Management—Project planning establishes a system to effectively plan, organize, implement, and control all of the resources and activities needed for successful completion of the quality program. It is at this stage that teams are formed to solve and carry out both process- and policy-related initiatives. Team activities are linked to operational objectives and improvement targets. They develop the critical success factors: control systems, schedules, tracking mechanisms, performance indicators, and skill analysis. The outcome of each is a vision of the project that is linked to the organizational objectives, a work plan with designated milestones, a communication process for documenting key decisions and improvements, and a project completed on time and within budget.

Personal Management—Quality planning provides all employees with the means to implement continuous improvement of the above processes and systems through development of individual work functions and control. Each individual is guided through the development of a personal mission and vision.

ENDNOTES

1. Tribus, Myron (1992). "Ten Management Practices." In Voehl, Frank (1992). *Total Quality: Principles and Practices within Organizations.* Coral Springs, FL: Strategy Associates, pp. IV, 20.
2. Deming, W. Edwards (1986). *Out of Crisis.* Cambridge, MA: MIT Center for Advanced Engineering Study.
3. Tribus, Myron (1992). "Ten Management Practices." In Voehl, Frank (1992). *Total Quality: Principles and Practices within Organizations.* Coral Springs, FL: Strategy Associates, pp. IV, 19.
4. Imai, Masaaki (1986). *Kaizen: The Key to Japan's Competitive Success.* New York: Random House. He also states, "The message of the kaizen strategy is that not a day should go by without some kind of improvement being made somewhere in the company" (p. 5).

ABSTRACT

ABSTRACT 5.1
THE BALANCED SCORECARD—MEASURES THAT DRIVE PERFORMANCE

Kaplan, Robert S. and Norton, David P.
Harvard Business Review, January–February 1992, pp. 71–79

"What you measure is what you get," begin these authors. "Traditional financial accounting measures like return on investment and earnings per share can give misleading signals for continuous improvement and innovation—activities today's competitive environment demands." The remedy, they say, is a "balanced scorecard," a group of measures that summarize progress toward the objectives most important to the organization. Anything else is like trying to fly a plane by watching just the altimeter and ignoring measures like air speed, remaining fuel, and so on. The authors conducted a year-long research project with 12 companies to explore ways of finding the combination of operational and financial measures that would constitute a "balanced scorecard." They concluded that there are four important measurement perspectives:

- Financial perspective (How do we look to shareholders?)

- Customer perspective (How do customers see us?)

- Internal business perspective (What must we excel at?)

- Innovation and learning perspective (Can we continue to create value?)

Each of these perspectives implies a set of goals that in turn imply measures of performance in reaching those goals. To illustrate possible goals and measures, the authors describe how a disguised electronics firm derived its own balanced scorecard of goals and measures from these four perspectives, and the authors supplement these examples with measures adopted by other businesses. They conclude with some suggestions on how to ensure that balanced scorecard measures will result in improved financial results. (©*Quality Abstracts*)

ABSTRACT 5.2
NEW ENGLAND TELEPHONE OPENS CUSTOMER SERVICE
LINES TO CHANGE

Clarke, J. Barry et al.
National Productivity Review, Winter 1992–93, pp. 73–82

When a consultant surveyed customers of the Interexchange Customer Service Center of New England Telephone, the results were not flattering. "The solution," say the authors, "was to reengineer the entire operation by establishing a customer-focused service team structure responsible for all processing and servicing support for a specific customer base." The company began by explaining the problems in very candid fashion to employees gathered in an auditorium. Reaction was extremely positive. Part of the program involved developing a vision statement which contained specifics regarding: customer loyalty, service quality, competitive edge, organizational effectiveness, job satisfaction, and training and participation. One of the key changes was involving service representatives in the billing and claims activity. Employees were offered a series of work effectiveness and change management workshops, and nonmanagement teams were formed to address job design, training, and mechanization. The redesigned workplace now includes the following elements, each of which the authors describe briefly: training, intern programs, career development programs, a mechanized report system, a managers' forum, professional development seminars, facilitator programs, support/supervisor monthly meetings, quality action teams, a quality notebook, a quality newsletter, a subject-matter expert process, a flexible work arrangements committee, and customer-centered work teams. Since 1989, the authors report, expenses have fallen, the workforce has been reduced 32 percent without any layoffs, overtime has been reduced, and the department has received quality awards for its achievements. (©*Quality Abstracts*)

ABSTRACT 5.3
QUALITY IN AMERICA: HOW TO IMPLEMENT A COMPETITIVE
QUALITY PROGRAM

Hunt, V. Daniel
Business One Irwin, Homewood, Illinois, 1992, 308 pp.

Quality in America is a readable volume that demystifies the quality movement and presents a clear plan to implement TQM in an organization. The author begins with an assessment of the global marketplace and the importance of TQM to a firm's remaining competitive. Next, he describes the fundamental concepts and vocabulary of quality. Chapter 3 is a helpful characterization of four of quality's pioneers: Deming, Juran, Robert Costello, and Philip Crosby. Then the author compares the emphases of the school of thought attributed to each of these people. "There is no one best way," says the author, but from that point on he describes and promotes his own synthesis of quality principles under the name *Quality First*™. A chart shows the relationship of Crosby's 14 steps, Deming's 14 points, and Juran's 7 points to *Quality First's* 8 tasks, which are summarized under the following major categories:

- **People-oriented tasks:**
1. Build top management
2. Build teamwork
3. Improve quality awareness
4. Expand training

- **Technically oriented tasks:**
5. Measure quality
6. Heighten cost of quality recognition
7. Take corrective action
8. Commit to a continuous improvement process

Chapter 4 describes the Malcolm Baldrige National Quality Award and recommends applying for it. This is followed by a chapter giving a thumbnail sketch of Baldrige Award winners: Federal Express, Globe Metallurgical, Motorola, Wallace Co., Westinghouse, and Xerox Business Products and Systems. Then the author provides a specific outline for implementing quality in an organization. Chapter 6 includes a complete self-assessment questionnaire and scoring evaluation system. After introducing his *Quality First* concepts and principles, the author outlines a 17-step implementation plan. The first ten steps are planning, followed by seven implementation steps. Chapter 10 consists of a brief survey of quality tools (e.g., bar chart, fishbone diagram, control chart, Pareto chart, etc.) and techniques (action plan, benchmarking, cost of quality, SPC, etc.). A final chapter reviews the steps and urges the reader to "act now." Three appendices provide basic resources: an executive reading list, a glossary of quality terms, and a list of information sources. This is a helpful "first book" to introduce the quality movement to corporate executives. (©*Quality Abstracts*)

CHAPTER 6

STRATEGY MANAGEMENT AND QUALITY PLANNING

The essence of management is...the art of mobilizing the intellectual resources of everyone working for the company. The intelligence of a group of executives, impressive as this might be, is no longer enough to guarantee success.

Konosuke Matsushita

STRATEGY MANAGEMENT

As indicated in Chapter 5, total quality is initiated at all levels of management. Implementing the principles of quality in an organization requires rethinking the very purpose of the organization. Without senior management's full support, it is impossible to provide the leadership, change the culture in which the organization operates, and potentially alter the direction of how to serve the organization's customers, shareholders, vendors, and employees.

Defining Strategy

Before proceeding, let's understand what strategy is. *Webster's New World Dictionary* defines strategy as "the science of planning and directing large scale military operations, skill in managing or planning, especially by using stratagem."[1] Stratagem is derived from two Greek words: *straos*, meaning army, and *agein*, meaning to lead. Basically it is a term used to describe a plan or trick to deceive an enemy. Eventually the concept of strategy spread to private businesses and then to public and nonprofit organizations. The term strategy in business has come to refer to the actions taken to establish and achieve the goals and objectives of an organization. Tregoe and Zimmerman[2] define organizational strategy as "the framework which guides those choices that determine the nature and direction of an organization."

Five basic functions of strategy critical for setting and maintaining direction are driven by the principles of total quality management and continuous improvement:[3]

1. Implement *leadership* for quality.

2. Develop an organizational *mission* for quality improvement.

3. Create a *vision* that inspires everyone to seek quality in all aspects of their work.

4. Generate a *culture* that encourages quality improvement efforts at all levels.

5. Establish overarching *goals and objectives* consistent with the principles of total quality and continuous improvement.

Each of these five points is briefly explained below. They should be used as guidelines to enrich planning and decision-making efforts.

Leadership: The Will to Change

Leadership is a catalyst for change, and total quality management efforts require positive change. Deming's seventh principle stresses the importance of leadership, and a review of all 14 principles shows that successful total quality implementations require leadership. The Baldrige Award criteria[4] describe the leadership category as examining "senior executives' personal leadership and involvement in creating/sustaining a customer focus with clear and visible quality values."

Becoming a manager does not automatically make one a leader. There is a difference between being a leader and being a manager. Bennis[5] summarizes the differences between management and leadership as follows:

Manager	Leader
1. Administers	1. Innovates
2. Is a copy	2. Is an original
3. Maintains	3. Develops
4. Focuses on systems and structure	4. Focuses on people
5. Relies on control	5. Inspires trust
6. Has a short-range view	6. Has long-range perspective
7. Asks how and when	7. Asks what and why
8. Has eye on bottom line	8. Has eye on horizon
9. Imitates	9. Originates
10. Accepts status quo	10. Challenges status quo
11. Classic good soldier	11. Own person
12. Does things right	12. Does right thing

Both management and leadership skills are necessary to produce an effective, efficient plan to guide the organization. A leader is receptive to change. Leadership practices should be adopted throughout the entire company, including the information technology (IT) organization. (For additional information, see Abstracts 6.1 and 6.2 at the end of this chapter.)

Mission

The mission is the basic purpose an organization seeks to accomplish—the reason why the organization exists. A mission statement is the formal expression of a company's purpose for its internal functions, customers, and employees. The IT mission statement should focus on complementing the overall company mission. IT should aid in developing the company mission. It is important that the mission statement identify the product produced or service performed and recognize the customers who are affected and their needs. The mission statement must be shared throughout the organization, with all its members, to be effective.

Vision

> Where there is no vision, the people perish.
> Proverbs 29:18

Vision is the direction or common belief of what the organization should be like five to ten years in the future. A vision should define what is to be created versus what is to be accomplished. A vision statement should be creative, clear, concise, positive, credible, reasonably obtainable, and shared throughout the company. The IT organization should have a vision that is in harmony with the overall company vision.

The concept of vision is often difficult for individuals to deal with because it defies conventional management approaches or the concept is unclear to them. Nanus[6] identified six things a vision is not:

1. While a vision is about the future, it is not a prophecy (although, after the fact, it may seem so).

2. A vision is not a mission. To state that an organization has a mission is to state its purpose, not its direction.

3. A vision is not factual. It does not exist and may never be realized as originally imagined. It deals not with reality but with possible and desirable futures.

4. A vision cannot be true or false. It can be evaluated only relative to other possible directions for the organization.

5. A vision is not (or at least should not be) static, enunciated once for all time.

6. A vision is not a constraint on actions, except for those inconsistent with the vision.

The benefits associated with a clear, positive vision for an organization include:

• Greater clarity of direction, which provides a framework for organizational decision making concerning desirable outcomes and actions and identification of opportunities and threats

• Greater unity of purpose and action

• Enhanced expectational guidance, which provides guideposts for determining appropriate behavior and assessing how individuals fit into the larger organizational picture

• Increased emphasis on innovation and anticipatory management, since the future direction is provided by the vision

• Increased motivation and commitment among the members of the organization; the creation of dynamic tensions between the present and desired future provides meaning and challenges for all

• Greater potential for decentralized decision making; when individuals and teams are aware of the vision and related mission, goals, and objectives, they are able to incorporate these factors into their decision making

Experience in strategic planning has shown that vision often ignores potential opportunity and lacks creative thinking. *Creating a vision requires playing the "anything goes" game, which involves using hindsight, foresight, and insight.*

Organizational Culture

Organizational culture refers to patterned ways of thinking, feeling, and acting throughout an organization. The specific characteristics of culture include behavior, structure, actions, attitudes, and roles. For the IT organization, this means transforming its image and conceptual ways of thinking about being merely computer analysts. IT professionals must also make an effort to help change the overall company cultural thinking and become business organizational allies and business analysts versus "an expensive department with technical people."

Table 6.1 lists nine key steps identified by Carr and Littman to ease the cultural transformation process. These nine steps are guidelines to follow. Organizational culture modification does not happen overnight. Culture change takes time, and it usually takes a long-term successful track record before transformation occurs. Old habits are hard to change, but time, consistency, and patience can make it happen. (For additional information, see Abstract 6.3 at the of this chapter.)

Goals and Objectives

The goals and objectives provide the linkage between the macro-level defined mission and vision statements of the organization. They identify how

Table 6.1 Carr and Littman[7] Steps in Easing the Cultural Transformation Process

---

1. Planning for cultural change
2. Assessing for cultural "baseline"
3. Training managers and the work force
4. Management adopting and modeling new behavior
5. Making organizational and regulation changes that support quality action
6. Redesigning individual performance appraisal and reward systems to reflect the principles of total quality management
7. Changing budget practices
8. Rewarding positive change
9. Using communication tools to reinforce TQM principles

---

the vision is going to be achieved. Goals and objectives can provide a larger picture and help unite everyone in the organization. Before developing plans and making decisions, the goals and objectives of the organization should be considered.

The quality planning process can begin when the overall company strategy has been established and communicated throughout the organization.

QUALITY PLANNING

Definition and Benefits

Quality planning is the business planning process used to formulate, deploy, and achieve business objectives by concentrating resources on high-priority items. This method of management links business activities to the long-term view of the company and provides the system that propels a company toward its vision while increasing the opportunity for competitive advantage.

Quality planning provides a systematic methodology to achieve the company vision once strategies have been defined. The processes and theories used to achieve success start with five basic business and personal management principles:

1. Always put the customer first.

2. Have true respect for people; treat others as you would want to be treated.

3. Deal with facts, not rumors or gossip.

4. Strive for continuous improvement.

5. Allow and encourage teamwork between *all* business functions and customers.

Life is not always as simple as we would like; complexity is a fact of life. However, if we look at the issues facing a company, apply the five principles listed above, and follow straightforward systematic approaches, we can solve complex problems and implement strategies to make our company successful.

Quality planning does not take the place of the organizational strategic plan; instead, it provides a bridge from strategy to operational actions. *Strategic plans concentrate efforts on particular markets and specify products to offer those markets. Quality plans focus on the business processes necessary to gain and maintain competitive advantage.* The differences between strategic planning and quality planning are shown in Table 6.2. Both strategic and quality planning work together to achieve the long-term goals of a company.

Table 6.2 Strategic Planning Versus Quality Planning

Strategic planning	Quality planning
Project oriented	Process oriented
Generally not well understood by everyone in the organization	Communicated throughout the organization
Projects selected by the knowledge and experience of those preparing the plan	Improvement areas selected by those most familiar with the processes
Difficult to link one year's plan to the next in most cases	Plan is built on the preceding year's plan
Targets are selected by intuition and reflect a top-down mentality	Targets are established based upon analysis and data

Quality planning breaks down barriers and opens lines of communication. Organizations establish breakthroughs by focusing the *entire* company on the vital few. All business functions and departments are able to understand where the objectives fit into the long-term company direction. The employees are given a clear sense of where they are headed. The firefighting mode prevalent in today's business operations is eliminated.

The quality planning model presented here follows the *hoshin* methodology. Management Systems International, Inc. (MSI), a firm that specializes in continuous improvement and planning, uses this methodology and has proved that it works.

Organizations that practice total quality deal with three interacting managerial systems: management, organizational, and educational. These systems were discussed in Chapter 5. The effectiveness of an organization is measured by its managerial system. Figure 6.1 displays quality planning and its interaction with the managerial system. It is through the managerial system that work is completed.

Components and Focus

Quality planning efforts consist of formation, deployment, and diagnosis. Formation is creating quality objectives based on understanding the organization from both customer and business viewpoints. Deployment is establishing methods to improve and assign resources (e.g., deciding to automate a manual process). Diagnosis is the ongoing review of the outcome (feedback) with emphasis not only on the results but on how the results were achieved.

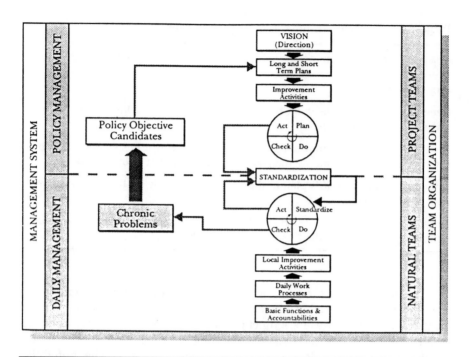

Figure 6.1 Quality Planning and the Managerial System.

Focus is the key in quality planning. There is often a difference between the apparent direction of a company and reality. It is important to understand the real focus rather than what is published in various plans. To ascertain the real focus, think back to last year's activities in your area. What items received the most attention? To assist in understanding, it is helpful to draw a pie chart divided into pieces proportional to how you spent last year. The largest slices are the real focus points.

FORMATION

Quality plan formation consists of three main sections. The sections produce customer requirements (voice of the customer), generate business requirements (voice of the business), and then develop objectives that are linked to the strategic plan. Where does IT fit into the picture during this process? Quite often, the IT professional does not have the opportunity to be involved in overall company planning or deal directly with customers, internal or external.

During the planning process, the business departments usually interact with their external customers to determine what is necessary to satisfy their business needs. IT must then rely on second-hand information and implement the technology requested without fully understanding the business need. Often the technology requested is more than what is actually needed or there may be other solutions, including preserving the status quo.

Including the IT function in the quality planning process and using cross-functional business teams will also improve the response time for delivery. It is faster, easier, and more cost efficient to make changes during the planning stage than it is to wait until product development or implementation. Every business function should be involved up front, before the customer is informed. It is embarrassing to tell customers that they will receive something at a set time and then, after discussing it with other departments, find that there is no feasible way to do it.

One suggested approach to aid in developing quality plans is to obtain the services of an outside facilitator. The facilitator is unbiased and can assure that all departments provide input and are fairly represented. Departmental representatives and the facilitator meet to determine requirements. The time required varies, but usually four to five dedicated days will suffice.

The first step in the formation of objectives is to determine the customer requirements by listening to the customer. It is important to equally weigh the customer and business interests so that one does not impinge upon the other.

VOICE OF THE CUSTOMER: CUSTOMER NEEDS

Many concepts regarding the voice of the customer fail to take advantage of information that exists within an organization. Most concepts begin with customer surveys but then do not use the information. Customers surveys are a useful tool but they should be used when customer requirements are already known.

In order to take advantage of the current body of knowledge, look for the various sources where customer requirements can be found. They include:

- Market research/surveys
- The sales force
- Warranty claims
- Customer complaints
- Customer service transactions
- Government regulations

- Technical and trade shows
- Customer site visits
- Focus/user groups

The key point is to *listen* to what customers say. It is amazing what knowledge can be gained by simply asking customers and listening to their responses.

Deriving Customer Requirements

In order to derive customer requirements, we must know how the customer views quality. The definition of quality with regard to planning and TQM is *conformance to customers' valid requirements*. This means that customer requirements are more than just quality issues; they reflect the customer's entire relationship with a company and its products and services.

Customer requirements can be broken down into four main categories: quality, safety, cost, and delivery. These categories have been derived by studying a significant amount of customer requirement data. The "Big Q" (quality) is derived from these four areas.

If we take time to reflect on the evolution of quality, from the days of the artisan craftsman, through the industrial revolution, to the present, we can see how quality consistently conformed to customer needs. When quality was controlled by the craftsman, he was responsible for building quality into the product. This was easily achieved since the same craftsman performed every step. Whether making a pair of shoes or cutting a gem, customer requirements were translated into product specifications, and the craftsman conformed to the specifications. Products were customized to customer requirements.

In some cases, customers did not know exactly what they wanted and relied upon the artisan's experience to develop specifications. Again, we see that the process involved translating customer needs into specifications and performing to specifications. The product was then either accepted or rejected by the customer. If the craftsman's interpretation of the customer need was valid, then the customer was satisfied. If not, the customer was unsatisfied.

The industrial revolution and mass production solidified the concept of conformance to specification. If the product was more complex, such as an automobile or piece of machinery, it was even more important to conform to specifications. This is also where the designer was forced to look at other aspects of quality, such as cost, reliability, and competition. If competitive pressure was light, a lower quality product could be produced and would be accepted by the customer. Once competitive pressure increased, cost became the main focus and cost reductions (many times at the expense of quality) were put in place.

The same concept applies to both services and products. Conforming to an internally derived specification will not always lead to satisfied customers. This is known as single-dimension quality, where achieving customer satisfaction is a function of conforming to specification. In actuality, there have always been two dimensions of quality. Instead of a single set of characteristics that govern quality acceptance, there are two: expected or required quality characteristics and unexpected or exciting quality characteristics.

Expected or required quality is a function of removing dissatisfaction. This means that supplying certain characteristics in a product or service does not create satisfaction but rather not supplying them can only create dissatisfaction. The best performance, or conformance to specification, only yields a neutral customer reaction. These are the items that a customer expects in the product or service.

As an example, let's consider a bank. A bank provides accurate statements to customers as an expected characteristic; by doing so, the bank does not gain customer satisfaction. When you received your last bank statement, did you call up the bank to say that it was doing a great job by providing you with an accurate statement? Of course not. But if the statement had been incorrect, how would you have reacted? You would have been dissatisfied with what you *expected* to be accurate. It is easy to see that providing an accurate statement does not create satisfaction, but *not* providing one creates *dis*satisfaction.

The question remains how to create satisfaction. Unexpected characteristics of a product or service create satisfaction. This stems from providing some feature or service that pleased and surprised the customer. By providing the *unexpected*, we can generate a sense of excitement that creates satisfaction. Looking at customer satisfaction from both points of view (*removal* of dissatisfaction and *creation* of satisfaction) is known as two-dimensional quality. This concept was developed by Dr. Noriaki Kano of the Union of Japanese Scientists and Engineers.

Let's return to our banking example. Suppose your bank manager called you and said that a review of your account showed that you could save money or time by subscribing to a new service. This unexpected service would make you feel good and give you satisfaction. (For additional information, see Abstract 6.4 at the end of this chapter.)

Obtaining Customer Requirements

The information to obtain customer requirements is usually available but, like most information, it must be translated into useful data. Gathering data

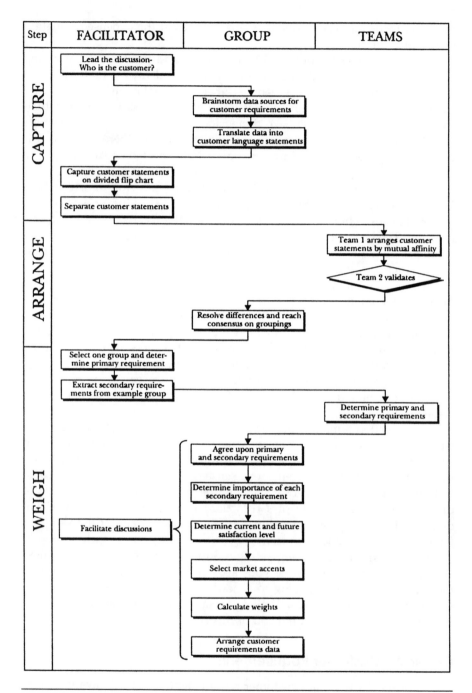

Figure 6.2 Process to Obtain Customer Requirements.

and arranging it in useful format(s) is the focus of this section. A three-step process is used to transform information into data:

- Capture the information
- Arrange the requirements
- Weigh the requirements

Figure 6.2 shows the process flow of the tasks to capture, arrange, and weigh customer requirements.

Step 1: Capture

In this step, a group brainstorms all possible data sources. All existing or potential customers are identified. The group basically asks, "Who are the customers and what do they require?" All ideas are written down and none are initially ignored. Each customer and the associated requirements are then translated into customer statements.

Step 2: Arrange

The customer statements captured in step 1 are arranged into common manageable groups. The affinity diagram is a recommended approach for documenting data. Figure 6.3 is a sample affinity diagram. The data are

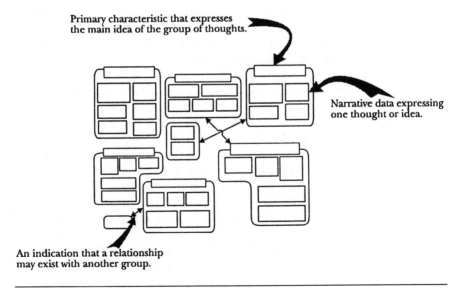

Figure 6.3   Affinity Diagram.

grouped by the primary characteristic that expresses the main idea of a group of thoughts. Each idea is documented with a narrative expressing the idea. Narrative data express one thought or idea of the group. These items are listed under the primary main idea. When primary ideas exist within another group, arrows are drawn to show the relationship.

Two teams should be created. Each team arranges the customer statements by mutual affinity. The teams then validate each other's work and resolve any differences before proceeding to step 3. The teams are a check and balance for one another and must arrive at a consensus.

Step 3: Weigh

The organization defines quality and the customer either rejects or accepts it. The customer provides two important components in determining the weight of a given requirement: importance and satisfaction. The customer indicates how important a requirement is, but this is somewhat skewed by performance, especially recent performance. The customer also indicates current level of satisfaction in terms of meeting requirements. Simply asking customers will not do, since recent performance will skew their responses.

Requirements should be weighed to achieve a balance between what the customer wants and good business practices. This means that the goal is to satisfy the customer, in fact even delight the customer, but to do so within the confines of good business practice. Anyone can throw money at a problem, but the challenge is to solve customer issues within constraints. *Throwing money at a problem rarely fixes it; it usually addresses the symptoms of the problem and not the true causes.*

Satisfying customer requirements poses certain problems, and it is a challenge to solve the problems, satisfy the customer, and maintain profitability. If a company goes out of business, it certainly will not satisfy customers. The balance between customer satisfaction and good business practice is achieved by utilizing four factors to weigh customer requirements: importance, current level of satisfaction, desired level of satisfaction, and market accent. Table 6.3 displays the weighing factors matrix and the weighing algorithm. By utilizing these factors, an organization can effectively weigh customer requirements and achieve a balance with good business practice.

Understanding what drives the weight is an important part of assessing customer requirements. In some cases, a relatively high importance, together with a rather dismal showing in performance, will make a weight high. In other cases, a significant gap between the current and desired levels of satisfaction will drive the weight. In still other cases, a combination of the above scenarios and a market accent will contribute to a highly weighted customer requirement.

The organization determines the desired level of satisfaction. For ex-

Table 6.3 Weighing Factors Matrix and Algorithm

Weighing factors matrix		
Factor	Description	Weight scale
Importance	The degree of importance customers place on a given requirement	1 2 3 4 5 low med high
Current level of satisfaction	The degree of satisfaction that customers are currently experiencing	1 2 3 4 5 low med high
Desired level of satisfaction	The degree of satisfaction that is needed to maintain competitive advantage or parity. This becomes your quality target for a given requirement	1 2 3 4 5 low med high
Market accent	Selected customer requirements, usually high in importance, that yield competitive advantage when satisfied	No accent = 1.0 Medium = 1.2 High = 1.5

Weighing Algorithm:

$$\text{Weight} = \text{Importance} \times \frac{\text{Desired}}{\text{Current}} \times \text{Market accent}$$

ample, it is not necessary to satisfy a given requirement at a level of five if customers only demand a level of three and the competition is at three. In this case, applying additional resources to achieve a higher than necessary level of satisfaction is poor business practice.

VOICE OF THE BUSINESS

Another key critical analysis, in addition to the voice of the customer, is to understand the voice of the business. This analysis is done to determine the current status of the business functions and identify which processes need improvement. The voice of the customer identifies key business functions that affect the needs of the system; the voice of the business evaluates the processes within these customer-identified business functions.

The business speaks to us differently than customers. Customers are sometimes very vocal in their demands. By watching certain indicators, such as market share, a company can get a good idea of what is needed. The voice of the business is assessed by looking at business problems in two main areas:

- *People*—Composed of employee-related issues
- *Waste*—Composed of efficiency- and cost-related problems

The voice of the business is very important because customers cannot always tell you what is wrong in the company. It is true that problem business processes generally manifest themselves through customer complaints, but many times this is too late. By thinking about the direction in which the company, business unit, or department is headed, the major problems in the organization can be assessed. What processes are broken with respect to achieving the long-term direction? What areas adversely affect the cost structure so as to make the business less competitive? (This question also applies to internal departments, since many of the functions performed by these departments are now outsourced.) Where can resources be gained by doing away with wasteful activities? These are the type of questions that assist an organization in determining the voice of the business.

All information is valuable when assessing business-related problems. Opinions are informative, but they can lead to working on the wrong things. When assessing business-related problems, one question always arises: "Compared to what?" Benchmarking can assist in identifying waste and can also help improve the situation. Finding and eliminating waste is a necessary and continuing effort.

The voice of the business analysis requires cooperation, openness, sharing, and understanding. Concerns which affect the business, such as personnel, competition, finance, technology, internal time cycles, and regulatory issues, are revealed and considered. All employee levels are included, and senior management must share future plans. The information captured is shared with work teams. This approach follows the capture-and-arrange steps identified in defining customer requirements.

IDENTIFYING THE PROBLEM

A problem well stated is half solved. This statement may sound trite but it is true. Individuals are often assigned a project and are not quite certain what is expected. A good problem statement is imperative to keep this from occurring. A good problem statement should be able to answer the following:

- *Who*—Who is affected by the problem, or the *customer* of the problem?
- *What*—What exactly is the "pain" the customer is experiencing?

- *When*—What is the time period associated with the information collected to support the problem?

- *Where*—*Precisely*, where is the problem being experienced?

Although these appear to be simple questions, they are often ignored when framing a business problem. The above checklist applies to any type of problem and should be used to assist in all improvement efforts.

DETERMINING BUSINESS PROBLEM PRIORITY

Today's business world is in a constant state of flux. Organizations must be concerned with change and change management. An inordinate amount of emphasis is sometimes placed on employee satisfaction when a company assesses the people side of the voice of the business. Satisfying employees is an admirable goal, but rapidly changing environments mandate a redefinition of people-related issues. The characteristics of the *new* organization are:

- Challenging work environment
- Encourages learning and employee development
- Values people as resources
- Encourages risk taking
- Leads rather than controls
- Leverages all parts of the organization
- Abolishes "not invented here"
- Achieves balance between processes and results
- Demonstrates consistency, integrity, and judgment
- Realizes that change is inevitable
- Seeks knowledge

An organization has many business-related problems. When prioritizing business-related problems, three factors should be considered:

1. *Urgency*—Must be solved in the next 18 months to 2 years in order to gain or maintain a competitive advantage. Weight scale is from 1 (problem does not affect competitive advantage) to 5 (problem significantly affects competitive advantage).

2. *Severity*—The level of impact the problem has on business operations. Weight scale is from 1 (problem does not take resources or time from other areas) to 5 (problem affects many areas and takes resources to support).

3. *Influence*—The level of influence the organization can exert in order to correct the problem. Weight scale is from 1 (problem is confined to one area of the organization) to 5 (problem will require involving many areas of the organization to solve).

These three factors are used to calculate the priority of the business problem using the following formula:

$$\text{Business Priority Weight} = \text{Urgency} \times \text{Severity} \times \text{Influence}$$

Recognizing business problems and reviewing business processes will identify areas that need improvement. The results will help management analyze the overall business and establish priorities for changing the business processes (especially those that require immediate attention). Downsizing is not always the best solution. Fewer employees may decrease customer satisfaction or eliminate resources that could be assigned to pursue new business opportunities. After all, the employees usually know the customers and the business problems.

BUILDING OBJECTIVES

Objectives are formed by taking data from the voice of the customer and the voice of the business and deciding where to focus efforts. There is no magic answer here. Only by utilizing the two voices can the confidence level be raised. There is no right or wrong choice, but some choices are better than others. Factual data, justification, and experience are the important tools.

Objectives merely provide a common focus. Each level is characterized by stating an objective and a corresponding means. An example is provided in Figure 6.4. One level's means becomes the next level's objective. In this manner, linkage is created from the formation stage through to implementation. The means to achieve objectives is through analysis based on data. Catchball is a useful technique to assist in quality planning. One of the most important aspects of quality planning is involving the individuals most familiar with the process in determining how it will be improved. This is where catchball is useful. Each level negotiates how it will support the company or departmental objectives.

The probability of achieving success is increased by having those closely associated with the work participate in the planning process. The concept is to select the most appropriate means to improve from all possible means. This is a key point of the *hoshin* planning methodology and separates it from other planning methodologies. Understanding how the results are achieved is as important as achieving the results. This allows good results to be replicated and eliminates undesirable results.

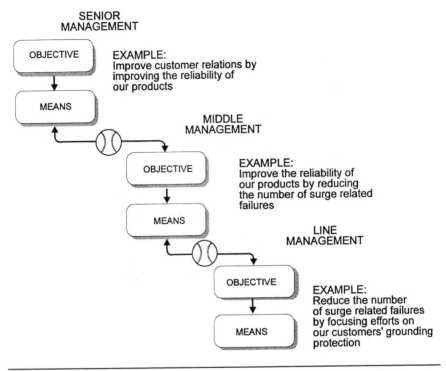

Figure 6.4 Example of Objective and Means Catchball and Leveling.

LINKING OBJECTIVES TO STRATEGY

The corporate strategy can be linked to the quality planning objectives. Figure 6.5 shows in further detail how the two interact. Monitoring and continuous feedback are important in the review process. Review steps include:

- Checking the long-term direction annually

- Building a one-year plan based upon the previous year

- Diagnosing throughout the year to provide midstream corrections and input to the next cycle

- Achieving the objectives through catchball discussions based on analysis

It is important to link the overall quality planning objectives to the business strategy plan. What use is defining objectives if the objectives are not considered in the overall planning effort? You must define what you want and be receptive to change.

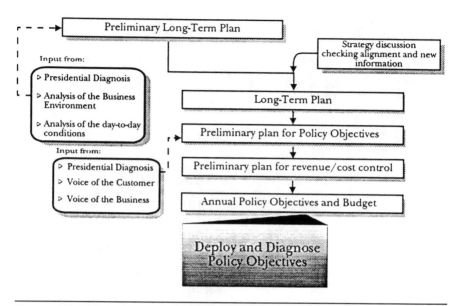

Figure 6.5 Objectives Link to Strategic Plan.

ENDNOTES

1. *Webster's New World Dictionary* (1992). Compact School and Office Edition. New York: Simon and Schuster.
2. Tregoe, Benjamin and Zimmerman, John (1980). *Top Management Strategy: What It Is and How It Works*. New York: Simon and Schuster, p. 17.
3. Lewis, Ralph and Smith, Douglas (1994). *Total Quality in Higher Education*. Delray Beach, FL: St. Lucie Press, p. 113.
4. 1993 Award Criteria, Malcolm Baldrige National Quality Award. Milwaukee: American Society for Quality Control, p. 16.
5. Bennis, Warren (1989). *On Becoming a Leader*. New York: Addison Wesley, p. 45.
6. Nanus, Bert (1992). *Visionary Leadership*. San Francisco: Jossey-Bass, pp. 31–32.
7. Carr, David and Littman, Ian (1990). *Excellence in Government: Total Quality Management in the 90's*. Arlington, VA: Coopers and Lybrand, pp. 190–203.

ABSTRACTS

ABSTRACT 6.1
WHAT IS LEADERSHIP?

Smolenyak, Megan and Majumdar, Amit
Journal for Quality and Participation, July–August 1992, pp. 28–32

What leadership type can empower employees to develop their inherent capabilities? The authors answer this question by describing three types of leaders:

- **The champion** is characterized by uncontested authority, usually resulting from a feat or event he or she has masterminded. This kind of leader is tough and determined and thrives in an autocratic, hierarchical world. The champion is normally patronizing toward followers.

- **The visionary** inspires others through a commitment to a vision of monumental proportions. This leader persuades people to follow by tapping their emotions. The visionary's relationship with followers can be described as paternalistic. The danger with this type of leadership is that the loss of the leader can mean the end of the movement.

- **The servant** attains stature through the accomplishments of followers by bringing out the "leader" in each of them. The servant is respected and admired but does not seek self-glorification. This type of leader is approachable and interactive, thriving on open communications. Most of all, the servant is an enabler who helps others develop their inherent capabilities in support of a mutually agreed upon mission. The followers then have a sense of ownership in the mission.

Many companies that practice TQM are already using servant leadership, say the authors, especially with self-managed work teams. When managers make the transition from boss to coach, they are adopting the servant style of leadership. Those who stubbornly resist this style may eventually have to leave for the good of the company. The good news, according to the authors, is that the supply of servant leaders as opposed to other types is very generous.   (©*Quality Abstracts*)

ABSTRACT 6.2
INSIDE THE BALDRIGE AWARD GUIDELINES—
CATEGORY 1: LEADERSHIP

Sullivan, Rhonda L.
Quality Progress, June 1992, pp. 24–28

This first in a series of articles on the guidelines for the seven categories of the Baldrige Award focuses on leadership. "The 1992 Baldrige Award criteria are built on 10 core values and concepts," says the author. She briefly discusses each: customer-driven quality, leadership, continuous improvement, full participation, fast response, design quality and prevention, long-range outlook, management by fact, partnership development, and public responsibility. "By completing the award application's leadership section," she says, "a company will determine whether its organizational structure will support its objectives." In addition to a copy of the actual Baldrige Award criteria for Category 1, and a table of scoring guidelines, the author offers advice on areas of importance in the leadership category, such as:

- Don't rely solely on management by walking around. Develop a formal structure and strategy to ensure that leaders are accessible.

- Insist on enthusiastic personal involvement from senior executives.

- Stress two-way communication.

- Develop multiple methods for accomplishing an objective to ensure validation.   (©*Quality Abstracts*)

ABSTRACT 6.3
BUILDING A TOTAL QUALITY CULTURE

Batten, Joe
Crisp Publications, Menlo Park, Calif., 1992, 88 pp.

"People want to be led, not driven," insists the author. Providing the kind of tough-minded leadership that will produce a total quality culture is the focus of this motivational book (which includes a foreword by Zig Ziglar). Rather than presenting a formula for TQM, the book aims at developing the attitudes which support successful TQM leaders. Chapter titles are:
1. The Path to the Future
2. The New Leaders

3. Making Quality Possibilities Come True

4. Peak Performance at All Levels

5. Winners Can Be Grown

6. Tomorrow's Culture

Some of the themes include tough-minded leadership (the title of one of the author's former books), servant leadership, being a winner, motivating one's subordinates, excellence, and dreams. The author draws on the upbeat quotations from a variety of individuals to bolster his points. The book concludes with a 14-page glossary of terms which serve to spell out Batten's philosophy of leadership. For example, he defines "builder": "The CEO who stands tall is, above all, a builder. Committed to vision, stretch, empowerment, synergy, responsiveness, flexibility—toughness of mind—a builder ensures that all dimensions of each P in the pyramid are intensely focused on creation, growth, and building." (©*Quality Abstracts*)

ABSTRACT 6.4
MIS + TQM = QIS

Keith, Richard
Quality Progress, April 1994

This thought-provoking article discusses the important role of information systems in implementing total quality systems and explains how one company, Lithonia, revamped its management information system (MIS) to create "quality information systems." With annual revenues over $700 million and a workforce of 4,500, Livonia enjoyed gains in product quality and cost reduction, but remained stagnant in the "office environment." Specifically, the general business processes were being maintained in the status quo while the total quality focus was on the plant floor.

The article discusses management's realization that MIS must occupy a central focus of the company's total quality movement and must be combined in a strategic way in order to achieve a new understanding of system and service. This involves expanding the scope of the "data processors" to include the entire business process, including those that have little to do with the information systems function or department. "QIS requires the systems department to develop, implement, and champion a methodology that looks at the business goals and develops activities that might or might not include a computer system to meet those goals. Service should be the MIS department's deliverable product. This service should include setting goals, facilitating and participating in process improvements, and implementing computer systems.

The MIS function took over the business reengineering activities, and a sister group to "applications development" was formed with senior business analysts from technical and nontechnical backgrounds. Three goals were formed: (1) everyone must understand the QIS initiative, (2) MIS/QIS is uniquely suited to facilitate process improvement, and (3) the goals of the company must be the same as the goals of MIS/QIS.

The group found success using the process mapping techniques described in *Improving Performance* by Rummler and Brache (Jossey-Bass, San Francisco, 1991). Flowcharts were developed to depict the customer/server relationships and the corresponding processes being performed. These flowcharts were based upon performance metrics and standards that focused on key processes of providing price quotes to customers, developing installation drawings, and entering orders. None of the standards set by the team were met once an order was received. The marketing division was reorganized into work cells, each having total responsibility for any job assigned to its area from start to finish. Each cell was measured and held responsible for errors, quality problems, and substandard performance. Supervisors were eliminated, resulting in better information flow between the company and the customer.

Also discussed are the long-term considerations for procedural improvement focused in two areas: education of the customer and automation of the remaining streamlined processes. One of the most important aspects of the overall effort was the buy-in by division management and staff. Six months after implementation, the prime objectives were being met in all areas, leading to the author's conclusion that the combination of QIS and an improved bottom line creates a win–win situation for all. Limited references are provided.

CHAPTER 7

PROJECT TEAMS AND METHODOLOGIES

After management has reviewed the business process objectives and set priorities, these priorities are then assigned to a project. *Webster's Dictionary* defines a project as "something that is contemplated, devised or planned; plan; scheme."[1] Project management consists of the tasks involved in planning, organizing, overseeing, scheduling, and implementing a project. Teams are formed made up of individuals whose activities are linked to the company's improvement objectives. The major tasks include creating the project-centered vision, identifying critical success factors and developing control systems and estimating, scheduling, and tracking mechanisms, as well as identifying skills required and performance indicators.[2] This approach allows the company to work with facts and gives all employees the opportunity to improve the quality and level of service provided to customers.

TEAM BUILDING: ROLE TEAMS PLAY IN QUALITY IMPROVEMENT

Companies have traditionally formed organizations around work groups and specific functional tasks. Each organization is accountable for its particular area and for meeting its budget. The company's top executives manage by functional unit as opposed to business process. This tradition is slowly changing as companies are beginning to manage accountability by *process*.

A major theme of this book is that the success of every company rests on the effectiveness of work group teams. The key differences between a work group and a team are displayed in Table 7.1. That view is the basis for the use of total quality management. If a house is being built by two different contractors and there is no teamwork or coordination, one contractor might build a contemporary style house while the other builds a colonial style. When a company is changing its work flow processes, *all* business departments must work together to consider appropriate technology. The entire company must work toward and be kept informed about achieving the same vision, goals, and objectives.

The term "team" has come to describe a group of people who are goal centered, interdependent, honest, open, supportive, and empowered. Team

Table 7.1 Groups Versus Teams

Groups	Teams
Members think they are grouped together for administrative purposes only. Individuals work independently, sometimes at cross purposes with others.	Members recognize their interdependence and understand that both personal and team goals are best accomplished with mutual support. Time is not wasted struggling over "turf" issues or personal gain at the expense of others.
People tend to focus on themselves because they are not sufficiently involved in planning the unit's objectives. They approach their jobs simply as hired hands.	Members feel a sense of ownership toward their jobs and units because they are committed to goals they helped establish.
Members are told what to do rather than being asked what the best approach would be. Suggestions are not encouraged.	Members contribute to the success of the organization by applying their unique talents and knowledge to team objectives.
Members distrust the motives of colleagues because they do not understand the roles of other members. Expressions of opinion or disagreement are considered divisive or nonsupportive.	Members work in a climate of trust and are encouraged to openly express ideas, opinions, disagreement, and feelings. Questions are welcomed.
Members are so cautious about what they say that real understanding is not possible. Game playing may occur, and communication traps may be set to catch the unwary.	Members practice open and honest communication. They make an effort to understand each other's point of view.

Table 7.1 (continued) Groups Versus Teams

Groups	Teams
Members may receive good training but are limited in applying it by the supervisor or other group members.	Members are encouraged to develop skills and apply what they learn on the job. They receive the support of the team.
Members find themselves in conflict situations which they do not know how to resolve. Supervisors tend to put off intervention until serious damage has been done.	Members recognize conflict as a normal aspect of human interaction, but they view such situations as an opportunity for new ideas and creativity. They work to resolve conflict quickly and constructively.
Members may or may not participate in decisions that affect the team. Conformity often appears more important than positive results.	Members participate in decisions that affect the team but understand that their leader must make a final ruling whenever the team cannot decide or an emergency exists. Positive results, not conformity, are the goal.

Source: Adapted from Maddux, R.B. (1988). *Team Building: An Exercise in Leadership.* Oakville, Ontario: Crisp Publications.

members develop strong feelings of allegiance that go beyond the mere grouping of individuals. The productive outcome is synergistic and the accomplishments often even exceed the original goals of the task.[3]

TYPES OF TEAMS

To effectively implement total quality improvement, four types of teams are necessary: the lead project team, functional team, cross-functional team, and task team.

Lead Project Team

The lead team, also known as the quality council, leads the project. It functions as the steering committee in that it sets policy, establishes guidelines, and handles overall communication for the other three types of teams. The other teams operate under the lead project team.

A lead team is formed for a specific purpose, either in the management area for policy or for a major business process activity. Members are selected by management and membership is determined by expertise and company background. Project team members consist of cross-functional representation from each business function, including information technology (IT). The level of membership can vary based upon the project and its effect on the organization. There are three types of project team membership:

- *Executive level*—For major, critical company-wide projects, usually composed of presidents and vice presidents (e.g., CEOs, CFOs, COOs, and CIOs).

- *Activity-centered*—For a specific activity that does not affect the entire company. Usually composed of vice presidents, managers, and directors.

- *Location-centered*—For region-specific projects. Consists of directors, functional managers, and the chief manager for the location.

Every lead project team must have a project leader. The leader coordinates activity, develops project plans, communicates, and ensures that project objectives are being met. This individual is a mediator and the central contact point for the project. The life cycle of the team varies from project to project; it may be as short as one week or as long as three years. The lead project team ensures the success of the project, no matter how small or large. Unless working on an internal IT project, an IT representative should not be the team leader. The function of IT representatives is to communicate technology concerns, to be aware of what is happening, and to support the company. They should not make business decisions.

Cross-Functional Team

Cross-functional teams are often created by the project team, depending on the size of the project and its effect on the organization. When the executive-level team is formed, a cross-functional team becomes a necessity, as communication, analysis, and research among the business processes are inevitable. Membership usually consists of (but is not limited to) directors and managers from each business function.

Functional Team

Functional teams are additional teams established by the lead project or cross-functional teams to further detail specific processes. A functional team has a eclectic membership and concentrates its efforts on specific functional processes. The functional team is a subset of the lead project team and sometimes the cross-functional team. A representative from the functional team communicates requirements and status to the lead project team. The idea is to ensure that all efforts are viewed as processes with measurable results. Numerous functional teams can be generated for a single project.

Task Team

Task teams include representatives from multiple areas and are formed to complete a specific task or problem. Suppose a major computer project needed to be converted. The task team would plan and implement the conversion. Its functions are similar to a project team and are part of the success of the project. Additional functional teams might be created if additional specialized planning and research are necessary. (For additional information, see Abstract 7.1 at the end of this chapter.)

INFORMATION TECHNOLOGY TEAM REPRESENTATION

IT team representation will vary from project to project. When the executive level is involved, the senior IT manager should always be a member of the lead team. If the team activity is location centered, the IT director, project manager, or a systems analyst can be involved, based on the criticality and importance of the project. IT management has the option of sending representatives from each IT functional area or assigning a central coordinator to communicate with all areas within IT. The central coordinator is usually the systems analyst or IT team manager responsible for the project assigned to the project team. A separate cross-functional IT team should be created for any project that involves technology to ensure that each IT functional area is aware of the project. Table 7.2 shows a sample internal IT cross-functional team, its membership, and the expertise that should be involved.

Table 7.2 Information Technology Team Interaction

Function	Skill
Applications support	Project lead Systems analyst
Data center	Scheduling Systems support
Telecommunications	Telecom analyst
Information	Security/audit Business administration

When the IT function is outsourced, someone with technical expertise should represent the project and coordinate with the outsource firm. This person can be either a company employee or a consultant who specializes in project management and planning. When using an outside technical service, it is wise to choose an advisor who does not represent a particular product or vendor. This eliminates the possibility of designing business requirements to meet a particular purchase.

The role of the technical representative is to guide and assist. For example, technology vendors sometimes announce a product and years pass before it is available, even in a test mode. The technical representative investigates the various technology solutions and informs everyone. IT professionals, usually management or systems analysts, also contribute their technical expertise by offering workflow enhancements. IT should avoid telling a business department that its request is not technically unfeasible. "Can't be done" is an unacceptable answer; IT should at least provide alternatives. Communication is enhanced when business functions and IT teams define requirements together. *All* business support functions must work together to ensure the highest quality and eliminate communication difficulties.

DEFINING PRELIMINARY PROJECT CRITERIA

Before starting any project, certain criteria must be agreed upon by top management and everyone involved in the project. These criteria are the team purpose, commitment, and review processes which are to be in place and enforced.

Team Purpose

Creating empowered, effective teams requires a four-step facilitative process, as described by Schultz.[4] The lead project team is responsible for creating the vision and mission for the project. This team is the guiding light that the other teams follow. The vision and mission statements should be consistent with the direction of the company. The first step is to create the vision statement using clear, unambiguous language that is endorsed by everyone on the team. The second step is to define the reason for the team's existence. The third step is to define the principles and values that will guide the team by answering the question: "What principles and values do we find most important in meeting the vision?" The fourth step is to develop a mission for the unit, based on the principles and values. This serves as a guideline for decision making by everyone on the team. It answers the question: "How do we fulfill the vision?" (For additional information, see Abstract 7.2 at the end of this chapter.) An opportunity to create team responses is provided in Exercise 7.1 at the end of this chapter.

Individual and Management Commitment

In total quality, managing is not limited to managers; managing falls on the shoulders of every employee. Senior management's sincere involvement and participation ensure that the policies of the organization are being implemented and that the departments are continually improving. While some people feel that total quality stifles creativity, with proper use, it can encourage creativity from all levels of the organization. Employees need to know the issues, however, in order to recognize problems and offer solutions.

Care must be taken to ensure that people do not use the quality tools for unimportant issues or to meet artificial or personal goals. Total quality is total because it considers cost, delivery, safety, etc., as well as quality. Time spent on useless quality stories, four-lane highways to nowhere, and busy work (which does not add value) simply wastes time and money.

Management must commit to providing whatever the project needs. This includes people and capital. A project cannot afford to have someone involved part-time when the effort requires full-time support and this support is continually being pulled from the project.

Senior management must also endorse the project and demonstrate its full support. Direct line managers and all personnel who report to them must know that deviations from team norms or lack of teamwork will not be tolerated.

Review Process

The project review process monitors the project, making certain its goals and objectives are being met. These reviews assist management in understanding how policies are being supported, keep management informed on the status and findings, show where funds are being spent, and indicate whether the project is within budget and on time. This type of review promotes cooperation among the functions and gives meaning to the company's plan, since senior management is in the communication circle.

During review, involved individuals must speak factually. When difficulties arise, the team should give an accurate status report and attack the process instead of the individual. If there are difficulties, management should be informed and help requested. If a top manager wants information about a project, that information should be available at any time.

The review should be scheduled based on the criticality and length of the project. It is difficult to set standard review schedules because each project is different. A guideline would be no less than a weekly written report from the project team. Each subteam formed from the lead project team should report its status to the team leader, who forwards the information to the project team. (For additional information, see Abstract 7.3 at the end of this chapter.)

PROJECT DEVELOPMENT METHODOLOGY CYCLE

After the lead project team has been formed, it is time to start the project development effort. There are various project development methodologies, but they all follow the same basic rules. A company should establish and follow a methodology customized to meet its quality standards and the way it conducts business. *No one methodology is right or wrong; companies have different guidelines and business directions. Each company must develop its own methodology.* It may be advantageous to obtain outside assistance in some situations. The point is that some *standard* project methodology must be in place and endorsed by everyone. Without senior management's commitment to support the methodology, the project is doomed, no matter how good the process is.

There is no one project development methodology for developing and maintaining automated systems; there are only guidelines. Figure 7.1 shows a comparison between manufacturing a product and software development.

When starting a project, the IT professionals and businesspeople must include all of the business work processes. When a project considers only one functional area and not the entire business process flow, integration is lost and redundant information occurs. The common high-level phases for project development are:

1. Planning and defining business requirements
2. Generating functional requirements
3. Designing and building the system
4. Testing
5. Installation
6. Ongoing maintenance and feedback review

Each project development phase has teams with assigned tasks. All teams work together throughout the entire project. There are checkpoints and sign-offs between each phase. This eliminates communication break-downs and ensures that what was requested is what is delivered. A description of each phase follows (see also Exhibit 7.1).

Phase I: Planning and Defining Business Requirements

This is the planning and business design phase. The requirements of the business and the customer are defined, feasibility determined, priorities established, and a project plan completed. Priorities are geared to company plans or, in some instances, are the result of government-mandated regulations.

MANUFACTURING PRODUCT DEVELOPMENT

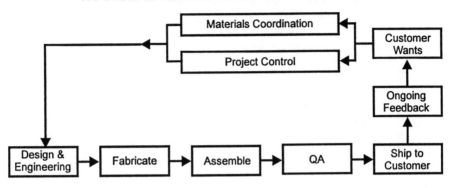

IT SOFTWARE DEVELOPMENT

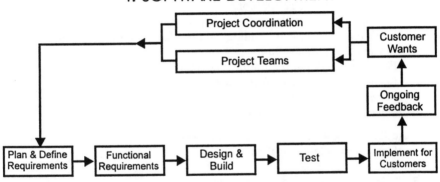

Figure 7.1 Comparison of Product Development to Information Technology Software Development.

The time needed to complete Phase I varies depending on the number of business functions involved and the complexity of the project request. There are a number of ways to conduct fact-finding sessions. The suggested method is to hold a master planning session, bringing all people involved together at the same time. Using an outside facilitator is recommended to keep the meeting on track and make sure that the objectives of the session are accomplished.

In most cases, within six to ten days, with the appropriate facilitator, complex business models can be designed, developed, and documented and "ownership" of business processes confirmed, with consensus reached as to strengths and weaknesses. Processes that deal with multiple markets

Phase I: Planning and Defining Business Requirements
1. Determine business objectives
2. Identify major business processes affected
3. Conduct fact-finding sessions
4. Document fact-finding results
5. Determine improvement areas
6. Prepare cost–benefit analysis
7. Prioritize processing requirements
8. Prepare requirements report
9. Receive management approval
10. Develop project plan
11. Receive management and user sign-off

Phase II: Generating Functional Requirements
1. Determine business process functions
2. Document business processing
3. Consider technology solutions
4. Document conceptual technology specifications
5. Determine conversion, training, and implementation requirements
6. Review alternative solutions
7. Produce functional requirements document
8. Review and update project plans
9. Receive management approval
10. Obtain user and management sign-off

Phase III: Designing and Building the System
1. Document detailed systems flow
2. Build a prototype
3. Select a package or develop in-house
4. Produce detailed systems specifications
5. Obtain user and management sign-off
6. Code and inspect programs
7. Review and update project plans

Phase IV: Testing
1. Develop testing scheme
2. Conduct technical testing
3. Conduct business process testing
4. Obtain user sign-off

Phase V: Installation

Phase VI: Ongoing Maintenance and Feedback Review
1. Conduct team review
2. Support maintenance requests

Exhibit 7.1   Project Methodology Phases.

or business departments require the same level of analysis as described for each of the initial business departments. Completing this phase takes longer, because it is usually more complex and requires outside customer information.

The information collected can be compiled in tabular format. These shared viewpoints will be the basis for identifying the system design. Evaluation of *shared* existing business strategies is critical in establishing the evolution of the system. Defining priorities for the first stage and the long-term goals of the process requires knowledge of the benefits to customers, departments, divisions, etc. This information will be integrated with appropriate technology and system architecture as the phases of the development plan are established.

This design allows management to see how the automated process aligns with its objectives and policies, as well as how it fits in with priorities within divisions and departments of the organization. It provides a shared view of the future and assures linkage to the long-term direction of the organization. When applied against four key indicators—quality, customer needs, safety, and delivery—the policy shows a balance between these factors.

Next, priorities are assigned. Management's approval follows and functional requirements can then begin.

The basic steps in planning and defining business requirements are:

1. *Determine business objective(s)*—Know what the objectives are for the business, what is important to customer service, and identify the financial bottom line.

2. *Identify major business processes affected*—Internal and external, by project request or process. Once the functions have been identified, a representative from each area is assigned to the cross-functional team for the duration of the project.

3. *Conduct fact-finding sessions*—Interview individuals involved in the business processes that are affected and learn how they conduct business.

4. *Document fact-finding results*—From all functional units using data models. Document the work flows and process; show where and how the functional units interact with each other in the process.

5. *Determine improvement areas*—Analyze facts documented for each business function. Identify the areas that are cross-functional and those that stand alone. Analyze and divide into subprojects by processing requirement.

6. *Prepare cost–benefit analysis*—Identify the costs and risks associated with each processing requirement identified in step 5. Technical con-

siderations must be included in this analysis. The risk of what would happen if nothing is done versus the risk of change must be considered.

7. *Prioritize processing requirements*—By using the company plans, cost–benefit analysis, and determining whether the requirement is mandatory or a "nice-to-have."

8. *Prepare requirements report*—Generate a report that will be presented to management for review.

9. *Receive management approval*—Review the findings with management for approval and commitment. Confirm the requirements that will be implemented and the order of priority.

10. *Develop project plan*—For the requirements that have been approved by management. This plan sets forth the tasks, what resources are needed, an estimated time frame, and the anticipated workload.

11. *Receive sign-off*—Distribute the project plan to all parties involved for sign-off and approval.

Phase II: Functional Requirements

The functional requirements phase identifies how the business requirements identified will be implemented. This phase analyzes business requirement(s) and determines particular actions within the business process affected. This may or may not include technology to enhance the process. In this phase, whether or not to automate is determined.

Always consider manual, less expensive solutions first.[5] Automating may be one solution, but it is not always necessary. If a process can be manually rearranged to meet acceptable quality standards, it may not be necessary to spend money to automate.

Team representation is revisited and any additional teams are created for the duration of the project. This phase primarily identifies the inputs and outputs on a business-user functional level. Process flows are generated by the business and technical areas. Business areas create detailed business work process flows and the technical area generates a detailed systems interface processing flow, showing the internal technical interactions. These are two separate tasks, although the efforts occur simultaneously.

The Plan-Do-Check-Act (PDCA) cycle of constant improvement (explained in Chapter 4) can be used to produce the system. Constant teamwork between the end users and the technical area is critical at this stage of the project. All planned activities are included in the continuous improvement cycle. Training requirements, conversion effort, and testing methodologies are fully explored and buy/build decisions are clearly delineated. Having defined customer needs and business issues, the natural question is: What is the best technological solution for this project? The technical area reviews available productivity tools in exploring ways to make the system more predictable and controllable.

IT evaluates currently available technology for present and future implementation. It is critical to match technology and the direction of the organization. *Business needs should dictate the technology used instead of technology driving the business.*

During this phase, quality measurements are defined and agreed to by each business process. Examples are given in Table 7.3, although the list is not comprehensive as there may be more or fewer measurements based on each individual project. The most important issue is to define standard methods for measuring the quality and overall success of the requirements and to build measurement criteria into the project. You cannot improve what you cannot measure. Measuring customer satisfaction should be included when considering technical requirements. This information will be the basis for the measurement criteria used to evaluate performance and quality at the end of the project.

Once the scope of the project is defined, it is reviewed and decisions are made about how to implement the system, in a phased, modular fashion.

Table 7.3 Functional Design Quality Measurements

Measurement considerations	Questions to ask when designing projects
System availability (up time)	When does the software/hardware need to be available to the users?
Response time	What is the turnaround time for obtaining results (online and reports)?
	Can processing be done in batch mode or must it be online in real time?
Ease of use	How user friendly is the software design?
	Is there a help function for online screens?
	Are the screens or reports easy to read and understand?
Performance criteria	How fast is the processing?
	Does the software function as the business requires?

Table 7.3 (continued) Functional Design Quality Measurements

Measurement considerations	Questions to ask when designing projects
Reliability	How responsive is the software?
	How long has the software/hardware been in use for similar situations?
	How dependable is the software/hardware?
Transferability	How easy is it to transfer to other types of computer equipment?
Upgradability	How easy is it to upgrade the hardware or software?
Ease to install	How easy is the software/hardware to install and learn?
Documentation	What documented information is available (vendor-purchased or in-house) and how detailed is it (i.e., user procedures, computer operating procedures, programming and restart/recovery directions)?
	Is the documentation easy to read and understand?
Peak load management	How will the software/hardware function during high-volume use?
Ease of maintainability	How flexible is the software design/code for handling future changes?
	Is the design in modular, reusable segments?
	Is the information integrated and documented?
Information redundancy	Is the information reoccurring, fragmented, or stored in a central location?
Cost to operate	How much will it cost to operate?
	How many users will access the software at the same time?
	Are the users all at one site?
	Is additional hardware/software needed to support the project (i.e., modems, terminals, larger computer)?
Security	Has the "owner" been identified?
	Have access privileges (i.e., who can access specific information and functions) been established?
Business recovery	Have the business recovery requirements been identified in terms of what is needed in case of a disaster or temporary disruption to the customer?

Whenever possible, it is best to divide a system into functional processes and conduct a phased installation. Benefits of the phased approach include:

- Less risk of failure when introducing production volumes
- Responsibility for each process step is clearly defined
- Easier to measure and debug manageable-sized pieces of a system
- Users start working with the system and provide feedback
- Ease of maintenance
- As progress is reported, management has confidence that there is some quick return on investment

The basic steps followed during the functional requirements phase are:

1. *Determine business process functions and activity*—Define each business activity within the process and the information (data elements) used or needed. Define the security and business recovery criteria and identify any other system interactions, manual or automated.

2. *Determine all the inputs and outputs to the business process*—Identify by function and show their interaction within the process. Compare existing and anticipated data elements to verify that all process activity has been identified.

3. *Build processing flows*—After determining inputs and outputs, document the processing flow and system interactions, including both automated and manual systems, for the anticipated process.

4. *Define hardware/software environments*—Identify the computer hardware and software environments currently being used and what is needed to support the project or task.

5. *Document conceptual technical specifications*—Create a functional narrative by process and flow that identifies any design constraints. Determine technical requirements by showing any inputs, outputs, and cross-system interactions.

6. *Determine conversion, training, and implementation strategies*—Find out whether any existing business process or computer system requires conversion or training to use. If conversion or training is necessary, a separate task team for should be created for each to support those activities. The conversion task team starts its own subproject using the project development methodology from phase I. When preparing a conversion project plan, conversion testing should be ready for user testing and installation concurrent with the new development. The implementation strategy is how and when this requirement will be introduced in the business.

7. *Review alternative solutions*—Contemplate and weigh any other possible choices that could be considered.

8. *Produce a functional requirements document*—Write a functional document that defines all the requirements identified for the new process.

9. *Review project status and update task plans*—Compare the original project task plan to the final document and update the project task plan and status.

10. *Receive user sign-offs and management approval*—Distribute the functional requirements document for review and receive approvals from all functional user areas involved. Update management on any changes and receive approval to proceed with the project.

Phase III: Detail Designing and Building

Once the functional requirements phase is under way, the detail design of the system begins. A system is a composite of information, equipment, skills, and techniques to support a business objective. This phase is primarily an IT responsibility. While IT is working on this phase, the business teams are completing their assigned tasks, including generating test schemes, training, and writing procedures. The technical task teams are formed by project functions (systems) and consist of systems analysts, programmers, and a project leader for each team, with key business interaction continuing. The individual IT teams communicate with one another, but are divided into separate teams to expedite the system development process.

The detail design phase is where the technological advances of today and the potential benefits of tomorrow are considered. Standards, philosophies, and methods are melded to build a foundation for future evolution.

The overall architecture and design are dictated by business requirements and the status of the process. The best technical solution is designed in detail, either by purchasing a software package or writing customized programs. Today, standardization is more important than ever before. Larger companies are taking either a centralized or decentralized approach to technology but all seek central integration of information. Standards must apply across company lines when regions come into play or there will be no information integration. These standards allow each IT region throughout a corporation to present a consolidated information base. This facilitates supplying information to a corporate parent and giving top management information for the overall corporation. It is helpful for all regions and subdivisions within a corporation to calculate and report information the same way. Matching the structure of information with the design of the organization is critical. Systems must provide the correct information to the appropriate people in a timely, dependable manner and must be designed to handle rapid change.

Although it is beneficial to have a set of standard modules for analysts to use, they are expensive to develop. Therefore, to be more cost effective, reusable modules should be evolutionary in application. It takes longer and requires greater discipline, standardization, and expertise to develop such reusable code, but long-term use and the ability to expand the product must be fully explored. Standard interfaces are a must to handle the linkage between modules, technical libraries, languages, and databases.

The steps in the design and build phase are:

- Document detailed systems flow
- Build a prototype
- Select package or develop in-house
- Produce detailed systems specifications
- Obtain user and management approval
- Code and inspect programs
- Review and update project plans

1. Document Detailed Systems Flow—Business processes are documented in detail, reflecting where and how the automated and manual systems will interact. The design should be modular and divided into maintainable, manageable pieces.

2. Build a Prototype—One good approach to use when designing a system is to develop a prototype, sometimes known as a pilot system. A prototype shows how the system will flow and what it will look like in the working environment. One difficulty with prototyping is that end users working with the prototype often believe that the system is almost complete. They do not realize that the core internal processing is not included in the working model. Prototyping is helpful when users find it difficult to state their information needs. A major cause of this difficulty lies in the users' inability to see how they might use an information system. Prototyping enables users to better perceive screens and reports in the proposed system.

The distinct features of prototyping are:

- Learning and experience are integrated into the design process for both IT and the user
- Faster feedback on whether the system is functioning as requested and less time to make changes
- User involvement and the opportunity to resolve any potential communication misunderstandings before coding begins

- Lower costs, because it costs less to change a system that has not been tested or coded

3. Select Package or Develop In-House—The final decision is made as to whether a software package will be purchased or the system will be developed in-house. In many instances, even though a package is selected, it must be integrated with existing systems. Often "hooks" are needed to interface packaged software with existing systems.

4. Produce Detailed Systems Specifications—Specifications are written on a program level and assigned to the appropriate IT project task team.

5. Obtain User and Management Approval—Distribute the detail specifications document for review and receive approvals from all functional user areas involved. Update management on any changes and receive approval to proceed with the project.

6. Code and Inspect Programs—Programmers write the code per the detailed specifications given to them. When completed, the IT project teams meet and inspect the code. This quality step ensures that standards are being met, the code is efficient, and the program is functioning as requested by the customer. This step saves time by desk-checking before testing begins.

When packaged software is selected, the code should be installed and reviewed by all team members, so they all understand the system.

7. Review and Update Project Plans—Compare the original project task plan to the final document's anticipated work and update the project task plan and status.

Phase IV: Testing

Thorough testing is critical to the success of any project. The business departments and IT must work together closely to ensure that the system requested is working properly and is exactly what was requested. The IT area is not the sole judge in determining that the project request is ready to be implemented in a production environment or that the system is what the business departments requested.

Basic Test Criteria

When testing, the following four steps should be completed:

1. *Develop a test scheme*—
   a. *Devise a test plan*—Identify what needs to be tested and how it will be tested. Determine the risk of the process change and the level of

testing required. For example, will it be necessary to test quarterly and year-end processing with this system change? Will both online and batch processing require testing?

b. *Create a test script*—Identify the specific functional activities that require testing and the sequence of testing steps.

c. *Build test data*—Establish controlled testing conditions and build test situations that will produce specific results.

2. *Perform the test transactions*—Enter the data for testing.

3. *Run any programs required to process transactions and generate reports*—Run the programs and process as they would run under actual conditions.

4. *Analyze the results*—Review and verify the expected test results for accuracy, both batch and online.

A controlled testing environment and test cases should be used to ensure quality results.

Every project request should meet the following testing criteria to ensure minimal difficulties when the system is implemented.

Types of Testing

There are two basic types of testing: technical only and combined business and technical involvement. Each step must to be completed before the next level begins.

Technical Only

At this level, the IT functional areas verify that the project functions as a system and that all the pieces work and fit together.

IT ensures that the project request delivers what the business user has requested. Technical involvement during the business requirement and functional requirement phases eliminates the miscommunication usually associated with not delivering what the user really wanted.

This criteria level includes:

1. *Unit test*—Programmers verify that the code for each program or component works (multiple programs are usually written for each project request).

2. *Systems test*—Programs or components that were unit-tested are migrated into the existing system process to ensure that all existing system interactions remain intact.

3. *Integrated test*—*All* systems and each IT function (such as telecommunications and the data center) involved are consolidated for a thorough systems integration test to ensure reliability.

Business Functionality

At this level, the business users and the technical teams work together to verify that the project request functions as intended. Users have the opportunity to "shakeout" or work with the system before it is installed in a production environment.

1. *User acceptance*—Business departments verify that the system request meets business requirements and that the system functions properly.

2. *Stress test*—Ensures that the system request functions efficiently using real-life business conditions and volumes. This test should always be conducted before implementing a new system. Without a stress test, a contingency plan should be in place, which may be "dropping back" to the original system or proven processing method. A three-minute response time is an unacceptable quality service indicator for most companies, and a stress test will help uncover this difficulty before installing the system.

3. *Conversion test*—This step is required only when existing information needs are converted into a new format. The business departments are responsible for verifying the integrity of information. The accuracy of this function is critical to implementation of the project request. If existing data are converted inaccurately, the new process starts off with incorrect information and the project will fail.

4. *Regression test*—This test ensures that no existing system functionality is affected when the changes are introduced. The ideal situation is to retain initial test cases created for new systems and test the system using those conditions. Maintaining test cases requires discipline because any new system functionality must be added as a test condition and any enhanced system functionality requires testing against original test case conditions.

Usual practice is for the IT area to conduct and verify all the technical testing before involving business users. This verification is conducted by technical teams first because technicians need to iron out any problems before involving business users (the IT organization has multiple functions which must be coordinated). Technical checking should be completed before business users see the system, because giving users a bad first impression due to technical problems can result in loss of confidence in IT and the entire effort. This loss of confidence, in turn, can lead to user resistance to change.

Mandated project delivery dates, such as government-mandated changes, may force testing steps to be combined. In such cases, business users may become involved in technical testing and verification of test results before IT completes its testing. This commonly occurs when projects are not given time to follow proper procedures. Users are then forced to play a more active role in technical testing. Under no circumstances should any IT changes be installed before users have approved or signed-off on the installation.

Phase V: Installation

Before a project can be successfully implemented, the following tasks must take place within both IT and the business areas:

1. Educating employees about the change
2. Training conducted
3. Knowledge transferred
4. Documentation and procedures written
5. Testing completed
6. Contingency plans developed

In this phase, the project request is implemented in day-to-day production processes. All conversions take place and processing is "live."

Phase VI: Ongoing Maintenance and Feedback

The implemented project request results are reviewed. This is also considered to be the continuous improvement phase.

Measurement Review

Pertinent team members review and discuss among themselves and with the customers:

1. What could have been done differently to improve the project request development process
2. How efficiently the process is operating, both for the business and within the technical area

Operating efficiency items which should be considered and measured include:

1. Malfunctions categorized by type and how many occurrences are due to:
   - Programming
   - Equipment
   - Incorrect or misleading requirements
   - Improper work flow
   - Business process misunderstanding
   - User input error
   - Data editing
   - Conversion

2. Generate a cost–benefit analysis for the new system.

3. Review overall system response time and availability.

4. Review feedback and compare the results to the measurement indicators set during the functional design phase.

5. Evaluate whether project was completed on time and within budget. If it was not, determine why for future reference.

6. Compare original estimated cost–benefit with new cost–benefit analysis. Compare the estimated payback period to what the project delivered.

Maintenance

System maintenance is a never-ending task and in total quality is continuous improvement. Maintenance is constant after any project request is implemented. It sometimes requires following all the project methodology steps, depending on the business change request. Someone must be responsible for making sure the system continues to run smoothly. Examples of maintenance include correcting technical difficulties ("program bugs") or enhancing the system with mandated requirements or requested improvements. All installation plans should include additional time for maintenance support, especially during the period immediately following installation. Maintenance usually impacts the technical area first, but the business departments must also allow time to learn the system before installing new quality measurements.

MEASURING AND ESTIMATING METHODS

Measurements Are Needed

The quality of technology is difficult to measure, and the quality of software development is even more difficult to assess. When measuring a physical product, it is relatively easy to quantify and compare. In addition to measuring physical attributes (such as disk space, memory, and response time), software measurement should consider user friendliness, maintainability, whether results meet customer requirements, and whether the system is problem free and was delivered on time and within budget. The number of lines of code produced by a programmer is not important. In fact, measuring by lines of code can be counterproductive if programmers include extra lines to make a project appear larger. The goal is to measure software efficiency and not the programmer's technical efficiency.

The total quality concept includes having a quantitative measurement standard; otherwise, you cannot know that you are improving your process. The Gardner Group[6] reported that:

- A TQM program that is not based on a measurement program will fail within 12 months of implementation (0.8 probability).

- A TQM program that is not based on standards will fail within 12 months of implementation (0.8 probability).

- TQM programs can reduce the amount of rework required to repair defects by 80 percent (0.7 probability) and increase information systems productivity by 30 percent (0.8 probability).

- The cost of correcting a defective requirement once code has been written is at least 30 times greater than the cost to correct the defect during the requirements definition process (0.8 probability).

- Formal, facilitated review sessions of requirements will identify 90 percent of requirements defects (0.7 probability).

The benefits of implementing a measurement program include:

- Determining what resources (people and machines) are being used

- Analyzing how much time is being spent on a system or project

- Producing more accurate time and cost planning estimates by comparing previous similar projects

- Improving the overall process

- Examining effectiveness of a methodology or tool

- Evaluating where defects are occurring throughout the process so they can be eliminated in future projects

When establishing and reviewing measurements, it is important to remember that the intent is to improve the process and not to attack the people involved. Productivity gains are usually lost when people feel they are being criticized. Also, improving communication in culturally diverse teams is an important consideration when breaking down the barriers that prevent success. (For additional information, see Abstract 7.4 at the end of this chapter.)

Getting Started

The measurement program should be a consistent, never-ending circle. The IT organization must initially set goals and review whether it has any existing measurements. Sample goals might be to achieve closer conformance to requirements or to reduce software development costs and delivery time.

A measurement should be meaningful, easily obtainable, consistently reproducible, pertinent, and have system-wide business applicability. A starting point *must* be established. It is suggested that a controlled activity be identified, a unit of measure chosen, a standard value used (to compare with the controlled activity), and a method chosen to measure the performance between the standard value and the created value. Each organization must establish its own guidelines according to what best meets its budget and quality control criteria. The findings should provide feedback to the entire organization for use in determining where there is potential room for improvement.

IT performance measurements should measure productivity gains, technical quality, and whether customer requirements were met. For example, if a larger computer is purchased to improve response time, the measurement would compare the original computer response time to the larger computer results using the same volumes and conditions. The Gardner Group[6] states that the measurement process must be integrated into development and maintenance environments, so that performing measurements becomes part of the way business is done. They also say that measurements can support strategic and tactical planning and can provide information for calculating the return on investment in IT.

IT measurement programs should include tracking work effort, evaluating project change activity, reviewing post-project problems, and surveying customers.

Tracking Work Effort

This method is good for measuring the time being spent on a new or existing project by task and individual. Based on the statistics, management is able to analyze actual versus estimated project time, provide improved estimates for future projects, monitor project estimates during project development, flag existing systems that continually require maintenance support, and schedule individual work assignments. Standard time reporting must be in place in order for this to be effective. When establishing a time tracking program, everyone must follow the same recording procedure. The following standards must be in place to measure accurately:

- Establish a standard work day, which is used to determine overtime
- Designate consistent project categories and tasks for all projects
- Determine the direct and indirect hours to be reported
- Define who records their time
- Design and implement a standard time reporting sheet or automated system

Tracking work effort can give the project team a history of project time and improve estimation accuracy. The estimation accuracy (EA) can be calculated using the following formula:

$$EA = \frac{\text{Estimated Value} - \text{Actual Value}}{\text{Actual Value}}$$

The estimation accuracy would then be compared to the quality standard set by the organization. Of course, in estimating projects the goal is 100 percent, but in the real world, the variance allowed is usually 10 percent (allowing for specific deviations).

Evaluating Project Change Activity

Change activity taking place during a project can be categorized into three different types:

1. Missed functionality/customer-need requirements
2. Deviations from the *expected* original functionality requirement
3. Problems discovered during the testing phase

Tracking the number and type of changes is a good measurement indicator to evaluate where there is room for improvement during each project methodology phase. During the project, a standard log should be generated tracking each change by type, phase within the project methodology, and time spent adding to or correcting the activity. These statistics can be used to measure against other comparable projects. (For additional information, see Abstract 7.5 at the end of this chapter.)

Reviewing Post-Project Problems

Post-project problems are situations that occur after the project is implemented and delivered to the customer. A standard log should be completed for each problem reported. Suggested information includes:

- *Type problem category*—Technology area where the problem occurred and where the problem should be forwarded (e.g., data center, applications support, telecommunications)

- *Severity level*—How much time until the problem must be corrected (e.g., now, within 24 hours, by week end and by month end)

- *Project*—The application project where the problem occurred

- *Date*—Date the problem was reported

- *Description*—A brief description of the problem

- *Contact*—Individual who reported the problem

- *Person assigned*—Individual assigned to correct the problem

- *Date corrected*—Date the problem was corrected

- *Problem resolution*—Description of what activity took place to correct the problem

- *Problem code*—Code indicating the cause of the problem as determined at resolution time (e.g., hardware failure, program bug, missed functionality, or scheduling)

- *Time spent*—Time spent correcting the problem (man-hours—time actually worked)

The problem log statistics can be used to measure software reliability. This includes how much time is being spent correcting problems and types of problems by project. Newer projects should have less problem reporting. This is a good measurement indicator to evaluate overall technical quality and to determine whether additional time is needed when conducting testing. These aspects can be used to anticipate the failure rate as software ages. Failure rate is defined as the number of problems reported divided by how much time it took to correct the problems.

The problem log tracking can be used to measure the number of new problems for a specified period of time and the turnaround time to service problems. Measuring the response time for open problems (RTOP) can be calculated using the following formula:

$$RTOP = \frac{\text{Total Time of All Problems Open}}{\text{Number of Open Problems}}$$

The average time taken to correct closed problems (TCCP) can be calculated using the following formula:

$$TCCP = \frac{\text{Total Time Closed Problems Were Open}}{\text{Number of Closed Problems}}$$

Comparing measurements is based on whatever specified time period is best for your organization. The specified time could be a daily, weekly, or monthly period.

Surveying Customers

A basic survey of IT customers is prepared and conducted, asking what they think of the IT organization and its service. A standard set of questions is generated and the results reviewed. The survey can be conducted and the results compared on a quarterly basis. The same customers are surveyed each time for consistent standard measurement. What better way to improve service to customers than by asking the customer directly?

Additional Measurement Considerations

When establishing IT measurements, it is important to consider effect on the business in addition to technical efficiency. This includes comparing functionality requested to what was delivered. During the functional phase of the project, customer needs and requirements were identified. During testing and after implementation, measurement criteria consist of reviewing the requirements and then comparing the expected results with the actual results. Table 7.3 provides a sample list of functionality requirement questions; the answers can be used to measure quality standards based on what was expected.

For most projects, a cost–benefit analysis is prepared before any project approvals are given. It is important to find out whether the anticipated savings and productivity gains were achieved. A projected cost savings is generally set before a project is initiated; this figure would be used as the measurement indicator.

Estimating Software Development Projects

It is difficult to create an accurate estimate for a software project. The situation is complicated by the fact that IT is often asked to provide an estimate before the business requirements are complete. IT should be given the opportunity to revise estimates after each step in the project methodology, especially after the business requirements (phase I) and functional requirements (phase II) steps. When the business requirements have been written, the final processing functional points still have not been determined and additional processes may be identified during the final conceptual design. When the functional phase is completed, all processing points should have been identified and the estimate can be measured against the result. This is a Catch-22, situation, however, as the software estimate is usually needed before IT knows how much work will be involved. To make matters worse, management usually will not allow changes to the estimate without good reason. Often the result is that management urges IT to assign extra people to the project, but there are limits. Remember, "nine women can't produce a baby in one month."

In addition to past history, the following should be considered: the size of the effort, company environment, IT staff, and other miscellaneous factors discussed below. (For additional information, see Abstract 7.6 at the end of this chapter.)

Size of Effort

The size of the effort can be estimated by counting the number of business process activities (called function points by IBM). The basic idea is to determine how many inputs, outputs, queries, processes, and files are involved. For example, suppose it takes an average of 3 man-days (working constantly) to create an input. If there are 10 inputs, then 30 man-days would be the estimate for inputs. The same procedure is followed for outputs, etc.

The sum-of-basic-function-points estimate should then factor in extra time for multiple locations, higher volumes, performance, complexity of processes, telecommunications, reusability, external customer involvement, and changes.

Company Environment

Any project estimate should consider company culture and customer involvement in past projects. When the customer is resistant to change or has not been involved in projects, extra time should be factored into the estimate. The requirements change rate will be higher when the end user does not participate in up-front planning and design.

Information Technology Staff

The expertise and size of the IT staff are factors which should be considered. Major projects using new technologies may require obtaining outside expertise to supplement staff skills. Additional IT staff training may be required, which adds to the estimate.

Miscellaneous Considerations

New projects often entail using new technologies. The estimate should consider whether the technologies have a proven track record.

When a pre-set deadline date is mandated, the existing staff size may not suffice and temporary help may be needed, adding to the estimate.

Misunderstandings most frequently occur between IT and its customers when the customer has a mental picture of what the final result will be but fails to communicate that image fully to the implementors. As part of any specification or plan, it is always a good idea to review a "mock-up" or prototype report, screen, or process flow. Unless IT has this information, it is difficult to estimate time and difficulty. The user also appreciates the thoroughness and a chance to participate in the planning process. This same method may be used when an existing process requires change or conversion.

Some projects require a conversion from an existing system to meet the new process requirements. When this is necessary, the estimate must include the planning, designing, building, and testing time required to convert the old process to the new.

WHAT CAUSES PROJECTS TO FAIL

Inevitably, some projects will fail. Factors that contribute to failure include:

- Inexperienced management and lack of skill
- Rudimentary planning techniques
- No previous situation to compare in order to accurately estimate the project
- Relationships between business functional areas, including IT, poorly handled
- Management did not follow through on meeting its commitment
- Poor planning, follow-through, and status reporting
- Appropriate knowledgeable people were not involved
- No communication or forewarning about the project
- Project was delivered to business areas before they were involved or trained
- New tools and techniques were used without proper training or outside expertise to help teach their proper usage

SUMMARY

Every project should have a project team and subproject teams that are responsible for the project request. The teams are responsible for ensuring the success of the project and are involved from start to finish. Before any project development methodology can be successful, commitment must be received from senior management and standard methodologies set in place. There are six basic phases in the project development methodology which must be completed when quality control standards are being meet. There is no single methodology a company must follow. A successful methodology complements how the company conducts business and is consistent with company goals and objectives. (For additional information, see Abstract 7.7 at the end of this chapter.)

ENDNOTES

1. *Webster's Encyclopedic Unabridged Dictionary of the English Language* (1989). New York: Portland House, a division of Dilithium Press, Ltd.
2. Shore, Joel (1989). *Using Computers in Business.* Carmel, IN: Que Corporation.
3. Lewis, Ralph and Smith, Douglas (1994). *Total Quality in Higher Education.* Delray Beach, FL: St. Lucie Press, p. 189.
4. Schultz, Louis E. (1989). *Personal Management.* Minneapolis: Process Management International.
5. Rowan, T.G. (1982). *Managing with Computers.* London: Heineman, p. 125.
6. Gardner Group Continuous Services (1993). "AD Metrics: A Foundation for Improved Quality and Productivity." *ADM Strategic Analysis Report,* January 4, 1993.

EXERCISE

EXERCISE 7.1   FOUR STEPS FOR DEVELOPING EFFECTIVE TEAMS

1. *Vision Statement*—Create a vision statement of the ideal team three to five years into the future. Answer the questions: "What can we do?" and "Where can we be?"

   Examples—To provide top quality customer service to our clients when they request information about any of the company's products or services. To be one of the top five companies in our industry according to customer surveys conducted by outside marketing firms.

2. *Purpose*—Define why the team is needed. Answer the question: "Why does the team exist?"

   Examples—Provide multiple customer services with one central customer support center. Provide integrated sales and marketing product offerings.

3. *Principles and Values*—Define the principles and values that will guide the team members' actions. Be certain they relate to company ethical standards and values. Answer the question: "What are the principles and values we consider most important in working toward our vision?"

   Examples—
   1. Continuously seek ways to improve business processes
   2. Develop and practice listening skills
   3. Encourage open discussion and welcome everyone's opinion
   4. Encourage initiative
   5. Work as a team and support each other
   6. Continue to learn
   7. Maintain a positive approach
   8. Assist with improving other teams and business processes
   9. Serve the customer's need
   10. Provide support in seeking and conducting research
   11. Encourage creativity and innovative ideas
   12. Maintain a positive attitude

4. *Mission Statement*—Develop a unit mission that will serve as a guideline for decision making by everyone on the team. Be consistent and identify areas for which the team will be responsible. Answer the question: "How will we move toward the vision?"

   Examples—Our mission is to plan for and implement the best customer support service center in our industry. Our services will allow customers to be served in a minimum of time. Customers will be able to receive product information from one central point versus having to call multiple service areas.

Our mission is to plan and install an intercompany employee growth and incentive program. This incentive program will fairly distribute information about company work positions and expectations and will provide a way to compensate employees and teams who are exceptional performers.

ABSTRACTS

ABSTRACT 7.1
STUDY SHOWS STRONG EVIDENCE THAT
PARTICIPATIVE MANAGEMENT PAYS OFF

Lawler, Edward E. III et al.
Total Quality Newsletter, September 1992, pp. 1–4

In this excerpt from a new book, *Employee Involvement and Total Quality Management: Practices and Results in Fortune 1000 Companies,* the authors present comparisons of surveys sent to Fortune 1000 companies in 1987 and 1990, with 51 percent and 32 percent response rates, respectively. The article includes several bar graphs and charts which compare 1987 and 1990 data. There seems to be little difference between the surveys in reasons for implementing employee involvement (EI) programs: improving quality and productivity are still at the top (about 70 percent each), followed by improving employee motivation and improving employee morale (about 55 percent each). "Most employees, in a 3-year period, did not receive training in interpersonal skills or in the kinds of technical/analytical skills necessary for an employee involvement or total quality program to work effectively," say the authors, the data showing little change from 1987. Only 9 percent of the organizations recently trained more than 60 percent of their employees in TQM and statistical analysis, and only 2 percent have trained 60 percent in understanding financial reports and business results. All but 10 percent of the corporations have some employees covered by individual incentives, but they usually cover less than 40 percent of the work force. Overall, the success ratings for the pay-for-performance reward systems associated with EI programs are extremely positive. Highest ratings were for profit-sharing and employee stock ownership programs, but 43 percent of respondents were undecided with respect to the success of gainsharing. Work group or team incentives indicated 51 percent undecided, but few reported failure. While support by top management retained its lead as a condition facilitating EI (50 percent), support by middle management dropped from 39 percent to 26 percent over 3 years, reflecting the ambivalence middle managers have toward EI when they see how the programs will force behavior changes and reduce their numbers. The greatest improvement in internal processes is reported in participatory management, technology implementation, trust management, decision making, and organizational processes and procedures. Quality, service, and productivity are reported improved as a result of EI efforts in about two-thirds of companies. The relationship between TQM and EI follows no clear pattern, with slightly more than one-third of companies managing EI and TQM as one integrated program, a third managing them as separate but coordinated programs, and the other third managing them separately. Still, respondents tended to view EI as part of quality (76 percent), rather than quality as part of EI.   (©Quality Abstracts)

ABSTRACT 7.2
THE QUALITY TEAM CONCEPT IN TOTAL QUALITY CONTROL

Ryan, John M.
ASQC Quality Press, Milwaukee, 1992, 272 pp.

"This book's intent," explains the author, "is to provide the reader with a comprehensive look at how various techniques, methods, and strategies fit together to restructure an organization's culture by building and implementing an overall team approach to total quality control/just-in-time (TQC/JIT)." The author focuses on a JIT approach to process improvement as a subset of TQC. In the first chapter, he relates JIT to TQC and discusses basic JIT terms and concepts, illustrating them with a variety of graphs. The second chapter explains how a company can organize the three types of teams required to implement and support a TQC/JIT system:

- *Top-level team (TLT)*—He explains how to select participants from the upper levels of management, and then he outlines and explains the specific responsibilities of this team to write and manage a plan for system implementation and maintenance.

- *Corrective actions teams (CATs)*—After the TLT identifies company-wide problems, it assigns CATs to solve the problems. This chapter outlines the basic guidelines by which a CAT runs.

- *Functional improvement teams (FITs)*—These teams are formed in every department to identify and correct problems which are more or less confined to their own operations. The author gives a list of guidelines for running FIT meetings, along with the responsibilities of the leader.

The next chapter gives a detailed description of how to implement a FIT. The principles, he explains, are nearly identical to those that govern the implementation of CATs. The author introduces flowcharting and the types of graphs through which to communicate information. This section also includes a number of forms and examples of implementation in various companies. The next chapter describes specialized CATs for solving specific problems, such as the pilot line, vendor relationships, value engineering, design for manufacturability, parts commonality, preventive maintenance, foolproofing, process layout and line balancing, lot size reduction, organizing and cleaning the workplace, *kanban,* line stop, SPC, visual signals (ANDON), training (certification), setup time reduction, automation review, and cycle time control. Chapter 5 deals with the principles of cost savings. A final chapter summarizes the commitment needed by top management to make the system work. This book provides practical, detailed help with team implementation. Though most of the examples are from a manufacturing setting, the author assures the reader that the principles also apply to non-manufacturing functions as well.   (©*Quality Abstracts*)

ABSTRACT 7.3
TQM: A STEP-BY-STEP GUIDE TO IMPLEMENTATION

Weaver, Charles N.
Quality Press, Milwaukee, 1991, 235 pp.

While it doesn't make sense implementing TQM like making "instant pudding," this book does offer a useful step-by-step approach. The author introduces a combination of TQM and a management information system called the "methodology for generating efficiency and effectiveness measures," and he proceeds to use the acronym TQM/MGEEM throughout the book to identify this system. He suggests beginning a comprehensive education based on Deming's and Juran's philosophies to help change the corporate culture a few months prior to introducing TQM/MGEEM. The book begins with a description of the quality problem in America. Then successive chapters describe in considerable detail the steps which need to be taken to implement TQM/MGEEM, down to the content of the leaders' talks and the group processes to be used. Briefly, the TQM/MGEEM program revolves around Blue Teams and Gold Teams for each organization within a company.

- The Blue Team for a department is composed of a facilitator, the manager, immediate superiors and immediate subordinates, and representative customers and suppliers. The team uses nominal group techniques to review the department's mission statement, and then it breaks the mission into measurable parts called "key result areas" (KRAs).

- The Gold Teams, formed from the manager's subordinates and key workers, are led by facilitators to develop indicators to measure the KRAs.

These teams also build a feedback chart for each indicator to be used for periodic feedback on the KRAs' progress.

- Members of each department participate in monthly feedback meetings, where they (1) review progress on their charts, (2) share ideas on how to improve the process by which work is accomplished, and (3) discuss how to eliminate unnecessary bureaucracy. Suppliers and customers can attend these meetings to provide input on their expectations and ideas for improvement. (©*Quality Abstracts*)

ABSTRACT 7.4
AFTER PRODUCT QUALITY IN JAPAN: MANAGEMENT QUALITY

Yahagi, Seiichiro
National Productivity Review, Autumn 1992, pp. 501–515

This is one of the most important new articles to come out of Japan in 1992, and the implications are enormous. The author proposes the use of expert systems featuring a 12-factor model organized into 41 "elements" of measuring subfactors. Japanese management has moved beyond product quality, says the author, to an emphasis on total integrated management (TIM)— management concerned about each facet of the company and interrelating them into a concerted, comprehensive corporate management policy of innovation. The author has developed an expert system which measures the 12 factors that determine management quality, divided into 41 subfactors:

- Corporate history: past, present, and future
- Corporate climate: core climate and culture
- Strategic alliances: objectives and coherence
- Channels: suppliers and buyers
- Management cycle: vision, strategy, planning, organizing and implementing, and controlling
- Environment: economic, societal, and global
- Management targets: inputs, markets, technologies, and products
- Business structure: business fields, business mix, and market standing
- Management resources: money, materials, information, and people
- Management design: system, organization, authority, and responsibility

- Management functions: decision making, interrelationships, and quality
- Management performance: growth, scale, stability, profit, and market share

He sees six factors as critical to the success of a company: management cycle, business structure, management resources, management design, corporate culture, and management performance. These six factors are interrelated in a circulatory system of Management Quality factors which have a cause-and-effect relationship as follows. The management cycle acts as the driver and influencer of the four factors of structure, resources, design, and culture, which in turn affect management performance. If the quality level of the management cycle is low, then the six factors generate a negative or bad feedback loop which finds management passively waiting until poor results of management performance force reactionary feedback into the management flow.* If the quality level of the management cycle is high, then these six factors generate an excellent feedforward loop in which management perceives the strategies and plans needed for success of each management factor and then proactively formulates and implements them.

The author's consulting organization conducts an annual survey of the management practices of Japanese firms, and in this article he presents the results of the most recent survey, which represents input from about 200 firms. Graphs and charts show comparisons between the worst-scoring and best-scoring companies, and he uses creative graphics to illustrate his analytical technique and to summarize questionnaire responses. From this comparison, he deduces a number of principles: (a) management quality factors must be well-balanced, (b) management cycle is the key to the management quality loop, and (c) the dynamics of TIM must be considered. He then goes on to describe the management cycle, which consists of the following key components: vision, strategy, planning, organizing, implementing, and controlling. The author recommends using an annual questionnaire to first analyze management factors within a company and then develop a multiphase action plan to restructure an organization for TIM. This article by Yahagi is must-reading for anyone who wants to remain on the leading edge of new application-oriented technology.

---

*According to Yahagi, the circulatory aspects of the management quality system are a key to understanding the relationships of this system to others, such as the Malcolm Baldrige National Quality Award.

ABSTRACT 7.5
THE PHASES OF DATA ANALYSIS

Cleary, Michael J. and Tickel, Craig M.
Quality Progress, February 1992, pp. 57–59

With Deming's claim that Japan's economic success has stemmed from the proper use of statistical analysis in its production process, U.S. organizations have developed a strong interest in statistical process control. But rather than making frantic efforts to master these particular skills, say the authors, an organization should expect to go through four distinct phases in implementing data analysis techniques:

1. *Hand calculation*—Manual data collection and preparation of control charts is a fundamental way to learn how a process works. However, it is prone to errors and does not make it easy to apply more advanced analysis techniques.

2. *Computer applications*—Readily available PC software packages will help the user chart more accurately, and they contain enhanced statistical tools for analysis.

3. *Data collection devices*—Data collection devices which allow data to be collected directly from the production process provide timely and accurate data.

4. *Online systems*—When automatic collection systems are connected directly to the computer, immediate analysis is available. The authors warn, however, against overcontrol from automatic adjustment systems.

The authors also caution against letting data collection become an end in itself. Successful programs emphasize problem solving and analysis, not charting. These should be seen as tools to address the issue of continuous improvement. (©*Quality Abstracts*)

ABSTRACT 7.6
QUALITY CONCERNS IN SOFTWARE DEVELOPMENT:
THE CHALLENGE IS CONSISTENCY

Perry, William E.
Information Systems Management, Spring 1992, pp. 48–52

Current software quality levels in the United States are 4.5 defects per 1,000 lines of code, compared to Japanese levels of 1.5 per 1,000. The difficulty in improving software quality, says the author, is in defining what quality is. "If quality means meeting specifications and standards, the definition of those specifications and standards is the definition of quality. In essence, every organization establishes its own quality definition." The remainder of the article concentrates on the information systems (IS) department's own internal standards. While critics argue that standards inhibit creativity, the author contends that standards produce a vital consistency. Internal characteristics of software which must be controlled by standards, according to the author, include: correctness, reliability, efficiency, integrity, usability, maintainability, and testability. However, in organizations with finite resources, these quality attributes must be prioritized so that programmers will emphasize those that reflect the users' needs rather than their own. Moreover, the author faults unrealistic scheduling with degradation of software quality. He concludes the article with three major suggestions:

- The IS standards committee should develop the standards it believes are necessary to meet each of the quality attributes listed above, making quality rather than uniformity its main objective.

- The user should be asked to prioritize each of the quality attributes so the developers can create the structure that best meets the user's needs.

- The estimating system should be designed to produce a schedule to build the software, but once the estimate has been established, meeting the estimate should not be the major concern of IS management. Instead, they should focus on those quality attributes.

ABSTRACT 7.7
TEAM DEVELOPMENT: THIS IS HOW IT'S DONE

Gold, Jeffrey (editor)
Executive Development, Vol. 5 No. 3, 1992, pp. 1–32

This entire issue of *Executive Development* is devoted to the process of developing teams—both training members of a management team and training members of work teams. The individual articles include:

- "Building Our Team—From the End of a Rope"—Explores training a management team through outdoor training.

- "Measures Which Help You Work Together as a Team"—Discusses three different feedback instruments: the Types of Work Index, the Team Management Index, and the Linking Skills Index.

- "Improved Teamworking Using a Computer System"—Reviews the computer-based Belbin *Interplace III Expert System* that is used to help determine and understand an individual's team role.

- "From Public to Private: The Team Approach at Scottish Hydro Electric plc"—Outlines a development program for 130 senior managers.

- "Management Team Building: An Experience at BT"—Explains a management team development workshop at British Telecom.

- "Organizational Change Through Team Development at BICC"—Describes a senior management team development exercise at a company implementing work teams throughout its organization.

- "Team-Built Teams"—Reviews three-day team-building workshops at Colworth House Laboratories as part of a total quality initiative.

- "Developing the Team at Northamptonshire Police"—Describes a management team development effort.

- "Know Thy Team—and Play Your Trump Card!"—Outlines the *TeamBuilder* analysis of five team roles used at a London-based design company.

- "Improvement Teams at Champion Spark Plug"—Describes workshops to train total quality management improvement teams at a manufacturing plant. (©*Quality Abstracts*)

CHAPTER 8

"HOW-TO"
TECHNIQUES
AND TOOLS

The purpose of this chapter is to present a "how-to" methodology to define and design processes using various techniques and tools available to implement quality. These tools and techniques are used internally and jointly by the business and information technology functions. It is important to mention at the outset that *methodology* is a *way for people to approach solving problems* in an organized, team-oriented fashion, whereas *techniques and tools* are *used to deliver improvements* that are envisioned and planned when using the methodology.

DEFINITION OF TECHNIQUES AND TOOLS

Techniques are a method used in performing functions or tasks. Tools are implements used to perform the functions or tasks. Techniques and tools work hand in hand to improve quality and productivity. A tool is usually given a name denoting the type of work performed. Tools can be equipment, computer software, or a standardized, codified series of steps to accomplish a specific end. Many other definitions are possible for both techniques and tools, but the above will suffice here. Even pencil and paper can be defined as tools.

CONSIDERATIONS WHEN USING TECHNIQUES AND TOOLS

It is important to remember that there is no one right or wrong way when deciding which techniques and tools should be used to improve business and technical functions. Each company must implement the techniques that will work best for that particular organization. Companies have different goals and objectives. Any technique being used should be periodically reviewed and modified to meet changes in philosophy, business, or technical areas. If the proper tools and techniques are carefully selected, a company can achieve success.

Companies of all sizes should use some type of technique or tool to document and standardize processing and communications methods. A technique can be as simple as a business plan. Every company, even the one-person owner, should have a business plan to define the goals and objectives of the business.

When a small company experiences sudden growth, the CEO can no longer keep tabs on all day-to-day events and processing. Without standard techniques, the employees and company no longer function efficiently. Once a firm reaches approximately 60 employees, the "way it's always been done" is no longer acceptable if the company wants to grow and develop. The company must reassess business plans and workflows to implement techniques and tools that complement business goals and objectives. Standard written communication methods and policies *must* be developed as the company outgrows the "word of mouth" communication that is no longer effective in a larger organization.

Smaller companies can use techniques and tools to a lesser extent, but since both communication and control are tighter, a small firm must beware of overkill when determining which methods to utilize.

There are many different products available representing various techniques and tools. Each vendor says, "We will meet your business needs!" or "You must have this; it's the newest thing out and everyone has it!" The reality, however, is that someone is trying to make a sale instead of addressing the company's best interests. Firms often purchase products that are inappropriate for their size and business processing needs or products that allow for future growth. Once a company identifies its business needs, a thorough vendor product evaluation and selection analysis should take place before investing money in any product. There are many products defined as techniques and tools from which to choose. These choices are *business decisions* that must take information technology into consideration (not the other way around). A firm can save money by knowing what it really needs and taking the time to do comparison shopping.

Whatever techniques and tools a company selects, they must be installed and used in a standardized storyboard fashion throughout all departments.

It is critical that every employee be thoroughly trained in the use of the tools, the techniques, and the storyboard before going into production mode. Any benefit is negated when one department uses one method and another department uses another method or an employee is told to use a tool or technique without being trained. This creates an organizational "Tower of Babel." *Consistency*—in communication, measurement, and method—can be lost in this manner and any attempt to achieve true progress is also lost. (For additional information, see Abstract 8.1 at the end of this chapter.)

TECHNIQUES AND NONSTATISTICAL TOOLS

The following represents a sampling of available techniques and tools. The list is intentionally not product name specific. Our purpose is to provide a guideline and create awareness that a product or method exists. The intent is not to endorse any product or vendor, since numerous companies offer these techniques and/or tools. A company should conduct a thorough analysis and feasibility study before implementing anything new in its quality control process. Not doing so only courts disaster.

Business Plan

A plan is a scheme for action to accomplish a specific purpose. A company may have many plans, each a part of the master corporate business plan. Each department should have its own plan. Departmental business plans must tie into the overall corporate plan and show appropriate linkage to corporate quality systems.

The goal of the business plan should be to:

- Provide a method to translate customer needs into specific action

- Focus business activities to achieve customer satisfaction

- Align control/improvement activities at all levels of the organization with corporate policy

- Communicate chronic high-priority problems and target them for improvement

Planning and communication of the plan gives everyone in the company a common direction.

Change Management

This methodology is used to track and communicate changes. A commonly understood plan for modification preserves a "business as usual" attitude as project development takes place within the company.

Information technology should have a separate change management process to handle software code, documentation, equipment, and data.

When everyone in the company knows what is going on and is aware of any changes taking place, fear and uncertainty are minimized.

Education and Training

TQM begins with education and training that never ends. The Japanese philosophy is to first train your employees and *then* you can make changes. The integration of training into system building and conversion is very important. There is a cost to good training, but any other alternative is more expensive.

Employees must be involved and educated before using any newly introduced processes or systems. Employees should be introduced to and trained in a new process before starting to serve customers. Quality service can be greatly affected when training occurs during process introduction.

Any company success is based on employee acceptance. You cannot please everyone, but most people can be less fearful and less resistant to change. Investment in education and training can pay rich dividends.

Management-by-Walking-Around (MBWA)

MBWA is a very positive management tool. Using the Plan-Do-Check-Act cycle, MBWA, and formal reviews educates everyone involved and creates understanding of issues/concerns faced by the entire organization. Senior managers, for instance, should not sit in their offices and only speak with their immediate links in the chain of command. If you really want to know what is going on within the company, talk to all employees, at all levels. It is surprising what information can be gained and the amount of feedback that is shared once trust is established. Managers should recall what it was like before they reached their present positions and stay in touch with employees. This is an excellent means to continually improve.

Benchmarking

Benchmarking is used to measure and to compare work processes, equipment, systems, or individual performance (of people or a department) with others either inside or outside the organization. This helps establish standards of excellence. Benchmarking helps groups/individuals to learn the innovations and best practices of other groups or companies, set targets based on data, and convince people that "we can do better, measure performance, and be a more outside-world-focused instead of inner-focused company." It leads to significant improvements in cost, quality, cycle time, and competitive ability.[1]

Brainstorming

In this technique, ideas are generated by a group. The ideas are not open to discussion and every idea is considered. A team of representatives from all areas, including information technology, is assembled for a brief period of time. The participants offer suggestions and consider "what if" situations. The reasoning behind the technique is "two heads are better than one."

Nominal Group Technique (NGT)

This tool is a structured group decision-making process used to assign priorities or rank order groups of ideas. NGT is used where agreement about a decision is lacking or where group members have incomplete knowledge of the details of a problem. It was developed by Delbecq and his colleagues in the 1970s[1] and has been used for a wide variety of organizational development and improvement activities. For example, it was used to obtain responses from a focus group of business faculty on the type and relative importance of changes that were needed in a comprehensive revision of an MBA program at a state university.

The process for performing the NGT is as follows:

- Silent (written) generation of ideas in response to a focused question

- Round-robin recording (usually on a flip chart) of one idea at a time from each group member by a designated recorder

- Clarify ideas through questions from group members as to the meaning of various listed items

- Vote on ideas to prioritize importance; uses a one- or two-stage process

- Closure on a decision of what to do about the prioritized items

For additional information, see Abstract 8.2 at the end of this chapter.

Joint Application Development (JAD)

In this method, all business and technology areas participate in planning and designing the system. It is usually divided into two separate phases which can consist of multiple sessions. A skilled outside facilitator should be used to facilitate the sessions. This technique is used during phase I (project development) and phase II (functional requirements) of the project development methodology.

The benefit is that everyone in the company is working in the same direction and toward the same purpose. All areas involved are working together, at the same time, planning and designing. This technique enhances the communication process and speeds development time because all participants are brought together as a company team.

Computer-Aided Software Engineering (CASE)

CASE is a collection of techniques and tools directed toward developing and maintaining software systems of all types. It provides project management as well as project development life cycle analysis, design, implementation, and maintenance support.

CASE is not recommended unless a company has already installed a proven project development methodology. A company can have the best CASE tools in the world to document and support product development, but if requirements are not defined in detail up front, the tools will not be effective. When CASE tools are used, they must blend in with some process and employees must be properly trained in their use. Numerous vendors sell CASE tools, but the tool purchased must meet a company's needs. Senior management must make an initial heavy investment and allow time for processes to be changed when using this new way of developing and maintaining systems.

Object-Oriented Design/Programming (OOD/OOP)

Object-oriented is "breaking into parts" functions that are performed in the same way and have common behavior. Each module is related to and communicates with another. Each module is considered "reusable," which benefits information technology by allowing the same modules (programs) to be used for other similar processes. Once the modules have been identified and the initial development efforts have taken place, reusing modules can expedite making changes and decrease maintenance time. This is similar to the top-down method, but there is more emphasis on how modules communicate and are related to one another versus emphasizing program development and testing modularity.

Structured Design/Programming

This was the trend in the 1970s, but it is being replaced by the object-oriented methodology. The method is directed more toward helping information technology program development and testing efforts. The overall process is designed, programmed, and tested in a modular fashion by function. The concept is to design programs that are reusable when performing common functionality. The premise is why reinvent the wheel when an existing process meets the need. Object-oriented methods expanded on this concept by including more information about how the modules communicate with and are related to each other. Top-down is mentioned only as a "nice-to-know."

Graphical User Interface (GUI)

This is a display format which enables the user of an online system to choose functions from pictures (icons). Instead of pressing a key to request an option, the user points to his or her request and clicks using a mouse. This method forces a modular design by business processing functions. This format is excellent, particularly when developing systems that support customer service inquiry.

Prototyping

Prototyping is the creation of a preliminary model that the business and technical areas try out to determine whether the system meets request objectives. This would be comparable to a sample in manufacturing. Everyone is given the opportunity to identify any difficulties before full technology development efforts are completed. An example would be designing the online screens and letting the customer navigate from one process to another. Prototyping saves time and money because the customer receives a preliminary preview and design problems can be addressed before coding begins. It should be used far more than it is.

Data Dictionary

This is a central repository for all the data elements. It can retain information about files, data definitions, fields, edits, and variables as well as whatever information the user wants to know about a data element. A company must generate standards for usage before a dictionary can be used efficiently and effectively. This is an excellent tool for decreasing information technology change-response time because it defines data element usage throughout the company. When developing a system, it can be an invaluable reference. It is difficult to see how earlier data processing existed without a data dictionary; in fact, COBOL was very popular in particular because it demanded a "data division" (at least on a program-by-program basis) that defined inputs and outputs in a dictionary-like manner.

Plan-Do-Check-Act (PDCA)

The PDCA cycle is a critical part of the management system and provides a means to gain knowledge from all employees, to communicate plans and activities, and to negotiate contributions to corporate policies.

Quality Function Deployment (QFD)

QFD is tied to customer needs and is an excellent method to systematically focus on the most important issues from the customer's viewpoint. What the customer wants and how this project will solve the problem are clearly stated, keeping technology in mind. This is an excellent method for helping to identify detailed project requests and for measuring improvement.

STATISTICAL TOOLS

Organization and resolution statistical tools are used when a project includes a large amount of varied data and the issue requires analysis. (For additional information, see Abstract 8.3 at the end of this chapter.) The basic statistical tools are as follows.

Control Charts and Graphs

Control charts and graphs are means to present information in the form of a picture. One example would be to show the variance between actual and estimated. This method monitors the ongoing performance of an activity. It can be immediate or over time. The type of analysis conducted and each presenter's personal preference determines which type of graph will be used. Each graph has its own application value. Some of the types of graphs are:

- Bar
- Line
- Circle or pie
- Radar

Flowchart

Flowcharts are commonly used and are a natural for the information technologist. They are not, however, an accepted way to stratify and recognize variation. Stratification is the arrangement of components within a whole.

A process flowchart is a visual representation of the steps in a given process (business or technical). The steps are sequential and the chart reflects how the process functions.

Upon reviewing a documented flowchart, it is easier to recognize redundant activities or missing steps. A flowchart shows:

- How the process works, like a factual "road map"
- Where there are interfaces with other key activities
- Where control points and measurements should be developed

Check Sheet

A check sheet is used to identify tasks and measure their status using a standard format. This tool is used when it is extremely important to capture the correct information in a timely manner and over a period of time. Check sheets provide a means to record events in a concise manner. The degree of accuracy achieved is dependent upon the number of people collecting the data and the level of detail they provide. It is a good tool for analyzing information.

The check sheet provides a means to simplify a process by preprinting the items to be checked. It serves three major purposes:

1. Makes the task easy
2. Standardizes and reduces variation
3. Arranges the information for future ease of use

Scatter Diagram

The scatter diagram is an analytical graph in which data items are plotted as points on an X–Y coordinate axis. Real-world conditions require us to study many variables. A scatter diagram is a graph showing the relationship between two variables. It helps to show:

- Cause and effect
- Relationship between characteristics
- Patterns and pictures of the variables

Histogram

The histogram is used to measure frequency of occurrence, which is displayed as a frequency distribution. It is represented as a vertical bar chart. The column widths are the interval ranges and the lengths are the frequencies.

If all data were constant and predictable, the world would be very orderly and probably very boring. However, data, like nature and people, do not always remain in a constant state. One of the basic principles of TQM and continuous improvement is management by facts. The histogram is a means to collect data and determine facts.

Pareto Diagram

The Pareto diagram is a technique to graphically display the ranking of causes from the most to least significant. It provides a means to break down the "countless many" in order to identify the "vital few."

Cause-and-Effect or Fishbone Diagram

The cause-and-effect diagram is a visual display illustrating the relationship of various causes and symptoms to a specific effect. It helps identify the root causes of a problem. The cause-and-effect and Pareto diagrams can be powerful allies when used properly.

Gantt Chart

This is a horizontal bar chart that shows the project plan over a period of time. It can show the tasks, areas of responsibility, milestones, critical paths, start and end dates—the list can go on and on. The content will be the factors that are necessary to manage and keep track of the progress of the project over time and ensure that it is on schedule and within budget. It a way to measure project status. A documented project plan keeps all involved parties aware of their deliverables and when their portions must be completed. It is a superior communication tool.

Program Evaluation and Review Technique (PERT)

PERT is commonly used to monitor large, long-term projects and their critical paths. It involves analysis of the time frame required for each step in a process and the relationship of the completion of each step to activity in previous steps. The chart is shown as circles (work elements against time) and connecting lines.

Graphical Evaluation and Review Technique (GERT)

This procedure is used for the formation and evaluation of systems using a network approach. The relationships between project activities, tasks, and events are documented. This method is used to organize data in artificial intelligence systems.

Data Flow Diagram

This is a graphical analysis and design tool that represents the flow of data through a system.

Hierarchy Plus Input–Process–Output (HIPO)

The standard format is divided into three basic categories using document work flows or system processes. All process inputs are shown, the process function(s) are delineated, and all outputs are defined in detail.

Affinity Diagram/KJ Method

This method organizes pieces of information into groupings based on the natural relationships that exist among them. It is used when large volumes of information are being gathered.

PERIODICALS AND NEWSPAPERS

The following is a list of nonindustry-specific periodicals and newspapers. They provide articles to assist management in remaining up-to-date with business and technology issues, services, and products.

- *Business Week*
- *BYTE* (sometimes more technical)
- *CIO (Chief Information Officer)*
- *Computerworld*
- *Datamation*
- *The Economist*
- *EDI World*
- *Entrepreneur*
- *Forbes ASAP*
- *Fortune*
- *Harvard Business Review*
- *IBM Systems Journal*
- *Information & Management Journal*

- *Information Week*
- *PC World* (sometimes more technical)
- *Profit*
- *Sloan Management Review*

ENDNOTE

1. Delbecq, A.L., Van de Ven, A.H., and Gustafson, D.H. (1975). *Group Techniques for Program Planning: A Guide to Nominal and Delphi Processes.* Glenview, IL: Scott Foresman.

ABSTRACTS

ABSTRACT 8.1
STORYBOARD: A CREATIVE, TEAM-BASED APPROACH TO PLANNING AND PROBLEM-SOLVING

Shepard, Dick
Continuous Journey, December 1992–January 1993, pp. 24–25, 31

The storyboard is a creative problem-solving tool which allows teams to assemble and process information and ideas in an efficient and effective way, says the author. An illustration pictures a typical storyboard layout on a wall or portable bulletin board, with colored cards affixed with pushpins. A *topic card* (5" × 7") defines the subject of the session. *Header cards* (4" × 6") provide column headings for major subjects under which *subber cards* (3" × 5") expand the ideas, with occasional *sider cards* (2 1/2" × 3") which modify other cards. Colored yarn is used to frame, divide, or connect ideas. The author recommends assigning one of the group to serve as facilitator, rotating this assignment every 30 to 45 minutes. The facilitator switches the group from creative (right-brained brainstorming) to critical (left-brained analysis) modes as the storyboard develops. During the creative times, participants write their ideas with marker pen on the cards and pin them to the board. The critical periods organize and provide opportunity for objection and countering. The article concludes with a discussion of four specialized types of storyboard approaches: idea, planning, communication, and organization.   (©*Quality Abstracts*)

ABSTRACT 8.2
TAKING QUALITY BEYOND THE AWARENESS STAGE

Wetzel, Charles F. Jr. and Yencho, Nancy M.
Journal for Quality and Participation, January–February 1992, pp. 36–41

"How can we get real performance with results from TQM?" The experiences of the RENEW team at Boeing Materiel exemplify how one can put the theory of quality into practical terms and actually improve work processes. Continuous quality improvement (CQI) is the term Boeing uses to represent its commitment to a total quality environment. When it set up the new entity of

Boeing Materiel, it saw an opportunity to pilot test innovations and extensions of the CQI concept. A team was assembled from eight Boeing Materiel employees and three consultants from the firm of IRD/Macro International. The primary objective of their pilot study was: "Improving the cycle time of major information processes, ensuring the effective utilization of people and improving information quality flow." To accomplish this, a PC-based software program called *RENEW* (from IRD/Macro International) was used to:

1. Gather and analyze data on organizational processes
2. Make recommendations for improvement
3. Create action plans to implement the improvements

Considerable detail is given here on the several surveys conducted, the functions the program performs, and the subsequent data analysis. Nonvalue activities were eliminated, processes were improved, and more emphasis was placed on "taking time to do the job right the first time." The pilot program allowed all the employees to see CQI in action with open channels of communication and a set of measurable goals. (©*Quality Abstracts*)

ABSTRACT 8.3
MEETINGS ANONYMOUS: IBM DOES IT WITH COMPUTERS

Grimaldi, Lisa
Meetings & Conventions, January 1992, pp. 100–102

This author suggests that trainers may find themselves as facilitators of "silent meetings," if IBM's *TeamFocus* software gains wide acceptance in corporate America. IBM developed the silent meeting to brainstorm and process ideas several years ago, but the company found it so successful—cutting the time of the average business meeting by 60 percent—that it has begun to market the computer program on which the silent meeting is based. The program, installed on a file server, links up to 24 desktop PCs. The typical meeting follows the sequence below:

1. During a brainstorming session, participants are given the topic to be "discussed" and are asked to type all their ideas into the computer.

2. The server collects and sorts the comments and sends them back to the participants so each can see what colleagues have written.

3. The facilitator and participants arrange these ideas into 10 to 15 categories.

4. Categories are then sent to participants who rank the categories in order of importance.

5. Finally the information and votes are printed out, eliminating the need for notetaking.

The power of the method seems to reside in: (1) allowing ideas to be shared without fear of reprisal and (2) saving time that would be taken up with socializing. However, computerphobia limits the enthusiasm of some top executives for this concept. (©*Quality Abstracts*)

CHAPTER 9

ELECTRONIC
DATA INTERCHANGE

Technology continually offers new and innovative techniques that affect companies and individuals. The cordless telephone, video games, facsimile (fax) machines, answering machines, notebook computers, electronic mail (E-mail), and calculators are a few examples that were not affordable or available ten years ago. With an ATM card, you can visit another state and obtain or transfer funds from your bank account. We are in the midst of the electronic communications era, which will determine how we communicate in the future. One innovation is electronic data interchange, which is causing major changes in how companies conduct business.

WHAT IS ELECTRONIC DATA INTERCHANGE?

The term electronic data interchange has many definitions. The description used by the Data Interchange Standards Association (DISA), a division of the American National Standards Institute (ANSI), is:[1]

> Electronic Data Interchange (EDI) is the transmission, in a standard syntax, of unambiguous information of business or strategic significance between computers of independent organizations. The users of EDI do not have to change their internal data bases.

EDI is the common "language" used to get information from one computer system to another. Users must translate this information to or from their own computer system formats, but this translation software has to be prepared only once.

In simple terms, EDI is computer-to-computer communication using a standard data format to exchange business information between companies. As an example, consider the postal system. A sender places a document in an envelope; the envelope is stamped and placed in a mailbox; it is picked up by a mail carrier, sent to the appropriate post office, and delivered by a mail carrier to your mailbox; you retrieve the mail from your mailbox, open the envelope, and read the document mailed by the sender.

EDI allows a company to rethink how it can improve its business processes and competitiveness. It is a means by which companies can become innovative in changing traditional methods used to conduct business. EDI allows companies to pursue new strategic business directions and visions. These efforts include reengineering business processes and implementing or revising the direction of total quality. Types of business processing improvements would be eliminating paper, faster turnaround, allowing data to be automatically entered into computer systems, and eliminating human data entry. The full benefits of EDI are realized when a company is creative in streamlining its business processes to make them more efficient and cost effective.

There are many definitions of EDI, and they vary based upon what article you are reading or who you are speaking with. Some people consider fax transmissions to be EDI, while others see it as using magnetic tape or diskettes. The key point when utilizing EDI is for a company to rethink how it conducts business and where it can continually improve.

EDI USERS AND TYPES OF ACTIVITIES

Who Uses EDI?

Companies of all types and sizes are able to utilize EDI. Some large corporations specify EDI as the communication method of choice. Businesses such as the federal government, K-Mart, and the Big Three automakers are nudging their suppliers to send all purchase orders and invoices electronically. EDI is being applied in many industries and is not limited to high-tech companies. Industry examples include banking, healthcare, retailing, travel, manufacturing, insurance, government, and utilities. Sample EDI application areas include purchasing, inventory, billing, distribution, price notification, financial, freight rate notifications, and sales and cash management, among others. A sampling of industries that are using EDI is provided in Appendix 9.1.

Based on a detailed study[2] conducted among firms using EDI, the majority suggested that EDI will be used as a competitive weapon. Dominant firms will choose to make alliances with a few suppliers rather than adopt an open market philosophy.

Types of EDI Activity

Currently EDI is primarily used for purchase orders, bills of lading, invoices, healthcare claims, and financial exchanges. The applications are limited only by imagination. As long as a standard data format is designed or in place and another company is willing to receive the information, any document can potentially be transmitted electronically. There is often confusion about the difference between EDI and electronic funds transfer (EFT), since EFT is also used to exchange information electronically. Financial EDI is the exchange of payment and bank balance information between a company and its bank or another company. EFT is the exchange of information between two banks that results in value being transferred.[3] It is possible for financial EDI to be bank to bank, but EFT does no bank-to-company exchanges. Examples of financial EDI would be bank account statements and payment orders; examples of EFT would be Automatic Clearing House (ACH) debit and credits or wire fund transfers. Realistically, EFT uses EDI as a means to transmit information.

One concern about using EDI arises when a company transmits information electronically and the receiving company does not simply print the information received. Someone in the process verifies and rekeys the information into another automated system, which means that the transaction continues to flow internally. Benefits of EDI should include elimination of paper and automatic information entry without manual intervention. Before this benefit can be achieved, companies must readdress their business processes and existing automated systems.

Business Processing Considerations

EDI is changing the way companies do business, shifting the ordering process from a snail-like, paper-intensive system to a computerized one.[3] One objective of using EDI is to align business transactions with business processes, not business functions. The nature of business relationships, both internal and external, is changing. EDI is evolving from transmitting orders and invoices to becoming a management tool used to reengineer business processes. Roles and tasks are changing as firms are changing their work process flows. A salesperson who used to receive and write orders has become a product advisor. Customers conducting business with firms that have multiple divisions now request centralized electronic transmission. These new concepts are forcing companies to build information technology (IT) organizational infrastructures that allow their divisions to exchange information and cooperate with one another.

Firms using EDI are in a position to consider reengineering various business activities, since EDI is faster and paperless. A company's information flow needs to be rethought. This change in thinking may necessitate revising operating procedures or eliminating procedures that do not support company strategies such as total quality management and just-in-time (JIT). With JIT, inventory is available as needed. EDI has assisted in this process by providing expedient inventory reporting to suppliers that continuously replenish stock. Many firms have eliminated warehouse space and allow manufacturers to resupply directly to the using location. Instead of storing products at a warehouse and having the location obtain inventory from the warehouse, the location is automatically stocked by the product manufacturer. (For additional information, see Abstract 9.1 at the end of this chapter.)

WHERE DOES INFORMATION TECHNOLOGY FIT IN?

EDI is not merely a technical tool or technique; it offers change and new ways of conducting business. The information provided and stressed throughout this text can also be applied to EDI projects. The involvement and role of the IT organization would be the same as for other business projects but entails crossing company boundaries. IT cannot be the sole implementor of EDI; it must be a business and technical team effort. An EDI effort involves thorough planning by the business and technical sides and requires technical functional support from all the IT areas identified in Chapter 2 (telecommunications, applications support, data center, and administrative planning).

EDI should have its own architecture tied to the company's strategic direction. This EDI architecture at a minimum should be designed to handle any system integration elements, systematically know the data format, address security levels, and know which communications connectivity to use. The real EDI world has many different criteria and needs; this preplanning allows for handling multiple data formats and multiple system interfaces and provides better support to the various business processing areas using EDI. It may be necessary to designate an EDI coordinator, who will be responsible for planning and coordinating all EDI activity within the company. The size of the firm and the extent of EDI activity are the basis for deciding whether an additional full-time position is necessary. It is recommended that someone coordinate the EDI effort, regardless of the size of the effort, so that results are not fragmented throughout the company.

An information architecture and systems integration should be in place to support the business before implementing EDI. In larger companies with multiple divisions, this interrelationship becomes even more critical, as the trend in customer service is "one-stop shopping" and dealing with a single entity for all products and services. Separate islands of information could easily be created as the result of EDI activity if there is no plan or technical platform to handle multiple data format standards and communication connections. Without planning within the IT organization, EDI will become fragmented and difficult to maintain, much like the antiquated computer systems many companies maintain today. When implementing EDI, or any new technology, planning is critical, to allow for business growth and to keep the systems modular and maintainable.

Using EDI for process reengineering and implementing a total quality program forces a company to examine itself by workflow process instead of functional unit. The business functional areas and technical functions must work together to develop an EDI strategy. EDI alone could be a company's mission that would generate numerous projects and subprojects for years.

WHAT IS NEEDED TO IMPLEMENT EDI?

Some companies and vendors make implementing EDI sound simple, but in reality there is more to it than electronically sending information to another company. In addition to top management's commitment (which is a *must* for all projects), other considerations include using a methodology, addressing standard data formats, and establishing electronic connections.

EDI Methodology

The EDI project methodology guidelines are the same as for any project. The stages are:

1. Planning and business requirements definition
2. Functional requirements
3. Design and build
4. Testing
5. Installation
6. Feedback and review

The above phases and their steps are the same as those discussed in the project development methodology presented in Chapter 7. The steps and considerations are the same, but the following are some additional factors to consider when implementing EDI.

EDI Implementation Considerations

Business Strategic Planning

Before starting any EDI adventure, it is important to establish a vision and mission for the company and its EDI commitment. The EDI project team should include a representative from each business functional area. No potential future user should be excluded. Questions that must be answered are:

- Why are we pursuing EDI?
- What do we expect from its usage?
- Who will be our EDI partners?
- What information do we want to exchange?

Based upon the answers to these questions, the scope of the project and the effort required to successfully implement EDI will vary. If the objective is solely to electronically communicate information but continue entering information into the existing business systems, then the project would not entail redesigning the work process to better utilize the technology. The effort would be minimal and the benefits of EDI would not be fully realized. On the other hand, a business may want to continually improve its work processes to take advantage of technological innovations, including EDI. In that situation, the firm's vision would be to phase in implementation of EDI by initially installing the data communications piece, which would eventually be incorporated into a new work process. It is always best to keep it simple by installing a project in small manageable pieces, using a pilot program.

Build External Company Relationships

One major factor that distinguishes an EDI project from other company projects is that EDI entails teaming with another company, known as a trading partner. When selecting a trading partner, it is important to survey potential firms to determine their level of interest in EDI and to find out if they are leaders or followers in implementing EDI. A trading partner must be an active participant in each phase and both partners must cover the same activities. A partner company must be included in the process as part of the project team and part of the project plan. EDI data formats and transmission method, checks and balances to confirm the receipt of information, volumes, and frequencies are critical requirements for both companies and must be defined and agreed upon up front. The user acceptance test must include both companies and must be signed off on by both before installation. Any EDI installation will be unsuccessful unless both parties involved are in sync with what is expected from the other. Timing, cooperation, and coordination between the trading partners are critical components of a successful implementation. (For additional information, see Abstract 9.2 at the end of this chapter.)

Ensure Commitment and Acceptance

It is important that all levels of management, employees, and team participants be educated on EDI and its capabilities. This helps define business requirements in solving business concerns. Education also helps in overcoming the fear of change and promotes eventual acceptance. The overall goals and objectives of the project must be explicitly defined and top management must commit to the project before moving on to functional requirements.

Legal and Tax Implications

Before implementing any EDI project that eliminates paper, a company should seek advice from legal and tax experts. The IRS is trying to help auditors eliminate paper files, but records must still be kept. IRS rules vary based on the company and its involvement with EDI. It is important to make certain the paper files can be eliminated when defining business requirements. Some basic questions (not an all-inclusive list) that must be answered are:

- Is the original document required?
- Are original signatures necessary?
- What information must be retained for tax or legal purposes?
- How long must the information be kept?
- How long does the company have to present the information?
- Will a copy of the document need to be recreated or will a report displaying the required information suffice?

One suggestion that should help in a tax audit or financial audit is to have well-documented processing explanations that include document flows and systems interaction flows.

It is better to be safe than sorry; consult appropriate authorities for clear, concise answers before eliminating paper. Microfiche and imaging are other alternatives when storing archival information.

Standard Data Formats

One benefit of EDI is that it forces industries to standardize terminology and usage and how information is recorded and presented by creating a dictionary of industry terms and usage. The data transmitted must be clear, concise, and unambiguous between companies. For example, on a bill of lading it would be important to clarify whether the port of discharge is the site where the product was unloaded or the location where the product was actually received.

EDI Data Standards History

The EDI data standards process began in the United States with the transportation industry during the mid-1970s. The transportation (ocean, air, motor, and rail) and other associated industries (banking, shipping, customs, freight forwarders, and brokers) created the Transportation Data Coordinating Committee (TDCC), which defined a standard electronic representation based on paper forms used within the industry. The initial effort created 45 transaction sets for the transportation industry. In the early 1980s, the American National Standards Institute (ANSI) initiated efforts to define a single set of standards for EDI that could be applied across industries.[4] These standards are known as the ASC X12 standards. Refer to Appendix 9.3 for an example.

Standardization is also growing internationally. The International Organization for Standardization (ISO) creates standards that are equivalent to the ANSI X12. This equivalent, called EDIFACT (Electronic Data Interchange For Administration, Commerce, and Transportation), was designated by the United Nations to support a global standard. Although the X12 and EDIFACT groups work together closely, the standards are different, which forces many companies to support multiple EDI formats.

Standard Group Types

Various standard groups have been formed to establish standards unique to their industries. These groups usually consist of major companies that communicate electronically with each other or compete with one another. The purpose is to establish a common language throughout the industry. This text will not attempt to explain all the different standards and meanings of the data. Appendix 9.2 provides a list of various industry standard groups and their addresses. Because each industry is unique and standards are rapidly changing, it is best to become involved with an industry standards committee to stay up to date.

Implementing Standards

An attempt to implement standard data formats is underway, but many firms still use proprietary formats. This forces companies to support multiple formats for the same business document. When implementing EDI, a company must be able to identify the sending company, determine the type of business transaction, and recognize the standard being used to translate the data into a format acceptable to the business system. When sending, the opposite occurs; the sender must "speak" in the format that the company addressed uses. Why have standards if multiple formats exist? One master format per business document would be the best of all possible worlds, and standards committees are striving to achieve that goal; however, some companies will insist on using proprietary formats, primarily because they have EDI formats in place and changes are costly. Another reason is that some firms are not team players and do not want a standardized format that would share competitive information. Regardless of any changes that may occur in the future, a firm should plan on handling multiple formats unless it has the clout to insist that it will only conduct business in its own format.

Data Standards Software

The cost of software that supports translating information into the standard data formats has dropped. As more and more firms pursue EDI software, vendors are offering products that perform this function. This eliminates the cost of developing in-house customized programs and maintaining reformat programs. As of this writing, it would take up to a year, at a cost of up to $60,000, to duplicate the function of a software package that retails for $4,000. The reason is standardization. The software vendor has already produced the product and has recouped initial development costs. (For additional information, see Abstract 9.1 at the end of this chapter.)

Some of the questions to ask when considering a software vendor are:

• Does the vendor provide current and future support of EDI standards?

- Does the software support handling multiple versions of the same standard, while going through the approval process?

- How long from approval of standards until the software is upgraded?

- How flexible is the communications support?

- How does the software handle auditing of the document life cycle?

- What mapping capabilities are supported (i.e., flat files, online, user-defined interface or menu driven)?

- Is the software upgradable for larger hardware (i.e., personal computer to mainframe)?

- What hardware platform is needed?

- What are the mailbox capabilities?

- What security features are offered and are they used at the recovery site?

- Are any formal software implementation plans available?

- How does the software handle network and/or mailbox transmission difficulties?

- What are the detailed guarantees and controls (checks and balances) that the entire transmission was delivered?

- What reports are available?

- What are the archive facilities? Where is the information stored? How available is it? How long must the information be retained? Can the information archived be selected by the user?

- What are the hours for support?

- What is the response time if difficulties arise?

- Will the vendor provide a complete client list that can be contacted?

- What is the maintenance cost after purchasing the package?

- Does the price include the entire package or is it modular?

- What is the cost to obtain multiple copies for other locations?

- Is the source code included?

- Can the package handle generating proprietary nonstandard formats?

Establishing Electronic Connections

In addition to a standard data format, it is mandatory that the companies' computers are able to "talk" to one another. This sounds simple but it can be complex. EDI entails the use of special translation and communications software. When connecting computers, companies must consider the communications method and protocol that will be used to transmit information, as well as security and business recovery. Much of this will be determined by the company with which a firm exchanges information. The following definitions are from the *Computer User's Dictionary*:[5]

- *Protocol*—A set of standards for exchanging information between two computer systems or two computer devices.

- *Communications protocol*—A list of communications parameters (settings) and standards that govern the transfer of information between computers using telecommunications. Both computers must have the same settings and follow the same standards to avoid errors.

- *Communications program*—An application program that turns your computer into a terminal for transmitting data to and receiving data from distant computers through the telephone system.

Protocol standards are different than data format standards. Protocol is used to communicate data formats. Industry groups are trying to implement protocol and communications standards.

Choosing the type of electronic connectivity is usually an economic decision. There are basically two choices: direct communication with a company or a value-added network (VAN). Recently, VANs have become compatible and more reliable, but it is important to make certain that the trading partners will be able to communicate. A firm may have to support multiple networks and communication connectivities. The most widely used VANs today are operated by such firms as AT&T, MCI, Sprint, General Electric, and IBM. Using a VAN usually eliminates concerns about protocol, security, data receipt acknowledgment, and recovery.

When deciding which type of communication connectivity to use, the following is a sampling of factors to consider:

- What are the data volumes?

- How often will data be transmitted?

- Will data be accumulated and transmitted at preset times or will transmission occur when processing activity takes place?

- Is data transmission dependent on system loads?

- Do security levels prevent data interception?
- Does data require encryption for security?
- What is the data recovery plan?
- How reliable is the connectivity?
- What are the costs?
- What equipment and software are necessary?
- What are the line speeds (BPI)?

Based on the answers to these questions, a company will be able to make a good decision. Often the trading company will dictate the choice.

Each situation is unique, and there is no way to choose the type of connectivity without knowing all of the details. The purpose of this discussion is to heighten awareness of the factors that must be considered. The telecommunications field is rapidly changing, and it is wise to include someone with a strong telecommunications background as part of the EDI project team.

INTERNATIONAL CONSIDERATIONS

Standards

EDI is not used only in the United States or North America. Data format standardization efforts are taking place in the United States (ANSI) and internationally (ISO). As mentioned earlier, ASC X12 is the American standard and EDIFACT is the international standard format. The committees work together but it will be years before one common standard is used throughout the world. This may seem like a simple task, but cultural differences, different ways of conducting business, different industry priorities, and egos must be taken into consideration. Until there is one common standard base, EDI implementation must be flexible enough to handle multiple standards for the same type of document.

Communication Connectivity

When dealing with international communications, there are numerous concerns other than the obvious language and cultural barriers. At the tenth annual EDI Strategies Conference, Dan Petrosky of EDI Partners stated: "As soon we leave North America, the involvement of governments in EDI becomes significantly important."[6] In some countries, telephone lines are

Table 9.1 Advantages and Disadvantages of EDI

Advantages	Disadvantages
Reduces the flow of paper between organizations	Standardizes programs and procedures
Improves productivity	Lack of a common understanding and limited education
Allows for more efficient disbursement of information (speeds up the transmission of information between organizations)	Complex to use
	Difficult to quantify return on investment
	Significant impact on organizational culture
Improves accuracy of information and reduces errors	Standards still in a state of flux
Allows for reduction in personnel	Requires a high initial capital investment
Enhances relationships with customers and suppliers by creating opportunities to take advantage of new technology	Lacks the security that some companies need
	Legal ramifications have not been tested
	Most trading partners do not use EDI
Reduces inventory and inventory costs	Impacts organizational structures, procedures, and controls
Complements and enhances marketing efforts	Requires high-level management commitment to be successful
Reduces data entry	Requires high-volume use before benefits are realized

Source: *Information & Systems Journal.*[7]

government regulated and are not as efficient as in the United States. When the government runs the show, acquiring permission from telecommunications authorities for equipment connection often causes delays. Another concern is the level of data security available and the right of ownership during transmission. Before conducting EDI business in other countries, regulatory requirements, hardware availability, types of telephone lines, etc. should be addressed on a country-by-country basis.

IS EDI FOR YOU?

EDI offers many advantages in addition to standardization and elimination of paper, but first a company must determine if it is ready for EDI. Table 9.1

shows the result of an industry study[7] to identify advantages and disadvantages of using EDI. The findings are self-explanatory.

Use of EDI is expected to continue to grow. More and more companies are being forced into the world of EDI as customers redesign processes to eliminate paper and to take advantage of the speed and ease of use of EDI. The initial capital cost to implement EDI can vary from $2,000 to over $500,000 depending on complexity and level of involvement. A firm must have data available in machine-accessible format, software to translate into data formats, communications connectivity, and computer hardware. Companies should be wary of vendors that try to convince them how easy and inexpensive it is to implement EDI. This is partially true, but before spending money, *all* implications and expenditures should be considered. Communication costs, ongoing maintenance, hardware costs, data volumes, and data availability should be investigated before investing. A word of warning: it is difficult to quantify costs and determine a return on investment for using EDI because it is a complex system which affects multiple business functional areas.

For firms interested in EDI, a list of organizations that support EDI or other electronic interfaces is provided in Appendix 9.2. Appendix 9.1 lists various organizations by industry that can assist with EDI standards and implementation.

ENDNOTES

1. Data Interchange Standards Association (DISA) (1994). *1994 DISA Information Manual*. Alexandria, VA: DISA, p. 6.
2. Blackman, Ian, Holland, Chris, and Lockett, Geoff (1992). "Planning for Electronic Interchange." *Strategic Management Journal*. Vol. 13, pp. 540–550.
3. Parkinson, Kenneth (1992). "It's Time to Get Involved in Financial EDI." *Corporate Cashflow*. July 1992, p. 46.
4. McGee, James and Prusak, Laurence, The Ernst & Young Center for Information Technology and Strategy (1993). *Managing Information Strategically*. New York: John Wiley & Sons, p. 83.
5. Pfaffenberger, Brian (1992). *Computer User's Dictionary*, 3rd edition. Carmel, IN: Que Corporation.
6. Sutton, Judy (1994). "In the Little Dragons: Varied EDI Use Calls for Different Approaches." *Global Trade & Transportation*. January, p. 42.
7. McGrath, Roger Jr. and Scala, Steve (1993). "Advantages and Disadvantages of Electronic Data Interchange." *Information & Systems Journal*. August, pp. 85–91.

APPENDICES

APPENDIX 9.1   EDI SOURCES BY INDUSTRY*

This list is by no means all-inclusive. If you require information about an industry not listed, contact DISA for assistance.

Automotive

Automobile Industry Action Group (AIAG), 26200 Lahser Road, Suite 200, Southfield, MI 48034; phone: (313) 358-3570

Motor and Equipment Manufacturers Association (MEMA), P.O. Box 13966, Research Triangle Park, NC 27709-3966; phone: (919) 549-4800

Educational Institutions

American Association of Collegiate Registrars and Admissions Officers (AACRAO), AACRAO SPEEDE/EXPRESS Project, One Dupont Circle NW, Suite 370, Washington, DC 20036-1110; phone: (202) 293-7383

Arizona State University (AACRAO) (post-secondary schools), Box 870312, Tempe, AZ 85287-0312; phone: (602) 965-7302

Council of Chief State School Officers (CCSSO), One Massachusetts Avenue NW, Suite 700, Washington, DC 20001-1431; phone: (202) 336-7054

Washington School Information Processing Center (WSIPC) (pre-kindergarten through grade 12), 2000 200th Place SW, Lynwood, WA 98036; phone: (206) 775-8471

Financial

Federal Home Loan Mortgage Corporation (Freddie Mac), 8609 Westwood Center Drive, P.O. Box 5000, Vienna, VA 22070; phone: (703) 760-2465

National Automated Clearinghouse Association (NACHA), 607 Herndon Parkway, Suite 200, Herndon, VA 22070; phone: (703) 742-9190

Treasury Management Association (TMA), 7315 Wisconsin Avenue, Suite 1250 West, Bethesda, MD 20814; phone: (301) 907-2862

Government

Department of Defense (DOD), Defense Information Systems Agency (DISA), DISPO-HVE, 5111 Leesburg Pike, 9th Floor, Falls Church, VA 22041; phone: (703) 681-0219

*Source: *1994 DISA Information Manual,* Data Interchange Standards Association (DISA).

Grocery

Uniform Communication Standard (UCS), c/o Uniform Communication Council, 8163 Old Yankee Road, Suite J, Dayton, OH 45458; phone: (513) 435-3870

Health and Healthcare

Health Industry Business Communications Council (HIBCC), 5110 North 40th Street, Suite 250, Phoenix, AZ 85018; phone: (708) 872-8070

Insurance

ACORD (Property and Casualty), One Blue Hill Plaza, 15th Floor, P.O. Box 1529, Pearl River, NY 10965-8529; phone: (914) 682-1700 ext. 421

Petroleum

Petroleum Accounting Society of Canada (PASC), P.O. Box 1403, Calgary, Alberta, Canada T2P 2L6

Petroleum Industry Exchange (PIDX), c/o American Petroleum Institute (API), 1220 L Street NW, Washington, DC 20005; phone: (202) 682-8491

Pharmaceutical

National Wholesale Druggists Association (NWDA), P.O. Box 238, Alexandria, VA 22313; phone: (703) 684-6400

Publishing

American Newspaper Publishers Association (ANPA), NAA, 11600 Sunrise Valley Drive, Reston, VA 22091-1412; phone: (703) 648-1224

Book Industry Systems Advisory Committee (BISAC), 160 Fifth Avenue, New York, NY 10010; phone: (212) 929-1393

Serial Industry Systems Advisory Committee (SISAC), 160 Fifth Avenue, New York, NY 10010; phone: (212) 929-1393

Purchasing

National Association of Purchasing Management (NAPM), P.O. Box 22160, Tempe, AZ 85285; phone: (602) 752-6256 ext. 401

Retail

National Association of Retail Dealers of America, P.O. Box 9680, Denver, CO 80209; phone: (303) 758-7796

National Retail Federation (NRF) (NRMA/ARF), 100 West 31st Street, New York, NY 10001-3401; phone: (212) 244-8451

Voluntary Interindustry Communications Standard (VICS) EDI, c/o Uniform Communication Council, 8163 Old Yankee Road, Suite J, Dayton, OH 45458; phone: (513) 435-3870

Transportation

Air Transport Association of America (ATA), 1301 Pennsylvania Avenue NW, Washington, DC 20004; phone: (202) 626-4000

American Truckers Associations/Management Systems Council (ATA/MSC), 2200 Mill Road, Alexandria, VA 22314-4677; phone: (703) 838-1721

Association of American Railroads (AAR), 50 F Street NW, Washington, DC 20001; phone: (202) 639-5544

Container EDI Council (CEDIC), 251 Lafayette Circle #150, Lafayette, CA 94549-4342; phone: (510) 763-9864

International Air Transport Association (IATA), IATA Centre, P.O. Box 672, Route de l'Aeroport 33, CH-1215 Geneva 15 Airport, Switzerland; phone: (41) (22) 799-2683

National Industrial Transportation League (NIT League), 1700 North Moore Street, Suite 1900, Arlington, VA 22209-1903; phone: (703) 524-5011

Rail Industry Group of National Association of Purchasing Management (NAPM), Subcommittee on Information Standards, c/o Union Pacific Railroad, 1416 Dodge Street, Room 200, Omaha, NE 68179; phone: (402) 271-5607

Utilities

Utility Industry Group, c/o Southern California Edison, P.O. Box 800-Procurement, Rosemont, CA 91170; phone: (818) 302-5347

APPENDIX 9.2   EDI ORGANIZATIONS

United States

ANSI Accredited Standards Committee (ASC X12), c/o DISA, 1800 Diagonal Road, Suite 355, Alexandria, VA 22314-2853; phone: (703) 548-7005
Formed in 1979 to develop interindustry standards for the electronic exchange of business transactions. The data areas are shipping and receiving information, order placement and processing, invoicing, payment and cash application, and so on.

Data Interchange Standards Association, Inc. (DISA), 1800 Diagonal Road, Suite 355, Alexandria, VA 22314-2853; phone: (703) 548-7005
Formed in 1987 as the secretariat and administrative arm of ASC X12. A nonprofit organization that handles the administrative functions and communicates with ANSI for ASC X12.

Electronic Data Interchange Association (EDIA), 225 Reinekers Lane, Suite 355, Alexandria, VA 22314-2853; phone: (703) 838-8042
Promotes and educates individuals about benefits and impacts of EDI. Does not specialize in standards such as ASC X12 but provides an overall EDI information base.

International

Pan American EDIFACT Board (PAEB), c/o DISA, 1800 Diagonal Road, Suite 355, Alexandria, VA 22314-2853; phone: (703) 548-7005
DISA undertook support in 1988. Provides a forum for representation and consensus for Pan American representation relating to EDIFACT standards development, promotion, and maintenance.

International Organization for Standardization (ISO) Technical Committee 154, U.S. Technical Advisory Group, c/o DISA, 1800 Diagonal Road, Suite 355, Alexandria, VA 22314-2853; phone: (703) 548-7005
Administrates the U.S. technical advisory board for matters pertaining to the EDIFACT syntax before ISO.

UN/EDIFACT UN/ECE, Trade Division Palais de Nations, CH-1211 Geneva 10 Switzerland; phone: (41) (22) 917-2457
Develops and maintains international EDI standards. Operates under United Nations sponsorship.

APPENDIX 9.3   ASC X12S/94-172 FORMAT*

ASC X12 FORMAT	SAMPLE INVOICE CONTENT/NOTES		
ISA*00*0000000000*01*01*PASSWORDME *01*123456789*bbbbbb*987654321*bbbbbb* 890714*2210*U*00204*000000008*0*P*N/L	**Outside Envelope** (Interchange Control Header, ISA)		
GS*IN*012345678*087654321*900509 *2210*000001*X*002040N/L	**Inside Envelope**		
ST*810*0001N/L	**Invoice**		
BIG*900713*1001*900625*P989320N/L	DATE ORDER DATE INVOICE # CUSTOMER ORDER #	7/13/90 6/25/90 1001 P989320	
N1*BT*ACME DISTRIBUTING COMPANYN/L N3*P.O. BOX 33327N/L N4*ANYTOWN*NJ*44509N/L	CHARGE TO	Acme Dist. Company P.O. Box 33327 Anytown, NJ 44509	
N1*ST*THE CORNER STOREN/L N3*601 FIRST STREETN/L N4*CROSSROADS*MI*48106N/L	SHIP TO	The Corner Store 601 First Street Crossroads MI 48106	
N1*SE*SMITH CORPORATIONN/L N3*900 EASY STREETN/L N4*BIG CITY*NJ*15455N/L	REMIT TO (Selling Party)	Smith Corporation 900 Easy Street Big City, NJ 15455	
PER*AD*C.D. JONES*TE*6185558230N/L	CORRESPONDENCE TO	Accounting Dept. C.D. Jones (618) 555-8230	
ITD*01*3*2**10N/L	TERMS OF SALE	2% 10 days	
	QUAN	UNIT	NO.	DESCRIPTION	UNIT PRICE
IT1**3*CA*12.75**VC*6900N/L	3	Cse	6900	Cellulose Sponges	12.75
IT1**12*EA*475**VC*P450N/L	12	EA	P450	Plastic Pails	.475
TDS*4395N/L	Invoice Total		
CAD*M****CONSOLIDATED TRUCKN/L	Via Truck		
CTT*4*20N/L	(4 Line Items, Hash Total 20)		
SE*21*000001N/L	Transaction Set—Trailer		
GE*1*000001N/L	Function Group—Trailer		
IEA*1*000000008N/L	Interchange Control—Trailer		

b = Space Character   ] = Data Element Separator   N/L = Segment Terminator

*Source: *DISA 1994 Publications Catalog*, Data Interchange Standards Association, Inc., Alexandria, VA.

Smith Corporation
900 Easy Street
Big City, NJ 15155
(618) 555-6765

INVOICE
No. 1001

CHARGE TO	INVOICE DATE 7/13/90	SALES PERSON NTO

Acme Distributing Co.
P.O. Box 33327
Anytown, NJ 44509

SHIP TO   The Corner Store
601 First Street
Crossroads, MI 48106

YOUR ORDER NO.	CUST. REF. NO.	ORDER DATE	TERMS
P989320	66043	6/25/90	2% 10 Days

QUAN.	UNIT	NO.	DESCRIPTION	UNIT PRICE	TOTAL PRICE
3	Cse	6900	Cellulose Sponges	12.75	38.25
12	Ea	P450	Plastic Pails	.475	5.70

Please direct correspondence to:

C.P. Jones

(618) 555-8230

PLEASE PAY THIS AMOUNT   43.95

DATE SHIPPED 7/13/89	SHIPPED VIA Truck

ORIGINAL (from paper format)

ABSTRACTS

ABSTRACT 9.1
HOW ARCHITECTURE WINS THE TECHNOLOGY WARS

Morris, Charles R. and Ferguson, Charles H.
Harvard Business Review, March–April 1993, pp. 86–96

The global computer industry is undergoing radical transformation, the authors wrote in 1993, and three years later the beat goes on. Success today flows to the company that establishes proprietary architectural control over a broad, fast-moving, competitive environment. The authors contend since no single vendor can keep pace with the outpouring of cheap, powerful, mass-produced components, customers have been sewing their own patchwork quilt of local systems solutions.

The architectures in open systems impose an order on the system and make interconnections possible. It is the architectural controller who has power over the standard by which the entire information package is assembled. The popularity of Microsoft Windows is used as an example to show how companies like Lotus must conform their software to its parameters in order to have market share. Thus, the concept of proprietary architectural control has broader implications in that architectural competition is giving rise to a new form of business organization. The authors contend that a small handful of innovative companies will define and control a network's critical design.

It is necessary to cannibalize old niches in order to evolve to occupy an ever-broader competitive space. The Silicon Valley model is used to show four important operational features that underlie the overall basic theme of the article: inventing—and reinventing—the proprietary architectures for open systems is critical to competitive success and can serve as the platform for a radiating and long-lived product family. Overall, the five basic imperatives that drive most architectural contests are: (1) good products are not enough, (2) implementation matters, (3) successful architectures are proprietary but open, (4) general-purpose architectures absorb special-purpose solutions, and (5) low-end systems swallow high-end systems.

Of added value are three sidebars featuring scenarios for architectural competition: (1) graphical user interfaces, (2) video games, and (3) page and image description standards.

The article ends with a look at Xerox's failure to capitalize on its pioneer xerography niche and create spin-off industries and business lines. The authors conclude with the challenge: "We think that similar strategies are available to companies in other complex industries—aerospace and machine tools, among others. If so, the information (technology) sector's strategic and organizational innovations might prove as interesting as its technology." This is one of the better *HBR* articles to come along in the information technology field in the 1990s. No references are provided.

ABSTRACT 9.2
THE ROAD TO 2015: PROFILES OF THE FUTURE

Peterson, John L.
Waite Group Press, 1994, 372 pp.

In this best-selling view to the future, Peterson takes us on a scientific and technological roller-coaster ride that often defies the imagination. The author is the founder of the Arlington Institute, a well-known futurist organization, and the issues are well developed and provocative. The basic theme is that scientific discoveries, information systems, and technological advances will push a renaissance toward a knowledge society that will dwarf every previous revolution in the history of mankind. Information access, on a parallel with lifespan extension, will reach unprecedented levels. Ironically, says the author, the very global system that sustains our basic life requirements will be in danger. The work revolves around three views as to how the world systems will shift: optimistic, pessimistic, and realistic. The book is illustrated and well researched and is must reading for every information systems professional.

CHAPTER 10

HORROR STORIES
AND HOW TO
AVOID THEM

This chapter presents real-life situations and the lessons learned: the do's and don'ts of implementing new projects using technology. The cases are real; only the names have been changed to protect the guilty.

SOFTWARE SELECTION COST OVERKILL

Rebe Enterprises is a small, growing manufacturing business with sales under two million dollars. The firm handled its inventory manually and decided it was time to automate the function. The owner, Kay Rebe, attended a trade show where she encountered a firm selling prepackaged computer software. The salesperson assured Ms. Rebe that his package would meet her company's inventory business needs, other manufacturing firms were using this package, and the software could be customized to meet any special requirements. She purchased the software for $10,000.

When the package was being installed, it was found to be incompatible with existing computer hardware (PCs), and additional money was spent to purchase new PCs. The package offered multiple inventory processing components, which allowed for expansion and company growth, but only one of these functions was used. The package was difficult to use and required continual vendor support in the form of training at an additional cost. More money was spent on vendor programming assistance and customization. Ms. Rebe, the managers, and the employees were unhappy with the software, especially considering the investment (over $20,000).

One day, while sharing her frustration with another company owner, Ms. Rebe found out that her peer was using a software package purchased for $75 which would have met her company's needs and anticipated growth through the next two years.

Lessons Learned

The owner purchased software processing capabilities that were unnecessary for her company's size, projected growth, and financial position. The owner did not realize that other software packages were available for substantially less money that could meet her company's existing volume and growth plans for the next two years. Due to the owner's lack of planning and computer knowledge, hardware compatibility was not taken into consideration, which cost extra unbudgeted dollars.

1. Comparison Shopping for Software Packages

The owner should have shopped around for other software packages instead of buying on impulse. The salesperson convinced her that other companies in the same type of business were using this software and that it was the best. The owner was also convinced that the salesperson had her company's best interests in mind, when in reality the salesperson was simply making a sale. The package purchased was overkill for the small business and money was wasted.

When selecting software, the purchaser has to consider functionality, type of hardware needed, and training offered, as well as maintenance/support costs. A complete product reference list should be obtained, and it is a good idea to speak with peers in the industry about their experience with technology in general. Companies share human resource information. Why not technology?

2. Hardware Compatibility

The ideal situation would be to purchase software and then buy the appropriate hardware, but often a company must utilize existing hardware. It is easier to find hardware that meets software needs than it is to find software that meets a specific business need. Evaluating software means considering the hardware needed to run it as part of the cost.

HIGH TECH TO BE HIGH TECH

Joe Sams, CFO of a retailing company, returned from a high-tech conference excited about the new voice-response systems he saw. His impression was that his company could realize immediate savings and easily eliminate two clerical support people and a receptionist. The company would also project an image as a state-of-the art organization. He decided to purchase a voice-response system immediately. After the system was installed, customers started to complain, and after six months the system was removed. Customers hated the automated system—they wanted to talk to a human being. Many customers decided to take their business elsewhere. Sales dropped 17 percent in one quarter.

Lessons Learned

A customer survey would have revealed that a voice-response system would not be readily accepted. Many customers still had rotary phones and could not use a system that required a touch-tone phone. The customer base was an older group that did not like high-tech machines; they wanted to talk to and place an order with a real live person. These customers decided to do business elsewhere.

BUSINESS END USERS NOT INVOLVED

The top management of JCB, Inc. decided that a new and improved accounting system was needed. The CFO approached the information technology (IT) manager and said, "Give us what we need and you have my support." The managers and the business users were informally asked what they wanted in an accounting application but were otherwise uninvolved until installation. The programmers evaluated accounting software packages and purchased one that met all the technical requirements. The package was installed and the users were suddenly told to start using the new system. There was no formal training or documentation before the system was implemented. Converted information was found to be incorrect, and customer service suffered until the difficulty was corrected three weeks later.

The business users hated the system and complained, "The technology people did it to us again! We asked for one thing and received something totally different."

Lessons Learned

The technical people thought they knew what was best for the business or may have felt that the business users did not want to be involved. It does not matter who was at fault; this type of miscommunication should never happen. IT professionals and businesspeople must work together as a team to consider both business and technical concerns. There must be coordination of information and a solid connection to the purpose of the organization. IT professionals must be both business and computer analysts. Businesspeople must get involved with the technology. If IT does not customarily include business users in planning, business users should express their concerns to senior management. Any project that succeeds will be the result of a team effort. (For additional information, see Abstract 10.1 at the end of this chapter.)

A QUESTION OF SIZE AND UPGRADING

Four manufacturing firms and one distribution firm were owned by a central corporate entity called Group, Inc., which in turn was owned by Havasu, Inc. Each of the five small companies had its own computer. Those computers were all of the same type with the same operating system software, although each company had different application software.

The officers of Group, Inc. did not know what to do about their data-processing needs. The computers at the five firms were aging and money would have to be spent to update the hardware. The officers also felt that new application software was needed. A committee was formed to investigate. The committee was made up of the financial officers from the five firms and the IT manager from Group. Group's IT manager supplied programming services and personnel from Group to the five companies; none of the five companies had IT personnel of its own.

The committee hired one of the big financial consulting firms to help in its search for hardware and software. For a year the committee traveled periodically to various other firms to see software and hardware in action. At the end of the year, both the committee and the consulting firm recommended that Group, Inc. buy one large computer and a well-known application software package and consolidate all computing at one site. The software vendor indicated that each of the five companies could "tweak" the software to customize it for their particular needs.

Before any decision was made, the IT manager from Group was fired. A new manager, Harris, came on board and learned of the plan. The initial cost of the projected system was $1.2 million. Since Group, Inc. did not have $1.2 million to spend, the money would be borrowed from Havasu, the parent company.

Harris was intimately familiar with the type of hardware at the five companies. Although he had only been on board a couple of weeks, he went to the CEO of Group, Inc. and told him that it made no sense to get rid of all the existing hardware and spend $1.2 million that Group did not have. Harris explained that they could spend $200,000 and be better off. With $100,000 they could buy a new computer for the largest of the five companies and send its old computer to the next largest firm. Each firm would, in turn, receive the hardware from the next largest firm. Every firm would end up with a larger computer, with the smallest old computer being discarded. With the other $100,000, they could buy new software that would be individually customized for each of the five firms. Harris added that if Group spent $1.2 million, it would probably have to spend another million for custom software and staff expansion. Also, once the expenditure of $1.2 million was agreed to, there would be no turning back. On the other hand, if spending $200,000 did not work, Group could still elect to spend $1.2 million. Harris was opposed by the financial officers of Havasu, who wanted a single large computer and new software. In effect, Harris was betting his job that the less expensive alternative would work.

Harris's idea was accepted by the Group CEO and, after some wrangling at Havasu, Group was allowed to spend $200,000. Installation of the new hardware and customization of new software began at all five sites. Havasu kept close watch on the software customization, which was incrementally installed and proved to work well.

Two years later, only one of the five companies was profitable, and Havasu decided to sell all five. Because each firm had its own self-contained computer and software, the sale of each company was easy to accomplish. Group, Inc. was dissolved, the CEO was forcibly retired, and Harris lost his job.

Lessons Learned

One knowledgeable man knew more about the company's IT needs than a big name consulting firm, a committee, and a group of financial executives. Studies, evaluations, and estimates by people who do not have pertinent experience are useless and expensive. The idea that one big computer can solve all problems is often an unreal but tempting fantasy. In most cases, small and distributed is better. Each of the five firms had its own IT needs and handling them separately would have been a better approach. Harris being hired was a fortunate coincidence. Havasu and Group should have originally outsourced their problem to an expert who knew their old hardware and software intimately, as well as what technology developments were taking place in regard to that hardware and software. There is no substitute for pertinent experience.

An additional lesson is that although an IT function may be solid, its continued existence and that of the company depends upon financial factors beyond IT's purview. It is also significant that Harris, who saved Havasu at least $2 million (and made the sale of the five companies much easier), made himself persona non grata with the financial executives from Havasu by doing a good job. It is worth noting that an individual who persists in doing what he or she knows to be correct sometimes loses out personally and financially.

REENGINEERING INFORMATION SYSTEMS

The corporate computer systems at XRAY, Inc. were antiquated; they were no longer in sync with the direction of the business, and they were difficult and costly to maintain. After conducting a thorough study and cost analysis, it was determined that the best approach would be to reengineer the information systems and business process workflows. XRAY, Inc.'s top management committed to becoming a state-of-the art organization and the effort began. Together IT and business management teams evaluated and chose a project development methodology which was standardized throughout the company. In addition, they purchased CASE tools, upgraded the computer hardware, obtained a data dictionary, and changed the database software.

A project team was formed to coordinate and monitor overall corporate departmental functions and to be responsible for the success of the project. Additional task teams were formed with representatives from each functional business department. The team members represented every facet of the business, including technology, business processing, and marketing. The initial plan was to convert all existing processes and implement them all at the same time. As the project moved along, most of the time and effort were spent in up-front planning and defining requirements.

Everything appeared to be working well except that the project was continually over budget and behind schedule. Three years passed and nothing was installed. Top management was naturally concerned about the lack of results, and the decision was made to phase in the new system. Implementation plans were changed. After a fourth year, user training was conducted, but only one piece of the new system was put into production.

Business users were unhappy with the lack of friendliness and business functionality of the new system. They were spending more time trying to get their work done. The audit controls of the new system were not as rigid as the old system, which led to extra work. When the new system could not handle mandatory processing requirements, "quick and dirty" techniques were introduced. The business support staff increased by ten people, although the new system was supposed to reduce head count. Special "SWAT" teams were created to analyze the new system and implement new audit controls and procedures. None of the remaining systems was ever implemented.

Lessons Learned

The project started off on the right track. All the proper studies were conducted, the right people were involved, and management was committed, but the project failed in three critical areas.

1. Failure to Review and Document the Processing and Information Capabilities of the Existing Systems

During the business planning and requirements identification phase, the capabilities of the existing system were not reviewed. True, the existing systems were antiquated and the way the company conducted business had changed since they had been implemented, but their information and processing capabilities should have been considered in the new design. No comparison between the old and new systems was ever made to determine whether any of the capabilities of the old system were still necessary.

2. Lack of a Project Change Management Methodology

Although IT had a change review process, there was no *change control* for enhancements made to transform activity from the old systems to the new systems. Sample enhancements included electronic data interchange for customers and improved quality control. These changes could have saved a lot of time and reduced costs, but they were never implemented.

3. Planning the New Project without a Modular, Phased Approach, or Pilot Project

The initial plan was to convert and install all systems at the same time. This puts a company at greater risk and does not show top management any ongoing return on investment. Modular implementation would have facilitated existing business users working with the new system sooner. Phasing in would have shown that required functionality was missing.

Roughly $20 million was expended in an effort that was largely ineffective. The main lesson learned in this debacle was there should have been teamwork between existing system personnel and the new project development teams. (For additional information, see Abstract 10.2 at the end of this chapter.)

THE MAGIC SOFTWARE SOLUTION

Complex, Inc. was a large utility company with many PCs in its main office and in the offices of its subsidiary companies. The IT director and the CFO were impressed by a demonstration of new PC financial software. As a result, they advocated buying the software for all of the company PCs. Upper management at Complex concurred with the CFO and the IT director.

All PCs had to be upgraded with more disk space and larger memory in order to use the new software. All employees who used the PCs had to attend training classes. All this was accomplished, but a year later very few people were using the new software. The conclusion was that the money spent for hardware, software, and training had been largely wasted.

Lessons Learned

This was a top-down decision, made without the benefit of consulting with the people who actually used the PCs and the software. The actual users had no personal stake in making the project a success. Also, management did not monitor the use of the software and did not mandate that any particular standard reports be generated. As the saying goes, "You can lead a horse to water, but you can't make him drink." Success does not "just happen"—it has to be ensured by involving the people who actually do the work and by management's insistence on, and measurement of, particular requirements. (For additional information, see Abstract 10.3 at the end of this chapter.)

THE SOFTWARE PURCHASE

Sudley, Inc. was a manufacturing firm that had outgrown its hardware and had a considerable investment in its customized software. Sudley called in a consultant to assist in its search for a new hardware/software configuration that would be able to use its existing application software. The consultant and the IT staff at Sudley concurred on the hardware decision. A new operating system also had to be purchased and there were two main vendors: Firm A and Firm B. Either operating system could do the job, but the consultant firmly backed Firm A.

Firm A offered a money-back guarantee. Firm B was $12,000 less expensive. A survey revealed that some other companies had changed from Firm B's product to Firm A's product; there was no evidence that any company had ever changed from Firm A to Firm B. Firm A's software had a much more open architecture with more options for future computing, but Sudley elected to purchase Firm B's less expensive software. The hardware and software were successfully installed and seemed to work well.

Lessons Learned

Most firms will choose hard-dollar savings over a technically superior product (even a superior product with a money-back guarantee) because everyone understands saving money now, but few understand the money to be saved by working with a better product that allows for technical expansion in the future. If one assumes that the consultant was correct in preferring Firm A's product, Sudley, Inc. will probably remain forever ignorant of the advantages it might have offered. If at some point in the future Sudley finds that Firm B's software cannot do something it needs, which Firm A's software would have been able to handle, it would probably be identified as a brand new problem with no reference to the past purchase. Firms often pay large sums of money for technical advice, only to ignore it. Also, no one can expect to succeed in business without compromise. Ideals are seldom realized.

ABSTRACTS

ABSTRACT 10.1
THE HIGH PERFORMANCE ENTERPRISE: REINVENTING
THE PEOPLE SIDE OF YOUR BUSINESS

Neusch, Donna R. and Siebenaler, Alan F.
Oliver Wight Publications, Essex Junction, Vt., 1993, 380 pp.

The promise of the 1980s was that if your company listened to the voice of the customer, implemented JIT and TQM, and empowered its people, it would achieve world-class success. But by the mid-1990s, ask the authors, what happened to the High Performance Enterprise? "We wrote this book," they explain, "because we deeply believe that opportunities for improved performance have been placed off limits for many companies. Not because they are powerless, but because they don't really know how to go about improving performance." The authors seek to integrate the "bits and pieces" of the High Performance Enterprise into a workable whole, and in doing so they present a book consisting of two parts. The first section describes the strategic process, gives an overview, and discusses how to establish an organizational context, a strategic direction, a habit of continuous improvement, and a new work covenant. The second section is built from chapters discussing each of the ten steps in the authors' High P·e·r·f·o·r·m·a·n·c·e·s People Systems™ Process:

1. Create the target and baseline organizational profiles.
2. Define flexibility.
3. Redesign work: redesign jobs and define teams.
4. Define the roles and scope of supervision.
5. Design a skills development process.
6. Design the p·e·r·f·o·r·m·a·n·c·e·s feedback system.
7. Design NewComp™.
8. Prepare a blueprint, and develop major design components.
9. Plan for implementation and implement.
10. Monitor, evaluate, and continuously improve.

What emerges is a step-by-step process purported to create a High Performance Enterprise. Several themes are key to the authors' approach:

- *Performance* needs to be addressed in terms of p·e·r·f·o·r·m·a·n·c·e·s, the thousands of daily performances, individual activities, decisions, and transactions taking place every day and at every level among the company's employees.

- *Leadership* is an acquired craft which comes from establishing a work environment that embodies strategic direction and empowers employees.

- *NewComp*™ is a compensation approach consisting of strategy-based pay, which reshapes base pay to ensure a return on human assets, and performance-based rewards, which reinforces shared business goals among all members of the organization.   (©*Quality Abstracts*)

ABSTRACT 10.2
THE JOBLESS FUTURE: SCI-TECH AND THE DOGMA OF WORK

Aronowitz, Stanley and Difazio, William
University of Minnesota Press, 1994, 392 pp.

The authors lay down the challenge to the popular belief of a utopian, knowledge-based, high-tech economy with plenty to go around. Instead, their message is that there will be massive displacement of workers at all levels in the future economy. The premise that the good life is possible based upon full employment must change radically, the authors assert. They offer alternatives for what they call our dying job culture in order to sustain ourselves and our well-being in a future economy based upon science and technology. Interesting reading.

ABSTRACT 10.3
QUALITY IN AMERICA: HOW TO IMPLEMENT
A COMPETITIVE QUALITY PROGRAM

Hunt, V. Daniel
Business One Irwin, Homewood, Ill., 1992, 308 pp.

Quality in America is a readable volume that demystifies the quality movement and presents a clear plan to implement TQM in an organization. The author begins with an assessment of the global marketplace and the importance of TQM to a firm's remaining competitive. Next, he describes the fundamental concepts and vocabulary of quality. Chapter 3 is a helpful characterization of four of quality's pioneers: Deming, Juran, Robert Costello, and Philip Crosby. Then the author compares the emphases of the school of thought attributed to each of these people. "There is no one best way," says the author, but from that point on he describes and promotes his own synthesis of quality principles under the name *Quality First*™. A chart shows the relationship of Crosby's 14 steps, Deming's 14 points, and Juran's 7 points to *Quality First*'s 8 tasks, which are summarized under these major categories:

People-oriented tasks:
1. Build top management
2. Build teamwork
3. Improve quality awareness
4. Expand training

Technically-oriented tasks:
5. Measure quality
6. Heighten cost of quality recognition
7. Take corrective action
8. Commit to a continuous improvement process

Chapter 4 describes the Malcolm Baldrige National Quality Award and recommends applying for it. This is followed by a chapter giving a thumbnail sketch of Baldrige Award winners: Federal Express, Globe Metallurgical, Motorola, Wallace Co., Westinghouse, and Xerox Business Products and Systems. Then the author provides a specific outline for implementing quality in an organization. Chapter 6 includes a complete self-assessment questionnaire and scoring evaluation system. After introducing his *Quality First* concepts and principles, the author outlines a 17-step implementation plan. The first 10 steps are planning, followed by 7 implementation steps. Chapter 10 consists of a brief survey of quality tools (e.g., bar chart, fishbone diagram, control chart, Pareto chart, etc.) and techniques (action plan, benchmarking, cost of quality, SPC, etc.). A final chapter reviews the steps and urges the reader to "act now." Three appendices provide basic resources: an executive reading list, a glossary of quality terms, and a list of information sources. This is a helpful "first book" to introduce the quality movement to corporate executives. (©*Quality Abstracts*)

INDEX

291

New directions in composition research

PERSPECTIVES IN WRITING RESEARCH
Linda S. Flower and John R. Hayes, *Editors*

NEW DIRECTIONS IN COMPOSITION RESEARCH
Richard Beach and Lillian S. Bridwell, *Editors*

In preparation

WRITING BLOCKS
Michael Rose, *Editor*

PROTOCOL ANALYSIS
Linda S. Flower and John R. Hayes

WRITING IN NONACADEMIC SETTINGS
Lee Odell and Dixie Goswami, *Editors*

New directions in composition research

edited by
RICHARD BEACH AND LILLIAN S. BRIDWELL
University of Minnesota

Foreword by Linda S. Flower and John R. Hayes

THE GUILFORD PRESS
New York London

© 1984 The Guilford Press
A Division of Guilford Publications, Inc.
200 Park Avenue South, New York, N.Y. 10003

Printed in the United States of America

Second printing, July 1984

LIBRARY OF CONGRESS CATALOGING IN PUBLICATION DATA

Main entry under title:

New directions in composition research.

  (Perspectives in writing research)
  Bibliography: p.
  Includes index.
  1. English language—Rhetoric—Study and teaching—
Addresses, essays, lectures. 2. English language—
Composition and exercises—Study and teaching—Addresses,
essays, lectures. 3. Language arts—Addresses, essays,
lectures. I. Beach, Richard. II. Bridwell, Lillian S.
III. Series. [DNLM: 1. Writing. 2. Research. PE 1408
N532]
PE1404.N48 1984   808′.042′07   83-5716
ISBN 0-89862-250-6

Contributors

Robert D. Abbott, PhD, Department of English, University of Washington, Seattle, Washington

Richard Beach, PhD, Department of Curriculum and Instruction, University of Minnesota, Minneapolis, Minnesota

Lillian S . Bridwell, EdD, Program in Composition and Communication, University of Minnesota, Minneapolis, Minnesota

Joyce Armstrong Carroll, PhD, Department of English and Writing, McMurry College, Abilene, Texas

Roger Cherry, BA, Department of English, University of Texas, Austin, Austin, Texas

Grant Cioffi, PhD, Department of Education, University of New Hampshire, Durham, New Hampshire

James L. Collins, EdD, Department of Learning and Instruction, State University of New York, Buffalo, Buffalo, New York

Charles R. Cooper, PhD, Department of Literature, University of California, San Diego, La Jolla, California

Marilyn M. Cooper, PhD, Rhetoric, Linguistics, and Literature Program, English Department, University of Southern California, Los Angeles, California

Barbara Copley, MA, Computer Task Group, Inc., Buffalo, New York

Colette A. Daiute, PhD, Department of Communication, Computing, and Technology in Education, Teachers College, Columbia University, New York, New York

John A. Daly, PhD, College of Communication, University of Texas, Austin, Austin, Texas

Sara Eaton, PhD candidate, Program in Composition and Communication, University of Minnesota, Minneapolis, Minnesota

Lester Faigley, PhD, Department of English, University of Texas, Austin, Austin, Texas

Stefan Fleischer, PhD, Department of English, State University of New York, Buffalo, Buffalo, New York

Linda S. Flower, PhD, Department of English, Carnegie-Mellon University, Pittsburgh, Pennsylvania

Sarah Warshauer Freedman, PhD, Department of Education, University of California, Berkeley, Berkeley, California

Lee Galda, PhD, Department of Language Education, University of Georgia, Athens, Georgia

Anne Ruggles Gere, PhD, Department of English, University of Washington, Seattle, Washington

Dixie Goswami, PhD, Bread Loaf School of English, Middlebury College, Middlebury, Vermont

Joy Lynn Hailey, BS, College of Communication, University of Texas, Austin, Austin, Texas

John R. Hayes, PhD, Department of English, Carnegie-Mellon University, Pittsburgh, Pennsylvania

Fern L. Johnson, PhD, Department of Communication Studies, University of Massachusetts, Amherst, Massachusetts

Kenneth J. Kantor, PhD, Department of Language Education, University of Georgia, Athens, Georgia

Michael L. Michlin, PhD, Department of Education, Duke University, Durham, North Carolina

Paula Reed Nancarrow, PhD candidate, Program in Composition and Communication, University of Minnesota, Minneapolis, Minnesota

Thomas Newkirk, PhD, Department of English, University of New Hampshire, Durham, New Hampshire

Lee Odell, PhD, Department of English, Rensselaer Polytechnic Institute, Troy, New York

Anthony D. Pellegrini, PhD, Early Childhood Education and Institute for Behavioral Research, University of Georgia, Athens, Georgia

Gene L. Piché, PhD, Department of Curriculum and Instruction, University of Minnesota, Minneapolis, Minnesota

Rita Pollard, BA, Faculty of Educational Studies, State University of New York, Buffalo, Buffalo, New York

Donald Ross, PhD, Program in Composition and Communication, University of Minnesota, Minneapolis, Minnesota

Donald L. Rubin, PhD, Departments of Speech Communication and Language Education, University of Georgia, Athens, Georgia

Michael Sartisky, PhD, Department of English, University of New Orleans, New Orleans, Louisiana

Brian F. Schuessler, PhD, Department of English, University of Washington, Seattle, Washington

Heidi Swarts, PhD, Department of English, Carnegie-Mellon University, Pittsburgh, Pennsylvania

Michael M. Williamson, EdM, Learning Center, Niagara University, Niagara Falls, New York

Stephen P. Witte, PhD, Department of English, University of Texas, Austin, Austin, Texas

Nina D. Ziv, PhD, Department of English, Seton Hall University, South Orange, New Jersey

Foreword

This volume is the first in The Guilford Press Perspectives in Writing Research series. In this series, we will attempt to present the best new research on reading and writing, drawn from diverse fields, in a form that is useful to teachers as well as researchers. We hope that the volumes in the series can serve as core readings in upper-class and graduate courses.

We feel that such a series is needed because the quantity of research on reading and writing is increasing dramatically and its sources are diverse, coming from such fields as linguistics, psychology, rhetoric, education, English, and computer science. As a result, relevant publications are scattered, so that it is difficult for an individual to keep abreast of current developments.

Further, with the diversity in fields, there is a corresponding diversity in method. Ethnographic techniques, protocol analysis, psychological research methods, computer simulation, and linguistic techniques all contribute importantly to the growing body of knowledge. Since the interested audience may be unfamiliar with some of these methods, tutorial volumes will be included in the series.

As the sources and the methods of research are diverse, so are the audiences. The study of reading and writing is of interest not only to researchers, but also to teachers and practitioners. Our attempt to bridge the worlds of theory and practice is very appropriate here. Reading and writing research is strongly applied in flavor, and that, we believe, is a peculiar strength worth supporting. Patricia Wright has argued that the best research on communication is conducted by starting with the knotty, interesting problems that confront practitioners, rather than by starting with theory and then turning as an afterthought to the practical world to see if there is a problem the theory can solve. By starting with practical problems, researchers already have their eyes on phenomena that matter.

The plan for the series, then, includes two sorts of books: (1) surveys, such as the present volume, which provide a broad overview of the current state of research; (2) volumes that focus on a single important issue—for example, forthcoming edited volumes by Michael Rose on writer's block and by Lee Odell and Dixie Goswami on the new field of nonacademic writing. Volumes are also projected by Linda S. Flower and

John R. Hayes on the psychology of the writing process and by Richard Young and John R. Hayes on quantitative methods in rhetoric.

The present volume is a particularly appropriate one with which to begin the series. Beach and Bridwell have brought together contributions from a wide variety of perspectives which bridge the interests of researchers and teachers. The four sections take us from the laboratory to the classroom. The first section, on research methods, includes chapters on protocol analysis, descriptive studies, and linguistic methods. The second section, on the composing process, includes chapters on important current issues such as revision, self-evaluation, the relations between reading and writing, and the constraints placed on writing by the limitations of short-term memory. The third section, on the writing situation, discusses topics such as writing in nonacademic settings, situational aspects of writing anxiety, and the influence of the writing task on how students write. The final section, on the instructional context, includes chapters on teacher training, teachers' attitudes toward writing, and the impact of word processors on composition.

In editing this volume, Beach and Bridwell have provided the reader with an excellent sampling of current research. In future volumes of the series, we will attempt to maintain the high standard set in this volume by encouraging contributions from the very best and most exciting researchers in the field.

Linda S. Flower
John R. Hayes

Contents

New directions in composition research

Introduction

LILLIAN S. BRIDWELL
RICHARD BEACH
University of Minnesota

The purpose of this collection is to present research studies that represent new directions in composition research, directions that have emerged in the last ten years as the result of a broadening in the scope of researchers' theoretical and methodological approaches. When we tell people outside of academia that we do "composition research," they often have no idea what we do. And with all of the new developments in the field, we ourselves have trouble giving a simple explanation. For our purposes here, we will define composition research as the investigation of writing behaviors, cognitive processes during composing, and the ways in which these behaviors and cognitive processes interact with written products and their contexts. While literary theory examines the stylistic, philosophical, structural, or aesthetic characteristics of texts in relation to authors' imputed intentions, authors' biographical experiences, and readers' responses, composition researchers are more concerned with the actual *production* of written language. Further, they study the writing and writing processes of all kinds of people of all ages—not just mature and widely read literary figures.

Certainly people in other disciplines have shown interest in what writers do. Cognitive psychologists study the decisions that writers make, seeing the decisions as reflecting certain problem-solving strategies or developmental levels. Text-structure linguists and reading researchers examine variations in writers' texts to determine variations in comprehension or readability. Educators examine the influences of various teaching techniques on students and their writing. In many cases, insights from one discipline are applied to another. An investigator in any of these fields could well be engaging in "composition research" as we have defined it. Thus, composition research is not a unique discipline but a hybrid of disciplines, each having something to offer to those who are attempting to understand the extremely complex process of writing.

In this introduction, we will briefly chart the trends over two decades of composition research (for a fuller view of the history, see

Braddock, Lloyd-Jones, & Shoer, 1963; Cooper & Odell, 1978; and King, 1978). Particular attention will be given to the theoretical assumptions underlying such research. We will also attempt to define the domain of composition research more fully here, in order to provide a context for the research summaries and reports in this book.

Underlying all the trends in composition research is one predominant theme: both proponents and critics of composition research are calling for a more valid and comprehensive theoretical base that would define, explain, and perhaps predict writing behavior. Some argue that this can only be done if researchers examine the total context within which writing occurs. Others feel that a unifying theory will come from a synthesis of studies of the *parts* of the writing process.

While the need for a valid theoretical base may seem obvious, much of the early research on written composition did not direct much attention to theory at all. Cooper and Odell (1978) have criticized the emphasis placed on the teaching methodology studies which assume that good writing can be defined simply as adherence to prescribed advice. Most of this research compared one method of teaching to another and based success or failure on global measures of "quality." Many assumptions went unchallenged:

- That classical rhetorical theory offered perhaps the best way of defining the "modes of discourse" (i.e., narration, description, exposition, and argumentation).
- That the standards for good writing (e.g., school writing) could come from static criteria derived more from logic than from any thorough, empirical study of the features of written language or the developmental characteristics of writing done by students at different ages.
- That linear models of logic also dictated the steps through which a writer should move during writing (e.g., pick a topic, narrow it, write an outline, flesh out the outline, edit, and proofread). Since these steps seemed to explain the final form taken by a paper and represented stages that a writer *might* go through, this kind of advice about composing enjoyed a long, unchallenged tenure.
- That if one knows the structure of a language and the abstract terms for describing it (at least the traditional school grammar versions), then one could use this knowledge to construct grammatically "correct" writing. Even better, a writer could memorize certain prescriptive rules for good form.

Certainly little of the research summarized in Braddock *et al.*'s (1963) review of composition studies challenged any of the assumptions. At that point, few people questioned the theoretical perspectives underlying composition research (at least not in print).

As with so many other disciplines, composition researchers began to question their assumptions in the late '60s and early '70s. The dramatic shift came when they began analyzing what writers really do when they write, not what they "ought to do" based on *a priori* logical assumptions. In her review of research conducted in the '70s, King (1978) noted that those who studied writing development had become increasingly concerned with "basic research." Although pedagogical questions were still recognized as important, most of the serious researchers were attempting to place "the process of writing within a larger, more cohesive framework" (p. 200). As researchers have studied what writers really do and what their language really looks like, many of the previous assumptions have proved invalid.

For example, Meade and Ellis (1970) published a small-scale study in which they examined one simple assumption: the prescriptive advice found in composition textbooks that "good" paragraphs should contain "topic sentences." They analyzed professional writing to find examples that might illustrate this standard advice and found few that conformed to the prescription. After Emig's landmark (1971) case study research on the composing processes of twelfth graders, this kind of iconoclastic research gathered momentum. Many myths about writing were shattered by the composing process studies which followed Emig's and which expanded her original model (Stallard, 1974; Pianko, 1979; Perl, 1979; Sommers, 1980; Flower & Hayes, 1981; Bridwell & Dunn, 1980). They found, for example:

- That many student and professional writers rarely employ outlines, but write first to discover a controlling idea.
- That many writers work from a set of goals or plans that constitute the direction or nature of a piece, but that these bear little resemblance to the traditional outline.
- That "good" or experienced writers' processes differ considerably from those employed by "poorer" or inexperienced writers, but that these differences are not centered on adherence to or deviation from much of the traditional lore concerning writing.
- That very few people outside of English classrooms actually follow the steps in writing that textbooks recommend.

In recent years, researchers have continued this reexamination of theoretical perspectives. Many (notably Flower & Hayes, 1981; Sommers, 1980; Perl, 1979) have found that some of the early insights about the sequential stages that came from composing process research do not adequately describe writers' actual composing processes. The linear "stage" model (prewriting, drafting, revising, and editing—in that order) which guided many of the early studies has given way to "recursive" models. Studies have shown, for example, that people may revise at any time during the writing process (Bridwell, 1981), or discover that they need to develop more material at the "editing stage."

In addition to challenging the logic of prescriptions about composing behaviors, researchers and theorists in the last decade have also begun to question the traditional classifications of written language. Moffett (1968), Britton, Burgess, Martin, McLeod, and Rosen (1975), Kinneavy (1971), Hirsch (1977), and others have proposed theories to account for the complex relationships between the writer and the reader, task, subject, or context. Even their work has been challenged as artificially separating writing into categories, as ignoring pragmatic constraints, and as ignoring recent developments in text linguistics. The traditional model of classical rhetoric—of writer persuading audience— has been modified by the "new" rhetoric (Burke, 1969; Steinmann, 1975), which defines an entirely different range of writer–audience relationships, for example, techniques by which writers gain the "identification" of their readers. Further, applications of psycholinguistics (Clark & Clark, 1977) and text linguistics (de Beaugrande, 1980) have further enhanced and complicated the writer–reader interaction with such factors as the writer's perceptions of the reader's knowledge (the "given-new" contract), the effects of long-term and short-term memory on language production and reception, and the nature of cognitive representations of meaning in writers' and readers' minds.

Those who studied the writing process were no longer content with the pat descriptions of writing from traditional rhetoric. As they designed assignments for research, for example, they found that they could not always predict the form the writing would take, even with explicit instructions such as "Write a narrative" (Perron, 1977). In contrast to the traditional descriptions, much published writing often contains well-integrated combinations of several traditional categories. Bridwell and Dunn (1980) have criticized the sterile writing that often results when inexperienced writers try to fill in formulaic patterns (i.e., the "500-word expository essay" complete with thesis statement) which they have learned from traditional writing instruction. Other researchers (such as Lloyd-Jones, 1977) have developed primary trait scales for assessing writing according to the rhetorical demands of a particular assignment. Global, preset criteria (e.g., "organization") for the text simply have not adequately accounted for the unique interactions among writer, form, content, and context. As researchers recognized the limitations of textbook prescriptions, they also recognized the limitations of their own definitions of writing genres. They discovered that distinctions among concepts such as "expository" and "descriptive" were arbitrary and vague.

Recent developments in text linguistics and applications of that work (Meyer, 1975; Kintsch, 1977; van Dijk, 1977; de Beaugrande, 1980) have provided more precise descriptions of how prose is organized than those prescribed in earlier category systems. For example, "opinion-example" or "problem–solution" describes the logical relationships among parts of texts more accurately than the concept "expository." Applications of pragmatics theory (Searle, 1969; Grice, 1975; Bach & Harnish, 1979) illuminate the type of interplay between the writer and the reader that makes for successful communication in both oral discourse and written texts. As the ability to describe cognitive processes merges with the ability to describe texts more accurately, develoment of a sound theory of written language production will continue.

Another major breakthrough has been the increased integration of research on writing and on reading (Shanklin, 1981; Galda, Chapter 9, this volume). In studying the writer's acquisition of text-structure schemata or self-assessing inferences, researchers recognize that these skills accrue from reading. The ability to summarize information while reading, for example, carries over to the ability to discern the gist or goal of one's own writing. The fact that writers acquire spelling, vocabulary, and various editing skills primarily from reading (Smith, 1982) may shift the emphasis from direct, didactic "bits and pieces" (Shuy, 1981)—which involve instruction in vocabulary, spelling, usage rules, and punctuation— toward instruction involving reading.

Much recent research has challenged the assumption that studying abstractions or rules about language has a direct effect on writing production. Such an assumption fails to distinguish between a theoretical "knowing-that" linguistic competence and a "knowing-how" competence (Lunsford, 1979). The extensive research on syntactic development and sentence combining points to a need for more practice with manipulating language and fewer drills on descriptions of language. It is an important step forward to recognize the limitations of direct, didactic instruction. However, some of the syntax research suffers from serious theoretical problems and misconceptions.

To take one example, sentence combining continues to be criticized by linguists (Kleine, 1983), who insist that the practice is not based on a systematic grammatical theory. Pragmatics theorists claim that the technique ignores the contingencies inherent in the rhetorical context. Even some proponents of sentence combining (Smith & Combs, 1980) have found that simply telling students to produce longer sentences yields similar results. While a more integrated theory is needed, instruction in sentence combining does improve certain kinds of syntactic fluency, something that cannot be claimed for traditional grammar instruction.

Sentence-combining research demonstrates how a plausible alternative can easily capture an audience among teachers and researchers who may not always consider the validity of the theory behind the practice. As information about written language production accumulates, perhaps there will be fewer premature applications of emerging theory. Researchers familiar with a variety of disciplines have a responsibility to cross-check their assumptions with those from other angles of inquiry.

We have seen, then, new directions and possibilities arising out of challenged assumptions. What is needed to guide future research is a model for writing production that represents a more global view of the factors affecting writers. A primary assumption of this model should be that we cannot isolate writing from the social, political, and psychological context in which it occurs. Studying the writer without taking the many dimensions of the context into account is a little like studying animal life by visiting zoo cages. A writer cannot be asked to suspend needs, attitudes, beliefs, prior knowledge, and intentions toward an audience so that his or her work can be studied in a "controlled" experiment. Researchers must therefore study or take into account the full range of variables that can be derived from the writer, the reader, and the contexts. Some of the main variables are shown in Figure 1.

Fig. 1. Composition research variables.

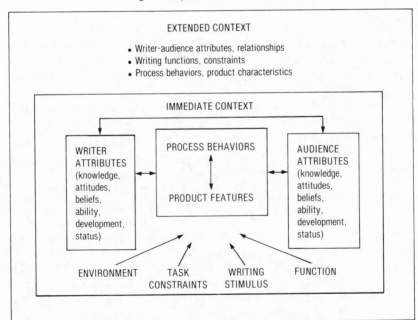

The figure refers to "writer attributes" and "audience attributes" rather than to "writer" and "audience." We mention specific attributes, such as knowledge and attitudes, because most writers do not think about "the reader" as a global conceptual entity. Rather, they focus on specific audience attributes in assessing their own writing, asking themselves, for example, "What does my reader know about this topic?" or "What does my reader believe?" As recent pragmatics theory suggests (Searle, 1969; Bach & Harnish, 1979), a speaker or writer succeeds or fails in accordance with the audience's prior beliefs, status, abilities, and so on. A writer may, for example, mistakenly expect a reader to have certain knowledge and thereby fail to make his or her point.

Figure 1 also distinguishes between the "immediate context" and the "extended context." For example, in writing a memo to a boss, a writer has an immediate, specific audience in mind and assesses the memo according to specific inferences about the boss's knowledge, beliefs, status, and so forth. In doing so, the writer is also drawing on tacit acquired knowledge about writing memoranda—appropriate styles of discourse, strategies for revision, and so on—that transcend the specific context. If writers lack tacit knowledge of the conventions appropriate for a specific writing context, they may have difficulty with the task. This distinction between the immediate and extended context is relevant to composition research because researchers often attempt to generalize from a writer's performance in a specific or immediate context to larger knowledge or skills. If our memo writer revises her memo extensively, a researcher may infer that she typically revises in an extensive manner, failing to recognize that she may vary her revising strategies with different immediate contexts. Thus, it is risky to generalize from immediate to extended contexts.

As Figure 1 shows, writers engage in various "process behaviors" that result in a product. They must cope with certain "task constraints": often they find they know so much about a topic that they have to pare the material down to what is relevant, or is dictated by the "writing stimulus." If an expert on nuclear energy is asked to write about a specific step in nuclear energy production for a general audience, he or she may have difficulty limiting the scope of the report.

Because a more comprehensive theory of writing is emerging, we need a systematic description of composition research methodology in order to define what aspects particular studies are designed to analyze. Before one can decide *how* to design a study, one must know what questions the study should answer, at least in experimental design and in statistical testing based on probability theory. Throughout the '60s and '70s, many researchers studied methods of experimental hypothesis testing and gained much-needed sophistication in employing the standard tools of social science and scientific research. While this was a positive step in many ways, researchers often tested whatever was convenient and could be easily quantified. Without investigating what writers really do in responding to unique rhetorical demands of a particular writing task, many researchers found it easy to operationally define variables (e.g., syntactic fluency, writing "quality," mechanical correctness) and to compare the effects of different, carefully controlled methods of teaching writing.

In a plea for more studies of the context for writing, Myers (1980) attacked many of these projects. He gave examples for three categories of research: rationalism, positivism, and contextualism. Myers made a timely call for research in the most neglected category, contextualism, but we see a need for all three kinds of research. If researchers attempt to synthesize work in all of these areas, we may then move forward toward an organized theory. Without insights from multiple perspectives the theory will be incomplete, and different varieties of research without theory will elude synthesis. Thus, we believe the focus of research must be enlarged as the focus of the theory is enlarged.

Rationalism, for example, is the kind of research that led Chomsky, Chafe, and other linguists to insights about the nature of language. The researcher begins with a collection of anomalies, or unusual cases, and by induction develops hypotheses that explain their existence. Without a comprehensive model of the composing process, this is all that most researchers can do. Consider, for example, a writer who does little or no revision. That writer may lack sufficient syntactic options to revise at the sentence level, may not have strong enough reading skills to make inferences about his or her text, may lack audience-analysis skills that would allow conversion of writer-based prose to reader-based prose, and so on. Without preconceived hypotheses, the researcher could observe this writer to determine what seems to account for the lack of revision. The strength of this approach is that a researcher is not initially bound to perceiving the data according to a set of predetermined questions or hypotheses, which means that he or she can inductively derive new insights from the data. On the other hand, not applying a set of predetermined questions or hypotheses may mean that a researcher does not attend to certain phenomena in any systematic manner according to his or her questions or hypotheses. This kind of study differs from contextualism in that the researcher has identified a limited set of cases that do not conform to typical patterns. The value of such research is that it may generate previously undefined variables. It lends itself to theory building rather than theory testing. The disadvantages are lack of control over variables and limited generalizability of the research.

Contextualism, for which Myers argues almost exclusively, also involves building theory rather than testing it. Nelson (1981), for example, has studied what happens when writers teach writing. Using ethnographic approaches, she took copious field notes on writers–teachers' classroom behaviors, making a great effort to ensure the reliability and validity of her perceptions, and attempted to synthesize her field notes into patterns that might lead to a hypothesis about how context affects writing. With contextualism, as with rationalism, the constraints of the *a priori* hypotheses necessary to positivism do not limit the investigator. Nelson and others (Graves, 1975; Bridwell, 1981) argue for a pyramid design in which the researcher collects layers of information, starting with generalizations about large groups and moving upward to collect more detailed information. At the apex are smaller, more detailed studies of individual cases; to some degree, it may be possible to generalize from those individual cases back to the initial experimental population, but not always beyond that group.

Positivism has its greatest value at the base of this system of describing composition research in that large numbers of subjects may be examined in their performance on a small number of variables. In this kind of work, the investigator clearly defines composing-process variables or text features to be studied, derives *a priori* hypotheses, and then tests the hypotheses for an entire sample. Studies of this kind (Beach, 1979; Bridwell, 1980; Crowhurst & Piché, 1979; Rubin & Piché, 1979; and others) focus on a particular variable or variables that can be clearly defined in advance. Herein lie both the strengths and weaknesses of these studies: they have generalizability because they go beyond the researcher's perceptions of individual cases, but the variables they isolate may function as described only with exact replications. We have learned much in the past about "particles" in the composing process (e.g., syntax, cognitive processes, text structures, specific behaviors) that can be integrated into a comprehensive model of written language production, but we must be careful to acknowledge the limitations of our research methods.

Anyone studying or planning research, then, must be aware of the trade-offs. Given the current interest in details of writers' composing processes, researchers often study a variety of pieces that a subject has written, observe the person during the writing process, and ask the subject what he or she was thinking while writing. Obviously, this kind of investigation is extensive and time-consuming. And without larger sample sizes, the researcher cannot be sure whether what is true for case study subjects is also true for larger groups. Without generalizability of findings, those who teach writing are left only with a theory of "individual differences." Obviously, not all writing instruction from kindergarten through graduate school can be done on an individual basis. Hence, we are led back to a need for generalizations: some composition researchers attempt to explain their results in terms of relationships or effects apparent in group behavior. They then try to fit these relationships or effects into a theoretical perspective.

Beyond the choice of a methodological approach, the researcher also faces trade-offs in what is to be studied. For example, much research in the past has attempted to determine what behaviors accounted for successful writing "quality." Early studies of the composing process used global or analytical scales such as the one designed by Diederich (1974), but such holistic measures are fraught with complications.

Rhetoricians, aestheticians, literary critics, and writing teachers posit different theories about what constitutes quality. Obviously, this implies that different criteria are used in making judgments. Some argue that quality is determined by a reader's subjective responses to or comprehension of the writing, a stance indicating that criteria other than text-based ones are being applied. Other theorists argue that it is possible to define objective, text-based criteria for judging quality, so long as those criteria are consistent with current distinctions being made among various text types. The criteria for judging a scientific report will differ sharply from the criteria appropriate for judging a piece of narrative fiction. Primary trait advocates argue that the criteria for judging quality should be based on all the ramifications inherent in a particular assignment or writing task, from text features to audience awareness. Because researchers have foreseen numerous problems in trying to determine quality according to these and other extrinsic factors, they have tended to employ intrinsic criteria.

Another problem, described by Hirsch (1977), is that some criteria fail to take into account the writer's own intentions. Hirsch argues that quality is a function of the degree to which a text fulfills these intentions. In his research, he trains judges who are adept at discerning intentions and has them rate the degree to which a writer's intentions were fulfilled. One problem with this method is that it is often difficult to discern intention and to attain interjudge reliability. The problem is alleviated if the judges are familiar with a set of clearly defined criteria; they are then more likely to arrive at the same ratings.

Thus, there is no simple way to define or ascertain writing quality. Those who stipulate their own definitions of quality—rhetoricians, literary critics, text-structure linguists, information-processing experts, and others—are working from their own unique assumptions about writing. Thus, common agreement about the nature of writing quality eludes the researcher.

Even the single example of how difficult it is to determine writing quality makes it clear that any reasonably comprehensive view of the composing process will have to emerge from the synthesis of much interdisciplinary work. Writing researchers must continue their recent efforts to integrate new (and old) information from at least four main areas of investigation: language study *per se*, psycholinguistics, sociolinguistics, and developmental studies.

Before we can adequately describe how a person writes, we must be able to describe more accurately the products of that process. For a long time we heard just the opposite—that researchers should focus on the process and not the products. However, until one can link behaviors to the emerging text, one has little more than a series of anecdotes about writers.

The best studies describing these behaviors went beyond anecdotes. But we still see a vast, uncharted territory between the writer and the text, not to mention the writer and the reader. The limitations of current linguistic theory are obvious. For the most part, linguists analyze small bits and pieces of language—sounds, words, idioms, syntactic relationships within sentences, and semantic propositions. Recent advances have been made in text linguistics, a field that involves the study of texts in units within and beyond the sentence. However, we have hardly progressed beyond the level of describing the glue that links one small proposition to another. The term "macrostructure" has cropped up in recent theory but it often refers to a proposition directly stated or implied in the text, to which smaller propositions are subordinated. So far, we lack a theory of text structure that goes beyond the immediate features of the language under the microscope; there is no comprehensive theory, for example, to explain the controlling glue that holds an entire book together. We can turn for help to literary theory and semiotics, to name only two sources. But we cannot as yet plot the interactions of static, text-bound features with those that are formed cumulatively as the human brain comprehends, stores, and responds to information, and then produces written language.

Similarly, much of the work in psycholinguistics hardly gets beyond the particle problem. We know a great deal about the limits of short-term memory with regard to items in a sequence, individual words or phrases, small units of syntactic and semantic structures, and other "bits." In order to understand texts beyond these bits, we need more information about how the human brain selectively stores and retrieves information, operates on information that is accessible, accommodates itself to shifting contexts, and reasons to solve novel problems.

Current information-processing theory and artificial intelligence systems offer mechanical models—embryonic forms of what human cognition might resemble if these forms were to grow into full-fledged computer programs capable of sustained discourse with humans. With future work we might, for example, be able to describe how a writer selectively searches memory for relevant information and how some processes take precedence over others at various times during composing. We might learn why a writer can sometimes ignore mechanical problems such as spelling and attend to overall content, while at other times mechanical concerns are in the foreground. Or we might discover why some typists react immediately to a letter reversal but have no idea of the sentence context within which the error occurred.

Another goal of composition research should be to describe the context and sociological implications of writing far more accurately than we have in the past—to get beyond the static, particle view and toward the dynamic patterns of language in action. Both the nature of the text and the nature of cognitive processing are altered as the purpose, the audience, the topic, and the mode of writing change. We could try to learn how writers alter their thought processes as such shifts occur; the degree to which a writer must be consciously aware of text structures and audience characteristics during the incubation phase; how this conscious awareness changes as the writer moves from task to task; and so on.

Finally, those in the area of language development have perhaps the heaviest burden of all. If we cannot accurately describe the mature writer or the mature text, we have tremendous difficulty describing their characteristics as they emerge or evolve. Some of the best work in development has proceeded on the assumption that child language is not simply inadequate adult language but rather has its own form and function categories, its own systems of pragmatic speech acts, and so on. This assumption frees the researcher from attempts to "scale down" models of the composing process for children, and it also means that the findings of a language development researcher can inform models of sophisticated language production.

Language development theory will have to function like a kaleidoscope if it is to account for the complexity of composing. It may be possible to define the array of variables that exist when one writes, to identify the chunks of colored glass that go into the child's toy. But such configurations will change as the writer, the task, and the context change. Even a longitudinal, contextual study carried out over a researcher's lifetime could not possibly analyze all the variables we can identify now, much less their interactions. Therefore, some researchers must continue to isolate pieces of the process for controlled studies; others will have to take in the broader range of the kaleidoscope. Still others will, through the process of induction, continue to generate rationalist hypotheses from introspection and intuition.

The mistakes of the past occurred because we grossly oversimplified the nature of written language and the processes by which humans create it. The methodological studies showed us one thing at least: our need for a comprehensive theory. When our methods for teaching writing did not work, we could often blame inaccurate or inadequate models of texts and writers' processes. When teaching methods did work, we weren't sure just why.

Undoubtedly, our own work and that of some of the contributors to this book could be faulted for shortsightedness and blind spots. It is for this very reason that we chose to put together a collection that would serve as a kaleidoscope of new directions. No one study or approach can stand alone as representative of composition research in the 1980s. The field is just too complex.

REFERENCES

Bach, K., & Harnish, R. *Linguistic communication and speech acts.* Cambridge, Mass.: MIT Press, 1979.

Beach, R. The effects of between-draft teacher evaluation versus student self-evaluation on high school students' revising of rough drafts. *Research in the Teaching of English,* 1979, *13,* 111–119.

Beaugrande, R. de. *Text, discourse, and process: Towards a multidisciplinary science of texts.* Norwood, N.J.: Ablex, 1980.

Braddock, R., Lloyd-Jones, R., & Schoer, L. *Research in written composition.* Champaign, Ill.: National Council of Teachers of English, 1963.

Bridwell, L. Revising strategies in twelfth grade students' transactional writing. *Research in the Teaching of English,* 1980, *14,* 197–222.

Bridwell, L. Rethinking composing: Implications from research on revising. *English Journal,* 1981, *77,* 96–99.

Bridwell, L., & Dunn, A. *Discourse competence: Evidence from cognitive development, reading, and writing.* Paper presented to annual meeting of National Council of Teachers of English, Cincinnati, 1980.

Britton, J., Burgess, T., Martin, N., McLeod, A., & Rosen, H. *The development of writing abilities (11–18).* London: Macmillan Education, 1975.

Burke, K. *A rhetoric of motives.* Berkeley: University of California Press, 1969.

Clark, E., & Clark, H. *Psychology and language: An introduction to psycholinguistics.* New York: Harcourt Brace Jovanovich, 1977.

Cooper, C., & Odell, L. (Eds.). *Research on composing: Points of departure.* Urbana, Ill.: National Council of Teachers of English, 1978.

Crowhurst, M., & Piché, G. Audience and mode of discourse of facts on syntactic complexity in writing at two grade levels. *Research in the Teaching of English,* 1979, *13,* 101–109.

Diederich, P. B. *Measuring growth in writing.* Urbana, Ill.: National Council of Teachers of English, 1974.

Emig, J. *The composing processes of twelfth graders.* Urbana, Ill.: National Council of Teachers of English, 1971.

Flower, L., & Hayes, J. The pregnant pause: An inquiry into the nature of planning. *Research in the Teaching of English,* 1981, *15,* 229–244.

Graves, D. An examination of the writing processes of seven year old children. *Research in the Teaching of English,* 1975, *9,* 227–241.

Grice, H. Logic and conversation. In P. Cole & J. Morgan (Eds.), *Syntax and semantics* (Vol. 3: *Speech acts*). New York: Academic Press, 1975.

Hirsch, E. D. *The philosophy of composition.* Chicago: University of Chicago Press, 1977.

King, M. Research in composition: A need for theory. *Research in the Teaching of English*, 1978, *12*, 193–202.

Kinneavy, J. *A theory of discourse*. Englewood Cliffs, N.J.: Prentice-Hall, 1971.

Kintsch, W. On comprehending stories. In P. Carpenter & M. Just (Eds.), *Cognitive processes in comprehension*. Hillsdale, N.J.: Lawrence Erlbaum, 1977.

Kleine, M. *Syntactic choice and a theory of discourse: Rethinking sentence-combining*. Unpublished doctoral dissertation, University of Minnesota, 1983.

Lloyd-Jones, R. Primary trait scoring. In C. Cooper & L. Odell (Eds.), *Evaluating writing*. Urbana, Ill.: National Council of Teachers of English, 1977.

Lunsford, A. Cognitive development and the basic writer. *College English*, 1979, *41*, 38–46.

Meade, R., & Ellis, W. Paragraph development in the modern age of rhetoric. *English Journal*, 1970, *59*, 219–226.

Meyer, B. *Organization of prose and its effects on recall*. Amsterdam: North Holland Publishing, 1975.

Myers, M. *A model for the composing process*. (National Writing Project Occasional Paper No. 3). Berkeley, Calif.: Bay Area Writing Project, University of California, Berkeley, 1980.

Moffett, J. *Teaching the universe of discourse*. Boston: Houghton Mifflin, 1968.

Nelson, M. *Writers who teach: A naturalistic investigation*. Unpublished doctoral dissertation, University of Georgia, 1981.

Perl, S. The composing process of unskilled college writers. *Research in the Teaching of English*, 1979, *13*, 317–336.

Perron, J. The impact of mode on written syntactic complexity. *Studies in language education* (Report No. 30). Athens, Ga.: Department of Language Education, University of Georgia, 1977.

Pianko, S. A description of the composing processes of college freshman writers. *Research in the Teaching of English*, 1979, *13*, 5–22.

Rubin, D., & Piché, G. Development in syntactic and strategic aspects of audience adaptation skills in written persuasive communication. *Research in the Teaching of English*, 1979, *13*, 293–316.

Searle, J. *Speech acts*. London: Cambridge University Press, 1969.

Shanklin, N. *Relating reading and writing: Developing a transactional theory of the writing process*. Bloomington, Ind.: Department of Reading, University of Indiana, 1981.

Shuy, R. A holistic view of language. *Research in the Teaching of English*, 1981, *15*, 101–111.

Smith, F. *Writing and the writer*. New York: Holt, Rinehart & Winston, 1982.

Smith, W., & Combs, W. The effects of overt and covert cues on written syntax. *Research in the Teaching of English*, 1980, *14*, 19–38.

Sommers, N. Revision strategies of student writers and experienced adult writers. *College Composition and Communication*, 1980, *31*, 378–388.

Stallard, C. An analysis of the writing behavior of good student writers. *Research in the Teaching of English*, 1974, *8*, 206–218.

Steinmann, M. Perlocutionary acts and the interpretation of literature. *Centrum*, 1975, *3*, 234–242.

van Dijk, T. A. *Text and context: Explorations in the semantics and pragmatics of discourse*. London: Longmans, 1977.

Research methods

1

In Part I of this book, we have included studies that seem to offer important new directions for methodological approaches in composition research. These studies present many of the theoretical assumptions that are treated in later chapters of the book.

Multiple Measures

In the first chapter, Charles Cooper and his colleagues discuss a number of measures currently employed in composition research: primary trait scoring, cohesion analysis, matrix analysis, and so on. They then illustrate the use of each measure by presenting data collected from a program study of college freshman writing. They initially divide the pieces into high- and low-quality writing groups and then apply each of the measures to each group to determine differences. Finally, they demonstrate that within each group, written pieces not only share linguistic, text-structure, and semantic features but have logical aspects in common.

In comparing the logical reasoning in high- and low-quality essays, Cooper *et al.* find that students in the low-quality group are restrained by faulty reasoning and rigid assumptions. These researchers' use of the established but often untapped disciplines of rhetorical and logical analysis, as well as the more current information/text-processing theories, represents a major new direction in composition research. Efforts to employ content-analysis categories or rating scales, as represented by the development of recent primary trait scoring systems, are beginning to shed important new insights on what makes a piece of writing succeed or fail.

Protocol Analysis

Another related direction in methodology has been the application of cognitive-psychological or problem-solving methods through analyses of writers' discussions about their composing processes. Drawing on previous problem-solving approaches, researchers ask writers to "think aloud" during the processes of formulating, planning, producing, and revising. These "spoken thoughts" are then analyzed according to the writer's strategies in defining problems, goals, plans, causal relationships, and so forth, as well as the writer's ability to cope with constraints imposed by the task. Previous composition researchers (notably Emig, 1971) had employed the "thinking aloud" method but were limited because they analyzed the behaviors from their own frame of reference: "formulating," "revising," "comparing," and so on.

In their chapter, Swarts, Flower, and Hayes explicate their methods for both eliciting and analyzing writers' open-ended thought processes. They also respond to some of the criticisms that have been leveled against their approach: that having writers think aloud while composing adds an artificial dimension to their writing, or that their approach superimposes a narrow problem-solving orientation onto a writer's processes. Their approach is certainly time-consuming and tedious, which limits the number of subjects who can be analyzed. On the other hand, because their content-analysis system generates empirical data, comparisons can be made between groups of subjects—between experienced and inexperienced writers, for example (see Flower & Hayes, 1981).

Ethnography and the Writing Process

Another new direction is the application of ethnographic research methods to the study of writing in particular social or cultural contexts. A major criticism of much composition research is that investigators know little about the writer's social and pragmatic perceptions or the task's rhetorical context. Subjects in a study may have performed poorly on an assigned task because they have ambiguous, conflicting feelings about the implied audience's needs—wondering, for example, if the reader really is concerned about what they say or is simply testing for some linguistic behavior.

Ethnographic research attempts to describe phenomena in the contexts in which they occur. While an experimental design may create a context, the ethnographic researcher studies the context as it exists in "the real world." The investigator, as an unobtrusive observer or participant, carefully records the specific social interactions that seem to be related to writing in a certain context. From these observations and from interview data, the investigator begins to determine subjects' perceptions—of themselves as writers, of their audience, and of the situation—and how these perceptions influence their writing performance. An ethnographic orientation, which draws on sociopsychological "constructivist" communications theory (Delia, O'Keefe, & O'Keefe, 1982), assumes that the meaning of any discourse act derives from the interpersonal perceptions shared by the writer and the audience— beliefs, knowledge, status, attitudes, needs, or abilities.

These perceptions are influenced by norms or conventions related to social behavior. By working with a larger group (classroom, business, family) to piece together a composite portrait of these shared perceptions, an investigator studies the ways in which a group's social norms influence an individual's behavior and perceptions. In Chapter 3 of this volume, Kantor argues for the significance of ethnographic studies in composition research.

Text Linguistics and Composing

Faigley and Witte propose a new method for linking composing process research to recent developments in text linguistics. They analyze one writer's revising processes and attempt to determine the effects of these changes on the text structure of the writing produced. Their work is suggestive of developments we hope to see. However, it is limited in that there is no comprehensive model of text structure which truly accounts for coherence in texts—no macrostructure beyond the ties that are discovered between propositions. The significance of Faigley and Witte's work is that it establishes a foundation for interpreting revisions, not just counting them. Future studies of revision and other composing processes will have to link revision not only to text structures but to the intentions of the writer and the effects of readers' responses during the composing process.

Pragmatics and the Writing Process

One such research methodology is the analysis of writing from a pragmatics or speech act perspective. Speech act theory (Austin, 1962; Searle, 1969, Grice, 1975; Labov & Fanshel, 1977) posits that the meaning of oral or written discourse acts is a function of the discourse conventions or conditions that constitute particular speech acts. For example, Searle (1969) proposes certain conditions that must be met if a speaker or writer is to make a request effectively: the speaker–writer must believe that the audience is able to fulfill the request, must have some status or power, and must be sincere. Labov and Fanshel (1977) propose a similar set of conditions for requests and other acts, emphasizing the underlying beliefs that speakers and audiences have about each other.

Drawing on his Cooperative Principle, Grice proposes several maxims having to do with "quantity" (say no more than you have to), "quality" (do not say what you believe to be false; do not say that for which you lack adequate evidence), "relation" (be relevant), and "manner" (avoid obscurity and ambiguity; be brief and orderly). Writers may violate these maxims, for example, providing irrelevant or insufficient information. Or, they may deliberately flout a maxim, calling attention to the fact that they are saying no more than is necessary in order to imply certain meanings. For example, in writing a letter of recommendation, a writer may deliberately imply an evaluation by saying no more than is necessary about a candidate.

Some researchers drawing on speech act theory (Tierney & LaZansky, 1980) have examined readers' perceptions of the writer's "ethos" by deliberately altering texts to create violations of speech act conventions. One limitation of this research is that it is often difficult to determine a reader's tacit knowledge of speech act conventions. A researcher must therefore assume that the reader's response to certain violations is a function of such knowledge. Moreover, it is difficult to separate a reader's prior knowledge of speech act conventions from knowledge of social conventions that come into play in judging appropriate discourse behavior. Marilyn Cooper's paper reviews current speech act theory and then applies that theory to an analysis of texts.

REFERENCES

Austin, J. L. *How to do things with words*. London: Oxford, 1962.
Delia, J., O'Keefe, B., & O'Keefe, D. The contructivist perspective on human communication. In F. Dance (Ed.), *Human communications theory*. New York: Harper & Row, 1982.
Emig, J. *The composing processes of twelfth graders*. Urbana, Ill.: National Council of Teachers of English, 1971.
Flower, L., & Hayes, J. The pregnant pause: An inquiry into the nature of planning. *Research in the Teaching of English*, 1981, *15*, 229–244.
Grice, H. Logic and conversation. In P. Cole & J. Morgan (Eds.), *Syntax and semantics* (Vol. 3: *Speech acts*). New York: Academic Press, 1975.
Labov, W., & Fanshel, D. *Therapeutic discourse*. New York: Academic Press, 1977.
Searle, J. *Speech acts*. London: Cambridge University Press, 1969.
Tierney, R., & LaZansky, J. *The rights and responsibilities of readers and writers: A contractual agreement* (Reading Education Report No. 15). Urbana, Ill.: Center for the Study of Reading, 1980.

1

Studying the writing abilities of a university freshman class: Strategies from a case study

CHARLES R. COOPER
University of California, San Diego
With
ROGER CHERRY
University of Texas, Austin
BARBARA COPLEY
Computer Task Group, Inc.
STEFAN FLEISCHER
State University of New York, Buffalo
RITA POLLARD
State University of New York, Buffalo
MICHAEL SARTISKY
University of New Orleans

Everybody has an opinion about the writing of school and college students. As I write these pages in August of 1982, nearly everyone seems to believe that students in America write very badly—indeed, that they are an illiterate bunch. Recent pronouncements from professors, from guardians of the language in the media, and from many others who mistakenly assume that verbal scores on the S.A.T. are tests of writing ability have declared a "writing crisis" and a "literary crisis."

High school English teachers blame elementary and middle school teachers. College English professors—offering generally unwelcome advice—blame high school English teachers. Professors outside of an English department blame the director of freshman writing; the latter is certain that these professors don't know how to give writing assignments and don't understand the relation of writing to learning. National commissions blame television, broken homes, elective courses, grade inflation, and students' disinterest in learning. Everywhere across the country the competency-testers and university admissions committees are planning to coerce high school teachers into raising writing standards. This chorus of blame and failure is now as familiar as a popular song we've begun to hum now and then because we've heard it so many times on the car radio.

This continuing "writing crisis" has created some especially awkward moments for chairpersons of school and college English departments and for writing program directors. We've been asked to explain, justify, and substantiate. We've felt obliged to learn something about evaluation, and we've actually become quite sophisticated about it. We now have more forms, models, and measures for collecting information about our programs and instructors than we can possibly use (Conference on College Composition . . . , 1982; Cooper & Odell, 1977; Davis, Scriven, & Thomas, 1981; Gere, 1980; Odell, 1981; Odell & Cooper, 1980; Meyers, 1980; White & Thomas, 1981). What we still lack, however—and what seems necessary in order either to challenge or to confirm pronouncements about a writing crisis—is comprehensive descriptions of the writing performance of groups of students. How many English department chairpersons or writing directors can offer anything more than generalities about the writing performance of an incoming freshman class?

The Need for Comprehensive Studies of Writing Performance

When students come to us for help, we need to know exactly what they can and can't do as writers—not just their degree of conformance to standard usage and spelling rules, but their syntactic fluency and variety, their ability to create coherent text, their strategies for achieving particular writing purposes, and their information and ideas as well. Any thoughtful, experienced writing director can look at a sample of placement essays or first essays from classes and reach conclusions about students' writing abilities. This director can lead a profitable discussion with instructors about the writing problems in selected papers. But even this specialized director may, if the papers are not analyzed more systematically, overlook or misinterpret features that could have important implications for instruction. If the director is to report to others how well students are writing, then he or she will certainly need a plan—a set of strategies or proceedings for analyzing written texts and producing a comprehensive assessment of writing performance.

Such a tool could serve many purposes. Obviously, it could display and discuss what students have learned in a secondary school or college writing program. It could also demonstrate to others the extent of freshmen's writing achievements, a demonstration that might be helpful to those who sent them to college (if tactfully presented), to instructors who will be teaching them, and to administrators who decide on funding for writing programs and who have broader concerns about core curricula and general education. Such an assessment tool could confirm or contradict any local pronouncements about a national literacy crisis.

This chapter presents a plan for a comprehensive description of writing performance. It illustrates only some of the presently available strategies for describing writing. (In the conclusion, I refer the reader to strategies besides those discussed here.) The plan will unfold itself as a narrative, a past-tense case study of a project I organized at the State University of New York (SUNY) at Buffalo in 1979.

At Buffalo, formal discussions were under way about a new undergraduate general education program. Everyone acknowledged that writing development was an important part of a general education, but nobody had any solid information on the writing abilities of our freshman students. Since they came from the top 12 percent of their high school graduating classes, could we expect that they would be competent writers? We needed an answer in order to estimate how much writing instruction might be required for most students in a general education program that included specific literacy goals.

Several of us planned a study that would help shape the specific proposals we would make to the committee studying general education. We had already felt that certain writing or literature courses should be recommended to incoming freshmen. Our study was designed to let us test that assumption, as well as to give us the writing samples we needed to assess comprehensively the writing abilities of freshmen. This chapter is an abridged and revised version of the original report on the study, "Writing Abilities of Regularly Admitted Freshmen at SUNY/Buffalo" (University Learning Center and Department of English). My coauthors on the original report were Stefan Fleischer, Roger Cherry, Barbara Copley, Rita Pollard, and Michael Sartisky. Of the sections included in this chapter, Cherry drafted the sections on cohesion analysis and error, Pollard the section on the special features of persuasive writing, and Fleischer and Sartisky the section on ideological assumptions and critical analysis. I drafted the section on syntactic fluency and edited the original report.

What follows, then, is an abbreviated report of what we learned from the Buffalo study, along with commentary on our procedures and methodology. Though they may be of general interest, the specific findings of the Buffalo report are not of central importance here. They are the local findings for a local problem. Most important are the particular advantages and limitations of each procedure we used in analyzing writing samples, and the model we offer of a comprehensive study of writing—a model that includes error and syntax but moves well beyond them.

Procedures Used in the Buffalo Study

We administered the following persuasive writing task to all fall 1979
freshmen attending orientation sessions at 8:00 A.M. on July 3 and
July 10, 1979.

A Test of Writing Ability

Your performance on this essay test will enable us to make specific recommendations about writing courses you might take. Your essay will be
scored by a specially trained group of raters and the results reported to
you in the mail by August 1.

Time yourself carefully so that by 9:30 A.M. you have completed the
essay. Use the attached pages for all the writing you do, including any
prewriting notes or plans.

You may use both sides of the paper if necessary.

Writing Task

At the place where you work, a woman has just quit her job, leaving
vacant the company's only executive position ever held by a female. The
Board of Directors have stated their preference that a woman replace her
in order to fulfill an Affirmative Action quota. As a member of the Hiring
Committee, it is your job to help choose a successor to the post.

The only woman who has applied for the job seems competent and
meets the written qualifications for the job but she is clearly less qualified
than both of the men she is competing with. Members of the Committee
disagree about what should be done: some say hiring a woman is absolutely
necessary for breaking down employment discrimination; others say hiring
a less qualified person would be foolish as well as unfair to those working
under the new executive.

To have a full hearing of all views on this critical issue, the Hiring Committee has asked each member to prepare a carefully written statement to
be distributed in advance of a meeting to discuss the issue. Write a statement which represents your position in the matter, making it as logical and
persuasive as possible. Your writing task is to persuade the Committee to
adopt your own view and to vote on the job candidates in accordance with
your view.

We decided to use a persuasive writing task, rather than an explanatory or expressive task, because we felt it came closest to the sort of
short paper or essay-exam question that students would encounter in
their lower-division general education courses. This writing task also
simulates the critically important brief position paper through which
policy is argued, shaped, and decided in business and the professions.
The task essentially asks students to take a position, generate arguments
to support it, and then discover ways to support their arguments.

On both orientation days, students had about an hour and twenty
minutes to write the essay in a large amphitheater-type auditorium.
After a very brief explanation of our purported reason for asking them
to write the essay—that is, the idea that the essay would help us to

recommend an appropriate writing course—we gave them the assignment along with several pages of writing paper. We did not read the assignment aloud or discuss it with them. We encouraged them to write the best essay they could and to use as much of the time as they needed up until 9:30 A.M.

We had asked all the students to write the same context-rich task rather than simply giving them a list of topics to choose among. We did this because we wanted to make a detaiied, comprehensive analysis of a subsample of the papers, an analysis that would be organized in part around a comparison of the performances of the best and poorest writers. We knew, also, that requiring all students to write on a single task would increase our ease in using a general-impression holistic scoring procedure and the reliability of the procedure.

Altogether about 400 freshmen, representative of the entire 3000 admitted for fall 1979, wrote essays, all of which were evaluated in a norm-referenced, general-impression scoring session. That is, papers were scored on a 1-to-6 scale against the range of performance displayed by the 400 papers, not against a general standard of quality. The scorers made their decisions quickly and impressionalistically, considering all the features of each paper simultaneously rather than analyzing separate features. The scorers were faculty members and advanced graduate students in English and education. All were experienced composition teachers. Each paper was independently scored twice, and papers on which scorers disagreed by more than two points were scored a third time. Such a procedure generally produces scores that are sufficiently reliable for screening or placement purposes. Certainly such a procedure —a written essay scored by a qualified, carefully trained reader— produces a more valid score than can be obtained from any nonwriting multiple-choice objective test (Cooper, 1977).

The holistic scoring was only preliminary to the real work of this study. The scores themselves would tell us nothing about the specific strengths of the best papers or the weaknesses of the worst. We needed a detailed, comprehensive analysis of a subsample in order to reach any conclusions about the writing abilities of the entire group. Consequently, we selected randomly 50 papers and planned an analysis that would let us view the papers from a great many different perspectives— from the word to the sentence to the discourse to the ideology behind the papers.

Errors

We began our analysis of the 50 papers with a look at the errors in usage, punctuation, and spelling. To get a sense of the entire range of problems in these areas—and, more importantly, to compare the writing of the best and the weakest writers—we examined the 10 papers scoring highest and the 10 scoring lowest in the holistic rating.

The greatest obstacles to error analysis are the sheer variety of errors and the fuzzy boundaries of some error categories. The best approach is to study only a limited number of errors and to collect enough examples of these from initial readings of essays so that readers doing the analysis will be clear on what counts as a particular kind of error. We decided to count all the designated errors in papers in the subsamples (10 lowest and 10 highest) and then report the results for each subsample as errors per 1000 words of writing. A reporting base of this size is required for a reliable sampling of error, and a standard base of 1000 words facilitates comparisons among subsamples. This number also represents the approximate length of many college papers—six to eight handwritten pages, or four typed pages—and hence is meaningful to other faculty members and administrators.

The procedure, however, is appropriate only for an efficient general indication of error patterns in *groups* of writers. It is inadequate as a teacher's diagnostic tool with regard to an individual writer, and certainly it is wholly inappropriate for a serious study of error—its patterns, causes, and cures—in the writings of college or adult writers. A good deal of sophisticated work has been done on this topic recently (Baddely & Wing, 1980; Bartholomae, 1980; Daiute, 1981; Hartwell, 1980; Harris, 1981; Hotopf, 1980; Kroll & Schafer, 1978; Shaughnessy, 1977; Stern-glass, 1974; Williams, 1981).

For our limited purposes in this evaluation study, we counted the incidence of errors in sentence end-stop punctuation, within-sentence punctuation involving commas, usage (verb tense and pronoun agreement), and spelling.

Errors in End-Stop Punctuation

Errors in sentence end-stop punctuation were of two familiar types: fragments and comma splices. A fragment is defined as a group of words that is punctuated as a complete sentence but cannot function independently, most often because the group is subordinate to another sentence or clause. In the example below, the fragment is italicized. (All examples given in this chapter are taken from the 50 essays.)

> The hiring committee should hire the male that best meets the qualifica-
> tions. *The reason being that the female is not the best qualified among the three applicants.*

The error of a comma splice—which occurs when two independent clauses are separated only by a comma, without a coordinating conjunction—is illustrated by this example:

It makes no difference what color, race or creed someone is from, the most qualified person should get the job.

Errors in Within-Sentence Punctuation Involving Commas

We counted two types of errors involving within-sentence punctuation: the omission of commas and the unnecessary use of commas. Commas were most typically omitted after introductory dependent clauses,

If the best isn't hired[,] discrimination has then taken place.

and before the coordinating conjunction in compound sentences:

I would hire the one who is better qualified for the job[,] and in this case the man would win.

Unnecessary commas made predictable appearances:

It is an injustice to the company and its consumers, to have anything but the best for the company.

Errors in Verb Tense and Pronoun Agreement

These errors are self-explanatory. Two examples are:

One cannot say that if the woman isn't *hire* they are being unfair.

The most important aspect in the final choice of an applicant is for *them* to be the most competent person.

Spelling Errors

Finally, we tallied spelling errors. We regarded a word that was misspelled more than once in the same paper as only one error.

The results of the error analysis, summarized in Table 1-1, demonstrate that not only had these writers made very few errors, but the incidence of particular kinds of errors per 1000 words for both groups is remarkably low. Surprisingly, the best writers made only three of the seven types of errors, with spelling errors occurring most frequently, followed by the omission of necessary commas and by errors in pronoun agreement. The most proficient writers, then, had no difficulty whatsoever with sentence end-stop punctuation. By comparison, the weakest papers contained two fragments and two comma splices per 1000 words of writing.

Table 1-1. Errors per 1000 Words in the Writing of 10 Fresh-men Who Scored Low and 10 Who Scored High on a Persuasive Writing Task

Type of error	Group	
	Low	High
Sentence end-stop punctuation		
Fragment	2	0
Comma splice	2	0
Within-sentence punctuation		
Omission of comma	6	4
Unnecessary use of comma	4	0
Usage		
Verb tense	3	0
Pronoun agreement	3	3
Spelling	13	6

Within-sentence punctuation, particularly the omission of necessary commas, presented more difficulties for both groups. The most capable writers omitted four commas per 1000 words, while the weakest writers omitted six. Whereas the writers in the low group used four unnecessary commas per 1000 words, the best writers did not use a single comma unnecessarily.

Usage errors occurred slightly less frequently than within-sentence punctuation errors. The most proficient writers made no verb tense errors, while the weakest writers made only three such errors per 1000 words. Both groups made three errors in pronoun agreement per 1000 words.

The most common mistakes in all the students' writing were spelling errors, and it is in this category that the clearest differences emerged between the high and low groups. Whereas the most capable writers made six spelling errors per 1000 words, the weakest writers made over twice as many. It must be noted, however, that dictionaries were not provided during the writing sessions, and this certainly inflated the number of errors that occurred.

What emerged most clearly from these data was the fact that regularly admitted incoming freshmen writers as SUNY/Buffalo *had no serious problems with the basic skills of written English—usage, mechanics, and spelling.* With regard to common errors, even the weakest writers had surprisingly good control of the written code. And, in this respect, the writing of the most capable students was virtually flawless.

From reading the papers many times, we knew that the pattern of error in even the poorest papers was not a barrier to communication with the reader. Even so, we certainly did not believe that the error rate was acceptable: for the weak writers a total of 33 errors in 1000 words, or an error in every 30 words; for the strong writers a total of 13 errors in 1000 words, or an error in every 77 words. Still, as teachers we believed that the problems we saw were easily correctable. And we knew that if students had been able to see their papers cold the next day, use a writer's handbook and a dictionary, and revise with care, the error rate would have been at least somewhat lower for even the weakest writers.

Syntactic Fluency

What about the syntactic fluency and versatility of these freshman writers? To answer that question we once again contrasted papers that had been scored low and papers scored high, but this time we also compared the high papers to an outside criterion—the syntactic fluency of published writers. Fortunately, there is a considerable amount of recent research (Hunt, 1965; Christensen, 1967; Cooper & Rosenberg, 1979; Watson, 1979) on the development of syntactic fluency, research that tells us exactly which features to examine if we want to describe the syntactic fluency of college students writing in a particular discourse type.

For this study we chose two features that are average *lengths* of syntactic units, and five that are specific *types* of syntactic constructions. We will define and give examples of each before discussing the results of the analysis.

Lengths of Syntactic Units

MEAN T-UNIT LENGTH

A T-unit (Hunt, 1965) is an independent clause and all its related modifiers. A sentence will always be a T-unit, but sometimes a sentence will contain two or even three T-units.

For analysis of the syntax of nonprofessional writers, the T-unit, rather than the orthographic sentence, is now the standard unit. The mean length of a novice writer's sentences is often inflated either by overcompounding or by orthographic sentence-punctuation errors. (The latter sometimes occur in first drafts when the need for consistent end-stop punctuation is overlooked, as in the test-like situation for writing used in this study.) Mean T-unit length overcomes these problems, since it is derived by segmenting a paper into a sequence of independent assertions (clauses), breaking compound sentences into two T-units, and ignoring the requirements of conventional sentence orthography.

And, of course, the use of the T-unit in this study enabled us to compare results with those from previous studies.

Here is a section from one paper that illustrates segmentation into T-units. The T-units are marked with a slash and numbered:

> It is my contention that the efficiency and quality of management should not be made to suffer in response to inessential yet worthwhile programs.[1]/ For members of a hiring committee it is the operation of the company to its best and fullest potential which should be our main concern,[2]/ and any or all decisions originating from this committee should be the result of our best assessment of the situation to that end.[3]/

While the first sentence is one T-unit, the second sentence has two T-units.

MEAN CLAUSE LENGTH

An even better index of the syntactic maturity of older writers like our college students is the mean length of all their clauses, both independent and dependent (Hunt, 1965). To obtain mean clause length we identified all dependent clauses within each T-unit and then added together the number of T-units (independent clauses) and the number of dependent clauses, dividing that total into the number of words in the paper. Here is a section of one paper with the dependent clauses underlined. The T-units are marked with a slash and numbered:

> The Affirmative Action quota should mean <u>that we employ people who have the best qualifications.</u>[1]/ We should not take into consideration the person's sex, religion, race or any other characteristic.[2]/ Just <u>because a person is a female,</u> it does not give her a better opportunity to obtain a job <u>if her competitors are men who are better qualified.</u>[3]/ It is unfair to the person with more ability.[4]/

Altogether there are five dependent clauses (two of them embedded in other dependent clauses) attached to four independent clauses, or T-units, for a total of nine clauses.

Types of Syntactic Constructions

FREE MODIFIERS

A characteristic of professional writing is the frequent occurrence of modifying structures (words, phrases, clauses) at the beginning of a T-unit, inserted within a T-unit, or trailing after the base clause in a T-unit (Christensen, 1967). Here are two sentences that illustrate all three types occurring within a T-unit: initial, medial, and final. The modifiers are underlined.

> Operation on all levels, [MEDIAL] whether production, management, or executive levels, must be maintained at the most practical and efficient levels possible, [FINAL] promoting the most competent and reliable leadership as well as personnel. (1)/ [INITIAL] While the female candidate may be well-qualified, it has clearly been stated that she is not as qualified as her male competitor. (2)/

FINAL FREE MODIFIERS

Since *final* free modifiers, like that in the first T-unit just above, are especially characteristic of professional writing, we made a separate count of these.

ADJECTIVE MODIFIERS

Another special feature of the sentences of older writers and professionals is the amount of nominal embedding—that is, the amount of adjective modification of all kinds (word, phrase, clause) around the nouns (Hunt, 1965). These two sentences illustrate word, phrase, and clause adjective modification:

> Just because a person is a female, it does not give her a better opportunity to obtain a job if her competitors are men who are better qualified. It is unfair to the person with more ability.

As simple as this sort of modification seems, it is surprising how rarely it appears in the writing of upper elementary and early secondary writers. We will see in a moment how sharply it separated the weak and strong writers in this study.

NONFINITE VERBS

A nonfinite verb is a verbal functioning in some way other than as a verb or predicate in a clause. If it is a gerund, it will be the subject or object of a clause. If it is a participle, it will be an adjective. A nonfinite verb is a kind of reduced clause, a way of packing more information into a single phrase. Noting these nonfinite verbs is a shorthand way of determining whether a writer's syntactic repertoire includes the invaluable option of the verb or verbal phrase (Watson, 1979). Here are some examples:

> They would like a woman to fill an executive position. Hiring her would not help the company.

That's discriminating against the more qualified, more deserving male.

The employees could also take us to court in an attempt to force us to fulfill our Affirmative Action quota.

Dismissing the girl would not be wise and just.

ADVERB PHRASES AND CLAUSES OF CAUSE, CONSEQUENCE, CONDITION, AND CONCESSION

We now come to a syntactic option that is especially important in persuasive writing: adverb phrases and clauses of cause, consequence, condition, and concession. These structures must necessarily do much of the basic work of persuasion, expressing such relationships as *if, since, because, in order to, because of, even though, provided that, whether or not, in spite of, contrary to,* and *depending on.*

From our analysis of the papers for all of these syntactic features, we arrived at results that are summarized in Tables 1-2 and 1-3. Table 1-4 compares these results with the results from a study of advanced writers at SUNY/Buffalo and of published writers (Cooper & Rosenberg, 1979), and this table is a good place to begin our discussion.

The first thing we noticed was the high degree of syntactic fluency of the best writers in the 1979 freshman class. They did about as well as juniors majoring in English at SUNY/Buffalo. (Note that we are discussing here only a very limited feature of writing ability: syntactic fluency, as measured by some conventional linguistic variables.) However, these writers still had a long way to go to match the performance of published professionals. The development of syntactic fluency—the slow expansion of the syntactic repertoire and the ability to use it confidently in various rhetorical contexts—continues throughout the undergraduate

Table 1-2. Syntactic Structures per 100 T-Units in the Writing of Five Freshmen Scoring Low and Five Scoring High on a Persuasive Writing Task

	Holistic scores	
Syntactic structure	Low	High
All free modifiers	33^a	49^b
Final free modifiers	15	9
All adjectival modifiers	149	263
Nonfinite verbs	56	75
Adverb phrases and clauses of cause, consequence, condition, and concession	31	42

[a]Incidence in 100 T-units, based on a sample of 55 T-units in five papers rated low in the holistic scoring.

[b]Incidence in 100 T-units, based on a sample of 67 T-units in five papers rated high in the holistic scoring.

Table 1-3. *Mean T-Unit Length and Mean Clause Length in the Writing of Five Freshmen Scoring Low and Five Scoring High on a Persuasive Writing Task*

Length in number of words	Holistic scores	
	Low	High
Mean T-unit length	14.68[a]	18.40[c]
Mean clause length	9.38[b]	10.94[d]

[a]An average of the mean T-unit length in five papers with a range of 12.0 to 17.3.

[b]An average of the mean clause length in five papers with a range of 7.6 to 11.2.

[c]An average of the mean T-unit length in five papers with a range of 16.5 to 24.9.

[d]An average of the mean clause length in five papers with a range of 9.5 to 14.8.

and graduate years. As good as the best incoming students were, they would all experience further growth in syntactic fluency.

The next thing we noticed was the large gap between the high- and low-scoring freshmen. The weakest freshmen writers lagged behind the strongest in syntactic fluency by nearly four words per T-unit (14.68 vs. 18.40) and by more than one word per clause (9.38 vs. 10.94). Given the developmental curve of growth in syntactic fluency that could be plotted from previous research, these are huge differences. In fact, the weakest freshmen writers had about the same degree of syntactic fluency as superior writers in Grade 8 (Cooper & Rosenberg, 1979), or as average writers in Grade 12 (Hunt, 1965).

Table 1-4. *Comparison of Low- and High-Scoring Freshmen with Junior English Majors and PhD Candidates in English at SUNY/Buffalo and with Adult Literary Critics*

	Syntactic variables	
	Mean T-unit length	Mean clause length
Freshmen in this study		
Low-scoring freshmen	14.68	9.38
High-scoring freshmen	18.40	10.94
Outstanding writers at SUNY/Buffalo		
Junior English majors	17.56	11.16
PhD candidates	19.40	11.57
Professional writers		
Adult literary critics	20.46	11.60

Table 1-2 reveals that the best freshman writers had a special advantage at the sentence level over the poorest writers: the best writers were able to pack more information into each T-unit, information that qualifies, elaborates, specifies, or modifies. In any given 100 T-units of their writing, the best writers among the 1979 class would use 387 free modifiers, adjectival modifiers, and nonfinite verbs, but the poorest writers only 238.

The only syntactic structure that professionals often use and that appeared more frequently in the poor freshmen writing than in the best freshman writing was the final free modifier (see Table 1-2). The incidence of this structure in the writing of both groups was low, however. And the types of final free modifier that professionals use— the absolute phrase and the participle phrase—almost never appeared in either group.

Examining the last row in Table 1-2, we can point to a difference between the two groups which, though not large in absolute terms, can be quite important in persuasive writing. As we mentioned earlier, phrases and clauses of cause, consequence, condition, and concession are especially useful in persuasive writing and, further, occur more often in the persuasive writing of mature writers (Watson, 1979).

But perhaps the most important thing to note about the results of our syntactic analysis is that in our random sample of 50 writers, *each one of the weakest five writers* (those with holistic scores of only 2 or 3) *used all of the syntactic structures we identified*. This meant that the very poorest writers among the regularly admitted freshmen had a relatively high degree of syntactic competence to use as a base for the growth they would need to make in syntactic fluency. Just as with our analysis of error, we found no lack of basic skills at the sentence level. Even the weakest writers knew what a sentence was. They wrote them regularly, signaling their orthographic boundaries (capitals and periods) in conventional ways. Certainly they did not need grammar instruction. They already had an adequate grammar—they could generate a variety of error-free sentences.

So far the analysis had taught us a good deal about the abilities of these writers and the possibilities for them at the sentence level, in terms of standard usage and syntactic fluency. Actually, we had expected much worse results, so we were quite surprised. We were encouraged that what they did need to know we could easily teach them. However, we wanted to move beyond the sentence to look at their control of text structure and their skills at argument. We wanted to know about their composing, as well as their editing. We began by examining systematically their strategies for creating coherent written text.

Cohesion of the Text

Cohesion analysis is a way of examining how written compositions are unified so as to be recognizable as complete texts. As a means of gauging the density or richness of texture in written pieces, cohesion analysis attempts to account in an objective or measurable way for the intuitive sense that some pieces are "more tightly structured," or perhaps "more coherent," than others.

Our discussion and analysis are based on the work of Halliday and Hasan (1976), who argue that "a text is best regarded as a *semantic* unit: a unit not of form, but of meaning." They claim that what bestows unity and coherence on individual texts is not the structural relations within sentences (determined by the constraints of grammar and syntax), but the *semantic relations* that hold between particular words *across sentence boundaries*. Individual writers achieve cohesion, then, by setting up links on a semantic (or meaning) level between a word (or words) in one sentence and those in another sentence. These links are referred to as "cohesive ties."

Examples from the student papers will illustrate the five major types of cohesive ties: reference, substitution, ellipsis, conjunction, and lexical. In the following examples, the words that form a tie are underlined.

Reference

The most frequent type of referential cohesion is the use of personal pronouns:

> In my opinion, hiring this particular woman to fill the executive position is harmful to the company. Her qualifications are not as high as the other applicants.

"Her" in the second sentence depends for its meaning upon the presence of "woman" in the first sentence. The two words together constitute one cohesive tie. Of course, demonstrative pronouns (*this, that, these, those*) function in a similar manner.

Referential cohesion is also achieved through the use of comparatives:

> Two weeks ago, the Supreme Court decided that Affirmative Action quotas are not examples of reverse discrimination. Another reason why it would be beneficial to hire a woman is that it would help and protect the image of our company.

"Another" in the second sentence presupposes the mention of a reason in the preceding sentence, this time forming a cohesive tie between a single word and an entire clause.

Substitution

Substitution and ellipsis occur much less frequently than the other types of cohesive ties, tending to be more common in speech than in writing. Here is an example of substitution:

> The solution to this problem may be solved in two ways. The first one I have mentioned already.

"One" in the first sentence acts as a substitute for "solution" in the second sentence.

Ellipsis

Ellipsis is defined as "substitution by zero." Whereas in the previous example "one" filled in for "solution" by occupying a grammatical slot, ellipsis occurs when the slot is left empty:

> In this manner, the workers would not suffer, and neither would the business [suffer].

Although "suffer" has been elided in the second clause, the meaning is clear because "suffer" in the first clause satisfies the presupposition created by the ellipsis.

Conjunction

Of the several types of cohesive ties achieved through the use of conjunction, the most common are the familiar coordinating conjunctions—*and, but, or, yet, for,* and *so.* The conjunctive verbs also function cohesively:

> The Affirmative Action quota is a solid step toward improvement. However, employment based merely upon sex, race or religion as the foundation of this person's qualifications is sheer folly.

Lexical

Since lexical cohesion proves to be one of the most interesting and important means through which writers achieve textuality, the four principal types all warrant exemplification. Perhaps the simplest kind of lexical tie results from the repetition of a particular word throughout a discourse.

> I feel that our company should employ the more qualified male. The company would run smoother with someone who knows what he is doing.

A second type of lexical tie results from the use of synonyms:

> There are good reasons for hiring a woman. If this company depends on any government contracts, it would be essential to have a female employee in an executive position.

A "general item" serves to classify or categorize a previously mentioned word, phrase, or clause:

> Therefore, in both ethical and practical perspectives, all factors related to government or corporate "suggested" guidelines, desires, or preferences should be secondary factors in dealing with the issue. Let me expand on that idea a little.

"Idea" in the second sentence makes explicit how the writer intends the information in the first sentence to be regarded.

The final type of lexical cohesion we will consider is brought about through the use of collocation. Any words that are closely associated with one another in the "language at large," when used together in a discourse, are said to collocate. Although this type of cohesion is more open-ended than the other types we have discussed, it is still readily identifiable:

> I feel our company should employ the more qualified male. If the female was chosen, it would take her awhile to adjust to a different situation at the job.

In juxtaposition here, *male* and *female* collocate very strongly with each other, as do *job* and *company*. Like all other kinds of cohesive ties, collocation establishes semantic links between sentences, thereby contributing to the coherence of the entire discourse.

Using a coding scheme developed by Halliday and Hasan (1976, pp. 333–355), we analyzed the papers of the five most competent and five least competent writers, classifying each cohesive tie according to a system that is considerably more detailed than has been suggested by our examples and too involved to report here. This analysis enabled us to see how many different kinds of ties were employed by the writers in each group, as well as how many times a particular type of tie was used. In keeping with previous research on syntax, we chose as our unit of analysis not the orthographic sentence but the more reliable T-unit. Thus we were able to calculate the number of cohesive ties per T-unit, giving us some indices of what might be thought of as "cohesive fluency."

Though the cohesive system in English is quite complex, the Halliday and Hasan presentation is accessible to nearly any patient reader willing to follow up a few technical terms in a good current grammar (e.g., Quirk & Greenbaum, 1973). Cohesion analysis will not fully explain the coherence of a text, but it will account for a major portion of the factors that contribute to coherence. Certainly for a descriptive evaluation like the present study, where *groups* of writers are being compared, the Halliday and Hasan scheme is a powerful tool. Recent work suggests that ties per 100 words would be a better base for reporting than ties per T-unit (or per 100 T-units) (Witte & Faigley, 1981). The problem with the latter measures is the positive correlation between T-unit length and ties per T-unit: better writers have more ties per T-unit in part just because there are more words in their T-units. Already a number of studies have been reported in which cohesion analysis has played a crucial part (King & Rentel, 1981; Rochester & Martin, 1979; Witte & Faigley, 1981).

What did our analysis reveal about the most competent and least competent incoming freshman writers? We will report only selected results from the complete analysis. First off, we noted that while the weakest writers formed cohesive ties using six different types of reference, the strongest writers employed six additional kinds of referential ties not used at all by the weak writers. And four of these six proved to be especially important, since they were not pronouns but comparatives. This suggested that the more mature writers were better able to provide explicit signals of the relationship between particular words or ideas. Saying that an issue was *the same as, similar to, different from,* or perhaps *better or worse than* another was a mark of sophistication that was simply not present in the writing of the weakest writers, whereas the best writers used approximately 10 such comparatives for every 100 T-units.

Neither substitution nor ellipsis appeared at all in papers by the weakest writers. The best writers, on the other hand, used substitution 2.90 times per 100 T-units and ellipsis 1.45 times. The best writers were more likely to tighten their syntax by eliding a word, or to avoid repetition by finding a substitute.

The use of conjunction for both the best and weakest writers was surprisingly similar: the most competent writers used five different types of conjunctive ties for a total of 17.39 per 100 T-units, and the least competent writers also used five different types for a total of 16.36 per 100 T-units. One notable difference was that the best writers used considerably more additive conjunctions (11.59 to 1.82 per 100 T-units), probably a result of their tendency to elaborate an argument more fully by coordinating several assertions or pieces of evidence on the same level of generality.

Finally, how did the best and weakest writers compare in their use of lexical cohesion? To review, the four principal types of lexical ties are repetition of the same word, use of synonyms, use of general items, and collocation. In the papers of the most competent writers, repetition of the same word accounted for 50 percent of all lexical ties, while for the weakest writers it accounted for 64 percent. Since the most competent writers depended less often on simple repetition to achieve lexical cohesion, they obviously employed alternative devices.

Perhaps the most striking difference was in the use of synonyms. Whereas the strongest writers used 11.59 synonyms per 100 T-units (accounting for 4 percent of all lexical ties), the papers of the least competent writers had no ties whatsoever resulting from the use of synonyms. Synonyms, along with nominal and verbal substitutes, add a degree of flexibility and variety to the writing of the most competent freshmen—features that were consistently and conspicuously absent in the weakest papers.

Both groups used general items to achieve lexical cohesion about the same percentage of the time (4 percent of all lexical ties for the weakest writers, 5 percent of all lexical ties for the strongest). However, the most competent writers used 2½ times as many general items (7.27 to 18.84 per 100 T-units).

Thirty-two percent of the weakest writers' lexical ties resulted from the use of collocation, whereas 41 percent of the strongest writers' ties were collocational. The texts of the latter were, as a result, richer in associations, variety, and creativity. Not only did the best writers rely less frequently on same-item repetition and more often on devices such as synonyms and collocation (in terms of percentage of all lexical ties), but there was a notable difference in number of collocational ties between the strongest and weakest writers. The least competent writers used 67.27 collocational ties per 100 T-units, while the best writers used over twice as many, with 144.93.

Altogether, the most competent writers used 69 percent more lexical ties per 100 T-units than the weakest writers. In considering the entire range of possible cohesive ties, we noted that the weakest writers used 15 different kinds of ties, whereas the strongest writers used 26. Among the ties not used at all by the weakest writers, as we have seen, were important synonyms and comparatives. Finally, we observed that the least competent writers used 2.80 cohesive ties per T-unit. By contrast, the best writers used 4.88 cohesive ties per T-unit.

As soon as we had looked beyond the sentence, then, the results were not nearly so encouraging. Since in the cohesion analysis we were not comparing the best writers to professionals, we could reach no overall conclusions about the performance of the best writers (as had been possible with regard to the syntactic analysis). However, we could still compare the best and weakest writers. It was troubling that the gap between the two was now much wider. The weakest writers used only half as many types of referential ties as the best writers, and the weakest never used substitution or ellipsis. Further, they avoided the use of synonyms as lexical ties. The texture of their essays was noticeably thinner. They seemed to lack some basic strategies for creating text.

Arguments and Elaborations

Up to this point, all of our analyses—dealing with error, syntax, and cohesion—could have been used with any kind of writing. Since we are dealing specifically with persuasive writing, we wanted next to look closely at discourse features unique to persuasion. Guided by the groundbreaking work of Klaus and Lloyd-Jones for the National Assessment of Educational Progress (Lloyd-Jones, 1977), we set out to classify the types of arguments the students had used to support their positions. We also wanted to evaluate their abilities to develop these arguments. Finally, we wanted to know whether they understood the requirements of written persuasion well enough to make all the moves a professional might make in the same writing situation.

We predicted that the most effective persuasive pieces would be those containing a wide range of well-elaborated arguments. We assumed that a more competent writer, in attempting to anticipate objections from readers, would use many kinds of arguments. In order to determine whether our prediction was accurate, we began with a content analysis of all 50 essays in the study, not just a subsample of high- and low-quality essays as was the case previously in this chapter. The most common arguments in all 50 essays were the following:

1. Arguments based on stereotyping
2. Arguments rooted in issues of legality
3. Arguments that dealt with sound business and financial practices
4. Arguments in favor of free enterprise
5. Issues about civil rights (i.e., the morality of discrimination and reverse discrimination)
6. Arguments grounded in a debate over competence
7. Concerns about public relations
8. "Altruistic" arguments—considerations of what was best or fair to employees and to the female job candidate

Roughly 70 percent of the writers relied on three or fewer of these arguments. This group of writers was distributed across holistic scores ranging from 3 points to 10 points. In other words, the more competent writers used about the same number of arguments as did the less competent writers. Overall, the two groups also used the same kinds of arguments: the most frequently recurring topics were competence, civil rights, and sound business practice. The remaining five of the eight kinds of arguments occurred with varying frequency in papers judged to be superior as well as in those rated low. Some of the arguments turned up in as few as 3 percent of the papers, while other arguments appeared in 30 percent or so of the pieces.

These results did not support our prediction that the better writers would use more arguments than the weaker writers. If the number of arguments was not a distinctive feature of the superior papers in our sample, then what was so different about the arguments forwarded by the more competent writers that motivated the judges to rate these freshman papers so high? Clearly, the superior papers seemed to have more substance. If the judges' sense that there was simply more pertinent information in the superior pieces could not be accounted for by the number of arguments, then we conjectured that depth of argument might explain the differences between papers written by more and less competent writers.

To study depth of argument, we used another simple kind of analysis on a subsample of the 50 papers. We examined the depth of arguments in the five papers scored highest and the five papers scored lowest. In order to measure this quality, we took a close look at the amount of elaboration of each argument. The method we used was developed by Rabianski (1979). Although her scale was originally designed to evaluate information contained in explanatory or informative writing, it was easily adapted for use with persuasive writing. Rabianski's scheme involves counting the number of both elaborated and unelaborated statements, and then assigning each statement a numerical score based on whether it receives no, some, much, very much, or outstanding elaboration. In presenting her scoring guide, Rabianski carefully laid out criteria for assigning points and for determining what, for example, constitutes "some" or "much" elaboration.

Our analysis of depth of elaboration yielded scores that showed a marked difference between papers written by more and less competent writers. The average elaboration score for the group of less competent writers in our sample was 2; the average score for the more competent group was 4.7. The 2.7 degree of difference means that the more competent writers included almost two and a half times the amount of information, or elaboration, in their papers as did the less competent writers. This volume of elaboration was what had given the superior papers their depth, and what had in part caused the judges to see them as so much more substantial than the papers scored low.

Papers with the lowest elaboration scores contained simply a single claim with no elaboration. Papers with the highest scores elaborated at least one claim, as in the following example. The claim and restatement of claim are italicized. The rest of the paragraph is elaboration or development.

Essay 155

. . . if the employees were in favor of hiring a woman, I believe that we should respect their wishes. Productivity would suffer if employees were hostile to our company. The employees could also take us to court in an attempt to force us to fulfill our Affirmative Action quota. This would be expensive and lead to antagonism between management and employees. Two weeks ago, the Supreme Court decided that Affirmative Action Quotas are not examples of reverse discrimination. Another reason why it could be beneficial to hire a woman is that it would help and protect the image of our company. Minority groups and consumer groups might boycott our company. The loss of sales would hurt our company. *I believe that for those reasons stated, we should hire a woman to fill the executive position in question.*

Argument, elaboration, summary: a very attractive piece of writing. Unfortunately, very few writers, even the most competent, were able to do this consistently. Surely, the elaboration of an argument is an important composing strategy. In this particular case, given the writer's purpose, "more" turns out to be "better."

Structural Features of Persuasive Writing

We wanted to deepen our analysis of persuasive writing by looking closely at certain features and structural relationships essential to persuasion. Through such an analysis we hoped to answer questions like the following: Just how close did these writers come to presenting their arguments and elaborations in patterns commonly used by professionals? And, to use terminology popular now in cognitive science: Had these writers internalized appropriate schemas or scripts for persuasive writing? More simply: When asked to argue for or against an important current social issue like affirmative action in employment, did these freshman writers have available any appropriate plans they could follow?

In order to find some answers to these questions, we carried out a structural analysis based on a subsample of five papers scored highest and five papers scored lowest in the holistic rating. Such an analysis allowed us to see what roles the individual parts of the persuasive discourse played, how those parts were interrelated, and how they functioned together to form the whole. We based our analysis on an established model by the philosopher Stephen Toulmin (Toulmin, 1969).

The model, which is grounded in a general theory of argument and persuasion, identifies six elements of rhetorical argument. It can be schematically diagrammed as in Figure 1-1.

In his discussion of the Toulmin model as an approach to teaching argument, Kneupper (1978) provides concise definitions for these six elements in the model. Three are absolutely essential to an explicitly developed argument, and three are used to support and qualify the argument. In order to qualify as an argument, an essay must contain at least a claim, some data, and a warrant. The claim is "the conclusion of the argument and the point at issue in a controversy. The data is evidence for the claim. The warrant provides the link which shows the relation between the data and the claim" (Kneupper, 1978, p. 238). The three additional elements in the Toulmin model function to justify or temper the argument, or to accommodate the writer's audience. The qualifier, Kneupper explains, "is usually an acknowledgment of the probabilistic nature of the claim, the reservation specifies conditions in which the warrant does not apply, the backing supports or justifies the warrant" (p. 238).

Fig. 1-1. An adaptation of the Toulmin model. From **The Nature of Proof** *(2nd ed.) by E. P. Bettinghaus, Indianapolis: Bobbs-Merrill, 1972. Copyright 1972 by The Bobbs-Merrill Company, Inc. Reprinted by permission.*

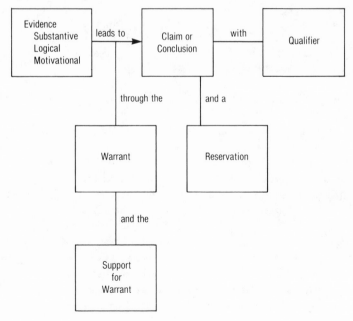

In analyzing the essays in our subsample, we first identified the six features from the Toulmin model, classifying every assertion in each essay in this way. Our analysis uncovered striking differences between the ways in which the more and less competent writers attempted to argue. We can illustrate here by looking at segments from two representative essays. Essay 179 scored low in the holistic scoring. Essay 155 (the same paper we examined for depth of elaboration in the previous section) was scored high.

Essay 179

[CLAIM] The task which lies before us, one of choosing a person for the job, is not a difficult one at all. [CLAIM] Clearly we should do what is best for the company. [CLAIM] Hiring the male is the most logical thing to do. [CLAIM] Why should we hire a woman just because she is a woman. [CLAIM] That's discrimination against the more qualified, more deserving male. [CLAIM] It makes no difference what color, race, creed someone is from, [CLAIM] the most qualified person should get the job.

Essay 155

. . . [WARRANT] if the employees were in favor of hiring a woman, [CLAIM] I believe that we should respect their wishes. [BACKING] Productivity would suffer if employees were hostile to our company. [BACKING] The employees [QUALIFIER] could also take us to court in an attempt to force us to fulfill our Affirmative Action quota. [BACKING] This would be expensive and lead to antagonism between management and employees. [DATA] Two weeks ago, the Supreme Court decided that Affirmative Action Quotas are not examples of reverse discrimination. [WARRANT] Another reason why it could be beneficial to hire a woman is that it would help protect the image of our company. [BACKING] Minority groups and consumer groups [QUALIFIER] might boycott our company. [DATA] The loss of sales would hurt our company. [CLAIM] I believe that for these reasons stated, we should hire a woman to fill the executive position in question.

What struck us immediately about the paper composed by the less competent writer was its lack of certain elements that are essential if the writing is even to qualify as an explicitly developed argument. Stringing claims together does not an argument make—a writer needs to support those claims with data and to suggest some connection (i.e., warrant) between the data and claims. Nowhere in Essay 179 do we find sentences that function as data or as warrants. We do get the sense that the statements about reverse discrimination and race, creed, and color could have functioned as warrants had the writer only included some backing or elaboration to make the connection between these statements and the conclusion more explicit. As they stand, however, these sentences are merely unsupported claims. In contrast, in Essay 155, data and backing are the principal means of elaboration.

Most important, we learned that none of the less competent writers and only two of the more competent writers in our subsample of 10 had included qualifiers or reservations in their pieces. The fact that a large majority did not address the probabilistic nature of their claims or mention instances in which their warrants would not apply indicates a failure to accommodate readers.

Thus, our multilevel analysis—word, sentence, text—had gradually disclosed more serious writing problems in the 1979 freshman class at SUNY/Buffalo. Only as we moved beyond the sentence to rhetorical features of persuasive writing did we begin to understand the nature of these problems. What any of us might have intuitively thought from reading several of the papers was now supported by systematic, specific information. We knew why even the best writers faltered when asked to write persuasively: they used a limited range of arguments, they lacked resources for elaborating and developing arguments, and they consistently failed to use important features of persuasive discourse (warrants, reservations, and qualifiers). In general, they didn't seem accustomed to writing with readers in mind.

But we wanted to know still more. We were curious to see how the students would analyze the problem-solving situation we had put them in. They had a specific and well-defined task to complete. We wanted to know whether their papers reflected a critical analysis of the task itself. And, of course, we were curious to see how much they knew about the social issue we had raised.

Ideological Assumptions and Critical Analysis

The intent of this part of the analysis was to determine to what degree and in what ways ideological assumptions that the students brought to the writing task had influenced their ability to analyze the facts of the situation as set before them in the task. We wished to learn how well students could address an assignment on the basis of the information presented to them rather than on the basis of preconceived notions about the subject. In other words, we wanted to know how carefully they could read and how well they could analyze objectively. For this analysis we used all 50 papers.

Our approach was to distinguish between material that was present in the writing task itself, such as certain facts or concrete alternatives, and concepts or assumptions that the students introduced to validate their positions. We also noted which facts in the writing task were emphasized by the students, and which were slighted or ignored.

For example, the fact that the woman was "less qualified" than the men was noted by 88 percent of the students. Yet only 16 percent displayed awareness that she had been described as "seems competent," and only 12 percent acknowledged the statement that she "meets the written qualifications." Not a single student undertook to distinguish between the terms "competent" and "qualified," or to consider whether it might be significant that the woman met the written requirements. In fact, 54 percent apparently assumed that "seems competent" meant "not really competent," and 62 percent assumed that "less qualified" meant "incompetent to do the job." These assumptions about these phrases also seemed related to two other assumptions that students brought to the task: 54 percent either stated or implied that affirmative action meant reverse discrimination, and 46 percent stated or implied that the company's major concern was to work at maximum efficiency. Neither of these ideas was derivable from the writing task itself. While it was stated that some people felt it would be "foolish" to hire the woman, that term was never further defined in the assignment. It was the students who decided it meant "economically inefficient." By the same token, it was stated in the writing task that some felt hiring the woman would be "unfair to those working under the new executive." However, nowhere was it stated that this would be unfair to the two men or would constitute reverse discrimination. Those two notions were brought to the assignment by the students themselves.

More than perhaps any other type of writing, the persuasive mode should invite a consideration of opposing points of view and involve a concern for the audience. Alternative views need to be examined, if only with the intent of disproving them and thus strengthening one's own position. What we observed instead was a consistent failure to do so: only 16 percent addressed the opposing point of view, the idea that hiring the woman was "absolutely necessary for breaking down employment discrimination."

The writing task itself supported the view that employment discrimination should be broken down, since it included the important fact that the vacant position was the "only executive position ever held by a female." Yet only 10 percent of the students made note of this fact at all, and none cited it as confirming one of the debated views. Having decided, as did 88 percent of them, that "quality" was the single important factor, they avoided considering the context, the alternative argument, or any facts inconsistent with their position.

Interestingly, none of the five students who mentioned the previous female executive assumed that she had been hired under an affirmative action mandate or that she had been given preference by the board of directors; rather, they assumed she must have been extraordinarily talented. This conformed with their belief that the woman who "seems competent" should not be hired.

Facts generally were carelessly observed, by students given a high holistic quality rating (scores of 8–10) as well as by those rated average (scores of 5-7) and low (scores of 2-4). As mentioned above, only 10 percent of the writers acknowledged the point that the executive position was the only one ever held by a woman. Only 12 percent noted that the woman was the board of directors' preference. Only 16 percent mentioned that she "seems competent," and only 12 percent acknowledged that she "meets the written qualifications." Of the group rated high, 40 percent noted at least one of these facts, while only one student noted all four. Of the group rated average, 43 percent noted one of the facts; only one student noted two of them. Of the group rated low, 27 percent noted at least one of these facts, and only two of these writers noted two facts each. Yet, as stated previously, 88 percent overall noted that the men were "more qualified" and made this argument the basis of their decision—doing so, in the vast majority of cases, without noting the extenuating facts. This seems to bode ill for the students' potential to perform carefully refined analyses of data. They seem inclined to observe only that which is most obvious, and which conforms to their preconceived notions.

While only 8 percent of the students actually asserted that social equality had been achieved, they displayed strong suspicion concerning the apparent unfairness of affirmative action plans. Meanwhile they did not show any capacity for considering the larger context of the problem which they had been asked to address, the "employment discrimination" that was supported by the fact of the single female executive. They did not conclude from this that prejudice existed which had affected and continued to adversely affect hiring practices. Instead, they lent greater credence to their own externally derived assumptions that the company's main goal was to work efficiently (46 percent), or they used the formula "I support equality but . . ." (16 percent) to rationalize their position. What we were seeing in the essays was *a systematic validation of general, external assumptions brought to the task, rather than a close analysis derived from the facts themselves.*

Reading and rereading the papers, we came to feel that this tendency to ignore the facts not only was detrimental to analysis of abstract ideas such as would be encountered in the humanities or social sciences, but was likely also to extend to analysis of hard data in engineering and the sciences. We felt that students who reasoned from preconceptions would do poorly in analyzing facts or evidence. It seemed likely that they would seek to confirm their own sense of what the conclusions *should* be rather than reasoning directly from the evidence. In addition, we feared that these students would be unlikely to take note of aberrations, qualifications, or extenuating circumstances—or, if they did note them, would probably not try to account for them.

It should be emphasized that it was not the content of these students' ideological assumptions that was most distressing (though the *uniformity* of attitude might be). Most important was the fact that these students had acquired a mode of thinking in which ideological presumptions and preconceptions predominated over factual analysis. Any particular ideological tenet might be susceptible to revision. However, the general tendency to think in such terms would determine how these students approached all experience and would severely limit their ability to understand and assimilate new material. And such assimilation was, after all, the function of the university they were to attend.

Of the sample selection of 50 papers that provided the basis for analysis, only two papers articulated a proaffirmative-action position. Because of the test setting, time pressure, unfamiliar surroundings, and some uncertainty on the part of students as to what might be expected of them, we did not expect their writing to be characterized by originality, intellectual acuity, flair, or indeed much of anything in the way of risk-taking. But even discounting such hindrances, the sample papers were nevertheless striking in their uniformity. The sample papers consistently expressed the range of intellectual stereotypes that the students had learned to feel most comfortable with and to incorporate as their own. To these stereotypes we gave the generic label "ideology."

As was demonstrated earlier, there was a distinct lack of variety to the students' arguments. Almost all the papers hinged on some basic, "common-sense" notion of fair play. But the task set before the students demanded—or at least would certainly allow for—extremely specific analysis of a problem in a particular context, with opportunity for careful attention to nuance and detail. For example, the fact that the board of directors wanted a woman candidate in order to fulfill an affirmative action quota was a subtlety most of the writers ignored. In the face of a possibly complex task of analysis, these students instead chose to interpret the problem as a simple one that would admit of a straightforward, common-sense solution. In their rhetoric the writers asserted simplicity. One said, "I feel there should be no dilemma"; a number said, in effect, "The solution is simple." We should note, however, that the writing assignment may have overcomplicated the students' task by insisting that the woman "is clearly less qualified than both of the men she is competing with." We wondered if a less absolute word than "clearly" would have changed the substance of the students' arguments in any significant way. We thought probably not, except that a substitution might have caused some students to tone down their rhetoric of absolutist simplicity.

What was missing from the students' arguments was a ready cognizance of *particular* social, historical, legal, and especially economic contexts—contexts in which they might have situated the question of just whom it was fair and proper to hire. Clearly, this group of students had only a dim awareness that affirmative action is, in fact, the law of the land. Those few students who alluded to the Supreme Court Bakke decision typically got the facts tangled and invariably used the allusion to support an antiaffirmative-action position, now knowing that the Court had used Bakke to support affirmative action principles.

Of great concern to us was the economic ideology that the vast majority of papers asserted with considerable heat and self-assurance. These students wrote as if they really knew what business was about: business is about competitive markets and profits. The following example is typical: "The basic ideas behind competition in today's business world dictate hiring the best, making the best product, and selling it for the lowest price you can." This is quite a strong sentence technically (note the active force of the verb "dictate"), with a good bit of rhetorical verve to it. But its analysis of "today's business world" is taken straight from the *laissez faire* economics of Adam Smith, a theory that represented a codification of established ideas when *The Wealth of Nations* was written in 1776, and is now reliable only as a cliché. Certainly the sentence contains some truth, but its ideology is constituted of stereotypes that often as not contradict the ambiguities of experience. This sentence about "selling for the lowest price you can" was written in the second summer when OPEC was in existence, with Exxon's gas price jumping a penny a day.

What can we infer from the fact that so many students mounted the same kinds of arguments, ignoring the intricacies of the situation for the sake of uniformity of doctrine—a doctrine that rests on "common sense" and "fair play"? It appears that these students were being taught to think alike, in their high schools, from their parents, and—we suspected—most importantly, from their television sets. The uniformity and naiveté of these essays persuaded us that these students had been *actively* taught to fear and shun complexity, and especially to deny moral and legal ambiguity.

Reflections on the Buffalo Study

In summary, our study of the writing performance of the 1979 freshman class at SUNY/Buffalo illustrates several procedures for examining writing, at levels ranging from error to ideology:

- Error
- Syntax
- Cohesion
- Types of arguments and depth of elaboration
- Special features of persuasion
- Ideological assumptions and critical analysis

What we learned from the analysis at each level was essential to a full view of the writing abilities of these freshmen. At each level we saw different implications for instruction and for general education. As we moved deeper into the writing, we found more and more evidence of truly substantive problems in composing and critical thinking. It was finally very clear to us—and to others who read the report—that even the best writers in the relatively selective 1979 class would need careful writing instruction.

It was also evident that the weakest writers had the basic writing competence necessary to participate in a challenging composing program in which some attention was given to usage, mechanics, and syntax. They certainly did not need a remedial course concerned mainly with grammar and error. This last point might be disputed by those who persist in defining the solution to "our literacy crisis" in narrow terms: consistent spelling, grammatical etiquette, stylistic flair. These are not small issues, but they are secondary ones. Composing, not editing, is the main problem. Such statements are truisms to informed writing directors, but they still have to be argued and demonstrated to others. Our findings support the point.

All of our conclusions about the Buffalo freshmen must be tempered by the limitations of our design and procedures, particularly the constraints of the writing task and the testing situation. Actually, we did not test the students' true writing abilities, but only their writing performance in a particular situation. We assumed that if they had had more time or a chance to revise or to use a dictionary they might have done noticeably better in some respects. It would be preferable to arrange a carefully planned sampling of first essays written under more flexible but still controlled conditions in course sections, though this approach might not satisfy some skeptics in a policy discussion. Such skeptics might wonder whether instructors had provided special help in order to make their students look as good as possible.

In reporting data like ours to other school or college faculty and administrators, strategies for quantifying and generalizing are very important. Certainly, a display of selected essays or common features in several essays, along with comments on the display, is effective and, in our view, essential. Such displays, with astute, jargon-free commentary, can be telling. But they are not enough for most readers of evaluation reports that relate to policy issues. We need to substantiate any generalizations we make about groups and subgroups, and this means quantifying at least part of our analysis. Notice that even our most general level of analysis in the Buffalo study—ideological assumptions and critical analysis—is based on counts and percentages. With some studies, and some readers, it might be necessary to test for the statistical significance of differences between subgroups.

One other feature of our design deserves comment. Though we wanted to generalize about the 1979 freshman class, we did not focus our study either on a random sample from the whole group or on some subgroup at the center of the score distribution in the holistic rating. By focusing on subgroups of writers at each end of the score distribution, we were able to specify the full range of writing abilities in the group. We sought to describe the *limitations* of the best writers, so that we could make a realistic assessment of the instructional needs of all the students. Since these limitations involved composing rather than editing, we had grounds for arguing that the goals for writing development in the general education program must be set quite high. Indeed, we had enough data to define writing proficiency in our way. Because we could describe the *strengths* of the weakest writers, we could head off any proposals for narrow, remedial instruction.

Further Sources of Procedures for Describing Writing Samples

The Buffalo study is only an evaluation model offered here for discussion, criticism, and refinement. It is not a model study. Copies of it have been in circulation too long and too widely for us to be unaware of its limitations of design and analysis. Since we planned the study and wrote up the results, we have become aware of many more possibilities for analyzing writing, not just persuasive writing but other types as well. As a conclusion to this chapter I will bring up some of these possibilities.

I have recently reviewed a number of procedures for describing written texts (Cooper, 1983). Besides the procedures in the Buffalo study, I discuss possibilities for analyzing abstraction levels of assertions and the patterning of subordinate, coordinate, and superordinate assertions in writing; information management in the placement of given and new information in each clause; thematic structure of written text; and sentence roles. I also suggest some ways of describing the structures of descriptive writing and personal-narrative writing.

Besides this review, I would recommend a new study from Andrew Wilkinson and his research group at the University of Exeter (Wilkinson, Barnsley, Hanna, & Swan, 1980). To study the writing development of children between the ages of seven and fourteen, the team devised four different models or systems of analysis:

> Cognitive. The basis of this model is a movement from an undifferentiated world to a world organized by mind, from a world of instances to a world related by generalities and abstractions.
>
> Affective. Development is seen as being in three movements—one towards a greater awareness of self, a second towards a greater awareness of neighbour as self, a third towards an inter-engagement of reality and imagination.

Moral. "Anomy" or lawlessness gives way to "heteronomy" or rule by fear of punishment, which in turn gives way to "socionomy" or rule by a sense of reciprocity with others which finally leads to the emergence of "autonomy" or self-rule.

Stylistic. Development is seen as choices in relation to a norm of the simple, literal, affirmative sentence which characterizes children's early writing. Features, such as structure, cohesion, verbal competence, syntax, reader awareness, sense of appropriateness, undergo modification (Wilkinson *et al.*, 1980, pp. 2–3).

The Wilkinson report provides a scheme of analysis and classification for each of these four models. Sternglass (1981) has used Wilkinson's cognitive model to study the writing of students in "basic" and "regular" classes at Indiana University.

The reports and released exercises of the National Assessment of Educational Progress—Writing are a particularly rich source of schemes for description, analysis, and scoring. Over many years and at considerable expense in three national writing assessments (a fourth is now being planned), NAEP has pioneered in writing evaluation, particularly with a descriptive-scoring procedure called primary trait scoring (Lloyd-Jones, 1977; NAEP, 1976, 1978, 1981). This procedure makes it possible to analyze writing in terms of the unique rhetorical requirements of the writing situation. At NAEP, many quite detailed guides have been developed for explanatory, persuasive, and expressive writing. All these guides, and a great many other valuable evaluation materials, are regularly reported and released for public use. They are not nearly so well known as they should be.

Of course, the starting point for anyone doing descriptive studies of writing remains Shaughnessy's *Errors and Expectations* (1977). Though the book concentrates only on spelling, usage, syntax, and vocabulary, it is a model of how writing samples can be analyzed in a vigorous yet careful manner.

REFERENCES

Baddely, A. D., & Wing, A. M. Spelling errors in handwriting. In U. Frith (Ed.), *Cognitive processes in spelling*. New York: Academic Press, 1980.

Bartholomae, D. The study of error. *College Composition and Communication*, 1980, *31*, 253–269.

Bettinghaus, E. P. *The nature of proof* (2nd ed.). Indianapolis: Bobbs-Merrill, 1972.

Christensen, F. *Notes toward a new rhetoric*. New York: Harper & Row, 1967.

Conference on College Composition and Communication, Committee on Teaching and Its Evaluation in Composition. Evaluating instruction in writing. *College Composition and Communication*, 1982, *33*, 213–230.

Cooper, C. R. Holistic evaluation of writing. In C. R. Cooper & L. Odell (Eds.), *Evaluating writing: Describing, measuring, judging*. Urbana, Ill.: National Council of Teachers of English, 1977.

Cooper, C. R. Procedures for describing written texts. In P. Mosenthall, L. Tamor, & S. Walmsley (Eds.), *Research in writing: Principles and methods.* New York: Longman, 1983.

Cooper, C. R., & Odell, L. *Evaluating writing: Describing, measuring, judging.* Urbana, Ill.: National Council of Teachers of English, 1977.

Cooper, C. R., & Rosenberg, B. *Indexes of syntactic maturity for superior writers in the expository mode.* Unpublished manuscript, State University of New York, Buffalo, 1979.

Daiute, C. A. Psycholinguistic foundations of the writing process. *Research in the Teaching of English,* 1981, *15,* 5–22.

Davis, B. G., Scriven, M., & Thomas, S. *The evaluation of composition instruction.* Inverness, Calif.: Edgepress, 1981.

Gere, A. R. Written composition: Toward a theory of evaluation. *College English,* 1980, *42,* 44–58.

Halliday, M., & Hasan, R. *Cohesion in English.* London: Longmans, 1976.

Harris, M. Mending the fragmented free modifier. *College Composition and Communication,* 1981, *32,* 175–182.

Hartwell, P. Dialect interference in writing: A critical view. *Research in the Teaching of English,* 1980, *14,* 101–118.

Hotopf, N. Slips of the pen. In U. Frith (Ed.), *Cognitive processes in spelling.* New York: Academic Press, 1980.

Hunt, K. W. *Grammatical structures written at three grade levels.* Urbana, Ill.: National Council of Teachers of English, 1965.

King, M. L., & Rentel, V. M. *How children learn to write: A longitudinal study.* Columbus, Ohio: Ohio State University Research Foundation, 1981.

Kneupper, C. W. Teaching argument: An introduction to the Toulmin model. *College Composition and Communication,* 1978, *29,* 219–227.

Kroll, B. M., & Schafer, J. C. Error-analysis and the teaching of composition. *College Composition and Communication,* 1978, *29,* 242–248.

Lloyd-Jones, R. Primary trait scoring. In C. R. Cooper & L. Odell (Eds.), *Evaluating writing: Describing, measuring, judging.* Urbana, Ill.: National Council of Teachers of English, 1977.

Meyers, M. *A procedure for writing assessment and holistic scoring.* Urbana, Ill.: National Council of Teachers of English, 1980.

National Assessment of Educational Progress. *The second assessment of writing, 1973–74 assessment: Released exercise set,* 1976. *The second assessment of writing: New and reassessed exercises with technical information and data,* 1978. *The third assessment of writing: 1978–79 released exercise set,* 1981. *Writing achievement, 1969–79:* Vol. 1, 17-year-olds, 1980; Vol. 2, 13-year-olds, 1980; Vol. 3, 9-year-olds, 1980. (All of the foregoing reports may be ordered from NAEP, Suite 700, 1860 Lincoln St., Denver, Colo. 80295.)

Odell, L. Defining and assessing competence in writing. In C. R. Cooper (Ed.), *The nature and measurement of competency in English.* Urbana, Ill.: National Council of Teachers of English, 1981.

Odell, L., & Cooper, C. R. Procedures for evaluating writing: Assumptions and needed research. *College English,* 1980, *42,* 35–43.

Quirk, R., & Greenbaum, S. *A concise grammar of contemporary English.* New York: Harcourt Brace Jovanovich, 1973.

Rabianski, N. *An exploratory study of individual differences in the use of free writing and the tagmemic heuristic procedure: Two modes of invention in the composing process.* Unpublished doctoral dissertation, State University of New York, Buffalo, 1979.

Rochester, S. R., & Martin, J. R. *Crazy talk: A study of the discourse of schizophrenic speakers.* New York: Plenum, 1979.

Shaughnessy, M. P. *Errors and expectations: A guide for the teacher of basic writing.* New York: Oxford University Press, 1977.

Sternglass, M. S. Dialect features in the compositions of black and white college students: The same or different? *College Composition and Communication*, 1974, 25, 259–263.

Sternglass, M. S. Assessing reading, writing, and reasoning. *College English*, 1981, 43, 269–275.

Toulmin, S. *The uses of argument.* Cambridge, England: Cambridge University Press, 1969.

Watson, C. *The effects of maturity and discourse type on the written syntax of superior high school seniors and upper level college English majors.* Unpublished doctoral dissertation, State University of New York, Buffalo, 1979.

White, E. M., & Thomas, L. L. Racial minorities and writing skills assessment in the California state university and colleges. *College English*, 1981, 43, 276–283.

Wilkinson, A., Barnsley, G., Hanna, P., & Swan, M. *Assessing language development.* Oxford, England: Oxford University Press, 1980.

Williams, J. M. The phenomenology of error. *College Composition and Communication*, 1981, 32, 152–168.

Witte, S., & Faigley, L. Coherence, cohesion, and writing quality. *College Composition and Communication*, 1981, 32, 189–204.

2

Designing protocol studies of the writing process: An introduction

HEIDI SWARTS
LINDA S. FLOWER
JOHN R. HAYES
Carnegie-Mellon University

One direction in writing research today is to look more closely at individual processes such as planning, invention, and revision, and to model the organization of these processes. Such close modeling is made possible by thinking-aloud protocols of writers performing a writing task: protocols give us a new window on the process and capture in rich detail the moment-to-moment thinking of a writer in action. Elsewhere we have looked at the theoretical implications of protocol analysis in contrast with other research methods (Hayes & Flower, 1983). Here we wish to focus on practical aspects of protocol analysis: What can protocol studies contribute to our understanding of the writing process? What kinds of studies can be done?

An experimental protocol is a sequential record of a subject's attempts to perform a task. Developed by cognitive psychologists, protocol analysis is an innovative and powerful research tool. One may study protocols of subjects doing an algebra problem, trying to read and understand a wordy government regulation, or performing any number of tasks. One may study motor protocols of a subject's actions, eye movement protocols that trace a subject's reading rate, or protocols of subjects performing a task while verbalizing what they are thinking. We are concerned here with thinking-aloud writing protocols and their use in writing research.

Protocol analysis is a particularly theory-driven form of research and is therefore quite demanding of the researcher. A protocol offers a wealth of unsorted information. While this profusion of unselective data may seem overwhelming, it is actually the method's hidden strength: the very completeness of the picture of the writing process provides a check on the researcher's hypotheses. In fact, a typical pattern in using protocols is to develop a hypothesis, derive from it a coding scheme, and then find the hypothesis disconfirmed because it doesn't fit all the data.

So protocols demand vigorous analysis. Their strengths are that they ruthlessly weed out half-formed initial hypotheses that cannot fully accommodate the reality of the writing process and that they can add substance and depth to a theory-driven analysis.

Techniques of Protocol Gathering

In a thinking-aloud writing protocol, the subject works in an experimental room with a desk, writing materials, and a cassette tape recorder and a tape (see Bond & Hayes, 1980). The experimenter gives the subject general instructions and the time limit (usually about an hour). The subject is given a rough idea of the task, such as writing a magazine article, and is told, "The most important thing about this experiment is that we want you to say everything out loud as you are thinking and writing your essay. Even if it has nothing to do with the task—stray remarks and irrelevant comments are fine. We realize it's impossible to say everything you're thinking while you're writing, so just try to say as much as you can." The last thing the experimenter tells the subject is the specific writing assignment, such as "Write about abortion, pros and cons, for *Catholic Weekly*." The experimenter can then choose to stay with the subject and make sure the tape recorder is working, the tape is turned over when the first side is used up, and the subject remembers to verbalize his or her thoughts. Or, the experimenter can choose to leave the subject so as not to create distractions or undue self-consciousness.

After the subject has finished the writing task, the essay and all written notes are numbered in order, and the tape recording of the subject's thinking aloud is transcribed (a process that takes a typist several hours with a transcribing machine). The transcript, which is usually 10–15 pages long, is the version of the writing protocol with which the researcher will probably spend the most time. This double-spaced, typed transcript of the writer's verbalized thoughts provides a unique window on the composing process. It allows the writing researcher to observe not only cognitive processes and their organization in the act of composing, but the development of the writer's ideas. Many people, however, wonder whether the act of verbalizing while writing might seriously distort the process. They also question the merits of protocol analysis relative to other research methods, such as introspection, retrospection, and observation of writing behaviors. These issues have been discussed at length elsewhere (Hayes & Flower, 1983) but deserve some mention here.

Those who ask whether the research technique interferes with the process it attempts to study share this valid concern with many social scientists and psychologists. Traditionally, there is a trade-off between the "reactive" and "nonreactive" research methods. Reactive research methods interact with (and possibly distort) the process studied but offer a close look at it; nonreactive research methods, such as examining a written product, have no effect on the writer's normal process but also offer far less information about it (Atlas, 1980). So *all* investigative techniques have some drawbacks. The value of any method is comparative: Is there any better alternative?

Protocol analysis gives us detailed information about the writer's processes of planning, goal-setting, decision-making, and revising. But does thinking aloud change the way one thinks? A recent series of studies by Ericsson and Simon (1979a, 1979b) indicates that the kind of verbalizing which protocol subjects are asked to do does not alter the writer's focus of attention, although it often slows the process down. To avoid significant alteration, the experimenter must be careful to remind the subject not to try to *analyze* what he or she is thinking, but simply to *think it out loud.* In contrast, the subject of an introspective study is not asked simply to express whatever he or she is consciously attending to, or whatever is retrievable from short-term memory, but must explain or comment on this information. As a result, an introspective report actually changes the subject's focus by imposing an additional task (Hayes & Flower, 1983).

In retrospective studies and famous writers' accounts, the person reports on his or her writing process after the fact. While this method doesn't interfere with the process itself, the information obtained has some important limitations. Most obviously, much of it may have already been lost from short-term memory. Also, subjects are often unaware of the subtle processes that lead to judgments. When asked about their decisions, they may provide causal explanations that are logical but are not always reports of the event as it actually occurred (Nisbett & Wilson, 1977). Subjects may also remember their processes selectively and give a distorted account of them, perhaps trying to say what they think the researcher wants to hear. In essence, retrospective and introspective reports include the writer's prefabricated theories; protocols simply reveal the writer's process itself (or as much as can be captured). This underscores the need for the researcher to bring theoretically based hypotheses to his or her analysis.

Studying objectively observable behaviors, such as pauses, avoids unreliable self-reports. But this process can be more informative if combined with methods that reveal the content of the writer's thought. For example, what is a writer actually thinking while he or she pauses? We can only guess. Thinking-aloud protocols, which provide some of the *content* of the writer's thoughts, give us many more data from which to draw inferences. Like all methods, protocol analysis is imperfect and misses information we would like to capture. But it has the advantage of gaining access to a deep and broad pool of information about the writing process without unduly distorting it.

The very advantages of protocol analysis are also the researcher's nemesis. Protocols offer so much information that it is sometimes hard to know how to design productive research questions that are also manageable. In the remainder of this paper, we would like to address these questions: How can one use protocol analysis to study cognitive processes in writing? And, once some protocols have been gathered, how does one begin to sort the data? We will start with some practical techniques for handling protocols as data and then discuss four types of analyses one might conduct.

Facing the Morass: Preliminary Parsing

The researcher who approaches a writing protocol with no idea of how to sort the data may well feel like someone who has never learned to float and is poised for a dive into the Atlantic Ocean. Some of the basic parsing techniques we have used may prove helpful. A protocol can be divided into various units, ranging from simple lines and clauses, to basic processes such as planning and translating, to composing episodes that reflect a writer's unit of concentration and changing goals. We find it useful to parse a protocol on several levels, with the approach naturally depending on the purpose of the study. It should be emphasized that there is no single, correct way to analyze protocols: one's method is ultimately determined by the task, the subjects, and the research questions to be answered. Bear in mind that any coding scheme which goes much beyond marking lines and clauses makes a theoretical statement. Many of the categories described here are based on our model of cognitive processes in writing (see Figure 2-1).

First, since there is no paragraphing in a protocol, it is helpful to have both the pages and the lines of a protocol numbered by the typist. This makes it easy to refer to a specific section or line—for example, 3.21 refers to page 3, line 21.

Clauses, rather than T-units or sentences, are the most *basic* precise unit with which to measure a writer's utterances. (For an example of the use of clauses in coding protocols, see Flower, Hayes, & Swarts, in press.) Our definition of a clause had two exceptions. Speakers use frequent relative clauses where writers would simply use a noun, and we wanted to limit our units to clauses that added new, independent information. Therefore, clauses in the subject or object position of a sentence (such as *"what I do as a teacher* is what I want to write about") that could easily have noun substitutes, and retrictive clauses (such as "students *who I talk with"*), were simply coded as part of the main clause.

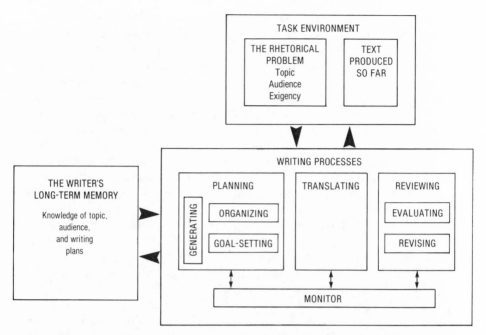

Fig. 2-1. *A model of cognitive processes in writing. From "A Cognitive Process Theory of Writing" by* L. S. *Flower and J. R. Hayes,* College Composition and Communication, December 1981, 35, 365–387. *Copyright 1981 by National Council of Teachers of English. Reprinted by permission.*

The next step is to match the protocol against the writer's notes and essay in order to distinguish what the person is *saying* while writing from what he or she is *reading*. (Writers normally say what they're writing as they copy it down.) For example, if the writer says, "Hmmm . . . can you imagine yourself spending the day . . . no, that's no good," one wants to know whether the writer was simply generating text verbally, writing it down, or rereading something already written. In effect, this step distinguishes the major processes of planning, translating, and reviewing before the protocol is analyzed further (Flower & Hayes, 1981a; Hayes & Flower, 1980a). It is helpful to compare the protocol with the writer's notes and manuscript and then underline in the protocol all comments that appear as written notes or prose. The next step is to underline, in a different color, all acts of rereading previously written material. When in doubt, we find that the most accurate way to distinguish "writes" from "reads" is to listen to the tape itself for intonation and the sound of writing.

Sometimes it is helpful to chart the first appearance of ideas, notes, or sentences in relation to their order in the final text. We number all notes and pieces of text that appear in the protocol by writing N_1 after the first note, T_3 after the third sentence of the final text, and so on.

Finally, we are interested in the units of activity in which writers compose, which we call "episodes" (Flower & Hayes, 1981b). Typically, four expert judges mark off what they feel are major and minor episodes—the points at which there is a shift in the writer's focus of attention or goal. In measuring reliability for this method, we found that two or more judges agreed on 70 percent of the boundaries of the episodes, as compared with 20 percent predicted by a multinomial probability test. We use a *de facto* definition of major episodes as units that at least two judges labeled as major and minor episodes as units that at least two judges coded as either major or minor. Episode boundaries are marked in the protocol with a slash.

Figure 2-2 shows a typical page from a protocol. The writer, a college instructor, was asked to describe her job for a theoretical audience of thirteen- to fourteen-year-old female readers of *Seventeen* magazine. Lines are numbered at the left, clauses are enclosed in parentheses and numbered above, "writes" are underlined with a straight line, and "reads" with a wavy line. Episode boundaries (all major on this page) are marked with slashes; generally we use different colors for major and minor episodes. Meta-comments, or remarks that do not relate to the assigned topic and often are concerned with the situation or process itself, are here noted by braces in the margin. Beyond these steps, the way in which a protocol is parsed depends in large part on what a researcher is looking for.

The writer in this example produced an eight-page protocol that illustrates the process by which she produced a fairly long essay in a comparatively short time. Her process was divided into 25 composing episodes, many of whose boundaries were signaled not by goal-related statements (as was typically the case with other instructors who worked on this task) but by quick, fluent shifts in process or topic. Often this writer interrupted her goal-directed thought flow with a comment on the process itself, or with a meta-comment (see lines 19 and 27 in Figure 2-2). This subject's protocol is also a good illustration of the "explore and consolidate" process (see Flower & Hayes, 1981a). She explores her knowledge, ideas, and memories with the underlying goal to "describe what I do to someone like myself . . . adjusted for 20 years later." The ideas and subgoals she generates ("I want to say something that would suggest the kind of -a- -a- inchoate -a- direction . . . ," lines 14–15) are periodically consolidated. She later stated: "I want to suggest that - that -um- the reader should sort of -what- what should one say - the reader should look at what she is interested in and look at the things that give her pleasure and things that make her feel autonomous and -a- and -a- optimistic and -a- effective . . . that the young woman should -um-

1   what I did as a) (—What I'm thinking of course is that this is becoming ambiguous) —
    (whereas—whereas I'm trying to compose a troche) — (I may be making something
    that is impenetrably vague) — (for pay and when I do — In a way I am able to continue
    doing as an adult...what I did as a teenager) — (why don't just leave it) — (take
5   out for pay) — (that I did as an adult what I did as a teenager for pleasure) —
    (only now my reading and writing and talking — and even talking — are part of —
    of...an endeavor I share with others and for which the state — [Why not...
    make a joke] — and for which I am paid...not grandly — though not grandly) .../
    (It's my sense that when we are thirteen or fourteen we have — [at least I know —
10 we have — at least I known I did.] .. -a- a- a sense — [I don't know] it's my sense
    that when we are thirteen or fourteen we have — at least I know I did — at
    lease I know I did — we have certain leanings or tendencies or we have certain
    inclinications or have certain — certain) -a- (I don't know) — (I don't want to say) —
    (I want to say something that would suggest the kind of -a- -a- inchoate -a-
15 direction) — (I mean a direction which is not chaotic except it's moving in a very
    purposeful way) — (In a sense we have — at least I know I did — a kind of
    individual purposiveness of -a- of individual — or say — personal personal
    purposiveness which really — which — which — which emerges from who we are and
    what's happened to us up to then...us — to then...) -a-/... (I notice as I'm doing this
20 that when I'm — when I'm writing under normal circumstances my — I often, when I
    go back to something that's not finished, I have a tendency to revise) -a- (I have
    a tendency to start over and over and over and over again) (and so that my essays
    often grow from the middle rather than in a kind of linear way.) (Here I'm — I'm doing
    this with sentences I think.) -a- (I think if I were working on a typewriter I
25 would be doing much more revision) / (-a- kind of purposiveness which emerges
    from who we are and what's happening to us up to then.) (My — What I'm thinking
    of is...is that a person of that age — is that a person — of that — age) — (It's
    (interesting,) (I just realized that I — when I spoke that sentence before I — I
    didn't know I hadn't written it down and I hadn't) (so I had to go back and write

meta-comment
meta-comment

Fig. 2-2. Sample page from a protocol.

kind of remain -a- in a very attentive posture towards her own history, abilities, and sources of satisfaction." As the excerpt in Figure 2-2 illustrates, the writer is quite attentive to audience (lines 1, 3, 11, 27).

The Coding of Writing Processes

After this initial parsing, the way in which the protocol is coded will be driven by the research question being asked and by the researcher's preliminary definition of what the phenomenon in question (such as awareness of audience) looks like. However, a particular approach we have often found useful is to go one step further in the preliminary parsing and to segment the protocol into the basic cognitive processes of *planning, translating, and reviewing,* and their main subprocesses. One advantage of this further coding is that it makes the writer's planning (specific plans, overall goals, and proposed content) stand out from the text that he or she actually produces. Such coding also distinguishes both planning and the actual text from the criteria and decisions used to evaluate and revise the text. Here, briefly, are some guidelines for making these distinctions.

A protocol can be coded at different levels of detail through use of the writing model, with the detail level depending on the researcher's purpose. At the most general level, the broad processes of planning, translating, and reviewing can simply be coded. These processes are defined as follows:

- Planning—includes generating and organizing ideas and goal-setting
- Translating—includes creating formal written text, as well as versions of the text that the writer tries out orally
- Reviewing—includes reading, evaluating, and making changes in the text

Planning

As the model in Figure 2-1 shows, planning involves several subprocesses: generating ideas, goal-setting, and organizing. (For a detailed discussion of these processes, see Flower & Hayes, 1981a.)

GENERATING IDEAS

This is a global process that includes retrieving information from long-term memory, drawing inferences, creating new ideas, and making connections. Examples:

Let's see, a waitress really has to know how to do several things well.
. . . [The writer's assigned topic was "my job"—in her case, waitressing.]
We have to address the fact that this girl is -a- what's she—seventh- or
eighth-grade girl. . . .

Instances of idea generation (which we mark "generates") fall into
two basic, though somewhat overlapping, categories: those providing
information on the topic alone, and those providing information about
the rhetorical problem. Some of the latter instances contain audience
information, as in the second example above and in this remark: "Would
a thirteen-year-old be interested in electrical engineering?" Alternatively,
the worker may supply information about his or her rhetorical problem
by generating ideas about the task, the genre, text features, grammar,
or the assignment itself. Note that topic information is often embedded
in this type of idea generation. Indeed, better writers often generate a
rich mix of information about topic, audience, and the rhetorical situation in the same phrase (see Flower & Hayes, 1980). The following
example is a response to the task, "You are a free-lance writer writing
about your job for *Seventeen* magazine": "Writing for *Seventeen*—the mention of a free-lance writer is something I've no experience in doing and
my sense is that it's a—formula which I'm not sure I know." Some
instances of generation contain old information that the writer regener-
ates as a prompt, as this writer does with the idea of "ethos, logos, and
pathos" he had considered earlier: "Okay . . . um . . . now how'd I
get all that—linked—that was that ethos–pathos–logos bit—linked to—
now I say my job."

Note that the main objective of this type of parsing is to identify the
process—to say that the writer is *generating* something. The "something,"
or content of that particular act, can be considered later. However, one
class of things that writers generate—their goals—is so major and
distinctive that we code it as a separate process, namely, goal-setting.

GOAL-SETTING

Goal-setting occurs in statements where a writer either explicitly states
objectives ("I want to explain what a PhD is") or states criteria for
evaluating the final text ("This needs to really wake them up," or "It'll
need to be short and snappy"). Goals fall into two categories: *content*
goals specify what one wants to achieve, and *process* goals describe how
to do it.

Content Goals
This broad category includes plans and goals for content, text structure,
and audience, as well as criteria for evaluating these things. These goals
may comprise anything that has to do with the writer's topic or essay.
Examples:

I want to change their notions of English teachers.

Why don't we just leave it—take out "for pay" [an objectionable phrase].

Process Goals

These goal statements could be shuffled and exchanged from one proto-col to the next, since they are generic statements about how to handle one's process, regardless of the topic. They include the instructions that writers give themselves to generate more ideas, jot down notes, take a break, or think the problem through again. The statements show an awareness of and control over one's own process—an alternative to being immersed in the act itself. Examples:

Now I should write some of that down . . . uh . . . but not right now.

All right, now let's see, is there anything else on the outline?

When coding, it is sometimes hard to draw the line between "gen-erates" and "goals," especially when topical information is embedded within a goal. Are decisions goals? We think of goals as the writer's own self-instructions on how and what to write. Decisions or choices among alternatives often reflect choices among goals.

ORGANIZING

This is the process of arranging information already generated (setting up lists, outlines, and so forth) and of creating superordination, subordi-nation, or coordination among ideas. The act of organizing most often appears in the form of a goal to organize, and is therefore usually coded under goal-setting. The information that has already arisen from the writer's memory will always have some organization of its own. The code "organizes" essentially refers to the *re*organization of information during composing.

Translating

In this process the writer generates either formal written text or tenta-tive versions of text that he or she tries out orally. Coded written text will already have been underlined (see Figure 2-2). If it sounds as if the writer was attempting to generate actual text, the utterance should be coded as a "translates" even if it is not ultimately written down or not written down the first time it is spoken. When, however, a writer generates an idea and notes it down but does not intend it to be finished text, it should be coded "generates" rather than "translates." In other words, we define translation as an attempt at finished text, generated either orally or in writing, *not* everything that the author has written down.

Reviewing

Reviewing includes reading (we underline all "reads" with red ink), evaluating, and making revisions in the text. The last two activities deserve additional comment.

EVALUATING

The act of evaluation can be a short interruption in the planning process (e.g., "No, that's no good") or a lengthy period of review after some text has been produced. As one might predict, evaluation often leads to goal-setting and as a result sends the writer back into planning. The following example leads to a process goal: "I don't like some of the formality of diction in that first paragraph, but I'm going to leave it for now." At other times evaluations are simply brief, automatically triggered interruptions or edits: "Oops, that's spelled 'end.'"

REVISING

A revision either may be a translate that is, new text, or simply an alternative that is generated but not formalized into text. Revision differs from a generate in this way: (1) what the writer is revising has already been articulated, and (2) time has elapsed. Sometimes it is difficult to say whether a writer is reviewing and evaluating old material or simply regenerating a thought as a memory prompt while working on the material. A simple rule of thumb here is to note the elapsed time between the repetition. If a long clause or significant length of time intervenes, it is reasonable to code the repetition of the same generate or translate as a review. In the example below, the final comment ("Okay—so—*First day of class*—let's see . . .") would be coded as a review. It will be recalled that reviewing processes can automatically interrupt any other process. For instance, an evaluation of a goal can occur in a generate. Or a revision of a text can occur in an extended translate. Example:

> So one question is where to begin—what kind of situation to start in the middle of—probably *the first day of class*. . . . They'd be interested—they'd probably clue into that easily because they would identify with first days of school and my first days are raucous affairs—it would immediately shake 'em up and get them to thinking a different context. Okay—so—*First day of class*—let's see. . . .

Some Things for Novice Coders to Remember

Keeping in mind a few general points about coding writing processes will make the task easier.

1. Remember that you are looking for the thinking process *behind* the text. When you encounter difficulty or ambiguity, remember you are trying to perceive intellectual actions through the sometimes cloudy medium of the writer's words.

2. Details of wording or syntax can be misleading cues. For example, the process of goal-setting is the same whether the writer expresses the goal in a future tense (e.g., "I think I will try to . . .") or in past tense ("I wanted to . . ."). The only difference between these two examples is that the writer chose different *times* to report a goal aloud—and that distinction is not particularly important. In fact, in data this rich there are an overwhelming number of fine distinctions one could make. The trick is to find the truly useful ones.

3. There are many instances in which you will wish to double-code a given clause. People are clever and manage to collapse a number of tasks into a given utterance, such as—in the same breath—generating content and giving themselves a process goal for presenting the content.

4. Many of the problems of beginning protocol coders stem from the mistaken assumption that phenomena to be coded in a protocol are objects to be examined and thrown into precisely marked bins, rather than being finely shaded processes shining through a screen of spoken words. Believing that the terms in a coding scheme can sum up the elusive reality of the processes partially revealed in a protocol is like claiming that the shimmering, ephemeral colors of a fish's scales can be summed up by a label such as "blue." Obviously we know better, as we know that an attempt to name, classify, and measure bits of protocol text—while valuable and informative—is inevitably reductionistic.

While aware of this in theory, many people, in their initial attempts to create or apply a reliable coding scheme, forget it in practice. They may ask, "How do I know whether this is a 'generate' or a 'goal' item?" The answer is, of course, that you don't, although you can be more sure in some cases than in others. The real question is, what was the writer doing? One important test of your coding scheme will be your inter-rater reliability. Can someone else, instructed in your scheme, see the same things you do with 80–95 percent reliability?

5. A related assumption is that there is a "correct" way to code a protocol. Many coders have asked, "How do I know whether I'm doing it right?" There is no given grammar for analyzing a protocol. A protocol is merely a tool for research; each group of researchers creates its own grammar, based on shared assumptions and research goals. A protocol is a pool of rich, complex data against which you test your theories.

We have noticed that protocol coders seem to go through a rough sequence in their relationship to the task. The first step is a "must pin it down exactly" attitude—probably a necessary phase as the researcher struggles to develop the categories in his or her own coding scheme, or apply someone else's unfamiliar one. Soon, however, awareness returns that labeling can never fully describe a protocol's complex reality, and the coder begins to double- or even triple-code items with abandon. Then he or she realizes that double-coding can be an easy way out and begins to make more pragmatic judgments, comfortable with the awareness that coding can only capture part of the reality of a protocol—but, one hopes, a useful and instructive part.

Using Protocols in Writing Research: Four Methods of Analysis

A protocol is a versatile research tool: it captures information from a writer while the writer is engaged in the whole range of composing subprocesses and behaviors. Therefore, protocols can be used for relatively limited studies of specific elements of the writing task (such as writers' concern with audience), for detailed studies of subprocess (such as the research we are currently conducting on revision), or for more global research. We will discuss four methods of analysis for protocol researchers: exploratory studies, studies that structure data by creating a taxonomy or testing a hypothesis, comparative studies, and studies that model writing processes.

Exploratory Studies

Protocols are a good resource for exploring uncharted territory. They are especially useful for researchers studying writing, a process that is complex, little understood, and difficult to see. Open-ended exploratory studies also provide the background needed to generate more specific questions.

Researchers may first want to ask, "What is actually happening in this protocol?" The answer will be different for each subject. One can investigate differences among writers or make more general observations of a group of writers. Some questions to investigate might be: What kinds of things are people doing? When? How often? Which people? When and where do writers have trouble? Graves and Calkins, for example, conducted a series of open-ended exploratory studies. Their case study of children writing over a period of two years has helped to fill in some of the gaps in our knowledge of children's writing development and provides background for future research (Graves,

1979a, 1979b). For example, Graves's studies have shown that the transition from drawing to writing is a critical and complex event—an event that will let us both understand and diagnose a young writer's development. Calkins has examined and isolated several stages in children's developing revision processes. Emig's landmark study of the composing processes of twelfth-graders is also a classic example of exploratory writing research; her work generated many of the questions guiding current studies in this area (Emig, 1969).

Studies That Give a Problem Structure with a Taxonomy or a Hypothesis

The richness of protocols can overwhelm a researcher at first. To interpret the data, one needs to impose a structure on them. The writing researcher can reduce the complexity of protocol data by creating a taxonomy with which to classify phenomena, or by formulating a hypothesis and using the data to test it. In some cases the goal might be to create an inclusive theoretical description of some process; in others, the taxonomy is a more open exploratory description in service of a question or hypothesis.

Two of the authors, in "The Cognition of Discovery: Defining a Rhetorical Problem," sought to describe the ways in which writers represented or defined their problem to themselves (Flower & Hayes, 1980). The taxonomy of *basic elements* of the writing problem was drawn from protocols of expert and novice writers who had been asked to "write about your job for the readers of *Seventeen* magazine, 13- to 14-year-old girls." The composite picture of the problem-definition process that was arrived at is shown in Figure 2-3. This taxonomy was then used to analyze and compare the ways different writers represented their tasks to themselves. However, the central goal of a study like this is to create a descriptive taxonomy of the problem-definition process itself.

An alternative method of protocol analysis is to develop a hypothesis and test it against the protocols. In one study, writers' concern with audience was investigated (Hayes & Flower, 1980b). It was hypothesized that role-playing (that is, the writer's identification with the audience) was a frequently used method of simulating audience response. However, after all references to audience in the protocols were coded, it was found that role-playing was much less frequent than other techniques for dealing with audience, such as imaginary dialogues ("If I said that, they would reply . . ."), identifying the audience with themselves ("I knew that word when I was their age"), or other techniques. From the process of testing the role-playing hypothesis, a starting taxonomy was

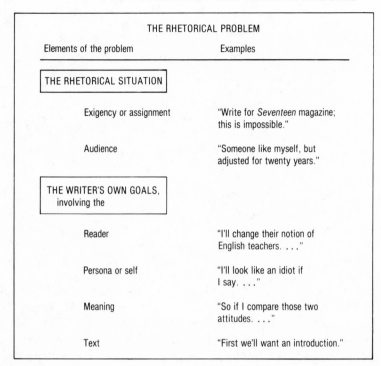

Fig. 2-3. Elements of the rhetorical problem that writers represent to themselves when composing. From "The Cognition of Discovery: Defining a Rhetorical Problem" by L. S. Flower and J. R. Hayes, College Composition and Communication, February 1980, 31, 21–32. Copyright 1980 by National Council of Teachers of English. Reprinted by permission.

developed. This taxonomy will lead to further questions, such as which techniques good and poor writers are likely to use.

Comparative Studies

Comparative studies introduce another dimension to the field of inquiry by examining differences among writers of different ages, skill levels, or other variables. In the study of the problem-definition process mentioned above (Flower & Hayes, 1980), the primary goal was to develop a general taxonomy of basic elements of the writing problem. However, the study also suggested performance differences between expert and novice writers: expert writers tended to consider all or most elements of a problem and create a rich network of goals, while poorer writers did not represent the rhetorical problem as fully to themselves, and their goal structure was correspondingly underdeveloped. A further study of writers generating ideas revealed that poor writers as a group generated only 28 percent of their new ideas in response to the rhetorical problem; the other 72 percent were in response to the topic and/or a current element in memory. For the good writers this 30/70 distribution was nearly reversed (Flower & Hayes, 1981c). Other differences among writers that researchers have studied include differences in age, particularly among children, and differences among individual writers over time (Graves, 1979a, 1979b; Calkins, 1980). Calkins, for example, has examined and compared third-grade children's revision processes.

Studies That Model Writing Processes

It is obvious that the methods discussed so far overlap to some extent and can be combined in the course of one study. We have generally focused on alternative methods of analysis to suit different purposes, but the methods are progressive and can funnel into a broad attempt to model the writing process. Perl (1978) has attempted to model behaviorial patterns within the writing process of individual Basic Writers. For example, her research has shown how the Basic Writer's heavy dependence on the assignment given and the already produced text as stimuli for writing produce a pronounced regressive pattern of constant rereading before writing. Our own efforts have been to model the cognitive processes in writing, that is, to describe key mental processes and their organization. Modeling not only creates a theoretical framework for studying writing, but tries to account for how people actually carry out the complex process of composing.

Reliability in Protocol Analysis

Reliability is a problem with any method of research, and particularly so with protocol analysis. People who look at protocols have the same problem as people looking at clouds: everyone might see something different. It is necessary that reports of what is happening in a protocol be more reliable than any one person's reports; without some assurance of objectivity, it would be foolish to try to prove a proposition through use of protocol analysis. Thus, obtaining agreement among investigators is vital. One way to achieve agreement is to develop a coding scheme for judges to use and then to measure their degree of agreement to see whether the categories are viable. Coding protocols is a hard job; if the phenomena that judges are asked to code are fairly complex, it may be a good idea to use only judges familiar with the researcher's theory or context. If more judges are needed, or if novices are to be used to further test a coding scheme's reliability, it is especially important that the coding scheme be teachable. Both kinds of coding are valid; which one is used depends on the study.

Figure 2-4 shows an initial coding scheme for a study of composing episodes. Judges were asked to determine what was happening at episode beginnings and classify them according to the categories listed. After discussing the categories in light of the data, comparing judgments, and analyzing borderline cases, we reduced the list of categories to a flowchart for novice judges (see Figure 2-5). Not only are there fewer categories, but the categories are arranged hierarchically, so the coder knows what to look for first. The coder sees whether a given sentence falls within the first (most likely) category; if it does not, the next category is considered. For example, the episode beginning "Let's see— but before I actually write that I think I'll give myself some notion of where I'm heading" would be coded as the setting of a process goal. An episode beginning "So one question is how to begin [the essay] . . . start in the middle of—of probably the first day of class . . ." would be coded as the setting of a content goal.

Whether it is fully articulated or barely conscious, we all bring a "model" or set of assumptions to research, which to a large degree guides our questioning. Protocols don't provide a theory or even a distilled description of the writing process, but are instead detailed accounts of writers in action. They are like any other form of data: the answers we get from them are only as good as the questions we ask. It is important for the analyst to bring theoretically based questions to protocol research. A potential pitfall for new protocol researchers to avoid is the temptation to think that since protocols offer so many hitherto inaccessible data, the sure way to knowledge is a really comprehensive coding scheme and a lot of protocols. Many composing behaviors can be observed, isolated, classified, and coded: protocol analysis can

Fig. 2-4. Coding categories for beginnings of composing episodes: First version.

EPISODE BEGININGS

CONTENT GOALS			PROCESS GOAL SET	GOAL INSTANTIATED OR CARRIED OUT		CHANGE IN PROCESS	NEW TOPIC	PARAGRAPH BOUNDARY
New goals set	Pop-up	Review goals		Above goal (latest goal)	Earlier, pop-up goal			

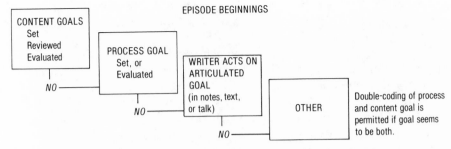

Fig. 2-5. Coding categories for beginnings of composing episodes: Second version.

generate hundreds of correlations and classifications, of everything from pauses to goal-setting. But perhaps *because* protocols offer such an overwhelming amount of information, it is especially important to try to use them to answer particular questions that we need and want to answer. Unlike interviews or retrospective accounts by writers, protocols do not offer ready-made theories of the writer's process. They let us test those theories. So the information a protocol yields is only as good as the questions we ask.

REFERENCES

Atlas, M. *A brief overview of research methods for the writing researcher.* Document Design Project Working Paper, Carnegie-Mellon University, Pittsburgh, 1980.

Bond, S., & Hayes, J. R. *Practical aspects of collecting a thinking-aloud writing protocol.* Working Paper, Carnegie-Mellon University, Pittsburgh, 1980.

Calkins, L. Children learn the writer's craft. *Language Arts*, February 1980.

Emig, J. *The composing process of twelfth graders.* Urbana, Ill.: National Council of Teachers of English, 1969.

Ericsson, K. A., & Simon, H. A. *Sources of evidence on cognition: An historical overview.* C.I.P. Working Paper No. 406, Carnegie-Mellon University, Pittsburgh, 1979. (a)

Ericsson, K. A., & Simon, H. A. *Thinking-aloud protocols as data: Effects of verbalization.* C.I.P. Working Paper No. 397, Carnegie-Mellon University, Pittsburgh, 1979. (b)

Flower, L. S., & Hayes, J. R. The cognition of discovery: Defining a rhetorical problem. *College Composition and Communication*, February 1980, *31*, 21–32.

Flower, L. S., & Hayes, J. R. A cognitive process theory of writing. *College Composition and Communication*, December 1981, *35*, 365–387. (a)

Flower, L. S., & Hayes, J. R. The pregnant pause: An inquiry into the nature of planning. *Research in the Teaching of English*, 1981, *15*, 229–243. (b)

Flower, L. S., & Hayes, J. R. *Process-based evaluation of writing: Changing the performance, not the product.* Working Paper, Carnegie-Mellon University, Pittsburgh, 1981. (c)

Flower, L. S., Hayes, J. R., & Swarts, H. Reader-based revision of functional documents: The scenario principle. In P. Anderson, C. Miller, & J. Brockmann (Eds.), *New essays in technical and scientific communication: Theory, research, and criticism.* Farmingdale, N.Y.: Baywood Series in Technical and Scientific Communication (Vol. 2), in press.

Graves, D. H. *Let children show us how to help them write.* University of New Hampshire, Durham, March 6, 1979. (a)

Graves, D. H. What children show us about revision. *Language Arts,* March 1979. (b)

Hayes, J. R., & Flower, L. S. Identifying the organization of writing processes. In L. Gregg & E. Steinberg (Eds.), *Cognitive processes in writing: An interdisciplinary approach.* Hillsdale, N.J.: Lawrence Erlbaum, 1980. (a)

Hayes, J. R., & Flower, L. S. *Writing with the audience in mind.* Paper presented at meeting of American Educational Research Association, Boston, 1980. (b)

Hayes, J. R., & Flower, L. S. Uncovering cognitive processes in writing: An introduction to protocol analysis. In P. Mosenthal, L. Tamor, & S. Walmsley (Eds.), *Research in writing: Principles and methods.* New York: Longman, 1983.

Nisbett, R. E., & Wilson, T. D. Telling more than we can know: Verbal reports on mental processes. *Psychological Review,* May 1977, *84*(3), 231-259.

Perl, S. *Five writers working: Case studies of the composing processes of unskilled college writers.* Unpublished doctoral dissertation, New York University, 1978.

3

Classroom contexts and the development of writing intuitions: An ethnographic case study

KENNETH J. KANTOR
University of Georgia

In their important study of the development of writing ability, James Britton and associates (Britton, Burgess, Martin, McLeod, & Rosen, 1975) pointed out that any classifications of writing with regard to rhetorical or other features should ideally be informed by knowledge of the specific contexts in which those writings were produced. Indeed, what has been lacking in many composition studies is a picture of the educational context: the conditions under which students write; the methods and styles of teachers; the personalities, attitudes, and learning processes of students; and the many interactions among these variables. Composition teaching is a multidimensional phenomenon, one which requires a research methodology that will account for its complexity.

Recently a number of researchers have turned to ethnographic and other qualitative approaches to help them discover these varied aspects of how writing is taught and learned. In this article I will discuss traits of ethnographic inquiry that make it appropriate to the study of writing instruction, and will then present a case study of a writing class in which ethnographic techniques were employed. To begin, then, five relevant features of ethnographic inquiry will be identified: contextuality, participant observation, multiple perspectives, hypothesis-generating, and meaning-making (see also Kantor, Kirby, & Goetz, 1981).

Features of Ethnographic Inquiry

Contextuality

Ethnographic researchers are concerned with events and relationships occurring within a particular context. Drawing from the traditions of anthropology and sociology, they seek to examine human behavior and beliefs as they are revealed in social and cultural settings. To properly assess these phenomena, they make use of "thick description" (Geertz,

1973), or concrete and detailed accounts of specific events, actions, and physical settings. Such researchers view context as an essential resource for understanding (Mishler, 1979), searching within it to discover significant patterns.

The work of Florio and her associates at Michigan State University (Clark & Florio, 1982; Florio, 1979; Florio & Clark, 1982) provides an excellent exemplar of the ethnographic attention to contextual features. These researchers have examined the functions of writing within elementary school classrooms, especially as these functions help students establish and maintain cultural membership. Particularly revealing are their findings regarding writing to a peer audience, which enables children to create connections between personal and social worlds and to develop shared meanings. Looking carefully at the context has also enabled Florio and her colleagues to describe a range of writing types, from mechanical exercises to letter writing to imaginative stories. We can see in their analysis the various functions of discourse—expressive, transactional, and poetic—as they actually occur within specific classroom situations.

Participant Observation

In varying degrees, ethnographers become both participant and observer in the settings they choose to investigate. What is important is that researchers do not detach themselves from objects of study; their perceptions become instead part and parcel of the investigation (Guba, 1980; Wilson, 1977). Typically researchers begin by assessing their own knowledge, experiences, and biases, and reevaluate those influences as their study proceeds. They adopt an attitude of "disciplined subjectivity" (Erickson, 1973) in considering participants' and their own affective responses and constructions of meaning. Ethnographers thus establish a dual identity of both insider and outsider, in order to represent authentically the perspectives and experiences of those being studied. A fine example of this dual role may be found in a study by Wotring (1981), who took a high school chemistry class along with the regular students so as to discover how writing might be used to learn that particular subject matter. Her combined perceptions as both student and researcher contributed greatly to the strength of her findings.

Multiple Perspectives

While recognizing the importance of their own points of view, ethnographers also seek to confirm, question, or add to their judgments by eliciting the judgments of others. This corroboration may be achieved by having more than one researcher in the setting, by teaming investigator and participant (Smith & Geoffrey, 1968), or by using key informant interviews (Jackson, 1968). An instance of effective use of key informant interviews may be seen in an examination by Martin (1980) of English instruction in schools in western Australia. Through such interviews Martin discovered a great deal about students' attitudes toward writing and ways in which they had been taught. Additionally, researchers may consider evidence from sources other than participant observation—for example, physical traces or historical information. The combining of multiple sources of data is termed "triangulation" by Denzin (1978), and results in greater claims for reliability and validity (LeCompte & Goetz, 1982).

Hypothesis-Generating

Ethnographic studies also require an open, eclectic stance on the part of researchers, who attempt to generate rather than test theories. They view emerging patterns with a skeptical eye until they have opportunities to reexamine and reevaluate these patterns. At the same time they may shape, alter, or refine their investigations as they proceed. An example of this process may again be found in Wotring's study, in which she changed her focus from "writing to learn" to "writing to think" as evidence led her to that conclusion. In similar fashion, Nelson (1981), in a naturalistic study of teacher–writers, identified several styles of teaching as she gathered and analyzed data from extensive interviews and classroom observations of her subjects. And Pettigrew, Shaw, and Van Nostrand (1981) used a procedure of "progressive coding" to establish and refine categories for an instrument designed to evaluate composition instruction.

As stated earlier, ethnographers generally enter settings with assumptions and predispositions, but maintain their options until the weight of evidence determines particular directions. This research process seems not unlike the discovery process in writing itself, in which individuals unlock their meanings as they actually write and revise (Murray, 1978; Perl, 1979). Eventually researchers seek to develop a grounded theory (Glaser & Strauss, 1967), based on the various hypotheses that have emerged from their analyses and interpretations.

Meaning-Making

Ultimately ethnographers are concerned with the ways in which individuals construct meanings for themselves, especially as members within a social or cultural group. In composition studies we need to be especially interested in how children develop concepts of what writing is about and what value it holds for them, and how they strengthen their knowledge and intuitions so as to write more effectively. The work of Graves and his colleagues at the University of New Hampshire (see Calkins, 1980; Graves, 1979; Sowers, 1979) has been enlightening in showing how children progress from an egocentric point of view to an awareness of audience, revision strategies, mechanics, and other aspects of the writer's craft, all within the context of a classroom in which such growth is nurtured. An observational study by Dyson (1981) reveals how young children develop their first notions about writing as they extend the resources of talking and drawing. Working with tenth-grade basic level students, Worsham (1980) documented gains in fluency, voice, syntactic complexity, sense of audience, and—most importantly— motivation to write. The processes by which young people formulate their ideas of and attitudes toward writing represent a crucial kind of meaning-making, one essential to their growth as writers.

In conducting the case study to be reported here, I attempted to incorporate as many of these features of ethnographic inquiry as was possible. Acting as both participant and observer, I sought to gather as much specific data as I could regarding the events occurring within the classroom context. I interviewed students and teachers in order to elicit their points of view, and although I admittedly entered the situation with a certain frame of reference (an awareness of research and theory in developmental rhetoric and composing processes), the information gained from the participants often served as a check on my own subjective impressions. Accumulating evidence also helped me to identify particular patterns as important and others as less relevant. Finally, on the basis of analysis and interpretation of the collected data, I was able to formulate some hypotheses regarding ways in which the students constructed meanings for themselves concerning their writing proc- esses. Specifically, I became interested in the question of how writers' intuitions, such as awareness of audience, revision strategies, modes of discourse, and writing as discovery, can be brought to light and strength- ened within a supportive classroom environment.

The Classroom Context

The setting for my investigation was a classroom in a nearby public high school, attended by students from varied socioeconomic and ethnic backgrounds. I had come to know the teacher through working with him in supervising student teachers, and in meeting with a group of local teacher–writers; he generously allowed me to enter the class as a participant–observer. The course was given twice a week, from August to December of 1979. I was able to attend most of the classes.

The course was titled Creative Writing and was offered to twelfth-grade students who had been identified by at least one English teacher as having some promise in writing. The course was officially listed as "independent study," and, while it was untypical for a high school, it enabled me to focus in on aspects of teacher–student interaction and writing development. In choosing this class, then, I was following the principle of "theoretical sampling" (Glaser & Strauss, 1967).

The structure and requirements of the course were the following: students were to submit one new piece of writing each week, to which the teacher would respond in written fashion, and share one piece with the class each week. Later, each student was asked to select one piece he or she liked and revise it as the "final exam." The teacher also suggested some readings to provide ideas for writing, in particular Peter Beagle's *I See by My Outfit*, but did not set these readings as requirements.

The teacher was Phil Butler, the English department chairman who had taught for seven years at the school. Phil is a writer himself, mostly in the genre of short stories, who had been inspired by an experience of sharing writing with friends and colleagues on Friday afternoons at a local gathering place. He hoped to build a similar sense of community among his student writers, at the same time realizing that he would need to provide certain kinds of structure and encouragement to move them in that direction. Phil's objectives, he told me, were to have students produce more writing and share their writing with their peers, thus building confidence with a secure group.

During the winter quarter, the seven students in Phil's class continued the course with Bruce Paulson, another English teacher and writer, who emphasized writing for wider audiences and submitting pieces for publication (as well as entering writing contests). During the spring quarter, the students participated in several voluntary reading sessions. I was able to observe only one of Bruce's classes but did join the group for two of the spring reading sessions. Thus my information regarding the progress of these students through the rest of the year is more limited than I would have wished.

The seven students who took the course were in general bright and academically successful individuals who had been identified by teachers as "closet writers"—talented but in many cases still unaware of their potential. They tended to be quiet and cautious with others but, as this report will indicate, became more outgoing and interactive as the quarter and year progressed. Following are thumbnail sketches of each individual, based on the combined perceptions of Phil, Bruce Paulson, and myself.

- Lori—strong poetic ability; had had several poems published in the school literary magazine; keen sense of imagery and poetic language; generally reserved in the class meetings
- Kevin—a thinker, read philosophical writers like Ayn Rand, Gregory Bateson, Dostoyevsky; enjoyed writing about ideas and deeper meanings
- Melissa—liked fantasy writing; stimulated by many things (books, television shows, conversations, Dungeons and Dragons game); hard worker, revised a great deal, responded positively to suggestions; always eager to share her writing
- Stan—serious, often intense in his writing; wrote about personal relationships and social interactions; poems often dealt with intimate topics; later revealed strong sense of humor in writing
- Alice—scientific thinker; admired science fiction writers; especially Asimov; craftsmanlike in her writing; concerned with character development and believability; admitted to sometimes writing deliberately to "please the teacher"
- Neal—wrote skillful and funny satires; used story or personal essay form; said he wrote humorous pieces to protect himself, avoid things too personal; uneasy about reading his writing, but gained more confidence within the group
- Mary—imaginative, "lighthearted" in her writing; artistic (primary interest in painting), keen eye for detail; personable and alert in her responses in class

As is obvious, many of these features of writing and behavior are related to personality traits. Being primarily concerned with their interactions and development *as writers*, however, I wish to avoid any unnecessary or cavalier psychological analyses.

Procedures

Three major ethnographic techniques were used in this study. The first involved acting as a participant–observer in the class itself, recording events in the form of field notes. At first I took notes on as many occurrences as I possibly could; as I began to see certain patterns and focuses for my study, I became more selective. For example, I grew interested in the students' talk about their personal experiences, and attended more closely to this kind of talk as the quarter progressed. Soon after each class session I would review my notes, sometimes with Phil's assistance. I added clarifications and placed brackets around comments that were more interpretive than reportorial, in order to separate out observations from more subjective judgments.

As a participant, I acted as both a co-teacher and a co-student, without intervening so much as to intrude or to prevent myself from taking adequate field notes. Sometimes I would ask questions to draw students out on aspects of their writing or to guide discussion along certain lines. On one occasion I became the teacher for the day, talking with the class about writing poetry and using some of my own poems as examples. Following is an account of part of that lesson, which Phil helped me reconstruct:

> I distribute copies of my poem "Aspiration," about riding the El train in Chicago as a child. Before reading it, I draw a sketch on the board to illustrate the first stanza. After I read it, Bruce (who is sitting in today) says he really enjoyed the poem. Melissa asks me about whether the second part of the poem is real or imaginary, and I answer that it's the latter—the experience is in the speaker's mind.
>   Kevin asks about whether the structure of the lines
>
>>   Soon, reluctantly
>>   slowing to a
>>   stop
>
> is intentional. I reply that it is, explaining that the form and sound of the words are intended to simulate the motion of the train. Melissa asks if I normally break poems into stanzas, and I tell her "not necessarily"—I do it sometimes to signal transitions, as a prose writer does with paragraphs. Alice wonders whether I think consciously about rhythm as I write—I respond that it's more an intuitive sense, the "auditory imagination." I've enjoyed being the poetry expert for the day.

At other times, when there was a lull in the proceedings, I would simply read a poem and ask for questions or comments. Phil identified me as the "poet-in-residence," viewing me as a resource person who could complement his own strengths in prose writing. Although the students were generally self-conscious, they seemed to be comfortable with me as a participant in the class. They responded to my poems with questions and comments, and two or three of them approached me individually to get my reaction to something they had written.

The second research method involved eliciting information from the teacher and students at the end of the course through the use of interviews and an open-ended questionnaire. The latter, which I had devised for use in a graduate methods course, included the following questions:

1. What kinds of things do you like to write outside of school? Why?
2. What kinds of school writing assignments do you like? Dislike?
3. How do you get ideas or inspirations for writing?

4. Is writing easy or difficult for you? Explain.
5. What conditions (time, place, etc.) for writing seem to be best for you?
6. Do you like to share your writing with others? If so, with whom?
7. How much revising do you do? What kinds of revisions do you make?
8. What teacher helped you most with your writing? In what ways?
9. What authors, if any, have influenced your writing? How so?
10. Do you have any career or life ambitions that involve writing? If so, what are these?

Data gathered from the questionnaires helped me plan the interviews, as I sought further information from each student. I met each student individually in an empty classroom and tape-recorded each interview. While I had particular questions in mind, I also tried to follow directions suggested by the interviewees and talk with them in a comfortable, conversational manner. These procedures enabled me to acquire a great deal of data about the students' attitudes toward writing, sources of inspiration, preferred conditions for writing, composing processes (especially revision), ways in which they felt the class had helped them develop their writing abilities, and feelings about teachers, peers, and wider audiences. I found the students to be generally open and honest in their answers to questions, perhaps in part because they had come to know me. I also interviewed both Phil and Bruce Paulson concerning their expectations for their courses and ways in which the students had progressed in terms of those expectations. In many cases the comments of the teacher would either confirm or add another perspective to my own impressions.

Third, I examined a number of the writings that the students had produced during the quarter to identify signs of growth. While I did not systematically analyze the syntactic or rhetorical features of these writings, I did note some improvements and even possible breakthroughs based on what I knew about the students' writing to that point and on confirmations by Phil and Bruce.

In reviewing field notes and transcripts of taped interviews, I used the method of "analytic induction" (Glaser & Strauss, 1967) to identify emerging patterns and categories. I marked what appeared to be revealing passages and made brief marginal notes as to rough classifications. I then searched for both repeated patterns and "negative cases" (inconsistencies, or divergent events or statements). Finally, using categories that had emerged as significant, I constructed charts, such as the one on composing processes that is reproduced in Table 3-1 (see p. 83). These charts enabled me to discover relationships among data drawn from interviews, field notes, and students' writings.

The combination of these ethnographic techniques thus produced a corroborative effect, or triangulation (Denzin, 1978). This allowed me to cite related evidence from several sources—my own as a participant-observer, the teachers', the students', and their writings. The triangulation of data sources and collection techniques contributed to internal validity (LeCompte & Goetz, 1982). As features of the educational context were verified by these "primary sources," so did they gain significance for me within that context. The following discussion of my findings is based on a synthesis of information derived from these sources.

Teacher Roles and Composing Processes

One of the more interesting aspects of this research involved looking at ways in which these students reacted to a situation unfamiliar to them. Most were accustomed to writing in school exclusively for a limited teacher audience (teacher as "examiner" or "generalized other"); the peer group represented a new and perhaps threatening audience. The students also had considerably more freedom than in most other classes, being allowed to write on whatever topics or in whatever modes they chose. The teacher gave no grades until the end of the quarter, and taking on the role of responder and fellow writer placed him in a position of more equal status with the students than is usually the case. The seating arrangement was circular, the mode of discussion low-key and informal—again, more like a gathering of friends or associates than an involuntary meeting of teacher and students. Many of them spoke in their interviews about the comfortable atmosphere in the class. I sensed that the students' previous conditioning, then, had much to do with their initial cautiousness and self-consciousness; it was only after a number of meetings that they became comfortable in the situation and trustful of one another. These perceptions are confirmed by Phil's comments:

> I had a great deal less frustration than in a regular class setting. This was due of course to the small size of the group and our commonalities. The problems, though, were in some ways similar:
> - how to establish myself as trusted adult
> - how to maintain that role
> - and then how to respond in formative ways to the things

they wrote. I had to read each piece on the author's terms rather than bringing in my own criteria, as a teacher does when he makes up a writing assignment.

I suspect that the students in this class might have had a more difficult time adjusting to the unfamiliar aspects of the situation had they not had a teacher who was so patient and accepting in his manner. What Phil did in effect was help students move from a perception of teacher as "examiner" or "generalized other" to one of "teacher, particular relationship" and "trusted adult" (Britton *et al.*, 1975).

To a great extent, he accomplished this by establishing himself as a fellow writer, by sharing his writing, admitting difficulties, and revealing his own processes. He would explain, for example, how he got ideas for writing, through either experiences or reading. Childhood incidents and Peter Beagle's works were favorite sources. He would talk with the students about conditions under which he wrote best, how he dealt with blocks, and how he revised. He shared with them how he had come to see writing as a discovery process, and how he had begun to trust his intuitions above what he had been taught in school about outlining and about writing structured, five-paragraph themes. Early in the quarter he read statements by various professional writers (Murray, 1978) attesting to ways in which they had discovered meanings and directions in the course of their writing. The following excerpt from my field notes reveals some of these methods:

> Phil reads more from his story about the man whose car breaks down in the desert. He tells the class he decided that what he read yesterday wasn't going to be the beginning of the story. Reading from his notebook he goes back and forth between the right-hand page and the back of the previous page (he told me later that he uses his left-hand pages for inserts, rearranging and reshaping as he writes).
>
> Neal says he liked the way Phil connected things from three different story lines. Kevin claims he liked the part about the man's hallucinations as the heat was getting to him. Phil mentions Ray, a "bully" he knew as a child, who formed the basis for one of the characters in this story. When one of the students asks him to tell more about Ray, Phil reveals how he got even with him.

For the most part Phil's teaching was nondirective, as he reacted spontaneously to the students' writings after they were read, giving suggestions rather than formulas, or guided discussion along lines that students were following, or simply waited for someone to respond. At times he would be more "didactic," as when he would give what he called a Sermonette. One of these was his communication theory speech, in which he discussed the importance of using concrete details, of appealing to the senses and helping the reader picture what the writer wished to convey. Most of the students commented in their interviews that he had also stressed these points in his written feedback on their papers.

Above all, Phil was encouraging. He would praise the students frequently, as individuals or as a group, pointing to specific features of their writing which he liked. He was sensitive to students' fears of being criticized, being careful not to put them on the defensive and using his genial sense of humor to help them relax and feel comfortable. Now and then he shared anecdotes from his own experience—for example, the time he got even with the school bully or an incident in the lives of his own children. All of these actions contributed to the students' image of him not only as a fellow writer but as an individual whom they could trust, a "real person."

My observations of Phil's interactions with students led me to perceive a possible connection between sense of audience and sense of writing as process. As students come to see the teacher as fellow writer and trusted adult, so do they realize that their own writing processes are valid and worthy of being cultivated. In their interviews these students showed insight into how they wrote, articulating a range of processes as varied as their personalities. Table 3-1, based on interviews and questionnaires, reveals the diversity of those processes.

Although I had no way of knowing how efficient their methods actually were, the students appear to have discovered processes that worked for them and did not apologize for those idiosyncrasies. At the same time they did not acknowledge any direct influence of the teacher on the formulation of those processes. Their comments about Phil tended to focus on his responses to their written products—for example, his recommendations about making ideas clearer or points of view more consistent. These responses were, in a sense, process-oriented, in that they represented suggestions for improving the pieces. Nevertheless, Phil's teaching of process was more implicit than explicit. Rather than talking prescriptively about aspects of composing, he tended to model writing processes and provide a structure wherein students could discover which processes worked best for them.

Some stereotypical notions appeared in the students' responses, especially concerning revision. As Phil commented, "Another problem I had was the students' previous conditioning with respect to writing processes: (1) You have to know what you want to say before you write. (2) Revision is merely proofreading." The students, even at the time the interviews were conducted, seemed to view revision more as the last stage of writing than as an ongoing activity during the process. Except for the final assignment, however, Phil did not involve the students in extensive revision activity during the quarter, being more concerned at

Table 3-1. Composing Processes

	Sources/stimuli	Prewriting/getting started	Writing: fluency/blocks	Revising
Lori	Not sure—places sometimes (e.g., art museum), dreams	Write one line, then think of rest	OK once I find rhythm; trouble with endings—many unfinished pieces	Usually don't revise unless required—may change first lines, or even whole poems
Kevin	Philosophical writers—unanswered questions	Jot down ideas when they hit me—start with line/sentence that sounds good; write at night	Write first draft all at once, build to whole, follow general direction; problems: structural, word level	Hard to change things—may revise words or images, but not basic plot
Melissa	Ideas from pictures, TV shows, family incidents, book titles, travel	Like to write at night, TV on, at dining room table, near picture window	Problems: grammatical, writing dialogue	Real life has to make sense; takes more revising, make many changes—small things or whole pages
Stan	Social situations—interactions, emotions	Once I get idea, I just write—late at night, quiet house	Usually satisfied with first draft; problems: getting ideas	Revise mostly as I write (in-process)
Neal	Get ideas while running—thinking is act of desperation; satirical writers (e.g., Jean Shepherd)	Write first chance I get; ideal conditions are comforts of home—TV, refrigerator	Process more fun than afterwards (between drafts); problems: planning strategies	Leave first draft for a while, then revise, rarely to my satisfaction
Alice	Science fiction writers (Asimov, Clarke); ideas from reading, TV	Start with several ideas, pick best one; if no ideas, may wait or switch modes (e.g., from poetry to prose)	OK if I like first paragraph, write without an end in mind, OK to go off in different directions; problems: making characters real	A lot of revising, both in-process and between drafts; won't change content—may change tone, structure, details, revision painful
Mary	Get ideas outside, anywhere	Try to think of what will shock, gain attention, be memorable	If I get idea, I want it to happen now, can't bother with details, afraid I'll forget plot	Write story, look at it, write it again without looking at first draft

83

this point with their developing fluency and their desire to share written pieces with peers. In more implicit ways, though, he was leading students to develop a motivation to revise, as he would give students suggestions for improving their writing:

> Melissa reads part of a story inspired by a picture on the cover of the game "Dungeons and Dragons." This section has to do with a battle between a fighter and the dragon. Phil comments on the effective description of the dragon's death, particularly the use of vivid colors. He asks if that's the way the game is played. Alice, who is a "Dungeons and Dragons" expert, explains that the players are characters in a story, and you take them through various strategies. The more you play, the more your character grows in experience. It represents a kind of fantasy role-playing in which you get into the personality of your character and interact with others.
>
> Phil tells Melissa that the narrator seemed like both characters at first, and that she might make the point of view more clear. Melissa nods and says she knows the story needs more detail. Phil points out that sometimes you don't know what's going to happen until you write.

One kind of classroom occurrence is important to note in this regard. Frequently the students would read unfinished pieces, even some they had just begun. They would claim that they weren't sure where the writing was going, having perhaps only a general sense of direction or, in some cases, being totally blocked. (Mary seemed to be the only one who consistently felt confident about her goals.) A few of them, Melissa in particular, would share "installments" of a story, or revisions of earlier drafts. Others in the class might ask questions or make recommendations to help the writer gain a clearer outlook. It struck me that this willingness to share writing in progress represented an important step for these students, as they were able to admit they were having difficulties and felt secure in sharing something not quite completed.

Additionally, the students indicated through their perceptions of their drafts that they were beginning to engage in what Perl (1979) calls "retrospective structuring"—looking back over what they had written in order to gain a sense of how to move ahead. Phil emphasized this kind of activity in another "Sermonette," and some of the students acknowledged it as occurring within their own processes. They were becoming, we thought, better readers of their own writing (see Bridwell, 1980; Sommers, 1979). They were developing an awareness of relationships among parts of discourse rather than succumbing to the "tunnel vision" —preoccupation with superficial aspects of texts—characteristic of less practiced writers. Again, Phil's reassuring style and the supportive comments of the peer group seemed to help build the confidence necessary for using these more successful revision strategies.

The Classroom as Writing Community

A closer examination of the nature of class interactions contributes further to an understanding of ways in which the students were developing audience awareness. As stated earlier, these particular students were at first cautious and reluctant to respond to one another's writing (perhaps for fear of being criticized themselves) and only very gradually became more comfortable and self-assured in doing so. I should note, though, that there was some "pairing" taking place outside of class— Alice and Melissa, Neal and Stan, Lori and Felicia (a friend in another class). For these students who appeared shy, sharing with this one-person audience provided a consultation, a trial run before reading to the larger class, and thus contributed to self-assurance.

Class discussion tended to focus on two kinds of concerns. The first was writing itself; the students' responses dealt with techniques, changes, structure, and the like. The second concern was talk about experiences and associations triggered by the writings. The following descriptions of classroom interactions excerpted from my field notes reveal these two kinds of emphases:

1. Mary reads a piece called "The Tree." Phil says he liked the beginning. Mary reveals that it was inspired by the trees during an ice storm. Melissa mentions a tree she has seen which she thinks would look good with carvings on it.
2. Neal reads a funny story about a fellow in a mobile house. It contains descriptions of a shower that looked like "stalagmites and stalactites" and a meal of "warm Coke, pancakes and Spam." The class laughs throughout. Melissa says that she likes Spam.
3. Lori reads a poem titled "Art Museum." The final image describes the colors of the paintings as "exposed like fish in the sun, baked dry." I tell her that this is a terrific image, and ask her how she thought of it. She replies that she was at the university art museum, and wondered how the artists would feel about 20th century people gawking at their work.
4. I read a poem titled "Fishing at Billy's Pond," based on a personal experience. We talk about fishing for a few minutes, Melissa showing special interest as a "fisherperson." Phil reads a poem titled "You Ever," the first part of which compares fishing to writing. A coincidence we had not planned.
5. Mary reads the first part of a murder mystery. Phil asks her if she knows what's going to happen next, and she replies immediately by relating the rest of the events in the story. She smiles as she finishes talking. I find her self-assurance refreshing.
6. Lori reads a piece about a visit to the dentist, after apologizing for having written it in only 50 minutes. The class gets caught up in a

lively discussion of things they associate with the dentist—the drill
(one student calls it a sandblaster), the spit sink, cotton in your mouth,
etc. Phil tells about his wife once having broken a $400 bridge.

Clearly, the first kind of discussion—dealing with process—is what
we would expect in a writing class. As students receive feedback on
their use of detail and imagery, the structure of their writing, and their
style and tone, they develop a sense of themselves as writers engaged in
a particular kind of craft. The second kind of talk, however, has been
exploited to a much lesser degree in most composition classes.

I would like to argue that talk about associations and experiences,
while it may appear tangential or irrelevant to objectives, is no less
important to the development of writing ability than direct discussion
of technique. Ultimately, I think, it is the qualities of experience that
inform and give richness and vitality to writing. If Lori had explored all
the varied dimensions of her visit to the dentist, she might have written
an essay or story that would place readers in this situation and thus
carry greater impact. Especially for students who are accustomed to
placing form before meaning, this kind of activity can help them discover
their content first and then suit the form to it. An exploration of
content contributes to audience awareness as students gain insight into
the qualities of experience that affect other people—that inform, entertain, or otherwise engage them. Moreover, the camaraderie engendered
when individuals share experiences helps to solidify a sense of community. Thus, while this particular class rarely had any free-wheeling
discussions about their personal experiences, they did begin to diverge
more often from discussion of the writing craft to talk about associations
triggered by the writings. Again, Phil encouraged this kind of talk by
modeling (often responding with "that reminds me of . . .") and allowing the students to discuss their experiences when they seemed so
inclined.

One important value of this experiential talk may be the fact that it
draws attention away from writing itself. Too often in school writing
becomes a self-conscious activity, performed for its own sake with an
emphasis on correct form and mechanics. This practice results in
students "writing writing" rather than writing to express meaning. As
Florio (1979) suggests, writing occurs most naturally when it is taken
for granted as a means for carrying out social roles and communications.
For students like those in the class discussed here, talk about experiences
might decrease the tensions they feel about their writings, by taking
the spotlight off those writings and placing it temporarily elsewhere.

In their interviews, the students revealed some of the specific
benefits they felt the class had for them. All agreed that the weekly
writing requirement helped them write more than they would have

otherwise. They expressed interest in what others were doing (Melissa claimed that the group gave her ideas) and in general came to trust the class as a "safe" group with which to share. A few stated that they wanted more feedback at times, but as Lori suggested, sometimes the facial expressions and other nonverbal behaviors of the class members would signal their responses sufficiently.

Several members of the group made telling comments about the peer group as audience. Kevin remarked that the class helped him build more concrete images and write more objectively, so as to get ideas across more effectively. Phil had of course reinforced this notion by his emphasis on engaging the reader at the level of the concrete. Stan said he liked receiving praise from the group, and Melissa claimed she enjoyed reading to the group because it appealed to her "ham" instinct. On the other hand, Neal and Lori admitted they sometimes held back on writing that was too personal or "weird," so as to protect them from being vulnerable to the group. In general, though, the students felt that they had profited from participating in the class, and that while they did not generally write with a peer group audience explicitly in mind, the experience had helped them formulate a better sense of what appealed to an audience outside themselves.

Apparently many of these growth processes that Phil had stimulated during the first quarter came along more dramatically than in the second quarter. Bruce Paulson observed that the group members became quite confident in sharing, began to give one another more criticism, and received the criticisms in a positive, nondefensive way. They explored creative processes more intensively and in preparing their writing for publication developed greater consciousness of the writer's craft, particularly revision strategies and the needs of wider audiences. I regret that I was unable to observe during this second quarter, so as to assess their continued growth and to corroborate Bruce's impressions.

Writing Development

Since my involvement in this situation was limited to a three-month period, my conclusions regarding growth in the writing abilities of these students must be very tentative. Some had entered the situation with strong writing talents and had used the course as an opportunity to refine those talents. Others began with lesser demonstrated abilities, but showed in their writing some significant gains. Again, both Bruce and Phil identified some signs of progress that revealed themselves later in the school year.

Some writings produced by the students, when related to information derived from observations and interviews, reflect important kinds of development. Kevin, for example, after writing several pieces in an abstract philosophical vein, suddenly produced two writings—a dream sequence and a story about a hunting accident—which contained strong sensory details to support his larger ideas.

> Kevin reads a passage from a story about a hunting incident. He claims it has symbolic significance, involving a young man being tested. It is more concrete than his earlier writings, and Phil and I praise it for that. I ask him how he might build the story, and he answers that he'll use this passage as a beginning, perhaps adding some background to it.

Phil responded positively to these writings, since he had been encouraging Kevin to include more concrete images in his writing. Later Phil revealed that he thought:

> . . . students often believe that depersonalization of writing improves it. This was especially true of Kevin, who was the most reluctant to shed the protection that this assumption provides the writer. It's easier to hide behind abstraction than behind the particular, and abstractions can be depersonalized more easily than particulars.

Kevin admitted in his interview that Phil had helped him see that if he was to convey his ideas more convincingly to his readers, he would need to write more "objectively," making greater use of specific detail. This comment reflects an increased awareness of the audience's needs—with the audience viewed not simply as the teacher or the peer group, but as readers in general.

Another instance of growth may be seen in Alice, whose earlier writings, while technically sound and craftsmanlike, lacked expressiveness and emotionality. We can see her concern for craft in the following:

> Alice reads a poem "At the Theater." Melissa asks whether the players are on stage or in the audience. Alice replies that it's some of both.
>
> I ask Alice how she feels about her poem. She says she hated it at first, but went on with it. This is her fourth draft, she claims, and she's still not sure about the first four lines.

A poem Alice wrote later, however, revealed some feeling and personal voice that had not been evident in her previous work. Again, Phil praised her strongly for this effort; she seemed a little embarrassed but at the same time pleased that he had liked it. Phil observed that Alice had perhaps sacrificed some control in this piece of writing for the sake of making a more personal statement, and thus deserved support for her risk-taking. I would cite this as an important dimension of teaching writing—the recognition that students need to be encouraged when they experiment with something new and potentially beneficial to their growth as writers. Again, this kind of support signals to students that their own intuitions are worth following.

Finally, Stan had been writing mostly serious pieces on quite personal topics, as reflected in my notes:

1. Stan reads a narrative about a family incident in which the father treated the sister in an arbitrary, unfair manner. Several others tell Stan that they know how that feels. Phil says something about his own sister, and tells Stan he liked the way he set the scene in this piece.
2. Stan reads a personal poem about a broken friendship. I tell him I like the balance between thinking about oneself and thinking about the other person. Phil notes the cinematic technique of shifting focus. The others are quiet, perhaps sensing the intimate nature of the poem.

During the second quarter, Bruce had asked the students to try writing a parody (he also believed in writers experimenting with new forms), and Stan wrote an excellent satire of *Star Trek*. The others enjoyed this parody greatly, and told him so. He seemed buoyed by this response, which was not surprising, since he admitted in his earlier interview to his pleasure at having others praise him for his writing.

The students also showed keen insight concerning writing in various modes. Melissa discussed her preference for fantasy writing, claiming that she liked having things come out the way she wanted them to; "real life takes too much revising." Others distinguished between poetry and fiction writing. Lori said she felt more comfortable with poetry, since it was "shorter"—she became impatient with prose writing. Neal, on the other hand, found prose to be more natural to him, saying that he had difficulty getting the rhythm and structure of poetry. Others, like Kevin and Alice, wrote both stories and poems, but acknowledged the more personal nature and compact form of the latter. Kevin revealed that it took longer for him to write a poem because of the effort required to shape and trim.

In their interviews, the students also made some perceptive distinctions between fiction or poetry writing and essay writing. Although they tended to classify the former as "creative" and the latter as "noncreative," they also noted some relationships between the two. Stan, for example, claimed that the organization required for essay writing helped him in structuring his "creative" writing. Lori and Mary agreed that they didn't mind writing essays if the assignments were open-ended and provided them some choice. Melissa claimed that since she had been writing more, essays had become easier for her; this attests to the importance of fluency. Reinforcing other statements he had made, Neal said that he liked to use the essay form because its "impersonal" nature helped him avoid themes that were too private. And Alice revealed that she found essay writing to be easier when she converted it to narrative form—the essays became more interesting when they had a "plot."

These perceptions suggest to me the need for students to discover forms that will bridge the gaps between creative and expository writing. The personal essay in particular represents a viable means for moving from expressive or poetic discourse to transactional discourse. Kevin's comments were perhaps the most insightful in this regard. He argued that writing a story or poem involved "suggesting" rather than stating a thesis; these forms were more an expression of a vision or a feeling than a straightforward argument. In effect, Kevin was making the same point as Britton and his colleagues (1975), who distinguished between transactional writing as explicit and poetic writing as implicit in conveyance of meaning.

Kevin's statement thus reassured me about claims made by almost all of the students that they wrote primarily for themselves. (Alice was the only one who said she often consciously wrote to please the teacher. She confessed to sometimes sacrificing her own intentions in doing so.) At first these revelations caused me to wonder whether I could cite any growth in audience awareness if the students themselves were not conscious of audiences when they wrote. I realized, though, that the kind of poetic or "spectator role" writing in which the students were principally engaged called for them first to please themselves and secondly to appeal to a wider audience. At the same time this writing was not the same as purely expressive writing, in that it required an increasingly internalized sense of audience, one that worked in subconscious, intuitive ways. As Ong (1975) suggests, effective writers "fictionalize" their audiences, sensing an image of a readership that will respond in anticipated ways. Again, the responses from the teacher and from fellow students in the creative writing class seemed to contribute significantly to that kind of image-making and audience awareness.

Summary and Implications

Although I am reluctant to recommend specific teaching procedures based on this investigation, I will describe some hypotheses that emerged during the course of the study. First, I perceived a relationship between roles that the teacher assumes and a development of a sense of audience and of writing as process. As a survival mechanism, students will write for the teacher. This need not be detrimental, however, if teachers are willing to expand their range as audiences. In effect, Phil's approach helped students move from a more limited view of the teacher as examiner or generalized other to a broader conception of teacher as trusted adult and one with whom they had a particular relationship.

This perception seemed to help them to begin taking some of the risks necessary to their development as writers. And in acting as a fellow writer modeling aspects of process, Phil helped the students build confidence in the worth of their own intuitions.

Second, my study helped me to see more clearly the possibilities of the classroom as writing community. Perhaps because we have stereotyped writers and other artists in our society as "loners," we have tended to make writing a solitary activity. Clearly, writing involves individual effort, but isolating writers from others who are undergoing similar developmental processes cannot be beneficial to them. More positively stated, students can experience growth, both cognitive and affective, from participating with others in a common social and intellectual enterprise. Audience awareness in particular is enhanced as students use their peer group as a transition from writing for themselves or teachers to writing for wider audiences, as they build images internally of those audiences.

Again, I would call attention to classroom talk as crucial to the development of the sense of community. In this case, the teacher encouraged students to discuss both writing itself and the qualities of experience that inform and give substance to writing. This kind of leadership requires judgment and patience; the teacher must assess when and how each kind of discussion should take place. As Mallett and Newsome (1977) assert, an open-ended-questioning and discussion-leading style will urge students to discover meanings for themselves, rather than trying to guess the teacher's agenda.

Third, we need to be alert to signs of growth in students' writing and intuitions about writing. This entails in particular identifying those moments when students have experimented with something new, have taken a risk which may mean a temporary loss of a control they had gained but reveals that they are stretching for something important to their development. In particular, we can watch for hints of movement from egocentrism to audience awareness (Kroll, 1978)—greater use of concrete detail, infusion of personal voice, or qualities of imagination and humor that suddenly appear in students' writing and indicate that they are seeking to engage their readers. As the teacher and other students respond positively to these features of writing, so are they reinforced as criteria for good writing in the writer's mind.

We can also look for indications that students are developing stronger intuitions about composing processes and modes of discourse. It is especially important for students to discover that revision is much more than proofreading and cleaning up, that it often involves many kinds of restructuring in order to make a piece of discourse more effective. Good teachers like Phil Butler and Bruce Paulson help students become aware of the range of revising strategies available to them.

Clearly, researchers can adopt more of a longitudinal approach than the one I have used here. Of course, growth in writing ability is a gradual process, with maturity often being achieved only in adulthood. Even if I had been able to observe the students and chart their progress for the full year, my conclusions would still most likely be tentative. But with young people much can occur in a year or less. Events over such a span deserve our attention.

Since the fall of 1979 I have continued this line of research, having acted as participant–observer in two additional writing courses taught by Phil Butler. Each group has had its own chemistry, and has provided a wealth of data. At present I am completing a report comparing the first and second groups, which differed considerably in the nature of class discussion. In the third class, a graduate student joined me as a second observer; her perspective has provided an important additional dimension. In all, this research has enabled me to discover a great many aspects of how writing is taught and learned.

Research in composition should be intensive as well as extensive; microanalysis should accompany macroanalysis. Further investigations can focus in on specific aspects of teaching and learning styles, composing processes (especially prewriting and revision), conferencing and evaluation strategies, oral language, and rhetorical development, as they occur within classrooms, schools, and larger social and cultural contexts. We need also to begin looking at other populations—younger (especially middle-grade) children, students classified as "basic" or "average," and minority students. The possibilities for discovering through ethnographic methods how writing is taught and learned are many and varied.

Ultimately, it is the *process* of conducting ethnographic research that holds the greatest fascination for me, and has contributed most to my development as a researcher (and indeed teacher and writer). The experience has been one of continual vision and re-vision, of bringing knowledge to bear on what is observed and at the same time remaining open to new and promising research directions. This seems to me essential to the business of teaching as well, as we look to discover meanings within the contexts of our own classrooms, and capitalize on these insights to improve our instruction.

REFERENCES

Bridwell, L. S. Revising strategies in twelfth grade students' transactional writing. *Research in the Teaching of English*, 1980, 14, 197–222.
Britton, J., Burgess, T., Martin, N., McLeod, A., & Rosen, H. *The development of writing abilities, 11–18*. London: Macmillan, 1975.

Calkins, L. M. Children learn the writer's craft. *Language Arts*, 1980, *57*, 207–213.

Clark, C. M., & Florio, S., with Elmore, J. L., Martin, J., Maxwell, R. J., & Metheny, W. *Understanding writing in school: A descriptive study of writing and its instruction in two classrooms.* Final Report of the Written Literacy Study (Grant No. 908040), funded by the National Institute of Education, U.S. Department of Education. East Lansing, Mich.: Institute for Research on Teaching, Michigan State University, 1981.

Denzin, N. K. *The research act: A theoretical introduction to sociolinguistic methods* (2nd ed.). New York: McGraw-Hill, 1978.

Dyson, A. H. *A case study examination of the role of oral language in the writing processes of kindergartners.* Unpublished doctoral dissertation, University of Texas, Austin, 1981.

Erickson, F. What makes school ethnography ethnographic. *Anthropology and Education Quarterly*, 1973, *4*(2), 10–19.

Florio, S. The problem of dead letters: Social perspectives on the teaching of writing. *Elementary School Journal*, 1979, *80*, 1–7.

Florio, S., & Clark, C. M. The functions of writing in an elementary classroom. *Research in the Teaching of English*, 1982, *16*, 115–130.

Geertz, C. *The interpretation of cultures.* New York: Basic Books, 1973.

Glaser, B. C., & Strauss, A. L. *The discovery of grounded theory: Strategies for qualitative research.* Chicago: Aldine, 1967.

Graves, D. What children show us about revision. *Language Arts*, 1979, *56*, 312–319.

Guba, E. *Naturalistic and conventional inquiry.* Paper presented at annual meeting of American Educational Research Association, Boston, April 1980.

Jackson, P. W. *Life in classrooms.* New York: Holt, Rinehart & Winston, 1968.

Kantor, K. J., Kirby, D. R., & Goetz, J. P. Research in context: Ethnographic studies in English education. *Research in the Teaching of English*, 1981, *15*, 293–309.

Kroll, B. M. Cognitive egocentrism and the problem of audience awareness in written discourse. *Research in the Teaching of English*, 1978, *12*, 269–281.

LeCompte, M. D., & Goetz, J. P. Problems of reliability and validity in ethnographic research. *Review of Educational Research*, 1982, *52*, 31–60.

Mallett, M., & Newsome, B. *Talking, writing, and learning, 8–13.* London: Evan/Methuen, 1977.

Martin, N., *The Martin report: Case studies from government high schools in western Australia.* Western Australia: Education Department, 1980.

Mishler, E. G. Meaning in context: Is there any other kind? *Harvard Educational Review*, 1979, *49*, 1–19.

Murray, D. Internal revision: A process of discovery. In C. Cooper & L. Odell (Eds.), *Research on composing: Points of departure.* Urbana, Ill.: National Council of Teachers of English, 1978.

Nelson, M. W. *Writers who teach: A naturalistic investigation.* Unpublished doctoral dissertation, University of Georgia, 1981.

Ong, W. The writer's audience is always a fiction. *Publications of the Modern Language Association*, 1975, *90*, 9–21.

Perl, S. The composing processes of unskilled college writers. *Research in the Teaching of English*, 1979, *13*, 317–336.

Pettigrew, J., Shaw, R. A., & Van Nostrand, A. D. Collaborative analysis of writing instruction. *Research in the Teaching of English*, 1981, *15*, 329–341.

Schatzman, L., & Strauss, A. L. *Field research: Strategies for a natural sociology.* Englewood Cliffs, N.J.: Prentice-Hall, 1973.

Smith, L. M., & Geoffrey, W. *The complexities of an urban classroom: An analysis toward a general theory of teaching.* New York: Holt, Rinehart & Winston, 1968.

Sommers, N. Revision strategies of student writers and experienced adult writers. *College Composition and Communication*, 1980, *31*, 378–388.

Sowers, S. A six year old's writing process: The first half of first grade. *Language Arts*, 1979, 56, 829–835.

Wilson, S. The use of ethnographic techniques in educational research. *Review of Educational Research*, 1977, 47, 249–265.

Worsham, S. E. *A naturalistic study of a basic writing program.* Unpublished Educational Specialist project, University of Georgia, 1980.

Wotring, A. M. Writing to think about high school chemistry. In *Two studies of writing in high school science.* Berkeley, Calif.: Bay Area Writing Project Classroom Research Series, 1981.

4

Measuring the effects of revisions on text structure

LESTER FAIGLEY
STEPHEN P. WITTE
University of Texas, Austin

When a house is to be remodeled, the owners have two options. First, they can simply change the appearance of the house by painting, wall-papering, adding siding, or making other external alterations. Second, they can change the structure of the house by replacing load-bearing walls or by adding rooms. Writers are faced with similar options when they revise what they write. Although recent research on the composing process (Flower & Hayes, 1980; Sommers, 1980) and statements by writing teachers (Hairston, 1981; Murray, 1978) indicate that experienced writers often make complex structural changes in their work during revision, no one has to date developed a reliable system for distinguishing between structural and surface revisions or for showing how text structure is affected by revision.

Several researchers have touched on some of the crucial issues. For example, scholars studying literary manuscripts have long noted that famous writers use sophisticated revision strategies. However, the few attempts, such as Hildick's (1965), to classify the types of revisions used during the writing of literary texts are largely impressionistic, limiting the applicability of the classification methods. Focusing on the revisions of elementary and secondary students, the National Assessment of Educational Progress (Rivas, 1977) attempted to gauge the effect of revisions on texts through a survey. Changes were categorized as "organizational," "stylistic," "continuational," "holistic," and so on. These categories overlap considerably with Hildick's and render the NAEP study equally impressionistic. The most rigorous studies of students' revisions to date have been those of Sommers (1978, 1980) and Bridwell (1980). Sommers classified changes by length and by type of operation, using the same categories (deletion, addition, substitution, rearrangement) that Chomsky (1965) had used to group transformations. Although Sommers's study advanced research on revision, measuring the effect of revision on the meaning of texts lies beyond the scope of her study. Bridwell employed a classification system like Sommers's, with one important difference: Bridwell included a category for broad, text-motivated changes, even though she found no examples in her twelfth-grade writing samples. While some descriptive research (such as Sommers, 1978, 1980) has shown that experienced writers revise more frequently and change longer units of text than do inexperienced writers, no study has been able to describe satisfactorily either the nature of these changes or the effects they have on the meaning of a text. Classification schemes based on syntactic theory are simply inadequate for these tasks.

The present study sets out a simple yet robust system for analyzing the effect of revisions on the semantic structure of a text. The theoretical basis for the system is described in detail, followed by an example of application of the system to a case study of a writer revising.

A Taxonomy of Revisions

Ten years ago, in seeking to explain the effects of revisions on text structure, there was little research to draw on. But that situation has changed. Research in several disciplines—primarily text linguistics, cognitive psychology, and artificial intelligence—now attempts to account for semantic relationships among elements in a text. As a result, several key properties of text structure have been isolated. This makes it possible to conduct more sophisticated research focusing on revisions.

One property that has been isolated is coherence. Researchers have found that besides internal, explicit cohesive devices (Halliday & Hasan, 1976), nonexplicit text inferences must also be analyzed in order to understand coherence (Clark, 1977; Crothers, 1978, 1979; Schank, 1975). Another such property is text hierarchy. Work in discourse comprehension demonstrates that readers stratify information according to levels of importance, remembering what is essential to the "theme" or "gist" of a particular text (van Dijk, 1980; Kintsch, 1974; Kintsch & van Dijk, 1978; Meyer, 1975; Thorndyke, 1977).

A classification system that accounts for the ways in which revisions affect text structure can now begin to take shape. Such a system must differentiate between changes that affect the meaning of a text and changes that do not. For example, the addition of a comma in sentence 2 does not change the meaning of sentence 1, even though placement of a comma after an introductory subordinate clause is considered standard usage:

1. Because the horse lost his shoe the rider was lost.
2. Because the horse lost his shoe, the rider was lost.

In other instances, the addition of a comma does change the meaning of a text. The difference in punctuating restrictive and nonrestrictive modifiers is a classic case in point:

3. The governors who took bribes abused the public trust.
4. The governors, who took bribes, abused the public trust.

Sentence 3, of course, refers only to those among a number of governors who took bribes; sentence 4 refers to all governors.

Thus the primary distinction in our taxonomy is between those revisions which affect the meaning of a text and those which do not affect meaning. This distinction is not a simple one, but neither is it impossible to make. Philosophers and linguists have described meaning as a *text base* with a formal language. Although the formal language most commonly used is a type of predicate calculus, other, more complex languages—such as Montague grammar (1974)—have also been advanced. Psychologists have used a simplified predicate calculus to represent a text base as a sequence of propositions containing a predicate or case relationship and one or more arguments (e.g., Frederiksen, 1975; Kintsch, 1974; Meyer, 1975). In the present system, we will use the notion of a text base to refer to the meaning of a text.

Explicit text bases are typically incomplete; that is, speakers or writers rely on the listeners' or readers' ability to make inferences. Consider the following short text with and without sentence 5a:

5. My teacher returned my essay on Tuesday.
5a. The teacher had graded the essay.
6. I received a "B."

Suppose sentence 5a does not appear in the text. Most readers would assume that the teacher had graded the paper, even though this assumption might be false. Crothers's model would represent sentence 5a as an implicit proposition if it were not stated explicitly, a procedure consistent with interactive models of text processing used in artificial intelligence research (see Schank, 1975; Schank & Abelson, 1977).

A completely explicit text is difficult to process, not only because such a text is verbose but because the reader or listener seeks to make additional connections that are not intended by the speaker or writer (see Shuy & Larkin, 1978). Crothers's (1979) model for representing a text base, which is sensitive to the inferential nature of texts, accommodates implicit propositions and connectives as well as explicit propositions. Such a text-base model permits us to distinguish between additions that make explicit what can be inferred and additions that bring new information to the text.

The basic distinction between the left and right branches in Figure 4-1 is not in the kinds of operations involved but rather *whether new information is brought to the text or whether old information is removed in a way that it cannot be recovered through inferencing.* Stated most simply, surface changes do not alter the meaning of a text; meaning changes do. Surface changes do not introduce new information, nor do these changes delete information that is not recoverable by inferencing. Meaning changes, on the other hand, introduce, delete, or alter information that cannot be inferred or recovered.

Surface Changes

Surface changes are detailed on the left branch of Figure 4-1. The first node under surface changes is *formal changes.* These changes include a variety of operations associated with copy editing, such as most (but not all) spelling changes; changes in tense, number, and modality; expansions of abbreviations to their full forms; internal and end-stop punctuation changes; and format changes. Here, capitalizations are considered to be spelling changes. Format changes are divided into two subcategories: paragraphing, and an "other" category that includes changes such as setting off a long quotation.

The second major subcategory of surface changes is *meaning-preserving changes.* These changes "paraphrase" the concepts in the text base but do not alter them. Additions are the first type of change; such changes raise to the surface thoughts that were previously inferred. Sentence 5a in the essay-grading example is a meaning-preserving addition. The

Fig. 4-1. A taxonomy of revisions.

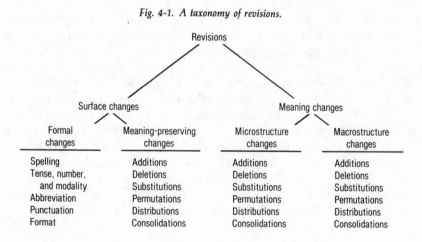

second type of meaning-preserving change—deletions—represents the opposite process, where a reader is forced to infer what had been explicit. These two types of meaning-preserving changes commonly involve the addition or deletion of single words.

Meaning-preserving substitutions involve trades of words, phrases, or sentences that represent the same concept. Permutations involve rearrangements or rearrangements with substitutions. Distributions occur when material in one text segment is passed into more than one segment. Consolidations do the reverse. In consolidations—the principal activity of sentence combining—material in two or more units is collected into one unit.

Meaning Changes

Meaning changes are the opposite of surface changes. We separate revisions that are simple adjustments or elaborations of existing text from changes that alter the gist of that text. Research in how readers comprehend texts has focused on how meaning in a text is processed as it is read and how a gist of that text—a global notion of what the text is about—is constructed in memory. Kintsch and van Dijk (1978), Kintsch and Vipond (1979), and Vipond (1980) have tested a model that describes how readers process texts at local and global levels. This model treats meaning at two levels: a *microstructure* level, where all ideas in the text are represented (including those ideas that can be inferred); and a *macrostructure* or summary level, which is abstracted from the microstructure (van Dijk, 1972, 1977a, 1977b, 1980). We do not find macrostructure theory entirely adequate for representing the gist of a text because it does not make sufficient allowance for world knowledge in interpreting texts (see Morgan & Sellner, 1980). We know, for example, that a junk mail flyer announcing a contest is an indirect attempt to get us to buy something. Nevertheless, for our purposes, macrostructure theory does give us systematic guidelines for obtaining a summary.

In Figure 4-1, the operations listed under micro- and macrostructure changes are the same six described under meaning-preserving changes. In the case of both micro- and macrostructure changes, however, the text base is altered.

Macrostructures are derived from a text base through three types of operations (see van Dijk, 1980, pp. 46–50). One operation, *deletion*, involves selecting propositions that will be retained in long-term memory. Propositions that are not necessary for the interpretation of another proposition, or propositions that have local relevance only, are not represented in the macrostructure.

A second operation is *generalization*, whereby a series of propositions is grouped into a *macroproposition*. A series of examples about a global topic can be subsumed into a single proposition at a higher level of abstraction:

> 7. Jane was wearing an orange print skirt. Linda had on a purple pants suit. Erin wore a red jumper.

According to van Dijk, such sequences neither are conditionally linked nor express stereotypical actions or settings. Yet from such details we can generalize a more abstract proposition, "The women wore colorful clothing."

A third operation is *construction*, in which a series of propositions is summarized in a *macroproposition* using the reader's conventional knowledge about the world. Researchers in discourse comprehension have represented conventional knowledge as *schemata* (Rumelhart & Ortony, 1977) or *scripts* (Schank & Abelson, 1977) or *frames* (Minsky, 1975). From a sequence such as this:

> 8. I walked out of the house and got in the car. It started rough, and I let it idle for a few minutes. I was late enough so that most of the traffic had cleared off of the freeway. I pulled into the parking garage under my building at 8:45.

we could construct the macroproposition "I drove to work."

Macrostructure changes, accordingly, are changes in the text base that would alter a summary of that text. In contrast, microstructure changes affect meaning but do not affect the summary of a text. A microstructure addition, for example, can be thought of as an extrapolation of the existing text base.

Applying the Taxonomy of Revisions

We coded numerically each of the subcategories in Figure 4-1 to facilitate our analysis. Table 4-1 lists the subcategories from the figure and their numerical codes.

One other dimension of revision needs to be addressed—the span of text involved in the change. Recent research studies of revision have all examined the length of each change. We decided to use Bridwell's (1980) system because it accounts for each sentence in a long revision. Six of her seven classes are:

1. Graphic changes
2. Lexical changes

Table 4-1. A Classification of Types of Revisions

I. Surface changes
  A. Formal changes (00)
    1. Spelling: 01
    2. Tense, number, and modality: 02
    3. Abbreviation: 03
    4. Punctuation: 04
    5. Format
      a. Paragraph: 05
      b. Other: 06
  B. Meaning-preserving changes (10)
    1. Additions: 11
    2. Deletions: 12
    3. Substitutions: 13
    4. Permutations: 14
    5. Distributions: 15
    6. Consolidations: 16
II. Meaning changes
  A. Microstructure changes (20)
    1. Additions: 21
    2. Deletions: 22
    3. Substitutions: 23
    4. Permutations: 24
    5. Distributions: 25
    6. Consolidations: 26
  B. Macrostructure changes (30)
    1. Additions: 31
    2. Deletions: 32
    3. Substitutions: 33
    4. Permutations: 34
    5. Distributions: 35
    6. Consolidations: 36

3. Phrasal changes
4. Clausal changes
5. Sentence changes
6. Multisentence changes

The above text-span taxonomy is based on surface features for ease of use. If the number of propositions involved in a given change were computed, there would be little hope of using this taxonomy for comparing different texts. Furthermore, representations of propositions often coincide with clause and sentence boundaries. *Clauses* in this taxonomy are defined as constructions with finite subjects and verbs. Constructions longer than one word without both a finite subject and a verb are classified as *phrases*. *Sentences* are determined by the writer's punctuation. If a phrase or subordinate clause is punctuated as a sentence, it is counted as a sentence. *Multisentence* changes are classified one sentence at a time. Thus, each sentence in a long macrostructure addition would be labeled with a 6 for a multisentence addition and with a 31 for the effect on text structure.

A Case Study of a Writer Revising

Before we give an example of how our taxonomy can be applied to a case study of a writer revising, two cautions need to be made. First, we found initially that the taxonomy could be applied reliably to examples of revisions in the texts of student writers. But after reviewing the comments of other researchers who have used the taxonomy, we now realize that our initial claim of high reliability (Faigley & Witte, 1981) was the result of our having worked closely with a few texts during the development of the taxonomy. When one of the authors attempted to apply the taxonomy to revisions in manuscripts of well-known novelists, he found that the distinction between microstructure and macrostructure changes often rested in judgments of literary criticism. Consequently, the reliability of the taxonomy depends upon the shared expectations of those applying it and the relative difficulty of the texts being analyzed. We expect reliabilities to deteriorate if raters have different notions of what constitutes the gist of a text or if the texts being analyzed exhibit unusual complexity. We wrote abstracts of the texts we examined to determine what was and was not a macrostructure change.

Second, researchers using our taxonomy will have to arrive at some consensus on how to distinguish potentially ambiguous changes. A particularly troublesome problem is deciding whether a span of text that includes several changes constitutes, say, a permutation at the sentence level or several individual changes at the word and phrase levels. Sentence 3024 in Draft 3 (see p. 106) is a case in point. Another similar problem is deciding how to classify when revisions occur. We did not become aware of this problem until we compared the results of a study using our taxonomy with those of Bridwell (1980). We wrongly concluded that Bridwell had not directly compared drafts because our figures for changes occurring between drafts were much larger than those of Bridwell (see Faigley & Witte, 1981, p. 414). What accounts for the differences between our results and Bridwell's is that we counted all differences between drafts as between-draft changes while Bridwell counted only those instances where the writer had annotated the previous draft. Neither procedure is necessarily correct, but our failure to recognize that Bridwell was using a slightly different procedure illustrates one of the potential difficulties in comparing the results of revision studies. We recommend that researchers using our taxonomy keep examples of particular kinds of changes and from these examples develop their own guidelines for scoring problematic cases. We tended to be conservative in ambiguous cases, scoring each change that we could identify as a separate change.

The following example includes sections from three drafts that were taken from a set of seven drafts collected from a student writer at the University of Texas. The student was given no special instructions other than to submit all drafts as part of a regular class assignment. This writer included nearly all types of revisions in doing complete rewrites of her manuscripts. We have reproduced the first twenty sentences of the first draft and the corresponding sections of the second and third drafts. The sentences are numbered for reference purposes. Changes between drafts are indicated by brackets ([ ]), changes within drafts by braces ({ }), and deletions by asterisks (*). The first element in a superscript number (such as 1 in 1-01) represents the span of text involved in the change and follows Bridwell's system; the second element in a superscript (01 in 1-01) follows the taxonomy of revisions given in Table 4-1. Errors have not been normalized in these drafts, nor have they been otherwise marked.

Draft 1

1001   I first heard of Dr Webb from my friend Elizabeth, already five months pregnant.

1002   He was the only doctor that would allow dim lights, warm water baths.

1003   I don't know how I was born but I know I survived, I decided to see him anyway, because of peer pressure, intrigue, or both.

1004   Any doctor open to new methods of the delivery of a baby must not be all bad, even if I didn't care for some of the methods.

1005   There was one catch, though.

1006   You had to drive to Georgetown where he practiced.

1007   I made the journey.

1008   Dr Webb looked like your favorite Teddy Bear—broad unassuming face, short stature overweight.

1009   His shortness probably also gave me this impression, anyway he looked like the kind of man woman would want to confide in.

1010   But a doctor?

1011   I am still trying to accept him as a doctor.

1012   Doctors carry a mistique few professions share.

1013   They cultivate a tough guy image, I don't know either in medical school or on the job.

1014   Perhaps their daily perceptions, so emersed with pain, sometimes life and death, forses them to block human reactions in order to perform the job.

1015   At any rate, Dr Webb did not instill me with the confidence I normally feel in doctors.

1016   As time passed Elizabeth had her baby.

1017   She didn't have enough to say about him.

1018   "I couldn't have done it without him."

1019   I though, "w{W}$^{1\text{-}01}$ell something must change as the time gets closer.

1020   I'm still too removed."

Draft 2

2001   I first heard of Dr Webb from my friend Elizabeth, already five months pregnant.

2002   [   ]$^{1\text{-}05\ 1\text{-}21}$ ["][He's]$^{1\text{-}02}$ the only doctor that [allows]$^{2\text{-}02}$ dim lights [and]$^{2\text{-}11}$ warm water baths.["]

2003   [   ]$^{1\text{-}05}$ I [didn't]$^{2\text{-}02}$ know how I was born[,]$^{1\text{-}04}$ but I know I survived, I decided to see him anyway, because of peer pressure, intrigue, or both.

2004   Any doctor open to new methods of the delivery of a baby must not be all bad, even if I didn't care for some of the methods.

2005 $^{5\text{-}16}$ [One catch, though, you had to drive to Georgetown where he practiced.]

2006   I made the journey.

2007   Dr [John R]$^{2\text{-}11}$ Webb looked like your favorite Teddy Bear—broad, unassuming face $_*$$^{1\text{-}04}$ [and pleasantly]$^{3\text{-}23}$ overweight.

2008   His shortness probably also gave me this impression, anyway he looked like the kind of man woman would want to confide in.

2009   But a doctor?

2010   I [still am] $^{3\text{-}14}$ trying to accept him as a doctor.

2011   Doctors [have]$^{2\text{-}13}$ a mistique few professions share.

2012   They cultivate a tough guy image, [learned]$^{4\text{-}23}$ either in medical school or on the job.

2013   Perhaps their daily perceptions, so emersed with pain [and]$^{2\text{-}13}$ sometimes life and death, fors[c]$^{1\text{-}01}$ e$_*$$^{1\text{-}02}$ them to block human reactions in order to perform the job.

2014   At any rate, Dr Webb did not instill me with the confidence I normally feel in doctors.

2015   As time passed Elizabeth had her baby.

2016   She didn't have enough to say about him.

2017   "I couldn't have done it without him."

2018   I though[t]$^{1\text{-}01}$, "Well something must change as the time gets closer.

2019   I'm still too removed."

Draft 3

3001   I first heard [about]2-13 Dr Webb from my friend Elizabeth, already five months pregnant.

3002   6-31["He's so-o wonderful.]

3003   6-35[Dr Webb's going to deliver our baby in the hospital room with dim lights.]

3004   6-35[Chucks going to give the baby a warm bath and everything.]

3005   6-31[You've just got to go to him to!"]

3006   6-31[I wasn't really prepared for the life of diapers much less doctors; I just wanted to finish school worrying about the baby when the time came.]

3007   6-31[I guess each generation will have some inside secret or try improvements on the last's attempts at the baby business—maybe because anyway you look at it delivering a baby is so incredibly violent and awesome, and whether the mother forgets from drugs or the job of seeing the baby, the experience will not be denied.]

3008   6-31[So behind all the blue and pink frills of the "ABC's" and "Boop-Peeps" lurks the spectre that birth can be difficult.]

3009   6-31[That must be why so many women look to the gynecologist as a savior and a trusted friend—only he and your husband, in most instances, will be the ones that share the labor.]

3010   [I know my mother was drugged heavily when]4-33 I was born, [and]2-23 *4-12 I survived, [but]2-21 I [went]3-16 to see [old Webb]2-13 anyway *1-04 [from]2-13 peer pressure, intrigue, [or perhaps the realizing that there really was something inside of me that would have to be delivered.]4-31

3011   Any doctor open to new methods *3-12 [couldn't]2-13 be all bad, even if I didn't care for [all]2-13 of [them].2-13

3012   One catch *1-04 though, you had to drive to Georgetown [to see him].3-13

3013   5-21[Every month at first, then two weeks, then every week, the intervals tightening, just like the time between the contractions until the last trip, not a check-up but the real thing.]

3014   I made [that first]3-23 journey.

3015   *2-12 Webb looked like [a cross between your favorite teddy bear and John Denver].3-24
        *[2008]6-22
        *[2009]6-22

3016   6-31[Was he the doctor Elizabeth raved about?]

3017   6-33[I tried to imagine that he could instill the confidence I hoped a doctor would bolster in me.]

3018   Doctors [mystify like few professions can, cultivating]6-16 a tough guy image learned *2-12 in medical school1-04 (or [maybe]2-11 on the job)1-04.

3019   Perhaps their daily perceptions *1-04 [are]2-11 so emersed [in]2-13 pain[,]1-04 [sometimes inflicting pain to relieve long-term suffering, and more startling,]3-21 *2-12 life and death [encounters]2-11 [that they are forced]4-14 to block [the]2-11 human [emotions]2-23 [on one hand]3-21 to perform the job [and on the other to rally the patient with his God-like presence].3-21

3020   At any rate, *2-12 Webb [didn't have this quality].4-16

3021   *4-12 Elizabeth had her baby.

3022   6-23[He's so-o wonderful."]

3023   6-23[Her words echoed.]

3024   *4-12 [Maybe]2-23 something *2-12 [changes]2-02 [biologically]2-11 as the time gets closer.

3025   "I'm still too removed," [I reassured myself].4-31

Even in these brief excerpts, we can see a pattern in this particular student's revising strategies. In Draft 2, she made three changes (see 2002, 2007, 2012) that affected the text base, which were all microstructure changes. None of these four changes was longer than a phrase. In Draft 3, she made twenty-seven changes that affected the text base, twelve of them macrostructure changes (see 3001–3010, 3016, 3017). Fifteen of the twenty-seven changes were sentence or multisentence changes. Only one *addition* to the text base appeared in Draft 2. (The writer added quotation marks to sentence 2002, directly attributing it to her friend Elizabeth.) The third draft, however, has fourteen additions that affect the text base. The most important of these additions are the ones that change the macrostructure. In Drafts 1 and 2, the writer's reasons for wanting to go to Dr. Webb are vague. She speaks of "dim lights and warm water baths," but it is not clear why this type of delivery would make a long drive to the doctor worthwhile. In Draft 3, we understand why the writer seeks Dr. Webb: she has postponed thinking about delivery, and now she is apprehensive. In Draft 2, the writer straightens up diction. In Draft 3 the writer begins to think about her audience. She begins to discover how much detail she needs to convey in order for her audience to understand her experience.

Even this brief case study suggests that many things students write are still in progress. It also shows revision as a recursive process, where, as Sommers (1980) has described, experienced writers attend to different concerns in different cycles. We see in this example what Murray (1978) calls "internal" and "external" revision. Our system, however, exposes just how internal and external revision are different. The tactics of Drafts 2 and 3 illustrate this difference. The changes in Draft 2 are text-bound; the changes in Draft 3 are motivated by the writer's sense of what is missing in the text. Many students, unlike this writer, cannot see what is missing. They cannot evaluate their texts in light of their intentions and revise to bring what they have written closer to those intentions.

The point for teachers is not to require such students to revise more, since unguided or misguided revision may actually be detrimental to the final product. The important thing is for students to discover what, exactly, they have to say and to think about how potential readers might react to their text. When writers are able to distance themselves from what they have written, to see their texts with new eyes, then they can perform the kinds of revisions that we associate with skilled writers.

ACKNOWLEDGMENTS

The research reported was supported by the National Institute of Education, Department of Education, under grant number NIE-G-80-0054. The opinions expressed herein do not necessarily reflect the policy of the National Institute of Education. We thank Margaret Kiersted for her assistance in analyzing revisions.

REFERENCES

Bridwell, L. S. Revising strategies in twelfth grade students' transactional writing. *Research in the Teaching of English*, 1980, *14*, 107–122.

Chomsky, N. *Aspects of the theory of syntax*. Cambridge, Mass.: MIT Press 1965.

Clark, H. H. Inferences in comprehension. In D. LaBerge & S. J. Samuels (Eds.), *Perception and comprehension*. Hillsdale, N.J.: Lawrence Erlbaum, 1977.

Crothers, E. J. Inference and coherence. *Discourse Processes*, 1978, *1*, 51–71.

Crothers, E. J. *Paragraph structure inference*. Norwood, N.J.: Ablex, 1979.

van Dijk, T. A. *Some aspects of text grammar*. The Hague: Mouton, 1972.

van Dijk, T. A. Semantic macrostructures and knowledge frames in discourse comprehension. In M. Just & P. Carpenter (Eds.), *Cognitive processes in comprehension*. Hillsdale, N.J.: Lawrence Erlbaum, 1977. (a)

van Dijk, T. A. *Text and context*. London: Longman, 1977. (b)

van Dijk, T. A. *Macrostructures: An interdisciplinary study of global structures in discourse, interaction, and cognition*. Hillsdale, N.J.: Lawrence Erlbaum, 1980.

Faigley, L., & Witte, S. P. Analyzing revision. *College Composition and Communication*, 1981, *32*, 400–414.

Flower, L., & Hayes, J. R. The cognition of discovery: Defining a rhetorical problem. *College Composition and Communication*, 1980, *31*, 21–32.

Frederiksen, C. H. Representing logical and semantic structures of knowledge acquired from discourse. *Cognitive Psychology*, 1975, *7*, 371–458.

Hairston, M. *Successful writing*. New York: Norton, 1981.

Halliday, M. A. K., & Hasan, R. *Cohesion in English*. London: Longman, 1976.

Hildick, W. *Word for word: The rewriting of fiction*. London: Faber & Faber, 1965.

Kintsch, W. *The representation of meaning in memory*. Hillsdale, N.J.: Lawrence Erlbaum, 1974.

Kintsch, W., & van Dijk, T. A. Toward a model of text comprehension and production. *Psychological Review*, 1978, *85*, 363–394.

Kintsch, W., & Vipond, D. Reading comprehension and readability in educational practice and psychological theory. In L. G. Nilsson (Ed.), *Perspectives on memory research*. Hillsdale, N.J.: Lawrence Erlbaum, 1979.

Meyer, B. *The organization of prose and its effect upon memory*. Amsterdam: North Holland, 1975.

Minsky, M. A. A framework for representing knowledge. In P. Winston (Ed.), *The psychology of computer vision*. New York: McGraw-Hill, 1975.

Montague, R. *Formal philosophy* (R. H. Thomason, Ed.). New Haven, Conn.: Yale University Press, 1974.

Morgan, J. L., & Sellner, M. B. Discourse and linguistic theory. In R. J. Spiro, B. C. Bruce, & W. F. Brewer (Eds.), *Theoretical issues in reading comprehension*. Hillsdale, N.J.: Lawrence Erlbaum, 1980.

Murray, D. M. Internal revision: A process of discovery. In C. R. Cooper & L. Odell (Eds.), *Research on composing*. Urbana, Ill.: National Council of Teachers of English, 1978.

Rivas, F. *Write/rewrite: An assessment of revision skills*. (Writing Report No. 05-W-04). Denver: National Assessment of Educational Progress, 1977.

Rumelhart, D. E., & Ortony, A. The representation of knowledge in memory. In R. C. Anderson, R. J. Spiro, & W. E. Montague (Eds.),*Schooling and the acquisition of knowledge*. Hillsdale, N.J.: Lawrence Erlbaum, 1977.

Schank, R. C. *Conceptual information processing*. New York: American Elsevier, 1975.

Schank, R. C., & Abelson, R. P. *Scripts, plans, goals, and understanding: An inquiry into human knowledge structures*. Hillsdale, N.J.: Lawrence Erlbaum, 1977.

Shuy, R. W., & Larkin, D. L. Linguistic consideration in the simplification/clarification of insurance policy language. *Discourse Processes*, 1978, *1*, 305-321.

Sommers, N. I. *Revision in the composing process: A case study of experienced writers and student writers*. Unpublished doctoral dissertation, Boston University, 1978.

Sommers, N. I. Revision strategies of student writers and experienced adult writers. *College Composition and Communication*, 1980, *31*, 378-388.

Thorndyke, P. W. Cognitive structures in comprehension and memory of narrative discourse. *Cognitive Psychology*, 1977, *9*, 77-110.

Vipond, D. Micro- and macroprocesses in text comprehension. *Journal of Verbal Learning and Verbal Behavior*, 1980, *19*, 276-296.

5

The pragmatics of form: How do writers discover what to do when?

MARILYN M. COOPER
University of Southern California

To begin, I assert the following proposition: Many texts contain— somewhere in their opening sentences, paragraphs, or pages—what is called a statement of purpose. Here is an example by my colleague Peter Manning, from a paper he delivered on the "Intimations Ode" and Vergil's *Fourth Eclogue* at the 1980 meeting of the Modern Language Association in Houston:

> I should like in this essay briefly to explore the effects of encountering the Ode in the Vergilian context, to consider some of the continuities and contrasts it suggests, and to speculate on the causes of Wordsworth's discarding it and the changes wrought by his substitution of "My Heart Leaps Up."

In saying that texts contain statements of purpose, I am asserting rather than informing, because I am reasonably certain that you have noticed this phenomenon yourself, in student papers as well as in scholarly articles. I can only inform you of something you do not already know; therefore, I had to assume something about your knowledge before I could know what I was doing (i.e., informing or asserting).

You might ask, "Why are you describing what you are doing while you are doing it?" I respond as follows (notice that I can only respond if there has been an inquiry, which is why I attributed one to you): here in the *exordium* part of my chapter I am trying to prepare you to receive my message by focusing your attention on the pragmatics of form: on my perceptions of the relevant conditions to be met in this communicative situation, on what I'm doing with what I'm saying, and on the order I'm doing it in.[1] I'm also saying something you already know about form in

---

1. Pragmatics is the general study of how language is used; the branch I am relying on in this paper is speech act theory, originated by the philosopher J. L. Austin. He makes the distinction I have just alluded to—the distinction between saying something (encoding a message in a linguistic form) and doing something with what you're saying (intending

order to establish a common ground between us—another function of the *exordium*.[2] Burke defines form as the "arousing and fulfillment of desires" (1931/1968). Thus, so as to avoid arousing desires that I do not intend to fulfill, I also (hereby) predict that I will not follow the classic arrangement discussed by Cicero in his *De Inventione*, but rather will take the option mentioned in his *Rhetorica ad Herennium* in which the speaker (or writer) varies the order when such an alteration makes the presentation more effective.

In having described what I'm doing in terms of Burke and Cicero, I performed another function of the *exordium*—that of establishing my authority to discuss this topic. And, finally, my *exordium* was intended to pique your interest in statements of purpose, to raise a question in your minds—something like "Why does she think statements of purpose are so important?"—that I could respond to. Statements of purpose serve several important functions. They set up a contractual relationship between writers and readers: writers promise to do certain things, commit themselves to performing certain speech acts in writing on the condition that readers also fulfill their end of the deal by reading what has been written.

Statements of purpose also help in clarifying writers' intentions for readers. Writers do not simply offer information neutrally, to no end, not even when they're simply fulfilling an assignment. They have specific purposes—to dispute or to confirm, to predict or to recount, to request or to command. Specifying what these purposes are at the beginning of a text facilitates the communication between writers and readers by relieving readers of the task of figuring out for themselves what's going on. Statements of purpose are also supposed to help writers make explicit to themselves what they are doing and to help them organize their texts. That is, students are told to write a statement of purpose in which they set up an order of steps and then to follow the order they set up in the rest of their paper. The instruction is deceiving in its simplicity: statements of purpose are not the beginning of the organizing process but rather the end result of a series of organizing decisions that are made throughout the writing process. Writers may

---

your utterance to have a particular function or purpose, such as informing or commanding). According to Austin, speech acts are composed of three separate acts performed simultaneously: a locutionary act (encoding a message in a linguistic form), an illocutionary act (the purpose the speaker has for speaking), and a perlocutionary act (the effect the speaker wishes to have on his or her audience).

2. That such strategies are not the sole property of writers is suggested by a P. Steiner cartoon published in *The New Yorker* (March 10, 1980): a collection of foreign dignitaries is seated around a conference table, and one man offers, "Look, everyone here loves vanilla, right? So let's start there."

start out with certain purposes and certain perceptions of the writing situation, but as they write, their purposes and the situation continually change in response to the acts being performed.

Sequences of Speech Acts

One thing writers do early in the planning of a piece of writing is to recast their purposes, which perhaps had been vague, into more specific speech acts. Writers order these acts into a sequence by taking into account the conditions for the successful performance of the acts and the conventional format associated with the genre of text that they wish to produce. Van Dijk explains how speech acts are sequenced:

> Two speech acts are connected if one is a *condition* (or consequence) of the other. Since each speech act, by definition, changes the (pragmatic) context, it is also able to influence the initial successfulness conditions of further (speech) acts. (1980, p. 181)

Van Dijk defines two ways in which speech acts are typically connected: by function and by conditional dependence. A speech act may explain a previous speech act, or draw a conclusion from a series of previous acts. More interestingly, a speech act may fulfill a condition for the performance of a subsequent speech act. Here is van Dijk's example:

> I have no watch. Can you please tell me the time?

As he explains, the first sentence in this sequence may, given the appropriate circumstances, function as an assertion, and the second as a request. But requests "must be motivated: It must be the case that the speaker cannot himself perform the requested action or give information asked for." Thus, the assertion of the first sentence provides the motivation that serves as a condition for the request (van Dijk, 1980, p. 182).

Van Dijk also explains that sequences of speech acts can form global speech acts, which can then be sequenced in the same ways as the individual speech acts of which they are composed. These global speech acts are the intentions writers begin with and/or work out in the course of writing; the statement of purpose represents their arrangement into a sequential and hierarchical structure. Sequences of global speech acts can become conventionalized, as with the conventional formats associated with genres of writing:

> . . . besides the usual conditional relations between speech acts we have more or less fixed functional categories. . . . functional relationships of this kind may become conventionalized to fixed *schemata*. . . . In that sense we could see the argumentation schema also as a pragmatic schema. . . . (van Dijk, 1980, pp. 183–184)

The parts of a speech described by Cicero and other classical rhetoricians are examples of such pragmatic schemata, as are their modern counterparts, which are offered to students as structures or "large frameworks" for persuasive papers.[3]

As yet, I have said nothing about organizing content as part of the planning of a piece of writing—a grievous omission, if the handbook I pull off my shelf at random is to be believed: "The best method for planning an essay is to devise an outline that shows major points as well as supporting information" (Fowler, 1980, p. 22). Although content certainly must be organized, I argue that the principles writers use to organize content come not from the content but from the writers' intentions, which are compounded of the writers' own desires and the characteristics of the particular communicative situation. The place to start in organizing a piece of writing is with these intentions and with an analysis of the writing situation. As van Dijk says:

> It may be the case that *the formation of semantic macrostructures* [whole message structures] *is determined by the pragmatic constraints of the context.* We assume that motivations, plans, interaction, and goals are often primary hence also the speech acts that are part of the interaction. What is relevant to the content, then, and hence also to the semantic macrostructure, depends on the specific global speech act(s) that must be performed. (1980, p. 195)

Intentions and Goals

The importance of both pragmatic and semantic intentions in writing has been noticed by other rhetoricians recently. Speaking at a conference on "Literacy and Language Use" held at the University of Southern California on November 14, 1981, Joe Williams maintained that the "crucial issue" in discourse is "pragmatic bite"—what the writer is doing with the discourse. Widdowson states that well-formed discourse is both coherent and cohesive, coherence being a property of the pragmatic structure of discourse and cohesion being a property of the semantic structure (1978, pp. 24–29).[4] Augustine and Winterowd distinguish rhetorical (pragmatic) and semantic intentions as two parts of writers' "superintentions" and conclude that "coherence results in large part from well formed intentions that are appropriate to audiences" (n.d., p. 26).

Flower and Hayes have incorporated an intuitive notion of this distinction into their model of the composing process. In the planning stage they advocate "shifting from focusing on your topic (what you

3. See Winterowd (1981, p. 267) and Lauer, Montague, Lunsford, and Emig (1981, p. 174).

4. Widdowson, like van Dijk, demonstrates in detail how speech acts can be sequenced, but he limits his discussion to the structure of paragraphs.

know) to focusing on your goal (what you want to do with what you know)" (1977, p. 453). They break down writers' goals into four groups, those focused on the reader, the writer (persona), the meaning, and the text (1980, p. 24), and they explain that writers make their goals operational by developing subgoals. Pointing to an example of a writer of a letter of application, Flower notes: "He established a goal ('I want to convince the congressman I'm the best candidate') and then made the goal operational by exploring *how* he could convince the congressman" (Flower, 1981, pp. 63–64). Unfortunately, Flower and Hayes never define their notion of "goal," other than to say that "the goals writers give themselves are both procedural . . . and substantive" (1981a, p. 372).[5] Nor do they explain how to distinguish the different types of goals.

A useful way to think about writers' goals is to see them as their intentions. There are three distinguishable types of intentions. Writers' intentions vis-à-vis the reader are among those that rhetoricians have studied since antiquity: how to persuade, how to arouse emotions, how to incite. These are all *perlocutionary* intentions, intentions to affect an audience in some way. Writers' intentions vis-à-vis their own desires involve having the reader understand that particular speech acts are being performed, such as informing, promising, or dissenting (and thus having readers understand that they are the kind of people who would perform these particular acts in this kind of situation); these are *illocutionary* intentions.[6] Writers' intentions vis-à-vis the meaning are to express propositions and to link them together in an overall semantic structure; these are the intentions that are usually made explicit in formal outlines of a piece of writing and that represent part of writers' *locutionary* intentions, intentions to be understood to be saying something. Another part of writers' locutionary intentions are intentions vis-à-vis the text: writers seek to ensure that the message is understandable by encoding it in the conventional phonetic, orthographic, morphemic, and syntactic structures of the language and by using conventional formats.

This taxonomy of intentions clarifies how past, present, and future rhetorical and linguistic investigations can be used to fill in Flower and Hayes's general model. In this chapter, I will demonstrate how the descriptions of writers' illocutionary intentions offered by speech act

5. For a more complete discussion of this and other problems in Flower and Hayes's model, see Cooper and Holzman (1983).

6. Specifying illocutionary intentions is a way of choosing a persona: it involves assessing the relationship between writers and readers, particularly in the areas of authority and knowledge, and assessing other aspects of the situation, such as the level of seriousness or formality. Thus, only writers who are in a position of authority can choose to command; only writers who know something readers don't know can choose to inform; and writers who have advice to offer might suggest or recommend depending on how sure they are of the advice and how seriously it appears the readers will take it.

theory help writers to generate plans to achieve the goals they have set themselves.

First, however, I want to emphasize something about the distinction between illocutionary and perlocutionary intentions. Illocutionary intentions are fully in the control of the writer or speaker; perlocutionary intentions are not. Of course, writers may (and often do) wish to convince, frighten, or arouse as well as to assert, forbid, or promise. But their success in convincing, frightening, or arousing depends heavily on the inclinations of their readers, some of which are knowable and some of which are not. (Note that statements of purpose that propose perlocutionary intentions sound odd: "In this paper I will convince you that. . . .") Success in asserting, forbidding, and promising depends completely on fulfilling known conditions. As long as you express a proposition along with your belief in the proposition and your intention that your audience form or hold a like belief, you will be taken to have asserted something.[7] Furthermore, the conditions on illocutionary acts explicitly dictate what to do to fulfill them. A condition on a recommendation, for example, is that you believe there is good reason for your reader to act. Thus, one thing to do before recommending something is to detail the reason or reasons you believe your reader should act as you are recommending.

Conditions on Speech Acts

At some level, everyone knows the conditions on speech acts, for they are the result of tacit agreements enabling communication within speech communities. But spelling out the conditions as they apply to the communicative situation of writing allows us to see more clearly how skilled writers create coherent, effective pieces of writing. I have derived the conditions on written speech acts from the taxonomy of speech acts developed by Bach and Harnish (1979, pp. 41–55; see Table 5-1) and from my adaptation of Grice's maxims for conversation (1975, pp. 45–46; see Table 5-2). Bach and Harnish propose four categories: constatives (expressions of beliefs), directives (expressions of attitudes toward actions), commissives (expressions of intentions to act), and acknowledgments (expressions of feelings toward hearers). Within each category they discriminate a number of types of speech acts; I have represented these types with one of the illocutionary verbs that typically are used to perform the act. Constatives are the largest category, containing fifteen types, and they are probably the most prominent category in writing.

7. This is not to say that speakers are never insincere or unsure of their assertions (or other speech acts), nor that they never wish to mislead their hearers. The conditions simply explain what speakers do *if* they wish their assertions (or other speech acts) to be considered sufficient, sincere, true, and relevant assertions.

Table 5-1. Taxonomy of Speech Acts

CONSTATIVES: Expressions of belief together with expressions of an intention that the audience form (or continue to hold) a like belief. In the particular descriptions below, belief and intention are considered to be tacit in the expression.

You *assert* if you express a proposition.

You *predict* if you express a proposition about the future.

You *recount* if you express a proposition about the past.

You *describe* if you express that someone or something consists of certain features.

You *ascribe* if you express that a feature applies to someone or something.

You *inform* if you express a proposition that your audience does not yet believe.

You *confirm* if you express a proposition along with support for it.

You *concede* if you express a proposition contrary to what you would like to or previously did believe.

You *retract* if you express that you no longer believe a proposition.

You *assent* if you express belief in a proposition already under discussion.

You *dissent* if you express disbelief in a proposition already under discussion.

You *dispute* if you express reason(s) not to believe a proposition already under discussion.

You *respond* if you express a proposition that has been inquired about.

You *suggest* if you express some, but insufficient, reason(s) to believe a proposition.

You *suppose* if you express that it is worth considering the consequences of a proposition.

DIRECTIVES: Expressions of an attitude toward some prospective action by the audience together with an intention that the attitude be taken as a reason to act.

You *request* if you express that you desire your audience to act.

You *ask* if you express that you desire to know whether or not a proposition is true.

You *command* if you express that your authority is reason for your audience to act.

You *forbid* if you express that your authority is reason for your audience to refrain from acting.

You *permit* if you express that your audience's action is possible by virtue of your authority.

You *recommend* if you express the belief that there is good reason for your audience to act.

COMMISSIVES: Expressions of intentions to act together with expressions of belief that such expressions obligate you to act.

You *promise* if you express that you intend to act.

You *offer* if you express that you intend to act if and when your audience desires it.

ACKNOWLEDGMENTS: Expressions of feelings toward the audience: apologies, condolences, congratulations, greetings, thanks.

A writer faces several important tasks in organizing a sequence of speech acts and successfully performing them: ensuring that the reader knows that the conditions on the act being performed have been fulfilled, and ensuring that the reader will accept the act as appropriate in form, relevant, sufficient, and sincere. How to ensure appropriateness and sufficiency has been written about extensively under other names.

Table 5-2. Grice's Maxims for Conversation

For a written illocutionary act to succeed, it must be clear to both writer and reader that these conditions have been fulfilled:

Appropriateness (Manner)
The act is as perspicuous, unambiguous, brief, organized, and consistent as is necessary in the situation in which it occurs.

Sufficiency (Quantity)
The act is as complete as is necessary for the reader to understand what act has been performed.

Relevance (Relation)
The act is connected to the needs and desires of the writer and reader.

Sincerity (Quality)
The act accords with the writer's beliefs, feelings, and capabilities and is supported by evidence and/or reasons.

Appropriateness is ensured by using formal organizational schemas, various devices for indicating connections, and syntactic devices for indicating the relations among and status of pieces of information.[8] Sufficiency is what audience analysis is largely concerned with; to ensure sufficiency the writer must be fairly certain of what the reader already knows. And because the sufficiency of successive illocutionary acts depends on whether information is offered in the right order, sufficiency is the central concern of most traditional outlines of content. How to ensure relevance and sincerity has received less attention; thus, in what follows, I will have more to say about them than about appropriateness and sufficiency.

Appropriateness

Achieving appropriateness in form can influence the overall organization of a piece of writing, especially in genres that have specified formats, such as newspaper stories and reports of scientific research. And, on a smaller scale, appropriateness in form is what writers are concerned with when they predict and summarize the organization of their writing, make transitions, and arrange given and new information within sentences. In the planning stage of writing, appropriateness is usually less of a concern than sufficiency, relevance, and sincerity; it becomes more of a concern in the revising stage.

8. For a useful summary of recent research on these schemas and devices, see Dillon (1981, Chapters 3 and 5).

Sufficiency

Fulfilling the sufficiency condition is notoriously difficult for beginning writers, and problematic for all writers. Providing enough information so that readers can understand clearly what writers believe or feel, what *writers want* readers to do, or what writers are committing themselves to do depends on knowing what readers know already and what they need to know. Writers try to analyze readers' knowledge and beliefs in advance, but, also, as writers and readers together progress through a text, some of what readers know is what they have read in the text so far. Thus, in writing this chapter, one thing I assumed about you at the outset was that you have some knowledge of speech act theory (though I do provide references to and notes on background information for those of you who don't, as I am ever anxious to please everyone). One thing I did not assume was that you have explicit statements of the conditions on various speech acts foremost in your minds. Only after I had asserted those conditions in Tables 5-1 and 5-2 could I successfully describe what I was doing by referring to the conditions.

Relevance

CONSTATIVES

Ensuring that an act is relevant is largely a matter of showing how it is motivated by the communicative situation. Constatives can be difficult to connect to a situation. The easiest cases are informing and responding, where readers' desires to have new information can be the motivation. Reporters' communications are predicated on the general public's desire to know what is happening in Washington, London, Rome, Hong Kong; gossips gain an audience by exploiting people's appetite for the intimate details of other people's lives. Abby Van Buren and Ann Landers ensure the relevance of their advice by responding to published letters from readers; memo writers often indicate the relevance of their memos by prefacing them with a heading such as *"Re:* Your request for information concerning application procedures."

The acts of conceding, retracting, assenting, dissenting, and disputing are not too difficult to make relevant; writers simply get a proposition under discussion somehow, and then their desire to express an opinion about the proposition can motivate the act.[9] And if the writing situation is one in which someone else has made a proposition the topic of

9. Cf. Bach and Harnish: *"Concessives, retractives, assentives, dissentives,* and *disputatives* all involve a presumption about the contextual relevance of the expressed belief" (1979, p. 45).

discussion, writers' acts will automatically be relevant: writing a letter to the editor is easier than writing the editorial to which the letter is a response. Getting a proposition under discussion is what is difficult, and the rest of the constatives all involve this task. Asserting, predicting, recounting, describing, ascribing, confirming, suggesting, and supposing —especially because they express beliefs not necessarily new to the reader—in themselves carry only the motivation of an individual writer's desire to express something. Writers in a position of authority, who know their readers must pay attention to their every utterance, can depend on this motivation to make constatives relevant. Supreme Court Justices' assertions of how laws are to be interpreted are relevant by virtue of their authority (though even these could be considered to be further motivated by the actions of lower courts). In letters to friends, writers can also depend on readers' willingness to accept their desire for self-expression as a motivation. But it is more often the case that writers must depend on something else in the communicative situation to ensure the relevance of their contribution.

Writers who can induce readers to want to know something can assert, recount, describe, ascribe, or inform by way of performing an act of responding. Indeed, writers can use these acts to induce readers to want to know something. If, for example, writers assert something well known to readers, readers may want to know why this was done (a strategy I used in the *exordium* of this chapter). If writers recount something not well known to readers, readers may want to know more about it. If a proposition addresses an unsettled or controversial question, writers can always confirm it, the motivation being our general desire to know the truth. At any point beyond the beginning of a piece of writing, these acts can be motivated by a need to sum up. Finally, writers can motivate an act of asserting, recounting, describing, ascribing, or informing if performing the act fulfills a condition for another act. For example, writers may inform in order to confirm, or ascribe in order to recommend. In van Dijk's example (p. 111), the speaker asserts in order to request.

Note that the difficulties involved in getting a proposition under discussion by making it relevant to readers' needs and desires account for some of the introductory strategies offered to beginning writers— the use of commonplaces; of interesting narrations, descriptions, or surprising facts; of the posing of controversial questions. And the difficulties of making assertions relevant, especially at the beginning of a piece of writing, may explain why writers are so reluctant to assert their theses in their opening paragraphs. Few writers are so confident of their command over their readers that they dare rely on it to secure the relevance of—and thus the successful understanding of—their main point. The role of authority in making assertions relevant is attested to by another introductory strategy, that of quoting an expert[10], and then assenting to his or her proposition.

DIRECTIVES AND ACKNOWLEDGMENTS

The condition that speech acts be relevant is most problematic with constatives because beliefs must somehow be tied to the needs and desires of writers and readers. Directives and acknowledgments, as they are expressions of attitudes and feelings, will be relevant if the attitudes and feelings they express are relevant in the situation. Writers can forbid others to quote them in notes attached to unpublished manuscripts, for their action can be seen to be motivated by their right to control the dissemination of their words. (Publication is a partial renunciation of this right in favor of some other desire—the pursuit of knowledge through the free exchange of ideas, for example—and thus writers' acts of forbidding any quotation of their published works would in most situations be considered irrelevant.)

COMMISSIVES

Commissives, as expressions of intentions to act, achieve relevance on the basis of either writers' or readers' needs or desires for the act. Promises are considered relevant when readers desire the act, whether or not writers desire it (for example, a guarantee) or when writers desire the act, whether or not readers desire it (for example, a threat). For offers to be relevant, writers must believe it possible that readers desire the act. Parents' letters of advice to their grown children are often unwelcome because such an offer implies that the child needs the advice.

Sincerity

CONSTATIVES

Fulfilling the sincerity conditions on constatives enjoins writers to express propositions they believe in and have evidence to support. Beginning writers often naively try to make clear to their readers that the sincerity condition is fulfilled by prefacing their constatives with the assertion "I believe." Of course, one reason this move fails is that it

---

10. Quoting can be an act of either asserting something well known or informing about something new.

betrays doubt of the "methinks she doth protest too much" variety. But the move is more fundamentally undermined by writers' lacking the authority over their readers needed to guarantee the success of their assertions. Unlike a doctor expressing belief in the efficacy of a new cure for cancer or a well-known literary critic expressing belief in a particular approach to literature, writers cannot ask readers to believe them on the mere basis of their own belief in their beliefs (unless, of course, the topic is one on which writers are expert—their own lives, for example).[11]

Demonstrating that there is evidence for the beliefs being expressed demands the most attention of a writer performing constatives. The evidence necessary varies with particular speech acts and includes appeals to authority and criteria, citation of sources, and references to experiments, observations, and reasoning processes. Assertions and predictions rely on the authority of writers to establish not only their relevance but also their validity: the personal knowledge, skill, and veracity of writers are the evidence offered in support of the assertion or prediction. No one believes writers who simply assert that capital punishment deters murder, just as no one believed David Stockman's economic predictions for some time after he revealed that his previous predictions had been largely fictitious. For this reason, texts rarely begin with assertions or predictions, but rather with some act that establishes the writers' authority. Writers may, for example, recount personal experiences with capital punishment to establish their authority to assert something about it. Or writers may inform readers of facts the possession of which gives them the authority to assert that capital punishment deters murder.

Assertions also vary in the strength with which writers hold a belief, from the relatively weak case of alleging to the strong case of avowing; thus the amount of authority writers must establish in order to assert successfully also varies. In contrast, establishing the authority to concede or retract is much easier: all writers have to do is make clear that they previously believed, or wanted to believe, a proposition they no longer believe, which is something they can assert on their own authority.

To ensure the sincerity of a description, writers must make sure that the criteria being applied to derive the description are known by the readers. Descriptions vary in what they apply to and what modes of

---

11. Writers also have difficulties making sure readers know when the sincerity condition is intentionally *not* being fulfilled, as in the case of irony. To succeed, writers must somehow ensure that their readers know enough about their beliefs to know when they are intentionally contradicting themselves to make a point indirectly. For further discussion of how writers say things indirectly, see Cooper (1981).

thought they appeal to. For example, diagnosing is aimed at finding causes; classifying, at fitting the object of description into a category; and evaluating, at measuring the object of description against a standard. But all descriptions depend for their credibility on readers knowing what criteria are being used, *and* on readers believing that these are the correct criteria to use.

Take, for example, the standard assignment to describe a place you are familiar with. If a student decides to describe her dormitory room, her familiarity with her room partly establishes the credibility of her description of it, but she must also describe the features her readers expect to read about. If she writes only about the floor and ceiling, her readers will not accept her writing as a description of her room (or will understand her act as something other than a description—an ascription of inadequacy as a room, perhaps). Sometimes writers can assume that the criteria for a description are shared knowledge between writers and readers. If this is not the case, writers must inform the readers of the criteria, or confirm the criteria (if they will be considered unusual by the readers), or dissent from or dispute the criteria that the readers would normally expect to be used.

Establishing the credibility of an act of recounting, informing, or responding is simply a matter of informing the reader of the source of the information. Of course, the reader must also accept the source as a reliable one, which is sometimes a problem when the writer is the primary source. But in recounting what happened when the local fire hall burned down, the writer need only assert that he or she was on the scene (and demonstrate that she was relatively sober and sane) to establish the credibility of the recounting.

When confirming a proposition, a writer must express support that is the result of a "truth-seeking procedure" (Bach & Harnish, 1979, p. 43). What truth-seeking procedure is appropriate depends in part on the field in which writers are writing; the procedure could be an experiment, an observation, or a logical argument. For example, when Jared Diamond confirmed the existence of the golden-crested bowerbird (long thought to be extinct), his procedure was personal observation: he saw thirty individual birds and discovered eight bowers. And he established the validity of his truth-seeking procedure by describing the birds, their bowers, and their courtship ritual in terms that most ornithologists will assent to. Interestingly, this confirmation was embedded in Lee Dembart's act of informing the readers of the *Los Angeles Times* that Diamond had confirmed the existence of the birds. Dembart ensured the credibility of his act by establishing the authority of his source: he described Diamond as "a UCLA scientist" (November 11, 1981, p. 1).

To establish the credibility of acts of ascribing, assenting, dissenting, disputing, or suggesting, writers may assert, inform, confirm, or suggest reasons that support their speech acts. In an article on the effects of "consciousness of correctness," Nutter dissents from any view that opposes "children's 'natural,' 'vigorous' language" to the "'artificial' language of the classroom" (1982, p. 167). She backs up her dissent by asserting that the more formal language used in classrooms is also used in many situations outside the classroom, and thus is not artificial.

Suggesting and supposing are the weakest types of constatives; Bach and Harnish note that these acts "express not even a weak belief that P, but only the belief that there is reason to believe that P or that (because it is possible or plausible that P is true) it is worth considering the consequences of P" (1979, p. 45). Writers may sometimes want to assert the reasons for supposing a proposition, just as they at times assert the reasons for suggesting a proposition. But more crucially, writers must assert, predict, describe, inform, confirm, or suggest the consequences of the proposition that is being supposed. Say a writer is asked to address a problem that will face her during the next year. If she supposes (with good reason) that clothing fashions will soon change radically, she must at least suggest consequences—the need to keep up with changing fashions will impose a further burden on her already shaky finances or will cause an identity crisis. The consequences establish the credibility of the supposition; changing fashions indeed cause a problem for her, which she may simply assert as a problem, go on to describe in more detail, or perhaps suggest alternate consequences to.

DIRECTIVES

Making sure that the sincerity conditions on directives are fulfilled involves providing information or instructions that will enable readers to perform the act specified and/or establishing reasons for performing the act. If writers sincerely request an action, ask for information, or make a recommendation, they also do whatever is possible to enable the reader to perform the action. For example, when organizations like the League of Women Voters send out communications requesting you to vote, they enclose information on the candidates and issues you will be asked to vote on and they tell you where to go to vote. Writers who ask whether a proposition is true or not may suggest sources in which readers may find the answer or may assert their criteria for a correct answer. And writers who recommend a particular diet explain the rules in order to enable readers to follow the regimen.

Readers must also understand that requests, queries, and recommendations are motivated by one or more reasons before they will take such directives as sincere. So writers inform or confirm the reason or reasons for the act before directing it (unless the reason is perfectly obvious). The person in van Dijk's example who requests information

about the time (p. 111) establishes the reason for the request by informing the hearer that he has not the means to discover the time for
himself; he has no watch. And in making a recommendation, writers not
only must enable readers to perform the recommended act but also
must confirm the proposition that performing the act will be somehow
beneficial. If writers wish to command, forbid, or permit, they must
first establish authority over readers (unless such authority is obvious
in the situation), for their authority is the reason for the act directed by
these illocutionary verbs.

COMMISSIVES AND ACKNOWLEDGMENTS

That the sincerity conditions on commissives and acknowledgments are
fulfilled is most often shared knowledge between writers and readers.
From our habitual analysis of communicative situations we find ourselves
in, we usually know whether writers can do the things they promise to do
and whether readers desire the act that has been offered. But promises
and offers can be prefaced with assertions of the reasons writers and/or
readers desire the act or should desire it. For example, because I assume
you want to know the research applications of my pragmatic theory of
form, I promise to spell them out for you, starting in the next paragraph.
And acknowledgments can be prefaced with assertions of the reasons
for the writers' feeling as they do. For example, because I know this
discussion of the conditions on speech acts is getting long, and thus is
taking up time you would probably rather be spending watching *Masterpiece Theatre* or fixing your car or worrying about whether the Dean likes
you, I sincerely apologize for monopolizing your attention.

Research Implications

Within any language community, the conditions on the successful performance of speech acts are well agreed on. This is just to say that
speech acts are conventional, and the employment of these conventions
by writers can be investigated in the same ways as other conventions
are. One line of research might analyze texts to see what standard
patterns of speech acts are being employed. Many questions arise. How
do these patterns interact with and support the conventionalized organizational schemata, such as Cicero's parts of a speech, or the modes of
development, such as cause-and-effect or analogy? How do the patterns
interact with other writing strategies, such as the three classical modes
of persuasion: ethos, logos, and pathos? How do the patterns interact
with lower-level writing conventions, such as punctuation, syntax, and
the organization of given versus new information in a sentence? How

do the patterns vary in different writing contexts as genre, audience, and writer change? Do individual writers develop idiosyncratic patterns that in part define their style? Do the patterns change over time? Do the patterns change from one language community to another—for example, from business writing to scientific writing?

A second line of research might simply test the hypothesis that training writers to be aware of speech act conditions as they write will improve their writing. One way to measure improvement focuses on the product: holistic scores of essays from students who have received instruction in how to form series of speech acts could be matched against scores of essays from students who have received traditional instruction in organization. Another way to measure improvement focuses on the process: students could be instructed not only to plan their writing in terms of illocutionary intentions but also to use these intentions as criteria in self-assessing their first drafts. Students could be instructed to ask these questions about their first drafts: What is my primary intention in this piece of writing? What conditions do I need to fulfill in order to successfully achieve this intention? Have I fulfilled these conditions? The same questions could then be asked about sections of the piece of writing.

Comparing the resulting self-assessing worksheets and changes between first and final drafts would reveal whether the questions had guided effective revisions. For example, a student whose primary intention was to confirm that aliens wishing to become U.S. citizens need better legal advice might discover in assessing her first draft that she had not supported her proposition with a truth-seeking procedure and thus had not completely fulfilled the sincerity condition on confirmations. In her revision, she might add the needed support. Or, if she found it impossible to muster the support necessary, she might change her primary intention from a confirmation to a suggestion, and make revisions in her draft that make clear to her readers that she is suggesting a proposition and, thus, that she believes the reasons offered in support of the proposition are sufficient only to make the proposition worthy of consideration.

Finally, a speech act model of writers' planning processes might be used to reanalyze data from other research, such as Matsuhashi's research on pauses (1981) and Flower and Hayes's protocol research. For example, in the third episode of one of Flower and Hayes's published protocols, an expert writer is discussing how he will describe his job (English professor) "for a young thirteen to fourteen year-old teenage female audience" (1981b, p. 235). He first considers explicitly how he will make his description relevant to his reader: "I suppose the most interesting thing about my job would be that it is highly unlikely that it would seem at all interesting to someone of that age" (p. 235). The sincerity condition is partly fulfilled by his presumed familiarity with his job, but he also uses one of several standard criteria for job descriptions: he describes a typical day's work: *"Can you imagine [. . .] starting to work*—to work *by reading*—*reading the manuscript*—*of a Victorian writer . . .* (p. 235). Such an analysis fills in some of the details of the "overall plan" Flower and Hayes see at work in this episode (p. 236).

The conditions on speech acts, because they offer a description of behavior, can guide the performance of the acts they describe. Writers juggle the whole range of goals—perlocutionary, illocutionary, and locutionary—as they write, and plans associated with all these goals help them to discover what they want to say and to structure their writing. But if van Dijk and Williams are right in stressing the importance of "pragmatic constraints" or "pragmatic bite," then plans for achieving illocutionary intentions may be the most essential part of writers' repertoires.

ACKNOWLEDGMENTS

A version of this chapter was presented at the Convention on College Composition and Communication in Dallas, March 27, 1981. It had its genesis several years ago in a discussion with Robin Brown and Robert Collins on what we would tell the instructors we were training to say about organization, and I hereby acknowledge my debt to them.

REFERENCES

Augustine, D., & Winterowd, W. R. *Intention and response: Speech acts and the sources of composition.* Undated manuscript.

Austin, J. L. *How to do things with words.* Cambridge, Mass.: Harvard University Press, 1962.

Bach, K., & Harnish, R. M. *Linguistic communication and speech acts.* Cambridge, Mass.: MIT Press, 1979.

Burke, K. *Counterstatement.* Berkeley: University of California Press, 1968. (Originally published, 1931.)

Cooper, M. M. Context as vehicle: Implicatures in writing. In M. Nystrand (Ed.), *What writers know: The language, process, and structure of written discourse.* New York: Academic Press, 1981.

Cooper, M. M., & Holzman, M. Talking about protocols. *College Composition and Communication,* 1983, *34.*

van Dijk, T. A. *Macrostructures: An interdisciplinary study of global structures in discourse, interaction, and cognition.* Hillsdale, N.J.: Lawrence Erlbaum, 1980.

Dillon, G. L. *Constructing texts: Elements of a theory of composition and style.* Bloomington: Indiana University Press, 1981.

Flower, L. S. *Problem-solving strategies for writing.* New York: Harcourt Brace Jovanovich, 1981.

Flower, L. S., & Hayes, J. R. Problem-solving strategies and the writing process. *College English,* 1977, *39,* 449–461.

Flower, L. S., & Hayes, J. R. The cognition of discovery: Defining a rhetorical problem. *College Composition and Communication,* 1980, *31,* 21–32.

Flower, L. S., & Hayes, J. R. A cognitive process theory of writing. *College Composition and Communication*, 1981, *32*, 365–387. (a)

Flower, L. S., & Hayes, J. R. The pregnant pause: An inquiry into the nature of planning. *Research in the Teaching of English*, 1981, *15*, 229–243. (b)

Fowler, H. R. *Little, Brown Handbook*. Boston: Little, Brown, 1980.

Grice, H. P. Logic and conversation. In P. Cole & J. L. Morgan (Eds.), *Syntax and semantics* (Vol. 3: *Speech acts*). New York: Academic Press, 1975.

Lauer, J., Montague, G., Lunsford, A., & Emig, J. *Four worlds of writing*. New York: Harper & Row, 1981.

Manning, P. J. *The Intimation Ode and Vergil's Fourth Eclogue*. Paper presented at annual meeting of Modern Language Association, Houston, December 29, 1980.

Matsuhashi, A. Pausing and planning: The tempo of written discourse production. *Research in the Teaching of English*, 1981, *15*, 113–134.

Nutter, N. The effects of "consciousness of correctness" on amount, fluency, and syntax of adolescents' speech. *Research in the Teaching of English*, 1982, *16*, 149–170.

Widdowson, H. G. *Teaching language as communication*. Oxford, England: Oxford University Press, 1978.

Winterowd, W. R. *The contemporary writer* (2nd ed.). New York: Harcourt Brace Jovanovich, 1981.

The composing process

11

The most important development in composition research over the last decade has been the study of the composing process: the ways writers discover ideas, formulate goals and plans, express their ideas, assess their own writing, revise, and edit. The initial case study research on the composing process was primarily directed toward defining global stages or components. Emig's (1971) landmark work generated categories such as reformulating, stopping, reflecting, and changing—categories that were used anecdotally to discuss high school writers' composing processes in case studies.

Since Emig's study, researchers have focused on more specific and carefully defined components of the composing process. They have developed elaborate content-analysis category systems derived from a variety of models of the process. As noted in Part I, Flower and Hayes's categories evolved from a problem-solving model of composing. Beach and Eaton's taxonomy of self-assessing strategies, which is presented in Chapter 7, partially stems from a pragmatic model of discourse. In addition to offering more concrete information about behaviors and cognitive processes during composing, these researchers and other argue that the composing process is not a linear sequence of stages, as suggested by earlier studies. They point to a recursive process during which the writer may consciously or subconsciously attend to a variety of constraints, sometimes balancing them almost simultaneously, sometimes shifting from a conscious awareness of one to a focus on another.

Voice in the Writing Process

The first chapter in Part II examines the quality of "voice" in writing. One of the charges leveled against writing instruction by Ken Macrorie, Peter Elbow, Donald Murray, and others is that much student writing is inauthentic, bland academic prose because students are not encouraged to write in a natural, communicative way. Students tend to distance themselves from their writing, adopting a somewhat strained, formal "voice." It remains unclear, however, what factors or incentives within an academic context could develop a sense of voice.

Newkirk's case-study analysis in Chapter 6 shows one student's evolution from the distanced, inauthentic "voice" to a stronger sense of involvement and purpose, particularly in writing about a personal incident. Using the student's own perceptions and writing, Newkirk demonstrates that a change can occur in attitude toward writing—that a student can discover how writing can be used to gain insights about personal experiences, and that an emerging power over voice significantly alters the writing process.

Revision and Self-Assessing

In recent years, revision has become a central focus in composing-process research. As Bridwell (1980) argues, the changes writers make as they compose are direct evidence of a dissonance model of composing. Writers attempt to reconcile their intentions with their texts; when their texts conflict with their intentions, they must resolve this conflict or dissonance by making revisions. Or writers may discover that they need to redefine their intentions because their text implies a different set of intentions. All of this reconciliation takes time. Unfortunately, the traditional outline–rough draft–edit model of writing forces students to collapse their production into one often relatively final drafting session that discourages extensive revision. Another reason for lack of revising is that students do not understand that revision can go beyond simple rewriting or correcting to involve extensive re-seeing of their ideas, organization, and style. Sommers (1978) describes a "cleanliness" theme in the definitions students give of revision, implying that they often see it as a tidying up of their initial efforts.

In their study in Chapter 7, Beach and Eaton drew on a cognitive-processing, problem-solving orientation as they analyzed self-assessing forms filled out by college freshmen for evidence of goals and judgments that might have influenced their revision processes. Their category system for analyzing descriptive and judgmental inferences is particularly appropriate for the study group data. Beach and Eaton also examined the effects of instruction on self-assessing, finding that students who had received instruction were more likely to make certain kinds of inferences than students who had not been taught to make them.

Children's Composing Processes

Donald Graves and his associates at the New Hampshire Writing Process Laboratory have conducted the most extensive investigations of children's composing processes (see Walshe, 1982). Employing an ethno-graphic approach, these investigators examined individual children's composing processes in the classroom context, carefully recording each child's behavior over periods of months or years and noting the stimuli that influenced them. Because growth in writing ability is a slow process, their work gives us documentation of development across significant periods of time, offering a major advantage over short-term experi-mental designs. However, some critics have charged that the results of the work are not explicitly grounded in child development or language development theory.

Cioffi's study in Chapter 8 is a part of the New Hampshire work. He examined the writing activities of two primary-age children over a two-year period in order to trace the development of their writing abilities and to study the connections between their reading and their writing. Basing the study on previous research in oral language develop-ment and using methods for studying the composing process developed by Perl (1979), he was able to explain some of his results in terms of previous research.

Reading and Writing Connections

Galda's report in Chapter 9, examines in detail the connection between reading and writing that is often alluded to in studies of revision or the development of writing ability in children. Very few studies have been carried out in this area. Further research on the connection between reading and writing is essential to understanding more about how writers read and assess their own writing. For example, one specific comprehension skill is retrospective summary—the ability to review pre-vious material in order to comprehend new material. Just as a reader infers the "gist" or essential points in order to predict the logical devel-opment or direction of the material, a writer infers the essential points of what he or she is writing, judges what has been written, and predicts further development. Perl (1980) has called this process "retrospective structuring." In a recent study, Taylor and Beach (1981) found that reading instruction had a stronger effect on writing quality than did writing instruction.

In her literature review, Galda summarizes a number of recent studies of the skills involved as writers read their own writing. One of these, by Atwell (1980), employed a "blind writing" technique and found that better readers could bind together propositions in a more coherent manner than poorer readers.

A Psycholinguistic Model of Composing

In Chapter 10, Daiute reports a study of the psycholinguistic constraints that affect student writers as they attempt to produce sentences. By analyzing a collection of their syntactically garbled sentences, she developed a theoretical explanation for these errors based on the limits of memory for various constructions. In addition to contributing to a model of sentence production, Daiute's work offers an important hypothesis to account for particularly resistant error patterns. Countless hours spent instructing students in the terminology that describes sentence structure may miss the point if she is correct. Even if students understand these abstractions, they may still produce erroneous constructions because of the limits of memory. Her approach suggests some new directions both for composing process research and for instruction.

REFERENCES

Atwell, M. *The evolution of text: The interrelationship of reading and writing in the composing process.* Unpublished doctoral dissertation, Indiana University, 1980.

Bridwell, L. Revising strategies in twelfth grade students' transactional writing. *Research in the Teaching of English,* 1980, *14,* 197–222.

Emig, J. *The composing processes of twelfth graders.* Urbana, Ill.: National Council of Teachers of English, 1971.

Perl, S. The composing process of unskilled college writers. *Research in the Teaching of English,* 1979, *13,* 317–336.

Perl, S. Understanding composing. *College Composition and Communication,* 1980, *31,* 363–369.

Sommers, N. *Revision in the composing process: A case study of experienced writers and student writers.* Unpublished doctoral dissertation, Boston University, 1978.

Taylor, B., & Beach, R. *The effect of text-structure instruction on seventh grade students' comprehension and writing of expository text.* Paper presented at National Reading Conference, 1981.

Walshe, R. (Ed.). *"Children want to write . . ." Don Graves in Australia.* Exeter, N.H.: Heinemann Educational Books, 1982.

6

Anatomy of a breakthrough:
Case study of a college freshman writer

THOMAS NEWKIRK
Univesity of New Hampshire

> *What interests me in the stimulus–response situation is the hyphen.* —William Barrett

Until the last decade the writer's mind was viewed as a "black box." Researchers could monitor what went in and what came out. But the actual workings of that box, because they were hidden, were not thought to be appropriate subjects of inquiry. This view has changed, the major impetus being Emig's study (1971) of the composing process. A number of researchers have followed her lead, most notably Flower and Hayes (1980) and Perl (1979), all working with students at the college level, and Graves (1975, 1978–1980), Calkins (1980), and Sowers (in press), working with students at the elementary level. Larson (1980) has deemed this research the most productive currently being conducted in the field of composition.

There are, however, two shortcomings in much of the writing-process research being conducted. The first one, noted by Larson (1980), is that most researchers begin by giving the student a topic. In doing so, they fail to explore the process of choosing a topic. Further, the topics presented may have elicited behavior that is uncharacteristic of students writing on self-chosen topics.

A second limitation of many writing-process studies is their static nature. They describe, often in amazing detail, the composing behavior of the subjects, frequently contrasting the processes of beginning and experienced writers (Stallard, 1974; Pianko, 1979; Sommers, 1980; Flower & Hayes, 1980). It is one thing, though, to describe the writing processes of these two groups of writers; it is another to describe how one becomes the other—how the beginning writer develops into the proficient writer—to depict the incremental steps that the maturing writer makes. Longitudinal studies such as those conducted by Graves (1978–1980) and Bissex (1980) have the virtue of depicting these steps and describing the instructional context in which the steps are taken. In effect, these researchers have viewed the writing process not as an isolated episode or set of episodes, but as a part of a larger process of intellectual growth. The research reported below is an attempt to adapt some of Graves's research techniques to the examination of college freshman writers.

I will report on a study of four students taking Freshman English at the University of New Hampshire during the eight-week summer session. I set out to explore the following three questions:

1. What criteria does each student use to evaluate his or her work at the beginning of the course?
2. How does this evaluation process change over the term of the course?
3. To what element of the course might this change be attributed?

As the study progressed it became apparent that the subjects were providing information that went beyond the initial question of evaluation. Larger issues of how writers view the writing process, and of how they view themselves as writers, were explored and will form part of this report.

For the course, students were required to write three to five typewritten pages each week, with a major revision of a previous paper counted as a new paper. Students were allowed to choose their topics and modes of development, the only exception being the short (six- to eight-page) research paper that was required during the sixth week of the course. Class time was spent on writing exercises, the sharing of writing, and discussions of the essays in *The Little, Brown Reader* (Barnett & Stubbs, 1979). No grades were assigned until the end of the course. At that time the research paper and the best weekly paper were graded.

The instructor for the course (whom I will call Judy) was an experienced teaching assistant who has consistently received superior student evaluations and who is considered by both the current and the previous directors of the Freshman English Program as one of its most able instructors. Each week, besides meeting with the class as a whole, the instructor met with each student for a fifteen-minute conference.

On the first class day, I explained the project to the class and asked for volunteers. On that day I also distributed two papers written by previous freshmen and asked the class members and the teacher to evaluate them (Newkirk, 1980). Five of the twenty-five students volunteered, and from those, I chose four—two whose evaluations agreed with that of the instructor, and two whose evaluations differed from the instructor's. In this way I tried to ensure some range of critical perspective in the small sample.

I met with each student for a weekly thirty-minute interview before the student conferred with the instructor on a particular paper. During the interviews, I would ask the same questions:

1. What did the instructor say about your previous paper?
2. What did you consider to be the strengths and weaknesses of this piece?
3. How does this paper compare in terms of quality with your previous work?
4. What major changes have you made in revising it? Why have you made these changes?
5. Are there other changes that you want to make? What are they?
6. Could you tell me how you went about writing this paper?

During the interviews I would not make any value judgments about the student's work, and this impassiveness proved initially frustrating to two of the subjects.

In addition to obtaining the students' own evaluations, I made copies of the papers and all the rough drafts. I conducted an initial interview during which Judy and I discussed the first papers the subjects had written and a final interview in which we discussed the changes the students had made over the eight-week course.

The Case Study: Anne

All four of the students in the study eventually were able to accurately evaluate their work and revise it. I will report on Anne, a seventeen-year-old student who seemed to cover the most ground, telescoping the greatest change into the eight-week period. Not only was the change extensive, it was abrupt; her resistance to changing her writing process was strong, but when the change came it was dramatic and complete. While Anne's experience is clearly not typical, it is at least possible that her case illustrates—in heightened and intensified form—the development of many freshman writers.

Anne's reaction to the screening essay indicated that she was a student well drilled in the rules of the five-paragraph theme. She was severely critical of one of the papers that did not follow this model:

First paragraph should introduce the topic of discussion. . . . First sentence *should* introduce the reader to the thought streamlined. . . . [the middle section] should carry it through . . . then create a type of conclusion.

In the opening interview Anne explained that she had picked up this introduction–body–conclusion model in fifth or sixth grade.

Her own writing process did not follow this model, however. In the initial interview, she claimed that she was a "poetic" writer who had to be in the right mood to write. Once she was in that mood, she would wait for the first sentence and the rest would simply come. She would write the night before the assignment was due and would not revise. She claimed to write only for herself and not for other readers.

Anne had, in effect, drawn a tight circle around herself as a writer. She wrote when inspired; what she wrote was good if it re-created a mood for her; and if anyone else failed to get the same meaning, that was just too bad. The view of writing she held and that of a course emphasizing revision could not have been more mismatched; it was inevitable that conflict would occur. What follows is an account of how that conflict evolved and finally was resolved.

The scope of the conflict became even more apparent when Anne brought her first paper to the interview. It was titled "Writing" and began:

> Anticipation, Inspiration, Constipation . . . writer's disease. Every writer trys to outdo another in information, creativity, and writing presentation; and unfortunately forgets his purpose for writing. Half the great writers were great because they had an appeal to a sympathetic audience, and the other half because they wrote so intensely of things we didn't understand and thus we all considered them geniuses. They didn't seem to experience writer's disease . . . they didn't seem to experience anything but the joy of writing, (whatever that is . . .)

Later in the paper, Anne makes clear her view of herself as a writer:

> Anticipation; knowing that I'm super intelligent, have the ability and the imagination to outdo everyone. . . . Dickens, Dewey, Marx, Bach, and all the others! Anticipation to see that "A" in bright red ink, in a little circle, in the right hand corner at the bottom of the last page. Anticipation; watching the teacher's face fall . . . when it realizes that I'm a better writer.

The rest of the paper exhibited these same qualities—erratic and unsupported assertions, flippant asides to the reader, and barbs thrown at the teacher.

When asked to evaluate the paper, Anne said that if she were to compare it to her previous work, she would grade it an A:

> It's not that it's better. I always write A's. This is almost as if I'm talking aloud, thinking on paper. In all my English courses, that's how I carried it through. It all depends on what mood I'm in, but it always comes out good.

Naturally, then, she didn't think anything should be changed:

I don't think I would want to do anything more to it. I wouldn't want to add anything or take anything out. I think it's as long as it should be.

She felt that readers could "identify" with the piece, but when I asked about the fact that she had used "obstinate" and "great" as synonyms, she replied offhandedly:

"Obstinate" and "great" are a little different, but they can be the same. I suppose you're going to take it however you're going to take it.

She implied that if the reader didn't get her intended meaning, that was the reader's problem.

As this first paper indicates, it could be said that Anne came to the first conference prepared for hand-to-hand combat. Yet both teacher and student claimed it went well. Judy ignored the baiting and viewed the paper as a plea for her to listen. "It's a paper about Anne and the fact that she really wants someone to look at her as a writer or to see her as someone who is interesting or witty or thoughtful." Yet, how might this be done when the paper demonstrates little of these qualities?

I tried to let her know in every small and large way that she already had my attention; that she didn't need to work so hard; that I was interested in what she had done. I appealed to her sense of herself as a good writer and tried to help her find standards that would allow her to meet that goal.

Some of this subtlety was lost on Anne, but she was still encouraged by the first conference. When I asked what Judy's opinion of the paper was, Anne replied, "I think she liked it."

The writing during the next two weeks of the course showed no improvement,[1] but it was becoming more and more difficult for Anne to maintain her previous view of writing and writing quality. Her second paper was a fictional story about going blind. While it showed brief flashes of believable insight and detail, it was for the most part maudlin and unconvincing. It began:

I went to the doctor's one day. And then I'm told I will go blind. I asked, "How long?" . . . and the reply was, "within two or three weeks." My mom asked all the others. . . . Any hope for operations? Eye transplants? . . . "No." Special care? There was but I didn't hear it. When it starts to become apparent that my . . . time has come . . . ? "Call doctor immediately, bring me to the hospital immediately. Keep moisture on the eyes at all times. Or else I will need glass ones." We went home. I couldn't see clearly, tears were in the way. I'm only seventeen . . . just only . . . I saw my mother, she looked fuzzy, and older, and I saw a tear fall down her cheek.

---

1. Evaluations are those of the instructor unless otherwise indicated.

Again, the writing process was one of waiting for inspiration and then writing nonstop the first and only draft:

> . . . it just went. . . . Once I sit down and get my mind saying, "I'm going to write," I just put the paper in and stare at it and just go from there—no rough drafts.

At this interview, Anne maintained her view of writing as poetic self-expression not amenable to conscious analysis. When asked to locate the strengths and weaknesses of the paper, she replied that she didn't think in those terms. "I don't think there are any strong or weak points. I think it all is just there." Here I realized that the question itself made an assumption about writing—that it can be evaluated by criteria more objective than the mood of the writer when writing. Anne simply rejected that assumption.

Anne did express some concern that there was "no lead to prepare the reader." She had, in effect, violated the rule she had dogmatically asserted in her reaction to the first paper. When I asked whether her present approach was a new experiment, she again backed off. "No. It depends on my mood. There is no new or old way of writing for me. It depends on my emotions." If she had admitted to conscious experimentation, she would have been denying her previous view of unconscious mood-determined writing. So she again was denying the premise of a question.

There were, however, signs of change. She was beginning to worry about how her audience might react, and grudgingly admitted that she couldn't really ignore the fact that both Judy and I read her papers. Anne worried:

> When I read this paper, I can feel myself into it. I don't know if anyone else can feel themselves into it. I try to write so I know they will, but I can't tell.

When asked if this was a new concern, she replied:

> It's not a real concern because it gets the feeling to me. I mean, I don't want any of my stuff published. The only problem is I've got you and Judy to read these papers and I want to transmit some of the feeling to you. But if you don't get it, I'm not going to cry over it. I'm just concerned with how I feel.

In the conference on the paper, Judy suggested that for the next paper Anne get away from first-person narratives because, "She'd just create fictions that were maudlin, hysterical, sentimental, and didn't have much connection with things she knew much about." Dutifully, Anne obeyed and next week wrote her poorest paper, "Five Positive Aspects of Inflation," an attempt at Art Buchwaldish humor. The piece was similar to her first paper on writing, but if anything, even more disconnected.

Anne herself was dissatisfied with the paper, and for the first time offered critical reasons for her opinion:

> It's kind of scatterbrained. . . . This paper seems to bounce back and forth. Like when I say that I can spend money on food and later I say you can spend the money you save on clothes. It doesn't follow. The paper's not logical. Someone could tear this paper up if they tried. I had no statements backing up what I'm saying. It's just kind of a lot of junk.

It would seem that a critical perspective is emerging. But just as quickly, she backed away. I asked about the previous paper on blindness, whether she had ever written on that type of topic before (putting herself in the position of another person with problems), and whether the blindness paper was better than her earlier papers of that type. Again she rejected the premise:

> I cannot say better. I don't choose that word. Because all of the papers I put myself into I really put myself into. I can't play one against the other because they are all so real to me. I've never written on blindness before, but I've written on other subjects and they come out just as good.

So we had a dilemma. She could be critical of papers like "Five Positive Aspects of Inflation" only because she had no commitment to them.

The conference during the fourth week marked the turning point in the course for Anne. Anne said that Judy had encouraged her to "write about something that really happened to me." Judy's memory of the suggestion was more complete:

> I told her, "You don't write about traumatic events [here referring to the blindness paper] unless you know something about them." I remember a sort of guarded question at the time about whether I'd really want to know something that was so bizarre that I'd probably believe it less than the blindness paper. Some of her questions were almost catty. I couldn't tell if she were just baiting me. I probably said, "Well, you have to write about the stuff you really care about—know about. If it's important to you, write about it."

Judy thought that for Anne, the distinction between fact and fiction was not clear because Anne felt her own true experiences to be so utterly unbelievable.

This motif, the relation between fiction and reality, appeared in the breakthrough paper, "A Story Is Only a Story until We Live It." It was twice as long as Anne's other papers. It begins by putting the reader in a movie theater to watch a film of the traumatic event of her life—the day her father shot her mother:

The theatre was in blackness, bodies were pressed against each other, voices were jumbled and the smell of popcorn filled the air. Suddenly blinding light covered the screen and illuminated the audience. A young teenage girl, a middle aged woman, and a small boy were shown driving down a main road.

The reel continues. The car is cut off by the father, who drags the mother from the car as Anne tries to flag down a passing car for help. Unsuccessful, she runs into a nearby house and on the way hears a shot. Her nine-year-old brother follows her. Another shot. Finally Anne and her brother are pushed into the master bedroom:

> The two youngsters sit on the large, white bed. The girl puts her arms around the boy, stroking his hair murmuring words of affection, love and, most of all of hope. The camera zooms down to the boy's blood-covered feet, then back to the faces of the two. Another shot is heard, and both children smile, a tremulous but hopeful smile.
>
> I am the girl, the boy, my brother John, the woman who was shot, my mother, and the man doing the shooting, my socially nomenclated father. John and I were smiling because we thought the last bullet was . . . in his head.

The rest of the paper recounts the waiting at the hospital and the eventual news that her mother was out of danger.

The interview on this paper was the most extensive of the study. Anne, rather than expressing satisfaction at clearly her best paper, is dissatisfied. I asked if the paper had been hard to write:

> Yeah, because there's so much I'm leaving out and there's so much more. I mean, we still get letters from him and there's the trial. One thing after another. I wanted to keep going but I couldn't. . . . There's so many little things you notice, but when you sit to type them out they don't have the significance that they had at the moment. Because when it happened you just took it in; you didn't analyze—you just accepted. And it was real hard to write.

Again, the opening presented the most serious problems, but the paper did not just flow once that opening had been determined:

> . . . in my mind I had to keep going through that sequence, what happened, where it happened, how it happened. What were other people's reactions as well as my own. And some of the sentences were really hard for me to get the ideas into them, the actual feeling, it's kind of like you feel and you don't have the words in your mind to say what you feel. The whole paper was like that. You know, looking for words.

Now also she is willing to "play" this paper against the others:

> I was satisfied with them. There was no great point to them. There was no emotional breakthrough. They were papers. But this, I would like to work

with this. I don't know how I would go about it, but I would like to work with it.

At this point in the course, the changes in Anne went beyond her concept of writing. According to Judy, she was a different student in class:

> . . . [before this paper] the only time she would say anything was if she *knew* it. She would especially say it so it would be ill-timed—which is just the voice in these early papers. But after she had been in the course a few weeks and especially after she'd written this paper [she and I both knew she had made a change, it was so obvious], she actually began to *ask questions* in class.

The next week, the sixth of the course, was the last I had with Anne, although I did see the two papers that she wrote subsequent to that interview. In the interview the motif of fiction versus fact reappeared. Anne stated that she had started to revise the earlier paper but had ripped it up. Why?

> I just wasn't able to get the feeling across. I showed it to a couple of friends, and they said that "this isn't the way you'd do it, Anne." But I told them, "That's what I did." It just wasn't coming across the way I wanted it to, so I got very upset and tore it up.

Five weeks earlier she had bragged about how her writing "always comes out good."

Anne made another change in her composing process, a change that would have been unthinkable five weeks earlier: she made an outline. She had decided that she wanted to interweave information about the trial with her account of the shooting:

> It's going to be flashbacks to the actual shooting. I was going to start off with news headlines and go from there to the basic facts about why there is a trial, the importance of the trial, then kind of go back to what we went through, kind of tie it in with the shooting, the injustice we felt when we were going through it and the actual trial. I'd like to mesh it all together.

Anne had set a problem for herself that would intimidate an experienced journalist. In explaining her strategy, she made a distinction that would prove crucial for her next paper. She said she would try to be more "presentational, facts, more or less," rather than "emotional."

At the end of the interview I asked her to summarize the changes in herself as a writer:

> I start questioning as I go through sentences. And so I start thinking, "Is this clear enough?" I'm starting to get into the habit, I guess, of writing for other people. But I'm still having a lot of problems reading as though I were

the reader and not the writer. But I'm trying, which is one thing I never did before. I think that's the major thing, the way I'm reading papers.

What has caused this change?

> I think it's this paper that I'm writing right now. Because I know how I feel, but I want other people to understand and it's that trying to get the idea across, you know, the thoughts that went through your mind, that's really driving me crazy. It's the last paper that's done it.

The next week Anne handed in her research paper. Given the complex plans she had spoken about in the last interview, the research paper was something of a disappointment. It contained six pages of text, with much of the information straight out of the source books. The language is impersonal and passive—the utterly detached style of the freshman term paper:

> Of primary importance in the correction of child abuse and neglect is the growing understanding of the reason "why" it happens and an improvement in the financial budget allotted those organizations that might, otherwise, decrease the steadily increasing cases of child abuse and neglect.

When I read the paper, I put it in the same category with the inflation paper. It was something that she had dutifully completed but that was unrelated to her major interests. In her words, "just a paper."

But there were indications that this paper, inadequate as it might be as a research paper, was far more important for Anne. She covered the title page with her poetry:

> His buttocks were burned
> by cigarette butts
> and someone laughed when
> he began to cry.

She also included pictures of abused children at the end of the report. These expressions of strong emotion seemed at war with the emotionless "presentational" text. Only with the next paper did the reason for the contradiction become clear—Anne had been an abused child.

The last paper, "Till Death Do Us Part," dealt with her own history of being abused and the relationship between her father and mother that had led to the shooting and the trial. In this paper she came close to resolving the problem that bothered her about the earlier paper on the shooting. She was troubled because that paper did not give the whole context of the shooting; it didn't explore the hell on earth that her home life had been before the incident. In "Till Death Do Us Part," she gave that context; she documented with chilling dispassion the abuse that went on before the shooting, beginning with a note she wrote to her mother when she was eight:

Report on Daddy—To: Mommy from Anne

Daddy was MEAN!

Report:

Daddy has been mean he would only let us have
apples and pears I told him that we could have
anything we want exip exsit exitep for to many
sweets

I went to bed hungrl hungry

I told him I would tell you I wrote this
right befour bed
from Anne

P.S.   Daddy was spanking Steve because he would not come down he
was in bed while daddy was yelling daddy gave him a bloody ~~noise~~ nose and
woke john

Childhood memoirs, not clear enough, but the meaning is there. Age eight:
the beginnings of first paternal rejection and second, my notes. Fights
between my parents were a common occurance by the age of nine. By
ten, I wanted my daddy dead. And now, at seventeen, my daddy's in
prison for attempting, and almost succeeding, to kill my mommy. I still
wish he were dead.

As a little girl, I spent hours crying in the bathroom because of my
daddy. He would call me names varying from "princess" to "stupid" or
"liar." He would hit me, bruise me in his father/child wrestling games. He
would swear and curse my mother one minute, act contrite the next
minute, and on the third, he'd be believing the lies with which he excused
his behavior. He'd ignore me one minute, cuddle me the next, and then
shove me away. It hurt. It always hurt.

What I found so striking about the piece was the distance she
maintained from the experience. There was none of the maudlin senti-
mentality that had marred her earlier piece on blindness. Instead, there
were objectivity and understatement. The effect is often horrifying, as
when she described her father's coming back for a meal after the
marriage had irretrievably broken down:

. . . He was "intent" upon saving the marriage and so would only
deposit [his checks] if mom would start socializing with him. She
refused.

However, one day, about a week before Christmas, he deposited
the checks, came home and demanded my mother "serve" him dinner
and sit with him while he ate. She refused to do both. It was 9:00. He
was a grown man capable of fixing his own meal.

He did, beer. He started pacing the kitchen saying, "I can't take
this anymore," repeatedly. His rage mounted, he smashed his fists at
the walls, kicked and broke the coffee table, and yelled at me to keep
my mother away from him or else he might kill her.

I called the police. It was the second time this week.

My mother was in her bedroom, holding my brother's baseball bat, in case he came after her before the police arrived. He was sitting in the kitchen cleaning the revolver and rifle.

This final paper was seventeen pages long, and was preceded by a full-page single-spaced outline. In retrospect, it became clear that the research paper had been an attempt to work in what she called the presentational mode. By going that far away from the experience, she may have been more able to move back into it.

And still she was not satisfied with the results. On the title page of "Till Death Do Us Part," she wrote a note:

I am still dissatisfied with this because it lacks total honesty. There are perspectives that I can't or am unable to express concisely on paper.

Anne

Discussion and Implications for Instruction

Any conclusions drawn on the basis of one case study must be tentative. The growth that Anne showed does, however, confirm other research on the composing process, especially the work of Calkins (1980). Calkins observed the revision processes of third- and fourth-grade students and noted a sequence of stages. Students begin by not revising, by simply moving on to new topics or different versions of the same topic. Next they "refine"—make minor word, spelling, and punctuation changes. Calkins then defines a phase that she calls a transition stage, which precedes the stage of true, substantive revision. In the transition stage, students sense that what they have written falls far short of their intention. They are no longer content to tinker (refine) because they see major problems. During the transition stage, they often experience great frustration because while they can see problems, they cannot diagnose the problems and adequately change the text. For a while the students' critical abilities outrun their composing abilities. Anne seemed to enter this stage when she began to explore the shooting of her mother.

Scardamalia and Bereiter (in press) suggest a three-part model of revision—compare, diagnose, operate—that could explain some of the frustration of this stage. Transition writers develop the capacity to compare their writing to the experience depicted and to an internal standard of good writing; they can detect discrepancies; yet they cannot diagnose the reasons for the discrepancy and act (operate) to change the text. At the beginning of the course, Anne was going through none of these stages. How could she? She was writing on topics she knew little about. There was no way to compare her text against the reality depicted when she had only a fuzzy idea of what that reality (the writing process, inflation, blindness) was.

Once she began writing on a topic that she knew a great deal about and cared about, the need for revision became obsessively evident. She was troubled by her omissions. She was worried by the fact that background information was not supplied. She worried that the emotions so vivid for her might not be vivid for the reader. The clarity of her memory gave her a standard against which she could test her writing. The tension between text and intention made revision possible, and by the end of the course she was able to go through the three steps defined by Scarmadalia and Bereiter.

Just as it is difficult to draw conclusions, it is difficult to draw hard teaching implications from a study of one writer. Anne's development, however, does illustrate practices and principles that may be of use to the classroom teacher.

1. Anne was responsible for choosing her own topics, and her decision to deal with the shooting eventually forced her to change her view of the writing process. As she dealt with the topic, she became aware of the disparity between the experience and the depiction of the experience. That disparity became the motivating force for revision.

2. Judy's reading of the first paper was critically important. It would have been easy (and technically justifiable) to focus on the many problems in that paper, to play, in Elbow's terms (1973), "the doubting game." Judy chose to play "the believing game," which Elbow describes as follows:

> By believing an assertion we can get farther and farther into it, see more and more things in terms of it or "through" it, use it as a hypothesis to climb higher and higher to a point from which more can be seen and understood—and finally get to the point where we can be more sure (sometimes completely sure) it is true. This was only possible by inhibiting the doubting game: if we had started doubting we would have found so many holes or silly premises we would have abandoned it. (p. 163)

Judy chose to believe, despite the abundant evidence to the contrary, that Anne could be the kind of writer she said she was. And by believing Anne's assessment to be true, Judy helped it become true.

3. Judy was able to play the believing game, in part, because she did not have to grade any of the early papers. Judy would probably have been unable to keep Anne in the course (let alone establish a good working relationship with her) if she had taken the evaluator role at the first conference.

4. To learn, a student must unlearn. In order to consider writing a conscious process, Anne had to give up an approach to writing that had served her well. She, and to a lesser degree other students in the study,

resisted change not so much because they could not understand the new skill demanded of them, but because they were reluctant to discard old opinions and approaches. William James described the process as follows:

> The individual has a stock of old opinions already, but he meets a new experience that puts them to a strain. Somebody contradicts them; or in a reflective moment he discovers that they contradict each other; or he hears of facts with which they are incompatible; or desires arise in him which they cease to satisfy. The result is an inward trouble to which his mind till then had been a stranger, and from which he seeks to escape by modifying his previous mass of opinions. He saves as much of it as he can, for in this matter of belief we are all extreme conservatives. So he tried to change first this opinion, and then that (for they resist change very variously), until at last some new idea comes up which he can graft upon the ancient stock with a minimum of disturbance of the latter. (1907/1954, p. 172)

As teachers we naturally determine what we want students to learn; too rarely do we ask—what must the student give up to meet our objectives? Perry (1970), for example, has shown the price, in loss of certitude, that a liberal education exacts. In order to meet the expectations of this writing course, Anne had to do more than master certain skills; she had to revise her view of what a student was.

Implications for Future Research: The Problem of Context

In this study I attempted to examine growth of the subjects in the context of a writing course where they could write on topics of personal importance to an interested audience. The importance of this communication context has, of course, long been recognized. Interest in such a context is as old as rhetoric itself. Yet those who have studied reading, writing, and the cognitive processes that underlie these activities have traditionally ignored the real-life contexts in which humans operate (Mishler, 1979). Bransford (1979), for example, demonstrates that traditional studies of memory that focused on list learning shed little light on the way memory is actually used. Donaldson (1978) has recently criticized Piaget for the artificial nature of many of his tasks and cites studies that show students performing operations successfully in meaningful situations while being unable to show a mastery of these operations in the more artificial tasks that Piaget used.

A similar division currently exists among those studying the composing process. Graves comes close to categorically rejecting the usefulness of traditional research that ignores context:

> Research about writing must be suspect when it ignores context or process. Unless researchers describe in detail the full context of data gathering and

the process of learning and teaching, the data cannot be exported from room to room. (1981, p. 99)

Graves argues for long-term observational studies that detail not only the classroom context but elements of the larger school, family, and community that affect writing development.

Bereiter (1980) has made the opposite argument. He claims that we know as much as we can expect to know about the normal development of writing abilities in classroom situations from definitive studies such as that of Britton *et al.*:

> . . . it is likely that research of this kind (i.e. research that looks at writing in the classroom) has yielded about all it can concerning the normal course of writing development. Further knowledge is more likely to come through the use of specialized tasks and other techniques that break through habitual school writing behaviors. (1980, p. 90)

Graves, then, is urging the researcher into the classroom, and Bereiter is urging the researcher back into the laboratory.

There are serious limitations to both arguments, however. Classroom-based studies of the magnitude that Graves describes pose logistical problems. Few researchers can realistically spend one to three years collecting data in the comprehensive fashion that Graves describes, nor can they expect access to the secretarial help necessary to process the data. Miller (1977), who conducted a naturalistic study of vocabulary development, details the difficulty and expense of the transcribing involved in his project. Miller's work also illustrates the difficulty of penetrating the developmental process through observational data-gathering. While able to document the growth in vocabulary that the subjects made, his techniques did not illuminate how that growth had occurred. Miller's study is a cautionary tale for anyone interested in the massive accumulation of observational data.

The emphasis on a natural context also constrains the researcher in two ways. First, he or she is limited by the curriculum of the school, and, as Bereiter (1980) notes in commenting on the work of Britton *et al.*, the results may say as much about the school system as they say about the students. Graves, for example, can say little about the development of story-writing skills, because in the school where he made his observations, story writing was not emphasized.

An effort to fully describe context creates problems in generalizing observations. As noted earlier, Graves claims that unless the entire context is described, results cannot be exported from room to room. Yet the more fully a context is described, the less likely it is that another classroom can match that context. And if contexts differ, how can observations and conclusions made in one context be made to apply in another? A possible answer might be that the entire context does not need to be duplicated, just the contributory elements of the context. But that only raises another question: How does the researcher separate the contributory elements from the peripheral elements?

There are equal dangers in approaches that rely exclusively on specialized tasks unrelated to any communicative need of the students being studied. The danger is that researchers will overgeneralize their findings, concluding that difficulties with the specialized tasks clearly illustrate basic deficiencies. This overgeneralization occurred in some studies of the oral language ability of minority students, whose problems with laboratory-based tasks were taken to indicate severe language deficiency. This view was refuted by Labov (1970), who studied similar students in natural settings.

Some of the tasks being used in the study of students' writing processes may also give misleading results. Flower and Hayes (1980), for example, asked college students to compose on the topic: "Write about your job for the readers of Seventeen magazine." They found that experienced writers used far richer problem-solving strategies than inexperienced writers. It is at least possible, though, that the assignment was so artificial that the inexperienced writers did not demonstrate the planning ability that they do normally use. If, for example, the same students were writing a job description to get work-study credit, would their planning have been so impoverished? Without dipping into the real world, the researcher cannot tell.

It can be argued that assignments like those used by Flower and Hayes are similar to assignments used in writing classes, and that the composing difficulties that they have uncovered are directly relevant to classroom instruction. Bereiter (1980) has implied that the norms of development should be established on the basis of work done to "ordinary task instructions." He writes that attempts, such as those of Graves and his colleagues, to look at development in terms of strongly motivated writing can "distort any normal developmental trends that might exist" (p. 81). Bereiter comes close to arguing, then, that the only true test of the development of rhetorical abilities is performance on arhetorical tasks, tasks with no real purpose or audience.

There is a second paradox here. Emig (1971), in the first major case study of student writers, argued that the assign–assess approach taken in many writing classes was part of the problem with composition instruction. She found that students had very little investment in many school writing assignments. We have come full circle when researchers justify their assignments by claiming that they replicate the "ordinary task instructions" that Emig condemned.

I have raised these questions not to belittle either the naturalistic or the laboratory approach. It does seem, though, that some cross-breeding is in order. Those researchers conducting observational studies can profitably use specialized tasks that can confirm impressions and provide quantifiable data. Calkins (1980) has demonstrated the usefulness of mixing approaches. And those researchers who specialize in laboratory techniques can profitably examine the match between student perform-ance on specialized tasks and student performance in more natural settings.

REFERENCES

Barnett, S., & Stubbs, M. *The Little, Brown Reader.* Boston: Little, Brown, 1979.

Bereiter, C. Development in writing. In L. Gregg & E. Steinberg (Eds.), *Cognitive process in writing.* Hillsdale, N.J.: Lawrence Erlbaum, 1980.

Bissex, G. *Gnys at wrk: A child learns to write and read.* Cambridge, Mass.: Harvard University Press, 1980.

Bransford, J. *Human cognition: Learning, understanding, and remembering.* Belmont, Calif.: Wads-worth, 1979.

Britton, J., *et al. The development of writing abilities, 11-18.* London: Macmillan Education, 1975.

Calkins, L. Children's rewriting strategies. *Research in the Teaching of English,* 1980, *14,* 331-341.

Donaldson, M. *Children's minds.* New York: Norton, 1978.

Elbow, P. *Writing without teachers.* New York. Oxford University Press, 1973.

Emig, J. *The composing processes of twelfth graders* (NCTE Research Report No. 13). Urbana, Ill.: National Council of Teachers of English, 1971.

Flower, L., S., & Hayes, J. R. The cognition of discovery: Defining a rhetorical problem. *College Composition and Communication.* February 1980, *31,* 21-32.

Graves, D. An examination of the writing processes of seven-year-old children. *Research in the Teaching of English,* 1975, *9,* 227-241.

Graves, D. *How children change in the writing process.* National Institute of Education study. Periodic reports have appeared in the "Research Update" section of *Language Arts* (1978-1980). The full set of papers from the study is available from the Writing Process Laboratory, Morrill Hall, University of New Hampshire, Durham, N.H. 03824.

Graves, D. A new look at research on writing. In S. Haley-James (Ed.), *Perspectives on writing in grades 1-8.* Urbana, Ill.: National Council of Teachers of English, 1981.

James, W. What pragmatism means. *American thought: Civil war to world war one* (P. Miller, Ed.). New York: Holt, Rinehart & Winston, 1954.

Labov, W. *The study of non-standard English.* Urbana, Ill.: National Council of Teachers of English, 1970.

Larson, R. *The writer's mind.* Keynote address at Skidmore Writing Conference, Saratoga Springs, N.Y., October 4, 1980.

Miller, G. *Spontaneous apprentices: Children and language.* New York: Seabury Press, 1977.

Mishler, E. Meaning in context: Is there any other kind? *Harvard Educational Review,* 1979, *49,* 1-19.

Newkirk, T. *Writing and critical reading.* Paper presented at Skidmore Writing Conference, Saratoga Springs, N.Y., October 4, 1980.

Perl, S. The composing processes of unskilled college writers. *Research in the Teaching of English,* 1979, *13,* 317-336.

Perry, W. *Forms of intellectual and ethical development in the college years.* New York: Holt, Rinehart & Winston, 1970.

Pianko, S. A description of the composing processes of college freshmen writers. *Research in the Teaching of English*, 1979, *13*, 5–21.

Scardamalia, M., & Bereiter, C. The development of evaluative, diagnostic, and remedial capabilities in children's composing. In M. Martelew (Ed.), *The psychology of written language: A developmental approach.* London: John Wiley & Sons, in press.

Sommers, N. Revision strategies of student writers and experienced adult writers. *College Compositon and Communication.* 1980, *31*, 378–388.

Sowers, S. Young writers' perferences for non-narrative modes of conception. *Research in the Teaching in English*, in press.

Stallard, C. An analysis of the writing behavior of good student writers. *Research in the Teaching of English*, 1974, *8*, 206–218.

7

Factors influencing self-assessing and revising by college freshmen

RICHARD BEACH
SARA EATON
University of Minnesota

Some composition research (Buxton, 1959; Sanders & Littlefield, 1975) indicates that students learn to improve their writing by revising. The pedagogical value of revision is further bolstered by research indicating that, for the most part, experienced writers engage in more substantive revision than do inexperienced writers. In one study (Stallard, 1974), twelfth-graders judged to be superior writers revised more than inferior writers. In another study, college freshmen judged to be higher-quality writers revised more extensively and employed more between-draft revision than low-quality writers (Bridwell, 1980). While substantive revision does not necessarily result in writing of higher quality, the research suggests that for inexperienced writers, this relationship often holds (Calkins, 1980; Beach, 1980).

Parallel to this research, there is much evidence that many secondary and college students engage in little substantive revision (Beach, 1976; NAEP, 1977; Perl, 1979; Sommers, 1978, 1980; Bridwell, 1980). In one examination of twelfth-graders' revision behaviors, Bridwell (1980) found that of seven different types of revisions, ranging from substantial reordering of material to minor editorial changes, the latter predominated. She also found that more substantive revision occurs between, rather than within, drafts. After completing drafts or draft sections, students could stand back and reflect in terms of their overall goals or audience considerations. From that larger or different perspective, the writing often seemed inadequate, and students perceived the need to revise.

One reason for the lack of substantive revision, particularly at the secondary grade level, may be students' inability to critically self-assess, which, in turn, may be related to cognitive development. Comparisons of revising at different age levels (Bracewell, Scardamalia, & Bereiter, 1978; NAEP, 1977; Bridwell, 1980) indicate that it is not until senior high school that students consistently engage in substantive revising. These age differences may be a function of developmental differences in students' audience awareness: it is not until late adolescence that writers are able to vary their writing behaviors according to inferred variations in audience characteristics (Bracewell *et al.*, 1978; Rubin & Piché, 1979). If secondary-school-age writers do not consider audience characteristics, they then may not critically assess their writing in terms of potential audience response (Sommers, 1980). They become so attached to the text that they focus their attention on wording problems rather than thinking about their readers.

In discussing the cognitive processes involved in revising, Bracewell *et al.* (1978) posit that in "decentering," writers do more than simply detach themselves from their original perspective. They acquire an ability to compare old and new potential material that allows them to improve the old rather than simply produce totally new material. This requires some degree of cognitive flexibility. When comparing old and new material, a writer needs to be able to assess the relative merits of two different and often opposing formulations. Persons who conceive of the world in rigid, absolute, either–or categories may have difficulty judging the superiority of the one over the other version because they simply perceive one version as different from rather than superior to another. Moreover, if they think in terms of absolute categories or "correct answers," they may assume that their expressed ideas or opinions constitute the "final word" on the topic. These students may avoid the truth–value dissonance that stimulates a need to revise (Della-Piana, 1978); they perceive versions as different without noting much of a difference in quality. However, while numerous studies have been made of cognitive flexibility, with use of different measures—for example, the Hunt Paragraph Completion Test (Hunt, 1971), a measure of "conceptual level"—there is little research on the relationship between cognitive flexibility and revising to substantiate these claims.

Students also may not revise because they have difficulty in *critically* assessing their own writing (Beach, 1976; Sommers, 1980; Bridwell, 1980). In a study by Beach (1976), judges rated students' drafts according to their revising behaviors. Students were categorized as being either "extensive revisers" or "nonrevisers," those who engaged in little or no revision. Analysis of taped, open-ended self-assessing indicated that "extensive revisers" were better able to define their own intentions and recognize the disparity between their intentions and the draft than "nonrevisers." In addition, some students' assumptions about the nature of revising—that revising is a matter of "polishing," of making minor editorial changes—limited the scope of their revisions.

Students may also have difficulty with self-assessing and revising because of their writing anxiety (Daly & Miller, 1975; Daly, 1979). Students scoring high on the Daly–Miller Writing Apprehension Scale had difficulty making decisions about their writing because they felt overwhelmed by the multiple and competing demands of the task. Some of the items on the Daly–Miller Writing Apprehension Scale concern attitudes toward teacher evaluation. Given their prior experiences with teachers' extensive correction of errors, students are often anxious about that themselves. Students are also concerned with impressing the teacher according to certain mandated criteria for success—criteria often limited to editorial matters. Students may assess their writing only in terms of those criteria, limiting the range of potential revisions.

Moreover, because highly apprehensive writers gain little satisfaction from writing (Daly, 1979), they may not be willing to devote much effort to revision. Highly apprehensive writers may also respond more negatively to a teacher–audience who poses more of a threat. For example, they may have difficulty writing for a teacher who knows more than they do about a topic.

In addition to the studies indicating reasons why students do not make substantial revisions, much research in composition has examined the effect on overall writing quality of certain global instructional methods—primarily training in critical analysis of texts, in sentence combining, and in descriptive versus prescriptive feedback. Often, these studies revealed no significant differences in writing quality as a consequence of instructional methods. Even when the instruction did improve quality, investigators often had difficulty explaining the results because it was unclear which aspects of the instruction influenced the change. Moreover, it is difficult to control, and as a result account for, the many other factors affecting quality.

Besides studying the effects of instruction on overall writing quality, another option is to study relationships between a specified set of teacher and student behaviors, one which may be directly influenced by instructional techniques. There is little research examining the effects of instruction on students' ability to make specific self-assessing inferences. For example, if a teacher gave instruction in describing rhetorical strategies such as giving support, linking, or contrasting, it would be possible, through the use of self-assessing forms, to determine which of the strategies was affected by instruction. Which strategies showed up on the self-assessing forms would be evidence of students' inferences about their drafts, and would begin to indicate the effects of instruction.

Guided Self-Assessing Forms

One technique for discerning students' perceptions of their drafts is to have them complete a guided self-assessing form. Different forms may be used for different stages or types of writing, or for different levels of student ability. Some forms employ only checklists or self-rating scales, while others include open-ended questions regarding students' intentions, perceptions, problems, predictions for revisions, and inferences about audience characteristics. Checklist or rating-scale forms are particularly useful in providing quantitative data for empirical research. Rating-scale forms can be used to discern changes in students' ability to critically self-assess or can be compared with judges' ratings to determine students' willingness to criticize their own writing. Objective scales also specify the criteria for ratings, which helps students who have difficulty making open-ended inferences. Herein lies a major pedagogical weakness of self-rating forms. Because students don't formulate their own responses to their drafts, they may never learn to self-assess on their own.

Another weakness of many self-assessing or checklist forms is that they generally ask students to assess their overall draft rather than to focus on specific sections. As Sommers (1978, 1980) found, many students have difficulty defining problems at the level of an overall draft. They made many vague, global inferences that don't help in dealing with specific parts. A more serious problem with focusing attention on only the overall draft is that students mistakenly assume that a draft should be in a relatively complete state, with the organizational sequence already well defined, before they complete the form. Rather than encourage a more recursive attitude toward composing, the forms serve to impose a premature organization on the draft. Another weakness of some self-assessing forms is that they employ the same questions or criteria regardless of differences in the text structure the student is employing. Criteria that are useful when assessing an autobiographical essay would be less appropriate when assessing a problem-solution essay.

An alternative to the global form is one that asks students to assess specific parts of their drafts. The students mark off sections and assess each section by answering questions in reference to their drafts. Such a form, which is the type we employed in this study, poses open-ended questions designed to encourage students to make inferences about their goals ("What are you trying to say or do?") for a particular section, followed by inferences about what they want their audience to do or think. Having defined their goals, students then make inferences about any problems they perceive in achieving those goals. Rather than being simply an unwarranted intrusion into the composing process, the form can be used by students as a device to help them learn to review. In completing the form, they learn to perceive reasons for making the inferences they do.

The questions on the self-assessing form we used are sequenced to mimic a problem-solving approach. Students first describe goals and strategies in each section. They then define audience characteristics, and then problems in fulfilling those goals and strategies. All of this leads up to proposing some resolution of the problems. The initial description of goals and/or strategies helps a student determine how he or she will assess a section. This initial description also implies criteria for judging the section. Knowing that a section is trying to support the main thesis implies that the material should be relevant to the thesis, should provide specific instances, and so on. If the section fails to meet those criteria, then a student might predict appropriate revisions.

This is not to argue that writers make these inferences in any definite chronological order. Writers may begin with a "felt sense" that something is amiss, and then try to define the nature of the problem. The self-assessing form may merely externalize, for some students, this felt sense of dissonance. For others, the inability to define goals, strategies, audience, and problems coherently may be their first indication that the draft fails their intentions. At any point in the describing, judging, and revising sequence, some breakdown can occur. A student may define a section as giving background information but then be unable to identify a reason for giving background information. Or, a student may define a problem but be unable to resolve it. These breakdowns may occur most frequently with certain types of inferences. For example, students may be able to describe their organization but not perceive any problems there.

Knowing which types of self-assessing inferences pose difficulty can help in explaining revision problems. Some research on revising (Beach, 1979, 1980) indicates that of the various types of revisions, students are most adept at supporting—adding examples or reasons for their contentions. One reason for this is the prominence of examples or reasons in an opinion/example text structure, one of the first organizational patterns they master. This suggests that in order to explain revising behaviors, it is necessary to examine the self-assessing inferences that precipitate those revisions.

On the other hand, there are a number of factors that could affect students' ability to use the self-assessing form. As they gain practice in using it, they may show improvement in their ability to self-assess, or improvement may occur as they receive instruction in how to define goals, strategies, or audience characteristics. Another factor that may influence students' self-assessing ability is their writing apprehension. As research on writing apprehension indicates, highly apprehensive writers are uneasy about receiving critical feedback. They may therefore be equally uneasy about critically assessing their own writing.

A student's sex may also influence self-assessing. Previous research on revision (NAEP, 1977; Beach, 1979; Bridwell, 1980) indicated that females revise more extensively than males. While there is little research on the relationship between sex role differences and writing attitudes, females may have more positive attitudes toward the kinds of self-assessing that result in more revising.

Unfortunately, there are few empirical data on the relationship between students' self-assessing ability and their ability to revise. Beach (1979) found that twelfth-grade students who rate their drafts more negatively were more likely to revise than students who rated their drafts more positively. Thus, if students can define problems, they are more likely to revise. It would be interesting to determine whether students who become better able to define certain types of problems then make more revisions in those problem areas. Some students, even if they can define problems, may simply be incapable of making certain revisions.

Purpose of the Study

The purpose of this study was to examine the effects of instruction in use of a guided self-assessing form on students' assessing of rough drafts. The study also examined the effects of sex and writing appre-hension on self-assessing as well as the relationship between students' self-assessing and their revisions. In addition to our quantitative analysis of the self-assessing and revision data, we subjectively analyzed the self-assessing forms to identify some of the difficulties in self-assessing that the students encountered.

The subjects in this study consisted of four intact classes of regular freshman composition students at the University of Minnesota. Two of these classes served as the experimental group. This group received training in use of the form and used the form on four assignments. The other two classes, the control group, did not receive the training and used the form twice—on the first and last assignments.

Procedures

The four classes were taught by two experienced freshman composition teachers. Each teacher taught an experimental and a control section; both teachers employed identical methods.

At the beginning of the course, subjects were administered the Daly–Miller Writing Apprehension Scale. Both the experimental and control group subjects then completed an initial assignment which was to define and analyze the audience of *Ms.* magazine.

After completing prewriting and a draft, students filled out a guided self-assessing form (Figure 7-1), which asked them to define their overall goal and audience. They then divided their drafts into sections

---

Before you hand in your draft, reread it and then fill out this form. It will help you think about ways to improve your draft. Attach this form to the draft.

1. What do you like best about your paper?
2. What is your goal in this paper? That is, what are you trying to say or show to the reader?
3. What do you want the reader to do or think?
4. Number your paragraphs or, if you don't yet have paragraphs, divide your paper into parts by putting a slash (/) at the places where you think you're beginning a new idea. Then reread the paper as if you were someone else reading it for the first time.
   a. In each paragraph, describe (list) what you did (the specific strategies you used). When you used each strategy, what did you want your reader to do or think?
   b. Then, in each paragraph or part, list the questions or problems that you have—places where you got confused, need more information, etc.

You should have some comment or criticism about every part. Use the back of this paper if necessary.

Fig. 7-1. Original self-assessing form.

according to paragraphs. For each section, they had to describe what they were trying to say in that section, the strategies they were employing, and specific audience characteristics. They then had to make judgments about any problems they encountered in the draft.

After completing the form, the subjects revised their drafts. For the next two major assignments in the class, the experimental group completed the self-assessing forms while the control group subjects did not. The teachers also provided the experimental group subjects with instructions based specifically on the form: ways of defining goals, specific strategies, and audience characteristics; methods of judging drafts; and ways of predicting revisions. Otherwise, the instruction and writing assignments given to the two groups were identical.

Analysis of Results

From reading over the forms, we determined which types of inferences or strategies students mentioned most frequently in answering questions 4a and 4b on the self-assessing form (Figure 7-1). We then derived categories for analysis of these strategy types. Next, two trained judges placed each writer's "statement" (defined as a clause and its modifiers) in one of the categories. If, for example, a student stated that a section was about the level of education of *Ms.* magazine readers, that was categorized as a "content summary." If a statement served to summarize the overall position of a certain section—such as, "This is my thesis about the MS. reader's education"—then that statement was categorized as an inference about "thesis."

The judges categorized references to other strategies: "supporting," "linking/sequencing," "backgrounding," and "contrasting," as well as "grammatical" or "lexical" items. The judges also categorized responses to the question "What do you want the reader to do or think?" (in question 4a) in terms of references to reader comprehension problems, prior knowledge about the topic, and reader needs.

Based on their responses to the self-assessing form's questions, the judges distinguished between two basic types of inferences: those that *described* the use of a particular strategy type (e.g., "I am providing some support") and those that *judged* the use of a strategy type, noting some problem or deficiency in employing the strategy (e.g., "I didn't provide enough examples to support my point"). Thus, for each content summary, strategy inference, and audience characteristic inference, the judges categorized instances of the students' *descriptions* of content, strategies, and audience characteristics and their *judgments* of problems in achieving their intended content summary or strategy. In the case of audience characteristics, the judges determined problems associated with audience emotional response, comprehension, prior knowledge, or needs. The judges were able to distinguish between descriptions and judgments because the form posed two different questions, asking students to first "describe (list) what you did (the specific strategies you used). When you used *each* strategy, what did you want your reader to do or think?" (question 4a), as opposed to "Then, in each paragraph or part, list the questions or problems that you have—places where you got confused, need more information, etc." (question 4b). The agreement between the two judges was high: .87.

Thus, for each strategy type, it was possible to determine the mean number of strategy descriptions and the mean number of problems inferred for each essay.

Effects of Treatment, Sex, and Apprehension

To determine the effects of treatment (training in use of the form vs. no training), sex, and apprehension on the mean number of instances of description and judgment inferences for the pre- and post-test essays, a three-way analysis of variance (Treatment × Sex × Apprehension) was run for each strategy type. The results are presented in Table 7-1.

The post-test essay results indicated only one significant main treatment effect for description, description of support ($F = 4.9, p < .03$), favoring the experimental group. In making judgments, treatment had a

Table 7-1. *Significant Effects of Treatment, Sex, and Apprehension on Mean Number of Descriptive and Judgmental Self-Assessing Inferences*

Pre-essay assignment (Ms. magazine)		Post-essay assignment (television program)	
Description	Judgments	Description	Judgments
	Significant treatment effects		
1. Content summary $(F = 5.6, p < .02)$		1. Treatment × Apprehension $(F = 4.0, p < .04)$	1. Background $(F = 3.7, p < .05)$
2. Support $(F = 11.2, p < .001)$		2. Support $(F = 4.9, p < .03)$	2. Support Treatment × Apprehension $(F = 6.1, p < .01)$
3. Organization × Treatment $(F = 5.5, p < .01)$			3. Organization $(F = 4.8, p < .03)$
			4. Syntax $(F = 6.2, p < .01)$
	Significant sex/apprehension effects		
1. Thesis Sex × Apprehension $(F = 4.5, p < .03)$	1. Thesis Sex $(F = 6.2, p < .01)$		1. Thesis Sex $(F = 6.8, p < .01)$
2. Organization Sex × Apprehension $(F = 4.3, p < .04)$			2. Organization Apprehension $(F = 7.3, p < .009)$
3. Contrasting Sex $(F = 5.5, p < .02)$ Sex × Apprehension $(F = 4.3, p < .04)$	3. Contrasting Sex $(F = 5.2, p < .02)$		3. Background Sex × Apprehension $(F = 6.3, p < .01)$
4. Syntax Sex $(F = 5.6, p < .02)$			
5. Audience Apprehension $(F = 4.3, p < .05)$	5. Audience Sex $(F = 7.2, p < .009)$ Sex × Apprehension $(F = 9.3, p < .003)$		

significant main effect on three areas: background $(F = 3.7, p < .05)$, organization $(F = 4.8, p < .03)$, and syntax $(F = 6.2, p < .01)$. There was also a significant Treatment × Apprehension effect: the low-apprehensive treatment subjects scored higher than the high-apprehensive treatment subjects. Scheffé tests on means favored the experimental group.

These results indicated that, contrary to our expectations, training and practice in using the form resulted in few differences in the ability to describe strategies. We had assumed that instruction in describing strategies would result in group differences in a number of areas.

However, the fact that the groups did not differ on the pre-essay but differed in four areas on the post-essay in judging problems could be attributed to the practice that the experimental group subjects had in using the forms. They had become more accustomed to making judgments than the control group subjects. The fact that treatment had a more pronounced effect on judgments than on strategy descriptions may mean that instruction in using the forms has more of an effect on describing problems than on strategies. Also, practice in filling out the forms may have helped students go through the stages of describing strategies and audience characteristics that lead up to definition of problems.

Both apprehension and sex had an influence on self-assessing. As indicated in Table 7-1, apprehension had a significant main effect on audience ($F = 4.3$, $p < .05$); the high-apprehensive students were more likely to make references to audience than the low-apprehensive students. There were a number of significant Apprehension $\times$ Sex interaction effects on organization ($F = 4.3, p < .04$), thesis ($F = 4.5, p < .03$), and contrasting ($F = 4.3$, $p < .04$). In all of these, low-apprehensive males and females made more inferences than high-apprehensive males or females. Low-apprehensive females made the greatest number of inferences, and high-apprehensive males, the least.

Sex had significant main effects on contrasting ($F = 5.5, p < .02$) and syntax ($F = 5.6, p < .02$). In making judgments, sex had significant effects on thesis ($F = 6.2$, $p < .01$), contrasting ($F = 5.2$, $p < .02$), and audience ($F = 7.2$, $p < .009$), with females making more judgments than males.

In contrast, in the last writing assignment, which involved analyzing a television program and/or its audience, neither apprehension nor sex had any significant main or interactive effects on descriptive inferences. In making judgments, sex had a significant main effect on thesis ($F = 6.8$, $p < .01$). Apprehension had a significant effect on organization ($F = 7.3$, $p < .009$). There were far more significant apprehension and sex effects with the initial *Ms.* magazine assignment than with the television review assignment. Without some data on students' perceptions of the task and of the teacher–audience, any explanation of these differences is purely speculatory. The fact that the *Ms.* magazine task was the first writing assignment may have meant that high-apprehensive subjects were more concerned about audience comprehension than low-apprehensive subjects.

Analysis of Revision

In order to determine the relationship between students' self-assessing and their revisions, a subgroup of 39 students was selected from both groups for analysis of revisions made in their drafts. (Given the time-consuming nature of the analysis—approximately 45 minutes per subject —all 90 subjects were not analyzed.)

Using the descriptions of the types of problems noted on each self-assessment form, judges read the student's rough draft in order to locate the type of problem referred to on the form. Then, comparing the initial draft with the revised draft, the judges recorded whether or not a subject had dealt with the problem in making a revision. For example, a student had noted on the form that the introductory paragraph lacked background information. In revising that paragraph, the student had not added any background information. The judge then recorded that no change was made regarding that particular problem. The judges achieved a high degree of agreement: .78.

The purpose of this analysis was to identify whether or not the students could deal with the problems they noted on their forms by attempting a revision. It would then be possible to determine those types of problems related to content summary and strategy inferences most often noted by these 39 students and to determine instances in which students could or could not make revisions related to a particular inference type. For example, if students could identify many instances of problems in supporting, it would then be possible to determine whether or not the students attempted to rectify those problems by adding support.

The group mean for each of the following was determined: the number of instances each subject noted a particular type of problem related to "content summary," "thesis," "supporting," "linking/sequencing," "backgrounding," and "contrasting" for each of two essays; the number of instances in which the student made a change related to a problem inference; and the number of instances in which the student did not make a change related to a problem. The mean number of instances related to audience characteristics was also determined. In addition to determining the mean instances of problems noted, changes made, and changes not made, we also determined the average proportion of changes made out of the total number of problems noted. This was determined by dividing the total number of changes made by the total number of problems noted for all subjects combined. This percentage provides some indication of students' ability to attempt some solution to the problems in their drafts. The results of these analyses are presented in Table 7-2.

The results as presented in Table 7-2 indicate that subjects were highly consistent in the mean number of problems noted, changed, and not changed, across the two essays. For example, for both their first and second essays, they noted .5 problems regarding content summary. For their first essay, they made .4 changes and for the second, .5 changes. This suggests that regardless of differences in the content of their essays, the students were consistently attending to the same types of

Table 7-2. *Mean Number of Problems Noted, Changed, and Not Changed, and Percentages of Changes Made Out of Total Attempts, for Each of Two Essays ($n = 39$)*

	Mean number of problems for each essay			Percentage of revisions made out of the total number of problems noted
	Noted	Changed	Not changed	
Content summary	.5	.4	.1	20%
	.5	.5	.3	22
Strategy inferences				
Thesis	.2	.2	.07	14
	.5	.1	.2	12
Supporting	1.3	.8	.5	45
	1.6	.7	.5	35
Linking/sequencing	1.2	.8	.4	30
	1.0	.8	.4	52
Backgrounding	.02	.00	.02	0
	.00	.00	.00	0
Contrasting	.1	.08	.02	10
	.02	.02	.02	2
Syntax	.9	.8	.1	42
	1.5	.6	.4	24
Audience inferences				
Emotional response	2.7			
	2.5			
Comprehension	.1			
	.2			
Prior knowledge	.05			
	.02			
Needs	.00			
	.00			

problems and were consistently attempting the same types of revisions. To some degree, the similarity in the means and the fact that students were most likely to cite problems of supporting (1.3 and 1.6) was due to the fact that students were writing opinion/example text-structure essays, in which the supporting evidence for their thesis was a particularly important component. They therefore devoted less attention to problems of backgrounding (.02 and .00) and contrasting (.1 and .02) largely because these strategies were less likely to be used relative to supporting in an opinion/example structure.

On the other hand, it could be argued that students were better able to cite problems of support because they had received more instruction in logical support than in problems of backgrounding or contrasting. They may have also noted few problems in providing background information because, as the data on inferences about audience characteristics indicate, they noted few, if any, problems related to audience comprehension (.1 and .2), prior knowledge (.05 and .02), or needs (.00 and .00). Lack of concern about audience may have been related to the lack of concern about providing background information.

As would be expected, students were most likely to make changes in the areas most frequently cited as problems: supporting (.8 and .7), link/sequencing (.8 and .8), and syntax (.8 and .6). At the same time, they did not make changes for a relatively high number of support problems (.5 and .5) and linking/sequencing problems (.4 and .4).

Because these means are relative to prominence of certain text features in an opinion/example essay, the percentage results across all students provide a more insightful indication of the overall group's willingness to attempt to deal with certain types of problems. The percentage results in Table 7-2 indicate that students were most likely to attempt changes in problems of supporting (45% and 35%), linking/sequencing (30% and 52%), and syntax (42% and 24%). They were less likely to deal with problems of content summary (20% and 22%), thesis (14% and 12%), backgrounding (0% and 0%), and contrasting (10% and 2%).

One reason that students were most likely to deal with problems of supporting, linking/sequencing, and syntax is that they may have been more accustomed to making these revisions, such as adding examples or altering syntax. Therefore, they may have been more likely to revise the problems they were most accustomed to dealing with. And, because they may have been more confident about making revisions in these areas, they may have initially been more likely to cite these areas as problems.

Subjective Analysis of Particular Assessment Problems on the Self-Assessing Forms

While these quantitative results provide some insights into the students' self-assessing behaviors, in reading over the students' forms, we also noticed certain consistent phenomena that were difficult to quantify. In order to deal with some of the deficiencies of the form used for quantitative analysis (Figure 7-1), we revised it, producing a new form (Figure 7-2). For example, on the original form, when students were asked to describe their strategies (question 4a), they often summarized their content. Perhaps they misunderstood the question and thought that restating content described the strategies employed. Because we suspected that the students did not know the difference between content and function or strategy inferences, the new form contained separate questions regarding content ("What does this paragraph say?"), function

---

Now that you have a conference draft done, spend some time thinking about your goals in this paper, your audience, what you have done so far, and what you need to do before you turn in a final draft.

In general, what do you want to say in this paper?

What do you want your reader to do or think after reading it?

Now for EACH PARAGRAPH, answer the following questions, using the space below and on the back:

1. What does this paragraph say?
2. What is this paragraph supposed to do in terms of the whole paper?
3. At this point, what do you want the reader to do or think?
4. What are you going to change?

Fig. 7-2. Revised self-assessing form.

("What is this paragraph supposed to *do* in terms of the whole paper?"), and audience ("At this point, what do you want the reader to do or think?"). For our subjective analysis, we wanted to determine if students could distinguish between these three questions; we were also interested in noting the range and complexity of their responses.

We administered the revised form to over 125 students in five different beginning composition classes. All of the writing assignments were different, but the students' responses were surprisingly similar and reflected some of the quantitative results previously discussed.

Case studies suggested that students still worry about organization, but they most often changed word choices and sentence structures. They added details or tinkered with sentences and words. Whole-text considerations, like changing the thesis, combining paragraphs, defining terms, or shifting paragraphs around, were subordinated to the smaller and more easily controlled parts of the essay—*when the students actually revised.* The students seemed able to add or to change only some aspects of their draft, and they rarely deleted material.

Most important, audience considerations in revision ranked very low. On the self-assessment form, most students showed concern with the reader's emotional responses and understanding—they wanted the reader to like them and be interested. Said one student, "I want the readers to think of their feelings and then see why it shouldn't bother them." Another student bleakly hoped that the reader would continue reading. However, few students related their concerns over syntax or details to a reader's obvious need for explanation or coherence. Often students' objectives with regard to the reader were illogical, considering the demands of the essays they were composing. For example, Sue, arguing in a persuasive essay that magazine quizzes are calculated to make even the truly mad seem sane, didn't want the reader to worry in some parts of her essay but to feel bad in others.

We wondered about these students' ability to critically read their own texts. Obviously, they saw themselves as communicating ideas to someone, since they were concerned about the reader's emotional responses. However, the students were primarily rereading their drafts and reconfirming, in a self-fulfilling manner, that the drafts said what they had intended. They were simply and literally rereading their paragraphs, egocentrically absorbed in their own ideas. They were not thinking about the functions of different sections of their drafts, and they simply assumed that their content summaries described the functions.

On the form that differentiated between description and function, students gave content summaries in response to all three questions on content, function, and audience. These summaries often did not make distinctions between content and function. For example, Julie said for (a) description: "Over 28 million women are beaten and something must be done." For the function (b), she responded, "Show that help is needed." Similarly, she wanted the reader to think that "help is needed." Julie's responses demonstrate her inability to come to conclusions, to make meaningful for even herself as a reader her statistic about beaten women. She was unable to move beyond the summarized surface of her essay to even use the code words like "introduction," "support," and "conclusion" that characterized other student responses. She had no larger frame or context for her essay. We think that writers like Julie, hesitant and confused over the requirements of an essay, and unsure about their intended meanings in their own texts, have limited options both as writers and as readers who are trying to rethink and revise essays.

Compare Julie to Tim. Where she repeats "something is needed," Tim said (a) "This is a case study—describes a young man's life and how he goes about ending it." (b) "First, to begin setting the mood, or rather the severity of the problem; secondly, by introducing the fact that suicide can happen to anyone"—he had at least two functions or reasons for this kind of introduction. (c) What he wanted the reader to think is, "Wow, this is really terrible; I'd better read on and find out what is going to happen to the rest of the people in this essay." Where Julie's responses demonstrated her inability to come to conclusions, Tim seemed to be controlling and dramatizing his reader's responses in terms of a topic he has already thought through. Yet his concern was also with the content of his essay; his considerations go beyond even the labeling of thesis and introductory parts. Tim understood and did not need to identify explicitly how his essay fulfills discursive requirements. Because he had mastered the frame for his essay, he wasn't guessing at context as much as he created it. Through himself, he had created the reader who governed his revision decisions.

Students' Self-Conceptions as Readers

A second pattern revealed by the self-assessment forms dealt specifically with how these students perceived themselves as readers. They recorded the story of the draft's production, seemingly following Mary McCarthy's dictum for the writer and reader of the novel: Guess what happens next? For example, Sharon's declared thesis was on the American family. Her answers to question (c), concerning audience, chronicle the disintegration of the family. She begins in paragraph 1 with courtship, and in the following paragraphs covers marriage and then divorce. She ends up asking the reader to "think of the hurt children if they are abused in remarriage." Sharon decided, on completing the self-assessing form, that she had tackled too much; she needed to refocus. She had portrayed the progression of her thinking on the form, and from this had been able to extrapolate and analyze her problem. Sharon's thinking, her reading of her text, follows the pattern described by theorists about story acquisition (Applebee, 1978). She recounted her essay and from that was able to generalize and come to some evaluative conclusions.

Students like Sharon seemed to be reconstructing their drafts into something like a summarized narrative in order to revise, to read their drafts from a reader's perspective. Developmental psychologists suggest that telling stories is one of the first cognitive operations mastered (Applebee, 1978). Some students may very well be reverting to this cognitive mode in order to move from the initial composing process to the stance of an evaluative reviser. But as their self-assessing strategies indicate, many students then perceived their revision options in terms of a narrative text structure. That is, they ignored whole-text considerations and paid attention to the things that matter in stories—addition of details, vivid descriptions, anticipations, and eliciting a reader's emotional responses—rather than considering the reader's need for explanations, coherence, or cogent argument. The self-assessing forms may encourage these students' tendencies to perceive their drafts as narratives, thus limiting their revision options.

Inability to Use Goal Inferences

Students often didn't apply their goal inferences to critically assess their writing. They would simply indicate that their drafts fulfilled their goals, but our own subjective analysis of the drafts indicated the contrary. It may have been that in reviewing their drafts, these students were not thinking about their goals. Or, they may have been thinking about their goals but not perceiving any tension or mismatch between their goals and their texts. Once a student had inferred "what I was trying to say" about a particular section, he or she seemed to have assumed that the inference was valid. However, we often found that the students were inferring what they *wanted* a section to say rather than what it actually said.

One reason students didn't critically assess their writing was that their statements of goals, even when referring to specific sections of a draft, were often too generous or global to be useful in a review. For example, in writing a paper on techniques for eliciting literary responses, a student stated that "this section shows that there are different ways to get students to respond." In fact, the section really discussed specific questioning techniques. The student's goal was only vaguely related to the text. This meant that the student didn't perceive any tension or disparity between goal and text. The goal statement is so irrelevant that no direct dissonance could occur; the student then simply assumed that the text fulfilled the goal.

Inferences about Audience

Even though the form explicitly asks the students to make references to their audience, students made relatively little mention of audience characteristics. Students may have had difficulty thinking about audience comprehension, prior knowledge, or needs because switching to a different perspective requires a relatively high level of role-taking ability (Rubin & Piché, 1979). In contrast, concerns with potential emotional responses—whether or not an audience would "like" the writing—reflect a more egocentric orientation.

One can only speculate about the relationships between audience inferences and self-assessing because students made few explicit links between their self-assessing and audience characteristics. The paucity of audience inferences may explain the small number of references to problems of backgrounding. If a student had inferred, for example, that the reader had little knowledge about a topic, he or she may have been more concerned about necessary background information. Also, students who were more "text-bound," or concerned with the text structure, cared most about whether their text conformed to the teacher's presumed dictates about format. They conceived of their audience as someone who would read primarily to check on whether or not they had used the proper form. Some of this derives from the assumption that there is one correct way of completing the assignment.

It would be useful to compare students' self-assessing strategies in writing for teachers and in writing for other audiences. Perhaps some students are more cognizant of certain audience characteristics in non-school writing tasks, while other students are consistently oblivious to audience considerations regardless of the rhetorical context.

Attitude toward Completing the Form

Another consistent pattern was that some students conceived of completion of the form as constituting an accomplishment. They assumed that they could simply report something that they had presumably accomplished in their draft: "I stated my main point," "I gave a number of examples to support my point," and so on. The implication was that such comments abrogated the necessity to do any more work on the draft.

While the forms were intended to encourage critical assessment, many students used them to tell the teacher that they had done what they assumed they were supposed to do. They may, therefore, have been reluctant to admit or divulge problems because they were concerned about the teacher's impression of their ability. The concepts these students used in describing their drafts suggest that they are thinking primarily in terms of a predetermined format derived from a textbook model. These students described the parts of their draft using the categories "introduction," "body," and "conclusion," and often cited few problems with overall organization of their draft. Further, once they had established the sequence in a draft, they rarely altered it. Described as "text-bound," such students were predominantly concerned with matters of text format and the extent to which a draft conforms to a preset organizational structure. Analysis of these students' drafts indicated that they did little substantive revision of content. Their concern with conforming to an organizational format often precluded an interest in developing ideas or content.

Moreover, examination of other students' responses to the "what are you doing" questions indicated that they didn't have the concepts for defining various functions. For example, Joe wrote a problem-solution paper. However, he wasn't familiar with ways of defining such functions as stating the problem or proposing solutions. If he could have defined a section as "stating a problem," he could have asked such questions as: Is the problem clearly stated; is this the only problem; is this a significant or solvable problem; and why does this problem exist? He could then assess the relationship between that section and other sections; defining one section as stating a problem would allow him to ask questions about how the problem statement relates to the background situation or proposed solutions. However, because he simply described the first section as his "introduction" followed by the "body" of the paper, he didn't assess the draft in these terms.

This kind of conceptualizing reflects an attitude toward revision and an attitude toward the assignment. When a student states that he or she has defined a thesis and given reasons to support the thesis, the implication is that the purpose of the assignment was to demonstrate an ability to write according to the textbook formula that every "good essay" states a thesis and gives supporting reasons. Because many students in this study assessed their drafts primarily in terms of conformance to a predetermined text-structure format, they tended to conceive of each section simply in terms of its contribution to the overall structure. For example, in an opinion/example structure, they were particularly concerned with how well each section referred back to the main thesis. As a result, they often didn't attend to problems unique to particular sections, such as poor internal development. Because they were prematurely concerned with establishing the overall sequence, they didn't delay or forestall decisions about this sequence. Instead of working on each section as a separate entity, they moved in a chronological path in order to complete the entire draft. As Sommers (1978, 1980) found, prematurely establishing an opinion/example structure often means that once a student has stated a thesis and given examples, he or she stops writing.

Some of this desire for a quick, premature closure reflects what learning-style theorists define as a "dualist" intellectual orientation (Perry, 1981). Dualists learn best in highly structured situations, in which requirements and expectations are clearly defined. Obsessed with following the rules and "doing it right," they assume that knowledge consists of absolute truths and have difficulty accepting conflicting opinions. They will conceive of "writing an essay" as conforming to an overall essay format. As our subjective analysis indicates, these students revise less than students who are able to recognize conflicting opinions.

Criteria and Assumptions Underlying Students' Inferences

In order to explain some of these self-assessing phenomena, we found it useful to examine some of the students' assumptions constituting their reasoning about goal–strategy–prediction relationships. For example, a student would state that a certain problem existed in a draft: "not enough support for my opinion." On the basis of that judgment, he or she would cite an implied solution:" add more support, examples, or reasons to support the opinion." In order to move from the judgment "lack of support" to the prediction "add examples," a writer draws on learned problem-solving techniques drawn from logic and the conventions for written language. These techniques underlie the reasoning: "given x goals and/or y problems, z change will solve the problem. Therefore, employ z revision."

To understand difficulties in self-assessment, one must understand the assumptions that constitute this problem-solving conditional reasoning. Often, students don't link problems and revisions. A student who doesn't tacitly know if the sections of his draft don't combine together effectively, he or she will need to add transitions, may not be able to fix disjointed sections.

Furthermore, a student's judgment about a problem plays a crucial role in implying revisions. That is, judging a section as irrelevant implies insufficient information, which then implies the need to add more information. If the student cannot judge a section as irrelevant, the revision process stops. As we saw on the self-assessing forms, students often cite quite rigid, outmoded assumptions about their writing. And some students simply aren't familiar with the conventions for writing that would allow them to translate their judgments into predictions for revision. As Shaughnessy (1977) found, many of her "basic writers" didn't know the conventions used in formal academic writing. Many students in our study seemed to be knowledgeable only about conventions regarding adequate evidence or support; the quantitative analysis and case studies indicated that they were most likely to focus on problems and make changes in this area. These students may be able to revise only text structures with which they are familiar.

Conclusion

This study examined the abilities of college freshmen to assess their own drafts. The study found that students receiving instruction in self-assessing made significantly more judgmental inferences in certain areas than did students who did not receive the instruction. Analysis of the pre-essay inferences indicated that the experimental and control groups did differ in a few areas, which suggests some limitations in interpreting the results. Sex and apprehension, in particular, had significant effects on the amount of self-assessing inferences.

Examination of the relationships between self-assessing inferences and degree of revision indicated that students were more likely to make revisions in areas initially identified as problems on the self-assessing forms. Particularly, students tended to identify and revise problems with support, organization, and syntax. The results of this study suggest that self-assessing forms can be used in helping students learn to critically assess and revise their drafts. Further research needs to examine the effects of specific teaching strategies (modeling the self-assessment process, problem-solving techniques, and so forth) on self-assessing.

Subjective analysis of responses to the self-assessing form indicated certain consistent patterns in students' self-assessing behaviors. Some students:

- Were incapable of describing various functions in their drafts, frequently confusing or conflating inferences about content with inferences about function
- Limited their perspectives as readers by conceiving of their writing primarily in terms of a narrative
- Were concerned simply about "what the teacher wants"
- Applied rigid assumptions about revision to their self-assessing
- Had difficulty applying their goal inferences so as to ascertain dissonance between their intentions and their text
- Had difficulty making inferences about specific audience characteristics and using those inferences to assess their writing
- Used the self-assessing form to cite accomplishments rather than admit problems
- Were cognitively bound to rigid conceptions of text-structure formats, an orientation that often limited their willingness to revise content

Because of these difficulties, we believe that students benefit from instruction in self-assessing strategies, and such instruction needs to be based on careful diagnosis of individual differences in the various self-assessing skills.

ACKNOWLEDGMENT

We wish to express our appreciation to Jane Telleen for her assistance with this project.

REFERENCES

Applebee, A. *The child's concept of story*. Chicago: University of Chicago Press, 1978.
Beach, R. Self-evaluation strategies of extensive revisers and non-revisers. *College Composition and Communication*, 1976, 27, 160–164.

Beach, R. The effects of between-draft teacher evaluation on high school students' revising of rough drafts. *Research in the Teaching of English*, 1979, *13*, 111–119.

Beach R. *Self-assessing strategies of remedial college students.* Paper presented at annual meeting of American Educational Research Association, Boston, 1980.

Bracewell, R., Scardamalia, M., & Bereiter, C. *The development of audience awareness in writing.* Paper presented at annual meeting of American Educational Research Association, Toronto, 1978.

Bridwell, L. Revising strategies in twelfth grade students' transactional writing. *Research in the Teaching of English*, 1980, *14*, 197–222.

Buxton, E. An experiment to test the effects of writing frequency and guided practice upon students' skill in writing expression. *Alberta Journal of Educational Research*, 1959, *5*, 94–99.

Calkins, L. Notes and comments: Children's rewriting strategies. *Research in the Teaching of English*, 1980, *14*, 331–341.

Daly, J. Writing apprehension in the classroom: Teacher role expectancies of the apprehensive writer. *Research in the Teaching of English*, 1979, *13*, 37–45.

Daly, J., & Miller, M. The empirical development of an instrument to measure writing apprehension. *Research in the Teaching of English*, 1975, *9*, 242–249.

Della-Piana, G. Revising strategies for the study of revision processes in writing poetry. In C. Cooper & C. Odell (Eds.), *Research on composing.* Urbana, Ill.: National Council of Teachers of English, 1978.

Hunt, D. E. *Matching models in education: The coordination of teaching models with student characteristics.* Toronto: Institute for Studies in Education, 1971.

National Assessment of Educational Progress. *Write/rewrite: An assessment of revision skills.* Denver: Educational Commission of the States, 1977.

Perl, S. The composing process of unskilled college writers. *Research in the Teaching of English*, 1979, *13*, 317–336.

Perry, W. *Intellectual and ethical development in the college years.* New York: Holt, Rinehart & Winston, 1970.

Rubin, D., & Piché, G. Development in synactic and strategic aspects of audience adaptation skills in written persuasive communication. *Research in the Teaching of English*, 1979, *13*, 293–316.

Sanders, S., & Littlefield, J. Perhaps test essays can reflect significant improvement in freshmen composition. *Research in the Teaching of English*, 1975, *9*, 145–153.

Shaughnessy, M. *Errors and expectations.* New York: Oxford University Press, 1977.

Sommers, N. *Revision in the composing process: A case study of college experienced adult writers.* Unpublished doctoral dissertation, Boston University, 1978.

Sommers, N. Revision strategies of student writers and experienced adult writers. *College Composition and Communication*, 1980, *31*, 378–388.

Stallard, C. An analysis of the writing behavior of good student writers. *Research in the Teaching of English*, 1974, *8*, 206–218.

8

Observing composing behaviors of primary-age children: The interaction of oral and written language

GRANT CIOFFI
University of New Hampshire

> *The speaker, and the schoolmaster, and the third grown person present, all backed a little, and swept with their eyes the inclined plane of little vessels then and there arranged in order, ready to have imperial gallons of facts poured into them until they were full to the brim.*—Charles Dickens, Hard Times (1854/1972, pp. 15–16)

Until recently, the overriding concern in teaching written language skills in the early elementary grades has been with receptive language, or reading. Teachers and researchers predicated writing ability on reading proficiency and delayed writing instruction until students learned to read (Graves, 1978). Recent research in composing (Bissex, 1980; Chomsky, 1971; Clay, 1975; Graves, 1982) challenges this practice. To delay instruction in writing until children learn to read underestimates both the sophistication of the child's use of oral language in composing and the degree to which reading and writing interact.

Written language is symbolic and conventional. Viewing written as solely the productive form of written language fails to capitalize on its symbolic nature. Vygotsky (1978, cited in Britton, 1982; Gundlach, 1982) recognized that when children draw, they seek to represent their world (first-order symbolism). Some discover that speech also can be drawn; when children represent speech (second-order symbolism), they discover the antecedents of writing. The early writing of children, while faithful to the symbolic nature of language, follows its own conventions of spelling, punctuation, and orthography (Graves, 1979). If the emphasis in writing is the graphic representation of speech and meaning—instead of, for example, proficiency in the conventions of written English—then writing need not follow reading: both may develop in parallel from proficiency in oral language.

Written Language and Oral Language Development

The preliterate five-year-old has acquired considerable competence in the use of oral language (Cazden, 1972; Gibson & Levin, 1975). Although it is beyond the scope of this paper to discuss the specifics of language development (interested readers may refer to a standard text, such as Cazden, 1972, or Dale, 1976), in general the linguistic components of "form, content, and use" (Bloom, 1978, p. 210) develop and interact.

> Language form is the mechanism, the code, the actual shapes and con-figurations of sounds and words and combinations—what children actually say. Language content is the meaning, gist, or semantics of messages—what children talk about, such as objects and relations between objects. Language use consists first of the reasons or functions for language be-havior and second of the selection process whereby individuals choose among alternative forms—how children learn to say what to whom and in which circumstances. (Bloom, 1978, p. 210)

As the child learns to use flexibly these components of language, explicitness in speech replaces the need to rely on a "physically present nonlinguistic context" (Cazden, 1972, p. 186) for communication. While preschool children are sophisticated language users, they are only beginning to demonstrate metalinguistic knowledge—knowledge about oral and written language (Ehri, 1975; Hiebert, 1981; Hiebert, Cioffi, & Antonak, 1983; Holden & MacGinitie, 1972; Mason, 1980, 1981; Mason & McCormick, 1979).

The interface between oral language and reading has been explored extensively (for reviews of research; see Gibson & Levin, 1975; Rubin, 1980); analogous investigations in writing are only beginning. Dyson (n.d.), Graves (1982), and Kroll (1981) all offer insights into the role of speech in writing. A review of their work provides a framework for investigating the subject of this chapter, the development of composing abilities in primary-age children.

Dyson, as a participant observer in a kindergarten classroom, con-structed five case studies to explore the role of talk in writing, to describe the early development of writing behaviors, and to chart the kinds of writing young children do. Building on Halliday's (1973) discus-sion of language functions, Dyson identified five uses of talk in writing. She found that children used talk while writing to provide additional information about the content of their writing and to direct their own actions and the actions of others. They also used talk to request in-formation, to express their feelings, and to regulate social relationships. When children wrote, they created messages, encoded messages, read messages, or drew letters. These recursive and overlapping activities accounted for all writing that children produced.

From her observations, Dyson postulated that the development of the use of oral language in writing moves from "graphic" to "orthographic" representation of speech (n.d., p. 22). Children initially draw language (letters) without concern for meaning; later, they represent language in writing to communicate a message. Of the five children Dyson studied, only two attempted to write messages, and even their writing needed to be explained orally and complemented with drawings to be understood. Dyson concluded that "children's first representational writing serves to label (organize) their world. Talk surrounds this early writing, investing the labels with meaning. Eventually talk permeates the process, providing both meaning (Representational function) and means (Directive function) for getting that meaning on paper" (p. 26).

While Dyson examined the beginnings of composing in kindergarten children, Kroll (1981) proposed a developmental model of the growth and integration of oral and written language in older schoolchildren. Drawing essentially from theoretical accounts of writing development—Kroll cites Britton specifically—and writing practices as described in language arts texts, he offered the following developmental sequence: "In the course of developing writing abilities, an individual progresses through 'phases' of preparing, consolidating, differentiating, and systematically integrating his or her oral and written language resources" (Kroll, 1981, p. 40).

Preparation consists of developing technical skills essential to writing (handwriting and spelling), practicing composition (primarily through dictation), and fostering growth in oral communication skills. During the phase of *consolidation*, the child's oral language ability provides the basis for early writing. Although "utterance" and "text" (Olson, 1977) differ along a number of dimensions, the early writing of children draws upon the similarities. In order to make progress in composing, however, children need to recognize the differences between speech and writing. This recognition occurs in the third phase, *differentiation*. Differentiation shifts the emphasis from tapping existing resources in oral language to learning the differences between oral and written modes of discourse; expository and persuasive writing replaces narrative and transactional writing. In the final stage of writing, *systematic integration*, children begin to use (flexibly) their resources from both oral and written language. As Kroll notes, they can "talk 'writing'" and "write 'talking'" (1981, p. 53). Writing also serves as a means of discovery. By representing complex ideas, writing permits an author to inspect and to manipulate those ideas.

The research of Graves (1979, 1982) and his associates, Calkins (1980), and Sowers (1981), also examined the developing composing abilities of children. Their research marks the transition between the kindergarten children whom Dyson studied and the older children about whom Kroll theorized. In the National Institute of Education funded research, Graves studied sixteen children over a two-year period: eight through grades 1 and 2, and eight through grades 3 and 4. The researchers selected children to represent low, middle, and high writing abilities. Using an ethnographic approach to gather data, Graves, Sowers, and Calkins videotaped children's composing processes, recorded children's spontaneous comments about their writing, observed composing behaviors, examined the writing that children produced, and informally questioned them about their composing. These naturalistic procedures netted a rich data base for the study of the growth of children's writing.

Graves views growth in writing as a process of solving problems:

> The learner perceives a gap, a problem to solve, and goes about trying to solve it. The problem is sometimes accompanied by tension, disillusionment —at least a halting to activity. In other instances the child isn't even aware the problem is being solved since the situation is only a quarter of a step away from what the child has been solving all along. Nevertheless, losing balance, regaining it, and going on, is the substance of learning. (Graves, 1983, p. 231)

As the child shifts from oral to written discourse, he or she uses oral competence to exert control over the text. In beginning writing, speech appears as an explicit problem-solving strategy. As children develop proficiency in writing, the manifestations of speech in composing become implicit (Graves, 1982). Graves defines this development as consisting of three stages (1982, pp. 21-22):

   I. Overt and early manifestations of speech
  II. Page-explicit transitions
 III. Speech features implicit in text

In children's earliest writing (Stage I), they use speech as did the kindergarten children Dyson studied. Speech directs and enhances their writing. Graves also found some evidence of social uses of speech but views conversation with others as more characteristic of Stage II writers. Eventually, children neither direct writing overtly with speech nor explain their stories. Text proves sufficient to carry meaning.

Drawing, which is characteristic of young children's composing (Clay, 1975), provides context in the earliest writing. Young writers draw before they compose. Stage II writers sometimes draw after composing, no longer relying on a picture for context. Graves found that drawing did not play an important role in Stage III composing.

Graves observed what he termed "para-language" behaviors, which included "kinesics, haptics, and proxemics" as well as "sound effects" (1982, p. 21). These activities diminished as children acquired writing proficiency. Their significance has not yet been verified, although Graves believes they are important.

Children also seek to represent prosodic characteristics of the speech stream in text. Early attempts include running words together by ignoring word boundaries, thus mimicking speech, and using "capitalization and blackened letters, [and] a mixture of upper and lower case letters" to represent the oral language features of stress and pitch (Graves, 1982, p. 21). These behaviors increased in frequency in Stage II and diminished markedly in Stage III.

Finally, Graves observed that as children's writing matures, the use of nonconventional writing features, such as drawing, speech, and prosodic representations, disappears. These are replaced by an increasing oral quality in the written product. As children's writing grows, it resembles more closely talk written down.

The work of Dyson, Graves, and Kroll may be dovetailed to suggest a more comprehensive model of the role of oral language in the development of composing. Kroll's scheme of phases—preparation, consolidation, differentiation, and integration—provides a structure for this synthesis. My focus in this chapter is on the first two stages, preparation and consolidation.

The phase of *preparation* consists of a period of *discovery* followed by *experimentation*. That speech can be drawn and that such drawings carry the messages of their authors constitute the first two major discoveries. These discoveries, which actually consist of metalinguistic knowledge, lead the child to experiment with this new form of communication. Children must solve to their satisfaction the problems of the relationship between speech and writing (phoneme–grapheme correspondences and prosodics), the mechanics of writing (left-to-right directionality, formation of letters), and communication through writing (and drawing and speech). Graves's first- and second-stage writers use oral language to solve these problems, thus gaining control over their composing.

The phase of consolidation begins with Graves's Stage III writers. They no longer need to direct their writing with speech, or provide context with drawings, or ensure the success of their messages with parallel oral texts. As Graves observed, these children speak less as their writing acquires an increasingly oral quality. It is paradoxical that while early composing benefits from the child's use of oral language abilities, later growth (in the phase of differentiation) may be hindered by the persistence of oral characteristics (see Collins & Williamson, 1981; Scardamalia, Bereiter, & Goelman, 1982).

Reading in the Development of Composing

Much as comprehension and production of speech seems to interact to promote growth in language acquisition (Bloom, 1978; Cazden, 1972; Dale, 1976), so may reading and writing—although, as already noted, the relationship is not typically exploited in schools. On a cognitive level, the two processes appear to employ similar linguistic and intellectual sources as the receptive and productive aspects of written language. On a practical level, as the child composes, he or she must also reread and reflect on what has been written. These connections between reading and composing have been widely acknowledged (Durkin, 1966; Moffett, 1968; Graves, 1979; Stotsky, 1982). However, the precise nature of this relationship remains to be defined.

An Observational Study of Early Composing Behaviors

This study sought (1) to confirm and to refine the role played by oral language in the development of the composing of two primary-age children over the first two years of elementary school instruction, and (2) to document and to categorize the kinds of reading that the composing required.

Method and Subjects

The students in this study were two first-grade students, Chris and Jenny. Their teachers and the researchers judged them to be of above-average and average ability, respectively. The data on these children were collected during a National Institute of Education funded study of children's writing directed by Donald Graves at Atkinson Academy, Atkinson, New Hampshire, from September 1978 through June 1980 (Graves, 1982). During the course of Graves's study, the children's writing episodes were videotaped. There was a total of thirteen and a half hours of writing videotaped for the two children—six for Jenny and seven and a half for Chris. The children were videotaped at their requests; therefore, the intervals between taping sessions were sometimes irregular. The child being videotaped sat at a table and wrote while the video camera was operated. The child wore a sensitive microphone and periodically responded to questioning by the experimenter. Both children were aware that they were being videotaped, but their behaviors appeared natural and spontaneous.

Coding of Behaviors

The purpose of this study necessitated examining the behaviors students exhibited while composing. In order to assess accurately the allotment of time, an observation instrument modeled on Perl's (1979) was developed. The instrument required a coding of observed behaviors every five seconds. In most cases, a single behavior was noted; in a few cases a number of behaviors were observed and recorded. These coding procedures provided a means of recording how students spent their time during composing as well as the sequence and duration of particular activities.[1]

When young children compose, they engage in a number of identifiable behaviors: drawing, writing orally, writing silently, reading orally, editing, and consulting other parts of their texts. They also engage in some covert and not directly observable activities: reading silently, planning, and reflecting on what they have written (see Graves, 1979, 1982, 1983; Scardamalia, Bereiter, & Goelman, 1982; Sowers, 1981). When the videotapes were analyzed, composing episodes were isolated. The percentages of time that the children spent on the overt and identifiable activities were tallied for each episode. The percentages of time they spent interacting with the experimenter and the time they spent on task-related but silent or covert activities were also recorded. An examination of the way in which the children distributed their time over this range of activities during the two years of the study provided insight into how the processes of writing were developing for these two children and a sense of how many activities observed during a composing episode were either reading-based or related.

While the names of the categories are reasonably indicative of the behaviors they describe, a more detailed description of each category follows.

DRAWING

Chris and Jenny spent a great deal of time drawing during their writing episodes. Any activity in which students created pictorial representations, or sketched or diagrammed some aspect of their stories, was coded as "drawing." Chris, for example, created a very elaborate diagram of a robot, from which he wrote a piece on how to build a robot. Jenny illustrated a piece on disco roller-skating with a picture of a roller skate. Both children sketched maps on occasion. Drawing occurred either before or after a child composed a particular segment of text.

WRITING ORALLY

Children frequently articulated words as they wrote them on the page. When speech accompanied writing, the behavior was coded as "writing

---

1. The experimenter's coding of composing behaviors was compared with another rater's results. Satisfactory agreement between the raters for a small sample of data indicated that the categories were well defined and identifiable.

orally." Sometimes a word was sounded out as it was encoded; at other times the child orally spelled the word; and at still others the child only said the word as he or she was writing.

WRITING SILENTLY

Writing that was not accompanied by audible speech was coded as "writing silently." From observation of the writing, the pauses examined recently by Flower and Hayes (1981) were evident. In coding writing behaviors, pausing was considered part of the writing category only if it was brief—less than three seconds. No attempt was made to distinguish between the covert intellectual activity required in composing and the physical effort and time employed in transcription. Performance factors probably either shaped or frustrated children's efforts in composing, but the character of the interaction was not accessible to direct observation.

ENGAGING IN READING-LIKE BEHAVIORS

The following three behaviors—reading orally, editing, and consulting texts—were coded separately for accuracy but were reported together in the data analysis as "reading-like behaviors" because these behaviors embedded reading in the composing process.

A percentage of the oral reading that was observed was done at the request of the experimenter; these instances were coded as interactions with the experimenter. Oral reading, however, did occur spontaneously and frequently. The reading could involve only a phrase or a sentence, or it could involve an entire passage or page. At times the oral reading prompted editing.

Students appeared to edit text when they decided that the words on the page were discrepant with their intentions. Often editing involved attending to spelling, although at times higher-level editing decisions regarding word choice, sentence construction, and paragraph organization were also observed. As with writing, editing involved both cognitive and physical activities. In coding this category, editing was judged to begin when a child either erased or crossed out a piece of text and to finish when the child either began rereading or continued writing. No distinction was drawn between editing and revising, for two reasons: (1) the videotape sessions usually involved the beginning of a new draft or the continuation of a piece begun earlier, rather than revision; and (2) students often began editing before they had finished writing a word, making it difficult to determine the reason for the change (e.g., incorrect spelling versus work choice). See Graves (1983) for a discussion of revision by young children.

Students sometimes interrupted their writing to read another portion of their texts or some other written reference source. Such behaviors were coded as "consulting texts."

ENGAGING IN COVERT BEHAVIORS

For a percentage of composing time, these children engaged in what appeared to be task-related but indeterminate behaviors. For example, they would look at the page with a pencil in hand but do nothing observable. One suspects that these periods of physical inactivity paralleled the intellectual activities of planning, reflecting, reading silently, or perhaps daydreaming.

INTERACTING WITH OTHERS

The Flanders–Amidon Interaction Scale (Amidon & Flanders, 1971) was used to account for the kinds of interaction that took place among the experimenter (who was always Graves, except in one instance), the child being videotaped, and occasionally another child in the classroom. The Interaction Scale distinguished among teacher talk, student talk, and silence and confusion. The coding permitted examination of the character and frequency of experimenter–student interactions, which were generally nondirective and student-centered.

Results and Analysis

The coding of composing behaviors permitted the students' development to be analyzed statistically as well as reported in qualitative terms.[2] Below, the statistical analyses of the percentage of time the children engaged in various composing behaviors are reported first, followed by qualitative accounts of the children's development as writers.

INITIAL DATA ANALYSIS

Initial analysis consisted of the tabulation of the percentage of time Jenny and Chris engaged in interactions with the experimenter or other students. The nature of the interactions was assessed by tallying the percentage of teacher talk (directive and nondirective) and student talk. In general, interactions accounted for a median of 13.9 percent of each writing episode for Jenny and 23.3 percent for Chris. The nondirective,

2. Readers unfamiliar with these kinds of observation instruments may find McNergney and Carrier (1981) helpful.

student-centered character of the interactions reflected the ethnographic approach employed by Graves and suggested that the children's behavior was natural and spontaneous. Subsequent analyses evaluated the percentage of time spent on composing behaviors exclusive of interactions.

QUANTITATIVE RESULTS

Median percentages and ranges for the five categories are reported in Table 8-1. A chi-square test of independence was used to determine whether the two children distributed their time equivalently over the five categories. A chi-square value of 43.474 ($df = 4, p = .001$) suggested that for the median percentages the two children distributed their time differently. Tables 8-2 and 8-3 and Figures 8-1, 8-2, and 8-3 show the patterns of behavior observed in the two years of videotaping.

In general, the percentage of time spent drawing and writing orally declined over the two years of the study, while the percentage of time spent in silent writing increased. In the first three sessions, for example, Chris spent a median of about 77 percent of his composing time either drawing or writing orally. In the last three sessions of the second year, this figure dropped to a median of 22 percent of his time. Silent writing increased from a median of 0 percent to 57 percent. The data on Jenny show a similar trend. Reading-like and covert behaviors appear to show no particular trend over the course of the study.

The rank correlation coefficient was used to confirm the direction and describe the strengths of the trends. To apply the statistic to Chris's drawing behaviors, for example, each episode was numbered chronologically. The drawing behaviors for each episode were then ranked in terms of the amount of time he spent drawing. The episode with the smallest percentage of time spent on drawing was ranked number 1, and the episode with the largest percentage was ranked number 19. Therefore, for each episode the rank correlation compared the relative amount of time spent drawing with that episode's chronological position.

Table 8-1. Medians and Ranges of Percentages of Time Spent in Various Task-Related Composing Behaviors

Composing behavior	Jenny		Chris	
	Median	Range	Median	Range
Drawing	3.1	0–53.3	23.2	0–65.7
Oral writing	6.1	0–36.9	24.6	4.2–57.1
Silent writing	46.7	1.2–61.2	22.2	0–62.7
Reading-like behaviors	23.3	13.5–31.7	7.4	2.5–19.3
Covert behaviors	15.5	10.7–24.1	14.3	4.7–35.4

Table 8-2. Percentage of Time Spent in Various Task-Related Composing Behaviors: Chris

	Grade 1: Number and date of session										
Composing behavior	1 12/20/78	2 1/3/79	3 2/1/79	4 2/15/79	5 3/15/79	6 3/16/79	7 3/20/79	8 4/6/79	9 4/9/79	10 5/4/79	11 5/14/79
Drawing	14.3	46.7	65.7	18.9	32.1	—	48.4	19.9	34.4	14.7	36.9
Oral writing	57.1	42.6	11.1	51.7	25.4	56.7	4.2	25.0	35.9	6.1	7.1
Silent writing	—	—	13.8	0.7	16.2	—	22.1	32.3	5.5	25.4	22.2
Reading-like behaviors	8.9	2.5	2.8	4.4	9.8	15.7	3.2	7.4	6.8	19.3	11.6
Covert behaviors	17.9	8.1	5.6	4.7	16.5	27.6	22.1	11.8	16.2	34.5	12.9

	Grade 2: Number and date of session							
Composing behavior	12 10/29/79	13 11/30/79	14 12/4/79	15 1/8/80	16 2/14/80	17 3/27/80	18 4/15/80	19 4/23/80
Drawing	23.2	28.1	30.4	20.7	20.1	13.9	1.2	—
Oral writing	23.2	25.0	34.1	24.6	24.5	7.6	21.9	6.1
Silent writing	39.3	29.2	18.5	39.1	34.4	28.5	57.4	62.7
Reading-like behaviors	5.4	6.9	8.3	8.0	6.6	13.9	4.0	10.5
Covert behaviors	7.1	10.0	7.8	7.2	14.3	35.4	15.5	19.7

Table 8-3. Percentage of Time Spent in Various Task-Related Composing Behaviors: Jenny

	Grade 1: Number and date of session		
Composing behavior	1 12/18/78	2 2/5/79	3 5/4/79
Drawing	53.3	9.2	1.3
Oral writing	15.8	36.9	24.4
Silent writing	1.2	4.1	31.3
Reading-like behaviors	14.5	26.7	31.3
Covert behaviors	15.2	21.5	11.9

	Grade 2: Number and date of session						
Composing behavior	4 11/5/79	5 11/28/79	6 2/13/80	7 3/8/80	8 3/27/80	9 4/15/80	10 4/21/80
Drawing	—	—	28.0	8.8	—	4.9	—
Oral writing	—	4.9	6.1	6.1	7.8	4.2	—
Silent writing	56.9	48.7	39.5	44.7	61.2	56.6	52.7
Reading-like behaviors	26.9	31.7	13.5	15.9	19.9	18.1	27.5
Covert behaviors	16.2	14.7	12.8	24.1	10.7	15.8	19.4

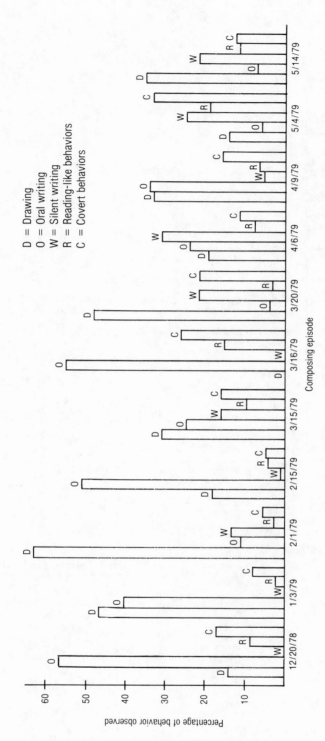

D = Drawing
O = Oral writing
W = Silent writing
R = Reading-like behaviors
C = Covert behaviors

Fig. 8-1. Development of composing behaviors in grade 1: Chris.

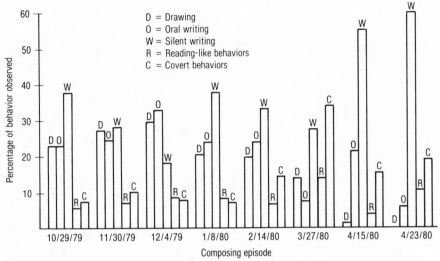

Fig. 8-2. *Development of composing behaviors in grade 2: Chris.*

Positive correlations would indicate a tendency for the behavior to increase in frequency over time, and negative correlations would indicate a decrease in frequency over time. Correlations close to zero would indicate little relationship between time and the frequency of behavior.

The rank correlations (R) confirmed the trends observed in Tables 8-2 and 8-3 and Figures 8-1, 8-2, and 8-3. For Chris, drawing and oral writing declined, with Rs of $-.59$ ($n = 19, p \le .006$) and $-.51$ ($n = 19, p \le .015$), respectively. Drawing and oral writing followed similar trends for Jenny, with Rs of $-.42$ ($n = 10, p \le .12$) and $-.62$ ($n = 10, p \le .03$).[3] Silent writing increased in frequency over time, with correlations of .85 ($n = 19, p \le .001$) and .71 ($n = 10, p \le .013$) for Chris and Jenny, respectively. Trends for reading-like behaviors and covert behaviors were less clear. Correlations for the observations on Chris for reading-like behaviors were .24 ($n = 19, p \le .15$) and for covert behaviors, .16 ($n = 19, p \le .25$). Jenny's correlations on these measures were .006 ($n = 10, p \le .50$) and .06 ($n = 10, p \le .45$), respectively.

Finally, in order to interpret the process measures used in this study, readability estimates (Spache, 1974) were calculated for three

---

3. Although the correlation coefficient for drawing was not significant at the .05 level, the observed frequencies reported in Figures 8-1, 8-2, and 8-3 do seem to reflect a trend. The nonsignificant correlation may have resulted from the inefficiency of the rank correlation in dealing with ties in ranking rather than from lack of a trend. The notable exception—session 6, in which 28 percent of the time was spent in drawing—involved Jenny diagramming a disco roller skate with care. This kind of drawing was uncharacteristic of Jenny, as well as being quite sophisticated.

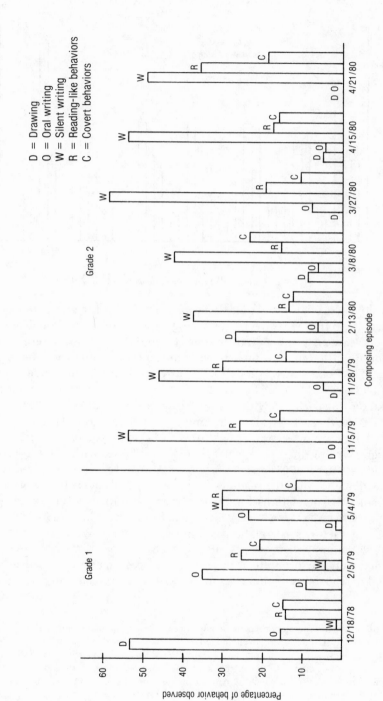

Fig. 8-3. Development of composing behaviors in grades 1 and 2: Jenny.

184

pieces of writing for each child. The pieces selected covered the span of the study and for the two children were matched chronologically. In April of grade 1, Jenny's story had a rated grade equivalent difficulty of 2.1; Chris's story was rated 2.0. In November of the second grade, Jenny wrote a story corresponding to a grade equivalent of 1.9 and Chris one corresponding to a 2.3 level. Finally, in April of the second year, the two children wrote stories corresponding to approximately 2.3 (Chris) and 2.4 (Jenny) readability levels. While these stories represented only a small sample of the children's writing, the data suggest that at least on this measure the children were keeping pace with each other. (However, see Bruce, Rubin, & Starr, 1981, for a discussion of the limitations of readability formulas.)

QUALITATIVE COMPARISONS

The quantitative analyses suggest that while Jenny and Chris showed similar trends in development, they differed from each other in important ways. An evaluation of the manner in which the two children drew, wrote, and read substantiated these differences.

Consider the differences observed in drawing. The earliest writing episodes of these students were characterized by a great deal of drawing. Jenny drew as much as 53.3 percent of the time and Chris 65.7 percent. Jenny, however, soon stopped drawing, while Chris continued to draw well into his second year. The differences in the use of drawing by Jenny and Chris seemed to result from Chris's approach of drawing before he wrote and using the drawing as a plan, and Jenny's use of drawing to illustrate her stories following composition. For Chris, drawing remained an important part of his prewriting activities well into the second year. Jenny seemed to use drawing to embellish her texts and discontinued its use rather early.

The two children also exhibited differences in their uses of oral writing. In the earliest episodes, Chris said a word, spelled it, and repeated it as he wrote. The volume of his oral writing decreased from virtually a conversational level to a whisper by the end of the first year. Chris continued to rely on oral writing to a substantial degree well into grade 2. Jenny provided a very different picture. Initially she sounded out the words as she wrote them, but soon she abandoned this strategy for silent writing. She continued, however, to use oral writing as an encoding strategy when she encountered a difficult word. She would sound out the word as she wrote, on one occasion spending nearly a minute writing a particular word.

Finally, differences were found in the children's frequency of reading-like behaviors. Jenny used reading about three times as frequently as did Chris (median of 23.3 percent, range of 13.5–31.7 percent; versus a median of 7.4 percent, range of 2.5–19.3 percent). Jenny frequently wrote a word or short phrase, reread it, and then edited. Chris's reading-like behaviors, although less frequent, were almost always rereading. When he reread, he usually read at least as much as a sentence and often a short passage.

Figures 8-1, 8-2, and 8-3 summarize the children's development. Jenny's early writing episodes could be characterized as drawing following composing, the use of oral writing as a default strategy analogous to the sound-by-sound decoding of words when reading, and frequent rereading and editing. In her later writing episodes, drawing declined markedly, oral writing was used only occasionally, and the majority of her time was spent writing silently. In contrast, Chris's early writing episodes included drawing before composing, a great deal of oral writing, and relatively little rereading or editing. While Chris also ended the second year by reducing the amount of drawing and oral writing in favor of silent writing, the shift was slower and less dramatic than Jenny's.

The Children's Attitudes

Both children enjoyed the writing sessions, although Chris remarked in the second year that he found writing to be "hard work." The children discussed classroom activities with the experimenter on occasion. Chris took a particular interest in classroom activity while he wrote. In a session during the first year, Jenny complained wistfully about missing words on a spelling test that she really knew how to spell.

Chris and Jenny wrote on a variety of topics and in different modes. Chris wrote, for example, about World War II, inserting spacecraft from *Star Wars* into a dogfight over Germany. He wrote a very long piece about the planets, narrative accounts of his activities with friends, and a science fiction piece in which he was the hero. A particularly memorable piece by Chris was a diagram and set of instructions for building a robot. When Graves asked a question about the piece, he was advised to pay more careful attention to the diagram and instructions. Jenny wrote an Easter play in the spring of her first year, took great care to explain and to diagram disco roller skates in grade 2, and near the end of the second year, began to write mysteries.

While the children enjoyed the videotaping, at least Chris was aware that Graves was interested in watching him write. Chris used to ask Graves to "cut" the videotaping so that he could take a break to go to the bathroom. He also asked Graves to erase an earlier portion of tape that contained an opinion about which he had changed his mind. Although both children had days when they were frustrated with writing, they seemed to have success in school and respond well to the demands of composing.

Discussion

Graves (1982) explained that as children develop as writers, they use less drawing and speech in their composing. The results of the study, described in this chapter support Graves's hypothesis. In the early stages of composing, Chris and Jenny drew and wrote orally; as they matured as writers, silent writing replaced these more overt approaches. In spite of the similar trends noted in the performance of the two children, stark individual differences were also observed. Instructional procedures in writing must take such differences into account.

The second purpose of this study was to examine the role of reading in the composing behaviors of young children. The children not only engaged in reading while they wrote, as suggested by the median percentages reported, but they also wrote orally—an activity that seemed to bear a useful relationship to reading. In the earlier composing episodes, oral writing represented a deliberate strategy for encoding speech as text—Chris spelled words orally as he wrote them, Jenny sounded out the words. Both children, although Jenny more so than Chris, appeared to use oral writing as a default strategy: when they could not immediately produce a word, they resorted to sounding out or attempting to spell the item. It appears that oral writing may have served as a link between speech and printed text.

Writing orally also resembled spelling. When students wrote orally, they were saying words, spelling them (orally or silently), and, as the incidence of editing suggested, reading to check the spelling. While the spellings were frequently not standard, they usually represented accurately at least initial and final sounds—as Sowers (1981) has observed. Carney (1981) has pointed out that the sequence noted by Sowers corresponds to the findings that Gibson and Levin (1975) reported in summarizing word-perception studies. Specifically, initial letters are most salient, followed by final letters and lastly by medial letters. Hence, the invented spellings found in the oral writings of children seem to capture those portions of words that readers find most visually salient. While this line of reasoning is only suggestive, oral writing may bear a particularly close relationship to decoding.

Conclusions

Developmental trends in composing behaviors demonstrate a movement from oral to silent writing and the disappearance of visual representations of information (drawings). The data summarized in this chapter also suggest that when young children compose, they do a great deal more than just transcribe words. Drawing, reading, and reflecting all seem to be linked to the composing task. Finally, the protocols of the two children reveal vast individual differences between two successful early elementary school writers.

The finding that two writers used markedly different procedures argues that one should eschew a curriculum or method that tries to teach composing to all children through a predetermined course of instruction or sequence of skills. It would be a mistake, for example, to prevent children from drawing before they write, or to require children to compose silently.

The role played by reading in composing leads one to expect that a writing program would benefit children's reading ability. While this premise needs verification, the finding that at least these two children spent a substantial portion of their composing time engaged in reading activities would justify devoting some of the time allocated for traditional reading instruction to composing. Implementation of a program like the Atkinson model (Graves, 1983) could well lead to improvement in reading ability.

ACKNOWLEDGMENTS

I would like to thank Mary Ellen Giacobbe, John Carney, and Donald Graves for their assistance in preparing this chapter.

REFERENCES

Amidon, E. J., & Flanders, N. A. The role of teaching in the classroom (Rev. ed.). St. Paul, Minn.: Association for Productive Teachers, 1971.

Bissex, G. GNYS AT WRK: A child learns to write and read. Cambridge, Mass.: Harvard University Press, 1980.

Bloom, L. The integration of form, content, and use in language development. In J. F. Kavanagh & W. Strange (Eds.), Speech and language in the laboratory, school, and clinic. Cambridge, Mass.: MIT Press, 1978.

Britton, J. Spectator role and the beginnings of writing. In M. Nystrand (Ed.), What writers know: The language, process, and structure of written discourse. New York: Academic Press, 1982.

Bruce, B., Rubin, A., & Starr, K. Why readability formulas fail (Reading Education Report No. 28). Cambridge, Mass.: Bolt Beranek & Newman, August 1981 (ERIC Document Reproduction Service No. ED 205 915).

Calkins, L. M. Notes and comments: Children's rewriting strategies. Research in the Teaching of English, 1980, 14(4) 331–341.

Carney, J. Personal communication, October 1981.

Cazden, C. B. Child language and education. New York: Holt, Rinehart & Winston, 1972.

Chomsky, C. Write now, read later. Childhood Education, 1971, 47, 296–299.

Clay, M. What did I write? Auckland, New Zealand: Heinemann, 1975.

Collins, J. L., & Williamson, M. M. Spoken language and semantic abbreviation in writing. Research in the Teaching of English, 1981, 15(1), 23–36.

Dale, P. S. *Language development: Structure and function* (2nd ed.). New York: Holt, Rinehart & Winston, 1976.

Dickens, C. *Hard times*. London: Collins, 1972. (Originally published, 1854.)

Durkin, D. *Children who read early*. New York: Teachers College Press, 1966.

Dyson, A. H. *The role of oral language in early writing processes*. N.d. Entry for National Council of Teachers of English 1982 Promising Research Award Competition.

Ehri, L. C. Word consciousness in readers and prereaders. *Journal of Educational Psychology*, 1975, *67*, 204–212.

Flower, L., & Hayes, J. R. The pregnant pause: An inquiry into the nature of planning. *Research in the Teaching of English*, 1981, *15*(3), 229–243.

Gibson, E. J., & Levin, H. *The psychology of reading*. Cambridge, Mass.: MIT Press, 1975.

Graves, D. H. *Balance the basics: Let them write*. New York: Ford Foundation, 1978.

Graves, D. H. *The growth and development of first grade writers*. Paper presented at annual meeting of Canadian Council of Teachers of English, Ottawa, May 1979.

Graves, D. H. *A case study observing the development of primary children's composing, spelling, and motor behaviors during the writing process*. Final report for NIE Grant G-78-0174, Project 8-0343/9-0963, February 1982.

Graves, D. H. *Writing: Teachers and children at work*. Exeter, N.H.: Heinemann Educational Books, 1983.

Gundlach, R. A. Children as writers: The beginnings of learning to write. In M. Nystrand (Ed.), *What writers know: The language, process, and structure of written discourse*. New York: Academic Press, 1982.

Halliday, M. A. K. *Explorations in the functions of language*. London: Edward Arnold, 1973.

Hiebert, E. H. Developmental patterns and interrelationships of preschool children's print awareness. *Reading Research Quarterly*, 1981, *16*(2), 236–259.

Hiebert, E. H., Cioffi, G., & Antonak, R. F. *A hierarchy of preschool children's print awareness concepts and reading readiness skills*. Paper presented at biennial meeting of the Society for Research in Child Development, Detroit, April 1983.

Holden, M. J., & MacGinitie, W. H. Children's conceptions of word boundaries in speech and print. *Journal of Educational Psychology*, 1972, *63*(6), 551–557.

Kroll, B. M. Developmental relationships between speaking and writing. In B. M. Kroll & R. J. Vann (Eds.), *Exploring speaking-writing relationships: Connections and contrasts*. Urbana, Ill.: National Council of Teachers of English, 1981.

McNergney, R. F., & Carrier, C. A. *Teacher development*. New York: Macmillan, 1981.

Mason, J. M. When *do* children begin to read: An exploration of four year old children's letter and word reading competencies. *Reading Research Quarterly*, 1980, *15*, 203–227.

Mason, J. M. *Prereading: A developmental perspective* (Technical Report No. 198). Urbana: University of Illinois, Center for the Study of Reading, February 1981 (ERIC Document Reproduction Service No. ED 199 659).

Mason, J. M., & McCormick, C. *Testing the development of reading and linguistic awareness* (Technical Report No. 126). Urbana: University of Illinois, Center for the Study of Reading, May 1979 (ERIC Document Reproduction Service No. ED 170 735).

Moffett, J. *Teaching the universe of discourse*. Boston: Houghton Mifflin, 1968.

Olson, D. R. From utterance to text: The bias of language in speech and writing. *Harvard Educational Review*, 1977, *47*, 257–281.

Perl, S. The composing processes of unskilled college writers. *Research in the Teaching of English*, 1979, *13*(4), 317–336.

Rubin, A. A theoretical taxonomy of the differences between oral and written language. In R. J. Spiro, B. C. Bruce, & W. F. Brewer (Eds.), *Theoretical issues in reading comprehension*. Hillsdale, N.J.: Lawrence Erlbaum, 1980.

Scardamalia, M., Bereiter, C., & Goelman, H. The role of production factors in writing ability. In M. Nystrand (Ed.), *What writers know: The language, process, and structure of written discourse*. New York: Academic Press, 1982.

Sowers, S. KDS CN RIT SUNR THN WE THINGK. In R. D. Walshe (Ed.), *Donald Graves in Australia—"Children want to write. . . ."* Rozelle, New South Wales, Australia: Primary English Teaching Association, 1981.

Spache, G. D. *Good reading for poor readers* (9th ed.). Champaign, Ill.: Garrard Publishing, 1974.

Stotsky, S. The role of writing in developmental reading. *Journal of Reading*, 1982, *25*(4), 330–340.

Vygotsky, L. S. *Mind and society* (M. Cole, V. John-Steiner, S. Scribner, & E. Souberman, Eds.). Cambridge, Mass.: Harvard University Press, 1978.

9

The relations between reading and writing in young children

LEE GALDA
University of Georgia

Research in composition has proliferated in the past decade as writing ability has joined reading ability as a criterion for literacy. Because writing became the focus of many researchers, we now have an idea of the process behind the product. Now that we do understand some aspects of writing, it is important to integrate what we know about writing with what we know about reading. It seems that children fluent in one area of language are often fluent in others (Loban, 1976). If this is true, then there might be certain similarities in the processes of each that would account for this simultaneous fluency. Further, it would seem that experience in one might influence facility in the other. In light of these assumptions, this chapter examines selected research in reading and writing to begin to determine possible relations between these two aspects of literacy.

First, the environments that produce early readers and early writers and these young children's concepts of print are discussed. The hypothesis-testing strategies underlying reading and writing are then considered. Following this is a discussion of the impact that experience with text has on both reading and writing. Finally, this chapter considers recent investigations of the relations between reading and writing, with special attention to the similarities between the two and the influence of reading on the writing process. These areas of inquiry—environmental influences, concepts about print, print-processing strategies, experience with text, and the integration of reading and writing—form the background for summarizing the implications for research and instruction.

Virtually all children enter school fairly fluent in their oral language (Bloom, 1970). However, only some of these children come to school ready to begin to read and write; others are far from ready. This disparity in readiness cannot be fully explained by differences in intelligence and language background (Clay, 1967). However, one feature common to the background of most of these children is their familiarity with and love for favorite books (Holdaway, 1979). Because of this similarity, Holdaway investigated the properties of the "bedtime story" model from an oral language acquisition perspective to determine just what influences it may have on early reading. He found that, like oral language acquisition, orientation to book language develops through exposure to language far beyond the child's immediate needs or abilities. The child who is read to is immersed in an environment in which the skill of reading is being used in a meaningful way. This environment is emulative rather than instructional; the *child* selects significant items to learn. These self-selected items are then practiced by the child at a pace and for a duration that are self-determined. Further, the purpose behind the bedtime story is pleasure, and strongly positive associations with books are developed.

Children who are frequently read to often exhibit reading-like behavior long before they are actually reading (Holdaway, 1979). This reading-like behavior consists of turning the pages of a book and "saying" a story that is based on the story contained in the book. Forester (1980) and King (1980) have suggested how the development of early writing might parallel oral language development, proposing that the scribbling phase of writing parallels the babbling phase of oral language acquisition. Reading-like activity would be the equivalent behavior in the progressive acquisition of reading ability. The behavior of reading is being approximated, and, as the child progresses in development, these approximations will come more and more to resemble the adult model. Further, because this practice is directed by the child and is a pleasant experience, a positive attitude toward reading is developed that should in turn positively influence the child's attitude toward reading instruction.

Research in early writing, or writing readiness, has also revealed the importance of the environment. Hall, Moretz, and Statom (1976) found that children who were in a home environment where writing was used in meaningful ways—for example, in letters to friends and notes to other members of the family—attempted to write at an early age. This environment, like that of children who perform reading-like actions, was emulative, not instructional. Like the "bedtime story" environment in reading acquisition and the supportive rewarding of approximations in oral language acquisition, the environment of these early writers was one in which children's productions were responded to with pleasure and their questions answered when asked (Hall *et al.*, 1976; Read, 1971).

A supportive environment in which reading and writing are used frequently and in meaningful ways seems, then, to aid in the development of a "literacy set" (Holdaway, 1979). This mental set sends some children to school ready to read and write, or already beginning to learn these processes. Those who are not ready may not have had the same environmental opportunities. As Birnbaum states, "While almost every baby capable of developing oral language receives sufficient information from observation and interaction with others to develop a model of the uses of oral language in his subculture, some children have little or no access to information about the uses of written language in their social environment" (1980, p. 203). This lack of information must then be addressed in the early school years.

Florio (1979a, 1979b) and Milz (1980) have documented two teachers' successful efforts to provide meaningful contexts for writing in the classroom. Building on the idea that children use and value language as a communicative tool, Milz and her first-grade children write notes to one another. The children also write in journals, to which the teacher responds, and write stories that become part of the reading material of the classroom. These children are using writing to communicate a message, and they learn to write from their immersion in a purposeful and print-filled environment. Florio (1979a, 1979b) showed how a second-grade teacher developed a similar meaningful context for writing by creating the classroom community of "Betterburg." Similarly, Holdaway (1979) has discussed how a group of teachers in Australia re-created the "bedtime story" environment found so effective in helping children develop positive attitudes toward reading at home, and has provided detailed plans for developing such an environment. Clearly, a meaningful pleasurable context for the communication of informational or poetic messages is a basic requirement for the development of both writing and reading abilities and can occur in both home and school environments.

In addition to similar environmental influences on the development of a "literacy set" for reading and writing, similarities in the concepts of print developed by early writers and early readers are also apparent. Although early writing may look like scribbling, certain powerful concepts about language in print inform the development of the child writer (Clay, 1975; DeFord, 1980; Harste & Burke, 1980). As children move from random scribbling to the writing of recognizable words and sentences, they are developing and employing several concepts about print. Children who are early writers learn that there is a certain directional arrangement which letters and words must follow and that a space must be placed between words to signal the end of a word. They progress from an understanding of the within-word direction to an understanding of within-page and within-story direction (Clay, 1975). Children who write do so from an understanding that words carry meaning and that what is spoken can be written down. They realize that there is a conventional way of writing a letter or word which is stable and may be repeated and combined with other letters and words to form a message that can be understood by others (Clay, 1975).

Children who are frequently read to develop similar concepts about print. They become familiar with directional and positional conventions, including front to back, top to bottom, left to right. They come to understand written symbols as signs and learn to attend to language without the support of concrete objects, relying entirely on print to carry meaning (Clay, 1975; Holdaway, 1979). They learn about letters and words. Immersion in an environment that provides information about print in a meaningful context helps children to acquire the knowledge about print necessary for learning to read (Goodman & Goodman, 1979; Hiebert, 1981; F. Smith, 1976).

Early contact with reading (being read to and reading-like behavior) and early contact with writing (seeing adults use writing to communicate and scribbling) influence the facility with which children learn these skills. Not only does the environment provide a purpose for these literacy behaviors, but the early and sustained contact with written texts also provides information from which children can develop concepts about print. Being read to should, therefore, facilitate writing as well as reading, just as early writing can serve "to organize the visual analysis of print" (Clay, 1975) so that children come to the reading task with an implicit knowledge of what to do with the words they encounter. Experience with one aspect of written language provides the concept-building child with information about the other.

One example of the interrelatedness of reading and writing is found in Gillooly's (1973) assertion that certain characteristics of the writing system itself have an effect on the early and intermediate stages of learning to read. The principles upon which our writing system rests, phonographic and orthographic representation, influence the reading process. As children work with language, manipulating it to encode the meaning they intend, they are internalizing principles about our writing system. English-speaking children, for example, learn that we have both phonographic (letter-sound correspondence) and orthographic (word families) regularities underlying the English spelling system (Gillooly, 1973). The exploration of this system through invented spelling can have a significant positive influence on both reading and writing ability (Chomsky, 1971). Invented spelling gives children access to print through the manipulation of preformed letters or through their own writing. This access to print influences writing fluency in that it allows children to say what they want to say without waiting to acquire spelling fluency.

At an even more basic level, however, invented spelling influences reading and writing fluency by giving the child practice in abstracting principles of language. Read has suggested that this may be a necessity: "Children can (and to some degree, must) make abstract inferences about the sound system of their language before they learn to read and write" (1971, p. 32). Another writer (F. Smith, 1981) has speculated that this influence is reciprocal, in that reading has a continued influence on a reader's knowledge of the spelling system by providing thousands of examples of correctly spelled words that the reader processes.

The hypothesis-testing behavior that allows children to abstract principles about language, be they phonological, orthographic, grammatical, or structural, is evident in the literature on oral language acquisition (Bloom, 1970; Brown, 1973). Children can and do actively process the linguistic information that they take in. It seems logical that the hypothesis-testing activities of children as they acquire oral language would be carried over into the acquisition and development of written language. That this is the case is clearly demonstrated by research in invented spelling. Read's (1971) study of preschool children's knowledge of phonology revealed that children's seemingly random choices in spelling were actually based on specific articulatory features. Their choices were clearly systematic as they moved from their initial hypotheses (based mostly on sound) about the way spelling works to more mature rule systems. Although children may begin with attempts at regular phoneme/grapheme correspondence, mature spellers, like mature readers, learn to look for underlying lexical principles and recognize lexical similarities even when there are phonetic differences (Chomsky, 1970). The studies of invented spelling in early writing clearly illustrate that children are actively processing information about language and its use as they work toward fluent writing.

Children also actively process information about language as they work toward fluent reading. Miscue analysis has demonstrated that "reading is an active, receptive process" (Goodman & Goodman, 1977, p. 325). As readers read, they do more than recognize sight words or combine known phonemes. Readers process several kinds of information. The fact that readers, like writers, are continually making hypotheses as they read can be seen by examining the miscues they make. For example, a reader is shown to be attending to and basing predictions on graphic information when he or she substitutes a word of similar graphic construction for the intended word. Readers demonstrate the processing of syntactic information when they substitute verb for verb or noun for noun (Goodman & Goodman, 1977). Similarly, substitutions usually "retain the morphemic markings of the text" (Goodman & Goodman, 1977), demonstrating readers' awareness of bound morphemic rules. These systematic choices by readers demonstrate that there are regularities operating in seemingly incorrect or random choices in oral reading, just as there are in invented spelling.

To summarize, both the acquisition of and the strategies employed in speaking, reading, and writing are similar. Fluency is acquired through the active processing of linguistic information in an environment that is supportive and provides many opportunities for both receiving and producing language. The concepts that children develop about language enable them to communicate with others in both the oral and written modes. The examples of active processing discussed above focus primarily on the "surface" concerns of encoding and decoding written language. However, just as children talk and listen in order to communicate and receive meaning, so do fluent readers and writers engage in those processes for the same reasons. Further, experience with the world and with language influences the meanings that children construct in both the decoding and the encoding processes.

Studies of oral reading indicate that readers read for meaning. For example, when they make miscues that are semantically acceptable to them within the context of the text, they often do not correct these miscues (Goodman & Goodman, 1977). Such miscues are not problematic, because readers are processing meaningful wholes and because semantically acceptable miscues do not interfere with meaning. The processing of written discourse is certainly influenced by the reader's experiences (Anderson, Reynolds, Shallert, & Geotz, 1976; Adams & Collins, 1977). It is also influenced by readers' expectations with regard to written discourse structure. A psycholinguistic view of reading sees the acquisition of experience with language and with the environment as the way in which beginning readers move toward fluency (Cooper & Petrosky, 1976). The acquisition of experience is necessary to attain fluency because reading involves making inferences based both on knowledge of the world and on knowledge of text. Fluent readers—rather than recognizing individual letters, translating the letters into sounds, combining sounds into words, and then stringing words together to form sentences—process information on a printed page in chunks of meaning, often not pausing to decode each word. As sentences and paragraphs unfold, readers form, reject, and confirm hypotheses about what is being read (Iser, 1972).

With this active hypothesizing the reader is adding to his or her storehouse of experience with print, thus increasing fluency. "One has to read, make mistakes, and test hypotheses in order to become a fluent reader. The experience of reading and attempting to read is the weightiest component of the process of reading development" (Cooper & Petrosky, 1976, p. 191). Thus, the psycholinguistic view of reading sees practice with texts as the major force in the acquisition of reading fluency. This practice, however, must be meaningful and thus requires whole texts rather than isolated skill drills.

So, too, practice with meaningful wholes is necessary for the development of fluent writers. When children begin to write on their own they produce "messages" that carry a meaning and are often indignant if someone cannot understand that meaning. Children become fluent in written discourse by producing writing that is important to them, writing that springs from an intent to communicate rather than from an attempt to write a neat, error-free paper (Graves, 1979; Milz, 1980). In a study involving fourth- and seventh-grade students, Birnbaum (1981) found that the more proficient writers wrote more than did the less proficient writers, with the more proficient writers reporting that they often engaged in self-initiated writing and viewed themselves as good writers. The practice in meaningful writing in which the proficient writers engaged gave them both the experience and the confidence from which to approach the writing act.

Meaningful practice develops fluency in speaking, reading, and writing. It gives children the opportunity to hypothesize about the way language works at the phonetic and syntactic levels while they are encoding or decoding at the semantic level. Further, using language also provides information about its pragmatic functions. Just as children learn to use their oral language for different functions (Halliday, 1975), so do fluent readers and writers learn to differentiate the functions of text.

Britton's (1970) discussion of how language is used in spectator and participant roles includes broad but clear comparisons among oral language, reading, and writing. Children learn to adopt the role of participant, and use language to get things done in the world. They also learn to talk about experiences that are not taking place at the time of the discourse, using this talk to construe, speculate, and evaluate. This is language in the spectator role. These two ways of using language are also applicable to writing and reading. Children move from writing primarily in an expressive mode, in which the roles of participant or spectator may be present but are undifferentiated, to being able to structure their written discourse according to their purposes (Britton, 1970). That is, if they want to convey information they do not write a story, and, conversely, if they want to construe an experience they do not write a report. Mature readers also are able to make the appropriate distinctions between spectator and participant roles. Children learn to adopt a participant stance and read certain texts for information, evaluating that information with reference to the external world. They learn to adopt a spectator stance toward other texts, notably stories, reading for vicarious experience and evaluating those texts in terms of the story world and their own responses (Galda, 1982). Children's growth in the ability to process written language in both roles necessarily depends on many factors, including cognitive development (see Applebee, 1978).

One other aspect of the development of an understanding of the functions of written texts is the influence of experience with those texts. The ways in which such experience affects the understanding and the production of texts have been examined from several different perspectives. The body of research grounded in story schema theory has provided examples of children using their knowledge about story, or narrative, as they both read and write. Mandler and Johnson (1977) found that recall of stories was best when the stories conformed to some kind of "ideal" story structure that readers had developed through contact with well-formed stories. Additions to a story were made during recall that reflected an ideal structure. Story readers (or listeners) come to "expect certain patterns of information, attend to informational sequences that match these patterns, and organize incoming information into similar patterns" (Stein & Glenn, 1978). This use of expected story structures extrapolated from experience also occurs in writing. Bereiter, Scardamalia, and Turkish (1980) investigated the relations between children's identification of Stein and Glenn's (1978) narrative elements and their use of those elements in their writing. They found that children "used significantly more text elements in their writing than they named" (p. 2), indicating that narrative discourse elements identified by attending to stories find their way into the production of story, even though the knowledge may not be fully articulated. As research in this area progresses, investigators should move beyond an inquiry into structure and address issues concerning other expectations that influence reading and writing. For example, when do children understand (or expect) motivations and causal relations in written discourse, and how does that understanding or lack of it influence their comprehension and production? Another promising avenue of inquiry lies in the interaction between children's exposure to texts that use a variety of rhetorical or literary devices and their ability to comprehend and produce these devices.

Investigations into the development of children's understanding and use of literary conventions have begun. Applebee (1978) found that readers of stories come to expect certain literary conventions, such as "once upon a time," use of past tense, and dialogue. Even very young children internalize forms of stories, and these forms can be observed in their own storytelling. Even two-year-olds use "at least some conventions in 70 percent of their stories" (p. 52). There is a developmental progression in the acquisition of those conventions, with the child's cognitive development and experience with story contributing to that progression (Applebee, 1978). King, Rentel, and Cook (1980) examined the oral retellings and the story writings of twenty first-graders to determine what story functions or conventions appeared. They found that the oral retellings contained "most of the functions typically found in the fairy stories to which they were exposed" (p. 8). As those same children gained control over their writing, they included more and more functions, both obligatory structures and structures that serve a primarily enriching function. What they heard or read was incorporated into what they told and wrote. The structures of stories that children internalized formed a background for the stories they produced. Britton (1970) has pointed out that, while children do have excellent examples of narrative structure and literary stylistic options in the children's literature they read, they have fewer models of good expository prose. This lack may be partially responsible for children's difficulty in learning to write expository texts.

Bissex (1980), in her discussion of the development of her son Paul's writing, demonstrated how other forms and functions encountered when reading were incorporated into writing as Paul became increasingly able to differentiate among forms, between writer and audience, and also among kinds of audiences. More research of this nature is necessary, research that looks closely at written language development and explores the relations among forms of languages. Such investigations should consider both the manner of language acquisition and development and the ways in which experience with one form of language influences other forms.

There have been other inquiries into the relations between reading and writing, although the number of theoretical models is greater than the number of empirical studies. (See Birnbaum, 1981, for an extensive review of this literature.) Those empirical studies which have been conducted have primarily involved measuring performance in reading and in writing and correlating the results, most often using syntactic complexity as a basis (Evans, 1979; W. Smith, 1970). Other studies have attempted to assess how instruction in one process influences growth in the other, as in the research centering on sentence combining and its effect on reading achievement and/or writing ability (Crews, 1971; Hughes, 1975; Combs, 1976). Only recently have we begun to look for relations between the processes involved in reading and in writing and to investigate the interactive nature of experiences in each.

The Bissex study mentioned above is the most intensive and extensive study to date of one child's development as a reader and a writer. Although they do not involve young children, three other recent studies (Atwell, 1980; Birnbaum, 1981; Shanahan, 1980) have specifically addressed the nature of the relations between reading and writing and are therefore of concern in this chapter.

The recursive nature of the writing process has been amply demonstrated (Emig, 1971; Perl, 1979; Pianko, 1979). Because of this recursiveness—that is, because reading is one way that writers retrieve and structure their texts—Atwell (1980) argued that one must study the reading process when studying the writing process. She manipulated the experimental conditions so that her participants were unable to read part of what they had written. Atwell found that both good and poor writers read their writing as they composed but that they read for different reasons. Good writers both preplanned and read, focusing on the overall meaning and coherence of their pieces. Not being able to read their writing did hinder the good writers' control of the structure of their writing, but this was not as disturbing to them as it was to the poor writers. The good writers could rely on their global plan to help them structure their pieces. Poor writers, on the other hand, were more surface-text dependent and relied more on reading than did good writers. Lacking a global plan, they had to read what they had written to know what else to write. Both good and poor writers read, but they read differently. It is this difference that seems to be the key to success in processing written language.

Perl (1979) noted that poor writers do not read effectively as they write. Atwell (1980) and Birnbaum (1981), in their discussions of good and poor writers, clarify what makes that reading ineffective. Quite simply, poor writers are also poor readers. They read for surface concerns such as mechanics and spelling without paying attention to the overall meaning of their texts. Poor writers also write at a surface level, showing more concern with editing than with their messages. On the other hand, good writers and good readers are concerned with wholes, with the sense of the text they are writing or reading (Atwell, 1980; Birnbaum, 1981). Not only are the ways in which they read their own writing different, but the general manners of reading vary between good and poor writers. Good readers, who are usually good writers, monitor their own responses as they read, much as they monitor their own writing (Birnbaum, 1981). Poor readers and writers don't. Another difference lies in their views of themselves. The poor writers felt that they were indeed poor writers; the good writers knew that they were good (Birnbaum, 1981). Further, good readers/writers indicated that they drew more upon past experiences as they planned and made predictions during both the reading and the writing processes (Birnbaum, 1981).

The differences between good and poor writers and readers might be reflected in how the relations between good reading and good writing change over time. Shanahan (1980) found that for children reading below third-grade level, the highest correlation between reading and writing was between word recognition and spelling. For those reading above fifth-grade level, the most significant relation was more global, occurring between reading comprehension and the structural complexity and lexical diversity of writing. Shanahan noted, however, that the relations he had identified only accounted for a portion of the variance.

What do these studies of older (second-, fourth-, fifth-, and seventh-grade and college undergraduate) writers/readers tell us about younger writers and readers? First, fluent readers and writers, young and old, are concerned with meaningful wholes rather than isolated parts. Just as children speak to convey meaning, so do fluent children read and write for meaning. Second, fluent readers and writers, at any age, draw upon their prior experience with and knowledge about both texts and the world. They also feel confident about their abilities as writers/readers. (See Harste and Burke, 1980, for an example of how that self-confidence can be shaken.) Fluent older readers and writers are aware of how print works, recognizing strategies and making predictions as they read and write. Young children also seek to discover how print works. This hypothesis-forming and -testing behavior is, then another characteristic of fluent readers/writers, although the focus of the hypothesizing seems to change over time.

Smith has suggested that extensive reading can facilitate learning to write, that "the secret of learning to write by reading [is] *by reading like a writer*" (F. Smith, 1981, p. 110). If this is the case, then one must first be a writer in order to know how to read like one. But writing doesn't simply spring, fully formed, on to paper. It is partially the result of prior experiences with print—and these experiences are experiences in reading. Reading experiences influence writing, and experiences as an author influence reading. We may never definitively state what comes first, but we can see that they are clearly related, both in origin and in process.

However, it is not sufficient to merely make the global statement that reading and writing are related. That relationship must be investigated, both by tracing the development of individual children as they learn to read and write and by studying large groups of children engaging in reading and writing. We need more precise information about environmental assistance. What factors in the home produce early readers/writers? What factors in the classroom encourage development in reading and writing? The emergence of reading and writing must be examined. Do children apply the same principles to their encoding and decoding of written language? What concepts about language are the most facilitative? Does the development of appropriate strategies for reading parallel the development of appropriate strategies for writing?

The interaction of what is being read and what is being written is another area for further research. We need to look more closely at how the reading of stories affects the stories children write as well as those they tell. Does the development of written narrative parallel that of oral narrative? Do children become aware of the potential connections between what they read and what they write? How do they learn to "read like writers" and use what they have observed in their reading to make conscious choices in their writing? Where do they acquire the information on which they base their decisions as authors? How do their experiences as authors influence the predictions and evaluations they make as they read? Are there adequate models of forms of writing other than stories, or even adequate opportunities to engage in these other forms at an early age? When do other forms emerge, and what seems to be the impetus for their use? Do children differentiate among forms only in structure, or do they make the kinds of sophisticated and systematic choices that they make in their oral language?

A third general area of inquiry might be the development of good and poor readers/writers. Information about environmental assistance and strategies is, of course, basic to answering questions about why some children learn to read and write more easily than others. However, there seems to be something in addition to attitude, ability, or environment that results in such different levels of expertise. It was suggested earlier that the differences between the strategies of older good and poor readers might be reflected in the development of good reading/writing skills. For example, is there a "critical period" when children move from at least a partial concern with parts (that is, spelling and mechanics) in writing, and from a focus on individual words and letters in reading, to a concern with wholes, with making meaning?

If there is, then teachers must learn how to recognize readiness for this transition as well as provide opportunities to encourage it. However, reading and writing for meaning needn't wait until the accompanying skills are acquired. Rather, a focus on meaning facilitates the development of skills. As children gain control of written language they can be encouraged to explore various forms of writing as the need to use those forms arises. Teachers can provide models of good writing in forms other than narrative as well as provide a meaningful context for the development of those forms. Children can be encouraged to look at what they are reading with a writer's eyes, through discussions of how and why different authors say different things.

In the midst of all of these words, two principles stand out clearly. Children who read and write well do so to create meaning. Children who read and write well also become aware of the choices they have and the strategies they use as they are making meaning. Perhaps the principles underlying the way we teach reading and writing should be the same: focus on meaning, and help children become aware of their choices as meaning-makers.

REFERENCES

Adams, M. J., & Collins, A. *A schema-theoretic view of reading* (Technical Report No. 32). Urbana, Ill.: Center for the Study of Reading, 1977.

Anderson, R. C., Reynolds, R. E., Shallert, D. L., & Geotz, E. T. *Frameworks for comprehending discourse* (Technical Report No. 12). Urbana, Ill.: Center for the Study of Reading, 1976.

Applebee, A. N. *The child's concept of story.* Chicago: University of Chicago Press, 1978.

Atwell, M. *The evolution of text: The interrelationships of reading and writing in the composing process.* Unpublished doctoral dissertation, Indiana University, 1980.

Bereiter, C., Scardamalia, M., & Turkish, L. *The child as discourse grammarian.* Paper presented at annual meeting of American Educational Research Association, April 1980.

Birnbaum, J. C. Why should I write? Environmental influences on children's views of writing. *Theory into Practice,* 1980, *19,* 202-210.

Birnbaum, J. C. *A study of reading and writing behaviors of selected fourth and seventh grade students.* Unpublished doctoral dissertation, Rutgers University, 1981.

Bissex, G. L. *Gnys at wrk: A child learns to write and read.* Cambridge, Mass.: Harvard University Press, 1980.

Bloom, L. *Language development: Form and function in emerging grammars.* Cambridge, Mass.: MIT Press, 1970.

Britton, J. B. *Language and learning.* London: Allen Lane, Penguin Press, 1970.

Brown, R. *A first language: The early stages.* Cambridge, Mass.: Harvard University Press, 1973.

Chomsky, C. Reading, writing and phonology. *Harvard Educational Review,* 1970, *40,* 287-309.

Chomsky, C. Write now, read later. *Childhood Education,* 1971, *47,* 296-299.

Clay, M. The reading behavior of five year old children: A research report. *New Zealand Journal of Educational Studies,* 1967, *2,* 11-31.

Clay, M. *What did I write?* Auckland, New Zealand: Heinemann, 1975.

Combs, W. E. Further effects of sentence-combining practice on writing ability. *Research in the Teaching of English,* 1976, *10,* 137-149.

Cooper, C. R., & Petrosky, A. R. A psycholinguistic view of the fluent reading process. *Journal of Reading,* December 1976, 184-207.

Crews, R. A linguistic versus a traditional grammar program: The effects on written sentence structure and comprehension. *Educational Leadership,* 1971, *29,* 145-149.

DeFord, D. Young children and their writing. *Theory into Practice,* 1980, *19,* 157-162.

Emig, J. *The composing processes of twelfth graders* (Research Report No. 13). Urbana, Ill.: National Council of Teachers of English, 1971.

Evans, R. V. The relationship between the reading and writing of syntactic structures. *Research in the Teaching of English,* 1979, *13,* 129-135.

Florio, S. The problem of dead letters: Social perspectives on the teaching of writing. *Elementary School Journal,* 1979, *80,* 1-7. (a)

Florio, S. *Learning to write in the classroom community: A case study.* Paper presented at annual meeting of American Educational Research Association, San Francisco, 1979. (b)

Forester, A. D. Learning to spell by spelling. *Theory into Practice,* 1980, *19,* 186-193.

Galda, L. Assuming the spectator stance. *Research in the Teaching of English,* 1982, *16,* 1-20.

Gillooly, W. B. The influence of writing-system characteristics on learning to read. *Reading Research Quarterly,* 1973, *8,* 167-199.

Goodman, K. S., & Goodman, Y. M. Learning about psycholinguistic processes by analyzing oral reading. *Harvard Educational Review,* 1977, *47,* 317-333.

Goodman, K. S., & Goodman, Y. M. Learning to read is natural. In L. B. Resnick & P. A. Weaver (Eds.), *Theory and practice of early reading* (Vol. 1). Hillsdale, N.J.: Lawrence Erlbaum, 1979.

Graves, D. Research update: A six-year-old's writing process: The first half of first grade. *Language Arts,* 1979, *56,* 829-835.

Hall, M. A., Moretz, S. A., & Statom, J. Writing before grade one—A study of early writers. *Language Arts,* 1976, *53,* 582-585.

Halliday, M. A. K. *Learning how to mean.* London: Arnold, 1975.

Harste, J. C., & Burke, C. L. Examining instructional assumptions: The child as informant. *Theory into practice,* 1980, *19,* 170-178.

Hiebert, E. Developmental patterns and interrelationships of preschool children's print awareness. *Reading Research Quarterly,* 1981, *16,* 236-260.

Holdaway, D. *The foundations of literacy*. Sydney: Ashton Scholastic, 1979.

Hughes, T. O. *Sentence combining: A means of increasing reading comprehension* (ERIC Document Reproduction Service No. ED 112 40), 1975.

Iser, W. The reading process: A phenomenological approach. *New Literary History*, 1972, *3*, 279–300.

King, M. L. Learning how to mean in written language. *Theory into Practice*, 1980, *19*, 163–169.

King, M. L., & Rentel, V. Toward a theory of early writing development. *Research in the Teaching of English*, 1979, *13*, 243–253.

King, M., Rentel, V., & Cook, C. *A longitudinal study of the influence of story structure on children's oral and written texts*. Paper presented at annual meeting of American Educational Research Association, April 1980.

Loban, W. *Language development: Kindergarten through grade twelve* (Research Report No. 18). Urbana, Ill.: National Council of Teachers of English, 1976.

Mandler, J. M., & Johnson, N. S. Remembrance of things parsed: Story structure and recall. *Cognitive Psychology*, 1977, *9*, 111–151.

Milz, V. E. First graders can write: Focus on communication. *Theory into Practice*, 1980, *19*, 179–185.

Perl, S. The composing process of unskilled college writers. *Research in the Teaching of English*, 1979, *13*, 317–336.

Pianko, S. A description of the composing processes of college freshman writers. *Research in the Teaching of English*, 1979, *13*, 5–22.

Read, C. Pre-school children's knowledge of English phonology. *Harvard Educational Review*, 1971, *41*, 1–34.

Shanahan, T. *A canonical correlational analysis of the reading-writing relationship: An exploratory investigation*. Unpublished doctoral dissertation, University of Delaware, 1980.

Smith, F. Learning to read by reading. *Language Arts*, 1976, *53*, 297–299.

Smith, F. Research update: Demonstrations, engagement and sensitivity—A revised approach to language learning. *Language Arts*, 1981, *58*, 103–112.

Smith, W. *The effect of transformed syntactic structures on reading*. Paper presented at the annual meeting of the International Reading Association, Anaheim, 1970.

Stein, N. L., & Glenn, C. G. An analysis of story comprehension in elementary school children. In R. O. Freedle (Ed.), *Advances in discourse processes* (Vol. 2: *New directions*). Norwood, N.J.: Ablex, 1978.

10

Performance limits on writers

COLETTE A. DAIUTE
Teachers College, Columbia University

Information-processing factors constrain writers as they compose (Daiute, 1980; Hayes & Flower, 1980). Writers generate ideas, form propositions, access lexical items, plan clause and sentence structures, translate from semantic and phonological representations to orthographic ones, and plan subsequent units. These mental activities occur simultaneously in limited short-term memory. The study described in this chapter builds on psycholinguistic theory for an understanding about the interaction between psychological factors and linguistic structure in the creation of first drafts.

I will discuss a psycholinguistic model of writing that outlines how the specific limits of short-term memory influence writers, especially as they compose sentences. Such information-processing concerns are considered in the context of other recent studies of writing as a cognitive process. The significance of this work is that it offers a model and methodology for studying writing in the light of twenty years of research on language performance. In addition, examining writing as it is constrained by cognitive processes highlights the unity of writing with other language behaviors, such as speaking and reading. This approach can help writing teachers gain insights about their students' general linguistic development and about their ability to write coherent sentences.

The data for this psycholinguistic study of writing are syntax errors, so it offers teachers information on ways of planning sentence structure exercises tailored to students' individual psychological capacities. The study offers insights on sentence-structure problems that have not yet been analyzed or explained. Also, the findings suggest reasons why sentence combining has been so successful. In addition, the study shows why writing perfect sentences in first drafts is psychologically difficult, suggesting that writers can benefit from postponing revising as they compose. Rather, in order to limit burdens on short-term memory, they should devote full attention to the processes separately. The study of errors offers specific information for teaching, but understanding errors is not the major goal of a psycholinguistic study of writing. Errors are clues to cognitive processes, and once we have a preliminary model of how one cognitive factor affects writers, we can apply it to understand processes involved in composing larger text units.

Psycholinguistics and Short-Term Memory

Recent psychological studies of writing have focused on the relationship between the development of general intellectual capacities and writing behavior (Kroll, 1978; Scardamalia & Bereiter, 1979). One of these capacities is the ability to take objective points of view. Studies of writing in the context of cognitive developmental theory have identified some reasons why revising abilities, for example, develop relatively late (Calkins, 1980; Bridwell, 1980). As children mature, they learn to take perspectives other than their own, which is crucial in evaluating their own writing. The psycholinguistic study of writing complements this work.

Psycholinguistics includes the study of how cognitive processes such as memory and attention influence linguistic performance. Most psycholinguistic research has focused on sentence-perception tasks such as reading and listening, but psycholinguists have recently begun to study talking. My aim is to show how psycholinguistic research on talking and the related analysis of ungrammatical sentences apply to writing, especially the writing of first drafts.

Talking and writing are both language-production processes, so it is reasonable to consider their similarities. The main similarity is that both writers and speakers form ideas into linguistic sequences. As the hand, rather than the mouth, expresses ideas, writing becomes different from speaking. Important differences have been discussed by current researchers of the writing process (Emig, 1971; Kroll, 1978; Rubin, 1978). The main differences between speaking and writing are the method, the speed, permanence of expression, and the reliance on independent context. In spite of these differences, it is important to consider the similarity of sentence formation in the mind of the writer and the mind of the speaker.

The Interactionist Model of Sentence Production

Psycholinguistically motivated studies of sentence production explore the interaction of linguistic and behavioral factors in talking (Fodor, Bever, & Garrett, 1974; Bever, Carroll, & Hurtig, 1976). The interactionist view is that sentences are produced via a set of memorized patterns that do not have to be reconstructed for each utterance because they represent the major surface structure forms of English (e.g., the subject–verb–object structure). The speaker uses such a pattern to guide the creation of each clause. Then the surface clause structure serves as the basic pattern, and the words fit into the pattern. The speaker monitors the meaning of the prior clause while producing subsequent clauses. Researchers working within the interactionist theory have found that the basic unit is the surface clause, which includes a limited number of words that can be held in short-term memory (Carroll, 1976, 1979; Bever et al., 1976; Carroll & Tanenhaus, 1978). During production of an utterance, a clause is recoded in semantic form; the exact wording of the clause fades, but the meaning is stored in memory.

The basic unit of sentence planning is also some form of the clause. Observational studies of the distribution of pauses and filler words (e.g., "um," "uh") indicate the relative integrity of clause-like sequences (Boomer, 1965; Goldman-Eisler, 1961; Osgood, 1963). A few experimental studies show that speakers exert the greatest mental effort just at the beginnings of clauses (cf. Ford & Holmes, 1978; Valian, 1971). In addition, the distribution of speech errors reflects clause structure. Almost all spoonerisms (exchanges of phonetic material between earlier and later words) occur within clauses (Fromkin, 1971; Garrett, 1975). Finally, stuttering tends to occur just at the beginnings of clauses (Wall, 1978).

Despite their theoretical differences, the major speech-production models all assume that speakers use set clause patterns as they plan and produce sentences. Evidence for this use of sentence-structure frames is both intuitive and observational. It is a common experience to find oneself saying an unintended phrase, apparently because of its frequency or structural simplicity. Set clause frames of the basic subject–verb–object canonical form seem to be the most basic and earliest learned full-clause structure (Bever, 1975). Furthermore, the systematic investigation of mistakes during speech production highlights the existence of such speech-production patterns. For example, a spoonerism like (1) may arise because the speaker is filling in a set surface structure within the clause.

(1) I didn't see the back trucking out. (should have been "the truck backing out")

(1a) I didn't see the "noun" + "verb" + "ing" "prep." ("back, truck, out")

(1b) I didn't see the back "verb" + "ing out."

According to Garrett (1976), such an error can occur because the speaker has the surface syntactic form of the sequence in mind ahead of time as represented in (1a). The lexical items are filled in to corresponding part-of-speech positions as the speaker talks. If the wrong lexical item, "back," is chosen for the noun position in (1a), the speaker is left with "truck" and inserts it according to the already-set syntactic form of (1a). Garrett suggests that such errors indicate that the syntactic form which one has in mind for a sentence is applied independently of the lexical items. An occasional error in accessing a lexical item from memory such as (1), reveals that the syntactic form can remain unaffected.

Sentences like (2) and (3) below illustrate how memory limits interact with language during the production of complete sentences. Sentence (2) is a miscombining of two sentences.

(2) That's the first time anybody ever sang to me like that before. (from Bever *et al.*, 1976)

The implied sentence (2a), "That's the first time anybody ever sang to me like that," overlaps with implied sentence (2b), "(Nobody) ever sang to me like that before." The speaker began one sentence and finished another. In overlapping sentences, there is a medial sequence that can go with the initial and final sequences of the sentence separately. The overlapping sequence in (2) is " . . . body ever sang to me like that."

Example (3) is a special case of phrase overlapping:

(3) The recent outbreak of riots are disturbing and upsetting to the peace efforts.

The sequence (3a), "The recent outbreak of riots," overlaps with (3b), "are disturbing and upsetting to the peace efforts." As the phrases overlap, the verb, "are," is based on the adjacent plural modifier "riots" rather than the singular head noun "outbreak." Such overlappings are called "gobbled verb" sentences. This is a common error type, made especially by people who do not make other types of errors in subject-verb agreement.

This kind of error gives further support to the claim that speakers use locally preset syntactic patterns as they talk. Such an example demonstrates that speakers can use set patterns, such as *plural-noun + plural-verb*, as part of the syntactic formation of utterances. Such a pattern is extremely powerful, and makes some speakers uncomfortable with the correct form of certain utterances, such as (3c).

(3c) The recent outbreak of riots is disturbing and upsetting to the peace efforts.

Bever *et al.* (1976) claim that such an error occurs because there is a limit to the specific information a speaker can hold in mind at one time; when a subject noun phrase or relative clause is far from its modifier or predicate, an anomalous structure can occur. As a matter of fact, listeners may not notice errors like (2) and (3) because the entire structure is difficult to hold in short-term memory at one time.

Short-term memory influences language performance in a specific way. Short-term memory holds a limited number of units, such as digits, pitches, and words, in exact form for only a limited time. Research has shown that between five and nine random units can be held (Miller, 1956). Related items may be stored together; thus, five to nine groups of organized material can be retained. After the exact units fade from short-term memory, their meaning is stored in long-term memory.

Language processing is responsive to these short-term memory limits. The perceptual clause, which is usually about six words, is the basic unit that is held in short-term memory. After perception or production of one clause, the exact words fade from short-term memory and the meaning of the clause is stored in long-term memory. This process is called semantic recoding. Research has shown that the basic perceptual clause includes a complete set of subject–verb–object relations (Carroll, 1976, 1979; Carroll & Tanenhaus, 1978). Perceptual clauses vary in strength as stimulators of semantic recoding, depending on how close they are to being grammatically complete clauses. For example, independent clauses are stronger perceptual units than dependent clauses, and thus more readily stimulate semantic recoding.

The findings about short-term memory constraints relate to writing errors. All English teachers recognize the errors in sentences (4) through (7) as ones that are frequent and persistent in writing. Like the structures in sentences (2) and (3), those in sentences (4), (5), and (6) have medial overlapping sequences. (The overlapping sequences are italicized.)

(4) Four years ago was the best time of my career which I *wasn't in a position to know* that then.

(5) This waste of *two intelligent women I know* would still be active if this boss never had such policies at work.

(6) The classic beauty of *the new Datsun models* are a big seller this year.

The similarity of these written sentences to the spoken ones analyzed by Bever *et al.* suggested a rationale for examining writing in the light of speaking (Daiute, 1978, 1979).

The Psycholinguistic Model of Writing

The psycholinguistic model of writing (Daiute, 1980) assumes that writers, like speakers, form sentences in clause-by-clause sequences. As each clause is produced, the writer monitors the prior clause. Monitoring helps the writer keep track of the meaning and the structure in order to complete the sentence grammatically, but as short-term memory is overtaxed, writers may suspend monitoring. After production of a strong perceptual clause, the clause is semantically recoded, which can lead to grammatical errors.

Writers who do not make syntax errors have ways of remembering important grammatical information from prior clauses that fade during recoding. They may store a variety of complex sentence structures in long-term memory. These structures may serve as patterns that guide the production of novel sentences, and patterns for entire sentences may aid in clause combining. Using such stored patterns would free writers from having to construct the details of complex sentences in ongoing short-term memory as they compose. Experienced writers have a variety of memorized complex-sentence-structure patterns that they automatically access as they write. For example, a writer who frequently writes sentences with several predicates may set up sentence patterns for parallel function phrases, which emphasize the endings of parallel phrases. "In the morning, I like ____ing, ____ing, and ____ing" would be the form of such a pattern. Such tagging can help the writer correctly combine clauses that are not simultaneously in immediate memory because the set pattern includes information that tends to fade after semantic recoding. Depending on the relative stability of sentence-structure patterns, writers are affected differently by the limits of short-term memory capacity.

The Memory Constraint Hypothesis

The memory constraint hypothesis is that errors occur after initial sequences have been semantically recoded. Difficulty in correctly completing multiclause sentences probably occurs as grammatical information in recoded clauses fades. The nature of errors suggests that, although the prior clause appears on the page during writing, the writer does not read it during production of the next one. This may occur because so much goes on during composing.

If the memory constraint hypothesis is correct, one ought to find that syntax errors are usually preceded in the sentence by strong perceptual clauses and large numbers of words. For example, sentence (5) on page 209 conforms to these characteristics. The sentence becomes ungrammatical in the predicate "would be active," which is after eight words and four strong perceptual clauses. A large number of sentences with syntax errors before the completion of any strong perceptual clause or before about six words would be evidence against the memory constraint hypothesis.

The studies described below showed that structural environments that have been independently shown to stimulate semantic recoding also occur before syntax problems in a large sample of error sentences.

Testing the Model of Writing

My colleagues and I did two types of studies to test the memory constraint hypothesis in writing. We analyzed a corpus of written syntax errors by college students for features suggesting that semantic recoding may have influenced the production of the errors. That analytic study was followed by a behavioral study of the relationship between the writing and short-term memory capacities of 171 sixth- to twelfth-grade subjects.

The Analytic Study

In the analytic study we identified twelve types of syntax errors (Daiute, 1980, 1981). Three types of structural characteristics show how short-term memory burdens could affect writers.

"Error sentences" are ones that do not conform to the forms of standard English syntax. Some error sentences are ungrammatical because they violate the basic rules of English syntax; other sentences violate the standard notions about syntactic precision and style. The classification includes all types of syntax errors we found in two error corpuses. It includes well-recognized errors like misplaced modifiers, nonparallel sentences, one type of subject–verb agreement error, and three types of errors that have formerly been grouped and labeled as incoherent or awkward sentences—sentences that have been said to "defy analysis" (Krishna, 1975, p. 43). We have also used this classification for all oral syntax errors by six-year-old children and adults (see Daiute & Wallace, in preparation). Although some of the error types have previously been considered simply careless mistakes (Shaughnessy, 1977), all of the types include problems that result in ill-formed sentences of consistent and predictable syntactic structures. Table 10-1 shows examples of the twelve main types of error sentences in the classification. (See Daiute, Allen, Jandreau, Chametzky, & Bever, 1981, for an extended version of the classification.)

An important fact to note about syntactically anomalous sentences such as those in Table 10-1 is that even the most highly educated speakers of standard English produce them in speech. Example (2), given on page 208 , was uttered by a college professor. My goal has been

Table 10-1. Error Sentence Taxonomy

Fragments
- Because the type of training a child gets from the computer is nothing compared to playing.
- Namely, younger people who are looking for a fresh new start.
- More and more people saying they want freedom.
- Politics, all those candidates wait for the public's approval.
- To know your children turned out okay.
- Similar to the way it is performed in Japan.

Overlapping sentences
- Double-function sequence sentences
  This waste of *two intelligent women I know* would still be active if this boss never had such policies at work.
- Gobbled verb sentences
  The recent outbreak of *riots are* upsetting and disturbing to the peace efforts.
- Split sentences
  They were too busy with being attractive *than taking time off and studying the mind's* riches.

Distant modifier sentences
- Misplaced modifier sentences
  The children were driven away in buses with big windows *laughing and singing.*
- Headless modifier sentences
  By working at home the unemployment of builders and office decorators would be tremendous.
- Feature match modifier sentences
  Secondly, schooling is not only *a place* of social development.

Nonparallel sentences
  The main purpose of government is *representation* and *to protect* the rights of citizens.

Gapped sentences
  Mechanical devices have tendency to lose student's attention.

Repetitious sequence sentences
- Written stutter sentences
  It is impossible to say the *the* younger workers are taking the jobs of the older workers. . . .
- Written echo sentences
  Your achievement in life can be very good *in life* but every American does not want to do a lot of work.

Multi-error sentences
  Most important to me is self-satisfaction of *myself* and the family that I have, *without one* is not successful.

to show why such structures occur and why they are often acceptable to the writers who produce them.

The error sentence corpus for the analytic study includes 450 error sentences in placement essays by 215 college freshmen at a well-respected branch of the City University of New York. One or more errors occurred in 11.3 percent of all the sentences in the corpus.

The main features suggesting that the memory constraint hypothesis may be correct are the relative numbers of words in the sentence, the numbers of words before the sentence goes awry (before error onset), and the syntactic environment of error onset. Table 10-2 shows the mean lengths of correct and error sentences and the numbers of perceptual clauses before error onset.

On average, errors occurred in sentences that were three words longer than correct sentences. (Error sentences by secondary school students are eight words longer, on the average, than their own correct sentences; see Daiute *et al.*, 1981.) This suggests that an error typically occurred after there was a burden on the writer's short-term memory during production of a sentence. The number of words before the error onset position was 11, on the average. This is just above the short-term memory limit for random words, which is between five and nine words (Miller, 1956). Although words in sentences are organized, which facilitates remembering them, writing may proceed in a word-by-word nature since it is so slow. Such word-by-word production would make it difficult for writers to use syntactic structure as an aid in organizing the words and thus holding more of them in short-term memory.

There is almost always more than one perceptual clause boundary before error onset (Table 10-2). There were, on the average, 3.6 perceptual clauses, including subject–verb–object sequences, not necessarily in grammatically complete form. This means that the mean number of potential spots of semantic recoding before error onset was 3.6. Thus, there is specific structural evidence that semantic recoding occurred before the sentence error.

A majority (64.5 percent) of the error sentences included error onset in optional or embedded sentence positions added on to the basic grammatical clause. Optional positions (Allen, 1974) are modifiers, second coordinate subjects, predicates, and nonrequired objects and complements. The significance of error onset in optional positions is that optional sections add extra complexity to the sentence, which increases the processing burden on short-term memory (Bever, 1975; Slobin & Bever, 1982).

The Behavioral Study

The behavioral study supported the analytic finding that short-term memory limits relate to the writing of error sentences. The subjects' abilities to remember sentences in the memory test correlated with their abilities to write correct sentences. In addition, error sentences written by sixth- to twelfth-graders conform to the classification and explanation developed from the college students' errors.

The subjects were 171 sixth-, eighth-, tenth-, and twelfth-graders in a suburban New York area public school. The students in the experiments did three tasks. They wrote essays describing a community

Table 10-2. *Mean Number of Words per Sentence, before Error Onset, and in Error Intervals, and Mean Number of Perceptual Clauses before Error Onset in Different Types of Error Sentences*

Type	Mean number of words per sentence	Mean number of words before error onset	Mean number of words in error intervals[a]	Mean number of strong perceptual clauses before error onset
Fragments	13.5	—	—	2.3
Overlapping sentences				
Double-function sequence sentences	18.4	11.5	4.6	4.4
Gobbled verb sentences	18.1	9.0	6.7	1.8
Split sentences	19.3	10.1	—	4.6
Total	18.6	10.2	5.7	3.6
Distant modifier sentences				
Misplaced modifier sentences	16.8	9.9	5.4	3.7
Headless modifier sentences	22.1	8.4	—	1.9
Feature match modifier sentences	15.9	10.4	8.0	2.6
Total	18.7	10.6	6.7	2.7
Nonparallel sentences	23.9	14.6	2.4	6.7
Gapped sentences	21.4	10.4	—	5.0
Repetitious sequence sentences				
Written stutter sentences	17.7	5.7	—	1.3
Written echo sentences	21.0	13.6	—	5.6
Total	19.4	9.7	5.8	3.5
Multi-error sentences				
Total	23.8	9.0	7.4	3.1
Error sentences	20.3	11.1	6.5	3.6
Correct sentences	17.9			

[a]Error intervals depend on the structure of the error type. Error intervals are the double-function sequence words: between the forgotten noun and the gobbled verb in gobbled verb sentences, between modifier and head noun in distant modifier sentences, between parallel and nonparallel phrases in nonparallel sentences, between written echo and original in written echo sentences, and between the two errors in multi-error sentences.

214

problem, such as traffic, and the effect it had on their lives. They also took two tests of short-term memory capacity—one for digits and one for sentences. The digit memory test included 22 sequences of random digits that ranged from 5 to 11 digit strings. The sentence memory tests included 16 sentences ranging from 11 to 18 words long. For each length, there was one sentence with a relatively large number of embedded perceptual clauses (7) and another with relatively few (8).

(7) *14-word sentence with few perceptual clauses*: The old state of Portugal has had rich land for almost four hundred years.

(8) *14-word sentence with many perceptual clauses*: Modern man learned that he could seek and often find the answers to problems.

The subjects heard the digit and word sequences on a tape recording at moderate speed. After hearing each sequence, they were to write the sequence exactly as they remembered it.

Although the frequencies of errors are different from those in the college sample (Daiute *et al.*, 1981), the sentences in this sample conform to the error sentence classification. The error sample collected from the essays includes 943 error sentences. Table 10-3 shows sixth- to twelfth-graders' sentences categorized according to the classification used for the college freshmen's sentences. These errors affected 39.5 percent of the sentences in the corpus.

There may be more errors in these papers than there were in those of the college students because the younger subjects had only fifteen minutes in which to write their first drafts and the college students had

Table 10-3. Typical Error Sentences in the Writing of Sixth- through Twelfth-Graders

Double-function sequence sentence
  We get the man from Public service has to come and fix the wires out side. (sixth grade)

Gobbled verb sentence
  The quitness on Sundays give people time to relax and clean the yard. (tenth grade)

Split sentence
  The other day my friend tried to get me to take something from a store but I convinced her out of it. (eighth grade)

Misplaced modifier sentence
  This particular instance has changed my attitude and behavior totally about my comminity. (twelfth grade)

Nonparallel sentence
  Another way pollution is caused is by forest fires, by cigarettes, or lightning striking fires left burning. (eighth grade)

Gapped sentence
  I also don't think it is right that there is violence in the area that we live. (tenth grade)

Written echo sentence
  Shouldn't we call the cops or not? (sixth grade)

fifty minutes, enough time to do some editing. Although the younger subjects later had time to revise and edit, the experimental sentences are from the quickly written first drafts, which presumably include the writers' most spontaneous sentence-structure styles.

As in the sentences by college students, error environments in the adolescents' sentences suggest that the sequences before error onset presented a burden to short-term memory. Error sentences were, on the average, eight words longer than correct sentences. Error onset occurred after about thirteen words, almost always after at least one strong perceptual clause boundary, and in optional sentence positions.

The results of the study suggest that short-term memory limits for sentences relate to ability to write correct multiclause sentences. There was a significant correlation (.35; $p < .001$) between the subjects' abilities to write grammatical multiclause sentences and their short-term memory capacities.

Figure 10-1 shows the correlation coefficients between short-term memory capacity for sentences and digits and the ability to write correct sentences in first drafts. The fewer errors subjects had in writing, the more words per sentence they remembered in the short-term memory test. This correlation does not necessarily show a causal relationship between short-term memory capacity and the ability to write grammatical sentences, but there is a significant correlation between memory capacity and correct sentence structure while there is not for other measures.

The results show that, depending on age, writers are affected differently by performance factors. Eighth- and tenth-graders' correlations between short-term memory capacity for word sequences and errors per word are stronger than those of the sixth- and twelfth-graders. The number of error sentences and the numbers of error sentences per word (number of errors divided by the total number of words the subject produced in the essay) correlate negatively .63 ($p < .001$) for eighth-graders and .45 ($p < .001$) for tenth-graders. (These correlations are presented positively in Figure 10-1.) Sixth- and twelfth-graders' scores on the memory test, on the other hand, showed weaker correlations (.24 for the sixth-graders and .11 for twelfth-graders, both $p < .001$). In spite of this difference in the correlation between short-term memory capacity and sentence-writing ability, the short-term memory scores increase steadily across the grades.

The finding that eighth- and tenth-graders show stronger correlations between short-term memory limits and the ability to write grammatical sentences than both younger (sixth-grade) and older (twelfth-grade) subjects may be interpretable in the light of findings

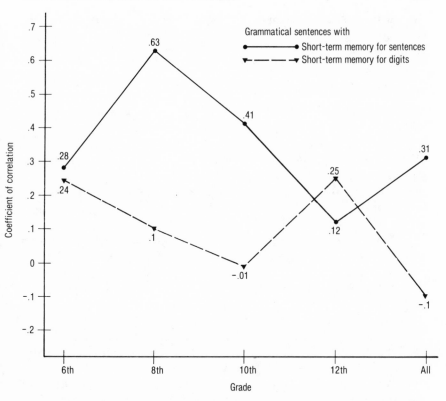

Fig. 10-1. The relationship between short-term memory capacity and the ability to write grammatical multiclause sentences.

in developmental psychology. The explanation offered by developmental theory is that twelve- to fourteen-year-olds are in a transition stage in cognitive development.

Development does not progress in a steady, incremental fashion across the grades. Rather, sometimes younger subjects seem to do better on certain tasks than do older ones. To explain this, I turn briefly to such phenomena in other areas of developmental research.

During transition stages in development, there is a reorganization of cognitive capacities and strategies (Langer, 1969, 1970; Bever, 1975; Carey & Diamond, 1977; Carey, Diamond, & Woods, 1980; Carey, 1982). Such reorganization is characterized by the separation of capacities and by apparent developmental lags. For example, two-year-olds are better at acting out complex cleft sentences like the following than four-year-olds[1] (Bever, 1975).

(9) It was the cow the pig kissed.

Similarly, eight-year-olds learned to pair letters with inverted faces almost as easily as with upright faces, which adults could not do (Goldstein, 1965). Such surprising lags in older subjects are presumably due to the development of new cognitive strategies for organizing stimuli in the world (Langer, 1969, 1970; Carey & Diamond, 1977). New cognitive structures may develop at certain points in development to help with a transition from relatively immature to mature cognitive strategies (Bever, 1975; Langer, 1969, 1970).

Some researchers think that stages are not clearly defined (Damon, 1981); rather, there may be developmental differences according to the type of skill in question. Damon explains that during one period, advanced aspects related to later stages may appear. For example, a child who generally reasons in an immature way may show more formal reasoning patterns with a specific task.

The eighth- and tenth-graders in our study show evidence that they are in such a transition stage. First, short-term memory capacities for words and digits are separate. The correlations between digit memory and the ability to write grammatical sentences were not significant for eighth- and tenth-graders, but were for sixth- and twelfth-graders. In other words, twelve- to fourteen-year-olds with particularly good memories for digits do not necessarily transfer this to sentence memory. These results suggest that short-term memory capacity itself is being restructured. Thus, short-term memory capacity for specific types of tasks differs during the time when other capacities are in flux.

Secondly, eighth- and tenth-graders wrote many more words in their essays than did the younger and older subjects. Table 10-4 gives the number of words and error sentences written in the essays by students in each grade. The eighth-graders' ratio of errors per word was slightly higher than the ratios of the sixth- and tenth-graders, indicating that they had not yet mastered the new structures. The twelfth-graders' rate of errors was high, but their ratio of complex to simple sentences is lower than that of the tenth-graders. The relatively higher number of words in eighth-graders' and tenth-graders' essays shows that they are in a period of greater expressive output. They seem to be experimenting with words and new structures. The students may be pushing them-

---

1. They performed equally well on simple declarative sentences.

Table 10-4. *Mean Number of Words per Essay, Percentage of Errors per Word, and Percentage of Complex Sentences per Essay in the Writing of Sixth-, Eighth-, Tenth-, and Twelfth-Graders*

Grade	n	Mean number of words per essay	Percentage of errors per word	Percentage of complex sentences
6th	45	206	3.6	27
8th	42	255	3.7	32
10th	47	223	3.6	37
12th	37	230	4.1	36

selves in sheer linguistic output, over which they do not have control, as they go on to a new stage in development.

At such a time, they would also be experimenting with new syntactic structures. From examining sentences by 20 subjects in each grade, we found that the eighth- and tenth-graders' ratio of complex to simple sentences is higher than that of sixth-graders, but the ratio for twelfth-graders is slightly lower than that of tenth-graders. This suggests that from age twelve to age fourteen, when students write more words, they are also experimenting with more complex structures. This period of experimentation is followed by a leveling off in the use of complex sentences.

During the period of experimentation with complex sentences, writers may be more influenced by performance factors such as short-term memory limits because their sense of grammatical correctness is not stable. They may have temporarily suspended automatic evaluation of commonly used syntactic patterns until they have developed set strategies for sentence production and perception of mature, complex sentence structures. This developmental explanation of the different results for the subjects in the middle grades suggests a trend that we are testing further.

In summary, syntax errors conform to consistent nonrandom patterns that can be organized into a classification. The analytic and experimental studies support the memory constraint hypothesis—the idea that sentence errors occur when short-term memory is excessively burdened or limited. Our results show that short-term memory capacity is significantly related to the ability to write complex sentences. This is especially true of eighth- and tenth-graders, who seem to be going through a stage in development when their cognitive strategies are in flux. At such a point, performance limits like those presented by short-term memory seem to be especially strong.

Implications

The psycholinguistic study of writing suggests ways in which writing teachers can apply an understanding of the psychological performance factors underlying all language behavior—reading, writing, speaking, listening. One type of psycholinguistic study is an examination of how performance factors influence writers. This is a unique way of studying *writing*, but psycholinguistics has been successfully used to understand the *reading* process for almost twenty years.

One specific contribution of the study described in this chapter is the classification of typical syntax errors. Teachers and researchers have noticed such error types before, but have not seen them as consistent structures resulting from the same psychological processes. The error sentence classification can help writing teachers and their students learn about the consistencies of the sentence structures that they have trouble using. Students have a penchant for specific syntactic forms (Arena, 1975; Daiute *et al.*, 1981). Consequently, they make systematic errors based on their preferred structures. If they can understand these consistencies in their errors, they may have an easier time recognizing and correcting them.

This study also shows that errors occur in specific environments that have independently been shown to burden short-term memory. For example, errors occur in longer-than-average sentences. This shows why the teachers who have been telling their students to write shorter sentences have been giving advice based on psychological behavior. This study suggests how such advice can be given in a way that will not limit students' syntactic development. Writers should feel free to compose sentences of all lengths, but when they revise they can analyze sentences that are longer than average because these are likely to include syntax errors. Thus, students should not be told to write short sentences, but to look in long sentences for errors. Such a procedure could sensitize students to details that they may not grasp because of the temptation to skim over a paper, recalling the content from long-term memory and not critically evaluating the precision of the wording.

The results with regard to the relationship between short-term memory capacity and the occurrence of syntax errors combine with the error classification to suggest plans for remediation. Since short-term memory limits relate to the ability to write correct multiclause sentences, students could benefit from increasing their short-term memory capacity for linguistic sequences. If students become familiar with a variety of specific sentence structures, they can devote less processing space to the mechanics of forming sentences as they compose. For example, a student who typically writes gobbled verb sentences could benefit from sentence-completion exercises, including increasingly longer subjects in the noun phrase. The head nouns would be followed by prepositional phrase modifiers with increasingly longer modifiers separating the head noun and the verb.

(9) The women of China _____ (use some form of the verb "work" to complete the sentence).

(9a) The women of the communes in China _____.

(9b) The women of the many productive communes in China _____.

Such exercises could increase students' control over the syntactic structures they use. This could, in turn, decrease short-term memory burdens during formation of such sentences, by making the pattern for that particular sentence structure automatic. This would leave more processing space for remembering other details. One of the benefits of sentence-combining exercises (see Mellon, 1978) may be that they help writers build automatic sentence-structure memories.

The experimental results suggest that at ages twelve to fourteen, writers should do sentence-structure exercises. Exercises in forming and analyzing a variety of sentence-structure types may be most useful at the time of the greatest increase in linguistic output and complexity. The teaching of framing and chunking strategies for use during sentence composing may transfer to help relieve some burden from writers' short-term memories. At this time, students may benefit especially from exercises involving a variety of sentence structures in ever increasing lengths and complexities. Students can develop strategies for using structure to overcome performance limits. Such instruction may transfer to become part of the stable grammatical knowledge they have in the twelfth grade.

The strong correlation between the production and perception abilities of adolescents, especially eighth- and tenth-graders, suggests that grammatical analysis and practice with sentence combining may be critical for several language activities—reading, writing and speaking. (The memory test is a measure of the students' performance on perception tasks; the error sentence measure indicates production ability.) These capacities are more closely related in eighth- and tenth-graders, so this may be the best time for coordinated reading and writing instruction.

It is important to present the error categorization and remediation procedures in the context of writing as a multifaceted process. Research has shown that writing is a multistage activity (Emig, 1971) but that the stages do not proceed in a linear fashion (Hayes & Flower, 1980; Perl, 1979). Elbow (1975) has suggested that writers compose and revise in separate stages. This should free writers to compose without worrying about correctness during the initial stage when they are generating ideas. The present study suggests that because of limits on short-term memory, it is difficult to produce perfect complex sentences on a first try. For this reason, writers should be encouraged to compose and then later to revise their sentences.

Conclusion

As writers compose spontaneously, they place burdens on short-term memory capacity, which is extremely limited. Beginning writers seem to be especially affected by such performance limits because they have to work consciously on all aspects of writing. Experienced writers, on the other hand, do not have to labor over forming sentences as well as deciding what to say; this limits the strain on immediate memory. The study of errors provides a test of the psycholinguistic hypothesis. We can now extend our data and scope by applying the theory to explain psychological burdens affecting writers as they create extended discourse. The psycholinguistic studies suggest that automatic access to discourse patterns could help writers compose by reducing some planning burdens on short-term memory.

ACKNOWLEDGMENTS

This research was supported in part by the National Institute of Education, Grant No. NIE-G-80-0014. My thanks go to Professors Walter H. MacGinitie, Thomas G. Bever, Joanna Williams, and Louis Forsdale, and to Dr. Jack Carroll, Steve Jandreau, Robert Chametzky, Ursula Wolz, Frank Secada, the experimental subjects, and their teachers for their participation in various aspects of the research and the analysis of results.

REFERENCES

Allen, R. L. *English grammars and English grammar.* New York: Scribners, 1974.
Arena, L. *Linguistics and composition.* Washington, D.C.: Georgetown University Press, 1975.
Bever, T. G. Psychologically real grammar emerges because of its role in language acquisition. In D. P. Dato (Ed.), *Georgetown University roundtable on language and linguistics, 1975.* Washington, D.C.: Georgetown University Press, 1975.
Bever, T. G., Carroll, J. M., & Hurtig, R. Analogy or sequences that are utterable and comprehensible are the origins of new grammars in language acquisition and linguistic evolution. In T. G. Bever, J. J. Katz, & D. T. Langendoen (Eds.), *An integrated theory of language behavior.* New York: Thomas Y. Crowell, 1976.
Boomer, D. S. Hesitation and grammatical encoding. *Language and Speech*, 1965, *8*, 148–158.
Bridwell, L. S. Revising strategies in twelfth grade students' transactional writing. *Research in the Teaching of English*, 1980, *14*, 187–222.
Calkins, L. M. Notes and comments: Children's rewriting strategies. *Research in the Teaching of English*, 1980, *14*, 331–341.
Carey, S. Face perception: Anomalies of development. In S. Straus (Ed.), *U-shaped behavioral growth.* New York: Academic Press, 1982.

Carey, S., & Diamond, R. From piecemeal to configurational representation of faces. *Science*, 1977, *195*, 312–314.

Carey, S., Diamond, R., & Woods, B. Development of face recognition: A maturational component? *Developmental Psychology*, 1980, 4(7), 257–269.

Carroll, J. M. *The interaction of structural and functional variables in sentence perception: Some preliminary studies*. Unpublished doctoral dissertation, Columbia University, 1976.

Carroll, J. M. "Mere length" and sentence comprehension units: An argument from ambiguity bias. *Papers in Linguistics*, 1979, *12*.

Carroll, J. M., & Tanenhaus, M. Functional clauses and sentence segmentation. *Journal of Speech and Hearing Research*, 1978, *21*, 793–808.

Carroll, J. M., Tanenhaus, M., & Bever, T. The perception of relations: The interaction of structural, functional, and contextual factors in the segmentation of sentences. In W. Levelt & G. d'Arcais (Eds.), *Studies in the perception of language*. New York: Wiley, 1978.

Daiute, C. A. *Overlapping and gobbled sentences: Insights from psycholinguistics*. Paper presented at National Council of Teachers of English convention, Kansas City, Mo., November 23–25, 1978.

Daiute, C. A. *Structural similarities between writing and talking*. Paper presented at Canadian Council of Teachers of English conference, Ottawa, May 1979.

Daiute, C. A. *A psycholinguistic study of writing*. Unpublished doctoral dissertation, Teachers College, Columbia University, 1980.

Daiute, C. A. Psycholinguistic foundations of the writing process. *Research in the Teaching of English*, February 1981.

Daiute, C. A. Psycholinguistic perspectives on revising. In R. A. Sudol (Ed.), *Revision: Process, product, pegagogy*. Urbana, Ill.: National Council of Teachers of English, 1982.

Daiute, C. A. The computer as stylus and audience. *College Composition and Communication*, May 1983.

Daiute, C. A., Allen, R. L., Jandreau, S. M., Chametzky, R. A., & Bever, T. G. *Psycholinguistic studies of the writing process in adolescents*. Report to National Institute of Education (Grant No. NIE-G-80-0041), 1981.

Daiute, C. A., & Taylor, R. P. *Computers and the improvement of writing* (Computing in Education Working Paper No. 10). Teachers College, Columbia University, October 1980.

Daiute, C. A., & Wallace, I. *Anomalous syntax patterns by six-year-old through adult speakers and writers*. In preparation.

Damon, W. Patterns of change in children's social reasoning: A two-year longitudinal study. *Child Development*, 1981.

Elbow, P. *Writing without teachers*. New York: Oxford University Press, 1975.

Emig, J. *The composing process of twelfth graders*. Urbana, Ill.: National Council of Teachers of English, 1971.

Fodor, J. A., Bever, T. G., & Garrett, M. F. *The psychology of language*. New York: McGraw-Hill, 1974.

Ford, N., & Holmes, V. M. Planning units and syntax in sentence production. *Cognition*, 1978, *6*, 35–53.

Fromkin, V. A. The non-anomalous nature of anomalous utterances. *Language*, 1971, *47*, 27–52.

Garrett, M. F. The analysis of sentence production. In G. Bower (Ed.), *Advances in learning theory and motivation* (Vol. 9). New York: Academic Press, 1975.

Garrett, M. F. Syntactic processes in sentences. In R. J. Wales & E. Walker (Eds.), *New approaches to language mechanisms*. Amsterdam: North-Holland Press, 1976.

Goldman-Eisler, F. Hesitation and information in speech. In C. Cherry (Ed.), *Information theory*. London: Butterworth, 1961.

Goldstein, A. G. Learning of inverted and normally oriented faces in children and adults. *Psychonomic Science*, 1965, *3*, 447.

Hayes, J. R., & Flower, L. S. Identifying the organization of writing processes. In C. W. Gregg & E. R. Steinberg (Eds.), *Cognitive processes in writing*. Hillsdale, N.J.: Lawrence Erlbaum, 1980.

Krishna, V. The syntax of error. *Basic Writing: Error*, 1975, 43–49.

Kroll, B. M. Cognitive egocentrism and the problem of audience awareness in the written discourse. *Research in the Teaching of English*, 1978, *12*(3), 269–281.

Langer, J. Disequilibrium as a source of development. In P. Mussen, J. Langer, & Carington (Eds.), *Trends and issues in developmental psychology*. New York: Holt, 1969.

Langer, J. Werner's comparative organismic theory. In P. Mussen (Ed.), *Revised Carmichael's handbook of developmental psychology*. New York: Wiley, 1970.

Mellon, J. C. *Issues in the theory and practice of sentence-combining: A twenty year perspective*. Paper presented at Conference on Sentence Combining and the Teaching of Writing, Miami University, Oxford, Ohio, October 1978.

Miller, G. A. The magical number seven, plus or minus two: Some limits on our capacity for processing information. *Psychological Review*, 1956, *63*, 81–97.

Osgood, C. E. On understanding and creating sentences. *American Psychologist*, 1963, *18*, 735–751.

Perl, S. The composing process of unskilled writers. *Research in the Teaching of English*, 1979, *5*, 317–336.

Rubin, A. D. *A theoretical taxonomy of the differences between oral and written language* (BBN Report No. 3731). Cambridge, Mass.: Bolt, Beranek & Newman, 1978.

Scardamalia, M., & Bereiter, C. From conversation to composition: The role of instruction in a developmental process. In R. Glaser (Ed.), *Advances in instructional psychology* (Vol. 2). Hillsdale, N.J.: Lawrence Erlbaum, 1979.

Shaughnessy, M. P. *Errors and expectations: A guide for the teacher of basic writing*. New York: Oxford University Press, 1977.

Slobin, D., & Bever, T. G. Children use canonical sentence schemas in sentence perception. *Cognition*, 1982, *12*(3), 229–265.

Valian, V. V. *Talking, listening and linguistic structure*. Unpublished doctoral dissertation, Northeastern University, 1971.

Wall, M.J. *Syntactic influences in the speech of child stutterers*. Paper presented at American Speech and Hearing Association Convention, San Francisco, 1978.

The writing situation

iii

Previous rhetorical or communications theories often defined "audience" in terms of a reader's relationship to the writer. Gibson (1969) discusses audience in terms of distance or formality, while Burke (1969) bases his rhetoric on the identification of writer and audience. Booth (1961) distinguishes between implied and actual readers. Similarly, in stylistics or linguistics, features in language have been described in terms of degrees of distance, familiarity, or identification between writer and audience.

A major limitation of much composition research is that writers, or "subjects," often write in a research vacuum with no implied or explicit context, a situation that can clearly diminish their involvement with the language being produced. Or, if writers assume that they are writing for a nebulous investigator or administrator, they may not have any notion of the criteria being used to assess their writing. While adding at least a hypothetical audience for a piece of writing sounds like an improvement, there is some evidence to suggest that specifying a fictitious audience may be counterproductive, detracting from overall writing quality (Brossell, 1982).

Sophisticated writers repeatedly report that they are concerned about their audience's potential response. But, because they do not receive immediate verbal and nonverbal feedback of the kind one gets in, for example, an oral dialogue, they must create a set of audience characteristics in order to make decisions about the level of information to be included, the background that must be provided, the tone of the language, and so on. One avenue of recent research examines the connections between audience awareness and the composing process or a student's writing development.

Current cognitive processing research in composition (Flower & Hayes, 1980) indicates that writers attempt to define very specific audience characteristics that apply to specific decisions about their writing—characteristics such as needs, beliefs, attitudes, prior knowledge, and comprehension level. While both classical and contemporary rhetorical theories include discussions of the relationship between writer and audience, and the cognitive processing research gives these theories

225

empirical support, there is very little focused research on how writers' inferring of audience characteristics affects either texts or the production of them.

One question is, how does one avoid limiting the writer in a research project while, at the same time, controlling enough of the context to make safe generalizations from one writing event to the next? Giving an assigned topic with a stipulated purpose and audience may limit a writer's potential response to the assignment, as does leaving the context undefined. (Is my reader a researcher in a white coat? A teacher with a red pencil? A "creativity" specialist?) Learning style may also enter in here; students who need structure may perform better with an assigned topic, while students who resist structure would do well without any constraints except those of their own making.

Most recent studies have used an artificial context to enhance the validity and reliability of the scoring instruments. When judges are rating the quality of 100 student essays, they need to agree on the criteria they are employing in order to achieve some degree of reliability. If students are all writing about the same topic to the same audience, perhaps even for the same reasons, the judges will have less difficulty agreeing on what constitutes a superior versus an inferior performance. Primary trait scoring systems prove highly reliable because they define specific criteria relevant to the particular task. Judges can more reliably detect minor deviations in performance because all the writers are following the same assignment. These scales also achieve a greater degree of construct validity because they define their criteria on features that should appear in the text rather than relying on amorphous judgments of "holistic" quality.

On the other hand, assigned topics may miss the target on one of the central goals of writing instruction: teaching writers to discover and develop their own topics (or, in the case of experienced writers, watching this happen and enhancing it). If writers are not able to choose what they write about, they may not give their best performance. Moreover, as one study found (Fox, 1980), apprehension about writing may *not* diminish if the demands of the task are made explicit. A further validity problem is that the writing that goes on in classrooms and research settings is often a strange variety that does not exist outside of these contexts. Hence, we have difficulty generalizing these phenomena to writing "in the real world."

In the following chapters, we have selected research of quite different kinds to illustrate the range of new developments in studying the influence of the context on writing. The first study, by Odell and Goswami, ventures out of the academic context and into a governmental agency. Next, Daly and Hailey's study presents a new focus on writing apprehension research—the ways in which context can raise or lower anxiety. The chapters by Pelligrini, by Collins and Williamson, and by Rubin *et al.* illustrate developmental characteristics—the effects of context on learning to write. These studies attempt to answer the questions: How does the context affect (or effect) learning to write? And when do young writers learn to accommodate to different audiences and writing situations?

Writing in Nonacademic Settings

Most writing research has been conducted with students in academic settings, probably because they are a captive pool of "subjects." However, in recent research some attention has been devoted to the examination of writing in nonacademic contexts. Much of the writing done in business, industry, and government consists of reports, letters, and memos. These generally have clear pragmatic ends: a memo from an employee to his supervisor arguing for a new training program, a letter from a supervisor to her salespersons urging them to turn in more orders. Because institutional roles and hierarchical relationships are often clearly defined, a writer learns that certain registers, or degrees of formality, are particularly appropriate for a given audience. It could also be argued that linguistic behavior actually creates differences in power, status, or class because of deliberate decisions on the part of the writer.

Odell and Goswami, in their analysis of memo writing in a governmental agency, examined the inferences that social workers and administrators made about their memos in order to determine which rhetorical considerations were most prominent in their writing decisions. The researchers also analyzed the memos themselves to determine the specific types of rhetorical strategies they contained. Through interviews, they isolated the reasons that writers gave for their choices, reasons that implied assumptions about the function of writing. This approach represents two important new directions: research that does not create an artificial writing context, and research that develops an in-depth profile of writers' perceptions about their composing strategies.

One finding of this study, that even "low-level" employees were able to vary their rhetorical strategies quite easily, suggests that most writers may be quite skilled in performing these highly pragmatic tasks— if they understand the audience for the writing and the purpose it serves, an ability that does not often reveal itself in academic writing tasks. While ethnographic case study research on writing (see Kantor, Chapter 3, this volume) is beginning to define the nature of pragmatic constraints in school writing, we find in Odell and Goswami's research some methods for generalizing about a group's performance that might be applied in school research.

Writing Apprehension

A number of studies have described the phenomenon of writing appre-hension (most recently, studies of "writer's block") and have revealed associations between a negative view of writing and job choices, willing-ness to take academic courses, and so forth. However, we do not completely understand what causes apprehension, nor do we know the best ways to reduce it. Some apprehension may come from a negative self-concept, manifested in an uneasiness about communicating to others or self-disclosing. Early unpleasant writing experiences with a hyper-correcting teacher may cause it, or it may be self-imposed by procrastination and attempts to finish a piece "in one shot" (i.e., un-realistic approaches to the writing process).

Much of the research on writing apprehension has employed the Daly and Miller (1975) scale, a scale for which there is a long track record of reliability and validity. This research defines writing appre-hension as a basic quality of an individual, so that subjects are ranked "high" or "low" in apprehension. However, this concept does not take into account the situational forms of apprehension. As Beach and Eaton (Chapter 7, this volume) found, writers may be more or less anxious, depending on the topic, the goals of a particular piece of writing, or the audience. Daly and Hailey, in their study reported in Chapter 12, analyzed the influence of situational variables on apprehension. While these researchers argue that some factors in the writing situation (such as the perceived levels of evaluation or the novelty of the task) generate anxiety, they retain interest in the dispositional nature of anxiety, examining the extent to which highly anxious writers may react more sharply to certain of these variables. By examining the variation in writing apprehension across different contexts, Daly and Hailey point to the need to consider how apprehension influences writing behavior in any context.

Dramatic Play and Early Childhood Writing

Recently researchers have also begun to study the complex relation-ships between oral and written discourse. (See Kroll & Vann, 1981, for a review of the research on speaking–writing relationships.) While there are obvious differences between oral and written discourse, the skills developed in oral language do transfer to writing. We know little about how and when this transfer occurs.

Pellegrini's report (Chapter 13) begins at an early stage of oral language development, the preschool years, in which children are beginning to engage in "symbolic functioning"—recognizing the symbols or signs that represent classes of objects or concepts. By engaging in dramatic play, preschool children are using language in a symbolic manner. For example, they may be defining roles for the players or objects used in role-playing. This symbolic play may in turn contribute to an increased ability to write isolated words, an ability that requires the use of decontextualized language. Such a shift from oral to written discourse requires an ability to write without the immediately reinforcing cues of an oral context; this ability may be acquired in part from symbolic play.

Cognitive Development and Audience Awareness

Much composition research consists of studies comparing writers at different grade or age levels, the most notable being the National Assessment of Educational Progress writing studies, which examine writing done by students at ages nine, thirteen, and seventeen. One contribution of this research is that it links writing development to larger developments in language. Many of Shaughnessy's (1977) explanations for writing errors in remedial writing trace errors back to syntactic development. As Loban (1976) demonstrated in his twelve-year longitudinal study, students within a grade level can differ by as much as five years in their syntactic maturity. While growth in syntactic maturity is relatively steady (Hunt, 1965; O'Donnell, Griffin, & Norris, 1973), other factors also contribute to improvement in writing ability.

For example, students develop tacit knowledge of certain discourse conventions at different age levels. Younger students are quite proficient in writing narratives, but have difficulty with more analytic, logical text structures. One explanation for this is suggested by developmental research on story production (Applebee, 1978). Children develop an oral storytelling competence at a relatively early age, and it transfers to their writing. Given their level of cognitive development, children learn to organize information or events in a concrete, linear, chronological pattern according to a central organizing point. They are also familiar with story genre conventions and schema acquired from reading and television.

A related factor that influences writing development is the writer's general level of cognitive development (see Barritt & Kroll, 1978; Higgins, 1977). There is little research that traces the interplay between changes in writers' evolving cognitive development and specific composing behaviors, particularly in terms of writers' use of logical strategies and audience awareness. Changes in developmental levels often result from conflict between different levels of thinking, conflicts that are resolved by movement to a more mature stage. As students are exposed to teachers' assessments or logical reasoning, they may begin to change their writing behaviors. Because this shift is gradual, longitudinal research needs to focus on points of dissonance that result in changes in students' writing.

An important issue in developmental research that has recently received attention is the relationship between egocentricity and audience awareness in writing (Kroll, 1978; Rubin & Piché, 1979). Research on children's role-taking capacity (Rubin & Piché, 1979) has examined children's ability to imagine audience characteristics, a task that requires the writer to break out of an egocentric perspective and assume the perspective of the reader. Younger writers, even up through high school, have difficulty adopting a perspective different from their own. By giving assignments with actual or hypothetical audience characteristics, it is possible to analyze the relationship between role-taking ability and audience inferences.

If a writer is aware of audience needs or prior knowledge, he or she may be more likely to provide background information that a reader might not possess. In their study reported in Chapter 14, Collins and Williamson developed a measure of "semantic abbreviation" in order to determine the extent to which students make this information explicit. Semantic abbreviation was operationally defined by combining features of spoken dialogue, namely, personal and demonstrative references and formulaic expressions. Because semantic abbreviation varies with the audience and purpose assigned in writing tasks, the researchers wanted to determine the extent to which superior adolescent writers, as opposed to inferior writers, would vary the rate of semantic abbreviation according to purpose and audience. The weaker writers in the study did not differentiate between two types of adult audience, parent and editor. These results indicate that while age is certainly related to developmental differences in audience awareness, better writers within age groups seem to be more sensitive to audience than poorer writers.

In an attempt to further explore the particular social and cognitive dimensions that influence audience awareness, Rubin, Piché, Michlin, and Johnson (Chapter 15) examined the relationships among social cognition and writing quality, fluency, and errors. On the basis of their findings, they argue that social cognitive ability predicts writing quality more accurately than do error or fluency counts. This study, in conjunction with the Collins and Williamson study, indicates that audience awareness is a crucial dimension of writing ability and suggests the need for further research on this dimension and an examination of whether audience awareness can be taught.

REFERENCES

Applebee, A. *The child's concept of story*. Chicago: University of Chicago Press, 1978.

Barritt, L., & Kroll, B. *Some implications of cognitive-developmental psychology for research in composing*. In C. Cooper & L. Odell (Eds.), *Research on composing*. Urbana, Ill.: National Council of Teachers of English, 1978.

Booth, W. *The rhetoric of fiction*. Chicago: University of Chicago Press, 1961.

Brossell, G. *Rhetorical specification in essay examination topics: An experimental study*. Unpublished manuscript, College of Education, Florida State University, 1982.

Burke, K. *A rhetoric of motives*. Berkeley: University of California Press, 1969.

Daly, J., & Miller, M. The empirical development of an instrument to measure writing apprehension. *Research in the Teaching of English*, 1975, *9*, 242–249.

Flower, L., & Hayes, J. The cognition of discovery: Defining a rhetorical problem. *College Composition and Communication*, 1980, *31*, 21–32.

Fox, R. Treatment of writing apprehension and its effects on composition. *Research in the Teaching of English*, 1980, *14*, 39–49.

Gibson, W. *Persona: A style study for readers and writers*. New York: Random House, 1969.

Higgins, E. T. Communication development as related to channel, incentive and social class. *Genetic Psychology Monographs*, 1977, *96*, 75–141.

Hunt, K. *Grammatical structures at three grade levels*. Urbana, Ill.: National Council of Teachers of English, 1965.

Kroll, B. Cognitive egocentrism and the problem of audience awareness in written discourse. *Research in the Teaching of English*, 1978, *12*, 269–281.

Kroll, B., & Vann, R. *Exploring speaking–writing relationships: Connections and contrasts*. Urbana, Ill.: National Council of Teachers of English, 1981.

Loban, W. *Language development: Kindergarten through grade twelve*. Urbana, Ill.: National Council of Teachers of English, 1976.

O'Donnell, R., Griffin, W., & Norris, R. *Syntax of kindergarten and elementary school children*. Urbana, Ill.: National Council of Teachers of English, 1973.

Rubin, D., & Piché, G. Development in syntactic and strategic aspects of audience adaptation: Skill in written persuasive communication. *Research in the Teaching of English*, 1979, *13*, 293–316.

Shaughnessy, M. *Errors and expectations: A guide for the teacher of basic writing*. New York: Oxford University Press, 1977.

11

Writing in a nonacademic setting

LEE ODELL
Rensselaer Polytechnic Institute
DIXIE GOSWAMI
Bread Loaf School of English

Researchers in oral language have a tradition of conducting naturalistic inquiries. They examine speech as it occurs spontaneously in the context of day-to-day activities, noting ways in which oral language is influenced by speakers' purposes and by their awareness of various cultural and interpersonal constraints. (See collections of essays edited by Giglioli, 1972, and Bauman & Sherzer, 1974.) At least one of these researchers (Basso, 1974) has suggested that written language should also be studied in a range of "sociocultural settings."

Some researchers (such as Scribner & Cole, 1978) have begun to conduct this sort of inquiry. But for the most part, research in composition has been done in academic settings where the writing task is assigned by a teacher or researcher in order to accomplish a pedagogical goal or provide data to answer a research question. Research done under these circumstances has provided valuable information about the composing process (Flower & Hayes, 1980; Perl, 1979; Matsuhashi, 1979) and about the features of written products (Rubin & Piché, 1979; Crowhurst & Piché, 1979). Since this information not only has implications for the teaching of writing but also provides an important test of assumptions from discourse theory, we think researchers should continue to explore writing done in these settings. Yet we also feel that researchers need to examine writing that is not assigned by a teacher or researcher and that has a purpose beyond improving writing skill or generating research data. More specifically, we feel that researchers need to examine writing done in nonacademic settings, especially the writing that adults do as a regular part of their daily work.

We have several reasons for our point of view. First, although adults often have to do a great deal of nonpublished writing as part of their day-to-day work (Goswami, 1978; Van Dyck, 1980), we know relatively little about the nature and functions of this writing. Indeed, we tend to speak of business writing (or government writing or bureau-

233

cratic writing) as though it were a single entity. We have limited information about the variety of tasks that adult, nonprofessional writers must perform and still less information about the types of stylistic and substantive choices writers make or the reasons why a writer chooses one alternative over another. This lack seems rather serious, since information about these tasks, choices, and reasoning might very well influence the teaching of composition. Furthermore, this sort of information provides a basis for testing theoretical assumptions, a basis quite different from that provided by school-sponsored writing.

It is true that there are apparent similarities between school-sponsored writing and writing that is done in nonacademic contexts. In both cases, the writer may seek the approval of a person (teacher or supervisor) who may not be the ostensible audience for the writing but whose good opinion is important to the writer. Yet these two types of approval are different in at least one respect: the approval of one's supervisor can have immediate economic as well as personal consequences. How a person is evaluated as a worker—and consequently his or her raises, promotions, and even continued employment—may be influenced by the supervisor's approval or disapproval. A teacher's evaluation of a given piece of writing may also have economic consequences, but those consequences are usually remote. Further, the consequences of nonacademic writing go well beyond gaining approval or disapproval. If the writer is careless, he or she may not accomplish a substantive, job-related goal. A reader may act or think in a way that will complicate the writer's job and perhaps the reader's as well.

Another apparent similarity is that both nonacademic writing and, increasingly, school-sponsored writing may be intended for a specific audience and purpose. However, it is relatively unlikely that school-sponsored writings will actually reach the intended audience. As a rule, they will be read by teachers or researchers, people who may not expect to learn something they do not already know or to have their feelings, thoughts, or actions influenced by the substance of the writing. In short, we feel that the consequences and contexts for nonacademic writing are substantially different from those of school-sponsored writing, a difference that justifies our careful inquiry.

This present study, part of a larger study of writing done in various nonacademic contexts, focuses on writing done in a government bureaucracy, a county social-services agency. In size and function, this organization seems typical of agencies that might be found in a great many counties and, at least so far as government bureaucracies are concerned, allows us to begin to answer these questions:

- To what extent are nonacademic writers sensitive to rhetorical issues such as their relation to their audience or the *ethos* conveyed in their writing?

- Assuming that researchers can identify points at which writers have made a choice about style or substance, what reasons do writers use in justifying those choices?
- Do their reasons reflect a sensitivity to, say, audience, or do those reasons suggest that writers are following pedagogical instructions (e.g., "Never use I") without regard to the specific situation they are confronting?
- When writers in nonacademic settings address different audiences or try to accomplish different purposes, are they likely to vary syntax or other linguistic features of their writing?
- When writers make judgments about style, does their sense of what is acceptable vary according to the type of writing they are examining (and, implicitly, vary with the audience and purpose)?
- Within a given institution, does writing vary from one group of writers to another? Assuming that researchers could identify workers who (1) were considered typical, competent workers; (2) did comparable types of writing; and (3) worked in offices that had quite different functions within a given institution, would one find that the two groups differed with respect to:
  —The types of reasons they used in justifying their choices?
  —The linguistic features that appeared in their writing?
  —Their sense of what constitutes acceptable style?

Procedures

Data Collection

SELECTION OF PARTICIPANTS

There were eleven participants in our study. Five were administrators, and six were caseworkers (three of the latter were from one agency unit, three were from another unit with quite different functions). Clearly, these participants do not represent all aspects of the agency. They do, however, have a range of responsibilities which assures us that the results of our study do not apply exclusively to a single unit of the agency.

Essential to our selection of participants were two key informants, administrators who were thoroughly familiar with all aspects of the agency and with agency personnel. We asked these informants to identify approximately thirty experienced, competent workers from several agency departments and at various levels of the agency hierarchy. Although we did ask the informants to select workers whose jobs were likely to involve a good bit of writing, we did not ask them to make judgments about workers' writing abilities.

Having identified prospective participants, we conducted a series of initial interviews in which we asked each worker about the amount of writing, the types of writing, and the importance of writing in his or her job. Almost all of these workers indicated an interest in taking part in our study, but the demands of workers' schedules and the complex, time-consuming nature of our research procedures made it necessary to reduce the number of participants to eleven.

DATA-GATHERING INTERVIEWS

After the initial interviews, each participant was interviewed on two additional occasions. At least two months elapsed between the first of these data-gathering interviews and the second. The purpose of these interviews was to elicit information about workers' reasons for making specific choices in their writing. We wished to answer two questions: When workers justify a stylistic or substantive choice in their writing, do their reasons indicate that they are sensitive to rhetorical considerations such as their relation to an audience? Are workers who have different types of jobs likely to have different types of reasons for the choices they make?

Prior to a data-gathering interview, we asked each worker to keep copies of all the writing he or she did during a two-week period. After collecting the writing from a worker, we proceeded as follows. First we tried to identify points at which the writer appeared to have made a stylistic or substantive choice. To do this, we looked for variations that actually appeared in the writing of each worker. We did not want participants to look upon us as English teachers and, therefore, as authorities on style. Consequently, we deliberately ignored variations (e.g., in syntax or level of diction) that we felt participants might associate with English classrooms.

In the letters and memos[1] of all the administrators, we identified the following types of choices, many of which involve matters of both substance and style.

1. *Form used in addressing the reader of a letter or memo.* In some situations the reader might be addressed as *Dear Mr. Smith*, in others as *Dear Bob* or *Dear Sir.*
2. *Decision to include or exclude introductory, context-setting information.* In some instances, administrators might begin with a phrase such as "As you will remember from our conversation of last Friday,

---

1. Although administrators occasionally wrote expository pieces that were labeled "Report," most of their writing took the form of letters and memos, some of which were, in effect, reports.

we have agreed to do X . . ."; in other situations administrators would omit such introductory material.

3. *Form of reference to self.* Sometimes administrators would use the pronoun "I"; in other pieces of writing, they would use the pronoun "we" or an expletive–passive construction, even though a sentence referred to what "I" had done or thought.

4. *Form used for commands or requests.* Sometimes an administrator might say "You must do X"; in other situations the same writer might say "It is imperative that you do X" or "State law requires that you do X."

5. *Decision to include or exclude elaboration.* In some instances, writers would shift level of abstraction or follow a general statement with a passage beginning "in other words. . . ." In other letters and memos, a writer would not shift level of abstraction even though he or she clearly possessed (as shown by interview comments) the information needed to elaborate on a general statement.

6. *Decision to include or exclude a concluding comment inviting further communication.* Some letters and memos concluded with this sort of invitation: "If you have any questions, please feel free to contact me." In other situations, this sort of statement would be omitted —rather pointedly, it sometimes seemed.

Though caseworkers occasionally wrote letters or memos, they were most likely to write reports on their contacts with clients or prospective clients. In these reports, we identified the following types of choices:

1. *Attribution of information.* In some reports a caseworker might write, "Mr. Smith *says* [our emphasis] his rent is . . ."; in other reports a caseworker might say "Mr. Smith's rent is. . . ."

2. *Decision to include or exclude reference to the writer's words or actions.*

3. *Decision to include or exclude reference to the client's or applicant's words or actions.*

4. *Form of reference to self.* In some instances a caseworker might refer to him- or herself as "worker," in other instances as "I."

5. *Form of reference to the client.* In some instances the caseworker might refer to the client as "client" and in other instances as "Mr. Smith" or "Joe."

Having identified types of choices in the writing of each caseworker and each administrator, we prepared interview sheets based on writing we had collected from these participants. To prepare an interview sheet for a given piece of writing, we would identify from four to six choices.

On the interview sheet we would list the choice that actually appeared in the piece of writing at hand. Underneath that choice, we would list one or two roughly comparable alternatives that appeared in other pieces of writing done by the worker we were interviewing. During the interview, we would ask each worker to reread a given piece of writing and would show the writer the interview sheet we had prepared. To reduce anxiety that might arise from being interviewed about one's writing by an English teacher, we repeatedly assured participants:

- That all the options listed on the interview sheet were equally "correct"
- That we felt that the interviewee was the expert on making appropriate choices in writing for the agency where he or she worked
- That we were interested solely on the reasoning that had led the writer to prefer one alternative to another

We would begin the discussion of choices by saying: "Here you chose to do X. It would also be possible to do Y or Z [the options listed on the interview sheet]. Would you be willing to substitute Y or Z for your original choice?" When the choice entailed a decision to include or exclude a particular statement, we would proceed as follows. If the statement was present, we would simply bracket it and ask whether the writer would be willing to omit it. If there was no statement, we would ask the writer to provide additional information and then ask the writer if he or she would be willing to include that information in the letter or memo.

Early in the interviewing process we became concerned that the form of our questions, even our tone of voice, might influence a worker's response. It is, for example, surprisingly easy to say "Why didn't you do Y rather than X?" in a tone of voice which implies that Y is the only acceptable alternative. There is also a danger of paraphrasing a worker's comments in such a way that they fit neatly with the interviewer's expectations: "Oh, so what you're saying is that you were very concerned with your audience at this point."

Inevitably, of course, the very presence of an observer has some influence on the phenomena being observed. But we tried to establish procedures that did not imply our values and that let us make our interviews as nondirective as possible. For example, after a worker responded to our initial question, "Would you be willing . . . ," he or she often paused. We would remain silent for a few seconds and allow the worker to elaborate. If no elaboration was forthcoming, we would begin a sentence with the words "So what you're saying here is . . ." and then pause, allowing the worker time to complete the sentence. If the worker did not do so, we would either say "I'm not sure I understand," ask the worker "Could you elaborate?," or paraphrase the worker's comment as closely as possible and give him or her a chance to modify our statement. When a worker used an unelaborated value term (e.g., "It seemed important to do X rather than Y"), we would attempt to get him or her to clarify the term. We might say, "How do you mean *important?*" or "*Important* in that . . . ?" and allow the worker to complete the sentence.

Usually, workers preferred their original choices and explained their preferences with little hesitation. Occasionally, however, a worker would say that alternatives Y and Z would be as acceptable as the original choice, X. In these cases, we would ask the worker whether he or she saw any difference between X and Y or between X and Z. Typically, the attempt to explain that difference would lead a worker to express a preference for one alternative and to give reasons for that preference.

WRITING SAMPLES

In addition to the writing that served as the basis for our interviews with participants, we collected samples of the types of writing that each worker typically performed on the job. Administrators' writing usually took one of three forms: pink memos, white memos, and letters on agency letterhead. The pink memos were relatively short, informal pieces that were usually addressed to one or two specific workers in the agency. Their purposes might vary, but their content usually concerned the day-to-day workings of the agency. White memos tended to be longer and more formal than pink ones. Usually, white memos were addressed to groups of workers (e.g., "All Caseworkers") and were used to announce and explain basic agency policy or regulations. Letters on agency letterhead had diverse purposes, but invariably these letters were written to people outside the agency whereas pink and white memos were written to workers within the agency.

From each administrator, we collected ten examples of each of the three types of writing. Since each participant in our study indicated that these three types of writing had different purposes and were addressed to different types of audiences, our analysis of the three types enabled us to answer this question: Do different rhetorical contexts (i.e., different audiences and purposes) prompt writers in our study to vary certain linguistic features of their writing? We will elaborate on this shortly.

Since caseworkers wrote reports much more frequently than they did letters or memos, we examined only caseworkers' report writing. From each caseworker, we collected six complete reports (the reports usually ranging from 10 to 20 T-units in length) on a specific meeting with a client. No more than two of a given caseworker's reports dealt with any one client, and no more than two of a writer's reports were written on the same date.

Three of the caseworkers, members of the Eligibility Unit, were responsible for screening prospective welfare clients. The other three worked with children who had been placed in foster homes. These foster-care caseworkers were responsible for helping children and their foster parents adapt successfully to the new relationship. Foster-care workers were likely to see foster parents and children several times a month, and they expressed strong personal interest in their primary clients, the children. Eligibility caseworkers rarely saw clients more than once, and they reported that their primary responsibility was to obtain factual information from prospective clients. Since these two groups of caseworkers had such different responsibilities and relations with clients (or prospective clients), an analysis of their writing enabled us to answer this question: Within a given institution, is the type of writing done by workers in one job significantly different from that done by workers who hold a quite different job?

JUDGMENTS ABOUT THE ACCEPTABILITY OF DIFFERENT STYLES

For this part of our study, we selected nine pieces of writing from our writing sample: three pink memos, three white memos, and three letters. All of these were relatively short, and none dealt with personal or controversial matters. Modifying procedures devised by Hake and Williams (1981), we prepared three versions of each of the nine pieces of writing. In one version, the "verbal" draft, all grammatical subjects were rewritten as agents, and all finite verbs were rewritten as actions performed by the agent in the subject slot. The second version was identical to the first except that there were five instances in which an active finite verb had been made passive. The third alternative was identical to the second except that it contained at least three instances in which verbs in the active voice had been nominalized. The three versions of each piece of writing were read by participants, who were asked to rate the alternative drafts as "most acceptable," "less acceptable," and "least acceptable." These ratings enabled us to answer these questions: Do participants consistently prefer one style of writing (e.g., the nominalized version) to another? Do workers' preferences vary according to the type of writing they are reading? For example, do workers prefer a verbal style in pink memos and a passive or passive-nominal style in the more formal white memos?

Data Coding and Analysis

INTERVIEW TRANSCRIPTS

In trying to categorize the reasons that writers gave for their choices, we were guided in part by our reading and rereading of interview transcripts and in part by assumptions from rhetoric and current theories about the purposes or functions of discourse. Our three main categories, *audience-based* reasons, *writer-based* reasons, and *subject-based* reasons, reflect distinctions made by Gibson (1969), Kinneavy (1971), and Halliday (1973).[2] We want to emphasize, however, that our terms do not refer to the functions of complete pieces of discourse (cf. Kinneavy, 1971). Rather, they refer to types of reasons given to justify several specific choices in any given text. Discussion of a single text—indeed, even discussion of a single choice—might elicit more than one type of reason.

Our categories and subcategories are as follows:

I. Audience-based reasons
  A. *Status of the audience.* Writer mentions reader's title, office, or place in hierarchy and expresses or implies deference or lack of deference.

> You're saying to the executive, "You *must* do this." And the executive is an important man.

> No, you're talking to your peers . . . and I don't think you have to say that.

  B. *Personal knowledge of or relationship with audience.* Writer says, in effect, "I know (or don't know) X audience personally," or "I have (or have not) had dealings with X audience in the past"; writer may recount an anecdote about past experiences.

> Well, see, I've called him [by his first name] all my life.

> We've never had any problems [before].

  C. *Personal characteristic of the audience.* Writer refers to some personal trait or to the reader's knowledge or lack of knowledge of a given topic.

> He tends to be a bit sensitive, and you have to be careful you don't offend him.

> Their purpose is not to know *why* your policy is such-and-such. They just want to know what [the policy] is.

2. Halliday's notion of *interpersonal functions* encompasses what we label *audience-based* and *speaker-based* decisions; his term *ideational functions* is comparable to our term *subject-based* decisions.

D. *Anticipated or desired action on the part of the audience.* Writer refers to overt actions or to changes in the audience's feelings or state of knowledge.

> But supposing I answered *yes*. And now they [the audience] come back and say, "Oh, we're very pleased with your *yes* answer. Would you please give us the cases in proof of the *yes* answer?"
>
> So that's the reason for the first paragraph . . . to let [the reader] know the background, that this is what's happening down here.

II. Writer-based reasons

A. *Writer's role or position in the organization.* Writer mentions him- or herself and specifically refers to individual scope of duties.

> [This is] not within my realm of authority to make—all I can do is recommend.
>
> The theme I'm trying to establish is that I am the one who is in charge of this deal.

B. *Ethos or attitude the writer wishes to project or avoid.* Writer uses a terminology that describes his or her attitude or personality.

> . . . *we* sounds . . . I don't know . . . too personal.
>
> I was trying to strike a somewhat casual note here.

C. *Writer's feelings about subject or task at hand.* Writer refers to feelings or attitudes that are not conveyed in the writing.

> When I wrote this I had had a really bad morning.
>
> I despise writing these [reports].

III. Subject-based decisions

A. *Importance of the topic dealt with in the writing.*

> I wouldn't say that because this [subject] is going to entail decisions and logic that are very profound dollarwise.

B. *Desire to provide an accurate, complete, nonredundant account.* Writer mentions alternatives and discards one as inaccurate, or simply asserts that a given piece of information needs to be in the text, without referring to an audience's need for that information.

> I wouldn't say that. That implies they have a choice, and they don't.
>
> I don't want to leave that out because that's what actually happened.

C. *Desire to document a conclusion the writer has drawn.*

> I guess the point I was trying to make here was that. . . .
>
> I wanted to show that their relationship really was a healthy one.

One might reasonably expect an additional category reflecting writers' sense of the formal demands of a particular type of writing. For example, we can imagine a participant saying, in effect, "When you write a pink memo, there are certain choices you make just because you are writing a pink memo rather than a white memo or a letter." Surprisingly, this type of comment did not appear in the transcripts we analyzed. It is quite conceivable, however, that such reasoning might appear in writing done in other nonacademic settings and that, consequently, our list of categories might need to be expanded.

WRITING SAMPLES

In determining which linguistic features we would consider, we drew upon recent research (Crowhurst & Piché, 1979; Watson, 1979) and upon theory (Gibson, 1969; Hake & Williams, 1981; Halliday & Hasan, 1976). For each piece of writing in our sample, we determined the following:

- Mean number of T-units
- Mean T-unit length
- Mean clause length
- Mean number of clauses per T-unit
- Mean number of passive constructions per T-unit
- Types of cohesive markers used and the mean number of each type per T-unit

JUDGMENTS ABOUT ACCEPTABILITY OF STYLE

The alternative drafts identified as "most acceptable" were given a score of 3, drafts rated "less acceptable" were rated 2, and the "least acceptable" versions were scored 1.

RELIABILITY OF JUDGMENTS

Each interview transcript was read by two judges, both of whom had done graduate work in English and had taught composition. Using the categories described earlier, these judges achieved an overall agreement of 80 percent in categorizing reasons that the workers gave for their choices. The results reported in the following section reflect only those instances in which the two readers agreed on the type of reason a participant had given.

The analysis of the linguistic features of writing samples was done by three judges. One judge did the analysis of cohesion. To check the reliability of this judge's scoring, another person made an independent analysis of cohesion in a subset of the total writing sample (10 letters, 10 memos, and 1 caseworker report). The percentage of agreement ranged from 91 (in the letters of one administrator) to 97 (in the caseworker report). Results for cohesion reflect the judgments of the reader who analyzed the entire sample. Analysis of the other linguistic features was done by two graduate students in English, each of whom analyzed one-half of the total writing sample. To assess the reliability of these judges, one of the principal researchers also scored 100 T-units from the writing sample scored by the two graduate students. On the marking of T-units and clauses, the agreement between principal researcher and graduate students was 99 percent. On the identification of other linguistic features, there was at least 97 percent agreement.

Results

Sensitivity to Rhetorical Context

REASONS USED IN JUSTIFYING CHOICES

Although we will present separate discussions of administrators and caseworkers, one observation applies to both groups. As Tables 11-1 and 11-2 show, it is very unusual for an administrator or caseworker to justify a given choice by citing an arhetorical rule that he or she follows in all circumstances. Instead, most of the reasons can be categorized as "rhetorical"; that is, the reasons reflect a concern for elements of the

Table 11-1. Frequency of Each Type of Reason Given by Administrators

		Type of reason	Number of instances of each type of reason	Percentage of reasons in each category
I	A	Status of audience	9	5%
I	B	Relation to audience	26	14
I	C	Characteristic of audience	31	16
I	D	Anticipated action	59	31
II	A	Writer's role in organization	4	2
II	B	Writer's ethos	40	21
II	C	Writer's feelings	4	2
III	A	Status of subject	2	1
III	B	Complete account	7	4
III	C	Document conclusion	1	1
IV		Arhetorical reason	8	4
			191	101%[a]

[a]Percentages do not total 100%, since the number for each type of reason was rounded to the nearest whole percent.

Table 11-2. Frequency of Each Type of Reason Given by Caseworkers

		Type of reason	Number of instances of each type of reason	Percentage of reasons in each category
I	A	Status of audience	0	0%
I	B	Relation to audience	0	0
I	C	Characteristic of audience	6	4
I	D	Anticipated action	38	23
II	A	Writer's role in organization	9	5
II	B	Writer's ethos	22	13
II	C	Writer's feelings	0	0
III	A	Status of subject	0	0
III	B	Complete account	59	36
III	C	Document conclusion	26	16
IV		Arhetorical reason	6	4
			166	101%[a]

[a]Percentages do not total 100%, since the number for each type of reason was rounded to the nearest whole percent.

rhetorical context: speaker, subject, and audience. Administrators were especially likely to be concerned with their audience. Thirty-one percent of their reasons were categorized as I D (writer's decision based on concern about audience's anticipated actions), and an additional 30 percent were categorized as either I B (decision based on writer's personal relationship with audience) or I C (decision based on writer's awareness of a personal characteristic of the audience). Caseworkers tended to favor subject-based reasons; 36 percent of their reasons were categorized as III B (decision based on writer's desire to provide an accurate, complete, nonredundant account) or as III C (decision based on writer's desire to document a conclusion he or she had drawn). Yet when we consider all reasons given by all administrators and all caseworkers, we find that no single type of reason appears more than 36 percent of the time. Moreover, again considering all reasons given by caseworkers and by administrators, we find that decisions about a single type of choice might be justified by a variety of reasons (see Tables 11-3 and 11-4).

Sometimes, a particular type of choice would elicit numerous references to a reason other than the primary one cited. When administrators gave a reason for preferring a particular way of making a command or request, they frequently (47 percent of all reasons given for this type of choice) indicated a concern for the audience's anticipated actions (I D). Yet 34 percent of their comments on this type of choice also indicated an awareness of the *ethos* they were creating (II B). When caseworkers justified their choice as to whether they would refer to their own actions, they frequently (43 percent of all reasons given for

Table 11-3. Types of Reasons Elicited by Each Type of Choice: Administrators

Type of reason	Type of choice	Form of addressing reader	Presence/absence of introductory material	Presence/absence of elaboration	Form of reference to self	Form of command or request	Presence/absence of concluding statement	Form of signature
I	A	26 (8)	0	0	0	0	0	3 (1)
I	B	19 (6)	15 (3)	17 (5)	5 (1)	3 (1)	10 (3)	23 (7)
I	C	13 (4)	30 (6)	20 (6)	11 (2)	13 (4)	24 (7)	7 (2)
I	D	7 (2)	45 (9)	38 (11)	37 (7)	47 (15)	41 (12)	10 (3)
II	A	3 (1)	0	4 (1)	5 (1)	0	0	3 (1)
II	B	19 (6)	5 (1)	10 (3)	16 (3)	34 (11)	17 (5)	37 (11)
II	C	0	0	4 (1)	0	0	4 (1)	7 (2)
III	A	3 (1)	0	0	0	0	0	3 (1)
III	B	3 (1)	5 (1)	4 (1)	11 (2)	0	4 (1)	3 (1)
III	C	0	0	4 (1)	0	0	0	0
IV		7 (2)	0	0	16 (3)	3 (1)	0	3 (1)
Total number of reasons given for each type of choice		31	20	29	19	32	29	30
Total of percentages		100	100	101	100	100	100	99

Note. In each instance, the number in parentheses is the number of times that questions about a given type of choice (e.g., form used in addressing readers) elicited a particular type of reason (e.g., I A). Numbers not in parentheses are percentages. These percentages were derived by dividing the total number of reasons given for one type of choice into the number of times a particular type of reason (e.g., I A) was mentioned for a particular type of choice. Some totals do not equal 100%, since numbers

246

this type of choice) indicated that they wanted to create a complete, accurate, nonredundant record (III B). Yet in 30 percent of all reasons given for this type of choice, they also indicated a concern for their audience's anticipated actions (I D). See Tables 11-3 and 11-4.

In summary, caseworkers and administrators rarely justified their preferences by referring to arhetorical rules. Instead, they gave rhetorical reasons. Further, one cannot assume that a participant's decision is always explainable by a single rhetorical reason.

ANALYSIS OF WRITING SAMPLES

The results reported here are based solely on an analysis of administrators' pink memos, white memos, and letters. Caseworkers wrote

Table 11-4. *Types of Reasons Elicited by Each Type of Choice: Caseworkers*

Type of reason	Type of choice	Form of reference to self	Form of reference to client	Reference to worker's acts	Reference to client's acts	Attribution
I	A	0	0	0	0	0
I	B	0	0	0	0	0
I	C	8 (2)	0	3 (1)	4 (2)	3 (1)
I	D	12 (3)	23 (5)	30 (12)	28 (13)	16 (5)
II	A	12 (3)	5 (1)	10 (4)	2 (1)	0
II	B	50 (13)	27 (6)	0	6 (3)	0
II	C	0	0	0	0	0
III	A	0	0	0	0	0
III	B	12 (3)	36 (8)	43 (17)	23 (11)	65 (20)
III	C	0	0	15 (6)	34 (16)	13 (4)
IV		8 (2)	9 (2)	0	2 (1)	3 (1)
Total number of reasons given for each type of choice		26	22	40	47	31
Total of percentages		102	100	100	99	100

Note. In each instance, the number in parentheses is the number of times that questions about a given type of choice (e.g., form used in addressing readers) elicited a particular type of reason (e.g., I A). Numbers not in parentheses are percentages. These percentages were derived by dividing the total number of reasons given for one type of choice into the number of times a particular type of reason (e.g., I A) was mentioned for a particular type of choice. Some totals do not equal 100%, since numbers were rounded to the nearest whole percent.

letters and memos so infrequently that we were not able to gather an adequate current sample for all of them. To determine whether administrators as a group varied linguistic features according to the types of writing they were doing, we performed a two-way analysis of variance (writer by product type) for each of the following: mean number of T-units, mean T-unit length, mean clause length, mean number of clauses per T-unit, mean number of between-T-unit coordinate conjunctions, mean number of passives per T-unit, and mean number of cohesive markers per T-unit. Some of this variation could be attributed to the practices of individual writers. Analysis of variance, reported in Table 11-5, showed that the writer him- or herself had a significant effect for eight of the ten features: mean number of T-units, mean T-unit length, mean clause length, clauses per T-unit, passives per T-unit, reference cohesive ties, substitution cohesive ties, and lexical cohesive ties. Furthermore, there were significant interactions between writer and type of writing for the following: mean T-unit length, clauses per T-unit, passives per T-unit, and lexical cohesive ties per T-unit. In spite of these interactions, all writers made the same types of distinctions among product types. Writers differed from one another only in the *degree* to which they made particular distinctions.

To assess the extent to which product type accounts for variation

Table 11-5. *Analysis of Variance in Administrators' Writing*

Variable	Writer $(4,235)$	Type $(2,235)$	Interaction of writer and type $(8,235)$	Pink versus white memos $(1,235)$	Memos versus letters $(1,235)$
Number of T-units	7.446^b	8.613^b	1.801	15.37^b	1.85
T-unit length	8.491^b	5.011^b	3.164^b	7.84^b	2.17
Clause length	5.107^b	1.022	1.682	.85	1.19
Clauses per T-unit	18.539^b	.983	2.041^a	1.76	.59
Between-T-unit coordination	1.715	1.399	1.081	.71	2.14
Passives per T-unit	2.477^a	8.728^b	3.832^b	16.41^b	2.07
Reference cohesive ties per T-unit	5.760^b	8.200^b	1.369	13.25^b	2.87
Substitution cohesive ties per T-unit	5.610^b	3.949^b	.937	.07	8.84^b
Conjunction cohesive ties per T-unit	1.502	3.475	1.508	6.43^a	2.12
Lexical cohesive ties per T-unit	17.511	26.607^b	2.728^b	51.88^b	1.12

[a]Significance at the .05 level.

[b]Significance at the .01 level.

among individual products, we partitioned products into independent, contrasting groups: pink memos versus white memos, and memos (both pink and white) versus letters. Planned orthogonal comparisons indicate that the administrators varied certain features of their writing according to the types of writing they were doing. Pink memos differed significantly from white memos with respect to these six variables: number of T-units, T-unit length, passives per T-unit, reference cohesive ties per T-unit, conjunction cohesive ties per T-unit, and lexical cohesive ties per T-unit (see Table 11-5). All memos, pink and white combined, differed significantly from letters with respect to two variables: passives and substitution cohesive ties (see Table 11-5).

JUDGMENTS ABOUT ACCEPTABLE STYLE

Since administrators tended to use more passive constructions in white memos than in pink memos, we wondered whether participants would prefer a verbal style in pink memos and a passive or passive-nominal style in white memos. They did not. The verbal versions of all types of writing (pink memos, white memos, and letters) were consistently assigned lower average ranks than were the passive or passive-nominal versions (see Table 11-6). Surprisingly, participants were more likely to give high rankings to the verbal versions of white memos and letters than to the verbal versions of pink memos (see Tables 11-7 and 11-8). But even in the case of white memos and letters, verbal versions never received as high an average ranking as did passive versions. And with only one exception, the average ranking of verbal versions was not as high as were average rankings given to passive-nominal versions.

The limitations of our sample size prevent our drawing strong conclusions. But verbal versions were consistently ranked lower than were passive ones. This suggests to us that the participants' judgments about passive and active style were not greatly influenced by the type of writing they were evaluating.

Table 11-6. Average Scores for Alternative Versions of Pink Memos, White Memos, and Letters

	Verbal	Passive	Passive-nominal	Percentage of times verbal version judged most acceptable
Pink	1.5	2.3	2.3	12% (4 of 33)
White	1.6	2.3	2.1	24% (8 of 33)
Letter	1.8	2.3	1.9	30% (10 of 33)

Table 11-7. Judgments about Style: Average Scores Given by Administrators, Foster-Care Workers, and Eligibility Workers

	Pink memos			White memos			Letters		
	Verbal	Passive	Nonpassive	Verbal	Passive	Nonpassive	Verbal	Passive	Nonpassive
Administrators	1.3	2.1	2.6	1.6	2.3	2.1	1.7	2.3	2.1
Foster-care workers	1.3	2.6	2.2	1.4	2.3	2.1	1.8	2.3	1.9
Eligibility workers	1.9	2.0	2.1	1.7	2.2	2.0	2	2.2	1.6

Table 11-8. *Percentage of Times the Verbal Version Was Selected as "Most Acceptable"*

	Pink memos	White memos	Letters
Administrators	0%	27%	27%
		(4 of 15)	(4 of 15)
Foster-care workers	11%	22%	33%
	(1 of 9)	(2 of 9)	(3 of 9)
Eligibility workers	33%	22%	33%
	(3 of 9)	(2 of 9)	(3 of 9)

Variations According to Job

REASONS USED IN JUSTIFYING CHOICES

The results of interviews with caseworkers and administrators indicated that there are at least some differences in the types of reasons most frequently given by workers in different types of jobs. Although both groups of caseworkers made use of the same types of reasons, foster-care workers occasionally justified a choice by expressing their desire to document a personal conclusion that they had drawn (III C) as a result of their dealings with a client (see Table 11-9). Eligibility workers almost never cited this type of reason. They were, by contrast, very likely to justify a choice by indicating the necessity of making a complete, accurate, nonredundant record (III B). And, to a lesser degree, they were likely to indicate a concern for the anticipated actions of their audience.

These basic distinctions are also apparent when we consider the types of reasons cited by caseworkers in commenting on different types of choices (Table 11-10). With only one exception (choices about attribution), eligibility workers consistently made more frequent use of reason I D (anticipated actions) than did foster-care workers. In commenting on three of the five types of choices, foster-care workers made use of reason III C (desire to document a personal conclusion), a reason that rarely appeared in interviews with eligibility caseworkers. One further distinction becomes apparent in foster-care workers' comments on four types of choices—reference to self, reference to client, workers' acts, and clients' acts. In these comments, foster-care workers indicated an awareness of the writer's role or status in the agency, an awareness that was not expressed by eligibility workers.

In addition to comparing reasons given by two different groups of caseworkers, we compared caseworkers' reasons with reasons given by administrators. In making this comparison, we must point out that interviews with caseworkers concerned only the choices reflected in one type of writing, reports of meetings with clients. By contrast, interviews with administrators were based on several different types of

Table 11-9. Types of Reasons Given by Two Groups of Caseworkers

Type of reason	Foster-care caseworkers	Eligibility caseworkers
I A	0	0
I B	0	0
I C	4	3
	(4)	(2)
I D	19	29
	(19)	(19)
II A	9	0
	(9)	
II B	13	14
	(13)	(9)
II C	0	0
III A	0	0
III B	29	45
	(30)	(29)
III C	23	3
	(24)	(2)
IV	2	6
	(2)	(4)
Total number of reasons	101	65
Total of percentages	99	100

Note. In each instance, the number in parentheses is the number of times that questions about a given type of choice (e.g., form used in addressing readers) elicited a particular type of reason (e.g., I A). Numbers not in parentheses are percentages. These percentages were derived by dividing the total number of reasons given for one type of choice into the number of times a particular type of reason (e.g., I A) was mentioned for a particular type of choice. Some totals do not equal 100%, since numbers were rounded to the nearest whole percent.

writing, ranging from informal notes to official letters. We cannot, therefore, refute or support this speculation: if administrators were writing caseworkers' reports, their reasoning might seem quite similar to that of the caseworkers. This idea seems plausible, since most of the administrators had previously served as caseworkers in the agency. But plausible as the speculation is, it is beside the point. Our study is based on the types of writing people regularly do as a part of the jobs they currently hold. In preparing for interviews, we found that caseworkers' report writing simply did not entail the same types of choices as did the administrators' memo and letter writing.

Moreover, as Tables 11-1 and 11-2 indicate, we found that administrators were much more likely to give audience-based reasons than were caseworkers. Further, administrators gave types of audience-based reasons (I A, status of audience, and I B, personal relation with audience) that never appeared in caseworkers' interviews (see Tables 11-1 and 11-2). Caseworkers, by contrast, were much more likely to use

Table 11-10. *Types of Reasons Cited for Each Type of Choice Made by Two Groups of Caseworkers*

Type of reason	Type of choice	Form of reference to self		Form of reference to client		Reference to worker's acts		Reference to client's acts		Attribution	
		Foster care	Eligibility	Foster care	Eligibility	Foster care	Eligibility	Foster care	Eligibility	Foster care	Eligibility
I	A	0	0	0	0	0	0	0	0	0	0
I	B	0	0	0	0	0	0	0	0	0	0
I	C	0	15 (2)	0	0	4 (1)	0	6 (2)	0	6 (1)	0
I	D	8 (1)	15 (2)	17 (2)	30 (3)	13 (3)	56 (9)	25 (9)	36 (4)	25 (4)	7 (1)
II	A	23 (3)	0	9 (1)	0	17 (4)	0	3 (1)	0	0	0
II	B	54 (7)	46 (6)	33 (4)	20 (2)	0	0	6 (2)	9 (1)	0	0
II	C	0	0	0	0	0	0	0	0	0	0
III	A	0	0	0	0	0	0	0	0	0	0
III	B	8 (1)	15 (2)	42 (5)	30 (3)	46 (11)	38 (6)	17 (6)	46 (5)	44 (7)	87 (13)
III	C	0	0	0	0	21 (5)	6 (1)	42 (15)	9 (1)	25 (4)	0
IV		8 (1)	8 (1)	0	20 (20)	0	0	3 (1)	0	0	7 (1)
Total number of reasons for each type of choice		13	13	12	10	24	16	36	11	18	15
Total percentages		101	99	101	100	101	100	102	100	100	101

Note. In each instance, the number in parentheses is the number of times that questions about a given type of choice (e.g., form used in addressing readers) elicited a particular type of reason (e.g., IA). Numbers not in parentheses are percentages. These percentages were derived by dividing the total number of reasons given for one type of choice into the number of times a particular type of reason (e.g., IA) was mentioned for a particular type of choice. Some totals do not equal 100%, since numbers were rounded to the nearest whole percent.

253

a subject-based reason to justify a given choice. We conclude that, for the agency in which our study was conducted, types of writing that are typically associated with different jobs entail different types of choices based on different types of reasons. Even when doing the same type of writing and commenting on the same types of choices, writers who hold jobs with different functions are likely to use somewhat different types of reasons in explaining their choices.

ANALYSIS OF WRITING SAMPLE

Differences between the two groups of caseworkers also appear in the linguistic features of their writing. As was the case with the administrators, the individual writer had a significant effect on several variables (see Table 11-11). But analysis of variance by job type also indicates that the writing of foster-care workers differed significantly from that of eligibility workers on the following variables: number of T-units, T-unit length, clause length, number of clauses per T-unit, between-T-unit coordination, number of passives per T-unit, reference cohesive ties, conjunction cohesive ties, and lexical cohesive ties (see Table 11-11).

JUDGMENTS ABOUT ACCEPTABLE STYLE

These judgments varied somewhat among the different groups of workers. For example, as Tables 11-7 and 11-8 indicate, eligibility workers rated the verbal versions of pink memos higher than did administrators and foster-care workers. But Table 11-7 also shows that one pattern appeared in the ratings done by all three groups of workers. On the average, all workers ranked the verbal versions lower than the passive versions. This holds true for all three types of writing—pink memos, white memos, and letters. Because of this overall pattern, we cannot claim that judgments about style vary according to the type of job a worker holds.

Discussion

The results of our study are based on three different sources of information: interviews, analysis of written products, and participants' judgments about acceptable style. Two of these sources lead to similar conclusions. Both interviews and analysis of written products indicate substantial variation in the writing of two different groups of workers. The two groups of caseworkers gave somewhat different justifications for choices they had made in their reports, and their writing differed significantly with respect to a number of linguistic features. Further-

Table 11-11. Analysis of Variance for Caseworkers' Writing

Feature	Foster-care workers				Eligibility workers				$F_{(1, 30)}$ Foster-care reports versus eligibility reports	$F_{(4, 30)}$ Interaction of writer and type
	Worker 1	Worker 2	Worker 3	Average	Worker 4	Worker 5	Worker 6	Average		
TUNITS	10.33	8.83	15.67	11.61	16.00	24.67	12.83	17.83	9.646[b]	4.188[b]
WPERT	17.18	10.45	20.74	16.12	8.98	7.07	8.36	8.14	128.639[b]	19.019[b]
WPERC	9.11	6.57	13.40	9.69	5.90	7.79	6.27	6.65	6.229[a]	2.904[a]
CPERT	.98	.40	.74	.71	.43	.13	.25	.27	23.305[b]	4.378[b]
BPERT	.13	.03	.16	.11	.06	.01	.03	.04	9.375[b]	3.281[a]
PPERT	.12	.04	.25	.14	.34	.57	.51	.47	35.979[b]	2.766[a]
RPERT	.54	1.03	.33	.67	.25	.07	.11	.35	8.713[b]	2.023
SPERT	.08	.29	.10	.16	.03	.04	.15	.07	2.705	2.268
JPERT	.15	.04	.17	.12	.04	.01	.00	.02	17.012[b]	3.018[a]
LPERT	1.47	1.44	1.87	1.59	.62	.79	.51	.64	14.198[b]	.404

[a] Significance at the .05 level.

[b] Significance at the .01 level.

more, both interviews and product analysis suggest that the writers in this study are sensitive to the rhetorical context for their writing. The administrators vary several linguistic features according to the type of writing they are doing. In addition, when giving reasons for preferring one alternative to another, both administrators and caseworkers showed a complex awareness of audience, self, and subject. They rarely justified choices by citing an arhetorical rule, and they never relied exclusively on one type of reason in justifying a given type of choice.

These conclusions find little support in our third source of information. When participants in our study made judgments about acceptability of style, those judgments varied only slightly according to the type of job a participant held. On the average, all three groups of participants (administrators, foster-care workers, and eligibility workers) preferred passages containing passive constructions. This preference held true for all types of writing. Thus, type of job had little influence on participants' judgments about what constituted "acceptable" style.

These results suggest several lines of inquiry. When we analyzed written products, we used a classification scheme (pink memos, white memos, letters) that was suggested to us by participants in our study. We think researchers should continue to consider participants' understanding of the principal types of writing done in a given setting, since this understanding is based on their familiarity with the job and with the functions that writing must serve on the job. Yet we also think researchers should consider other ways of classifying written products. That is, researchers might group writings according to their various purposes or speaker–audience relationships and then determine whether writers vary linguistic features according to their purpose or the speaker–audience relationship.

Another line of inquiry arises from our attempt to investigate participants' sense of "acceptable" style. Although we asked participants to comment on writing that had actually been done in the agency, we provided them with no information about the context of the pieces of writing. Since the participants had no specific information about audience and purpose, their judgments about style may not have been influenced by the same considerations that guide their stylistic choices in their own writing. Given this possibility, we suggest consideration of these questions: What stylistic preferences would workers exhibit if they were asked to judge alternative versions of pieces that the workers themselves had written? What stylistic preferences would workers display if, in judging something written by others, they were given specific information about the writer's sense of audience and purpose?

Two final suggestions for research are based on our awareness of the rhetorical considerations that participants mentioned in the interviews. Many of the choices apparent in workers' writing (e.g., choices about the form of a request or the inclusion of elaboration) are also important in speaking. Thus we wonder: Are there other types of choices that appear in both oral and written language? A second set of questions arises from the fact that all participants in our study were experienced workers. All the caseworkers had worked in the agency for at least two years, and all the administrators had worked there for ten or more years. Since we have no information about the writing of inexperienced workers, we wonder: Do inexperienced workers make the same types of choices as do the more experienced workers? Would their reasons be comparable to the reasons given by more experienced workers? Do the reasons change as workers become more experienced? If so, are there factors in the working environment that influence those changes?

We are interested in these kinds of questions because it appears that writing in nonacademic settings will continue to be a significant area for study. Many people must write with some skill in order to succeed at (or indeed, to retain) their jobs. Part of this skill entails the ability to make complex rhetorical decisions. As we gain increased knowledge about those decisions, the reasons that govern them, and the means by which workers come to make them more skillfully, our basic understanding of our discipline—and our ability to teach writing—will be enhanced. To repeat a familiar phrase: further research is clearly indicated.

ACKNOWLEDGMENTS

This chapter is adapted and reprinted by permission from "Writing in a Non-academic Setting" by L. Odell and D. Goswami, *Research in the Teaching of English*, October 1982, *16*(3), 201–223. The study was supported by a grant from the National Institute of Education. We are very grateful to Ronald J. Kerwin and Judith B. Marks, whose advice and assistance at all stages of the study made our task much easier.

REFERENCES

Basso, K. H. The ethnography of writing. In R. Bauman & J. Sherzer (Eds.), *Explorations in the ethnography of speaking*. London: Cambridge University Press, 1974.

Bauman, R., & Sherzer, J. (Eds.). *Explorations in the ethnography of speaking*. London: Cambridge University Press, 1974.

Crowhurst, M., & Piché, G. L. Audience and mode of discourse effects on syntactic complexity in writing at two grade levels. *Research in the Teaching of English*, 1979, *13*, 101–110.

Flower, L. S., & Hayes, J. R. The dynamics of composing: Making plans and juggling constraints. In L. W. Gregg & E. Steinberg (Eds.), *Cognitive processes in writing*. Hillsdale, N.J.: Lawrence Erlbaum, 1980.

Gibson, W. *Persona*. New York: Random House, 1969.

Giglioli, P. P. (Ed.). *Language in social context*. Harmondsworth, England: Penguin, 1972.

Goswami, D. *Rhetorical occurrences in occupational writing*. Paper presented at National Council of Teachers of English conference, Kansas City, Mo., November 1978.

Hake, R., & Williams, J. Style and its consequences: Do as I do, not as I say. *College English*, 1981, *43*, 433–451.

Halliday, M. A. K. *Explorations in the functions of language*. New York: Elsevier, 1973.

Halliday, M. A. K., & Hasan, R. *Cohesion in English*. London: Longman, 1976.

Kinneavy, J. *A theory of discourse*. Englewood Cliffs, N.J.: Prentice-Hall, 1971.

Matsuhashi, A. *Pauses and planning: The tempo of written discourse production*. Unpublished doctoral dissertation, State University of New York, Buffalo, 1979.

Perl, S. The composing process of unskilled college writers. *Research in the Teaching of English*, December 1979, *13*, 317–336.

Rubin, D. L., & Piché, G. L. Development in syntactic and strategic aspects of audience adaptation skills in written persuasive communication. *Research in the Teaching of English*, December 1979, *13*, 293–316.

Scribner, S., & Cole, M. Literacy without schooling: Testing for intellectual effects. *Harvard Education Review*, 1978, *48*, 448–461.

Van Dyck, B. *Partial taxonomy of writing demands on bank executives*. Paper presented at Conference on College Composition and Communication, Washington, D.C., March 1980.

Watson, C. *The effects of maturity and discourse type on the written syntax of superior high school seniors and upper level college English majors*. Unpublished doctoral dissertation, State University of New York, Buffalo, 1979.

12

Putting the situation into writing research: State and disposition as parameters of writing apprehension

JOHN A. DALY
JOY LYNN HAILEY
University of Texas, Austin

During the past few years, considerable attention has been focused on a dispositional tendency of people to avoid writing and writing-related activities. Research concerning this construct, labeled writing apprehension or writing anxiety, has yielded a variety of important correlates. Writing apprehension has been related to occupational and academic choices (Daly & Shamo, 1976, 1978), enrollment in advanced writing courses (Daly & Miller, 1975c), performance on standardized tests of writing competency (Daly, 1978; Daly & Miller, 1975c; Dickson, 1978; Faigley, Daly, & Witte, 1981), actual writing performance and rated quality of messages encoded (Book, 1976; Daly, 1977; Daly & Miller, 1975a; Faigley *et al.*, 1981; Garcia, 1977; Richmond & Dickson, 1980), a variety of self-esteem and personality dimensions (Daly & Wilson, 1981), various developmental differences (Harvley-Felder, 1978), performance on counter-attitudinal tasks (Toth, 1975), and different attitudinal measures of people's willingness to write, success expectations in writing, and student evaluations of classes that center on writing (Daly & Miller, 1975c; Scott & Wheeless, 1975). Additional work has focused on the reduction of writing apprehension (Fox, 1980; Powers, Cook & Meyer, 1979), its role in composition program assessment (Witte & Faigley, 1980), and sex differences (Daly, 1979; Daly & Miller, 1975c; Dickson, 1978; Jeroski & Conry, 1981).

Dispositional versus Situational Anxiety

One of the defining characteristics of writing apprehension as it is currently conceived is its dispositional nature. The construct assumes that people can be ranked in some consistent fashion in terms of their apprehension about writing: some people are more anxious than others in enduring ways. This "trait-like" nature of the construct clearly limits its practical and theoretical applicability: The empirical use of the construct is restricted to situations where an individual's apprehension can be assessed in comparison with the apprehensions of others. Further, the construct is highly person-specific; it ignores the situational characteristics that can affect how anxious an individual feels regardless of his or her dispositional apprehension. Certainly people have dispositional variations in their apprehension about writing, but situations also carry with them some propensity to make people more or less anxious about activities that occur within them. There are, in other words, at least two distinct forms of writing anxiety. One form is the dispositional sort measured by self-report and reflecting a stable and enduring difference among people. Another form is situational anxiety. This sort is transitory in nature and depends on the particular characteristics of a writing situation. The two notions are complementary. In any writing situation an individual will experience, to some extent, both dispositional and situational anxiety. While a substantial body of literature has focused on dispositional anxiety, virtually no attention has been paid to situational anxiety.

Tied to this lack of research on situational anxiety is the observation that empirically grounded writing research has often ignored the situational aspects of writing. Yet clearly the situation in which people write affects both their writing process and their written product. Two papers, on the same topic by the same person written in different situations, will often be very dissimilar. The critical point here is not only that situations can affect writing but that the important dimensions of situations which impact on writing have not been carefully specified. Situations, of course, vary along certain dimensions. Exactly what those dimensions are, and how relevant each is to writing, are important questions that to date have received little attention.

Conceptually, this chapter introduces the "state" dimension of writing apprehension and emphasizes the critical role of situations in writing. The underlying assumption is that an individual, placed in different situations that vary along certain dimensions, might experience differing levels of anxiety about writing regardless of his or her dispositional response to writing. That is, the contextual nature of the situations in which writing takes place may profoundly affect how a person both approaches the act of writing and actually writes.

Thus, this chapter extends the apprehension construct beyond the dispositional model. It reports the initial development of measures of situational anxiety specific to writing, offers some characteristics of writing situations that may affect an individual's situational anxiety, and summarizes a preliminary study examining the role of these situational characteristics in creating or mitigating anxiety associated with the act of writing.

To measure situational anxiety, we adapted to the writing situation various measures that are used in psychology to assess "state" or transitory anxiety. Since situational anxiety may involve responses to both the writing assignment and the writing environment (e.g., class), two measures of situational anxiety were needed. The hypothesis was that the two would be significantly related to each other. Also of importance was our examination of the relationship between writing apprehension as a disposition and writing anxiety as a situational response. Conceptually they are different. It is possible for a person low in apprehension to feel anxious in a particular environment, and for a highly apprehensive person to feel comfortable in another environment. Generally, however, a positive relationship would be expected. Highly anxious people ought to find situations that require writing more anxiety-producing than their counterparts who are low in apprehension. The critical issue is not the direction of correlation, which seems obvious; rather, it is the magnitude of the relationship. The entering hypothesis was that there would be a small to moderate, but significant and positive, correlation between dispositional and situational anxiety.

Situational Dimensions

In this investigation, five situational characteristics were hypothesized to affect how situationally anxious an individual would feel. The five, drawn conceptually from observations of writing classrooms and reports by students and teachers, were considered to affect situational writing anxiety both individually and jointly. The first situational dimension was the level of perceived *evaluation* present in the writing situation. The expectation was that the greater the perceived evaluation, the greater the reported anxiety. When people perceive that they are in highly evaluative situations, they should feel less comfortable and more anxious than they would in situations where less evaluation is perceived to be present. The second characteristic was the *novelty* of the situation. People should feel more anxious in an unfamiliar, novel writing situation than in a familiar one. When people have previously experienced a situation, they may have devised strategies for coping with the requirements of the environment; they are less uncertain, less anxious. The third characteristic was the situation's perceived *ambiguity*. Ambiguity should produce anxiety responses, while clarity should lead to less anxiety. When people know what is required and how to do it, anxiety is expected to be lower. The fourth characteristic was the perceived *con-

spicuousness of the situation. When people believe their work is going to be viewed by others, they should feel more anxious about the work than when they know no one will see it. Privacy, or at the very least inconspicuousness in creating written materials, should make people less anxious about the activity. The final characteristic was *previous experience*. When people feel that previous efforts on similar tasks have been successful, they should approach the situation with less trepidation than when earlier encounters have been less than successful. These five variables—evaluation, novelty, ambiguity, conspicuousness, and previous experience—were hypothesized to affect people's anxiety responses to writing.

Methods

Subjects

Three hundred and ninety-nine undergraduate students enrolled in basic communication courses at a large Southern university participated in the study as part of a classroom project.[1]

Procedures

Each subject received a booklet that included a set of directions, the experimental manipulations, two measures of situational anxiety, and the writing apprehension measure.

The directions told subjects to imagine they were in a situation where a writing task was assigned. We opted to describe hypothetical situations for two reasons. First, the procedure allowed us to cleanly manipulate the situational dimensions. Second, given the exploratory nature of the investigation, this approach permitted multiple independent variables that, while occurring naturally in some situations, are not likely to co-occur very often (in the specific patterns we chose) in everyday settings.

The imaginary situation was described on the next five pages. Each page offered a description of the setting in which one of the five situational characteristics described above was varied. For each characteristic, two descriptions were potentially available to the subject. One was expected to elicit low anxiety; the other, high anxiety. Descriptors were pilot-tested to ensure their clarity. Each subject received

---

1. Sample sizes for individual analyses varied because of incomplete data. No systematic biases existed.

only one level of each characteristic. The individual descriptions are presented in Table 12-1. The order of presentation was random within and across subjects and conditions.

After reading the five descriptions, subjects completed two measures of situational writing anxiety. Both were constructed for this investigation. The first, a seventeen-item measure, assessed how anxious the respondents felt they would be about the particular writing assignment (ASSIGN). The second measure, a ten-item instrument, assessed how anxious respondents felt they would be immediately after the assignment within the classroom setting. This scale was labeled CLASS. Items comprising both scales were drawn from Spielberger's A-state measure (Spielberger, Gorsuch, & Lushene, 1970), Buss and Gerjouy's (1957) adjective scales for personality, and Zuckerman's (1960) affect adjective checklist. Items were piloted with teachers of writing

Table 12-1. Situational Variables Manipulated in the Study

Conspicuousness

You are to turn in your paper in a folder with no name visible to anyone. Only the teacher will read it. No one else will see it.

You are to turn in your paper with your name on top of each page. You must run off copies of your paper for everyone else in the class to read.

Evaluation

The assignment carries with it no grade or any other sort of evaluation. It is done on a pass–fail basis where you pass if you turn the assignment in. No one evaluates your writing; the assignment is a practice exercise, even the teacher won't read it.

The assignment carries with it a grade and quite a bit of evaluation. Grades are very strictly given and it is easy not to do well. The assignment is an important one. The teacher will carefully read and completely analyze it.

Novelty

The assignment you are given is a familiar one. You've done many of the same type before. The subject of the assignment is something you are familiar with.

The assignment is not a familiar one. You've never done anything like it before. The subject of the assignment is something you are unfamiliar with.

Ambiguity

The instructions on what and how to write are very clear. You know what the teacher wants and how it will be graded. You're given a topic area to write about. The teacher's instructions are very clear.

The instructions on what and how to write are very unclear. You don't know what the teacher wants or how it will be graded. The topic area you are to write about is unclear. The teacher's instructions are very vague.

Prior experience

In previous writing assignments you've done well. You have received positive evaluations on your work.

In previous writing assignments you have not done well. You have received poor evaluations on your work.

and students in order for us to select the best ones. Figure 12-1 contains both instruments, along with the instructions subjects received. While the two instruments have good face validity and are derived in part, from measures designed and validated for a purpose similar to the one we had in this study, no construct validity exists at this time for either measure. Indeed, our study represents the first attempt at validation insofar as the hypothesized effects were observed.

Subjects also completed the twenty-six-item version of the Daly and Miller (1975b) writing apprehension measure. Whether they completed the measure at the start or end of the exercise was random. Approximately half the subjects completed the apprehension measure prior to reading the test booklet; the other half completed it after filling out all other instruments. Finally, subjects completed a five-item questionnaire assessing the effectiveness of the experimental manipulations. Subjects were asked to indicate on nine-step scales the degrees of evaluation, conspicuousness, ambiguity, novelty, and prior success experiences that were present in the situation in which they had imagined themselves.

Data Analysis

The data were analyzed in a series of related steps. First, the internal consistency of each measure was assessed through use of Cronbach's alpha coefficient. Alpha provides an indication of the reliability of a measure. Only if alpha was suitably larger ($>.80$) can further analyses be justified.

Second, tests were made on the effectiveness of each manipulation. Five analyses of variances were computed, one for each manipulation check. Only if significant and large main effects for the manipulations appeared could they be considered successful. Obtaining these effects would indicate that subjects correctly perceived the manipulations.

Third, the three measures of anxiety were intercorrelated. The expectation was for a large and significant positive correlation between the two situational measures. In addition, to the extent that situational anxiety is truly different from dispositional anxiety, we expected small but positive correlations between writing apprehension and the two situational measures. If large correlations were obtained, doubt would be cast upon the extended conceptualization of apprehension that emphasizes the impact of contextual cues on anxiety.

Fourth, a five-way multivariate analysis of covariance was computed. The two dependent variables were the two situational anxiety measures (assignment and class). The covariate was dispositional writing

You have just completed reading some descriptions of a writing situation. Imagine that you are in that situation. The following statements are about how you would feel in that situation. Please indicate whether you (1) strongly agree (SA), (2) agree, (A), (3) neither agree nor disagree (UN), (4) disagree (D), or (5) strongly disagree (SD) with the statement. There are no right or wrong answers. Just respond thinking about how you would feel in the situation described.

	SA	A	UN	D	SD
1. I feel terrified about the writing assignment.	1	2	3	4	5
2. I feel comfortable about the writing task.	1	2	3	4	5
3. I feel panicky about the writing project.	1	2	3	4	5
4. I feel calm about the writing assignment.	1	2	3	4	5
5. I feel apprehensive about the writing task.	1	2	3	4	5
6. I'm uneasy about the writing assignment.	1	2	3	4	5
7. I'm tense about the writing task.	1	2	3	4	5
8. I feel secure about the writing assignment.	1	2	3	4	5
9. I feel at ease about the writing task.	1	2	3	4	5
10. I feel upset about the writing project.	1	2	3	4	5
11. I'm worrying about the writing assignment.	1	2	3	4	5
12. I feel anxious about the writing task.	1	2	3	4	5
13. I feel self-confident about the writing task.	1	2	3	4	5
14. I feel nervous about the writing assignment.	1	2	3	4	5
15. I am jittery about the writing assignment.	1	2	3	4	5
16. I am relaxed about the assignment.	1	2	3	4	5
17. I am worried about the writing task.	1	2	3	4	5

Now consider how you would feel about the entire classroom day. Indicate how you think you would be feeling immediately after the assignment overall.

1. I feel calm.	1	2	3	4	5
2. I feel secure.	1	2	3	4	5
3. I am tense.	1	2	3	4	5
4. I feel at ease.	1	2	3	4	5
5. I feel upset.	1	2	3	4	5
6. I feel anxious.	1	2	3	4	5
7. I feel comfortable.	1	2	3	4	5
8. I feel self-confident.	1	2	3	4	5
9. I feel nervous.	1	2	3	4	5
10. I am jittery.	1	2	3	4	5

Fig. 12-1. Situational anxiety measures.

apprehension. The independent variables, each having two levels, were evaluation, novelty, conspicuousness, ambiguity, and prior experience. The covariance procedure was used to adjust for differences among subjects in writing apprehension. In essence, this procedure offered a statistical control for apprehension and thus allowed us to study situational differences while dispositional apprehension was held constant. When significant effects were encountered, we completed two separate follow-up analyses. First, univariate analyses of variance were computed on each of the two dependent measures. On an *a priori* basis, only significant multivariate effects were probed. Second, when significant interactions were encountered, the two dependent measures were weighted by their associated discriminant weights, which were drawn from the analysis to form a composite variable. The composite variable was used in interpreting the pattern of means. For significant main effects, weighting was used only when the direction of effect was not clear.

Results

Reliabilities

The alpha coefficients for the three measures were all above .90. The alpha coefficient for the writing apprehension measure was .95; for the class anxiety measure, .92; and for the assignment anxiety instrument, .96. Thus, each measure was deemed sufficiently reliable for further analysis.

Manipulation Checks

The one-way analysis of variance on the manipulation checks indicated that each manipulation was perceived as expected. The high-evaluation condition was perceived as significantly more evaluative than the low-evaluation condition, the novel situation was perceived as significantly less familiar than the non-novel one, and so on. Table 12-2 contains the means and F values.

Correlations

The Pearson product–moment correlation between the two situational anxiety measures was .72 ($p < .00001$). The correlations of the two situational anxiety instruments, assignments and class, with apprehen-

Table 12-2. Manipulation Checks

Evaluation	High	$\bar{x} = 6.73$	$F(1,363) = 154.03$
	Low	$\bar{x} = 3.75$	
Novelty	High	$\bar{x} = 6.33$	$F(1,359) = 48.16$
	Low	$\bar{x} = 4.62$	
Ambiguity	High	$\bar{x} = 6.97$	$F(1,362) = 64.45$
	Low	$\bar{x} = 5.05$	
Conspicuousness	High	$\bar{x} = 5.85$	$F(1,348) = 44.26$
	Low	$\bar{x} = 4.17$	
Experience	Poor	$\bar{x} = 5.53$	$F(1,354) = 67.46$
	Good	$\bar{x} = 3.68$	

sion were .31 ($p < .001$) and .26 ($p < .001$) respectively. There was no significant difference between these two latter correlations, but both were significantly smaller ($p < .001$) than the correlation between the two situational anxiety measures. Writing apprehension as a dispositional construct and the situational writing anxiety construct, as measured by the two instruments, are not the same. They are related, but not in a large way. The average correlation between dispositional and situational anxiety was .28, which, while statistically significant, is not of sufficient magnitude to assume equivalence.

Multivariate Analyses

The five-way multivariate analysis of covariance yielded five significant main effects and three significant interactions. The first significant interaction was among prior experience, conspicuousness, and evaluation ($F(2,332) = 2.87, p < .06$). Both univariate analyses were statistically significant (class: $F(1,333) = 5.03$, $p < .03$; assignment: $F(1.333) = 4.31$, $p < .04$). Means for the three-way interaction are summarized in Table 12-3. The most anxious situation was the high-evaluation, low-conspicuousness setting with prior poor experience. This finding needs to be considered in light of a multiple comparison which indicated that the mean value for this cell was not significantly different from the values of three other cells. The least anxious condition was the low-conspicuousness, low-evaluation condition with positive prior experience. Within the high-evaluation condition, prior experience played a significant role when subjects felt that they were inconspicuous. Similarly, when prior experience was poor in the nonconspicuous conditions, evaluation was a significant dimension.

The second significant interaction was among evaluation, ambiguity, and prior experience ($F(2,322) = 3.24$, $p < .04$). The univariate analyses indicated only that the class variable approached significance

THE WRITING SITUATION

Table 12-3. *Means and Standard Deviations for Evaluation × Conspicuousness × Experience Interaction*

	Low evaluation		High evaluation	
	Prior good	Prior poor	Prior good	Prior poor
Nonconspicuous	$3.02(.84)_a$	$3.07(.88)_a$	$3.33(.75)_{ab}$	$4.07(.82)_c$
	$43.07(13.45)_a$	$45.09(14.38)_{ab}$	$49.66(12.39)_{ab}$	$60.70(11.15)_c$
	$24.49(7.75)_{ab}$	$23.84(7.16)_a$	$25.67(6.71)_{abc}$	$31.43(7.32)_c$
Conspicuous	$3.27(.87)_{ab}$	$3.60(.88)_{abc}$	$3.81(1.08)_{bc}$	$3.95(.96)_{bc}$
	$43.73(12.59)_a$	$52.18(13.24)_{abc}$	$54.07(13.73)_{bc}$	$60.44(13.06)_c$
	$26.29(7.28)_{abc}$	$28.18(7.30)_{abc}$	$29.93(9.23)_{abc}$	$30.18(8.38)_{bc}$

Note. The first row for each level is the weighted composite, the second the assignment variable, the third the class variable. Means were compared using Scheffé's procedure. They were compared only within-variable. Means that share a common subscript letter are not significantly different from one another ($p < .05$).

($F(1,333 = 2.75, p < .09$). Subsequent multiple comparisons in which the composite measure was used indicated no significant differences; the conservative Scheffé test was employed. Using Tukey's more liberal procedure, we found that the high-ambiguity, high-evaluation, and poor-prior-experience condition created significantly greater anxiety than did the condition with low evaluation, low ambiguity, and positive prior experience. Table 12-4 summarizes the means.

The third significant interaction was between experience and conspicuousness ($F(2,332) = 2.42, p < .09$). The univariate analyses indicated that only the class variable was significant ($F(1,333) = 3.96, p < .04$). Multiple comparisons made with use of the composite measure indicated that the major effect was for the nonconspicuous conditions where prior experience was good, contrasted with either of the conditions where the person felt conspicuous. Table 12-5 contains the means.

All five of the main effects were statistically significant. The high-evaluation condition created significantly more reported anxiety than the low-evaluation condition. This effect held for both dependent meas-

Table 12-4. *Means and Standard Deviations for Evaluation × Ambiguity × Experience Interaction*

	Low evaluation		High evaluation	
	Prior good	Prior poor	Prior good	Prior poor
Unambiguous	$2.49(.84)_b$	$2.62(1.02)_{ab}$	$2.76(.94)_{ab}$	$2.65(.98)_{ab}$
	$23.94(7.75)_a$	$25.41(8.38)_a$	$26.92(7.58)_a$	$28.27(8.05)_{ab}$
Ambiguous	$2.84(.98)_{ab}$	$2.64(1.20)_{ab}$	$2.75(1.38)_{ab}$	$3.22(1.03)_a$
	$27.07(6.98)_{ab}$	$27.61(6.15)_{ab}$	$28.38(8.84)_b$	$32.90(7.12)_b$

Note. The first row for each level is the weighted composite, the second the class variable. Means for the composite were contrasted using Tukey's method, while Scheffé's procedure was used in the comparisons for the class variable. Means that share a common subscript letter are not significantly different from one another ($p < .05$).

Table 12-5. *Means and Standard Deviations for Experience* × *Conspicuousness Interaction*

	Prior good	Prior poor
Nonconspicuous	$3.27(1.03)_a$	$3.64(1.21)_{ab}$
	$25.10(7.21)_a$	$27.76(8.15)_{ab}$
Conspicuous	$3.80(1.24)_b$	$3.80(1.18)_b$
	$28.09(8.46)_{ab}$	$29.08(7.83)_b$

Note. The first row for each level is the weighted composite, the second the class variable. Means were compared using Scheffé's procedure. Means that share a common subscript letter are not significantly different from one another $(p < .05)$.

ures in the follow-up univariate analyses. The high-conspicuousness condition yielded significantly greater reported anxiety than did the low-conspicuousness condition. Univariate analyses indicated only a significant effect for class. The more novel situation elicited significantly more reported anxiety than the more familiar one. Both univariate effects were statistically significant. The more ambiguous situation led to significantly more reported apprehension than did the less ambiguous one. Both univariate effects were also significant. Finally, the more positive prior experience led to significantly less reported anxiety than did prior poor experience. Both univariate effects were significant. The means, standard deviations, and F values for significant effects are reported in Table 12-6.

Table 12-6. *Means and Standard Deviations for Main Effects*

		Assign	Class
Experience	Good	47.83(13.89)	26.37(7.79)
$(F(2,332) = 34.46)$		$(F(1,333) = 68.88)$	$(F(1,333) = 23.59)$
	Poor	54.50(14.37)	28.43(8.04)
Novelty	Low	48.62(13.98)	26.14(7.22)
$(F(2,332) = 9.48)$		$(F(1,333) = 18.30)$	$(F(1,333) = 11.66)$
	High	53.78(14.60)	28.66(8.47)
Conspicuousness	Low	49.63(14.53)	26.16(7.63)
$(F(2,332) = 3.13)$			$(F(1,33 = 6.19)$
	High	52.81(14.36)	28.63(8.13)
Ambiguity	Low	47.53(14.74)	25.83(7.88)
$(F(2,332) = 21.22)$		$(F(1,333) = 42.24)$	$(F(1,333) = 20.67)$
	High	55.22(13.19)	29.13(7.74)
Evaluation	Low	46.62(14.07)	25.81(7.42)
$(F(2,332) = 15.23)$		$(F(1,333) = 29.72)$	$(F(1,333) = 7.52)$
	High	56.03(13.40)	29.10(8.20)

Note. All F values reported were statistically significant $(p < .05)$.

Discussion

The results of this research provide evidence for the potential importance of examining the situational nature of writing and writing anxiety. Briefly, the results showed that, first, highly reliable measurement of situational anxiety about writing can be obtained through a series of self-report questions. Second, dispositional writing apprehension and situational anxiety about writing are not equivalent. While the correlation between them is significant, it isn't large. Third, the hypothesized main effects of various situational characteristics were consistently observed. High evaluation, conspicuousness, ambiguity, novelty, and a history of poor experiences in similar situations lead—individually and in some cases jointly—to greater anxiety about writing. Finally, the study provides an initial piece of evidence for the construct validity of the situational anxiety construct, in that the hypothesized effects were observed.

Of critical importance in this study is the nature of the variables selected as situational characteristics of writing environments. All five are parameters of virtually every situation where writing might be required. In some situations they may be more salient than others; in some, they may produce more anxiety than in others. But whatever their level or relative importance, each can be used to specify some situational or environmental set that a person must deal with in the act of writing. Other variables clearly exist. We believe that the procedure we opted for in this chapter yields more meaningful findings than does the generation of individual situations without any consideration for the parameters that define them. Attempts at individual comparisons could continue indefinitely without any final conclusions being reached.

The relationship between dispositional apprehension and situational anxiety was probed further in a *post hoc* fashion. It will be recalled that half the subjects completed the writing apprehension measure after reading the situational manipulations and completing the situational questions. Situational characteristics failed to affect dispositional apprehension to any measurable degree. Further, apprehension was not observed to be affected significantly by any of the situational manipulations. This lends strength to the conclusion that apprehension, as measured by the Daley and Miller instrument, is actually an enduring disposition. However, it should be noted that the average correlation between dispositional apprehension and situational anxiety was larger when the writing apprehension measure came last (.33 with Daly–Miller test last; .22 with Daly–Miller test first). This may indicate some minor effect for both the situational manipulations and the situational anxiety questionnaires.

The most telling limit to this study is the nature of the manipulation of situation. The approach of asking subjects to imagine themselves in a situation where five separate characteristics are clearly present may raise questions about the validity of the findings. At present we make no claim for the realism of the experiment. Further, we doubt that one could find classrooms that actually vary in the manner designed in this study. While every writing situation contains each dimension, the dimensions are not generally as straightforwardly present as they were in this design. In addition, other dimensions, not considered here, may be present. We do, however, make a case for considering situational parameters of writing and suggest, through the analysis in this chapter, that there is strong potential for the five variables we identified to play a role in writing.

Note that we have not emphasized the significant interactions among the independent variables. At this point we don't feel confident in interpreting them, for two reasons. First, they were not hypothesized *a priori*, and the magnitude of their effects was small. Second, we are not sufficiently confident that our procedures match reality to draw any extensive conclusions other than the main effect statements made above. Certainly some interactions exist in writing situations. But the specific nature of these joint effects must be left to further study.

It is important to note the potential extensions of this research. First, a more comprehensive examination of the situational parameters of writing could be made. In work on interpersonal communication, Forgas (1980) and Wish and his colleagues (1979) have begun complex explorations into the characteristics of situations in which people communicate. Scholars concerned with writing have the opportunity to do the same. Second, exploration of how situational variables, such as those examined in this study, affect actual writing performance seems an obvious and very important future focus. Classroom teachers consistently report that the degree of tension students perceive in a situation affects how and what they write. Clearer specification of these effects is quite important. Third, continued concern with situational anxiety may permit a number of heuristic advantages to accrue for the writing classroom. For example, within classrooms the things teachers do to shape the situation where writing takes place can be examined for their impact on student anxiety. Additionally, advice can be offered on ways of establishing classroom environments that are relatively anxiety-free. Instructions, tasks, and projects can be presented to students in various ways. Some styles of presentation may induce more anxiety than is desired. Structuring situations with anxiety repercussions in mind may be useful. Fourth, investigations are needed into what might be the optimal levels of anxiety for effective performance. We may seem to have suggested by our procedure that less is better. Not necessarily so. Research in a number of fields indicates that the relationship between anxiety and performance is nonlinear. Moderate amounts enhance performance; too much or too little anxiety detracts from the quality of the product. Perhaps this is so in writing as well.

ACKNOWLEDGMENT

The investigation was supported in part by a grant from the Department of Education, Fund for the Improvement of Postsecondary Education.

REFERENCES

Book, V. *Some effects of apprehension on writing performance.* Paper presented at annual conference of Western Speech Communication Association, San Francisco, 1976. (Available from Daly.)

Buss, A., & Gerjouy, H. The scaling of adjectives descriptive of personality. *Journal of Consulting Psychology*, 1957, *21*, 366–371.

Daly, J. A. The effects of writing apprehension on message encoding. *Journalism Quarterly*, 1977, *54*, 566–572.

Daly, J. A. Writing apprehension and writing competency. *Journal of Educational Research*, 1978, *72*, 10–14.

Daly, J. A. Writing apprehension in the classroom: Teacher role expectancies of the apprehensive writer. *Research in the Teaching of English*, 1979, *13*, 37–44.

Daly, J. A., & Miller, M. D. Apprehension of writing as a predictor of message intensity. *Journal of Psychology*, 1975, *89*, 175–177.(a)

Daly, J. A., & Miller, M. D. The empirical development of an instrument to measure writing apprehension. *Research in the Teaching of English*, 1975, *9*, 242–249.(b)

Daly, J. A., & Miller, M. D. Further studies in writing apprehension: SAT scores, success expectations, willingness to take advanced courses, and sex differences. *Research in the Teaching of English*, 1975, *9*, 250–256.(c)

Daly, J. A., & Shamo, W. Writing apprehension and occupational choice. *Journal of Occupational Psychology*, 1976, *49*, 55–56.

Daly, J. A., & Shamo, W. Academic decisions as a function of writing apprehension. *Research in the Teaching of English*, 1978, *12*, 119–126.

Daly, J. A., & Wilson, D. *Writing apprehension, self-esteem, and personality.* Paper presented at annual conference of American Educational Research Association, Los Angeles, 1981. (Available from Daly.)

Dickson, F. *Writing apprehension and test anxiety as predictors of ACT scores.* Unpublished Master's thesis, West Virginia University, 1978.

Faigley, L., Daly, J. A., & Witte, S. *The effects of writing apprehension on writing performance and competence.* Paper presented at annual conference of American Educational Research Association, Los Angeles, 1981. (Available from Daly.)

Forgas, J. P. *Social episodes.* New York: Academic Press, 1980.

Fox, R. Treatment of writing apprehension and its effects on composition. *Research in the Teaching of English*, 1980, *14*, 39–49.

Garcia, R. J. *An investigation of relationships: Writing apprehension, syntactic performance, and writing quality.* Unpublished doctoral dissertation, Arizona State University, 1977.

Harvley-Felder, Z. C. *Some factors relating to writing apprehension: An exploratory study.* Unpublished doctoral dissertation, University of North Carolina, 1978.

Jeroski, S. F., & Conry, R. F. *Development and field application of the Attitude Toward Writing Scale.* Paper presented at annual conference of American Educational Research Association, Los Angeles, 1981. (Available from S. Jeroski, Department of Educational Psychology, University of British Columbia, Vancouver, B.C., Canada V6T 1 W 5.)

Powers, W., Cook, J. A., & Meyer, R. The effect of compulsory writing on writing apprehension. *Research in the Teaching of English*, 1979, *13*, 225–230.

Richmond, V. P., & Dickson, F. *Two studies of the validity of the writing apprehension test.* Paper presented at annual conference of Eastern Communication Association, Ocean City, Md., 1980. (Available from V. P. Richmond, Department of Speech Communication, West Virginia University, Morgantown, W.V. 25904.)

Scott, M. D., & Wheeless, L. R. *An exploratory study of the relationship of three types of communication apprehension to student attitudes, levels of satisfaction, and achievement.* Paper presented at annual conference of Speech Communication Association, Houston, 1975. (Available from M. D. Scott, Department of Speech Communication, West Virginia University, Morgantown, W.V. 26904.)

Spielberger, C. D., Gorsuch, R. R., & Lushene, R. E. *State-trait anxiety inventory test manual for Form X.* Palo Alto, Calif.: Consulting Psychologists Press, 1970.

Toth, D. *The effects of writing apprehension on attitude change in the counterattitudinal paradigm.* Unpublished Master's thesis, West Virginia University, 1975.

Wish, M. Dimensions of dyadic communication. In S. Weitz (Ed.), *Nonverbal communication.* New York: Oxford University Press, 1979.

Witte, S., & Faigley, L. *Assessing composition programs.* Unpublished report, 1980. (Available from S. Witte, Department of English, University of Texas, Austin, Tex. 78712.)

Zuckerman, M. The development of an affect adjective checklist for the measurement of anxiety. *Journal of Consulting Psychology*, 1960, *24*, 457–462.

13

Symbolic functioning and children's early writing: The relations between kindergartners' play and isolated word-writing fluency

ANTHONY D. PELLEGRINI
University of Georgia

The development of children's writing skills has been subjected to interdisciplinary examination by psychologists (e.g., Olson, 1977), educators (e.g., King & Rentel, 1979), and ethnographers (e.g., Florio, 1979). The development of the writing process has been characterized by Wheeler (see King & Rentel, 1979, p. 243) as having children first generating designs and pictures, later generating isolated letters and words, and finally using word phrases and words in sentences. Luria's (1977) research supports this general developmental trend. He has shown how children's ability to use socially agreed-upon signs (written words) develops during the early childhood period (three to five years of age). Young children's written words start off as scribbles, then resemble pictures, and finally take the form of adult-like written words. Most of the research on children's development of writing competency, however, has focused on the higher end of continuum; that is, the emphasis has been on how children learn to write words in sentences. The general intent of this chapter is to examine factors related to an earlier stage of writing development—writing isolated words.

Clay (1975) stated that children construct individual words only after they discover that individual letters carry meaning (the sign concept) and that words are built out of these same individual letters. This specific skill of noting sign-meaning relations develops during the preschool period, as part of the more general development of representational competence. That is, during this period children come to realize that symbols, or signs, represent other classes of objects or concepts (Sigel, 1970). Fein (1979) refers to this symbolic function, giving the example of a boy who strums a broom to represent his playing a guitar. As the boy's symbolic competence develops, his representations for objects become more abstract; that is, the representations resemble the objects less or not at all. For example, the child may now symbolize his playing the guitar by strumming an invisible guitar. In the area of writing, this symbolic function takes place when preschoolers begin to use socially agreed-upon signs (letters) to represent concepts. The specific purpose of the study presented in this chapter was to investigate the relations between kindergartners' symbolic functioning in free play and their ability to generate isolated written words.

Developmental psychologists such as Piaget (1962) and Fein (1979) have suggested that insight into children's ability to symbolize—that is, to consciously separate symbols from concepts—can be gained by observing children's pretend play. Smilansky (1968) has developed a system, based on Piaget's thought (1962), that enables an observer to categorize children's play along a cognitive–symbolic hierarchy. This hierarchy, empirically verified by Rubin and Maioni (1975), consists of: functional play, where the child simply exercises his or her muscles (with or without objects); constructive play, where the child creates something; dramatic play, where the child uses language to take on a pretend role; and lastly, games-with-rules, where the child's play is subordinate to a prearranged set of rules. In order to move through this continuum, children must utilize progressively more demanding cognitive processes. That is, to move from functional to constructive play, children must coordinate the movements used in functional play toward a goal. Both dramatic play and games-with-rules are yet more demanding cognitively, because they not only require children to be goal-oriented but also require that socially shared symbols be used to sustain play. Dramatic play requires children to use a symbolic medium, language, to define symbolic roles for objects and players. For example, a doll may be used to represent a live child. Finally, games-with-rules require children to accept an arbitrary, or symbolic, set of rules and to subordinate their behavior to the rules in order to sustain play. Thus, players in both dramatic play and games-with-rules must define symbol–concept relations—for example, identify real roles and play roles—in order to sustain play.

Research has shown that engaging in symbolic play facilitates cognitive processing by preschoolers (e.g., Saltz, Dixon, & Johnson, 1977; Sylva, Bruner, & Genova, 1976) and by school-age children (Smilansky, 1968; Zammarelli & Bolton, 1977). The research of Bruner and his colleagues suggests that the tension-free atmosphere of free play enables children to become more efficient problem-solvers. During problem-solving tasks in free play contexts, these children experimented with many self-generated solutions to the tasks. The children exposed to problem-solving in a play context were more adept at solving novel problems than children who had previously followed adult suggestions for problem solutions.

A recent study showed that training elementary school children to do fantasy play raised their mathematics functioning (Zammarelli & Bolton, 1977). Zammarelli and Bolton argued that fantasy play enables children to abstract rules from context (e.g., make object transformations) and to apply the rules to different situations.

Saltz et al. (1977) found that training lower-socioeconomic-status children to do sociodramatic play about a story read to them raised their story comprehension and verbal IQ. The studies by these researchers indicate that the symbolizing processes used in play are also used in school learning tasks.

The symbolic processes used in dramatic play seem to be similar to the symbolic processes used to write individual words. In both writing and symbolic play situations, children are using socially defined symbols to represent concepts. For example, in one dramatic play episode in this study a child used a stick to represent a gun. The symbol, stick for gun, was socially defined when the symbolic transformation was announced to other players: "This is my gun." If the child had not defined the transformation of stick to gun, other players may not have been able to respond appropriately to the role assigned to that prop in the play episode; play probably would not have been sustained. Research has shown that children engaged in dramatic play, as opposed to lower forms of play, tend to explicitly define player and prop roles at the beginning of play episodes to avoid role confusion (Pellegrini, 1982). For example, a child observed in this study initiated a play episode by clearly defining players' roles: "I'll be the Mommy and you be the Daddy." Play is not sustained when roles are not explicitly defined.

Simons and Gumperz (1980) point out that children must learn to use literate oral language before they are able to write. By literate language they mean language that is not dependent on context to convey meaning. This decontextualized language is characterized by linguistically defined pronouns and lexically defined objects. In short, children are conveying meaning with words, not through context (e.g., pointing). As was previously stated, research has shown that children engaged in dramatic play use literate language (Pellegrini, 1982). The language of dramatic play, as opposed to language generated by children in constructive play, is highly cohesive. That is, pronouns are typically linguistically defined, explicit topic introductions are used, and listeners are asked for clarification of roles when ambiguity does exist. Dramatic play, then, may facilitate symbolic functioning by giving a child practice at explicitly separating symbols and concepts. Furthermore, children must define socially these symbolic representations. Thus, symbolic play and word writing both may be related to the children's general representational competence—ability to use socially defined symbols to represent concepts.

It will be argued here that the symbolism exhibited by kindergartners in free play is related to the symbolic processes involved in writing isolated words; both processes involve using socially accepted symbols to encode concepts. The specific hypotheses posed are:

1. Children's play will be the best predictor of word-writing fluency.
2. Play will have a significant main effect on isolated word-writing fluency.
3. Symbolic forms of play (dramatic play and games-with-rules) will have the largest effect on isolated word-writing fluency.

Method

Subjects

The sample consisted of 65 children from mixed socioeconomic backgrounds (37 males, 28 females) attending morning and afternoon kindergarten classes in a rural public school. The sample consisted of all the children whose parents had consented to their involvement in the study. The age of the sample ranged from 67 to 78 months ($\bar{x} = 71.523$, $SD = 3.833$).

Procedures

All kindergartners in the school were given the Metropolitan Readiness Test Level II, Form P (Nurss & McGauvren, 1976) in the beginning of May as part of the school district's regular testing program. Robinson's test of writing fluency (1973, reproduced in Clay, 1975) was also administered to all children at this time. Raw scores from Robinson's test were used in regression analyses and analyses of variance. The total writing fluency score was composed of the following subscores: writing one's own name, writing others' names, writing names of colors, and a miscellaneous category.

Two weeks after the districtwide testing ended, two experimenters observed each child for five twenty-minute periods during the children's free play periods. The observers classified each observed play episode according to Smilansky's (1968) cognitive hierarchy of play: functional play, constructive play, dramatic play, or games-with-rules.

Functional play, coded 1, was defined as repetitive muscle movement, with or without objectives. Constructive play, coded 2, was children's manipulation of objects to build something. In dramatic play, coded 3, the children pretended to be somebody else and imitated that person in speech and action; language was used to define objects, activities, and situations. In games-with-rules, coded 4, children adapted their behavior to a set of prearranged rules. Inter-rater agreement between the two observers for the categorization of play episodes was 84 percent. The overall play rating for a child was the type of play most often observed (the mode of all five of the ratings). The order in which each child was observed was determined by random assignment.

Children's socioeconomic status (SES) was ranked as follows: upper-middle class (coded 1), middle-middle class (coded 2), lower-middle class (coded 3), and lower class (coded 4) ($\bar{x}$ SES rank = 2.309, SD = .949). Parents' average level of education was the criterion on which SES was based. Children's sex was coded 1 for male and 2 for female. Age was coded as age in months.

Results

Dramatic play was the most commonly coded play category (32), followed by constructive (22) and functional play (11). No instances of games-with-rules were observed; therefore, this category was not included in subsequent analyses.

Intercorrelation Analyses on Total Writing Fluency

The intercorrelations for play and demographic predictors (SES, age, and sex) and the achievement variable (total writing fluency, $\bar{x}$ = 6.166, SD = 4.449) are as follows: play and writing, r = .50 ($p < .001$); writing and sex, r = .02 (ns); play and SES, r = .21 (ns); play and age, r = .05 (ns). These data suggest that intercorrelation between play and total writing fluency was significant. The correlation, $r(65)$ = .36, $p < .01$, for SES and writing, though significant, was quite low; it accounted for only 12 percent of the variation in total fluency.

The intercorrelations among play, sex, and age, were nonsignificant. This finding was desirable because the ability of the predictors to explain, or account for, the variance in the achievement variables was thereby maximized. In short, the three levels of play (functional, constructive, and dramatic) were highly related to the achievement variable (total word-writing fluency), whereas the demographic variables (SES, age, and sex) appeared to be minimally related to the achievement variable.

Multiple Regression Analyses on Total Writing Fluency

To obtain a better understanding of the relations among these variables, stepwise multiple regression analyses were employed. The purpose was to identify the variables that were the best predictors of writing, as measured by each of the writing subcategories and the sum of the subcategories (total fluency). The regression analyses show the relations among the predictor variables (play, SES, age, and sex) and the criterion variables (own name, others' names, colors, miscellaneous, and total fluency). The multiple correlations (R) obtained for the four criterion variables with total fluency ($\bar{x}$ for the total fluency = 6.166, SD = 4.49) were: .46 ($p < .01$) for play alone with fluency; .523 ($p < .01$) for play and SES with fluency; .529 ($p < .01$) for play, SES, and age with fluency; and .530 ($p < .05$) for play, sex, age, and sex with fluency. The multiple correlations (R) for the four predictor variables (play, SES, age, sex) with each subcategory are given in Table 13-1.

Summary of Regression Analyses

Inspection of these data indicates that in all cases play was the most significant predictor variable related to achievement in writing. In fact, the play variable alone, in step 1 of the various regression analyses, predicted between 21 and 5 percent of the variance for the criterion variables. Inspection of the F statistics for the analyses further substantiates the importance of play; the correlations obtained for play were found to be significant across the following achievement measures: total fluency, others' names, and colors. These findings suggest that a child's level of play is a powerful predictor of writing achievement in kindergarten.

Table 13-1. Multiple Correlations for Predictors on Writing Subcategories

Writing own name	($\bar{x}$ = 1.547, SD = .550)
	Play = .246
	Play and SES = .327
	Play, SES, and sex = .34483
	Play, SES, sex, and age = .34938
Writing others' names	($\bar{x}$ = 1.428, SD = 1.416)
	Play = .249[b]
	Play and SES = .288[b]
	Play, SES, and age = .312[b]
Writing names of colors	($\bar{x}$ = .500, SD = 1.173)
	Play = .326[a]
	Play and sex = .362
	Play, sex, and age = .384
	Play, sex, age, and SES = .399
Writing miscellaneous words	($\bar{x}$ = 2.690, SD = 3.211)
	SES = .279
	SES and play = .369
	Ses, play, and age = .400
	SES, play, age, and sex = .408

[a]Significance of $p < .05$.

[b]Significance of $p < .01$.

Play and SES together were found to be significantly related to total writing fluency ($R = .523$, $p < .011$) and to writing others' names ($R = .288$, $p < .01$). The increase in the multiple correlation due to the inclusion of SES in the regression equation was .05 and .03 for total fluency and others' names, respectively. This finding indicates that play and SES together were useful predictors of writing achievement. However, the contribution of SES to the explanation of the variation in writing achievement should be considered minimal, given the small increments in explained variance.

Analyses of Variance

Separate one-way analyses of variance were computed to analyze the effect of play on achievement in total writing fluency and on each of the writing subcategories. No significant main effect for play was detected on the following subcategories: own name writing, $F(2,39) = 1.270$, $p < .292$; color, $F(2,39) = 2.746$, $p < .076$; miscellaneous, $F(2,39) = 2.585$, $p < .088$. A significant main effect for play was detected on others' names, $F(2,39) = 6.475$, $p < .003$, and on total writing fluency, $F(2,39) = 6.626$, $p < .003$. Newman–Keuls *post hoc* analyses, set at the .05 level, were subsequently computed on each significant main effect. For the others' names subcategory there was a significant difference between dramatic play ($\bar{x} = 2.00$) and both constructive play ($\bar{x} = 1.083$) and functional play ($\bar{x} = .142$); the difference between functional and constructive play was not significant. Newman–Keuls analyses on total fluency set at the .05 level, were similar: there was a significant difference between dramatic play ($\bar{x} = 8.173$) and both functional ($\bar{x} = 3.428$) and constructive play ($\bar{x} = 3.916$); the difference between functional and constructive play was not significant.

Results of multiple regression analyses and analyses of variance were consistent to the extent that in both analyses play accounted for a significant amount of the variation in total writing fluency. Analyses of writing subcategories indicated that play had a significant effect only on the writing of others' names. A possible explanation for this may be that the form of play most often observed (sociodramatic play) required children to interact socially with peers. Because of this, children who engage in such play may be more aware of peers' names and thus more likely to write them.

An alternate explanation for these results might hold that it was merely children's knowledge of others' names, not play, which affected children's ability to write others' names. This counterhypothesis is clearly not supported by the data, however. If children's general familiarity with others' names, but not propensity to engage in symbolic play, was responsible for fluency in writing others' names, one would not expect significant differences between the different types of play. Children who tended to engage in sociodramatic play also tended to write significantly more others' names. This finding suggests that there is a specific relation between sociodramatic play and fluency in writing others' names.

The specific aspect of sociodramatic play that affects ability to write others' names probably is the social interaction among peers. Research by Pellegrini (1982, in press) suggests that when children engage in sociodramatic play, as compared to functional and constructive play, they tend to interact more with peers, both socially and linguistically. Often these interactions are characterized by initial disagreement between players as to who can do what. For example, two players may both want to play the father. Players typically negotiate a compromise between their conflicting views. In Piagetian terms, they accommodate to others' views. Thus, in sociodramatic play, children are aware, often abruptly, of the existence of peers. The highly social nature of such play may be the reason why the players are more aware of others' names than is the case in functional and constructive play. The symbolic aspect of sociodramatic play (i.e., the ability to have objects or words signify other entities) may be responsible for the ability to actually write the words.

In summary, the analyses of variance and *post hoc* analyses of total fluency and writing others' names indicate that the mode of play requiring social and symbolic functioning (sociodramatic play) had the largest effect on children's individual word-writing fluency. Those children most often engaging in sociodramatic play were also the most fluent writers. The social and symbolic processes used in sociodramatic play and in writing individual words seem to be related. More specifically, in sociodramatic play the symbolic roles of players and props are verbally negotiated among players. For example, if a child wants a chair to represent an automobile seat, he or she must define explicitly this symbolic transformation of chair to auto seat, as in "This is my car." In word writing, children are using socially agreed-upon symbols (words) to represent concepts.

Pooled variance estimate *t* tests, comparing sexes, were computed for each writing subcategory and for total fluency. No significant differences were detected.

Implications for Teaching

In order for teachers to facilitate the development of young children's representational competence, they must view children as active, not passive, learners. An active learner engages in an activity with other players and chooses the objects that are to be symbolically transformed.

He or she then must define the transformation for other players so that the play theme is sustained. In this way children become competent in the *process* of symbolic transformation. In some symbolic transformations, the child uses a sign to represent a concept. For example, a child may first draw a picture to represent an object. In a more abstract transformation, a child uses a written word to represent an object. Similarly, in symbolic play children may use objects, or props, to help them define a play role (e.g., wearing a dress and hat to symbolize an older woman). A child who employs a more abstract transformation of this play role would verbally define players' roles (e.g., "I'll be the teacher").

The passive-learner model of symbolization has a teacher supplying children with symbolic transformations and corresponding labels and asking them to repeat the labels (e.g., "Let this shoe be a telephone"). In the passive model, the children themselves are neither doing the symbolic transformations themselves nor having to define the transformations for other players. As the data suggest, the symbolizing process itself is related to a number of cognitive achievement skills, such as conservations skills. Other researchers (e.g., Rubin & Maioni, 1975) have reached a similar conclusion. In the active-learner model, children themselves transform and socially define the transformations. They are motivated to do so because they typically want to sustain play episodes; without socially defined symbolic transformations, dramatic play cannot be sustained.

Teachers can use dramatic play to enhance children's active symbolizing. Field trips and literature can provide basic experiences that form the themes of dramatic play episodes. Initially teachers should provide realistic play props, such as dress-up clothes and dolls. Teachers themselves should take part in play episodes as players, not as instructors. Adults also need to help children define role transformations, by saying, for example, "I'll be the mother. What will you be?"

As children become competent dramatic players, teachers should withdraw themselves and explicit props from the play arena. Children should be encouraged to use props that are less realistic representations of the concepts used in the play themes. For example, a teacher could take a doll out of the housekeeping corner and replace it with a block. The block could then be used as a more abstract representation of a baby. In this way children gain practice at having more abstract objects represent concepts. Children who are most competent at dramatic play are typically not dependent on props for the sustenance of play episodes. They use language to replace props: for example, "I have my baby with me today."

The research reported in this chapter, and the research of others (e.g., Luria, 1977), can be used by teachers attempting to facilitate children's writing competence. Children are motivated to write when they see it as a useful process. They should realize that written words are used to communicate meaningful ideas. Luria suggests having children write titles under their art works in order to convey meaning to peers and teachers. With practice, the form of individual written words will develop to approximate socially agreed-upon standards.

A final implication of the study relates to the suggested use of Smilansky's (1968) cognitive hierarchy of play as an instrument for assessing children's symbolic play. Research has shown (Smilansky, 1968; Rubin & Maioni, 1975; Sponseller & Jaworski, 1979) that the progressions from functional to constructive play and from dramatic play to games-with-rules is indeed cognitively hierarchical; that is, children must go through the lower stages of play before they are capable of reaching the higher stages. Teachers can use the Smilansky model to chart children's ability to engage in cognitively demanding forms of play. Charting this progression, along with more traditional measures of representational competence (letter–sound correspondence, word writing, and sight vocabulary), should provide teachers with a multifaceted system for evaluating children's symbolizing processes.

The intent of this chapter was to illustrate how the young child's symbolic functioning in free play is related to achievement in a more traditional academic area, isolated word writing. Strong relations have been suggested. Teachers of young children can use dramatic play, in conjunction with the more usual activities, to facilitate achievement in reading and writing. This study, along with others previously cited, suggests that the symbolizing skills acquired and refined in play are related to more traditional measures of achievement.

ACKNOWLEDGMENTS

I would like to thank Bill Ripley, of the University of Georgia Educational Research Lab, for his help in data analyses; Raymond Pecheone of the University of Rhode Island for help with data collection and analyses; and Lee Galda of the University of Georgia, and Martha King of Ohio State University, for their critical reading of the manuscript.

REFERENCES

Clay, M. *What did I write?* Auckland, New Zealand: Heinemann, 1975.
Fein, G. Play and the acquisition of symbols. In L. Katz (Ed.), *Current topics in early childhood education* (Vol. 2). Norwood, N.J.: Ablex, 1979.
Florio, S. *Learning to write in the classroom community.* Paper presented at annual meeting of American Educational Research Association, San Francisco, April 1979.

King, M., & Rentel, V. Toward a theory of early writing development. *Research in the Teaching of English*, 1979, *13*, 243–253.

Luria, A. The development of writing in the child. *Soviet Psychology*, 1977, *16*, 65–114.

Nurss, J., & McGauvren, M. *Metropolitan Readiness Tests*. New York: Harcourt Brace Jovanovich, 1976.

Olson, D. From utterance to test: The bias of language in speech and writing. *Harvard Educational Review*, 1977, *29*, 257–281.

Pellegrini, A. D. The generation of cohesive text by preschoolers in two play contexts. *Discourse Processes*, 1982, *4*, 101–108.

Pellegrini, A. The effects of classroom ecology on preschoolers' functional uses of language. In A. Pellegrini & T. Yawkey (Eds.), *The development of oral and written language in social context*. Norwood, N.J.: Ablex, in press.

Pellegrini, A., & Galda, L. The effects of thematic-fantasy play training on children's story comprehension. *American Educational Research Journal*, 1982, *19*, 443–452.

Piaget, J. *Play, dreams, and imitation in childhood*. New York: Morton, 1962.

Robinson, S. *Predicting early reading progress*. Unpublished Master's thesis, University of Auckland, New Zealand, 1973.

Rubin, K., & Maioni, T. L. Play preference and its relationship to egocentricism, popularity and classification skills in preschoolers. *Merrill-Palmer Quarterly*, 1975, *21*, 171–179.

Saltz, E., Dixon, D., & Johnson, J. Training disadvantaged preschoolers in various fantasy activities: Effects on cognitive functioning and impulse control. *Child Development*, 1977, *48*, 367–380.

Sigel, L. The distancing hypothesis. In M. R. Jones (Ed.), *Miami symposium on the prediction of behavior, 1968*. Coral Gables: University of Florida Press, 1970.

Simons, H. & Gumperz, J. *Language at school: Its influence on school performance*. Paper presented at annual meeting of American Educational Research Association, Boston, April 1980.

Smilansky, S. *The effects of sociodramatic play on disadvantaged preschool children*. New York: Wiley, 1968.

Sponseller, D., & Jaworski, A. *Social and cognitive complexity in young children's play*. Paper presented at annual meeting of American Educational Research Association, San Francisco, April 1979.

Sylva, K., Bruner, J., & Genova, P. The role of play in the problem solving of children 3–5 years old. In J. Bruner (Ed.), *Play*. New York: Basic Books, 1976.

Zammarelli, J., & Bolton, N. The effects of play on mathematical concept formation. *British Journal of Education Psychology*, 1977, *47*, 155–167.

14

Assigned rhetorical context and semantic abbreviation in writing

JAMES L. COLLINS
State University of New York, Buffalo
MICHAEL M. WILLIAMSON
Niagara University

Every teacher of writing has been frequently confronted with inexplicit student writing. Such writing suggests what the writer means, but it does not state that meaning adequately, as in this tenth-grader's sentence: "One kid have a bag of candy and this boy took the bag and eatin a piece of his candy he hit him in the arm." The burden of meaning is on the reader in that sentence; indeed, the writer seems to be holding back information by referring to characters, objects, and actions only in vague terms. The sentence asks the reader to complete the writer's meaning because the writing is inexplicit.

This chapter reports the second in a series of studies designed to investigate inexplicit meaning in student writing. In the first study (Collins & Williamson, 1981), we found that inadequately stated meaning can be understood as abbreviated meaning. In the tenth-grade writer's sentence above, for example, certain items represent fuller meanings for the writer than for readers. These items are demonstrative pronouns ("one" and "this"), personal pronouns ("he," "his," and "him"), and formulaic language ("hit him in the arm"). Each suggests that the writer could be more specific, could provide more precise information and more meaningful connections between words and their referents. Certainly the writer, for example, could say more about his characters than is conveyed by the labels "one kid" and "this boy." We refer to this underrepresentation of the writer's meaning as semantic abbreviation, a term we have borrowed from Vygotsky (1934/1962, 1978).

In Vygotsky's theory, semantic abbreviation is characteristic of inner speech, a level of verbal thought developed from children's private or egocentric speech. Inner speech functions to direct activity and expression, and it does so by taking the form of highly condensed, trim, efficient language. For Vygotsky, words in inner speech are condensed and compact highlights of meaning; speaking and writing involve processes of transforming these abbreviated semantic highlights into communicative spoken or written language. Inner speech, Vygotsky adds, is the opposite of written speech. In inner speech, meaning exists fleetingly; it is abbreviated and only personally comprehensible. Writing must represent meaning much more permanently and completely, so that the meaning will be comprehensible to others. In inner speech, words have no clear social reference. Instead, they are saturated with personal sense, with all of the associations that the words might call to mind (see Markova, 1979). Sentences have no clear subjects in inner speech. Instead, the emphasis is on predication, since the subject of thought is known and accessible to the thinker. In inner speech, a personal, implicit course of reasoning takes the place of the discernible, explicit logic necessary to communicate in writing. Accordingly, Vygotsky argues that the semantic abbreviation characteristic of inner speech is never found in writing (1934/1962, p. 145).

Our studies, however, suggest that there is an important exception to that rule. The exception is the writing of inexperienced or unskilled writers. We argue that in these individuals' writing the semantic abbreviation characteristic of inchoate verbal thought has not been transformed into the explicit, autonomous meaning characteristic of written language. Instead, the transformation has at times stopped at the level of spoken dialogue. Like Flower (1979, p. 19), we are saying that semantic abbreviation is part of an "undertransformed mode of verbal expression" typical of the writing of unskilled writers. Unlike Flower, though, we believe that such writing is not only based in the workings of the writer's verbal thought; it is based also in the form of spoken dialogue and the function of interpersonal communication.

The main theoretical assumption that our studies examine is that inexplicit meaning in student writing is at least in part the result of the writing having been produced through the mediation of spoken language. Unskilled writers might represent meaning in writing in a manner appropriate to the way meaning is represented in spoken dialogue (Vygotsky, 1934/1962, 1978; Elsasser & John-Steiner, 1977; Hirsch, 1977; Collins, 1979). In our work, we have reasoned that inexplicit meaning is context-dependent meaning (see Malinowski, 1923; Bernstein, 1975; Goody & Watt, 1976; Olson, 1977; Hirsch, 1977; Collins, 1979) and that context-dependent meaning is characteristic of everyday spoken dialogue. To return again to our sample sentence, we can say that the identities for "one kid" and "this boy" might be as clear as they need to be for effective oral communication between intimate parties who share situational and cultural referents for those labels. Given a certain sociocultural context, such as a neighborhood peer group, the sentence "One kid have a bag of candy and this boy took the bag and eatin a piece of his candy he hit him in the arm" takes on a fuller meaning than when the sentence is written for a non-intimate audience.

In our studies, then, we have been examining the assumption that inexplicit meaning in student writing is associated with the influence of spoken language. The assumption holds that in unskilled writing, private verbal thought has often been transformed into "one-half of a dialogue written down," that is, into writing that abbreviates meaning by requiring familiarity with the situational and cultural contexts of language that the writer has in mind. Inexplicit meaning, in this conception, is characteristic of writing that is close to context-dependent spoken dialogue.

Purpose and Method

Our initial study (Collins & Williamson, 1981) supported the theoretical assumption that inexplicit meaning in student writing is attributable, at least in part, to the influence of spoken dialogue. In that study we used writing in a descriptive mode for a peer audience as a data base. At the outset of the present study, we wondered if our findings could be extended to student writings that were in a persuasive mode and were intended for other audiences.

The foregoing question is important for at least two reasons. First, it seems plausible that explicitness of meaning would vary with assigned purpose and audience. Syntactic complexity does vary in this manner (Crowhurst & Piché, 1979), and semantic complexity, in the form of "self-contained messages for remote audiences" (Rubin & Piché, 1979, p. 313), ought to increase as audience intimacy decreases. The variance of semantic explicitness with audience, furthermore, seems to follow a developmental pattern: in the Rubin and Piché study, only expert adults substantially adapted persuasive strategies to audience differentiation. This finding suggests that the ability to differentiate among audiences might be related to writing ability and to explicitness of meaning. It is worth asking, then, whether inexplicit meaning, measured in terms of semantic abbreviation, varies according to assigned rhetorical context, grade level, and general writing ability.

Secondly, our question has its theoretical ramifications. Proponents of the theory that unskilled writers tend to produce writing through the mediation of spoken language attribute that tendency to key differences between speaking and writing. Unskilled writers are unfamiliar with ways to meet the demand for explicit, context-independent meaning in written language. Instead, they use familiar spoken language to produce writing. Speaking, because of the proximity of situational contexts and the participation of an interlocutor, can represent meaning less fully than writing and still achieve the same degree of communicative effectiveness. The crucial distinction, then, would seem to be between dialogue and monologue, not among audiences and purposes assigned by task. Unskilled writers, regardless of assigned rhetorical contexts, write as if they were speaking. Abbreviated meaning, cryptic and context-dependent, is the result.

Recent research, however, suggests that we examine this assumption of the weak writer's rather constant dependence on the mediation of spoken language. Certain studies (Collins & Williamson, 1981; Cayer & Sacks, 1979; Shaughnessy, 1977; Britton, Burgess, Martin, McLeod, & Rosen, 1975) support the assumption. Other studies, though less concerned with relationships between speaking and writing, suggest that the assumption is too simple. These studies indicate that factors such as mode of written discourse and audience (Crowhurst & Piché, 1979; Rubin & Piché, 1979), cognitive development (Kroll, 1978), and task difficulty (Krauss & Glucksberg, 1977) can influence the degree of explicitness in language, so that a change from dialogic to monologic modes is not the only explanation for inexplicit meaning in weak student writing. From the many variables suggested in these studies, we selected writing ability, grade level, mode of discourse, and audience as the ones most likely to help decide whether the rate of semantic abbreviation is constant or variable. We combined mode and audience, and we asked whether persuasive writing to parent and editor audiences might show different rates of semantic abbreviation in comparison with descriptive writing to a peer audience. We also asked whether the rates would vary according to writing ability and grade level.

We analyzed samples of writing[1] from grades 8 and 12 in which writers had responded to three tasks: a description of a place for a peer audience, a persuasive letter to a parent audience, and a persuasive letter to the editor of *TV Guide*. For the peer audience task, ten writing samples were assigned to each of the categories "strong" and "weak," in the following manner. Sixty writers in each grade had responded to a series of four explanatory writing tasks. These essays were read and rated by each of two raters, using primary trait scoring on a scale of 1 to 3. A total score on explanatory writing was established for each writer,

1. These data came from the Cross-Sectional Sample of Writing Performance, which was planned as a data base for descriptive studies of writing performance. The design for the sample and the specific writing tasks were developed in early 1976 by Charles Cooper, Lee Odell, and Cynthia Watson. During the 1976–1977 school year, Cooper and Watson coordinated the gathering of the sample from school districts in New York, Michigan, and Illinois. Subsequently, Cooper and Odell supervised the primary trait scoring of the sample.

and writers were ranked from high to low on the basis of these total scores. At each grade level the ten highest- and ten lowest-scoring writing samples, as determined both by total explanatory score and by peer audience essay scores assigned by both raters, were placed in "strong" and "weak" categories respectively. We assigned the same twenty writers at each grade level to the same categories for the parent audience essays and editor audience essays, a move justified by separate ratings and rankings of four persuasive tasks that showed a correlation with the explanatory tasks of .98. Thus, a total of 120 writing samples was analyzed, and the samples were distributed three ways: 60 in each of two ability groups, 60 at each of two grade levels, and 40 in each of three rhetorical context categories.

Two measures of semantic abbreviation were combined to analyze the writing samples for features of spoken language. The first, personal and demonstrative exophora (Halliday & Hasan, 1976), measured a writer's tendency to refer outside of the written text to situational contexts necessary to make the writing more explicit. The second measure was formulaic expression (Ong, 1979), a category that included commonplaces, clichés, adages, proverbs, and epithets. Formulaic expression concerns a writer's tendency to refer outside of the written text to cultural or social contexts that are needed if the meaning is to be understood. The identification of exophoric and formulaic features was made less arbitrary through reliability checks with independent raters. The raters made a distinction between missing information that is necessary to understand the writer's main line of meaning (information that *should* have been supplied) and missing information that is not necessary to follow that line (information that *could* have been supplied).

This twelfth-grade student's sentence will illustrate the manner in which the semantic measures were employed: "In the TV shows or police shows, I think these people (not to just entertain us) but to show us how some people react when they see a crime committed." The rather peculiar syntax in that sentence provides a clue to the writer's intended meaning. The parenthetical expression is an apparent attempt to indicate that television programs inform as well as entertain. The reader cannot tell, however, which shows or which people the writer has in mind; this information is not in the text. "These people" is an instance of demonstrative exophora; we can tell that the writer means people who are responsible for television programs, but not which members of that class (writers, producers, sponsors, or some combination) the writer wants to include. Similarly, "some people" is used formulaically; it refers to a class of television viewers, but the members of that class are not specified. Finally, the pronoun "they" is an example of personal exophora, since it refers back to "some people." Thus, the sentence abbreviates meaning by depending on a particular situation (the viewing of certain television programs) and on a particular sociocultural context (in which certain television viewers would be identifiable).

Data Analysis and Results

The following research hypothesis guided the analysis of the data:

H_1: Rates of semantic abbreviation will vary in student writing for differing assigned rhetorical contexts according to grade level and to writing ability.

Calculations of rates of semantic abbreviation were figured as frequency per total words. The first step in the data analysis was to examine the mean number of total words per essay written by each group for each audience. Table 14-1 contains the mean number of words per essay for each group in the study. Differences between these means were found to be significant (multivariate $F(2, 35) = 6.507, p < .004$). It is interesting to note that the differences are much greater for the strong writers at each grade level.

Frequency of semantic abbreviation was converted to rate of semantic abbreviation, and the research hypothesis was examined through a repeated-measures analysis of variance (Finn, 1974). This analysis allows simultaneous interaction between the groups in the study and between the rates of semantic abbreviation for each rhetorical context. Table 14-2 presents these mean rates of semantic abbreviation.

The test for interaction of quality of writing, grade, and rhetorical context was not significant (multivariate $F(2, 35) = 1.83, p < .1755$). Thus, we did not conclude that writing ability, grade, and rhetorical contexts vary simultaneously. Two main effects tests, however, were found to be significant when tested separately. These tests were for the interaction of grade and rhetorical context and for the interaction of writing ability and rhetorical context. Results of these tests are presented in Tables 14-3 and 14-4.

Table 14-1. Mean Number of Total Words per Essay by Ability Groups and Grades

Purpose/audience	Weak ability		Strong ability	
	Grade 8	Grade 12	Grade 8	Grade 12
Describe/peer	164.4	145.8	218.9	174.1
Persuade/parent	112.6	141.9	233.7	247.6
Persuade/editor	98.8	167.8	271.9	210.0

Table 14-2. Mean Rate of Semantic Abbreviation by Ability Groups and Grades

Purpose/audience	Weak ability		Strong ability	
	Grade 8	Grade 12	Grade 8	Grade 12
Describe/peer	11.9%	12.6%	5.0%	4.9%
Persuade/parent	7.8	11.1	2.4	9.5
Persuade/editor	9.3	10.2	1.9	3.1

Table 14-3 presents the mean rate of semantic abbreviation for the two grade levels. The differences in this table were found to be statistically significant ($F(3, 34) = 11.9007$, $p < .0001$). This confirms the part of our hypothesis which states that rates of semantic abbreviation will vary according to assigned rhetorical context and grade level. In Table 14-3, eighth-grade writers produced the lowest rate of semantic abbreviation for the parent audience and a very similar rate for the editor audience. The rate increased for the peer audience, indicating that for eighth-grade writers in the study, audiences are differentiated into peer and adult categories. The twelfth-grade writers, on the other hand, made an additional distinction between types of adult audiences. These writers produced the highest rate of semantic abbreviation for the parent audience. The next lowest rate in the twelfth-grade samples was for the peer audience, followed by the editor audience. The results for writing ability were almost identical, as Table 14-4 indicates.

Table 14-4 presents the mean rate of semantic abbreviation for weak and strong writers. Differences in this table are significant ($F(3, 34) = 49.9479$, $p < .0001$). As in Table 14-3, differences between writers and measures (rhetorical contexts) represent other than random variation. The extremely interesting finding is that the pattern of rates of semantic abbreviation for ability is exactly the same as that for grade level. Weak writers produced nearly the same rate for the two adult audiences, parent and editor, and their writing for the peer audience showed the highest rate. As with the twelfth-grade group, strong writers produced their highest rate for the parent audience, a slightly

Table 14-3. Mean Rate of Semantic Abbreviation by Grades

Purpose/audience	Grade 8	Grade 12
Describe/peer	8.5%	8.8%
Persuade/parent	5.1	10.3
Persuade/editor	5.6	6.7

Table 14-4. *Mean Rate of Semantic Abbreviation by Ability Groups*

Purpose/audience	Weak ability	Strong ability
Describe/peer	12.2%	5.0%
Persuade/parent	9.4	6.0
Persuade/editor	9.7	2.5

lower rate for the peer audience, and a rate close to zero for the editor audience.

These data support the model of semantic abbreviation stated in the research hypothesis.

Discussion

This study determined that the rate of semantic abbreviation, a measure of inexplicit meaning in student writing, varies with assigned purpose and audience. The variation was in accordance with writing ability and grade level for groups in the study. Twelfth-grade writing samples and writing samples that had been judged to be strong showed rates of semantic abbreviation that decreased by audience categories in this order: parent, peer, editor. Eighth-grade writing samples and writing samples that had been judged to be weak showed almost the same rate of semantic abbreviation for both parent and editor audiences and a higher rate for the peer audience.

In our previous study of inexplicit meaning in student writing (Collins & Williamson, 1981), we concluded that a higher rate of semantic abbreviation is a defining characteristic of weak student writing. In light of the present study, the conclusion must be modified to include assigned rhetorical contexts. The rate of semantic abbreviation varies for both weak and strong writers, and it varies more for strong writers. Strong writers, according to intimacy with an assigned audience, are more able to vary the extent to which their writing includes the situational and cultural contexts of their language. Weak writers are less able to do this. It is not simply a higher rate of semantic abbreviation that characterizes weak writing. Rather, it is a rate of semantic abbreviation that is inappropriate for the assigned audience.

Strong writers in the study distinguished among parent, peer, and editor audiences, and they adjusted explicitness of meaning accordingly. Strong writers, in terms of grade level and writing ability, produced the most semantic abbreviation for the parent audience, which was the most familiar audience of the three. They produced less for the peer audience, which was socially familiar but less intimately known. Finally, the strong writers produced the least semantic abbreviation for the least familiar audience, the editor of *TV Guide*. Weak writers, on the other hand, made a distinction only between peer and adult audiences. They produced more semantic abbreviation for the unknown peer audience than the parent and the editor, and their writing revealed a similar rate of inexplicit meaning for the latter.

Apparently, weak writers in the study did not differentiate between the two adult audiences, as was the case with the strong writers. For weak writers, familiarity with an assigned audience did not influence the rate of semantic abbreviation as sharply as for the strong writers. Thus, an inappropriate rate of semantic abbreviation can be said to characterize weak writing. We do not intend to imply that semantic abbreviation is always an inferior mode. When the audience is intimately known (a parent), the rate can be higher than when the audience is less familiar (an unidentified peer), and the rate must be low when the audience is not known at all (an editor). The more intimately known audience needs less explicit writing. Strong writers in the study adhered to that rule of appropriately explicit meaning; weak writers did not.

This conclusion supports the theoretical assumptions that the study examined. The fit of the results to the theory seems quite plausible: weak writers at times produce meaning in writing through the mediation of spoken language, and inner speech is transformed into writing that abbreviates meaning by replicating some of the context-dependence of spoken dialogue.

We want to clarify what we believe this theory means. In claiming that weaker writers produce writing through the mediation of spoken language, we are choosing our words carefully. We are not claiming that basic writers are limited to spoken language habits and patterns (a linguistic-deficit hypothesis), or that basic writers are limited to thinking in context-dependent ways (a cognitive-deficit hypothesis). Our argument that weaker writers resort to spoken dialogue, or depend on speaking while writing, means only that at times conversational features show up inappropriately in writing, and these times are more frequent in weak than in strong writing. We stop short of causal analysis here, both because our methods were correlational and, more importantly, because we suspect that the causes of writing problems reside neither in cognitive nor in linguistic deficits, but in difficulties particular writers have with particular writing tasks.

This distinction between deficit and difficulty sets our theoretical stance apart from two others. In this study and our previous one, we found that exophoric reference is more characteristic of weak writing than of strong writing at grades 8 and 12. That finding supports the theory that weak writers resort to the forms and function of spoken dialogue while writing. British researchers, however, used exophoric reference and inexplicit meaning to support a somewhat different theory. Research by Hawkins (1977) showed that significantly more working-class children use items of exophoric reference, particularly third-person pronouns, than do middle-class children. Hawkins concluded that these findings support Bernstein's (1975) theory of socially determined restricted and elaborated codes. This is the linguistic-deficit hypothesis. In American research relating to basic writing, we have been more inclined toward cognitive-deficit hypotheses, such as Piaget's (1926/1955) concept of egocentrism. Some examples: Basic writers have not attained a concept-forming level of cognitive development (Lunsford, 1979); in matters of coherence, some adult writers are like young children (Brostoff, 1981); problems in basic writing beyond the syntactic level are attributable to the writer's egocentricity (Shaughnessy, 1977). Who is right, those who claim that social or linguistic factors cause weak writing, or those who claim that the cause is cognitive?

Closer analysis shows that this is not the right question to ask. We need to ask how difficulties inherent in writing tasks lead writers to produce inexplicit writing. To illustrate, one of the authors (Collins) conducted a subsequent pilot study. An illustrated narrative was used (from Hawkins, 1977) that tells a story of three boys playing soccer, breaking a window, getting yelled at, and running away. While the Hawkins research used an oral interview method, in this study students (in grades 9, 11, and 13; total $n = 114$) were asked to write to someone who could not see the illustrations. The question was whether this instruction would prompt them to write in a relatively explicit manner.

Subjects in the study were described as weak writers by their teachers. Their texts supported that description in terms of not being informationally full, well formed, and interesting—but not in terms of calculated rates of exophoric reference. The latter was again figured as frequency per total words. Mean rates of exophoric reference (grade 9 = 2.7%; grade 11 = 2.3%; grade 13 = 1.9%) stayed about the same across grade levels, suggesting that writers in the study had very little difficulty writing about the assigned illustrated narrative in a context-independent manner. It seems that the writing task this time reduced the level of difficulty inherent in writing about an assigned topic so that exophoric references were reduced to a minimum. The task presented writers with a complete and coherent universe, and writers were told that their reader would not have direct access to that universe. This is tantamount to telling writers all they need to know about a situational context and instructing them to represent that context adequately in a written text.

Apparently it is a writer's ability to manage difficulties inherent in a writing task that makes a text more or less dependent on readers' familiarity with contexts of situation and culture. When difficulty is at a low level, as in the pilot study that asked writers to represent a simple illustrated narrative for an absent reader of their choice, then even weak writing is relatively context-independent. The only problem in specifying referents adequately in this task was the need to distinguish among characters; most writers solved this problem by including relative heights or positions, or by naming characters. When the level of difficulty increases, as in the tasks used in the major study reported here, weaker writers produce context-dependent writing.

A text containing dialogic features does not mean that the writer is speech-dependent. Basic writers do not suffer from cognitive egocentricism, nor do they consistently produce context-dependent writing. These are, in a sense, as much labels for problems with writing tasks as they are labels for problems with writers. Our studies lead to the conclusion that perhaps researchers (and teachers) evoke a tendency toward "egocentric, context-dependent, dialogic" writing when they assign tasks that call for rather specialized writing that is simply too difficult for some writers to produce in isolation from necessary contexts. These contexts include the rhetorical (topic, purpose, audience), the environmental (schooling and other conditions surrounding the writer), and the societal (the sociocultural backgrounds of writers and audiences). Certainly we need to know more about how these levels of context interact with the cognitive dimensions of writing processes.

REFERENCES

Bernstein, B. *Class, codes, and control* (Vol. 1). New York: Holt, Rinehart & Winston, 1975.

Britton, J., Burgess, T., Martin, N., McLeod, A., & Rosen, H. *The development of writing abilities, 11-18.* London: Macmillian Education, 1975.

Brostoff, A. Coherence: "Next to" is not "connected to." *College Composition and Communication*, 1981, *32*, 278-294.

Cayer, R. L., & Sacks, R. K. Oral and written discourse of basic writers: Similarities and differences. *Research in the Teaching of English*, 1979, *13*, 121-128.

Collins, J. L. *Teaching writing: An interactionist approach to abbreviated and idiosyncratic language in the writing of secondary school students.* Unpublished doctoral dissertation, University of Massachusetts, Amherst, 1979.

Collins, J. L., & Williamson, M. M. Spoken language and semantic abbreviation in writing. *Research in the Teaching of English*, 1981, *14*, 23-35.

Crowhurst, M., & Piché, G. L. Audience and mode of discourse effects on syntactic complexity in writing at two grade levels. *Research in the Teaching of English*, 1979, *13*, 101-109.

Elsasser, N., & John-Steiner, V. P. An interactionist approach to advancing literacy. *Harvard Educational Review*, 1977, *47*, 355-369.

Finn, J. D. *A general model for multivariate analysis.* New York: Holt, Rinehart & Winston, 1974.

Flower, L. Writer-based prose: A cognitive basis for problems in writing. *College English*, 1979, *41*, 19-37.

Goody, J., & Watt, I. The consequences of literacy. In J. Karabel & A. H. Halsey (Eds.), *Power and ideology in education.* New York: Oxford University Press, 1976.

Halliday, M. A. K., & Hasan, R. *Cohesion in English*. London: Longman, 1976.

Hawkins, P. R. *Social class, the nominal group and verbal strategies*. London: Routledge & Kegan Paul, 1977.

Hirsch, E. D., Jr. *The philosophy of composition*. Chicago: University of Chicago Press, 1977.

Krauss, R. M., & Glucksberg, S. Social and nonsocial speech. *Scientific American*, 1977, *236*, 100–105.

Kroll, B. M. Cognitive egocentrism and the problem of audience awareness in written discourse. *Research in the Teaching of English*, 1978, *12*, 269–271.

Lunsford, A. Cognitive development and the basic writer. *College English*, 1979, *41*, 39–46.

Malinowski, B. The problem of meaning in primitive languages. In C. K. Ogden & I. A. Richards, *The meaning of meaning*. New York: Harcourt, Brace & World, 1923.

Markova, A. K. *The teaching and mastery of language*. White Plains, N.Y.: M. E. Sharpe, 1979.

Olson, D. R. From utterance to text: The bias of language in speech and writing. *Harvard Educational Review*, 1977, *47*, 257–281.

Ong, W. J. Literacy and orality in our times. *Profession 79*. New York: Modern Language Association, 1979.

Piaget, J. [*The language and thought of the child*] (M. Gabain, trans.). New York: New American Library, 1955. (Originally published, 1926.)

Rubin, D. L., & Piché, G. L. Development in syntactic and strategic aspects of audience adaptation skills in written persuasive communication. *Research in the Teaching of English*, 1979, *13*, 293–316.

Shaughnessy, M. P. *Errors and expectations: A guide for the teacher of basic writing*. New York: Oxford University Press, 1977.

Vygotsky, L. S. [*Thought and language*] (E. Hanfmann & G. Vakar, Eds. and trans.). Cambridge, Mass.: MIT Press, 1962. (Originally published, 1934.)

Vygotsky, L. S. *Mind in society: The development of higher psychological processes* (M. Cole, V. John-Steiner, S. Scribner, & E. Souberman, Eds.). Cambridge, Mass.: Harvard University Press, 1978.

15

Social cognitive ability as a predictor of the quality of fourth-graders' written narratives

DONALD L. RUBIN
University of Georgia

GENE L. PICHÉ
University of Minnesota

MICHAEL L. MICHLIN
Duke University

FERN L. JOHNSON
University of Massachusetts

The construct of audience awareness has assumed major significance in contemporary composition research and teaching (Britton, Burgess, Martin, McLeod, & Rosen, 1975; Ede, 1979; Kroll, 1978: D. Rubin, in press). Competent writers engage in social cognition, representing to themselves their audiences' interests, values, prior knowledge, and experiential associations, as well as readers' linguistic skill and ongoing information-processing operations. Writers apply the conclusions of their social inferences to anticipate the effectiveness of persuasive strategies (O'Keefe & Delia, 1979; D. Rubin & Piché, 1979), the adequacy of informational content (Kroll, 1978; Higgins, 1977; Scardamalia, Bereiter & McDonald, 1977), the appropriateness of syntax (Crowhurst & Piché, 1979; D. Rubin, 1982; Smith & Swan, 1978), and the aptness of organizational cues and patterns (Bracewell, Scardamalia, & Bereiter, 1978). Investigations of composing processes reveal that social cognitive considerations—concern for audience needs—are operative in all phases of writing, during invention (Flower & Hayes, 1980) as well as revision (Sommers, 1980).

Research seeking to explicate the dependency of composing skill on social cognitive ability suffers, in the main, from several shortcomings. First, many studies infer social cognitive activity from aspects of writing performances, that is, from the criterion variable itself. This approach constitutes a type of circular reasoning. (To whit, social cognitive ability is presumed to underlie audience-adapted communication. A script ap-

297

pears to be well adapted. Therefore the writer is judged skillful at perspective-taking.) Such inferences about social cognitive ability have been drawn on the basis of global strategies (Kantor & Rubin, 1981) as well as on the basis of specific discourse features such as amount of information (Kroll, 1978), amount of discriminating information (Higgins, 1977), and use of context-creating statements (Bracewell, Scardamalia, & Bereiter, 1978). When specific discourse features are taken as indicators of social cognitive ability, researchers run the risk of operating on uncorroborated assumptions (see D. Rubin, in press). For example, one might postulate that a high density of useful information is a sign of audience awareness in descriptive writing tasks; however, such information presented in the form of a list is likely to be lost to an audience. Therefore a writer may manifest regard for readers' needs, on occasion, by presenting a low density of useful information. Moreover, an additional danger is incurred when these discourse features are also designated *a priori* as indicators of overall composition quality.

A more adequate approach to the exploration of links between social cognitive ability and adapted communication requires that subjects be administered social cognitive measures independently of the criterion writing task. D. Rubin (1982) and O'Keefe and Delia (1979) correlated aspects of writing performance with indices of social cognition derived from measured cognitive complexity and impression organization (Crockett, 1965). Rubin and Piché (1979) employed a "metapersuasion task" (Howie-Day, 1977) in a similar manner. These studies, however, examined persuasive writing. No independent measures of social cognitive ability have been used in conjunction with other modes of writing— narrative, for one—in which audience salience is less obvious.

An additional weakness in research on social cognition and writing is the prevailing treatment of social cognitive ability as a unitary, monolithic construct. That is, composition researchers have rarely engaged in detailed analyses of the various social cognitive tasks underlying particular writing performances. Cognitive developmental psychologists investigating the ontogenesis of communication skills in general have similarly neglected to treat social cognition as a multidimensional construct. As a result they have failed to resolve such issues as pinpointing the age of onset of social decentration (Urberg & Docherty, 1976) or empirically establishing the relationship between role-taking and moral reasoning (Kurdek, 1978).

Indeed, both conceptual and empirical inquiries reveal the multidimensional character of social cognition (Piché, Michlin, Johnson, & Rubin, 1975; K. Rubin, 1973, 1978; Kurdek, 1977, 1978). In a discussion of social inferential processes in composing, D. Rubin (in press) outlines the following framework for conceptualizing the dimensions and components of social cognition:

1. *Subskills*
   - Perspective differentiation: S (message source, self) recognizes that O (audience, other) may have a different point of view than S.
   - Construct repertoire: S possesses diverse categories for construing Os.
   - Sense of instrumentality: S recognizes that social cognitive activity will contribute to effective communication.
   - Cue selection: S acquires or retrieves information about O.
   - Representation: S infers O's perspective on the basis of available information in conjunction with general expectations culled from experience.
   - Maintenance: S preserves the integrity of S's representation of O against the press of egocentric intrusion.
   - Sense of applicability: S attempts to utilize the representation of O's perspective in selecting appropriate communication strategies and options.

2. *Structure*
   - Egocentric: S assumes that O's perspective coincides with S's own.
   - Sequential: S apperceives O's perspective only when S and O are not participants in the same objective event.
   - Simultaneous: S recognizes that O's subjective experience differs from S's subjective experience of the same event.
   - Recursive: S understands that O is engaged in inferring S's perspective, including S's representation of O.

3. *Content domain*
   - Perceptual: S represents O's perceptual field.
   - Cognitive: S represents O's knowledge, values, opinions, associations, linguistic skills.
   - Affective: S represents O's emotional state.

4. *Content stability*
   - Dispositional: S represents O's enduring traits, predispositions.
   - Episodic: S represents O's internal state at the time of the interaction.
   - Processual: S represents O's ongoing decoding processes as a function of text properties.

5. *Audience determinateness*
   - Determinate other—generalized other: S calls forth different sets of operations depending on the degree to which O constitutes a well-defined entity.

Given the multidimensional nature of social cognition, researchers may select perspective-taking assessments that emphasize those components corresponding most closely to the demands of criterion communication tasks (Clark & Delia, 1977; Enright & Lapsley, 1980). Alternatively, researchers may adopt multivariate methods, measuring social cognitive ability by means of a battery of instruments that collectively span the entire range of this construct (Kurdek, 1977, 1978).

Empirical investigations link independently measured social cognitive ability to certain writing behaviors in which various strategic and syntactic discourse features are adapted in accordance with audience characteristics (O'Keefe & Delia, 1979; D. Rubin, 1982; D. Rubin & Piché, 1979). These stylistic features might be presumed to affect overall quality of written expression. No studies, however, have undertaken the logically prior, if less sophisticated, task of directly demonstrating that social cognitive ability does contribute to composition quality. On the other hand, composition length or fluency is well documented as a predictor of judged quality (Page, 1968), and contemporary popular concern with transcribing conventions (standard usage, syntax, punctuation) suggests that writing "correctness" is another variable likely to influence perceived writing quality. Recent advances in writing assessment point to the utility of some form of holistic rating as a measure of overall composition quality (Cooper, 1977).

The purpose of the present investigation was to determine the contribution of social cognitive ability to judged overall quality of composition. The influence of social cognitive ability is assessed relative to that of other likely predictors, fluency and error incidence. Social cognitive ability is measured by means of a battery of four previously developed instruments. Writing samples were elicited in the narrative mode, with the expectation that these would yield a conservative indication of the impact of audience awareness.

Method

Subjects

Data for the present study include observations made in conjunction with a previously reported investigation of role-taking and oral referential communication accuracy (Piché et al., 1975), as well as additional observations collected concurrently from the same subjects. Complete sets of data were obtained from 19 children, all fourth-graders randomly selected from a predominantly middle-class public school in suburban Minneapolis. The children scored within one-half of a standard deviation of the mean for the entire fourth grade on the Peabody Picture Vocabulary Test ($\bar{x} = 104.3$, SD $= 16.18$), a measure of verbal IQ (Dunn, 1965).

Predictor Variables

Social cognitive ability was assessed by a battery of four instruments. In the Concrete/Abstract Word Association Test (CAWAT), developed by Milgram and Goodglass (1961), subjects are presented with a series of stimulus words, each followed by an adult-typical and a child-typical word associate. They are asked to respond as adults for one-half of the items, and as younger children for the remainder. The number of role-appropriate responses is summed to arrive at a total role-taking score. The CAWAT is thus a measure of accuracy in taking the perspectives of indeterminate others.

In contrast, the Dymond Empathy Test, or DET (Dymond, 1949), measures accuracy in predicting the episodic internal states of peers participating in face-to-face interaction. The DET and similar techniques have been severely criticized for confounding a variety of judgmental processes in a single score (e.g., Gage & Cronbach, 1955). Nevertheless, the DET was selected for use in this study because its very dimensional complexity confers on it a degree of ecological validity. A person's understanding of everyday social occurrences is likewise an amalgam of diverse judgments based on many sources of information. In this study, groups of four children first engaged in unstructured group interaction. They then filled out semantic differential scales predicting each of the other three children's self- and other-perceptions. Scores were obtained by summing the differences between each predicted rating and the corresponding target rating.

The Chandler Role-Taking Task, or CRTT (Chandler, 1973), is also largely a measure of perspective-taking accuracy, but utilizes materials contrived to reflect the degree to which subjects can maintain the integrity of another's point of view without intruding their own egocentric perspective. Subjects tell a story depicted in a cartoon sequence, and then retell the story from the perspective of a late-coming bystander who is not privy to preceding events. In this study, stories were transcribed and scored for the degree of egocentric intrusion, as opposed to role-appropriate narration. The children's total CRTT scores were derived from their performances on six such cartoon narratives.

The Feffer Role-Taking Task, or FRTT (Feffer & Gourevitch, 1960), is a measure of social cognitive activity that emphasizes the structure of social representations (egocentric, sequential, simultaneous, or recursive). Subjects tell an original narrative and then retell their initial stories twice, from the perspective of a different character in each retelling. In this study, stories were transcribed and scored for thematic consistency between telling and retelling, for role appropriateness of narration, and for depth of elaboration of characters' internal states

(Schnall & Feffer, 1960). Subjects participated in two such sequences of storytelling.

In addition to the four social cognitive instruments, two textual variables derived from analyses of writing performances served as predictors. The first, fluency, was a simple word count of composition length. The second, error rate, was derived by dividing the incidence of nonstandard spelling, usage, punctuation, and syntax by the total number of words for each composition.

Criterion Variable

Overall composition quality was assessed by a ten-interval holistic scale that corresponded to general impression mark (A–F) to be assigned to each student paper. Raters were thirteen pre-service teachers enrolled in a middle-school language arts methods class. Writing quality scores were the mean of the thirteen ratings.

Procedures

The Peabody Picture Vocabulary Test and the CAWAT were administered to intact classes from which the subjects were ultimately drawn. Children were randomly assigned to four-person groups for the DET. The FRTT and CRTT were individually administered and recorded on audiotape. Writing samples were obtained in intact classes by means of an elicitation procedure developed in the National Assessment of Educational Progress (1970). A color slide depicting an elderly woman handling tomatoes was projected on a screen. The children were instructed to "Write a story that tells what is happening in the picture and what is likely to happen next." Students were permitted to take as much time as they wished for their writing.

Analysis

Zero-order correlations among predictor variables and between predictors and the criterion were calculated. Next, social cognitive ability was treated as a single canonical variable, a composite of the four perspective-taking assessments. With the canonical correlation procedure, composite variables are constructed by weighting component measures in such a way that the correlation between the resulting composite and the criterion variable is maximized. Through a multiple linear regression procedure, social cognitive ability, thus composed, was used as a predictor of composition quality ratings along with fluency and error rate.

Results

Table 15-1 shows the zero-order Pearson product–moment correlations between measures of social cognitive ability, textual variables, and judged composition quality. The canonical correlation between the composite social cognitive variable and composition quality was .6024. That between social cognition and fluency was .2512, while the correlation between social cognition and error rate was .4277.

Multiple regression confirmed that social cognitive ability accounted for 36.29 percent of the variance in quality ratings. Adding fluency to the model produced an R^2 change of .0748. When error rate was added as the third predictor, the further increment in R^2 was .0392, with this three-predictor model accounting for a total of 47.69 percent of the variance in composition quality ratings.

Discussion

This study examined the contribution of measured social cognitive ability to overall quality of writing in fourth-graders' narrative composition. We employed a battery of social cognitive instruments representing the multidimensional nature of subjects' ability to assume various social perspectives. The study provides some basis for comparing the influence of social cognitive ability on composition quality relative to the influence of fluency and of transcriptional "correctness."

Table 15-1. Zero-Order Correlations between Measures of Social Cognitive Ability, Textual Variables, and Composition Quality

	Quality	Fluency	Error	CAWAT	DET	CRTT	FRTT
Quality		.3908	−.2658	.5393[a]	.2381	−1808	.1265
Fluency			−.1127	.2140	−.0403	−.0567	.0174
Error				−.3000	−.2668	.1652	.0006
CAWAT					.2774	.1195	.2850
DET						.0731	.2544
CRTT							.1291
FRTT							

[a]Significance of $p < .05$.

The results unambiguously sustain the view that social cognitive ability contributes substantially to overall quality of written composition. The canonical correlation between social cognitive ability and quality ratings exhibited roughly twice the predictive value of either fluency or error rate. Interestingly, the strongest univariate predictor of quality was the measure that asked subjects to respond from the points of view of different age groups (CAWAT). The particular writing task employed in this study did not specify a determinate audience. Rather, writers were addressing an indeterminate reader. It makes sense, therefore, to find that the instrument which taps sensitivity to indeterminate others exhibited the strongest relationship to writing quality in this investigation. These results support methodological suggestions about selecting tests of social cognitive ability (e.g., Enright & Lapsley, 1980). Researchers ought not expect that any measure of social cognition will correlate with any indicator of communicative effectiveness. Instead, researchers would be well advised to first analyze the social inferential demands of the communication tasks assigned to subjects. An appropriate social cognitive instrument can be selected by narrowly targeting the instrument to the nature of the communication task.

While these results do demonstrate a link between social cognition and writing quality, they do not reveal the mechanism whereby audience awareness is instantiated in texts. Clearly raters were responding favorably to some discourse feature (or features) that was, itself, positively related to audience awareness. That feature was neither fluency nor control of writing conventions; its identity remains obscure. In a *post hoc* attempt to identify discourse features that mediate between social cognitive ability and judged quality of composition, texts were reanalyzed for several variables of potential interest. An index of modification, the Noun–Verb/Adjective–Adverb ratio, was computed. Density of pronominalization was also tabulated, since pronominalization increases the risk of faulty reference and also inherently limits elaboration of nominal groups. Neither of these latter variables was significantly related either to judged composition quality, on the one hand, or to social cognitive ability on the other. It remains for future research to identify those textual variables which reflect underlying audience awareness and trigger judgments of writing quality. Promising candidates for investigations of this nature include discourse structures beyond the sentence level, such as explicit encoding of story grammar elements (Applebee, 1978; Pradl, 1979; Stein & Glenn, 1979; Sutton-Smith, Botvin, & Mahony, 1976).

The four social cognitive measures did not exhibit strong interrelatedness among themselves. In this regard the present study also confirms previous research, which suggests multidimensionality rather than convergence within the construct of social cognition (K. Rubin, 1978; Kurdek, 1977). Designs that employ a battery of social cognitive instruments and exploit multivariate analyses appear to have utility (Kurdek, 1978).

Finally, these results bear on issues pertaining to the organization of writing instruction, at least in the lower grades. They lend support to rhetorically motivated writing programs such as Moffett's (1968), in which matters of audience awareness and adaptation are given precedence over usage and grammar drills isolated from the context of communicative writing. Programs designed to enhance social sensitivity in general (e.g., Chandler, 1973; Cooney, 1977) may do more to promote composing skill than does didactic training in writing conventions.

REFERENCES

Applebee, A. N. *The child's concept of story: Ages 2 to 17*. Chicago: University of Chicago Press, 1978.

Bracewell, R. J., Scardamalia, M., & Bereiter, C. *The development of audience awareness in writing*. Unpublished manuscript, York University, 1978.

Britton, J., Burgess, T., Martin, N., McLeod, A., & Rosen, H. *The development of writing ability (11-18)*. London: Macmillan Education, 1975.

Chandler, M. J. Egocentrism and anti-social behavior: The assessment and training of social perspective taking skills. *Developmental Psychology*, 1973, *9*, 326–332.

Clark, R. A., & Delia, J. G. Cognitive complexity, social perspective-taking, and functional persuasive skills in second- to ninth-grade children. *Human Communication Research*, 1977, *3*, 128–134.

Cooney, E. W. Social cognitive development: Applications to intervention and evaluation in the elementary grades. *Counseling Psychologist*, 1977, *6*, 6–9.

Cooper, C. R. Holistic evaluation of writing. In C. R. Cooper & L. Odell (Eds.), *Evaluating writing*. Urbana, Ill.: National Council of Teachers of English, 1977.

Crockett, W. Cognitive complexity and impression formation. In B. Maher (Ed.), *Progress in experimental personality research* (Vol. 2). New York: Academic Press, 1965.

Crowhurst, M., & Piché, G. L. Audience and mode of discourse effects on syntactic complexity at two grade levels. *Research in the Teaching of English*, 1979, *13*, 101–109.

Dunn, L. M. *Peabody Picture Vocabulary Test manual*. Circle Pines, Minn.: American Guidance Service, 1965.

Dymond, R. F. A scale for the measurement of empathic ability. *Journal of Consulting Psychology*, 1949, *13*, 127–133.

Ede, L. S. *Audience: An introduction to research*. Unpublished paper, State University of New York, Brockport, 1979.

Enright, R. D., & Lapsley, D. K. Social role-taking: A review of the constructs, measures, and measurement properties. *Review of Educational Research*, 1980, *50*, 657–674.

Feffer, M., & Gourevitch, V. Cognitive aspects of role-taking in children. *Journal of Personality*, 1960, *28*, 383–396.

Flower, L., & Hayes, J. R. The cognition of discovery: Defining a rhetorical problem. *College Composition and Communication*, 1980, *31*, 21–32.

Gage, N. L., & Cronbach, L. J. Conceptual and methodological problems in interpersonal perception. *Psychological Review*, 1955, *62*, 411–422.

Higgins, E. T. Communication development as related to channel, incentive and social class. *Genetic Psychology Monographs*, 1977, *96*, 75–141.

Howie-Day, A. M. *Metapersuasion: The development of reasoning about persuasive strategies.* Unpublished doctoral dissertation, University of Minnesota, 1977.

Kantor, K. J., & Rubin, D. L. Between speaking and writing: Processes of differentiation. In B. Kroll & R. Vance (Eds.), *Exploring speaking–writing relationships.* Urbana, Ill.: National Council of Teachers of English, 1981.

Kroll, B. M. Cognitive egocentrism and the problem of audience awareness in written discourse. *Research in the Teaching of English*, 1978, *12*, 269–281.

Kurdek, L. Convergent validation of perspective taking: A one year follow-up. *Developmental Psychology*, 1977, *13*, 172–173.

Kurdek, L. Perspective taking as the cognitive basis of children's moral development: A review of the literature. *Merrill-Palmer Quarterly*, 1978, *24*, 3–28.

Milgram, N. A., & Goodglass, H. Role style versus cognitive maturation in word associations of adults and children. *Journal of Personality*, 1961, *29*, 81–93.

Moffett, J. *Teaching the universe of discourse.* Boston: Houghton Mifflin, 1968.

National Assessment of Educational Progress. *1969–1970 writing: National results* (Report No. 3). Denver: Education Commission of the States, 1970.

O'Keefe, B., & Delia, J. G. Construct comprehensiveness and cognitive complexity as predictors of the number and strategic adaptation of arguments and appeals in a persuasive message. *Communication Monographs*, 1979, *46*, 231–240.

Page, E. The use of the computor in analyzing student essays. *International Review of Education*, 1968, *14*, 253–263.

Piché, G. L., Michlin, M. L., Johnson, F. L., & Rubin, D. L. Relationships between fourth graders' performances on selected role-taking tasks and referential communication accuracy tasks. *Child Development*, 1975, *46*, 965–969.

Pradl, G. M. Learning how to begin and end a story. *Language Arts*, 1979, *56*, 21–25.

Rubin, D. L. Adapting syntax in writing to varying audiences as a function of age and social cognitive ability. *Journal of Child Language*, 1982, *9*, 497–510.

Rubin, D. L. Social cognitive dimensions of composing processes. *Monographs of the Duke University Writing Project.* Durham, N.C.: Duke University, in press.

Rubin, D. L., & Piché, G. L. Development in syntactic and strategic aspects of audience adaptation skills in written persuasive communication. *Research in the Teaching of English*, 1979, *13*, 293–316.

Rubin, K. H. Ego-centrism in childhood: Unitary construct? *Child Development*, 1973, *44*, 102–110.

Rubin, K. H. Role-taking in childhood: Some methodological considerations. *Child Development*, 1978, *49*, 428–433.

Scardamalia, M., Bereiter, C., & McDonald, J. D. S. *Role taking in written communication investigated by manipulating anticipatory knowledge.* Paper read at annual meeting of American Educational Research Association, April 1977.

Schnall, M., & Feffer, M. *Role-taking task scoring criteria.* Unpublished manuscript, Brandeis University, 1960.

Smith, W. L., & Swan, M. B. Adjusting syntactic structures to varied levels of audience. *Journal of Experimental Education*, 1978, *46*, 29–34.

Sommers, N. Revision strategies of student writers and experienced adult writers. *College Composition and Communication*, 1980, *31*, 278–388.

Stein, N. L., & Glenn, C. G. An analysis of study comprehension in elementary school children. In R. O. Freedle (Ed.), *New directions in discourse processing* (Vol. 2). Hillsdale, N.J.: Ablex, 1979.

Sutton-Smith, B., Botvin, G., & Mahony, D. Developmental structures in fantasy narratives. *Human Development*, 1976, *19*, 1–13.

Urberg, K., & Docherty, E. Development of role-taking skills in young children. *Developmental Psychology*, 1976, *12*, 198–203.

The instructional context

iv

One question that continually confronts composition teachers is: Does writing instruction really have any effect on students' writing? Some would argue that one can't really teach writing *per se*—that students improve in their ability to write simply with practice, wide reading, and encouragement. It is argued that students don't learn writing, but rather thinking, and this can best be accomplished in courses where there is something to think about, as, for example, in critically responding to literary texts. Others disagree, arguing that inexperienced writers need to be taught how to organize their thinking, define their intentions, find sources of information, employ rhetorical strategies, rearrange early attempts, or edit for errors in usage and mechanics. These two perspectives reflect one of the many difficulties that arise in demonstrating that writing instruction does make a difference—the fact that it is difficult to isolate writing as a unique cognitive enterprise that can be taught as a separate skill.

Much early composition research attempted to determine the effectiveness of different teaching methods. The implied value of this work was obvious: some teaching techniques did make a difference, and some were better than others. However, questions about the validity and theoretical underpinnings of the instructional research pushed many serious researchers away from such work and into "basic research" on the processes of reading and writing. Now, with increasing attention to research on composing processes, questions arise about the benefits of understanding the nature of writing behavior. The days of "basic research" without pragmatic payoffs may be numbered unless researchers begin to make connections with the world that is supposed to benefit from their work.

As many of the studies in this volume demonstrate, writing is a complex and difficult process involving a range of cognitive, linguistic, and social strategies, and writers attend to these parts of the process in different ways. There may be direct benefit from just this insight alone, as teachers appreciate the difficulty of the tasks they and their students face and adopt new attitudes toward their role in the composition classroom. They may be more reluctant to accept the model of writing contained in many textbooks: outline, draft, polish. Given recent research documenting the recursive nature of composing, they may encourage students to conduct prewriting, revising, and editing at a variety of times during composing, rather than in a linear, lockstep fashion. Teachers may also recognize the range of different writing styles within one class and refrain from having everyone follow the same steps in an assignment in unison, twenty-five or thirty at a time. Thus, in the long run, this research can shape teachers' attitudes and influence their methods, even though no simple "solutions" to writing problems have emerged.

The studies in this section focus on teachers—their training, their responses to students' writing, the attitudes they bring to the classroom, and the new technologies available to them. We have excluded a large body of research that examines the effects of different instructional methods—for example, comparing a direct presentation method (a lecture on rhetorical concepts) with a more indirect, facilitative method (conferences on students' writing).

Many of the methodological studies have design and validity flaws that continue to concern us. For example, it is virtually impossible to distinguish clearly between an "experimental" and a "traditional" instructional method, unless one subjects students to practices that could hardly be condoned in this age of "human subjects" rights. If one method proved to be statistically superior in such a study, it would be nearly impossible to claim a direct cause–effect relationship between the "treatment" and the results, given all the factors that can affect a writer in a controlled and somewhat "unnatural" environment. Other problems arise because of the chief outcome measure used in much of this research, the writing-quality rating. Not only can many influences beyond the classroom affect students' performances, but they also affect judges' ratings. With pre- to post-essay ratings, for example, students may perform poorly on the first assignment because it is a novel, unfamiliar writing experience. Then, when students complete the posttest essay, they may improve in their performance simply because they have had practice with a particular writing task, rather than because they were provided with a particular instructional technique.

Concurrent with the changes that have occurred in writing research, there has been a sharp increase in the demand for writing inservice workshops. If there ever was a time when we need to be able to say "research proves . . . ," it is now, but because of the developments we have described, solving immediate practical problems has not been a top priority in research. Without much empirical testing for results, projects modeled after the Bay Area Writing Project have proliferated across the country. They serve a direct need—to provide help to teachers who face the "writing crisis" (or literacy crisis"), many of whom never received training in methods of teaching writing, particularly some of the more current practices.

Measuring the Effectiveness of Instruction

A few studies, often a result of state assessments or mandated assessments of projects funded through grants, have attempted to determine what effects in-service instruction in writing methods has had on teachers' and students' performance in the classroom (Donlan, 1980; Dilworth, 1980). One difficulty that has emerged in trying to measure the effectiveness of this training is an old one—the influence of other variables (students' basic verbal ability, the slowness of language development, attitudes, interest, etc.). Given the real world of classrooms, obtaining "matched pairs," which might help to isolate some of these confusing factors, is difficult at best.

This work is nonetheless important, given the need to test claims for the efficacy of currently popular insights from some of the "basic research." For example, one of the assumptions behind much current theory about how to teach writing is that with more emphasis on the "process" and less on the individual "products" that result from a writing class, students will produce better writing—eventually, if not immediately.

In Chapter 16, Carroll's study examines the effects of instruction that teachers received as participants in the New Jersey Writing Project, a project Carroll describes as emphasizing a "process" orientation. By comparing the writing performances of students who had "process"-oriented teachers with those of students whose teachers had not been trained, she argues for the benefits of the project. Her study illustrates how a variety of measures that form a composite of what has gone on during and as a result of instruction can be used, rather than simply examining the effects of a globally defined method on a global outcome measure (writing quality ratings). The advantage of the multivariate design is that it allows an investigator more sensitivity to fine-grained explanations of the phenomena under study. For example, modeling high-level self-assessing or revising strategies may be successful with cognitively advanced students, but not with basic writers for whom elementary orthographic skills are a higher priority.

Teacher Attitudes and Writing Assessment

The attitudes that teachers have toward writing strongly influence their own teaching practices, particularly their evaluation of student

writing. Their beliefs about the importance of such things as organization, logic, syntax, wording, or neatness serve as filters that train their
attention to these qualities (or lack thereof) in student writing. Thus, a
growing body of research is concerned with the relationships between
teachers' assessments of students' abilities and the factors that influence
their judgments. A number of studies indicate that a student's sex, level
of apprehension, race, and learning style influence writing evaluation
(Beach, 1979; Piché, Rubin, Turner, & Michlin, 1978). Teachers are
often biased against students with deficient school language skills, for
example. Such an assessment may simply reinforce low-ability students'
negative self-images as writers.

Some research suggests that teachers' attitudes about appropriate
style for academic writing influence their evaluation of student writing.
In one study, Hake and Williams (1981) rewrote passages, deliberately
making them more wordy and abstract than the originals. They then
asked high school and college composition teachers to rate the passages.
They found that the high school teachers rated the more verbose
versions higher than the original versions. The college teachers were
more inclined to judge the passages according to logical organization
rather than language. One explanation for the high school teachers'
predilection toward the more verbose passages is that they assumed that
more formal writing was more acceptable. This suggests that these
teachers had definite assumptions about "appropriate" school writing
that guided their assessments.

In a similar study, reported in Chapter 17, Freedman gave college
freshman composition teachers essays written by both freshmen and
professional writers. The essays were written on the same assigned
topic, and the teachers did not know that they were written by two
different groups. There were few significant differences between the
teachers' ratings. In some cases, the teachers were critical of the professional tendency to adopt a personal, assertive, somewhat opinionated
tone, which they considered inappropriate for college freshmen's writing.

Gere, Schuessler, and Abbott analyzed teachers' attitudes toward
writing instruction (see Chapter 18). Their analysis provides some
explanations for the results of the Williams and Freedman studies. They
developed an attitude inventory based on a range of items representing
possible approaches to composition instruction. Using factor analysis to
sort out common orientations in the ratings, they found that the
teachers tended to fall into two basic groups: those who valued activities
which fostered expressive use of language through extensive writing in
a range of genres, and those who valued specific elements of syntax,
usage, and organization. This basic difference is often reflected in dis-
agreements regarding the value of certain teaching methods. Further

research should explore the question of how teachers acquire these attitudes and what can alter them if they should be altered.

One Method: The Writing Conference

Despite the increased use of one particular approach, the writing conference, we have seen little empirical research on its effectiveness. That is, whether it results in better papers or better revising strategies is unclear. An obvious problem is the difficulty of generalizing across different conferences with different students, assignments, and writing strengths or weaknesses. It is also difficult to predict what approach will work with students. Sometimes a direct approach works well with students who lack the ability to assess their own writing, particularly if they see what the teacher does as a model for what they should do. At other times, the teacher robs the student of the opportunity to do his or her own assessing when that might be more beneficial than listening passively (or resentfully but silently) to the teacher's directives.

Given these variations in student ability and development, a teacher needs to be able to diagnose students and their writing in order to determine appropriate approaches. A teacher will therefore have certain intentions—intentions that many content-analysis schemes may not pick up, particularly if the schemes rely exclusively on what is said or done. Despite the foregoing limitations, categories developed for conference activities can be useful in training teachers to recognize their own patterns. In one study (Beach, 1979), teachers who used a category system allowed students to talk more and gave more indirect feedback over a one-year period.

Ziv's report (Chapter 19) discusses the development and application of one set of categories for analyzing teacher feedback. One positive feature of Ziv's categories is her attempt to determine the intentions of both the students and the teachers in the conference. As expected, students differ in their perceptions of a teacher's feedback. Once these and other category systems for analyzing conference behaviors are refined, we may improve our understanding of the often complex verbal and nonverbal interactions that occur in a writing conference.

Word Processors and Writing

In Chapter 20, Bridwell, Nancarrow, and Ross review the state of the art in word processing, which is, in a sense, the newest direction in instructional research reported in this collection. Five years ago, few people believed that a computer had an important place in a composition classroom. With the advent of word processing software and relatively cheap microcomputers, however, everything changed. The computer was no longer just a screen that could give immediate responses to a student's multiple choices. It became a system that now makes it possible to create "fluid texts"—electronic sentences that can be added, deleted, expanded, reduced, and rearranged with a few strokes on a keyboard without any need for retyping. Bridwell, Nancarrow, and Ross not only discuss this development but also describe the software that has been developed to interact with the writer during the composing process, often providing instant analyses of writing. Several studies are reported, including one on how the use of word processors affected experienced writers. The researchers conclude with their plans for incorporating microcomputers and word processing systems into their writing program. They maintain that writing teachers must prepare students to use the new technologies that are revolutionizing the ways in which much written language is produced.

REFERENCES

Beach, R. *The effects of between-draft teacher feedback, apprehension, sex, and conceptual level on students' self-assessing and revising.* Paper presented at annual meeting of National Council of Teachers of English, San Francisco, 1979.

Beach, R. *The development of a category system for analysis of student conferences.* Paper presented at annual meeting of Conference on College Composition and Communication, Washington, D.C., 1980.

Dilworth, C. Locally sponsored staff development for English teachers: A survey of methods and results. *English Education*, 1980, *12*, 98–105.

Donlan, D. Teaching models, experience, and focus of control: Analysis of a summer inservice program for composition teachers. *Research in the Teaching of English*, 1980, *14*, 319–330.

Hake, R., & Williams, J. Style and its consequences: Do as I do, not as I say. *College English*, 1981, *43*, 433–451.

Piché, G., Rubin, D., Turner, L., & Michlin, M. Teachers' subjective evaluations of standard and black nonstandard English compositions: A study of written language and attitudes. *Research in the Teaching of English*, 1978, *12*, 107–118.

16

Process into product: Teacher awareness of the writing process affects students' written products

JOYCE ARMSTRONG CARROLL
McMurry College

In the summer of 1977, a group of English teachers were trained in writing as a process and in the teaching of that process. These participants were members of the New Jersey Writing Project (NJWP)—a consortium of Rutgers University, the Educational Testing Service, and New Jersey school districts. Also, by extension, they were part of NJWP's sponsor: the Bay Area Project (BAWP), which is now known as the National Writing Project.

NJWP officially began as a summer institute conducted by Janet Emig, director, and Joyce Carroll, co-director. Volunteering teachers from project schools had been interviewed before the institute began, after district administrators had recommended them as being committed to writing and to NJWP's goal of improving student writing by improving the teaching of writing. This goal was predicated on the following assumptions:

1. Teachers of writing should write.
2. Writing is a mode of learning.
3. Teachers teaching teachers accomplish efficient curricular change.
4. Theories about and assessment of writing enhance classroom practices.

NJWP participants, therefore, engaged in prewriting, writing, and re-writing activities. They wrote, shared, and discussed what they had written, and studied writing theory, pedagogy, and research findings. Returning to their classrooms, they generally modeled these experiences, taught their students writing as a process, initiated multiple drafting, and encouraged collaboration.

Problem Definition

Writing samples from these students and from control students were taken in October 1977 and May 1978. The major purpose of the research was to answer the question: Would the writing of students taught by teachers who had been trained in writing as a process improve more than the writing of students taught by teachers who had not received such training?

Related Literature

There is little previous research in the area of teacher training in composition and the effects of that training on students' writing. Bragle's (1969) review of the College Entrance Examination Board Summer Institutes, and Hook, Jacobs, and Crisp's (1969) report on the Illinois Statewide Curriculum Study Center in the Preparation of English Teachers (ISCPET), were pioneer attempts to ascertain the extent and kind of preparation teachers were receiving in composition (as well as in language and literature) in order to help bridge the gap between practice and preparation. Recommendations included a call for more research in the area of teacher training in composition. However, ten years of research reveals little heeding of that recommendation.

Studies such as those by Tovatt (1965) and by Tovatt and Miller (1967) describe the results of the oral–aural–visual (OAV) stimuli approach when applied to the teaching of general skills in English to ninth-graders. While these studies deal with a specific kind of process, they reveal nothing about the teachers' experience prior to teaching OAV. Others, such as Moslemi (1975) and Denman (1978), stress evidence supporting a particular aspect of writing—the former focusing on teacher evaluation of creative writing, the latter taking a humanistic, noncognitive approach to the teaching of writing. Neither researcher deals in any way with teacher training. Nor does Bamberg (1978). In her thorough study she concludes that composition instruction does make a difference, but she investigates how the quality and quantity of instruction affect students (regular and remedial), not how the quality and quantity of instruction affect teachers.

Blake (1976) reports the results of attitude changes (using an attitude scale of his own construction) after a five-week summer course on the teaching of writing. While the attitude changes are generally positive, there is no account in the report of any transference of the summer course training or of ways in which the changed attitudes about writing influenced subsequent student writing. Also dealing with teacher attitudes, Schuessler, Gere, and Abbott conclude that the development of their four scales represents a "first step in investigating the relationship between teacher attitudes and student achievement in written composition" (1981, p. 62). They recommend further research into how teachers attitudes are related to amount and types of course-work assigned and to personal work in composition.

One other recent study, by Donlan (1980), probes two staff de-velopment models—developmental and deficit. The attitudes of twenty-four composition teachers toward an in-service education program were assessed. Once again, however, possible transference of the training to the writing of these teachers' students was not studied.

This somewhat neglected area of teacher training and transference may account in part for Witkin's contention that teachers, whether habitually or intentionally, remain on the periphery of students' writing and note only externals. In discussing the process of creative expres-sion, he suggests that this traditional concern with product may be due to the incomprehensibility of process to the praxis of teachers. Witkins insists that involvement is so essential to the setting, making, holding, and resolving of expressive acts that teachers must "enter the creative process at the outset" (1974, p. 69).

Britton and the members of the University of London Writing Research Unit agree:

> Teachers have many reasons for being interested in writing processes. Their involvement with all the learning processes of their pupils requires that they understand how something came to be written, not just what is written. They can bring to their reading of a pupil's work all their knowl-edge of his context, realizing, perhaps intuitively, that what they already know about a child and his thinking when they read his work enables them to understand and appreciate something that may be incomprehensible to another. In this respect, many teachers are far in advance of anything educational research has been able to offer them. (Britton, Burgess, Martin, McLeod, & Rosen, 1975, p. 21)

Bullock concurs: "If a teacher is to succeed in this he will need to learn all he can about the process involved in writing and above all the satisfactions to be derived from it" (1975, p. 165).

Yet when O'Donnell (1979) systematically surveyed ten volumes of the journal *Research in the Teaching of English*, he recorded that 51 of the 176 articles focused on composition but less than half a dozen dealt specifically with the preparation of English teachers. His data support the significance of the present study, which addresses a question here-tofore unposed about teacher training in the writing process while probing the impact of that preparation on students' writing.

O'Donnell's (1979) observations and questions, raised to spur fur-ther research in the teaching of English, juxtaposed with the Fagan and Laine (1980) study, which shows that only 34 percent of the English teachers surveyed in Pennsylvania believed their undergraduate preparation could be improved, underscore the fact that composition, evaluation of student writing, study of dialects, and usage remain areas where teachers feel inadequately prepared. Quisenberry, in an article entitled "English Teacher Preparation: What's Happening?," justifies both encouragement and impatience for "major stirrings which are resulting from genuine attempts to meet perceived needs in the profession" (1981, p. 77).

Procedures for Training Teachers: Overview of the Institute

Writing

The institute, which consisted of a morning and an afternoon session five days a week for three weeks, held to the basic premise that teachers should learn the composing process by composing themselves. Thus, the twenty-five participating teachers wrote for at least one hour every morning; the free, self-sponsored writing activated the process and kept it going. Many of the teachers kept journals, recording their individual responses to the dimensions of the composing process: context, stimuli, prewriting, planning, starting, stopping, contemplating, and reformulating. As the institute progressed, other stimuli activated writing: peer suggestions, conferences, presentations, and the assignment of two polished pieces of writing due at the institute's end.

Sharing

After writing, the participants formed small groups and each person freely read his or her piece of writing aloud twice. No one was coerced to read; no one was pressured. Other group members responded by using the pointing, telling, summarizing, and showing techniques gleaned from Elbow (1973) and by using and thereby testing criteria sheets of their own design. If a piece of writing would not work, the informal workshop nature and the constructive responses of peers encouraged the writer to invite specific criticism. Gradually, group evaluation deductively moved from general comments to specific analyses of grammar, style, tone, purpose, syntax, sentence structure, and so forth; thus, collaboration spurred meaning.

While sharing with peers provided one important and immediate type of audience and evaluation, conferences with the institute's instructor provided another. Such meetings allowed participants to have one-on-one discussions of working papers with the instructor.

Reformulating

Next reformulation occurred. This process was individual, not prescriptive: while peer advice was taken into consideration, personal purpose and style arbitrated final decisions. The task of correcting, revising, and rewriting, which are often theorized as separate functions in the composing process, naturally grew out of continual writing practice, not out of some remote mechanical rules.

In her article "Writing as a Mode of Learning," Emig builds on the work of Vygotsky, Luria, Bruner, and Revesz when stressing her thesis that writing is unique because it enables immediate "feedback, as well as reinforcement . . . because information from the *process* is immediately and visibly available as that portion of the *product* already written" (Emig, 1977, p. 125). In addition, Stallard (1976) points out that cognitive processes seem to be inherent in the composing process. During the NJWP institute, this immediacy and cognition fulfilled two purposes: it enabled self-evaluation, and it heightened awareness of the composing process. So writing became a mode of learning about writing as well as a mode of learning about the teaching of writing.

Presentations and Theory

Activities during the institute—which included listening to visiting speakers, viewing and discussing videotapes, attending brief lectures, and presentations, engaging in interactive dialogues, and participating in large and small group discussions—revolved around theory, research, and practical experiences. Question and answers depended upon group needs. Three examples: teachers studied Francis Christensen's generative rhetoric of a paragraph, applied this theory to their writing of a paragraph, and evaluated the results; teachers replicated the stylistic and syntactical characteristics of a classic literary excerpt, shared their writing with the class, and discussed the implications and extensions of this type of assignment; teachers' lessons, in which a proven writing technique was used with the group simulating grade level, were followed by an analysis of the theoretical basis of what they had done. Because of this procedure, many discovered firm foundations for methods they intuitively had been using, while some discovered that their methods were nothing more than baseless gimmicks.

Resources

The participants used Emig's *The Composing Process of Twelfth Graders* (1971), which provided theory; Elbow's *Writing without Teachers* (1973), which furnished practical suggestions for composing, sharing, and evaluating; Winterowd's *Contemporary Rhetoric* (1975), which added the breadth of recent rhetorical research; and Smith, Goodman, and Meredith's *Language and Thinking in School* (1976), which presented both theory and suggested classroom applications. Reprints and photocopies of selected articles and a bibliography were distributed for further reference.

Procedures for Implementation of the Institute Training

Classroom Implementation

WRITING

Returning to their classrooms, the institute-trained teachers generally followed the institute's design, though there were many individual variations. The same ratio of time that had been spent writing during the institute was now spent writing in the classroom. For example, in some classes each student wrote for 15 to 30 minutes two or three times a week; in others, students wrote for 5 to 10 minutes daily, usually in journals. Also, these teachers became models for their students by writing when their students wrote. Finally, these trained teachers ingeniously integrated writing into all phases of their curricula. In every case there was more writing activity going on in the classrooms of the trained teachers than in other classrooms.

SHARING

In their classrooms, trained teachers allocated more time for group sharing and various kinds of peer evaluation. In many cases, students heard and systematically responded to one another's writing for the first time.

That the teacher is usually the only audience for the student writer is a point of common knowledge. Noise levels, fear that students will "talk about something other than the writing," lack of training in group processes, and teacher-centered curricula all foster this tendency not to see others as an audience. Yet the trained teachers, because they had experienced group processes themselves, returned to their classrooms equipped to shift from the teacher as the only audience to a situation providing a range of audiences. They were also able to use the criteria sheets they had developed and tested during their own group sessions in meaningful ways with their students.

Another component of the institute that found its way into the classroom was the conference. As students became involved in the group processes, and as the interactions progressed, teachers situated themselves in the room so that students needing assistance or encouragement could visit about their writing. Some conferences were brief (a nod, a smile, a quick diction check); others required more time (an in-depth reading of an excerpt, help in unblocking). Some students conferred often, some rarely, some never.

REFORMULATING

"The question is as always, what does one wish to achieve? At present in the teaching of English, it is not a matter of returning to grammar as much as it is a matter of returning to composition" (Mellon, 1976, p. 74). Assumptions harkening back to inadequate or inappropriate theories and pedagogies have led to ideas about grammar *as* composition. To the uninformed, writing means what is done to words, phrases, clauses, and sentences in isolation. This atomistic approach emphasizes exercises, and often these exercises do not transfer into student's writing. Sometimes because of this emphasis, the product never comes to be; if it does, it is stilted, lacking style, often syntactically immature.

The institute teachers returned to composition teaching not by way of product but by way of process. They realized that fragmented drill work in isolation or atomistic approaches must be replaced by integrated instruction about grammar, style, tone, syntax, and so forth during the writing process itself. They worked with their students on multiple drafting, using Emig's reformulating categories: correcting (elimination of mechanical errors and stylistic infelicities), revising (shifting larger segments of material), and rewriting (completely redoing a piece). Going through this process with their own work, and seeing their peers go through it, had provided the teachers with at least one explicit, teachable method that was transferable to their students.

District Implementation

Fitting development programs to the needs of district curricula, these teachers conducted mini-institutes, in-service programs, and workshops for their English departments or, in some cases, for the entire faculty. They often visited other project schools. NJWP administrators also participated. In short, there was a consistent inter- and intrasupport system operating among all levels of the consortium. Control schools, while part of the consortium, were not part of the 1977 institute, in-service training, or any phase of the staff development in 1977–1978.

Assessment of the Implementation

The third component of NJWP involved the development and use of assessment instruments and procedures. Evans Alloway, Director of Programs for the Assessment of Writing at the Educational Testing Service in Princeton, New Jersey, worked closely with members of the consortium. This stage encompassed (1) students' writing samples, (2) teacher and student writing attitude surveys, (3) classroom observation sessions, and (4) the Written English Expression Placement Test. This chapter deals only with the results of the students' writing samples.

Students' Writing Samples

PROCEDURES OF ANALYSIS

For the purpose of analysis, 15 students from each district were chosen at random from all participating students. This sampling was conducted in order to weight each district's contribution equally. Additionally, since the argument can be made that the district should be the unit of observation, the resultant n of 225 strikes a middle ground between the highly conservative n of 15 (using the district as the unit) and the liberal n of 1400 (using all students). Fifteen students were chosen as the base number because this number ($n = 15$) represents the largest number of students with complete scores in a given district. Students from the other school districts were then randomly selected. Consideration was given to a balance according to sex (S). There were approximately 7 or 8 males and 7 or 8 females from each district, resulting in a total of 112 females and 113 males. At the time of the investigation, these students were enrolled in grades 7 through 12 in the English classrooms of 8 project and 7 control school districts. There were 120 subjects from project TG-1, 105 from control TG-0. Subjects were coded to indicate district identification and to protect their anonymity.

Socioeconomic status (SES) is so closely aligned with New Jersey's District Factor Grouping (DFG) that often these two labels are used interchangeably. DFG is determined by factor analysis. The eight variables in the composition of the factor are educational background, occupational background, per capita income, percentage poverty level, unemployment rate, population density, degree of urbanization, and population mobility. In New Jersey, the letter A signifies the lowest level of socioeconomic status; the letter J signifies the highest. School districts designated A, D, E, F, G, H, and J were represented in this study.

The prewriting sample (PREWRIT) was obtained in October 1977 from all the subjects in this study who responded to Writing Topic I:

> Write on this topic for twenty minutes.
> Use the bluebook(s) provided.
>> Write about an object that is really important to you, something that has become a part of your life. You might want to write about how you discovered it or what it has come to mean to you. You may write a journal entry, a letter, a story, a brief autobiography, an essay, or a poem.

The nature of this stimulus, field and mode of discourse, involved nonlimiting options. The nature of the conditions for testing—a timed, impromptu piece of writing—provided the limitations (Hogan, 1977).

The postwriting sample (POSTWRIT) was obtained in May 1978 from all the subjects in the study. This writing sample also was a response to Writing Topic I. Between October and May, subjects in the project group were taught writing by the teachers previously trained. No attempt was made to alter the control school district teachers' usual manner of approaching the teaching of writing.

The method of assessing the writing samples was holistic scoring. This type of writing evaluation enables trained readers, in this case trained by Alloway, to rank writing samples quickly, as a whole, according to a predetermined four-point scoring range: 1 (low quality) to 4 (high quality). A scale of this type works because:

> . . . readers are forced away from a middle, or uncommitted, score. Readers must first decide whether the paper is above average (in the 3–4 category) or below average (in the 1–2 category). After making this first decision, readers must then judge whether the paper is enough above average to rate the highest score (4) or enough below average to rate the lowest score (1). (Conlan, 1976, pp. 3–4)

Mellon writes that reliable and valid "holistic scoring techniques have been extensively researched over the past twenty years, particularly by personnel of ETS in connection with essay exercises used in various College Board examinations" (1975, p. 23). As such, holistic techniques help establish comparisons of large numbers of papers written at different times.

All the writing samples were coded and mixed, and the information pages were taped back. From these, random samples were chosen, read, and rated by Alloway and a group of four experienced readers in order to establish an accurate representation of the total set of papers for baseline data. The ratings were made in accordance with this dictum: "Raters must judge individual essays relative only to the other essays in the group being rated rather than to outside norms" (Mellon, 1975, p. 23). Next, these representative samples were reproduced for use in the training session of the other readers. After the training, readers, identified only by number, progressed through all the writing samples with occasional breaks for consistency checks and rest periods until each writing sample had been read and rated once. Then each writing sample was read and rated a second time by a different reader. Discrepant papers (those with a difference of two points) were given a third reading by another reader. The scores were checked, then summed to provide a scale ranging from 2 to 8. Inter-rater reliability was .72.

Multiple regression allowed for investigation of the experimental factor of teacher training in writing and its effect on students' written products. The following formula provided the procedure for the statistical multiple regression computations.

$$POSTWRIT = \beta_0 + \beta_1 TG + \beta_2 SES + \beta_3 S + \beta_1 PREWRIT$$
$$n = 225$$

Postwriting sample score (POSTWRIT) was the dependent variable, and type of group (TG), socioeconomic status (SES), sex (S), and prewriting sample score (PREWRIT) were the independent variables.

RESULTS

The simplest way to look at the data is to examine post-test differences for control and for project (experimental) students. Control students dropped $-.20$ between the pre-test and post-test, whereas the project students increased $+.60$. These are presented in Table 16-1.

This, however, is an oversimplification and slightly overestimates the effect of the intervention. A more sophisticated and justifiable approach is the multiple regression analysis described above. The results of this analysis are given in Table 16-2.

Table 16-1. Pre-test and Post-test Sample Scores

	Pre-test	Post-test	Difference
Control ($n = 105$)			
$\bar{x}$	4.89	4.69	$-.20$
SD	1.45	1.29	
Project ($n = 120$)			
$\bar{x}$	4.64	5.24	$+.60$
SD	1.65	1.49	

Table 16-2. *Regression Analysis of Writing Scores*

	Analysis of variance					
Source	df	SS	MS	F	p	R^2
Regression	5	202.34	40.47	35.08	$\leq .0001$	.44
Residual	219	252.6	1.15			
Total (corrected)	224	454.96				

	Coefficients			
Parameter	Regression coefficient	t	p	Standard error of coefficient
PREWRIT	+ .396	6.67	$\leq .0001$	.059
Sex	−0.068	−0.47	.6401	.145
SES	−0.059	−1.57	.1182	.038
TG	+0.674	4.66	$\leq .0001$	.145
INTERCEPT	+1.499	4.55	$\leq .0001$	.329

The project variable regression coefficient was significant at $p < .0001$. Thus the statistical significance of the project is clear. Since the project was coded 1 and control was coded 0, the coefficient may be interpreted as the direct additional contribution of being a project student as opposed to a control student. This effect was .67 points of the holistic scoring scale of 2 to 8. Since the standard deviation of the postwriting sample was 1.43, this represents an effect of 45.5 percent of the sample's standard deviation.

An alternative method of assessing the educational impact of the experimental factor is to compare two students who were average on all independent variables except the project/control dichotomy. The average control student would score 4.633 on the postwriting sample, while the average project student would score 5.306, an increase of 14.5 percent.

Prewriting was entered in the multiple regression in order to control, in part, for differences that may have existed between the two groups. The purpose of this inclusion was to reduce bias. Sex is not significantly related to the postwriting test. SES is marginal ($p = .12$) and in an anticipated direction (Loban, 1976; Tucker & Smithers, 1977).

Additionally, the means and standard deviations for SES and grade level broken down by project/control type group and sex, as presented in Table 16-3, show that the project students were slightly younger and from slightly lower socioeconomic conditions than the control students.

It is reasonable to conclude that these results are not only statistically significant but educationally important. The training in process was a potent influence on the development of writing ability. Students of teachers so trained showed statistically significant and educationally important increases in their writing performance.

Table 16-3. Mean SES and Grade by Sex and Group Type

Type of group	Sex	Mean grade level (SD)	Mean SES (SD)	n
Control	Male	10.80 (1.31)	4.54 (2.44)	52
	Female	10.71 (1.32)	2.44 (2.39)	53
Project	Male	10.54 (1.39)	4.28 (1.57)	60
	Female	10.43 (1.51)	4.00 (1.52)	60
Total		10.61 (1.39)	4.33 (1.99)	

Implications of this Study

Writing

In presenting suggestions that will help teachers develop necessary strengths as teachers of writing, Larson is explicit:

> . . . *writing* (writing in varied forms: journals, narratives of personal experience, editorials, news stories, poetry, pieces of dialogue; using their own voices and assumed voices; addressing different audiences) . . . doing, themselves, the activities they expect students to perform . . . and analyzing at some point the processes they pass through in doing these things. (1978, p. 79).

The present study reinforces Larson's suggestions by indicating that when teachers experience process, when they write and experiment in different forms, they broaden their praxes. This enables them to interact meaningfully with their students, especially in certain crucial phases of the writing process. Conversely, perhaps, they do not interfere at other crucial times. In his survey of the 1977 NCTE achievement award winners in writing, Applebee observes that their "teachers found ways to get involved during the writing process" (1978, p. 341). He suggests that class size affects a teacher's opportunity to sponsor this type of interaction. The present study suggests training in process as another important factor. Further investigation of these two suggestions would prove enlightening.

If writing more and experiencing various forms help improve teachers' writing and their understanding of the process, then it follows that students should also write more often. Since research indicates that writing frequency and writing aptitude have been declining, the implications—that increased student writing is needed—seems clear.

Increased frequency encourages practice in all facets of the composing process. This practice, in turn, often leads to improvement of the written product (Stallard, 1974). While the results of the present study cannot be attributed solely to increased frequency, the data suggest that (1) writing may be a mode of learning about writing; and (2) writing may be a sharper shaper of experience than speech, since the former is more deliberate, more demanding, and more permanent.

The fact that writing frequency does not entirely account for the results of this study suggests that thinking about the act of writing fixes the experience by adding the dimension of cognitive reflection. Therefore, as Mandel (1978) posits, it is important for teachers to investigate their own composing processes and those of their students in order to lead their students into realizations about writing as a complex of processes and into analysis of their own writing in that context.

Finally, as Graves noted in his report to the Ford Foundation, students rarely see adults writing. Hence, students have few adult writing models. Often they wonder aloud, "Why all this fuss about writing?" Graves calls for more research on "how adult models affect children's writing" (1978, p. 16). Since the trained teachers often wrote when their students wrote, the positive results of this study echo his call.

Sharing

After training in myriad sharing techniques, the teachers shifted more easily from the traditional teacher-centered audience to situations providing what Britton *et al* (1975) termed "a wide range of audiences." The implications of that shift support training that involves the experiencing of classroom groups, peer evaluation, self-evaluation, and conferences. Also, the institute, rich with theory and practice on self or peer as audience, provided teachers with the security to reduce the amount of time they were spending writing comments on students' papers and to increase the amount of time students were spending writing comments on one anothers' papers. Clarke's study (1969) of 141 eleventh-grade students found that the number of teachers' comments written on themes produced little effect. Further, purely negative comments produced lower scores in reinforcement, satisfaction, and confidence than completely positive ones. These findings made sense to the trained teachers, who knew from their peer group experience the importance of positive remarks. This realization carried over into the classroom.

By reducing written comments and by expanding peer evaluation, the teachers discovered that time was available for conferences. But conferences are not new. At the Yale Conference in 1968, for example, James Squire requested more class time for individual conferences. More recently, Graves stated that the "process-conference approach is a proven workable way to reverse the decline of writing in our schools" (1978, p. 19). The implication seems clear. Despite urgings, even those based on research, teachers seem to adopt a technique more readily if they themselves have experienced the technique and have internalized it.

Whether through self-evaluation, peer group evaluation, or conferences, the teachers recognized the need for immediate feedback on writing and honest, positive teacher comments (see also Beach, 1979; Stoen, 1976). The teachers also continued to seek theoretically sound and interesting exercises to heighten students' self-awareness of weak areas in their writing, and they continued perfecting their criteria sheets, fitting them appropriately to the reflexive and extensive modes of discourse.

Reformulating

Although no one aspect of the teacher training can be isolated to account for the statistical significance of the findings, the results seem to support Bullock's assertion:

> It has not been established by research that systematic attention to skill and technique has no beneficial effect on the handling of language. What has been shown is that the teaching of traditional analytic grammar does not appear to improve performance in writing. This is not to suggest that there is no place for any kind of exercises at any time and in any form. It may well be that a teacher will find this a valuable means of helping an individual child reinforce something he has learned. What *is* questionable is the practice of setting exercises for the whole class, irrespective of need, and assuming that this will improve every pupil's ability to handle English. What is open to question is the *nature* of some of these exercises. . . . Most give the child no useful insight into language and many actually mislead him. (1975, p. 171)

Teachers trained in the institute reevaluated their approach to reformulating—considered by most, before the institute, as recopying. Fragmented drill work was replaced in a variety of ways. Grammatical problems were dealt with in conference, or through small groups. Self-evaluation techniques enabled some students to catch some of their own errors. Reading aloud to peers helped some students "hear" their mistakes, "hear" different styles and tones. Usage and syntax problems were extracted from papers and shared with the class as a large group, through use of an overhead projector or the chalkboard. Sentence combining was often done as a class. Students soon realized that many of their problems were shared ones, and that helping one another was mutually beneficial.

All was not perfect during this stage, however. Students unaccustomed to sharing and taking responsibility for their own writing demanded drills. These seemed safer, perhaps. Teachers often expressed frustration, reverting back to traditional approaches and short-circuiting groups. Trying to deal with instruction when the students were in the middle of the writing process often led them to doubts, especially if all did not work as it had during the institute. Again the implications are clear. More research is needed on the relationship of grammar and usage to composition (Fraser & Hodson, 1978; Kolin, 1981; Newkirk, 1978). Theoretically the teachers understood that instruction had to be integrated with the writing, but few explicit strategies exist.

The teachers did create ways of preserving multiple drafts. Some kept a folder for each student, which was accessible at times of collaboration or for self-evaluation. Others preferred notebooks, portfolios, or, for prewriting, journals. A packet of teacher writing visible on a desk or in a file enabled students to see that their model also had to correct, revise, and rewrite.

Training

If training teachers through a process orientation results in more teacher and better student writing, more college and universities should offer courses, experiences, and programs to complement the process approach to writing. The surprising lack of training in the teaching of writing compounds existing problems.

For instructors teaching composition, cooperative college and school district training such as NJWP seems necessary. The London Schools Council's development project, proposed as early as 1966 and approved in 1971, was a corroborative experience (Britton et al., 1975). That project, as well as the one upon which this study is based, proves that a multi-leveled participative venture is feasible. Robert Bush, Director of the Center for Educational Research at Stanford University, supports such collaboration. "Beginners, experienced school teachers, researchers and developers, all working together in a problem-solving mode in a school setting proved an exciting environment for training" (1977, p. 7).

Another neglected area is on-site in-service training, with teachers having a greater amount of content control. Administrators and school boards need to consider general professional development training and retraining of existing teachers. Teachers' centers might be established within school districts, especially since extra space is often available because of declining enrollments.

Theory

The word "theory," second only to the word "writing," seems to strike fear into the hearts of most teachers. Because of their predominantly literary backgrounds, English teachers "need to examine the training and socialization which shape our responses. Although we may define ourselves as composition teachers, our origins lie in literature study" (Gere, 1978, p. 258). Therefore, teaching writing without explicit theory and thorough training is a flabby affair, often resulting in either a stubborn attachment to outmoded methods or a continual vacillation between the latest method and the newest "in" gimmick. Yet in most reactions there is some sublimated truth. Perhaps the negative reaction to theory is not caused by ignorance, fear, stubbornness, or weakness, but by abstractness—that is, by the general lack of never having the theoretical merged with the experiential.

Through NJWP, and by actively engaging in composition's complex of processes, the institute teachers began structuring their own theories of composing upon theories engendered during the readings, research, lectures, presentations, discussions, and writing itself—in general, all the experiences of three weeks. In short, the teachers learned theory by experiencing theory; they learned its validity by applying it to their own writing; they learned its value by employing it in their classrooms.

The major implication of this study is the necessity of merging theory and practice when training teachers in composition (Applegate & Newman, 1978; Donlan, 1974). As Graves puts it, "Teachers do not teach a subject in which they feel unprepared, even when the subject is mandated by the school curriculum. Writing is such a subject" (1978, p. 15).

Clearly, most teachers were product-oriented before the institute. Their approach to composing had been one generated by the teacher and foisted upon the student. Most admitted that they taught writing "as I was taught." The major movement from this *what* of composing (product) to the *how* (process) affected their perceptions of themselves, of their students, and of composition in general. This new perceptivity, which had been influenced by their process orientation, nudged them to ask new questions, which in turn gave rise to another, perhaps much more subtle implication of this study—the idea that teachers of composition become also researchers of composition (Berthoff, 1979; Goswami & Odell, in press). Processes ebb and flow to different rhythms during different stages and at different levels of development. More research into each of these dimensions is needed, and who is better equipped to conduct some of this research than trained composition teachers themselves?

In conclusion, this study presents new challenges. Since training in the writing process produces positive results, teachers are provided with new direction and support. What is necessary for writing to improve, a necessity apparently recognized, in view of the popularity of writing projects, is for a deep change to occur within the writing classroom—a deep change within its teachers—a deep change training can bring about. Writing is a complex process; it is a dynamic, unique, highly individual yet participatory venture. Students profit most when teachers engage in this complex process with them. When that happens, all levels of the academic structure are served best.[1]

REFERENCES

Applebee, A. N. Teaching high-achieving students: A survey of the winners of the 1977 NCTE achievement awards in writing. *Research in the Teaching of English*, December 1978, *12*(4), 339–348.

Applegate, J. H., & Newman, K. K. Now that I think about what I said: A language reflection approach to educating language arts teachers. *English Education*, December 1978, *10*(2), 67–74.

Bamberg, B. Composition instruction does make a difference: A comparison of the high school preparation of college freshmen in regular and remedial English classes. *Research in the Teaching of English*, 1978, *12*, 47–59.

Beach, R. The effects of between-draft teacher evaluation versus student self-evaluation on high school students' revising of rough drafts. *Research in the Teaching of English*, May 1979, *13*(2), 111–119.

Berthoff, A. *The teacher as researcher*. Paper presented at meeting of California Association of Teachers of English, San Diego, February 16, 1979.

Blake, R. W. Assessing English and language arts teachers' attitudes toward writers and writing. *English Record*, 1976, *24*, 87–97.

Bragle, G. W. *An evaluation of the 1962 CEEB workshops in New York State*. Unpublished doctoral dissertation, State University of New York, Albany, 1969.

Britton, J., Burgess, T., Martin, N., McLeod, A., & Rosen, H. *The development of writing abilities (11–18)*. London: Macmillan, 1975.

Bullock, Sir A., F. B. A. *A language for life*. London: Her Majesty's Stationery Office, 1975.

Bush, R. N. We know how to train teachers: Why not do so! *Journal of Teacher Education*, November–December 1977, *28*(6), 5–9.

Clarke, G. A. *Interpreting the penciled scrawl: A problem in teacher theme evaluation* (ERIC Document Reproduction Service No. ED 039 241). Chicago: University of Chicago, May 1969.

1. After the year of testing (1977–1978) and the year of analyzing the data (1978–1979), the director, co-director, statistician, and two district representatives met with the Deputy Commissioner of Education and members of the Joint Dissemination Review Panel in Washington, D.C., for a full review of the project and the data presented in this study. On May 23, 1979, NJWP was endorsed by this body and was subsequently validated through the National Diffusion Network (NDN) as Developer/Demonstrator Project. The NJWP was, as of January 1983, the only national project within the National Writing Project complex to receive this distinction.

Conlan, G. *How the essay in the college board English composition is scored*. Princeton, N.J.: Educational Testing Service, 1976.

Denman, M. E. The measure of success in writing. *College Composition and Communication*, 1978, *29*, 42–46.

Donlan, D. Teaching writing in the content areas: Eleven hypotheses from a teacher survey. *Research in the Teaching of English*, Summer 1974, *8*(2), 250–262.

Donlan, D. Teaching models, experience, and locus of control: Analysis of a summer inservice program for composition teachers. *Research in the Teaching of English*, December 1980, *14*(4), 319–330.

Elbow, P. *Writing without teachers*. New York: Oxford University Press, 1973.

Emig, J. *The composing processes of twelfth graders*. Urbana, Ill.: National Council of Teachers of English, 1971.

Emig, J. Writing as a mode of learning. *College Composition and Communication*, 1977, *28*, 122–128.

Fagan, E. R., & Laine, C. H. Two perspectives of undergraduate English teacher preparation. *Research in the Teaching of English*, February 1980, *14*(1), 67–72.

Fraser, I. S., & Hodson, L. M. Twenty-one kicks at the grammar horse. *English Journal*, December 1978, *67*(9), 49–54.

Gere, A. R. Writing well is the best revenge. *College Composition and Communication*, October 1978, *29*(3), 256–260.

Goswami, D., & Odell, L. *Studying writing: Theories, contexts, and applications*. Rochelle Park, N.J.: Hayden Book Company, in press.

Graves, D. H. *Balance the basics: Let them write*. New York: Ford Foundation, 1978.

Hogan, C. Let's not scrap the impromptu test essay yet. *Research in the Teaching of English*, Winter 1977, *2*(3), 219–225.

Hook, J. N., Jacobs, P. H., & Crisp, R. D. *Illinois state-wide curriculum study center in the preparation of secondary school English teachers* (USOE Project No. HE-145; USOE Contract No. OE-5-10-029). Chicago: University of Illinois, 1969.

Kolin, M. Closing the books on alchemy. *College Composition and Communication*, 1981, *32*(2), 139–151.

Larson, R. A statement on the preparation of teachers of English and language arts. *College English*, September 1978, *40*(1), 70–82.

Loban, W. *Language development: Kindergarten through grade twelve*. Urbana, Ill.: National Council of Teachers of English, 1976.

Mandel, B. J. Losing one's mind: Learning to write and edit. *College Composition and Communication*, December 1978, *29*(4), 362–368.

Mellon, J. C. *National assessment and the teaching of English*. Urbana, Ill.: National Council of Teachers of English, 1975.

Mellon, J. C. Round two of the national writing assessment—interpreting the apparent decline of writing ability: A review. *Research in the Teaching of English*, Spring 1976, *10*(1), 66–74.

Moslemi, M. H. The grading of creative writing essays. *Research in the Teaching of English*, 1975, *9*, 154–161.

Newkirk, T. Grammar instruction and writing: What we don't know. *English Journal*, December 1978, *67*(9), 46–54.

O'Donnell, R. C. Research in the teaching of English: Some observations and questions. *English Education*, February 1979, *10*(3), 181–183.

Quisenberry, J. D. English teacher preparation: What's happening? *English Education*, May 1981, *13*(2), 70–78.

Schuessler, B. F., Gere, A. R., & Abbott, R. D. The development of scales measuring teacher attitudes toward instruction in written composition: A preliminary investigation. *Research in the Teaching of English*, February 1981, *15*(1), 55–63.

Smith, E. B., Goodman, K. S., & Meredith, R. *Language and thinking in school* (2nd ed.). New York: Holt, Rinehart & Winston, 1976.

Stallard, C. K. An analysis of the writing behavior of good student writers. *Research in the Teaching of English*, Summer 1974, *8*(2), 206–218.

Stallard, C. K. Composing: A cognitive process theory. *College Composition and Communication*, 1976, *28*, 181–184.

Stoen, D. Stuttering pencils. *English Journal*, November 1976, *65*(8), 40–41.

Tovatt, A. Oral-aural-visual stimuli for teaching composition. *English Journal*, 1965, *54*(8), 191–195.

Tovatt, A., & Miller, E. L. The sound of writing. *Research in the Teaching of English*, 1967, *7*, 176–189.

Tucker, R. W., & Smithers, A. G. Cognitive style and linguistic style. *Educational Review*, 1977, *29*(4), 6.

Winterowd, W. R. *Contemporary rhetoric*. New York: Harcourt Brace Jovanovich, 1975.

Witkin, R. W. *The intelligence of feeling*. London: Heinemann Educational Books, 1974.

17

The registers of student and professional expository writing: Influences on teachers' responses

SARAH WARSHAUER FREEDMAN
University of California, Berkeley

Would teachers evaluate expository prose written by professional writers as better than that written by college students? The answer to this question seems obvious. Professional writers are generally thought to be more skillful as writers than college students (Atlas, 1979; Flower & Hayes, 1980; Sommers, 1980). Thus, teachers who are thought to value such skill should prefer professionals' essays to those of college students. The real answer, however, is not so clear-cut. I found that when I asked professional writers and college students to produce essays under similar conditions (assigned topic, 45-minute time limit) and that when teachers judged these essays, thinking they all had been written by students, the teachers did not evaluate the professional essays as better across the board.

Two explanations for this unexpected finding seem plausible. First, professionals, given a constrained writing situation, may not be able to demonstrate their skill and thus may not produce better essays than many students. Atlas (1979), Flower and Hayes (1980), and Sommers (1980) found that professionals, even on constrained, assigned tasks, exhibited different problem-solving and revision strategies than did the nonexpert student. However, no one has examined in detail differences in the quality of the essays that these two groups produce. It may be the case that professionals' essays do not deserve to be judged as better across the board. A second conceivable explanation for the finding that teachers in general did not give higher ratings to professional essays has to do with the teachers. If the professionals wrote superior essays, teachers, when blind to whose writing they are judging, may not value the generally more skillful professional writing because something within the essays biases them. For example, Markham (1976) has demonstrated that handwriting features may bias raters. And Hake and Williams (1981) have found that syntactic style and black English vernacular may be sources of bias. Certainly, professionals who assume a student role might write in ways that could bias raters.

These two explanations, one focusing on the writer and the other on the evaluator, are not mutually exclusive. Evidence from two sources, the patterns of the teachers' judgments and the essays themselves, lends support to both. However, most of the evidence supports the second explanation—that the teachers often did not value the greater skill demonstrated by the professional.

For this study, I first had 64 college students write essays. Each wrote on one of eight expository topics, with eight students writing on each topic. Half of the topics asked students to compare and contrast two quotations; the other topics asked them to argue their opinion on a current controversial topic. A sample of each type of topic follows:

1. A Founding Father said: "Get what you can, and what you get hold: 'Tis the Stone that will turn all your Lead into Gold." A contemporary writer said: "If it feels good, do it." What do these two statements say? Explain how they are alike and how they are different.
2. Do you think the drinking age in California should or should not be lowered to 18? Give reasons for the position you take.[1]

I chose the expository mode since this is the mode most commonly taught in college-level required writing classes and is the mode most frequently called for in proficiency and placement essay tests.

The students were enrolled in required writing classes at four San Francisco-area colleges ranging in type from highly select private schools to open-admissions public schools. Thus, the student writers exhibited a wide range of abilities.

I next recruited eight professional writers from different parts of the United States, each to write on one of the eight topics. Initially, all eight agreed to write; only five completed the task. Although I agreed to keep the identities of these writers confidential, the following information indicates their caliber. All have published books and articles, and all have had extensive experience teaching composition at the college level. One is a novelist and poet; one is a literary scholar and the author of a freshman rhetoric text and has directed a freshman composition program at a major university; one is an eminent researcher on composition; another has authored a bestselling text on teaching writing and is a literary scholar.

Four experienced college writing teachers, who also were experienced with holistic rating, evaluated the essays. First, all four teachers rated each essay with a four-point holistic scale. They judged each essay

1. All topics are detailed in Freedman (1977, pp. 73–75, 198–200). The balanced design for assigning a particular topic to a given student is also elaborated there (pp. 76–77, 201).

independently and read the essays in topic sets. In each set, there were the eight student essays on the topic and one professional essay if it was available. The professional essay was always placed at the end of the set so that it would not influence how the raters reacted to the student essays. I feared that if the professional essays were placed early and were too good, they might raise the raters' expectations to unrealistic heights for the subsequent student essays. If no professional essay was available, an extra student essay was included in the set so that the raters would be reading the same number of essays in every set. After the holistic ratings were completed, two raters evaluated each essay with an analytic rating scale.[2] The scale, modeled after Diederich's (1974), contained six categories: voice, development, organization, sentence structure, word choice, and usage. The two raters independently gave each paper a score of 1 to 6 in each of the categories, so that the highest summed analytic score a paper could receive from each rater was 36 and the lowest was 6.

The patterns of the teachers' judgments for the students and for the professionals proved quite different. First, I will examine the scores the teachers gave the different groups on the two rating scales, and then I will look at differences in their reliability as they rated the two groups of essays.

On the holistic scale, the teachers rated reliably. According to Cronbach's alpha, the reliability of the differences in papers was high ($\alpha = .84$) and the consistency of differences between readers was low ($\alpha = .20$) for ratings with the holistic scale. On this scale, the teachers did not give the professionals much better scores than they gave the students. The average score given a professional on a four-point holistic scale was 2.65; the average score given a student was 2.24. According to a t test, the difference in the mean holistic score for the professional versus the student groups was insignificant ($t = 1.19$). Although professional holistic scores were slightly better on the average, students received the three highest holistic scores.

On the analytic scale the professionals fared better. The averaged summed analytic score given the professionals as 30.2; the average for the students was 19.5. According to a t test, the difference in the mean analytic score for the professional versus the student groups was significant at the .02 level of confidence ($t = 2.43$). Whereas on the holistic scale students received the three highest scores, on the analytic scale professionals received the three highest scores. Since the professional papers would receive consistently higher scores when rated analytically than when rated holistically, those professionals who received the same

2. The complete design for the rating system can be found in Freedman (1977, pp. 80–83, 204).

ratings as the students on the holistic scale could expect to receive ratings higher than their student counterparts on the analytic scale.

Table 17-1 compares the analytic scores for each professional paper with the range of analytic scores for the student papers that received holistic scores identical with the professionals'. In the table, the scores are summed across both raters. So, for the holistic rating, across four raters, with the top score given by each rater being a 4, a paper could receive a high holistic score of 16 if it received a 4 from all four raters. And on the analytic scale, a paper could receive as many as 36 points from each of two raters for a maximum of 72 points. Notice, in Table 17-1, that the professional papers that received a summed holistic score of 9 received summed analytic scores of 55 and 59; the student papers receiving a holistic score of 9 were given analytic scores between 34 and 54. Actually, only one of these students received a 54; the others received scores below 49. The other holistic/analytic comparisons in Table 17-1 bear out the discrepancy between students' and professionals' holistic and analytic scores.

A breakdown of the analytic scale by categories revealed that the professionals had received outstanding scores on voice, sentence structure, word choice, and usage. But they were not judged so consistently high on the categories of development and organization. The boost in the analytic scores came primarily from high scores in the more technical, style-oriented categories (sentence structure, word choice, and usage) and from the style/personality category (voice). It is interesting that the directions to the raters regarding the voice category instructed them to give a high score to anyone who wrote with a distinctive voice or personality; the directions did not include anything about liking that

Table 17-1. *Professional versus Student Scores*

	Analytic score range	
Holistic score	Professional	Student
4	—	22–28
5	—	12–38
6	—	31–42
7	—	26–42
8	—	24–47
9	55–57	34–54
10	59	27–55
11	67	37–57
12	—	39–49
13	—	43–58
14	64	52
15	—	47–56

voice or personality. So it was possible for a rater to give a high score to a paper with a distinctive voice even if the rater disliked the voice that was there. This breakdown of scores on the analytic scale shows that the raters gave the professionals credit for their technique (sentence structure, word choice, and usage) and for the presence of a voice.

In another study I had average-quality student essays revised to be either weaker or stronger in development, organization, sentence structure, and mechanics (Freedman, 1977, 1979a, 1979b). I then presented the revised essays to raters to see how strength or weakness in the different categories would influence their holistic scores. I found that the traits of an essay that contribute most to a rater's holistic judgment are development and organization as opposed to sentence structure and mechanics. In the present study, the raters' lower judgments of the professional essays in the development and organization categories of the analytic scale indicate that they would be inclined to give lower holistic scores. These low analytic and holistic scores led me to suspect that either the development and organization were inadequate in the professional essays, and thus had caused the lowered scores, or that something else within these essays had caused the raters to rate them low in these areas. Certainly, these two analytic categories and the holistic scale provided a convenient channel through which the raters could indicate bias, since these parts of the rating system allowed more subjectivity than the other parts.

The following reliability pattern also supports the conclusion that some factors common in the professional essays but not in the student essays had led raters to respond differently, and sometimes in a negative way, to the professional essays. As I noted earlier, the four raters were very reliable when rating the 64 student essays holistically; that is, they agreed well with one another on holistic scores for the student papers. However, about the professional essays, the raters disagreed violently with one another. The four holistic scores for each of the five professional essays are shown in Table 17-2. For every essay, there was at least one two-point disagreement, and two essays (1P and 5P) received the lowest score possible from one rater and the highest score possible from another.

In contrast, the scores for five randomly selected student papers in Table 17-2 demonstrate the raters' usual reliable pattern. Notice that in four out of five cases (1S, 2S, 3S, and 5S) three of the four raters gave identical scores, with one rater just one point off from the other three. In only one case (4S) was there a two-point discrepancy, and then the two agreeing raters gave scores in the middle. For the professionals the two-point discrepancies followed a different pattern. In all cases when raters agreed (2P, 3P, 4P, and 5P), their scores were higher than the

Table 17-2. Holistic Scores—Individual Raters

	Professional essays					Student essays				
Rater	1P	2P	3P	4P	5P	1S	2S	3S	4S	5S
1	1	2	1	2	1	3	1	2	2	3
2	2	4	3	1	4	3	1	1	2	3
3	4	4	3	3	4	3	1	2	1	4
4	3	4	2	3	2	2	2	2	3	3

other raters', indicating perhaps that these other, lower scores should have been higher and were given because the raters were inappropriately biased. Only one of the raters, rater 3, liked all of the professional essays, giving them all scores of 3 or 4. Rater 1 generally was displeased, giving all the professionals scores of 1 or 2. The other two raters gave the professionals the whole range of scores, liking some essays and disliking others, but not agreeing on the essays they liked and the ones they disliked. Some qualities in the professional essays seemed to attract attention, enough attention to jar the raters and make them all, except rater 3, give low holistic scores on some occasions.

The holistic/analytic scale differences combined with this odd reliability pattern at least indicate that the raters generally responded to the professional essays differently from the way they responded to the student essays. Because something within the essays produced erratic scoring and probably some biased responses from most raters, my next step was to analyze the student and professional essays in order to account for the scoring. Others who have examined the differences between student and professional prose have counted the frequency of occurrence of particular linguistic features in student writing and published professional prose (e.g., Hunt, 1965; Christensen, 1967). Since the teachers in this study gave the professionals lower scores for development and organization, I was not as interested in syntactic features as in the larger features of the text that might have influenced the teachers' judgments. So I examined the essays as a literary critic, looking for major differences in development and organization as well as for differences in style or approach that might have biased the raters. I also informed my observations with work in discourse analysis in linguistics.

As I began my critical examination of the essays, I found that the professional essays were well developed but that their organizational patterns were, at times, unconventional. Since essay length may be considered a rough measure of development, it is interesting to note that the professional essays averaged 694 words. The number of words averaged 416 for the two top-scoring student essays on each topic for which there was a professional essay. Interestingly, essay length usually correlates strongly and positively with raters' scores (e.g., Nold & Freedman, 1977; Grobe, 1981).

However, what stood out more than either the development or the organization was an obvious difference in the tone of the sets of texts. The professionals' writing seemed more informal and casual than the students'. The professionals did not distance themselves from their readers; rather, they tried to establish closeness with their informality. One important marker of this informality was the professionals' frequent use of the first-person pronoun "I," with four out of five using the first person throughout their papers and with three of the five beginning their essays with the focus on themselves. The first words of these three essays were:

> 1P. I feel most strongly that . . .
> 2P. First, I want to answer . . .
> 3P. You've asked me to comment on . . . and I've made a goodfaith effort to do so.

Students, by contrast, tend to begin differently. The following openers are typical of the top-ranked student essays:

> 1S. Different assumptions underlie the two quotes presented.
> 2S. The two statements from topic B are spoken from two different points of view . . .
> 3S. In recent years a great controversy has been raised concerning abortions.

Certainly, students use the first-person pronoun, even to open their papers. But they generally do so only in response to the demand of a topic asking whether or not they agree with a particular point of view, and then they are quick to depersonalize. An example:

> I agree with the court's decision, although it may lead to many problems. Mercy killing is a question which is, in most instances throughout history, handled by individual decisions.

Besides the use of the first-person pronoun, the professionals conveyed a familiar tone by seeming actually to speak to the reader directly. The third professional writer (3P) begins directly with a statement to "you," the reader. The one writer who did not use the first-person pronoun spoke to the reader inside parenthetical remarks, which he punctuated with dashes: "In a commercial civilization—and American civilization is just that—language is, more often than not used deceitfully. . . ." As a matter of fact, four of the five made frequent use of the dash in this way, while the fifth writer put long segments of discourse in parentheses. Interestingly, these punctuation conventions usually are associated with less formal, more personal forms, such as the letter. Every professional writer used one or more of these punctuation devices to establish informality and familiarity. I could find no instances when high-scoring student writers attempted to establish familiarity with the reader in these ways. Hayes and Flower (1979) and Atlas (1979) both noted that their experts wrote in a more personal style than their novices, and Atlas identified these differences "especially in the personalization of the opening paragraph" (p. 18).

By applying the concept of speech registers to written language, one can see why the professional writers may have chosen such an informal style. Speech registers are marked in three key ways: by their context, by the relationship between the speaker and the hearer, and by their linguistic form.[3] An example of a speech register is nurse–patient talk in a hospital. The social context is the hospital; the nurse is in a superior role to the patient, who is often helpless and dependent on the nurse; and the linguistic features typical of baby talk are rampant in the nurse's speech as he or she addresses the patient with a line such as: "Did we have our dinner tonight?" Writers, it seems, parallel speakers by writing in certain social contexts (e.g., the school), establishing certain role relationships with their readers (e.g., inferior student writer to superior teacher), and marking their prose linguistically to indicate the register they are using (e.g., the professionals' already described marks of informality, which they perhaps used to indicate that they were not subordinate to their readers).

In comparing the student and professional prose written within the context of this study, I believe that the professionals' display of informality and the students' usual formality can be traced back to their natural or usual registers. The normal context for professional prose is the nonschool world. The professionals' role is usually superior to that of his or her readers, who consist of uninformed strangers whom the professional expects to inform. The professional writes to this audience about deeply held beliefs and novel ideas. For students, on the other hand, the normal writing context is the school. The student generally writes for a teacher–reader and is in a subordinate role to the teacher since the teacher will evaluate the prose and instruct the student. The student writer is necessarily in a subordinate role to the teacher–evaluator, who possesses all the power and most of the knowledge. Rarely is the student's audience wider than the teacher, and then it commonly includes only other members of a writing class. When writing, the student, as a subordinate, must use linguistic forms that show respect, deference, and the proper degree of formality. Just as the

3. This concept of speech register is derived from the work of Bloch (1974, 1975) and Olson (1980).

student cannot assume that it is all right to call the teacher by his or her first name, the student cannot presume to establish too much closeness or be too informal with the teacher–reader. So the students in this study wrote formally as they usually do for school writing.

But the professionals were unused to writing as subservient students and could not easily assume this role. They knew they were at least the peers of their readers and thus felt free to write informally and casually. Some even seemed to be rubbing in their status, writing too casually. The professionals' prose took on the tone of a friendly letter, full of dashes, addressed to a reader of equal or lower status.

The teacher–readers in this study, expecting prose from student subordinates, may well have reacted against the professionals' too familiar tone. In the context of this study and of other school writing, students who write informally do so because they do not know what the appropriate formality level is for the occasion or because they do not know how to show the appropriate degree of formality as they write. As a matter of fact, students who write too formally may be trying to achieve the proper formality level, but like students who write too informally, they do not know how to achieve the level they desire, and so they write gobbledegook that seems to parody academic prose.

A second striking difference between the student and professional essays in this study was that three of the five essays by professionals were marked by an initial defiance of the task that ended in acceptance of the task. One of the professionals who began his essay defiantly said, "First I want to answer 'damned if I know.' Then 'who cares?'" In the third paragraph, he made a transition to his acceptance: "What is more interesting to me than the answer is the reasoning I'm forced to go through to achieve my considered indifference. For the issue is full of things to which I am not indifferent." And with the beginning of the fourth paragraph, he writes more conventionally, "First of all it is clear to me that drinking *is* a problem in our society." This initial defiance resulted in what the teachers may have judged as weak organization, but the organization of such essays was not weak once the defiant first section had ended.

Students usually accept assigned tasks without rebelling on paper, but the few times that they take a defiant stance in an essay they generally carry through with their defiance adamantly. And in doing so, they expect to be penalized by the teacher–reader. The initial defiance on the part of the professionals seemed to occur when they felt alienated by their topics and by the situation. The defiance did not take the form of a diatribe from which they could not recover; rather, the professionals seemed not to be able to write without first overcoming their honest alienation. Some reacted to the time limitation and to the overwhelming initial alienation they felt by expressing their feelings on paper as they tried to cope with the constraints of the writing situation and to find something within the topic that was personally meaningful, to discover an honest approach. Most students do not go through this process of establishing a serious commitment to the topic, especially when writing an in-class assigned essay, and so they would never show such a step on paper. The initial musings of the professionals on paper did seem inappropriate content to be included in a polished essay. Since the musings were so unconventional and were inappropriate to a finished product, some raters may have penalized the professional writers for them. And since some of the writers honestly admitted their hostility toward the task, this admission easily could have been comprehended as a student's overstepping his or her role instead of as a struggle by a professional to cope with a difficult situation.

Searle's (1969) differentiation between two types of questions, "real questions" and "exam questions," may clarify why the professionals were compelled to find meaning in these topics. "In real questions S [speaker] wants to know (find out) the answer; in exam questions S wants to know if H [hearer] knows" (p. 66). In the context of the present study, S is the teacher who assigns the topic—or, in Searle's terms, asks the question—and H is the student or professional who receives the topic and then responds to it. When a teacher in a classroom assigns an essay topic, he or she is assigning an "exam" question. In this case, the teacher wants to know not what the student knows, but how well the student knows how to write. And as Horner (1979) has noted, students interpret such topics as "exam" topics. In the real world, when professional writers assign themselves a topic, they generate "real" questions to which their readers presumably do not know the answers. The professionals in this study seem to have approached their teacher-assigned "exam" questions as though they were "real" questions. The raters did not expect the writers to answer "real" questions; rather, they expected them to answer "exam" questions. And all five writers, whether they were initially alienated by their topic or liked their topic, wrote as though the topics posed "real" rather than "exam" questions.

A third general difference between the two sets of papers surfaced in the level of emotional commitment the professionals exhibited toward the topics. Once they accepted the task, they wrote with passion, with feeling, and with definiteness. This emotional commitment may stem from the fact that the topics were or became "real" to the professionals. One professional attacked the author of a quotation about which he was writing as "the self-assured, moralizing, and to me, pompous sort of person who delights in highly generalized pronouncements to an audience. . . ." Another said about politicians and advertisers, "Both groups of language-mongers twist words and phrases—and communication distortion be damned!—to achieve their desired ends." Another author concluded his argument in favor of abortion with, "But niceness about the idea that the embryo is a sacred life—at any point during gestation—is a sentimental fastidiousness that we cannot as a society afford—not if we intend to have a society fit to live in for our children's children." The professionals did not argue irrationally. They wrote emotionally and definitely because they were able to develop a commitment to their assigned topics and because their role as an authority demands this style. Although the teachers should not have penalized the professionals for writing definitely, they may have, since they would not expect students to exercise such authority. Students mitigate their statements or give the expected cliché-like responses. Professionals typically make unexpected points and offer strong, decisive statements about these points.

A fourth and final difference that marked the professional essays was that the writers exhibited evidence of varied and broad experience with the world. One of the writers used many scholarly references to lend support to his opinions—Forrester, Schumacher, Mills, and Rawls. Another referred to Aristotle. Scholarly reading formed a significant part of the professionals' personal experience. Even the examples from personal experience that the professionals brought to the task were, at times, different in kind from the examples the students brought. Because the teacher-readers had less experience, the scholarly allusions and personal experiences marked the writer as more powerful and statusful than the reader. The evaluators, thinking the professionals were students, could not believe the extent of the scholarly experiences that the professionals displayed.

In some manifestation, all four of these distinctive markers of professional written discourse—familiarity with audience, task defiance/acceptance, commitment to topic, and scholarly experience—could have influenced some teachers to evaluate a given essay more negatively than they should have. By examining the role relationship between the reader and writer, one sees a plausible explanation for why the teacher-readers sometimes reacted negatively to the professional writers' essays. With all four markers, the professionals violated their expected student roles: they were threateningly familiar, some defied the task, they wrote too definitely about novel ideas, and they displayed a literally unbelievable amount of knowledge. Although the teachers may have been justified in penalizing the writers for an inappropriately familiar tone and for the task defiance, they might have overreacted to these features. This may have caused them to react against the other features of definiteness and knowledge, and thus sometimes not to give credit to the professionals for what they had done well (e.g., development).

Whenever writers violate their expected roles, their readers are prone to react negatively, just as hearers do when speakers violate their roles. Such violations can even cause miscomprehension. Searle (1969) discusses how our social roles "infect" the ways in which our speech acts are comprehended. He explains how only someone in authority over someone else can issue a command. If the speaker does not have authority over the hearer, a command will not be comprehended as such. Likewise, if a reader (teacher) does not perceive the writer (student or professional) to have authority and if the writer takes authority, much of the writer's language can be misinterpreted and misevaluated. The teachers thought they were rating student papers, papers written by writers who were their subordinates. Since the professionals did not write as subordinates, the teachers could well have miscomprehended the intent of the writers and evaluated the papers in a biased way. For example, the informal dashes might have signaled to the evaluator that the writer lacked knowledge about the expected expository form. Indeed, in an informal discussion after the ratings, one rater accused one of the professionals, who had used quite a few scholarly references in his piece, of "obnoxious name-dropping." I doubt that the rater, an advanced graduate student, would have entertained this thought, much less expressed it, had he been aware that the essay was written by one of his most admired professors rather than by the lowly student whom he understood to be dropping names.

The writing and rating situations in this study were admittedly special and unusual. Teachers usually know whose writing they are reading, and professional writers usually do not write solely to be evaluated. Nevertheless, the results of the rating and the analysis of the essays bring up some issues for writing teachers to consider.

First, teachers may have biased responses to prose, especially when we feel that our role as an authority has been threatened. Like the professionals in this study, students probably overstep their roles from time to time when they write. As teachers we may tend to overreact to this overstepping, taking it as a threat to our authority, misunderstanding the writer's intent, and thus penalizing the student unfairly. Teachers must guard against this source of bias when evaluating student writing, especially since shows of authority are marks of professional prose.

Second, one of the problems that many students exhibit when they write is a lack of force, a lack of commitment to their topics. I do not believe that most of us take into account how much the teacher–student role relationship militates against the student's ability to write with force and authority. The amount of force a student can show is most likely directly related to the student's power over the topic and the audience. The more the student thinks he or she knows as opposed to what the audience knows, the more forceful the student will be able to be. As teachers we must remember that part of a strong self-concept and force comes from knowledge. Students must become intimate with and committed to their topics. We should teach students to become flexible enough to develop commitments even to topics that at first may seem uninteresting, as the professionals in this study did. Most important of all, once we ask for and get forceful writing, we must be careful not to show bias and penalize the writer inadvertently for what may appear to be a student's overstepping of his or her role. As teachers, we must be secure enough to help our students, as they advance, become better, yes better, writers than we ourselves are.

REFERENCES

Atlas, M. *Writer insensitivity to audience: Causes and cures.* Paper presented at annual meeting of American Educational Research Association, San Francisco, 1979.

Bloch, M. Symbols, song, dance and features of articulation. *Archives Européenes de Sociologie,* 1974, *15,* 51–81.

Bloch, M. (Ed.). *Political language and oratory in practitional society.* London: Academic Press, 1975.

Christensen, F. *Notes toward a new rhetoric: Six essays for teachers.* New York: Harper & Row, 1967.

Diederich, P. B. *Measuring growth in English.* Urbana, Ill.: National Council of Teachers of English, 1974.

Flower, L., & Hayes, J. R. The cognition of discovery: Defining a rhetorical problem. *College Composition and Communication,* 1980, *31,* 21–32.

Freedman, S. *Influences on the evaluators of student writing.* Unpublished doctoral dissertation, Stanford University, 1977.

Freedman, S. How characteristics of student essays influence teachers' evaluations. *Journal of Educational Psychology,* 1979, *71,* 328–338. (a)

Freedman, S. Why teachers give the grades they do. *College Composition and Communication,* 1979, *30,* 161–164. (b)

Grobe, C. Syntactic maturity, mechanics, and vocabulary as predictors of quality ratings. *Research in the Teaching of English,* 1981, *15,* 75–85.

Hake, R., & Williams, J. Style and its consequences: Do as I do, not as I say. *College English,* 1981, *43,* 433–451.

Hayes, J. R., & Flower, L. *Writing as problem solving.* Paper presented at meeting of American Educational Research Association, San Francisco, 1979.

Horner, W. Speech-act and text-act theory: "Theme-ing" in freshman composition. *College Composition and Communication,* 1979, *30,* 165–169.

Hunt, K. *Grammatical structures written at three grade levels* (Research Report No. 3). Urbana, Ill.: National Council of Teachers of English, 1965.

Markham, L. Influences of handwriting quality on teacher evaluation of written work. *American Educational Research Journal,* 1976, *13,* 277–283.

Nold, E., & Freedman, S. An analysis of readers' responses to essays. *Research in the Teaching of English,* 1977, *11,* 164–174.

Olson, D. On the language and authority of textbooks. *Journal of Communication,* 1980, *30,* 186–196.

Searle, J. *Speech acts: An essay in the philosophy of language.* London: Cambridge University Press, 1969.

Sommers, N. Revision strategies of student writers and experienced adult writers. *College Composition and Communication,* 1980, *31,* 378–388.

18

Measuring teachers' attitudes toward writing instruction

ANNE RUGGLES GERE
BRIAN F. SCHUESSLER
ROBERT D. ABBOTT
University of Washington

Research on teacher effectiveness is not new. Brownell (1948) suggested criteria for teacher effectiveness research, and his suggestions have been echoed by educational researchers of succeeding generations. Although research in the area has long existed, we still know little about what constitutes effective composition instruction. For example, the relatively recent establishment and preliminary investigations of the Conference on College Composition and Communication's Committee on Teaching and Its Evaluation, attest to how little is known about effective composition instruction.

One explanation for this paucity of knowledge lies in the state of teacher effectiveness research generally. Few studies of teacher effectiveness have considered all of Brownell's (1948) three criteria: (1) presage variables (teacher personality, knowledge, attitudes, status characteristics); (2) process variables (classroom activities); and (3) product variables (measures of student change/learning). In the case of research on the effectiveness of composition instruction, investigations are hampered by inadequate measures of presage variables among composition teachers. The new direction here, then, is a measure of teachers' attitudes toward the teaching of composition, a measure that can contribute to presage variables in evaluating composition instruction.

Existing measures of writing teachers' attitudes lack evidence of construct validity. One such instrument is the Knowledge and Attitude in Written Composition, Test B (Jacobs & Evans, 1969). This test elicits attitudes with respect to two issues: emphasis on form and emphasis on content. Lin's (1974) survey measures three dimensions of teacher attitudes toward language function. The Attitude Scale: Writers and Writing (Blake, 1976) measures attitudes in three areas: skills of writing, varieties of writing, and kinds of writers. Finally, Klinger's (1977) essay

348

questionnaire investigates teacher recognition of and response to mechanical and structural faults in a 435-word student paper.

Three other measures (Zemelman, 1977; Behrens, 1978; Donlan, 1979) examine several dimensions of instruction. Zemelman's (1977) interview protocol considers five major areas of composition ranging from context for writing to evaluation. Behrens's (1978) survey solicits response to eight categories of questions that include several aspects of teaching practices. Donlan's (1979) Methodology Inventory, which solicits response on five stages of writing and three categories of language development, measures several dimensions of composition instruction, dimensions that parallel the current range of instructional approaches. However, all of these measures ignore a more important issue in the design of measurements.

This more important issue is validity. Measures of individual differences should be designed to provide evidence of convergent validity—that is, an indication that two independent measures of the same dimension produce similar information. It is also important to show that a measure had discriminant validity—that is, it is not simply an extension of some test with which the measure was intended to differ (Campbell & Fiske, 1959). Little evidence of convergent and discriminant validity was provided in studies designed by Jacobs and Evans (1969), Lin (1974), Blake (1976), Klinger (1977), Zemelman (1977), Behrens (1978), and Donlan (1979).

In order to sample a wide domain of attitudes toward the instruction of writing, items from the Composition Opinionnaire (NCTE, 1971) were grouped into a questionnaire. These items were originally developed by a committee of the National Council of Teachers of English and were designed to sample salient dimensions in the instruction of writing. Items of the opinionnaire that did not conform to rules for stating items in attitude scales (Nunnally, 1978) were rewritten or if their content overlapped with other items, discarded. The final questionnaire consisted of 47 items on composition instruction and the 26-item Writing Apprehension scale (Daly & Miller, 1975). Subjects responded to all 73 items on a 5-point Likert-type scale: (1) strongly disagree, (2) disagree, (3) no opinion, (4) agree, and (5) strongly agree. The content of the items was distributed throughout the questionnaire. The questionnaire and a self-addressed, stamped return envelope were mailed to 675 members of the Washington State Council of Teachers of English.

Results

Data were obtained from the 311 of the 675 questionnaires that were returned. One hundred subjects were male, 198 were female, and 13 did not indicate their gender. The mean age of the teachers was 41.5 years, and the mean number of years spent teaching English was 12.91. Thirty-five elementary, 227 secondary, 16 community college, and 33 college or university teachers completed questionnaires.

On the basis of rational construct definitions, earlier research (Schuessler, Gere, & Abbott, 1981), and the intercorrelations of the responses to the items, scales were developed. This was an iterative process that resulted in four scales of 10 items each. The four scales dealt with: (1) attitudes toward the importance of standard English in the instruction of writing (Standard English); (2) attitudes toward the importance of defining and evaluating writing tasks in the instruction of writing (Defining and Evaluating); (3) attitudes toward the importance of student self-expression in the instruction of writing (Student Self-Expression); and (4) attitudes toward the importance of linguistic maturity in the instruction of writing (Linguistic Maturity). Table 18-1 lists the items in each scale and the mean and the standard deviation of ratings for these items. High ratings on an item represent agreement, and low ratings represent disagreement. Three items were added to the Student Self-Expression scale that had not been used in the corresponding scale in the earlier research (Schuessler, *et al.*, 1981). These new items are the last three in the Student Self-Expression scale in Table 18-1. One item in the Linguistic Maturity scale that appeared in the scale in the earlier research—"Correct English should be required of all students in the high school"—was dropped. The last item in the Linguistic Maturity scale was added. Rational and empirical criteria were used to determine the changes.

Table 18-2 indicates sample sizes, mean scores, standard deviations, and Cronbach alpha reliability coefficients for each of the four scales. Here again, high scores on the scales represent agreement, and low scores represent disagreement. All analyses in this chapter were based on all available data. Failure to respond to specific items accounts for differing sample sizes. However, no systematic tendencies to omit certain items were noted.

Scores on each of the four scales were intercorrelated, and these correlations among scales are shown in Table 18-3. Interpretation of these correlations indicates that the scale scores are relatively independent and thus are not measuring a unidimensional attitude. The degree of convergent and discriminant validity was investigated further by correlating a teacher's response to an item with a score based on all the other items in the scale. These item remainder correlations are shown in column *r* of Table 18-1. If we interpret a teacher's response to a single item as a separate measure of the attitude, then the correlation between a rating on the item and response to the remainder of the scale can be interpreted in terms of convergent validity of item and scale.

Table 18-1. Items in Each Scale, Mean and Standard Deviation of Item Responses,[a] and the Correlation between the Item and Its Scale (Excluding the Item)

M	SD	r	Item
			Standard English scale: The importance of standard English in the instruction of written composition
1.81	.93	.40	1. In order to avoid errors in sentence structure, weak students should be encouraged to write only short, simple sentences.
1.54	.82	.34	2. High school students should be discouraged from using figurative language because their efforts at metaphor so often produce only clichés.
2.22	1.14	.44	3. Students should not be allowed to begin sentences with *and, or, for,* or *but.*
2.40	1.13	.43	4. Students should be discouraged from using the first-person pronoun in their composition.
3.03	1.30	.12	5. The English course for junior high school should include a research paper so that students can learn how to use the library and source materials for papers in their own courses.
2.75	1.21	.30	6. Correct English is established by logical grammatical relationships within the language.
2.71	1.15	.42	7. Students' oral language should be corrected so that the forms will appear in their writing.
1.49	.84	.17	8. High school students who are able to consistently write correct English should not be required to do further work in composition.
2.64	1.26	.43	9. Students should be required to prepare written outlines before they begin writing expository papers.
2.49	1.18	.26	10. There is little research evidence that knowledge of grammar and usage will produce improvement in student writing.[b]
			Defining and Evaluating scale: The importance of defining and evaluating writing tasks in the instruction of written composition
2.04	.99	.47	1. Successful writing is achieved only if all themes are carefully corrected by the teacher.
1.90	.99	.48	2. Grades are the most effective way of motivating students to improve their writing.
2.96	1.29	.42	3. The major obligation of instruction in composition is to help students learn and practice the convention of standard, educated English.
1.75	.90	.46	4. Every error on a student's composition should be indicated.
2.82	1.05	.27	5. Assignments during the last two years of high school should require primarily expository writing.
2.24	1.02	.30	6. Rhetoric as it is pertinent to the composition course concerns only the manner of writing or speaking, not the matter.
1.90	.99	.60	7. Grades are the most effective way of evaluating compositions.
2.15	1.08	.34	8. Students should rewrite each paper regardless of the number or kind of errors.
3.53	1.14	.23	9. By the time they leave high school all students should be able to distinguish clearly among the four forms of discourse: narration, description, exposition, and argumentation.
1.87	.94	.06	10. The major purpose of evaluating compositions is to guide individual student growth and development.[b]

(continued)

Table 18-1. (Continued)

M	SD	r	Item

Student Self-Expression scale:
The importance of student self-expression in the instruction of written composition

M	SD	r	Item
3.13	1.12	.29	1. Teachers should write all compositions they assign to students.
2.10	1.04	.16	2. Compositions written in class should never be given letter grades.
2.80	.98	.20	3. Growth in written self-expression depends in part upon a wide range of first-hand experiences.
3.43	1.07	.33	4. Composition programs in the elementary grades should be directed primarily at encouraging students to self-expression.
4.43	.84	.12	5. Writing assignments should be more extensive than the specification of a topic or list of topics.
3.58	1.09	.33	6. Composition programs in the elementary grades should be designed primarily to help students learn to discipline their writing and develop awareness of accepted standards of good prose.[b]
2.66	1.13	.35	7. Teachers should correct errors on students' papers.[b]
2.87	1.19	.32	8. Strict conformity to rules of standard English inhibits student growth in writing.
3.23	1.08	.27	9. Students given freedom in composing will discover various types of writing for themselves.
3.95	.91	.34	10. Creative dramatization, role-playing, and pantomime have little effect on written composition.[b]

Linguistic Maturity scale:
The importance of linguistic maturity in the instruction of written composition

M	SD	r	Item
4.02	.83	.35	1. The experience of composing can and should nurture the pupils' quest for self-realization and their need to relate constructively to their peers.
4.52	.70	.35	2. The teacher–pupil conference can and should aid learners in finding their strengths and encourage them in correcting some of their weaknesses.
4.04	1.14	.17	3. The techniques of writing and documenting a formal research paper should be taught in high school to all college-bound students.
3.67	.97	.27	4. Students should have freedom in selecting the topics for their compositions.
3.54	1.12	.09	5. Differing teaching approaches must be used for teaching factual writing or objectively oriented writing and for teaching subjectively oriented or imaginative material.
4.29	.94	.29	6. Growth in writing in the elementary school is enhanced by a broad and rich program of literature.
3.85	.86	.25	7. Students should often "talk out" their compositions prior to the writing.
3.67	1.04	.12	8. Able pupils tend to explore different forms and styles of expression and show more variation in quality from one written product to another than do less able pupils.
3.99	1.15	.10	9. Grading a paper or a course with a single letter grade informs no one as to the values sought, whether those of style, content, mechanical accuracy, or a combination of these elements.
3.06	.99	.16	10. Students who speak freely, fluently, and effectively are generally good writers.

[a]Item responses are scored (1) strongly disagree, (2) disagree, (3) no opinion, (4) agree, and (5) strongly agree.

[b]Item responses are reversed in scoring these items, since they correlated negatively with the other items in the scale.

Table 18-2. *Number of Teachers, Means, Standard Deviations, and Alpha Reliability Coefficients for Four 10-Item Scales of Teacher Attitudes toward Instruction in Written Composition*

Scale name	n	M	SD	α
Standard English	277	23.12	5.51	.66
Defining and Evaluating Writing Tasks	286	23.14	5.44	.70
Student Self-Expression	283	33.11	4.88	.60
Linguistic Maturity	290	38.80	4.15	.49

An examination of the means, standard deviations, and Cronbach alphas for various subgroups suggested that these features differed according to the teacher's gender and level of teaching. Consequently, responses were also analyzed separately for teaching level and gender. Scale means, standard deviations, and sample sizes for males and females are shown in Table 18-4; the same for elementary, secondary, community college, and university teachers are shown in Table 18-6. Tables 18-5 and 18-7 show the scale intercorrelations for these two groups.

Discussion

One of the functions of a survey study such as this is to contribute to theory building about teacher attitudes. To this end we considered patterns of correlation in light of current theories about composition. The high positive correlation between Standard English and Defining and Evaluating and between Linguistic Maturity and Student Self-Expression, coupled with the negative correlations between, for example, Defining and Evaluating and Linguistic Maturity or Student Self-Expression (see Table 18-3), suggests that the four scales fall into two subgroups that identify discrete teacher characteristics. Teachers whose scores are high on both the Standard English and the Defining and Evaluating scales agree strongly with items concerning correctness,

Table 18-3. *Intercorrelations of Scales, Based on Total Sample*

	Writing Apprehension	Standard English	Defining and Evaluating Writing Tasks	Student Self-Expression
Standard English	.31	1.00		
Defining and Evaluating Writing Tasks	.10	.58	1.00	
Student Self-Expression	−.12	−.42	−.49	1.00
Linguistic Maturity	−.33	.04	−.17	.25

Table 18-4. Scale Means, Standard Deviations, and Sample Sizes for Males and Females Separately

		Standard English	Defining and Evaluating Writing Tasks	Student Self-Expression	Linguistic Maturity	Writing Apprehension
Male	M	22.41	23.44	32.31	38.35	47.58
	SD	5.50	5.46	4.82	3.42	10.92
	n	97	105	101	102	99
Female	M	23.47	23.02	33.66	39.02	49.51
	SD	5.49	5.45	4.85	4.51	14.80
	n	177	176	178	184	181

usage, and form. They see evaluation as a means of assuring adherence to these. In contrast, teachers who score high on both the Linguistic Maturity and the Student Self-Expression scales agree strongly with items emphasizing the importance of experience, exploration, personal relationships, and individual development in the teaching of writing.

The attitudes of these two groups of teachers are consistent with the two paradigms identified in Kroll's (1980) discussion of composition instruction. According to Kroll, two competing theories of human development—"nature" and "nurture"—underlie most composition instruction. Interventionists, following the nurture principle that environment provides the essential source of development, emphasize the content and agent of instruction, text-centered evaluation, comprehensive error marking, and tightly controlled assignments. Teachers in the interventionist mode, according to Kroll, focus on "such topics as standard usage, sentence structure . . . paragraph structure (methods of development), and written conventions (punctuation and mechanics)" (p. 744). An interventionist program "places priority on teaching the

Table 18-5. Intercorrelations of Scales for Males and Females Separately[a]

	Standard English	Defining and Evaluating Writing Tasks	Student Self-Expression	Linguistic Maturity	Writing Apprehension
Standard English	1.00	.56	−.43	−.02	.40
Defining and Evaluating Writing Tasks	.62	1.00	−.49	−.24	.22
Student Self-Expression	−.47	−.50	1.00	.31	−.21
Linguistic Maturity	.16	−.03	.12	1.00	−.33
Writing Apprehension	.07	−.17	.04	−.36	1.00

[a]Correlations for males are below diagonal, and correlations for females are above diagonal.

Table 18-6. *Scale Means, Standard Deviations, and Sample Sizes for Elementary, Secondary, Community College, and University Teachers*

		Standard English	Defining and Evaluating Writing Tasks	Student Self-Expression	Linguistic Maturity	Writing Apprehension
Elementary	M	22.81	20.83	35.76	39.00	47.23
	SD	3.75	3.62	3.92	4.14	10.89
	n	31	35	34	34	34
Secondary	M	23.75	23.79	32.74	38.80	49.83
	SD	5.56	5.52	4.84	4.29	14.19
	n	208	207	207	213	207
Community college	M	21.30	22.38	33.46	37.54	45.20
	SD	6.23	4.96	5.03	2.63	13.45
	n	10	13	13	13	12
University	M	19.43	21.97	32.52	39.13	44.52
	SD	5.04	5.97	5.38	3.68	10.77
	n	28	30	29	31	31

Table 18-7. *Intercorrelations among Scales Separately by Level of Teaching*

	Standard English	Defining and Evaluating Writing Tasks	Student Self-Expression	Linguistic Maturity	Writing Apprehension
Elementary and secondary[a]					
Standard English	1.00	.49	−.10	.18	.04
Defining and Evaluating Writing Tasks	.56	1.00	−.35	−.15	−.09
Student Self-Expression	−.45	−.43	1.00	.36	−.08
Linguistic Maturity	.03	−.19	.25	1.00	−.43
Writing Apprehension	.30	.13	−.13	−.34	1.00
Community college and university[b]					
Standard English	1.00	.60	−.42	.27	.60
Defining and Evaluating Writing Tasks	.80	1.00	−.74	−.39	−.02
Student Self-Expression	−.64	−.76	1.00	.03	.04
Linguistic Maturity	.08	−.02	.30	1.00	.20
Writing Apprehension	.19	−.10	−.13	−.38	1.00

[a]Correlations for elementary teachers are above diagonal, and correlations for secondary teachers are below diagonal.

[b]Correlations for community college teachers are above diagonal, and correlations for secondary teachers are below diagonal.

basic skills which the students lack, assuming that once students acquire control of such skills their written products will show marked improvement, and therefore, their self-esteem as writers will improve as a matter of course" (p. 750).

Maturationists, on the other hand, follow the "nature" principle that organisms contain the seeds of their own growth. They emphasize personal writing, "writing centered on the experiences and emotions of the students and aimed at fostering personal growth" (Kroll, 1980, p. 746). Further, maturationists conceptualize writing as artistic expression, focus on the process of composing, and try to enable students to experience that process rather than to impart specific knowledge or skills as interventionists do. For the maturationist, evaluation is context-centered. "A student's paper is judged in the context of that student's intentions, effort, and past performance . . . [and overlooks] many specific errors because they are trivial features of a composition and tell little about an individual writer's progress in sincere, self-confident expression" (p. 750). A maturationist writing program "focuses on the self-confidence of the students, assuming that only when these writers are able to engage freely in the process of composing will they produce the quantities of writing necessary for improvement" (p. 751).

Kroll's categories, based on careful examination of educational philosophy and on close observation of composition instruction, are the theoretical counterpart of the two statistical subgroups identified in this study. Comparison of Kroll's description of the maturationist paradigm with items eliciting strong agreement on the Student Self-Expression and Linguistic Maturity scales reveals parallel attributes. Likewise, items with high scores on the Defining and Evaluating and Standard English scales parallel Kroll's description of the interventionist paradigm of composition instruction. This correlation between composition theory and subgroups of items identified by statistical evaluation of the opinionnaire suggests that the opinionnaire can contribute to the development of theories about the relationship between teacher attributes and student achievement.

While the identification of these subgroups and their correspondence with theoretical paradigms is significant, we must also determine that the two scales within each subgroup identify different qualities or the scales have no discriminant validity. The Student Self-Expression and Linguistic Maturity scales may appear to identify dimensions similar to Kroll's maturationist category, but they have a low degree of correlation ($r = .25$), and rational examination of the items in each scale illustrates their theoretical differences. For instance, experience and drama figure in the Student Self-Expression scale, while language itself, or "talk," is more important in the Linguistic Maturity scale. The Student Self-Expression scale's emphasis on growth through exploration and experiences has much in common with Moffett's (1968) views on the development of writing abilities. Moffett emphasizes the importance of drama and experimentation for young writers. Two items in the Student Self-Expression scale mention elementary students specifically, and a number of others refer to developing writers and their need for exploration.

The two items (4 and 5) in the Linguistic Maturity scale that have the highest intrascale correlation both describe students' language use in relation to others. This suggests one of the differences between the Student Self-Expression and Linguistic Maturity scales. Items in the Linguistic Maturity scale refer more frequently to language in relation to others, whereas those in the Student Self-Expression scale refer more to language for the self. In Moffett's terms, Student Self-Expression items describe egocentric uses of language, while the Linguistic Maturity scale describes more decentered language. Thus, we can say that the two scales do identify different qualities.

Differences between the Standard English and Defining and Evaluating scales of the interventionist subgroup are more immediately apparent. Although both focus on the content of a composition course rather than on the student, they address different aspects of that content. Items in the Standard English scale deal with issues of form and usage, while those in the Defining and Evaluating scale speak to the teacher's responsibility for assessing writing. Thus from both an empirical and a rational perspective, we can claim that the four discrete scales in this opinionnaire have sufficient reliability and construct validity to be useful in future investigations of teacher attitudes.

Although the two scales measure different dimensions of language, the relatively low (.49) alpha (see Table 18-2) for the Linguistic Maturity scale raises questions about the reliability of this scale. In an earlier study (Schuessler, et al., 1981), items from this scale produced an alpha of .73. We interpret this difference in alphas as a result of the samples that responded to the opinionnaire. The sample for the earlier study was homogeneous and knowledgeable about linguistic processes in writing. The sample in the present study was more heterogeneous and was probably less knowledgeable about linguistic processes. These factors may have contributed to the lower alpha in the second study because linguistic issues usually divide teachers more than any other issue (Gere & Smith, 1979).

When we turn from constructs represented by the scales to the teacher groups within the sample, we find that while the four scales measure discrete attributes, they are not monolithic. We refer to the previously mentioned differences in means, standard deviations, and alpha according to gender and level of teaching. For example, the negative correlation between Standard English and Student Self-Expression decreases from university to secondary to elementary teachers, which suggests that the two constructs are more distinct for teachers at higher levels of education than for teachers in the elementary school. Likewise, intercorrelations of scales according to gender reveal variations in the relationships between scale constructs. Specifically, correlations between the Writing Apprehension scale and other scales vary according to gender. As Table 18-3 indicates, the correlation between Standard English and Writing Apprehension for the whole sample is .31, but, as Table 18-5 shows, the correlation is .40 for females and .07 for males. For men this correlation is not significant ($r = .07$, $p > .05$), but for women it is significant ($r = .40$, $p < .05$).

This statistically significant correlation supports the hypothesis that female teachers' concern for issues of form and usage in teaching writing may be tied to anxiety about their own writing. Research (Gilley & Summers, 1970; Barron, 1971; Key, 1972; Lakoff, 1975; Kramer, 1974; Thorne & Henley, 1975) has indicated differences between the language of men and women, and an analysis of these differences suggested that women are more sensitive than males to linguistic indicators of lower status and are less likely to use syntactic features characterized by such connotations. This sensitivity to appropriate usages may arise, as Lakoff (1975) suggests, because a woman's position in society depends on how others view her. "She must dress decoratively, look attractive, be compliant, if she is to survive at all in the world. Then her overattention to appearance and appearances (including, perhaps overcorrectness and over gentility of speech and etiquette) is merely the result of being forced to exist only as a reflection in the eyes of others" (p. 27).

Thus the sociological forces that shape women's perceptions of themselves and the language they use may contribute to their anxiety about writing and the related concern with the importance of Standard English demonstrated by women in this study. Other researchers (Campbell & Williamson, 1973) have suggested that teachers may reduce their anxiety by becoming more dogmatic, and a relationship between anxiety and dogmatism is evident in the correlation between the Writing Apprehension and Standard English scales. The correlations for female teachers in our sample are consistent with the Campbell and Williamson hypothesis.

Implications

As is true with much research, this study raises more questions than it answers. For example, the differences in responses to a particular scale according to gender or teaching level suggest the importance of considering subgroups in examinations of teacher attitudes. At the same time, this information poses questions about which demographic features should be considered, how many subgroups should be created, and what weight should be given to whole-group responses as opposed to subgroup responses. In other words, careful examination of teacher attitudes toward composition instruction is complex, and future studies must allow for these complexities.

Just as this study demonstrates the complexity of investigating teacher attitudes toward composition instruction, so it points to the importance of doing this kind of work. The close correspondence that emerged in this study between Kroll's theoretical constructs of interventionist and maturationist approaches to composition instruction and the Standard English/Defining and Evaluating and Linguistic Maturity/Self-Expression groups suggests strong links between empirical and theoretical work regarding views of composition instruction. These links are essential to the theory building that must precede fuller understanding of what constitutes effective composition instruction.

While it is true that teacher attitudes constitute just one small part of the presage variables essential to evaluation of writing instruction, attitudes do play a significant part. In particular, our finding that the Standard English and Writing Apprehension scales correlate significantly for female teachers suggests that anxiety about writing may influence other attitudes toward writing. Since males and females do not differ significantly overall on the Standard English, Defining and Evaluating, Linguistic Maturity, and Self-Expression scales, we need an explanation for the fact that a statistically significant correlation between the Standard English and Apprehension scales appears for female respondents but not for males. One explanation is that for women at least, responses to the Standard English scale are predictable from the Apprehension scale. From this we conclude that anxiety about writing may influence attitudes toward teaching. We recognize that our interpretation of the finding may be confounded by the teaching level of the majority of our sample population. Responses to the Apprehension scale were highest among secondary teachers, the majority group in our sample, and the ratio of females to males at this teaching level in our sample was nearly 2 to 1. However, having acknowledged potential difficulties with our data, we affirm that the construct of anxiety about writing is an important one to consider in research on effective composition instruction because such anxiety appears to predict other attitudes more closely linked to teacher behavior.

Because this study focuses on attitudes only, it suggests little about teacher behaviors. Research indicates that the degree of generality of a statement influences the types of behavior that can be predicted. While items in this study are closer to what Fishbein and Ajzen (1975) define as statements of behavioral intention than to traditional attitude meas-

360 THE INSTRUCTIONAL CONTEXT

ures, they still may not predict teacher behavior in a specific situation. Therefore, presage variables such as the ones identified in this study must be combined with process and product variables to provide a complete picture of writing instruction.

REFERENCES

Barron, N. Sex-typed language: The production of grammatical cases. *Acta Sociologica*, 1971, *14*, 24–27.

Behrens, L. Writing, reading, and the rest of the faculty: A survey. *English Journal*, 1978, *67*, 54–60

Blake, R. W. Assessing English and language arts teachers' attitudes toward writers and writing. *English Record*, 1976, *27*, 87–97.

Brownell, W. A. Criteria for learning in educational research. *Review of Educational Research*, 1948, *18*, 106–112.

Campbell, D. T., & Fiske, D. W. Convergent and discriminant validation by the mutitrait-multimethod matrix. *Psychological Bulletin*, 1959, *56*, 81–105.

Campbell, L. P., & Williamson, J. A. Dogmatism in student teachers. *Educational Forum*, 1973, *37*, 481–489.

Daly, J. A., & Miller, M. D. The empirical development of an instrument to measure writing apprehension. *Research in the Teaching of English*, 1975, *9*, 242–248.

Donlan, D. A methodology inventory for composition education. *English Education*, 1979, *11*, 23–29.

Fishbein, M., & Ajzen, I. *Belief, attitude, intention, and behavior.* Menlo Park, Calif.: Addison-Wesley, 1975.

Gere, A. R., & Smith, E. H. *Attitudes, language and change.* Urbana, Ill.: National Council of Teachers of English, 1979.

Gilley, H. M., & Summers, C. S. Sex differences in the use of hostile verbs. *Journal of Psychology*, 1970, *76*, 33–37.

Jacobs, P. H., & Evans, W. H. *Illinois tests in the teaching of high school English* (U.S. Office of Education Project No. HE-145). Washington, D.C.: Department of Health, Education and Welfare, 1969.

Key, M. R. Linguistic behavior of male and female. *Linguistics*, 1972, *88*, 15–31.

Klinger, G. C. A campus view of college writing. *College Composition and Communication*, 1977, *28*, 343–347.

Kramer, C. Women's speech: Separate but unequal? *Quarterly Journal of Speech*, 1974, *61*, 14–24.

Kroll, B. M. Developmental perspectives and the teaching of composition. *College English*, 1980, *41*, 741–752.

Lakoff, R. *Language and women's place.* New York: Harper & Row, 1975.

Lin, C. C. *The analysis of teachers' attitudes toward students' writing.* Unpublished doctoral dissertation, Rutgers University, 1974.

Mitzel, H. E. Teacher effectiveness. In C. W. Harris (Ed.), *Encyclopedia of educational research.* New York: Macmillan, 1960.

Moffett, J. *Teaching the universe of discourse.* Boston: Houghton Mifflin, 1968.

National Council of Teachers of English. *Composition opinionnaire.* Urbana, Ill.: NCTE Commission of Composition, 1971.

National Council of Teachers of English. *The student's right to write* (ED 068 938). Urbana, Ill.: NCTE Commission of Composition, 1972.

Nunnally, J. *Psychometric theory.* New York: McGraw-Hill, 1978.

Schuessler, B., Gere, A. R., & Abbott, R. D. The development of four scales measuring teacher attitudes toward written composition: A preliminary investigation. *Research in the Teaching of English*, 1981, *15*, 55–63.

Thorne, B., & Henley, N. (Eds.). *Language and sex: Difference and dominance.* Rowley, Mass.: Newbury House, 1975.

Zemelman, S. How college teachers encourage students' writing. *Research in the teaching of English*, 1977, *11*, 227–234.

19

The effect of teacher comments
on the writing of four college freshmen

NINA D. ZIV
Seton Hall University

English teachers have always been concerned with how to help their students to become better writers. While lectures and class discussions about good writing have their place in the composition classroom, one of the most direct methods of affecting students' writing performance is that of writing comments on their papers.

Research has shown that teachers have different priorities when they respond to student writing. Some studies indicate that teachers respond primarily to mechanics, grammar, usage, and vocabulary (Kline, 1973; Harris, 1977; Searle & Dillon, 1980). In contrast, Freedman (1978) found that teachers were more concerned with content and organization than with mechanical errors. Though the emphasis of their responses may vary, most teachers do comment on the finished products of student writing and consider these comments to be evaluations of their students' work. In such a model of teacher response, the teacher acts as a judge who grades students' papers and writes comments suggesting how the students can "fix up" their essays. When a teacher responds in this manner, he or she assumes that the students will learn what "good writing" is from the comments and will thereby improve in future papers.

Students who receive such comments on their papers may read them; however, they often do not write subsequent drafts in which they can act upon the comments, and thus the improvement desired by their teachers rarely occurs. Along with not being able to react to teacher comments immediately, students may not see a need to respond to these comments because they view them as *evaluations* of their work and not as the *responses* of an interested adult reader.

It is evident that teacher responses on the final products of student writing may not be reaching their goals in helping students to improve their writing. Indeed, Pianko (1979) wrote that if teachers are to effect a positive change in students' written products, they must change their focus from evaluating and correcting finished papers to helping students expand and elaborate on the stages of their composing processes. Researchers who have studied the various stages of the composing process (Emig, 1971; Stallard, 1974; Graves, 1975; Perl, 1978) have identified revision as a stage of the process which is of vital importance. Murray (1978) defined revision as what the writer does after a draft is completed in order to understand and communicate what has begun to appear on the written pages. The writer reads to alter and develop what has been written and eventually after several drafts, develops a meaning which can be communicated to the reader.

Though revision is a major aspect of the writing process and one that students should engage in when writing their compositions, teachers frequently equate revisión with what Murray (1978) called its external variety—that is, writers' efforts to communicate what they have found to a specific audience. In doing external revision, writers edit, proofread, and use the various conventions of form and language to put the finishing touches on their pieces of writing. Thus Beach (1976) found that if teachers evaluated any drafts, their comments usually concerned matters of form and language. In her work on the revision process, Sommers (1978) compared the writing of college freshmen with that of experienced adult writers and found that adult writers were concerned with revising the composition as a whole and had developed their own revision criteria, while student writers were more concerned with changes on the word or phrase level, and were using specific criteria they had learned from teachers or textbooks.

If teachers are to help their students to revise their papers on the conceptual and structural level as well as on the lexical and sentential levels, they need a model for commenting on student papers. Yet no such model has been established. One reason for this is that the few students that have been done on the effects of teacher response during the writing process have yielded inconclusive results.

The purpose of this exploratory study was to explore the effects of teacher comments on successive drafts of student compositions in order to generate hypotheses concerning effective kinds of responses and thus begin to develop a model of teacher intervention. Such a model would include categories of teacher response which teachers could use to classify their comments. They could then correlate these comments with their students' actions on final drafts in order to see how students used particular kinds of comments to revise their papers.

The following questions were addressed in this study:

1. What is the effect of teacher comments on the conceptual and structural levels of a student's composition?
2. What is the effect of teacher comments on the lexical and sentential levels of a student's composition?
3. What is the effect of teacher comments on the overall quality of a student's composition?

Related Literature

The research on teacher response has been primarily concerned with determining the effects that different types of responses have on the overall quality of student writing and on student attitudes toward writing. Several researchers, for example, used experimental designs to compare the effects of comments which praised student writing with the effects of comments which criticized the writing (Taylor & Hoedt, 1966; Seidman, 1967; Clarke, 1969). These investigators found that one type of comment is no more effective than another in helping students to write better compositions. Other studies in which various methods of commenting were compared also failed to yield any conclusive evidence about the kinds of responses which would be most helpful for student writers (Bata, 1972; Wolter, 1975; Maranzo & Arthurs, 1977). The lack of significant conclusions in these studies may have been due to inadequate research designs. However, they may have also been the result of basing these designs on a model of teacher response in which comments only appeared on student papers that were already completed. Such feedback, not integrally built into the writing process, is of questionable value.

Yet studies on the effect of teacher responses during the writing process are rare. Buxton (1958) studied the writing development of two groups of college freshmen over the course of an entire year. One group received no grades on their papers and no comments except for a few general ones at the ends of their papers suggesting ways in which they might improve their future essays. When their papers were returned, these students were told to look at the comments and not to revise their papers in any way. A second experimental group received extensive marginal and interlinear comments, final comments suggesting ways they could improve their papers, and two grades reflecting their teachers' assessments of the content and "accuracy" of their papers. These students received their annotated papers and revised them during a class period while teachers went from student to student and helped them. Buxton reported significant differences between the revision and writing groups, leading him to conclude that college freshmen whose writing is criticized and who revise in light of this criticism can improve their writing more than students who receive a few general suggestions but do not revise. While Buxton's results appear to be significant, the comments were only part of the treatment variable, and thus it was impossible to know what their relative influence was on student writing improvement.

Kelley (1973) investigated the effects of two types of responses on student writing. In her study, one class of 28 twelfth-graders was randomly divided into two groups. One group received clarifying responses on the rough drafts of their essays, and the other group received directive responses. Kelley defined the clarifying response as "a question or series of questions designed to help the student evaluate the nature of his ideas and consider alternatives in relationship to the writing skills he is expected to demonstrate in his writing" (p. 141) and the directive response as "a written comment which gives a specific direction to the student regarding improvement of the writing skills which he is expected to demonstrate in his writing" (p. 141).

During the experiment, the classroom teacher wrote either clarifying or directive comments on each student's papers concerning the ideas, wording, flavor, and organization, and used a mechanics chart to indicate to the student the frequency of mechanical errors—spelling and punctuation. After the appropriate comments were written, the students revised their papers during two class periods and then returned them to the teacher. Kelley found that while neither type of response significantly influenced the amount of growth in writing performance of students on between-draft revisions, there was a strong indication that "the clarifying response may be more effective than the directive response for expository essays" (1973, p. 116). Although Kelley's conclusions indicate that one type of response may help students to improve their writing more than another, her categories of commenting were very general and no attempt was made to ascertain how particular comments within these categories affected specific aspects of student writing.

In addition to the Buxton and Kelley studies, some research has focused on whether teacher corrections between drafts and subsequent revisions by students have any effect on the elimination of mechanical errors in student writing (Fellows, 1936; Arnold, 1963). King (1970) studied the effects of three different types of comments on specific errors frequently made by students in their writing and found that students understood teacher corrections less often than comments which named the error or stated the rule that the student had violated. King also began to divide the comments into well-defined categories instead of the general categories of previous studies. However, like her predecessors, she did not investigate how student writing performance is affected by specific teacher responses.

Procedures

The foregoing survey of the literature on teacher intervention indicates that further research needs to be done in order to find out how teachers can best help their students during the writing process. Since experimental studies in which researchers compared the general effects of different types of comments yielded somewhat inconclusive results, I decided to use the case study method to explore how four college freshmen perceived the specific comments I wrote on their papers and how they used these comments in revising. The writers, Linda, Mark, Vincent, and Joann, were four students enrolled in a regular section of the New York University Expository Writing Program. All entering freshmen are required to take two semesters of Expository Writing and are randomly assigned to a section of the course. Sections of the Writing Program are limited to fifteen students and are taught by graduate students or faculty members from NYU.

During the fall semester of the 1979–1980 academic year, I taught two regular sections of Expository Writing. At the beginning of the semester, I asked all my students to write an essay on a topic of their choice, and on the basis of these first papers, I selected two male and two female freshmen from one section who exhibited problems of organization, focus, and logic in their writing. After obtaining their consent to participate in the project, I met with each of them and interviewed them about their previous writing experience.

Students in the Writing Program attend writing classes for an hour and fifteen minutes twice a week. During a semester, they write and revise several expository essays on assigned topics, react and comment on other students' writing, and read and react to various published essays. Instructors also hold class discussions on revision strategies, style, and other writing problems that the students in a class might have. An important feature of the Program is the three-stage draft process that the students go through when writing their papers. The students in a section are divided into groups of four or five, and after they have written their first drafts, they bring in their papers with copies for all the students in their group. The students read their essays aloud, and their peers comment orally and then write their comments on the copies. After the peer group meetings, the students use the comments they have received to write a second draft outside of class. Finally, the students use the instructor's comments to write a final draft, which is typed and handed in for a grade.

During the semester in which the study was conducted, the research participants attended regularly scheduled classes and participated in classroom activities which included writing seven papers in a series of three drafts and completing one in-class assignment. While I did follow the course outline of the Expository Writing Program, I deviated from the general procedures by not giving students specific assignments. Instead, I used a variety of techniques to stimulate them to think about topics for their papers. Thus, the students kept journals and from time to time I responded to their journal entries and suggested topics for their papers based on what they had written. Other sources of topics were writing inventories which the students filled out at the beginning of the semester, and prewriting sessions in which they discussed a variety of topics they were interested in developing. In addition to not assigning topics, I did not give grades on the final drafts of the papers. Rather, at the end of the semester, I asked the students to choose five of their final drafts and hand them in to me so that I could give each student one composite grade.

Collection of the Data

In order to assess how teacher comments were affecting student writing, I asked the research participants to react aloud and tape-record their reactions to the comments which appeared on the second drafts of their papers. Initially, I met individually with the participants in my office and returned the second drafts of their first papers to them. I then asked the participants to read their papers aloud and when they came to a comment I had made to record their reaction to it. Before a participant started to record, I demonstrated what I wanted him or her to do by reading a comment from the papers and giving my reaction to it. During each recording session, I remained in the room and did not interfere with the taping except to remind the participant to react to each comment aloud.

After the recording sessions were over, the participants took their second drafts home and revised their papers. They then typed final drafts and handed in all three drafts to me. The process described above was repeated five more times during the semester. However, for the remaining five papers, the participants reacted to my comments at home, and after revising their papers turned in all three drafts to me. At the end of the semester, the participants met individually with another instructor in the Expository Writing Program, who interviewed them about their writing experiences during the semester and their views on teacher intervention during the writing process.

Analysis of the Data

The data that I analyzed consisted of the comments I had made on the research participants' papers, their perceptions of my comments, and their actions in preparing the final drafts of their papers.

Teacher Comments

Since the categories in previous studies such as Kelley's were general in nature and not well-defined, I developed my own taxonomy of teacher comments by inductively sorting my comments into various categories. The major categories of this taxonomy are explicit cues, implicit cues, and teacher corrections. Explicit cues are those in which the teacher indicates to the student exactly how he or she might revise a paper or points out a specific error. Examples of explicit cues on the macro level are:

- *Conceptual level.* Substitution: Student writes a paper in which she discusses how she uses her imagination to cope with the monotony of riding the subway every day. One of her final lines is: "The faculty of the mind to conjure up adventures in order to deal with the monotony of routine is fascinating." Teacher comment intending that the student make a major conceptual change by changing the focus of the paper: *You could expand your essay with (1) as your central idea and use the subway as one example. Other monotonous chores may come to mind.* (1) refers to the sentence "The faculty of the mind. . . ."
- *Structural level.* Rearrangement: Student writes a paper about his composing processes and has a paragraph near the end of the paper about when he writes his essays. Teacher comment intending that the student rearrange the paragraphs: *You should put the last paragraph near the beginning where you set the scene for your composing processes.*

Examples of explicit cues on the micro level are:

- *Sentential level.* Deletion: Student writes the following sentence in a paper on the sensual nature of monsters: "He has so many different parts about him that could turn a female on." Teacher comment intending that the student delete a phrase: *The words "about him" are unnecessary in the sentence and make it sound awkward. In your rewrite, I suggest that you delete "about him" so that the sentence reads "He has so many different parts that could turn a female on."*
- *Lexical level.* Substitution: Student writes the following sentence in a paper on juvenile delinquency: "Juveniles are thirty percent of the population but they *constitute* almost 50% of the crimes in the United States." Teacher comment intending that the student substitute a word: *It does not make sense to say that juveniles constitute crimes. Try using "commit" or "are responsible for" and see what different meanings are conveyed when you substitute one of these words for the one you have written.*

    Grammar: Student writes the following sentence in a paper on the New York City blackout of 1977: "Finally, we drove out to Howard Beach, I spotted a church bazaar right before the toll booth to enter Rockaway." Teacher comment intending that the student change the punctuation: *This is a comma splice.*

- *Format conventions.* Spelling: Student writes the following sentence in a paper in which she compares life to a game of Monopoly: "The roll of the dice he controlls." Teacher comment intending that the student substitute the correct spelling of the word "controls": *Spelling.*

Implicit cues are those in which the teacher calls attention to a problem, suggests alternative directions for the student to pursue, or questions the student about what he or she has written. Examples of implicit cues on the macro level are:

- *Conceptual level.* Addition: Student writes a paper in which she compares life to a game of Monopoly. She does not give enough examples to make her analogies vivid to the reader. Teacher comment intending that the student elaborate on her ideas: *You apparently like to use analogies in your writing, which is a good technique. Somehow this paper is a little abstract. Perhaps some concrete examples for your generalizations would help.*
- *Structural level.* Substitution: Student writes a paper on the isolation people experience in New York City. Her concluding paragraph is about the suicide rate in this country. Teacher comment intending that she substitute another conclusion: *Do you think your conclusion follows logically from the ideas you discuss in the body of your paper?*

Examples of implicit cues on the micro level are:

- *Sentential level.* Deletion: Student writes the following sentence in a paper on the New York City blackout of 1977: "Most of the middle class citizens moved out of this area and moved to other places." Teacher comment intending that the student delete the phrase "and moved": *This is awkward.*
- *Lexical level.* Substitution: Student writes the following sentence in a paper on stereotypes: "Stereotypes not only enslave but reduce equality." Teacher comment intending that the student substitute another word for "reduce": *This word is inappropriate here.*

Actual teacher corrections, the third category, include the rearrangement, addition, and deletion of phrases and sentences, and the addition, deletion, and substitution of words in a paper.

Student Perceptions

I also categorize the perceptions of the research participants. Examples of these categories are:

- *Perceives teacher intention:* Teacher writes "Is this the right word?" next to "view" in the sentence "He'd view his apartment and punch the walls in frustration." Teacher's intention is for the student to substitute another word for "view." Student *perceives teacher intention:* "'View' is circled. 'Is this the right word?' I guess I could change that. Well, when you say he viewed his apartment, it sounded as if he's standing on top of a mountain looking down. It's not too clear, and I wasn't sure I was using the word in the right context."
- *Does not perceive teacher intention:* Teacher writes "Do you like the way this sounds?" next to the sentence "All that is seen is a uniform and according to preconceived notions, he is a lacky." Teacher intention is for the student to change the sentence into active voice by substituting "all people see" for "all that is seen" so that the sentence reads "All people see is a uniform, and according to preconceived notions, he is a lackey." Student *does not perceive teacher intention:* "You asked me do I like the way that sounds. Yeah, I like the way it sounds. Because I was talking about stereotypes and stereotypes are preconceived notions, and I thought that it sounded pretty good myself."
- *Explains own intention:* Teacher writes "What do you mean?" next to the word "impressionable" in the sentence "In him you can see the young impressionable of today as he will appear tomorrow." Participant *explains own intention:* "You asked me what I meant by 'impressionable.' What I meant was that here was a young man, a young person, who really hasn't had too many experiences and that he's looking at the world all wide-eyed and bushy-tailed and eager and that being as young and naive and unknowing as he is, he is very impressionable."
- *Suggests course of action:* Teacher writes "spelling" over the word "pandimonium" in the sentence "Now all out pandimonium broke out, people were raiding every store." Student *suggests course of action:* "You have that I spelled 'pandemonium' wrong. You didn't correct it so I'll go to the dictionary and see if I can look it up and correct the spelling."

Student Actions

In addition to categorizing teacher comments and student perceptions, I developed a taxonomy of actions taken by students on the final drafts of their compositions. The taxonomy includes categories on the macro and micro levels. Examples of student actions on the macro level are:

- *Conceptual level.* Addition: In the final draft of a paper on juvenile delinquency, the student discusses why juvenile offenders receive such light sentences, a new idea he had not written about in his previous drafts.

- *Structural level.* Deletion: In a paper on the crisis in Iran, the student writes a paragraph about the Pope's role as an intermediary between the United States and Iran. In the final draft, he deletes this paragraph from the text.

Examples of student actions on the micro level are:

- *Sentential level.* Addition: Student writes the following sentence in a paper on stereotypes: "Why do these invisible chains refuse to judge a man by the content of his character not the color of his skin?" In the final draft, the student adds the phrase "the people who enforce," so that the sentence reads: "Why do the people who enforce these invisible chains refuse to judge a man by the content of his character not the color of his skin?"
- *Lexical level.* Substitution: Student writes the following sentence in a paper on a "left-over hippie" from the '60s: "His life seemed to have ended in the last cycles of that era." In the final draft, the student substitutes "years" for "cycles" so that the new sentence reads: "His life seemed to have ended in the last years of that era."

Method of Analysis

Using these taxonomies, I coded each of the comments that I had written, the perceptions of the research participants, and their actions on their final drafts. When I coded my comments, I also wrote down the intention of each of them. For example:

Comment	Perception	Action
"This is a comma splice." Refers to "It was a warm July evening, my mother, father, and I had finished dinner and were deciding what we could do for that nights entertainment."	"You have a comment that this is a comma splice." (Direct response—rereads comment)	Makes sentence into two sentences so that they read: *"It was a warm July evening. My mother, father and I had finished dinner and were deciding what we could do for that nights entertainment."*
(Explicit—sentence-phrase grammar Teacher intention —punctuation change)	"I'm not sure what a comma splice is . . ." (Direct response—does not perceive teacher intention)	(Sentence-phrase-grammar-punctuation change)
	. . . but I'll look it up in my little handbook." (Direct response—suggests course of action)	

After coding the data, I correlated my comments on the second drafts of the research participants' papers with their actions on their final drafts and analyzed what changes, if any, had been made as a result of my comments. The participants' reactions were an important part of this analysis because they indicated whether the participants had understood the intentions of my comments and why they had made particular revisions.

On the macro level, I compared drafts to see whether as a result of my comments the research participants had made any structural changes in their paragraphs or in the text as a whole. Similarly, on the conceptual level, I compared drafts to see whether the participants had rearranged, deleted, or added ideas. On the micro level, I compared sentences and lexical items I had commented on in the second drafts with parallel sentences and lexical items in the final drafts in order to see what changes had been made. Another part of my analysis on the micro level concerned the corrections I had made on the research participants' papers. In order to analyze the effect of these comments, I compared the sentences and lexical items that I had corrected in the second drafts with the parallel sentences and lexical items in the final drafts. The majority of my corrections concerned grammar, spelling, and punctuation. I had also written explicit cues on the participants' papers pointing out errors in these areas, and thus was able to compare the research participants' responses and actions to teacher corrections and explicit cues on similar errors.

Using the results of my analysis of the effect of particular comments on individual papers, I charted the patterns of responses and actions of each participant to particular categories of comments and compared the responses and actions of all participants across the various categories of comments on both the macro and micro levels.

Discussion and Results

An analysis of the data on the structural and conceptual levels indicated that the research participants, who were inexperienced revisers, responded favorably to explicit cues in which I gave them specific suggestions about how they could strengthen or reorganize the ideas they had already formulated in their papers. For example, Vincent wrote a paper on the hostage crisis in Iran. One of his arguments concerned the Soviet Union's possible reaction to United States military intervention. I thought Vincent's argument was a weak one and suggested that he elaborate on it. Vincent added a paragraph about this issue and wrote a more convincing argument.

When students were still in the process of discovering what they were trying to say, explicit cues also helped them to make major conceptual revisions. For example, earlier (see p. 368) I gave examples from a paper written by Joann, in which she discussed how people cope with their daily ride on the dirty subways of New York by imagining more pleasant experiences. The paper was clearly written and well-organized, but, as noted previously, I thought she might be able to expand on her idea by writing about how people use their imaginations to cope with other monotonous chores. Thus, I suggested in my final comment:

> Joann—this is well-organized and I enjoyed it. You could expand your essay with 1 as your central idea and use the subway as one example. Other monotonous chores may come to mind.

The number 1 referred to one of the last lines in the paper, which read: "The faculty of the mind to conjure up adventures in order to deal with the monotony of routine is fascinating." Joann's response was:

> I see where it would be more interesting if I focused in on the mind fantasizing and brought about various situations in which one does that, like the various routines—the various circumstances which cause one to start daydreaming. I picked the New York subways because I guess that's where I daydream the most.

In her final draft, Joann began with the sentence I had suggested and turned the paper into a general discussion of how people cope with monotonous chores. Thus she wrote about the subway rider as well as the student listening to a boring lecture and the housewife trying to finish her housework.

Implicit cues, in which I questioned the participants about the ideas they had presented or suggested alternative directions for them to pursue, helped them to clarify their ideas or stimulated them to think about ways they could further develop the topics. Responding with these kinds of cues was also appropriate when the participants presented well-developed ideas or when I wanted to suggest alternative ideas for them to pursue in future papers. For example, one of Joann's papers, a character sketch of a "leftover hippie from '69," was clearly written and well-developed. My response was to suggest that she write another paper dealing with the general problem of leftover "flower children."

On the sentential level, my implicit cues were not helpful because the research participants frequently did not recognize what the problems were in the sentences I had commented on and/or didn't have the strategies needed to revise them. Thus in response to cues such as "Can you rephrase this?" and "Rewrite this sentence" they either deleted the sentences, made no revisions in them, or wrote revisions which were just as awkward as their original sentences or did not fit into the context of the paper. On the lexical level, only two of the research participants responded favorably to my implicit cues. The other two participants did not perceive the intentions of such cues. Thus, when I wrote "wrong word" next to "constitute" in the sentence "Juveniles are thirty percent of the population but they constitute almost 50% of the crimes in the United States", Vincent substituted "compose" for "constitute." Linda reacted to "Is this the right word?" by challenging my comment and making no revision at all in her final draft.

The data also indicated that while the research participants readily accepted by corrections, they did not always understand why I had made such changes. For example, in one paper Vincent wrote: "Remington is owned by Dupont, *who* is one of the wealthiest families in America and Standard Oil is owned by Rockefeller." I substituted "which" for "who" in the sentence and the writer commented:

> Okay, I have "Remington, who is owned by Dupont, who is one of the wealthiest." You changed the word "who" to "which is one of the wealthiest." Okay, I guess that's correct English. That's good. I appreciate that because, uh, I'm not sure when to use words like that.

Though in the final draft, Vincent made the substitution I had indicated, in his next paper he still did not know how to use relative pronouns. Thus he wrote, "I quote Wolfgang and Cohen which states exactly what I would like to say." In this case, I substituted "who" for "which" and crossed out the "s" in the word "states" so that the sentence read: "I quote Wolfgang and Cohen who state exactly what I would like to say." Vincent's response to my comment was: "Okay, yeah, it doesn't sound right so I'll fix that up"; in the final draft, he wrote the correct version of the sentence.

Linda wrote this sentence in one of her papers:

> Instead of that innocent and naive look, his face clearly shows his experiences: from that speculative, glassy look in his eyes; to his nose that has been knocked out of joint in youth; to those hard, unyeilding lips, with their cynical smirk and that condescending leer.

I changed the semi-colons to commas in the sentence, and Linda made the changes I had indicated in her final draft. In a later paper, she wrote:

> When one takes away the pride of a race by portraying it as second class citizens; when one race insults the dignity of another race by treating it in deed and manner as inferior; when one race displays blatant disregard of another by seeing it only through stereotypes; it not only takes equality but also freedom.

I again changed the semi-colons to commas, and Linda questioned me about it:

> Then I say "when one takes away the pride of a race by portraying it as second class citizens" and then I use a semi-colon, and then I say "when one

race insults the dignity of another race by treating it in deed and manner as inferior" and I use a semi-colon, and "when one race displays blatant disregard of another by seeing it only through stereotypes" and I use a semi-colon. All those times you made my semi-colons commas, and I'm not really sure why because I always thought that commas weren't right when a sentence was so long but you did it so I guess that I was wrong.

Linda's response and use of the semi-colon in this paper indicated that she had not learned anything about the use of semi-colons from my corrections on her previous paper. From these examples it is evident that teacher corrections alone are not helpful kinds of comments because students frequently revise their papers according to the corrections without understanding why they have been made.

Along with being ineffective in helping students to understand their errors, teacher corrections reinforced the participants' perceptions of the writing process and the teacher's role in the process. Indeed, two of the participants viewed revision as a matter of correcting errors and had always looked upon the teacher as someone who would show them how to "fix up" their papers. Because of the passive role they had played in the writing process, they preferred when I made the necessary corrections on their papers. Yet they and the other participants were capable of correcting their errors when I just wrote explicit cues on their papers, in which I pointed out errors and left it to them to make the revisions. For example, when I wrote "subject and verb do not agree" next to a sentence, the participants were able to correct this error. Likewise, when I wrote "sp" over a misspelled word, the participants corrected their mistakes.

Implications for Teaching

What emerge from the analysis of the data on both the macro and micro levels are continua of commenting along which a teacher might respond to her students' writing. Thus on the macro level, students who are inexperienced revisers will respond favorably to explicit cues which indicate to them how they may strengthen the ideas they have already presented in their papers. For example, teachers might write comments in which they suggest how students may rearrange paragraphs in a more logical order, elaborate on specific points in their papers, or add more examples to support generalizations they have made. If students are still in the process of discovering the topics for their papers, then explicit cues suggesting how they can make major conceptual changes can be helpful. When students become more experienced at revising, teachers may want to be less explicit in their comments and instead suggest alternative directions for them to pursue or question them about various aspects of the ideas they have presented in order to stimulate them to make conceptual changes.

On the lexical and sentential levels, explicit cues may also be effective in helping inexperienced revisers during the writing process. Thus if a word choice is inappropriate, a teacher might suggest a number of alternative words that the student can use in place of the original one. On the sentential level, a teacher might respond to an awkward sentence by suggesting a way of rewriting it. It is also important to note that while explicit cues telling students why sentences are awkward may be helpful, such students may also need to listen to their sentences aloud so that they can hear why a sentence is awkward and to learn some stylistic options for revising such sentences.

The research participants' responses and subsequent actions on their final drafts indicated that teacher corrections did not help them to understand their errors and that in fact they were capable of revising their papers if errors in punctuation, spelling, and grammar were pointed out to them. Therefore, teachers might refrain from correcting the grammar, punctuation, and spelling errors in student papers and instead name the errors so that the students can make the necessary changes themselves.

It is evident that inexperienced revisers need specific directions from their teachers about how to revise their papers. However, at some point when students are more experienced revisers, teachers might move along the continua on both the macro and micro levels and write more implicit cues. The continua of commenting, then, can be used as a guide for writing comments on student papers.

Yet, comments can only be helpful if teachers respond to student writing as part of an ongoing dialogue between themselves and their students. In order to create such a dialogue, teachers might begin by responding to student writing not as evaluators and judges but as interested adults would react to such writing. For example, in response to one of Mark's papers I commented that after reading the paper I wasn't sure of the point he was trying to make in it. Mark's response to my comment indicated that his perception of himself as a writer was a poor one. He said: "I really didn't know what I was doing and you sort of told me you didn't know what my main topic was." In trying to help a student such as Mark, teachers might comment in an encouraging and supportive manner instead of reinforcing the student's poor self-perception.

To further diffuse the student's perception that the teacher's role in the writing process is that of an evaluator, teachers might write comments on the final drafts of papers encouraging students to pursue further some of the ideas they have presented. For example, one way I responded to the paper on a "leftover hippie" was to suggest that Joann write another paper on the general problem of "leftover flower children." Though Joann chose not to pursue this idea, my comment indicated my interest in the idea she had presented, and encouraged her to think of me as a participant in a dialogue about her writing.

Another way teachers can help to create a dialogue with their students is for them to become more sensitive to the intentions of student writers. Indeed, as a result of my research, I became aware that I often did not perceive the intentions of the student's text but rather wrote comments reflecting my stylistic preferences. For example, when Vincent wrote "The budget crunch was felt by my school so they cut certain activities one of which was the track team," I commented "Rewrite the sentence" intending that he change the sentence into the active voice. In retrospect it was evident that Vincent's intention in the sentence was to emphasize the words "budget crunch," so the passive voice was appropriate there. Because of my stylistic preferences, however, I did not consider his intentions and thus asked him to rewrite his sentence.

Along with writing comments in a positive and empathic manner and becoming more sensitive to the intentions of student writers, teachers might try to find out whether their comments are having a favorable effect on their students. Using the taxonomies developed in this study, teachers can categorize their comments, correlate them with their students' actions on subsequent drafts, and then see what kinds of comments are being understood by their students. For example, if a teacher moves along the lexical continuum and writes a comment such as "Is this word appropriate here?" on several student papers, then she can correlate her comments with her students' actions on their final drafts and be able to see whether such comments are being understood.

When creating a dialogue with their students, teachers might follow the suggestions that I have made. Teachers should be aware, however, that many students have never written papers in a series of drafts and therefore may not be receptive to such an approach and to teacher comments during the writing process. Thus, Vincent said in his final interview that at first he had reacted negatively to the idea of a draft process because he had been used to writing a paper once and handing it in to the teacher for a grade. Since other students may have similar attitudes, teachers might discuss the value of revision and show their students samples of their own writing and revising processes.

Teaching students the value of revision may help them to change their perceptions of their roles in the writing process. At the beginning of my study, the participants rarely challenged my comments and preferred to play a passive role in the writing process. However, as a result of their experiences with teacher responses during the process, they began to change their attitudes and play a more active role. Thus, all of the participants went beyond the intentions of my comments on either the macro or micro levels in papers that they wrote in the latter part of the semester. Indeed, Joann's remarks during her final interview indicated that her attitude toward teacher comments had changed and that, in terms of her role in the writing process, she viewed herself as a participant in a dialogue between herself and her teacher:

> I guess the reason teacher comments never really influenced me before was because I got fairly good ones. You know, before it was always a mark or a statement. The teachers never went into any big descriptions about your writing. If you fulfilled the task, you know, it was okay. Suddenly this year, I see it. I can question it. I can disagree with it. I can see, you know, the different aspects of it. That did make sense.

Suggestions for Further Research

While their reactions to my comments and their actions on final drafts did vary among the research participants, it was possible to generalize about the effect of my comments on all four students. It was evident that they responded favorably to my explicit comments on the conceptual and structural levels. It was also apparent that they did not respond well to my implicit comments on the lexical and sentential levels, and therefore might respond more favorably to explicit comments on these levels. Based on the results of my study, I have hypothesized:

1. Students who are inexperienced revisers will improve on the structural and conceptual levels if they receive explicit cues about how to revise their papers.
2. Students who are inexperienced revisers will improve on the lexical and sentential levels if they receive explicit cues about how to revise their papers on these levels.

Using an experimental design, these hypotheses could be tested on a larger population. The distinction I have made between two major types of comments, explicit and implicit, should enable a research to control closely the comments that are written on papers in such a study. In addition to testing my hypotheses, researchers might also use the dimensions of composition annotation suggested by King (1979) as a guide for studying the effect of other types of comments on student writing. For example, research might be done to investigate student actions in response to whether a comment is interlinear, marginal, at the beginning/end, or on a rating form.

Although the analysis in this study concerned the changes that occurred between the drafts that the research participants turned in to me and their final drafts, they actually wrote three drafts. They got an initial response to their work from their peers and then wrote a second draft, to which I responded. This progression of reactions was sometimes confusing to the participants because my responses often contradicted those of their peers. On the conceptual level, for example, I often pointed out the lack of focus in a paper and suggested a major conceptual change, in contrast to the peer group which had had a positive response to the idea that the participant had presented. Since the three-stage draft process in which both peers and teachers respond to student writing is an integral part of many composition classrooms, the problem of how these two sets of responses interact with each other might also be the subject of future research projects.

Most of the previous research that has been done in the area of teacher response to student writing has been concerned with how teachers evaluate the finished products of student writing. The model of teacher response which emerges from such research is one in which the teacher's role is that of an evaluator who comments on the strengths and weaknesses of her student's papers. When a teacher writes comments, the underlying assumption is that the students will respond to them and thus improve their writing performance. However, these implied dialogues rarely happen because students invariably look upon their teacher as a judge and, consequently, see themselves as participants in a "dialogue" in which they can do little but accept their teacher's criticisms. In this study I have suggested a different model of teacher response, in which teachers are no longer evaluators and students are no longer passive recipients of their teachers' judgments. Instead, teachers have an effect on the immediate products of student writing and through their supportive responses during the writing process, begin to establish an on-going dialogue in which both they and their students are active participants.

REFERENCES

Arnold, L. V. Effects of frequency of writing and intensity of teacher evaluation upon performance in written composition of tenth grade students (Doctoral dissertation, Florida State University, 1962). *Dissertation Abstracts International*, 1963, *24*, 1021A. (University Microfilms No. 63-6344)

Beach, R. Self-evaluation strategies of extensive revisers and non-revisers. *College Composition and Communication*, May 1976, *27*(2), 160-164.

Bata, E. J. A study of the relative effectiveness of marking techniques on Junior college freshmen English composition (Doctoral dissertation, University of Maryland, 1972). *Dissertation Abstracts International*, 1973, *34*, 62A (University Microfilms No. 73-17028)

Buxton, E. W. An experiment to test the effects of writing frequency and graded practice upon students' skills in written expression (Doctoral dissertation, Stanford University, 1958). *Dissertation Abstracts International*, 1958, *19*, 709A. (University Microfilms No. 58-03596)

Clarke, G. A. *Interpreting the penciled scrawl: A problem in teacher theme evaluation.* Unpublished doctoral dissertation, University of Chicago, 1969. (ERIC Document Reproduction Service No. 039 241)

Emig, J. *The Composing processes of twelfth graders.* Urbana, Ill.: National Council on Teachers of English, 1971.

Fellows, J. E. *The influence of theme reading and theme correction on eliminating technical errors in written compositions of ninth grade pupils.* Unpublished doctoral dissertation, University of Iowa, 1936.

Freedman, S. *The evaluators of student writing.* Research prepared at San Francisco State College, San Francisco, 1978. (ERIC Document Reproduction Service No. ED 150 079)

Graves, D. H. An examination of the writing processes of seven year old children. *Research in the Teaching of English,* Winter 1975, *9*(3), 227–241.

Harris, W. H. Teacher response to student writing: A study of the response patterns of high school English teachers to determine the basis for teacher judgment of student writing. *Research in the Teaching of English,* Fall 1977, *11*(2), 175–185.

Kelley, M. E. Effects of two types of teachers responses to essays upon twelfth grade students' growth in writing performance (Doctoral dissertation, Michigan State University, 1973). *Dissertation Abstracts International,* 1974, *34*, 5801A. (University Microfilms No. 74-6068)

King, J. A. Teachers' comments on students' writing: A conceptual analysis and empirical study (Doctoral dissertation, Cornell University, 1979). *Dissertation Abstracts International,* 1980, *40*, 4872-A. (University Microfilms No. 80-03942)

Kline, C. R., Jr. *Instructors' signals to their students.* Paper presented at a meeting of Conference on College Composition and Communication, New Orleans, 1973. (ERIC Document Reproduction Service No. 083 600)

Maranzo, R. J., & Arthurs, S. *Teacher comments on student essays: It doesn't matter what you say.* Study prepared at University of Colorado, 1977. (ERIC Document Reproduction Service No. 147 864)

Murray, D. M. Internal revision: A process of discovery. In C. R. Cooper & L. Odell (Eds.), *Research on composing: Points of departure.* Urbana, Ill.: National Council of Teachers of English, 1978.

Perl, S. Five writers writing: The composing processes of unskilled college writers (Doctoral dissertation, New York University, 1978). *Dissertation Abstracts International,* 1978, *39*, 4788A. (University Microfilms No. 78-24104)

Pianko, S. A description of the composing processes of college freshmen writers. *Research in the Teaching of English,* February 1979, *13*(1), 5–22.

Searle, D., & Dillon, D. The message of marking: Teacher written responses to student writing at intermediate grade levels. *Research in the Teaching of English,* October 1980, *14*(3), 233–242.

Seidman, E. Marking students' compositions: Implications for achievement motivation theory (Doctoral dissertation, Stanford University, 1966). *Dissertation Abstracts International,* 1967, *28*, 2605A. (University Microfilms No. 67-17503)

Sommers, N. I. Revision in the composing process: A case study of college freshmen and experienced adult writers (Doctoral dissertation, Boston University, 1978). *Dissertation Abstracts International,* 1979, *39*, 5374A. (University Microfilms No. 79-05022)

Stallard, C. K. An analysis of the writing behavior of good student writers. *Research in the Teaching of English,* Summer 1974, *8*, 208–218.

Taylor, W. F., & Hoedt, K. C. The effect of praise upon the quality of creative writing. *Journal of Educational Research,* 1966, *60*, 80–83.

Wolter, D. R. *The effect of feedback on performance on a creative writing task.* Unpublished doctoral dissertation, University of Michigan, 1975. (ERIC Document Reproduction Service No. 120 801)

20

The writing process and the writing machine: Current research on word processors relevant to the teaching of composition

LILLIAN S. BRIDWELL
PAULA REED NANCARROW
DONALD ROSS
University of Minnesota

When Mark Twain wrote *The Adventures of Tom Sawyer* in 1875, he wrote it on a Remington typewriter, and it was one of the first novels, if not *the* first, to be so produced. The story goes, however, that he suppressed his method of composing because he did not want to offer any testimonials or answer any questions about the "new fangled thing." Our experiences with microcomputers and word processing systems have been just the opposite. We can hardly escape the "new users" who have a habit of offering up testimonials about how word processors have changed their lives as writers. (We have to admit we've said some similar things.) However, we have yet to see many significant changes in writing instruction result from this dramatic new technological development. Admittedly, the advent of the typewriter hardly revolutionized the way people learned to write. But despite the rather limited exploration to date of ways to use word processing technology for writing, micro-computers afford their users more revolutionary methods of producing written language than typewriters have ever permitted.

For the last decade, writing researchers—working with approaches they learned from cognitive psychology, linguistics, and sociology—have been studying "composing processes," the ways writers (sometimes experienced, sometimes novice) produce written language. At the same time, we have seen tremendous advances in the development of micro-computers, small terminals or self-contained minicomputers—found on office desk-tops and even in the home—that use the power of a computer to store, retrieve, and operate on huge masses of data. Perhaps because of these rapid developments in both fields, computer-aided instruction (CAI) for composition classes has not, for the most part, caught up with either current composition theory or the potential of technology. Since the profit motive for large corporations has not extended to composition classrooms, those responsible for producing software for writing have either opted for relatively easily programmed, mechanical packages or developed software for business and industry in which, until recently, those using the microcomputers were usually typists reproducing someone else's writing, rather than writers originating their own texts.

The first composition teachers to be bitten by the computer bug wrote exercise programs primarily by analogy, knowing how computers were used in other courses and in other fields. These programs were built around simple stimulus–response patterns, not unlike those in printed "programmed-instruction" workbooks, except that the computer could provide almost instantaneous feedback. (For reviews of some of the best—and some of the worst—of these programs on the college level, see Packert-Hall & Burke, 1981; and Kline, 1980.) But the last ten years have seen a new development in microcomputer technology—the word processor—that is just beginning to enter the writing classroom. Word processing systems afford a unique opportunity to develop computer-aided instruction that teaches writing strategies *and* assists in implementing them, for now the writing machine itself is a heuristic tool. The word processor's "editing" capabilities, designed initially not for writers doing original work but for typists transcribing someone else's prose, provide a means for making written text more fluid and changeable than ever before, and can also assist in prewriting, drafting, and revising.

Even though the composition classroom would seem the logical place for word processors, they are not yet extensively used there. At colleges and universities where students have regular access to microcomputers, growing numbers of students learn the advantages of text editors as writing and typing tools on their own, or as a fringe benefit in a computer science course, and can turn in flawlessly printed papers for any class in which writing is required (R. Burns, 1982). Students who don't happen to be taking computer science courses may thus find themselves at a disadvantage in producing polished pieces of writing.

Since revising can be done more quickly and easily (without retyping whole papers), writers have more opportunities for revision. Some, as a result, find it a more rewarding task. On the other hand, the writer without access to a word processor may, in some ways, be better off. The admittedly mechanical "editing" capabilities of a text processing system, especially when a student is given no guidance as to how these individual functions could be used in a comprehensive re-vision of the subject, may induce the student to produce *less* coherent text than his nonprocessing peers, text that is not so much rewritten as it is manipulated. The size of a CRT screen (the display) may also pose difficulties for text coherence. Even the word processor's chief drawing card—the ability to change text almost instantly—may cause problems for writers who insist on crafting perfect drafts, sentence by sentence. For these individuals, word processors may make Flaubert's comma an epidemic syndrome.

The fact remains, however, that word processors and microcomputers with word processing capabilities are proliferating, not only on college campuses but especially in business and industry. We argue that unless those who understand writing *and* computers work together, in the immediate future, we will see even more mindless software and very few significant instructional materials. Either the writers themselves or the employers of writers must demand "principled use" of the power of word processing, our term for systematic study of the ways in which word processors can be used to meet the writer's needs.

If composition classes are to keep pace with the writing habits of their students, and if the machine itself is to be used by writers with full awareness of its capabilities and limitations for producing better prose, writing instructors must begin to incorporate word processors into their curricula, at least as an option. Furthermore, those involved in composition research and theory must examine the impact of computers on writing. Research concerning the effects of word processors on writing behavior is almost nonexistent, in spite of the pressing need to explore these effects. If instructors are to teach writing using word processors, they must know whether significant differences in writing behavior and quality of final products result from having this tool at a student's disposal.

At the University of Minnesota, projects to study the effects of word processors on writing and writers are presently under way: one a controlled study of experienced writers, and the other a study of undergraduates in composition classes. A working bibliography of research relevant to the use of word processors in the composition classroom has been compiled, and is being regularly updated. We will now provide an overview of the research on CAI applications to writing that our search has yielded so far, describe in more detail the work we are doing in our composition program, and discuss the long-range plans for continuing this work.

Relevant Research on CAI for Writers

Schwartz (1982a), in an article entitled appropriately "Monsters and Mentors: Computer Applications for Humanistic Education," has divided available computer writing programs into four areas: (1) text feedback—

that is, programs which provide statistical information (often in the form of "readability formula" data) that allegedly serves to stimulate revision; (2) practice exercises, which concentrate on rote learning of grammar and sentence structure; (3) "simulations," which allow students to "create" their own texts, usually pseudo-poetry, by selecting elements of content that are then applied to a preprogrammed poetic formula; and (4) tutorials, the newest type of CAI, which attempt to "converse" with the student and aid her in exploring a topic by means of various prompts. Schwartz shows how each is presently being used and concludes with a section on selecting computer programs for composition use and applying them in the classroom. Her discussion has significant implications for those interested in how word processors and their software can best serve the needs of student writers.

Schwartz's article, while it provides the teacher or researcher with a good overview of what has been done in computer-aided instruction in composition, does not touch on word processors themselves. In addition, the categories she selects under which to group various CAI programs are useful for those unfamiliar with CAI, but they necessarily focus on these programs' distinguishing features as computer-aided instruction, not on which CAI program addresses the needs of students engaged in what portion of the writing process. Dividing research relevant to word processing and the writer along the lines of the writing process itself may be a better way to delineate the stronger and weaker areas of CAI applications for writing instruction. We do not see writing processes as "linear" in the sense that each stage is completed before another is begun. However, we do think that certain labels—invention, drafting, revising, and editing—are useful for identifying the kinds of activities that go on, sometimes separately, sometimes simultaneously, and in many orders, when a writer composes.

Invention

In the area of invention, the most important work we know presently is that of Hugh Burns (1979, 1980b, 1981a). In his doctoral dissertation (1979), Burns studied four freshman composition classes to determine the effectiveness of what Schwartz calls "open-ended" CAI (i.e., the "tutorial" variety) in helping students to generate material for a paper. "Dialogues" between computer and student were made possible by programming the computer to ask the student a question about his topic. Then, key words in the student's response (such as the "how" in "How does my comp teacher teach and do all that research at the same time?") cue a generally applicable encouraging comment and another prompt for further exploration of the subject. The questions used as prompts for invention were based on Aristotle's topoi, Burke's pentad, and tagmemics.

Burns's findings should be examined by anyone interested in designing word processing software for invention purposes. Schwartz (1982a) critiques Burns's work and summarizes work of her own in progress (1982b) that attempts to provide heuristic strategies for students writing about literature. "Writing" poetry by computer, what Schwartz calls "simulation," also prompts the student to provide content, but it is questionable whether this is a means to stimulate invention. Nevertheless, it is important to mention the early work of Della-Piana (1971), Bailey's review article on the subject of computer-assisted poetry (1974), and the recent work of Marcus (1981, 1982).

Software designed to promote generation of content may prove very useful for beginning writers, but the capabilities of the system commands themselves for stimulating invention are still relatively ignored. This is because we tend to think of microcomputers primarily as intelligent terminals, not as text processors. The system being used is generally taken for granted as an incidental means of entering data so one can *do* something to it, not as a tool in its own right, although anyone who has used word processors to write and rewrite knows differently. Fast typists, for example, might do their rush writing on the machine, and use "find" and "boldface" options to highlight key ideas in their texts for further exploration. One program in the Bell Labs' *Writer's Workbench* package, TOPIC, is intended to provide key words or index entries by locating frequent noun phrases in the text and capitalizing them. Perhaps future software would work in a similar way, and could be modified to locate verbs and adjectives as well. *Writer's Workbench* is discussed further later in this chapter.

In addition to this form of highlighting or "looping," block-moving functions might be used to regroup lists of details and better reveal patterns in prewriting. This type of writing assistance, the most fundamental type that word processors are capable of providing, is what the undergraduate project at the University of Minnesota is presently beginning to explore, for all areas of the writing process.

Nothing has been done specifically by composition theorists to see how treeing (i.e., drawing diagrams to illustrate either emerging or existing text structures) might be done on a word processor. Obviously, the lines and arrows that allow trees to show relationships between ideas and potential paragraph organization and sequence would require a word processor with graphics capability to depict them in the way that is most familiar to us. We have not found this capability in existing systems. However, any editor's ability to move and regroup details might make it possible to discover hierarchical relationships more easily and express them without lines and arrows; one of the word processor exercises devised for one of our freshman composition courses makes use of this option. But software designed specifically for organizing a writer's notes prior to producing a first draft would be a significant supplement to the editing capabilities of a word processor.

In our explorations of ways to develop such software, we have found analogies between the treeing done in composition classrooms now, and that described in data processing literature and in the literature of text formatting. The latter has been especially valuable for scientific and technical documents, where formulas for organizing text are so specific that a writer need only plug in new ideas or even old documents to the structural model provided and let the automatic formatting commands arrange the result in suitable combinations. Allen, Nix, and Perlis (1981) describe a hierarchical document editor called PEN that uses tree structures, nodes, leaves, and so forth. However, the rigidity of the system would probably make a paltry heuristic for writing something as complex as most essays. The editor described by Strömfors and Jonesjö (1981), ED3, also uses the idea of a "tree" as a preliminary outline for inserting blocks of text. The ED3 command language, written in Pascal, seems a bit cryptic for the ordinary writer, but the idea might be emulated in a more "user-friendly" environment.

Hegarty (1980) of Bell Laboratories also has done work with tree structures as aids in text reformatting. The fact that his report concerns the need to make frequent design changes in a text may make its algorithms more analogous to those which student writers would need to organize and structure their material. Such systems could probably be modified to prompt content by indicating under- and overdeveloped nodes and runaway branches; tree structures that could distinguish different types of information and recognize gaps and violations of hierarchical structure would have to be rather sophisticated and are further down the pike. However, whenever an assignment with a predictable organizational structure is appropriate, programs could be developed that would move the student through that structure.

Drafting

One of the few studies we found that deals with writers drafting on the word processor is an IBM Research Report and subsequent article in *Human Factors* by Gould (1981). In this study, writing behaviors of two groups of mature writers were compared on and off the word processor. Gould found that word processing writers actually spent more time writing than did writers composing letters in longhand. However, the extra revising on the machine accounted for only one-fourth of the additional time spent; the remainder may have been taken up in part by formatting the letter (e.g., setting up the return address). The word processor writers, therefore, ended up getting time charged to them for formatting, while longhand writers had typists formatting their text with no additional time added to their composing totals. Gould concludes that this particular machine seems to have been a barrier for writers. Various reasons are suggested, including the writers' inability to see the entire document at one time, the lure of gadgetry to put things down instead of planning first, and the design of the editor itself. The study, interestingly, does not draw any conclusions about differences in quality of writing between the two groups. One obvious omission in the comparison is the fact that the longhand writers had to use the services of a secretary to type and retype drafts, something the word processing writers could do without.

Preliminary reports from experienced writers involved in a study we have done (discussed later in this paper) indicate that they find similar problems: the lure of the gadgetry, the compulsive need to correct as they go along, the speed of text production, and the need for paper copies. But they accommodate to the word processing system and either change their own habits of drafting or control the system's power to change their habits.

Revising

Despite the most obvious characteristic of word processors as "writing processors"—that is, their facility in revising text—few studies have been made of how use of the machines might alter the revising strategies of student or experienced writers. In Collier's (1982) study of students using word processors in a writing lab, the results were mixed. Revisions were done more efficiently but were not sufficiently different from revision paradigms that the students already had for Collier to state that there were immediate instructional effects. He calls for more "user-friendly" systems that would not get in the way of the beginning student's concentration on the task of composing. The bulk of computer-aided instruction and research on revising, as in Schwartz's analysis, is "text feedback"; the student types in her text and runs a program on it, the text itself being "data" from which various statistics are calculated—the number of passive constructions in the text, the average number of words per sentence, the overall "readability" of the material (based on formulas like the Flesch index), and so on. The 1980 review article by Moe is a very useful survey in this area, as are the reports of Holland (1981) and Frase (1981) on the limitations of readability formulas, which were originally designed to provide a means of doublechecking the grade levels of student textbooks, and have limited applicability to other forms of writing.

Predictably, when one considers that most text processors are in offices, current programs being developed for revising (notably by Bell Labs) are not primarily instructional. Instead, they focus on the professional needs of business and technical writers. The *Writer's Workbench* package was programmed by a number of researchers, including several who have written about it and, to varying degrees, critiqued it: Cherry (1981), Macdonald, Frase, Gingrich, and Keenan (1982), and Frase (1981). Although Macdonald *et al.* claim that these programs have potential for writing instruction, only Colorado State University has begun to test them as pedagogical tools. However, since these programs are the most comprehensive package of computer writing aids now availabe, they are worth discussing in some detail here.

STYLE, the most elaborate of these programs, provides an analysis of the text through use of readability formulas and quantifies certain kinds of stylistic information, in the manner of Schwartz's "text feedback" category for CAI. It gives statistics for variations in sentence and word length, type of sentence (simple, complex, compound, and/or compound-complex), how sentences begin, and, finally, how often various parts of speech appear. STYLE has definite limitations in terms of grammatical accuracy: most significantly for college writers, it cannot distinguish legitimate sentences from fragments and run-ons. DICTION, another program in this package, prints out sentences containing frequently misused or verbose phrases. DICTION works in conjunction with a program called SUGGEST, which provides alternative phrases for those which DICTION has listed as possible problems. There is even a program similar to DICTION called SEXIST, which identifies words that could potentially be considered such. DICTION makes no attempt to group similar errors in usage together, to explain errors, or to distinguish between different types or degrees of inappropriate usage. These are all areas for further development in an instructional setting.

PROSE uses some of STYLE's statistics to compare the text under examination to standards calculated from good examples of the same type of document: Although Cherry insists that all these programs "may be applied to documents on any subject with equal accuracy" (1981, p. 11), so far only technical papers and training manuals have such standards calculated for them. PROSE is useful mainly in those fields where a rigorous set of expectations about the text is defined independent of content; it would not be highly supportive of the type of writing instruction that seeks to let form develop *from* content. However, to the extent that a teacher's expectations about a particular assignment (e.g., primary trait analysis from writing research) could be defined, analogous programs could be developed.

Most of this type of text feedback, unless modified considerably to explain itself in greater detail to a student, or given considerable attention in class, is not really suitable for beginning writers. Indeed, for them such a formulaic approach might be detrimental. There are several programs in the *Writer's Workbench* package, however, that are more amenable to beginning writers. With these, microcomputers are used as text processors, from which revising exercises might be developed. One program, REWRITE, locates prepositions, "to be" verbs, and empty phrases (using DICTION) in order to isolate passive constructions and wordy sentences, and highlights them by capitalization. Another program ORG, excerpts the first and last sentence in each paragraph as a test for text coherence. There is also a program (ABST) that identifies abstractions. TOPIC, mentioned earlier as a program with potential as an invention heuristic, might also be used as a revising tool to find overused words. The other programs in the *Writer's Workbench* package are primarily editing or surface-level tools.

As opposed to STYLE, smaller programs like REWRITE, ORG, ABST, and TOPIC put out a manageable amount of information, which might be more easily grasped and tested against a student's developing sense of the pragmatic priorities of context that affect stylistic decisions. The instructor may then be better able to devote time to discouraging absolute judgments about writing style. In fact, any of the *Writer's Workbench* programs may be made more suitable for use by beginning writers if they are used first to create exercises demonstrating particular revising options, rather than being presented as a prescription for revising the student's text. An important tenet of our approach to instruction, for example, is that the strategies a student learns for future writing tasks are more important than the revision or editing of individual papers, even though this practice may be what a student needs to learn useful strategies. It might be difficult for a student using the *Writer's Workbench* programs on individual papers to generalize about principles she could use for revising or editing.

At this point it is important to mention a program developed by Hordowich (1979), who built upon Hewlett Packard's IDAF (Instruction Dialogue Author Facility) program. Hordowich's program for teaching stylistic awareness by clause analysis is a promising revising tool. Its chief usefulness, in connection with the text-moving capabilities of the word processor, would seem to be in the area of sentence combining. Hordowich bases her study in tagmemic theory. Williams's work on computer-generated sentences (1980) may also be useful for sentence combining.

Two other feedback programs we've come across may be useful. First, the RSVP program developed by Anandam (1981) focuses specifically on student writing and combines prescriptive "letters" that identify mechanical and rhetorical errors at various skill levels with the option to call up explanations of basic grammar and sentence structure. Second, IBM's EPISTLE system (L. A. Miller, 1980; Miller, Heidorn, & Jensen, 1981) is primarily for editing business correspondence. Both these feedback programs seem more designed to correct surface errors than to provide food for thought on revising. The RSVP program has limited objectives, being admittedly a "content- and context-free" system for feedback about general error patterns noted by instructors. In addition to these programs, Macdonald et al. (1982) mention two others: the JOURNALISM program developed at the University of Michigan for analyzing the content of news stories and pointing out missing details, and the CRES system, which the U.S. navy uses to improve the readability of its technical documents and training manuals.

Editing

Several programs in *Writer's Workbench* aid the writer in editing. Included in the larger program PROOFR are SPLITINF, which locates split infinitives; SPELLWWB, a dictionary spelling checker; and PUNCT, which checks for unbalanced quotes or parentheses, fixes spaces around dashes, and so on. (Interestingly, the DICTION and SUGGEST programs are also run under PROOFR, and are considered to involve editing rather than revising problems.) Most word processing units come with the option to purchase spelling checkers or to communicate with a larger operating system that has a spelling checker. Miller (G. Miller, 1979), Peterson (1980), and Turba (1981) have written articles surveying some of these editing aids. Some portions of these articles, especially Turba's, provide a more technical analysis than one would need simply to purchase a spelling checker. But anyone interested in the design of spelling software should probably read all three.

The writing category "editing," naturally, has been the object of the largest amount of research on word processors. The machines were originally created not for originating text but for typing it, for correcting errors easily, and for varying form letters—all basically editing concerns. Consequently, most industry research on "optimal user interface" focuses here. Riddle's early report (1976) comparing text processors and formatters, while somewhat dated, remains a useful study for anyone becoming acquainted with text processors for the first time. The study is devoted, however, to on-line editors. The continuing work of Card and his colleagues in analyzing text processing as a routine cognitive skill and experimenting with various editors to speed up editing is significant, although Card's subjects are typists, not writers (Card, 1978; Card, Moran, & Newell, 1979, 1980).

Wimmer's early study (1978) also uses office staff as subjects, as does Good's (1981) study on the recently developed ETUDE editor. Although he discusses mainly secretarial uses of ETUDE, Good brings up many user–interface considerations which composition theorists will find significant. Hammer and Rouse's study of the same editing system (1979), however, uses researchers and programmers keying in their own work as subjects. Hammer and Rouse found significant differences in keystroke performance between those subjects using the editor to produce documents and those using it for programming purposes, though the differences between the two groups were no larger than differences in performance within the groups themselves. The modifications in keyboard and CRT design for this editor are themselves interesting. The editor features command syntax in simple declarative sentences; Good (1981) cites Ledgard, Singer, Seymour, and Whiteside (1980) on the advantages of natural language commands versus notational commands in editing systems, a study that is in itself important. Significantly, Ledgard's research was with advanced computer science majors who had various degrees of "hands-on" experience—a group somewhat closer to the writers we wish to study. Overall, even these computer science majors preferred the English-based text editor to the notational editor.

Work in Progress at the University of Minnesota

Several research projects at the University of Minnesota are presently being conducted to examine writers' reactions to word processors and ways of integrating these machines into the composition classroom. We have developed a three-year plan to produce both basic research and instructional designs using word processors. With the basic research, we are studying the differences word processors make in writers' composing processes; with the instructional designs, we plan to apply the results of the basic research and develop software for student writers.

Research on Composing Processes

Our composition program is now using a commercially available word processing software package which runs on a microcomputer. Thus we have opportunities to preserve all kinds of information on writers' composing processes as they use the system. To date, we have developed two programs, one that yields a time recording of the text and control keys the writer used to produce a text, and one that enables us to do an "instant replay" of the images the writer sees on the video screen. The recording program gives an absolute time record, in one-second intervals, of all the keystrokes the writer produces. For research purposes, this means that many elaborate methods used in the past (e.g., videotapes and electronic pencils) are no longer necessary for studying exact behaviors during composing. The writer simply learns to use a word processing system, and the recording program captures what occurs without interfering with the process. In addition to the "iconic" representation of composing processes that the program yields, it also synthesizes some of the data for us (e.g., histograms and exact frequency counts of all control keys). Using frequency counts, for example, we can determine such things as how often writers delete or add text, read back over lines or pages (screenfuls, to be exact), or move blocks of text around within a composition. The exact occurrence and duration of pauses during composing are also easily determined from the recording program.

The second program, the playback feature, enables us to watch the text evolve. While this is somewhat redundant because we already have the time tracks on paper with the recording program, we find that watching the text unfold makes analysis far more precise. We are able to determine the relationship between changes and text structure far more accurately than we could when we depended on a "paper trail" left by the writer composing with paper and pen or typewriter. (See Bridwell, 1980, for an example of a "pre-microcomputer" study of revision processes.) While we have not yet done extensive analysis beyond the text, we plan to use this playback feature for what we call retrospective protocol analysis.

In the past, researchers (notably Flower & Hayes, 1981) have used a "composing aloud" method to determine what concerns the writer had while generating text, or what problem-solving strategies were employed. The advantage of composing-aloud protocol analysis over retrospective interviews is obvious: it does not depend on the writer's memory of what was going on during composing. However, many critics have suggested that the talking aloud destroys the validity of the information gathered in terms of generalizations about silent composing. Writing and talking, and writing and thinking, are simply not analogous processes. With retrospective protocol analysis, we show the writer the "instant replay" of her composing process and, as words appear on the screen, ask her to talk aloud about what she was thinking. We can stop the replay for an extensive comment, slow it down, or speed it up, depending on the degree to which the writer can articulate problem-solving concerns. While we do not claim that we capture all that was occurring at any given "point of utterance," we do believe that we get a more accurate representation of the silent composing process, at least for writers using word processors.

In the first study, we had eight "experienced writers" (PhD candidates with writing experience beyond academia) engaged in four writing tasks. For the first task, they used "typical processes" and, in two interviews, gave us insight into what their normal approaches to such a writing task were. For the next three tasks, they used word processors and we tracked their processes with the recording and replay programs and with interviews. None had ever used word processors before, but they were experienced typists. With a minimum of two hours of training, all felt confident that they could compose on the word processor. Obviously, one of our hypotheses was that their facility with the word processing system would increase and that their methods of composing would change over time as they learned to use all of the text processing functions available to them. A second hypothesis was that as they gained facility with the word processors, their writing processes would still not return to "normal" because of the effects of the fluidity of the text when one composes and revises in a paperless medium. Finally, we also speculated that the shape of their texts and certain stylistic features might not remain the same as they learned to write in this new way.

Our preliminary findings have suggested that we were correct in some of our assumptions. A number of the writers reported that they were unable to duplicate their old methods on the word processor. Drawing diagrams, for example, is not easy with the word processing system as it is currently configured. Many found that they had to use paper for this step. Others found that they could ignore the need to plan on paper and simply compose to see the shape of their ideas. Nearly all reported that they revised more because it is so easy to do with a word processor. Some said they had to force themselves not to tinker as they went along in order to build up forward momentum. All the writers in the study have begun to use word processors for their own personal work. Not all feel comfortable abandoning paper completely, but they do like the speed of organizing a polished manuscript with the microcomputer.

Long-Range Planning for Instruction

Our long-range plans include studying the composing processes of advanced undergraduates to determine the specific needs they have which can be addressed with microcomputers, functioning both as interactive instructional systems and as word processors. We believe word processors can be far more powerful tools for interacting with the composing process than most of the currently existing software mght suggest. Presently we are purchasing additional software and developing new software and disk file sytems that would offer students a variety of options for prewriting (e.g., free-writing, brainstorming, tagmemic analysis), for revising (e.g., audience analysis, text-structure analysis, "given–new" information levels), and for editing (e.g., surface mechanics, spelling).

Word Processors and Writing for Special Purposes

Our second line of inquiry is concerned with ways to design instruction in upper-division courses developed for "writing for special purposes." Features of some commercial word processing packages allow the writer to use preset formats for minor elements such as foot-notes, but none directly addresses the more important structural or stylistic features of the kinds of texts that are expected in various disciplines. While some software we have reviewed does provide students with *post hoc* descriptions of their texts, we are beginning a three-year project (funded by the Fund for the Improvement of Postsecondary Education) to help students with invention heuristics, drafting, and revising for features beyond surface-level editing.

Word Processors in Classroom Contexts

At the present time, we are conducting pilot studies on the third area of inquiry: how students and teachers can best use word processors in classroom contexts. For example, in the spring of 1982, members of our staff taught three undergraduate courses using Xerox 820 microcomputers and the WordStar editing system: an introductory course in freshman composition, a course in business writing, and a course in technical writing for engineering students. Each student received approximately four hours a week in lab time, in two two-hour blocks. One block was fixed, and the student signed up for the other two hours on a weekly basis. Students used the word processors primarily for drafting and revising their papers; in none of the courses was composing a paper on the word processor required. Occasionally writing exercises were given in the business and technical writing course that had to be done on the word processor, and the freshman composition course included word processor writing exercises on a regular basis. The freshman exercises, which were designed to complement a popular composition textbook, are not interactive; they merely use the text-altering capabilities that WordStar provides to teach heuristics for prewriting, drafting, revising, and editing. Such exercises might be easily modified for any word processing system or for any textbook that emphasizes the writing process.

From these pilot studies, we have gathered some valuable information and have already developed methods for accommodating writing instruction to the use of word processors. For example, all three of the instructors whose students used word processors for their writing have developed new ways of handling files, responding to student writing, and developing exercises. We can already foresee the need for a screen arrangement that would allow a teacher's comments to "float" along with the changing text and not become incorporated into that text as the student rewrites and reformats a section.

Conclusion

Many composition instructors, seeing the initial promise of word processing microcomputers for writers, are eager to proclaim their value from the academic rooftops—to students, to fellow faculty members, and, perhaps most fervently, to departmental budget directors. But our review of relevant literature suggests that little research has yet been done to substantiate that claim. If we are to make such proclamations more than temporary outbursts of enthusiasm for an "innovative" approach to teaching writing, instructors must begin to take a larger part in ergonomics research and in the design of word processing software, and they must begin to formulate, out of their theoretical knowledge and practical experience, new or modified methodologies for integrating word processors into the context of writing classrooms. Unless this occurs, the word processor will become not a valuable heuristic tool, but just one more gimmick in computer-aided instruction for writers; like Mark Twain, we may then be forced to conclude that premature testimonials to "new fangled" gadgets cause more trouble than they're worth.

REFERENCES

Allen, T., Nix, R., & Perlis. A. Pen: A hierarchical document editor. *Proceedings of the ACM SIGPLAN*, 1981, 74–81.

Anandam, K. *RSVP: Response system with variable prescriptions, applications of a computer system for individualizing instruction and advisement*. Miami–Dade Community College, Instructional Development and Research, March 1981.

Bailey, R. W. Computer-assisted poetry: The writing machine is for everybody. In J. L. Mitchell (Ed.), *Computers in the humanities*. Edinburgh: University of Edinburgh Press, 1974.

Bridwell, L. S. Revising strategies in twelfth grade students' transactional writing. *Research in the Teaching of English*, 1980, *14*, 197–222.

Burns, H. *Stimulating invention in English composition through computer-assisted instruction.* Unpublished doctoral dissertation, University of Texas, Austin, 1979.

Burns, H. Education's new management: The personal computing underground. *Pipeline*, Fall 1980, 20, 41. (a)

Burns, H. *A writer's tool: Computing as a mode of inventing.* Paper presented at New York College English Association Conference, Saratoga Springs, N.Y., 1980. (b)

Burns, H. Computing as a way of brainstorming in English composition. In D. Harrid (Ed.), *Proceedings of the National Educational Computing Conference, 1981.* University of Iowa, Iowa City, June 1981. (a)

Burns, H. Pandora's chip: Concerns about quality CAI. *Pipeline*, Fall 1981, 15–16, 49. (b)

Burns, H., & Culp, G. Stimulating invention in English composition through computer-assisted instruction. *Educational Technology*, 1980, *20*, 5–10.

Burns, R. E. *Designing learning modules for the micro computer.* Paper presented at Conference on College Composition and Communication, San Francisco, March 1982.

Card, S. K. *Studies in the psychology of computer text editing systems.* Palo Alto, Calif.: Xerox Palo Alto Research Center (SSL-78-1), August 1978.

Card, S. K., Moran, T. P., & Newell, A. *The keystroke-level model for user performance time with interactive systems.* Palo Alto, Calif.: Xerox Palo Alto Research Center (SSL-79-1), March 1979.

Card, S. K., Moran, T. P., & Newell, A. Computer text-editing: An information-processing analysis of a routine cognitive skill, *Cognitive Psychology*, January 1980, *12*(1), 32–74.

Cherry, L. L. *PARTS: A system for assigning word classes to English text* (Computing Science Technical Report No. 81). Murray Hill, N.J.: Bell Labs, 1980.

Cherry, L. Computer aids for writers. *Proceedings of the ACM SIGPLAN*, June 1981, *16*(6), 61–67.

Cherry, L. L. Writing tools. *IEEE Transactions on Communication*, 1982, *30*, 100–105.

Cherry, L. L., & Versterman, W. *Writing tools: The "Style" and "Diction" programs* (Technical Report). Murray Hills, N.J.: Bell Labs, November 1980.

Collier, R. M. *The influence of computer-based text editors on the revision strategies of inexperienced writers.* Paper presented at Northwest Regional Conference on the Teaching of English in the Two-Year College, 1982.

Cottey, P. *Research in computer-assisted writing instruction: An overview.* Paper presented at Conference on College Composition and Communication, San Francisco, March 1982.

Della-Piana, G. M. *The development of a model for the systematic teaching of the writing of poetry* (BR-O-H-004). Salt Lake City: Bureau of Educational Research, Utah University, August 1971.

Flower, L., & Hayes, J. A cognitive process theory of writing. *College Composition and Communication*, 1981, *32*, 365–387.

Frase, L. T. *Writer's Workbench: Computer supports for components of the writing process* (Technical Report). Murray Hills, N.J.: Bell Labs, 1980.

Frase, L. T. Ethics of imperfect measures. *IEEE Transactions on Professional Communications*, March 1981, *24*(1), 49–50.

Frase, L. T., Keenan, S. A., & Dever, J. J. Human performance in computer aided writing and documentation. In P. A. Kolers, M. E. Wrolstad, & H. Bouma (Eds.), *Processing of visible language* (Vol. 2). New York: Plenum, 1980.

Frase, L. T., Macdonald, N. H., Gingrich, P. S., Keenan, S. A., & Lollymore, J. L. Computer aids for text assessment and writing instruction. *NSPI Journal*, November 1981, *20*, 21–24.

Good, M. Etude and the folklore of user interface design. *Proceedings of ACM SIGPLAN/*

SIGOA Symposium on Text Manipulation, Association for Computing Machinery, New York, June 1981.

Gould, J. D. Composing letters with computer-based text editors. *Human Factors,* 1981, *23*(5), 593–606. Also IBM Research Report, RC 8446 (#36750), September 2, 1980, available from IBM Research Center, Box 218, Yorktown Heights, N.Y. 10593.

Hammer, J. M., & Rouse, W. B. Analysis and modelling of freeform text editing behavior. *Proceedings of the International Conference on Cybernetics and Society,* Denver, 8–10, October 1979. New York: Institute of Electrical and Electronic Engineers, 1979.

Hegarty, J. *Text reformating algorithms* (Bell Laboratories Technical Report). Paper presented at annual meeting of American Educational Research Association, Boston, 1980.

Holland, V. M. *Psycholinguistic alternatives to readability formulas* (Document Design Project A, Technical Report No. 12). Washington, D.C.: American Institutes for Research, May 1981.

Hordowich, P. M. *Developing stylistic awareness on the computer: A tagmemic approach.* Paper presented at annual meeting of Midwest Modern Language Association, Indianapolis, Ind., 1979.

Kline, E. A. *Computer-aided review lessons in English composition.* 1980. Paper available from Notre Dame University, Freshman Writing Program, Notre Dame, Ind. 46556.

Ledgard, H., Singer, A., Seymour, W., & Whiteside, J. A. The natural language of interactive systems. *Communications of the Association for Computing Machinery,* October 1980, *23*(10), 556–563.

Macdonald, N. H., Frase, L. T., Gingrich, P., & Keenan, S. A. The Writer's Workbench: Computer aids for text analysis. *IEEE Transactions on Communication,* 1982, *30*, 105–110.

Marcus, S. COMPUPOEM: A computer writing activity. *South Coast Writing Project Newsletter,* 1981, *1*(3), 3.

Marcus, S. COMPUPOEM: A computer-assisted writing activity. *English Journal,* February 1982, *71*(2), 96–99.

Miller, G. Automated dictionaries, reading and writing. *Chairman's report of a Conference on Educational Uses of Word Processors with Dictionaries,* June 14–15, 1979.

Miller, L. A. Project EPISTLE: A system for the automatic analysis of business correspondence. *Proceedings of the 1980 AAAI Conference,* Stanford, Calif., August 1980.

Miller, L. A., Heidorn, G. E., & Jensen, K. Text-critiquing with the EPISTLE system: An author's aid to better syntax. *Proceedings of National Computer Conference,* Anaheim, Calif., May 1981.

Miller, L. H. A study in man-machine interaction. *AFIPS Conference Proceedings* (Vol. 46). Montvale, N. J.: AFIPS Press, May 1977.

Moe, A. J. Analyzing text with computers. *Educational Technology,* July 1980, *20*(7), 29–31.

Packert-Hall, M., & Burke, R. C. *An index to Plato lessons on composition.* 1981. Available from Language Learning Laboratory, University of Illinois, Urbana, Ill.

Peterson, J. L. Computer programs for detecting and correcting spelling errors. *Communications of the Association for Computing Machinery,* December 1980, *23*, 676–687.

Riddle, E. A., *Comparative study of various text editors and formatting systems.* Washington, D.C.: Air Force Data Services Center/Air Force Automation Agency (AD—A029 050), August 1976.

RSVP: Feedback program for individualized analysis of writing. Manual for faculty users, Part I: Analyzing students' writing. New York: Exxon Education Foundation, 1979.

Schwartz, H. J. *A computer program for invention and audience feedback.* Paper presented at Conference on College Composition and Communication, San Francisco, March 1982. (a)

Schwartz, H. J. Monsters and mentors: Computer applications for humanistic education. *College English,* February 1982, *44*(2), 141–152. (b)

Strömfors, O., & Jonesjö, L. The implementation and experiences of a structure-oriented text editor. *Proceedings of ACM SIGPLAN/SIGOA Symposium on Text Manipulation*, Association for Computing Machinery, New York, June 1981.

Turba, T. N. Checking for spelling and typographical errors in computer-based text. *SIGPLAN Notices*, June 1981, 16(6), 51–60.

Williams, R. L. Sentence construction with a computer. *Creative Computing*, April 1980, 6(4), 52–58.

Wimmer, K. E. *Research on human interface considerations for interactive text generation.* Conference on Evolutions in Computer Communications, Kyoto, Japan, September 26–29, 1978. Amsterdam: North-Holland, 1978.

Author index

Subject index